WAR

A CLASSIC COLLECTION OF 56 GREAT WAR STORIES OF OUR TIME

EDITED BY JON E. LEWIS

WAR

A CLASSIC COLLECTION OF 56
GREAT WAR STORIES OF OUR TIME

EDITED BY JON E. LEWIS

Galahad Books • New York

First Galahad Books edition published in 1995.

Galahad Books
A division of Budget Book Service, Inc.
386 Park Avenue South
New York, NY 10016

Galahad Books is a registered trademark of Budget Book Service, Inc.

Published by arrangement with Carroll & Graf Publishers, Inc.

Library of Congress Catalog Card Number: 95-78588

ISBN: 0-88365-909-3

Printed in the United States of America.

Jon E. Lewis is a writer and critic. He was born in Hereford, England, in 1961 and educated at the Universities of Kent and Wales. His previous books include the anthologies *The Mammoth Book of True War Stories*, *The Mammoth Book of the Western*, and *Red Handed*.

Contents

Foreword

In this century war writing and war reporting grew up and entered an era of realism. No longer is combat the experience of a bold few, often fighting in remote corners of Europe and empires overseas. With the advent of telegraphy, mass circulation newspapers, the newsreel and finally radio and television, it is now something everybody can witness.

Yet the experience of the man and woman caught up in fighting and its aftermath is often intimate and elusive—and tests the skill of the writer in fiction and journalism. Often war writing in prose and poetry can have the precision and realism of reportage. As this volume shows, the best writing about action is from those who have been through the turmoil of combat themselves—like the former U-Boat commander Lothar-Günther Buchheim, whose *U-Boat* was rightly such a success in print and film twenty years ago.

War journalism often has the creative intensity of art—the war reporting of a Hemingway or Graham Greene became a vital ingredient in their novels. *The Quiet American* still remains one of the greatest works on the Vietnam conflict, a war which endured for more than thirty years and broke the will of two great powers, France and the United States.

The intimate link between creative writing about war and war reporting makes the appearance to *The Mammoth Book of Modern War Stories* the natural partner to Jon Lewis's anthology *The Mammoth Book of True War Stories*. He has confined the collection to pieces written during the last hundred years, the era of the new realism in war writing. It is also the era of mass participation in wars, where millions would be recruited, actively or passively, whether as the conscripts for Kitchener's new army for the Somme campaign, or the appalled witnesses to the quagmire of Vietnam through myriad television tubes.

Many modern writers, some represented here, have proved brilliant observers of the phenomenon of combat. They are excellent war reporters. Take Tolstoy describing the Hussars coming under fire for the first time during the Austerlitz campaign in *War and Peace*: ". . . there arose the smoke of a shot, and a cannon ball flew whizzing over the heads of the squadron of hussars. The officers, who had been standing together, scattered in different directions. The hussars began carefully getting their horses back into line. The whole squadron lapsed into silence. All the men were looking at the enemy in front and at the commander of the squadron, expecting an order to be given." This has such a stark brilliance that it could not have been an invention from Tolstoy's head; it must have been a scene he witnessed during his service in the Crimean War.

Some pieces are very much the idealised view of the propaganda and the recruiting poster. Captain W. E. Johns is the master of this genre—but Biggles and Algie and co., like Sapper's Bulldog Drummond, were the beaux ideals of the time—how war was supposed to be in the heroic idiom. They are the prose equivalent of the over-romantic battle scenes of Lady Butler, such as the Scots Greys at Waterloo, and are valid for all that as the mirror of taste and attitude of a past age.

For nearly all participants, with pen or sword, combat has a peculiarly private aspect, and for many of us it can bring the most indelible experience, whether excitement or trauma, of a lifetime. This is caught brilliantly by the Australian writer David Malouf in his *The Great World*, sadly not represented here. "Billy Keen had run off to France when he was fifteen. By the time he got home again, a survivor of Pozières and Villers Bretonneux, he had already, at just eighteen, had the one great adventure of his life. Though married and more or less settled as chief ferryman at the Crossing, he continued to live in spirit, since he was barely out of his lively boyhood, at that intensified pitch of daring, terror and pure high jinks that would forever be his measure of what a man's life should be when he is at full stretch. Anything else was a tameness he could not endure."

The sheer intimacy and muddle of human contact in battle is precisely caught by two outstanding World War II novelists, both in their way brilliant journalists, Joseph Heller and Evelyn Waugh. *Catch-22* and 'The Sword of Honour' trilogy are masterpieces of their war as surely as Remarque's *All Quiet on the Western Front* and *The Good Soldier Švejk* are of the Great War. They all show war as chaos, with large bouts of boredom between the spasms of terror and pain. Waugh's depiction of the Crete debacle is one of the best evocations in prose of what happens to an army breaking up in defeat, where units suddenly become loose groups of individuals scrambling for safety.

Waugh's deftest touch was in the dialogue of his soldiers: he could represent the mutterings and musings of Tommy Atkins as well as Kipling. His Halberdiers were the Royal Marines, with whom he served with distinction. The Marines in the Falklands were still the same Marines or Halberdiers Waugh portrayed. The jargon, the chat were the same, and so was the inner and private battle of each with his fear. I well remember the sight of Royal Marines of 40 and 42 Commandos on the sun deck of the *SS Canberra*, steadily sharpening their bayonets, as the ship ploughed the waves to the South Atlantic. They were unnaturally quiet, each busy with his thoughts, for he knew that his honing of the blade on the whetstone meant that action was not far off. Only a few bright sparks started muttering about 'breaks for nutty' and the prospects for 'a good proff' in the battle to come.

The astonishing range of emotion experienced in war, so eloquently evoked in this collection, is the strange attraction of the subject to many war reporters like myself. Like it or not, and it is not a moral judgment, all human life is here. War has to be discussed, portrayed, analysed, and if necessary condemned. It is as much part of the human condition as love, sex, politics, food, fashion and religion. To ignore it is to ignore what we are. We need to understand why and what wars are, and in whatever form—as these pages show—if only to avoid them. From the swamps of Vietnam, to battered Beirut, and the bloodied snows of Sarajevo, they are part of our collective memory and conscience.

Robert Fox *is the leading war reporter and Mediterranean Correspondent of the* Daily Telegraph. *In 24 years in journalism for the BBC and the* Telegraph *he has covered five wars and a dozen conflicts, including the Falklands (for which he was awarded the MBE), the Gulf, Afghanistan, the Middle East, the Red Brigades terrorist campaign in Italy, and the fighting in Bosnia. He has written a best-seller about the Falklands* Eyewitness Falklands *and his latest book is an account of the upheavals in the modern Mediterranean* The Inner Sea.

Introduction

This anthology of stories is neither for nor against War. It is about it. It won't tell you how to stop War, or how to wage it, but it will show you what War has been, and is, like in the Twentieth century and how writers have viewed it.

War is the ultimate, the most extreme of human experiences. The job of the soldier—or sailor, or airman—is to kill or be killed. No other human activity is like it, or so pervaded by the imminence of Death. War is perhaps the supreme theatre for asking the questions about what it means to be human.

It is not surprising, then, that War with its attendant big themes of courage (or lack of it), suffering, and barbarism has fascinated many of the century's greatest authors, and produced some of its finest novels: Erich Maria Remarque's *All Quiet on the Western Front*, Norman Mailer's *The Naked and the Dead*, Hemingway's *For Whom the Bell Tolls*, to name but three.

There are excerpts from all of the above books in this anthology, along with extracts from such other classic war novels as Gustav Hasford's Vietnam story, *The Short-Timers* (the basis for the movie, *Full Metal Jacket*). It has been one of my intentions, more or less ambitious, to give a representative sampling of modern war fiction in these pages.

So the anthology commences with a short story by Stephen Crane, "The Upturned Face", from 1900. It was Crane who virtually invented modern war fiction, when he published in 1895 his novel of the American Civil War, *The Red Badge of Courage*. The book depicts with graphic realism what soldiers go through in combat, both in body and mind. It was the first true war novel. (Occasionally, claims are made for Tolstoy as the father of modern war fiction, but *War and Peace*, 1869, is actually a family saga played out against the Napoleonic conflict, not a novel of war.)

The importance of Crane to modern war fiction can be gauged by the fact that virtually all the other writers in the anthology are indebted to him, knowingly or not. The best war fiction of the century has retained his realism, his concern for truth.

Not truth in details of fact, but in the relating and intrepreting of experiences. War fiction at its worst—the "With a savage flick of his wrist he cut the Nip's throat" school of writing—is not concerned with truth, but propaganda.

Crane's achievement with the *The Red Badge of Courage* was all the more remarkable in that he had, at the time of its writing, no direct experience of War (although he was afterwards a war correspondent). To write the novel he talked to Civil War veterans and imagined what combat in the Civil War had been like.

This makes Crane almost unique as a writer of war fiction. Most of the rest of the stories in the anthology are based, in some degree, on the personal experience of the author. War fiction is, in fact, an unusual sort of fiction: it is invariably fictionalised autobiography.

This element of autobiography means that war fiction has changed as War itself has changed. There are two World Wars of difference between Rudyard Kipling's 1902 story of the Boer War, "The Comprehension of Private Copper", and the Vietnam stories which close the anthology.

Also, the fiction of particular wars tends to have a particular tone. In retrospect, World War I stories—like World War I poems—are a distinct body of literature, imbued with a sense of disillusion, and contempt for the slaughter through which the troops were put. Stories from World War II, on the other hand, often convey a feeling that it was a just and necessary war (for the Allied side, at least). In Studs Terkel's phrase, it was "The Good War".

To give some sense of all this, the changes and differences in modern war fiction, the stories and selections which follow are arranged in rough chronological order, grouped by the war concerned.

I don't wish to suggest, however, that some there is some didactic purpose behind this book; there is not. The pieces in this anthology are in it because they are, in my opinion, the best War stories—the most vivid, the most painful, the most exhilarating. Pieces which show how War is, in all its faces.

There are good scenes of fighting, for instance, like Norman Mailer and Eric Lambert's stories of combat against the Japanese in the jungles of the Far East. Most of the accounts are about warfare on land—which is, after all, where most twentieth century wars have been fought—but there are also stories of warfare in the air, and at sea.

Included in the latter category is an excerpt from *U-Boat* (filmed as *Das Boot*) by the German author, Lothar-Günther Buchheim. Although this anthology is primarily for an American and British readership I have, in the pursuit of a total picture of War, used authors from other nationalities: French, Nigerian, and Russian among them.

In the same vein, the collection includes stories about the Home Front and Boot Camp, as well as the Combat Zone, since War is not restricted to those on the killing fields alone. Seventy-eight million people were killed or wounded in World War II alone, most of them civilians.

I said earlier that War was the stuff of big themes. There are, consequently, stories here of sacrifice, bravery, and human loss. And, of course, the question asked by the infantrymen in Frederic Manning's "Her Privates We": Why are we fighting?

Yet War is also about small things, like the lucky charm in Tim O'Brien's Vietnam tale, "Stocking". And it can be bizarrely, blackly funny, as in the story from Joseph Heller's *Catch-22*. These things have not been forgotten either.

This is to the best of my knowledge the biggest collection of war fiction from our century. I can only hope that it is also the best.

Jon E. Lewis

STEPHEN CRANE
The Upturned Face

*Stephen Crane (1871–1900) was born in
Newark, New Jersey, and educated at
Harvard. His psychologically realistic short
novel of the American Civil War,* The
Red Badge of Courage *(1895), virtually
invented modern war fiction. He was briefly
a war correspondent, reporting both the
Greek and Spanish-American Wars. He
died, aged 28, from tuberculosis.*

*"The Upturned Face" is from 1900. The
setting is an imaginary country in Europe.*

"WHAT WILL WE DO NOW?" said the adjutant, troubled
and excited.

"Bury him," said Timothy Lean.

The two officers looked down close to their toes where
lay the body of their comrade. The face was chalk-blue;
gleaming eyes stared at the sky. Over the two upright figures
was a windy sound of bullets, and on the top of the hill
Lean's prostrate company of Spitzbergen infantry was firing
measured volleys.

"Don't you think it would be better—" began the adjutant.
"We might leave him until tomorrow."

"No," said Lean. "I can't hold that post an hour longer.
I've got to fall back, and we've got to bury old Bill."

"Of course," said the adjutant, at once. "Your men got
entrenching tools?"

Lean shouted back to his little line, and two men came
slowly, one with a pick, one with a shovel. They started in
the direction of the Rostina sharpshooters. Bullets cracked
near their ears. "Dig here," said Lean gruffly. The men, thus

caused to lower their glances to the turf, became hurried and frightened, merely because they could not look to see whence the bullets came. The dull beat of the pick striking the earth sounded amid the swift snap of close bullets. Presently the other private began to shovel.

"I suppose," said the adjutant, slowly, "we'd better search his clothes for—things."

Lean nodded. Together in curious abstraction they looked at the body. Then Lean stirred his shoulders suddenly, arousing himself.

"Yes," he said, "we'd better see what he's got." He dropped to his knees, and his hands approached the body of the dead officer. But his hands wavered over the buttons of the tunic. The first button was brick-red with drying blood, and he did not seem to dare touch it.

"Go on," said the adjutant, hoarsely.

Lean stretched his wooden hand, and his fingers fumbled the bloodstained buttons. At last he rose with ghastly face. He had gathered a watch, a whistle, a pipe, a tobacco-pouch, a handkerchief, a little case of cards and papers. He looked at the adjutant. There was a silence. The adjutant was feeling that he had been a coward to make Lean do all the grisly business.

"Well," said Lean, "that's all, I think. You have his sword and revolver?"

"Yes," said the adjutant, his face working, and then he burst out in a sudden strange fury at the two privates. "Why don't you hurry up with that grave? What are you doing, anyhow? Hurry, do you hear? I never saw such stupid—"

Even as he cried out in his passion the two men were labouring for their lives. Ever overhead the bullets were spitting.

The grave was finished. It was not a masterpiece—a poor little shallow thing. Lean and the adjutant again looked at each other in a curious silent communication.

Suddenly the adjutant croaked out a weird laugh. It was a terrible laugh, which had its origin in that part of the mind which is first moved by the singing of the nerves. "Well," he said humorously to Lean, "I suppose we had best tumble him in."

"Yes," said Lean. The two privates stood waiting, bent over

their implements. "I suppose," said Lean, "it would be better if we laid him in ourselves."

"Yes," said the adjutant. Then, apparently remembering that he had made Lean search the body, he stooped with great fortitude and took hold of the dead officer's clothing. Lean joined him. Both were particular that their fingers should not feel the corpse. They tugged away; the corpse lifted, heaved, toppled, flopped into the grave, and the two officers, straightening, looked again at each other—they were always looking at each other. They sighed with relief.

The adjutant said, "I suppose we should—we should say something. Do you know the service, Tim?"

"They don't read the service until the grave is filled in," said Lean, pressing his lips to an academic expression.

"Don't they?" said the adjutant, shocked that he had made the mistake. "Oh, well," he cried, suddenly, "let us—let us say something—while he can hear us."

"All right," said Lean. "Do you know the service?"

"I can't remember a line of it," said the adjutant.

Lean was extremely dubious. "I can repeat two lines, but—"

"Well, do it," said the adjutant. "Go as far as you can. That's better than nothing. And the beasts have got our range exactly."

Lean looked at his two men. "Attention," he barked. The privates came to attention with a click, looking much aggrieved. The adjutant lowered his helmet to his knee. Lean, bareheaded, stood over the grave. The Rostina sharpshooters fired briskly.

"O Father, our friend has sunk in the deep waters of death, but his spirit has leaped toward Thee as the bubble arises from the lips of the drowning. Perceive, we beseech, O Father, the little flying bubble, and—"

Lean, although husky and ashamed, had suffered no hesitation up to this point, but he stopped with a hopeless feeling and looked at the corpse.

The adjutant moved uneasily. "And from Thy superb heights—" he began, and then he too came to an end.

"And from Thy superb heights," said Lean.

The adjutant suddenly remembered a phrase in the back

of the Spitzbergen burial service, and he exploited it with the triumphant manner of a man who has recalled everything, and can go on.

"O God, have mercy—"

"O God, have mercy—" said Lean.

"Mercy," repeated the adjutant, in quick failure.

"Mercy," said Lean. And then he was moved by some violence of feeling, for he turned upon his two men and tigerishly said, "Throw the dirt in."

The fire of the Rostina sharpshooters was accurate and continuous.

One of the aggrieved privates came forward with his shovel. He lifted his first shovel-load of earth, and for a moment of inexplicable hesitation it was held poised above this corpse, which from its chalk-blue face looked keenly out from the grave. Then the soldier emptied his shovel on—on the feet.

Timothy Lean felt as if tons had been swiftly lifted from off his forehead. He had felt that perhaps the private might empty the shovel on—on the face. It had been emptied on the feet. There was a great point gained there—ha, ha!—the first shovelful had been emptied on the feet. How satisfactory!

The adjutant began to babble. "Well, of course—a man we've messed with all these years—impossible—you can't, you know, leave your intimate friends rotting on the field. Go on, for God's sake, and shovel, you."

The man with the shovel suddenly ducked, grabbed his left arm with his right hand, and looked at his officer for orders. Lean picked the shovel from the ground. "Go to the rear," he said to the wounded man. He also addressed the other private. "You get under cover, too; I'll finish this business."

The wounded man scrambled hard still for the top of the ridge without devoting any glances to the direction from whence the bullets came, and the other man followed at an equal pace; but he was different, in that he looked back anxiously three times.

This is merely the way—often—of the hit and unhit.

Timothy Lean filled the shovel, hesitated, and then, in a movement which was like a gesture of abhorrence, he flung the dirt into the grave, and as it landed it made a sound—plop. Lean suddenly stopped and mopped his brow—a tired labourer.

"Perhaps we have been wrong," said the adjutant. His glance wavered stupidly. "It might have been better if we hadn't buried him just at this time. Of course, if we advance tomorrow the body would have been—"

"Damn you," said Lean, "shut your mouth." He was not the senior officer.

He again filled the shovel and flung the earth. Always the earth made that sound—plop. For a space Lean worked frantically, like a man digging himself out of danger.

Soon there was nothing to be seen but the chalk-blue face. Lean filled the shovel. "Good God," he cried to the adjutant. "Why didn't you turn him somehow when you put him in? This—" Then Lean began to stutter.

The adjutant understood. He was pale to the lips. "Go on, man," he cried, beseechingly, almost in a shout.

Lean swung back the shovel. It went forward in a pendulum curve. When the earth landed it made a sound—plop.

RUDYARD KIPLING
The Comprehension of Private Copper

Rudyard Kipling (1865–1936) was born in Bombay, India, of English parents. He was the unofficial laureate of the British Army in the quarter century leading up to World War I, celebrating the service in such volumes as Soldiers Three *(1889)* and Barrack Room Ballads *(1892). His other works include the children's classics, the* Jungle Books *and the* Just So Stories. *He was awarded the Nobel Prize for Literature in 1907.*

The short story "The Comprehension of Private Copper" (1902) is set during the Boer War in South Africa. The war was occasioned by the attempt of the Boer Republics of the Transvaal and the Orange Free State to secure independence from Britain.

PRIVATE COPPER'S FATHER WAS A Southdown shepherd; in early youth Copper had studied under him. Five years' Army service had somewhat blunted Private Copper's pastoral instincts, but it occurred to him as a memory of the Chalk that sheep, or in this case buck, do not move towards one across turf, or in this case, the Colesberg kopjes unless a stranger, or in this case an enemy, is in the neighbourhood. Copper, helmet back-first, advanced with caution, leaving his mates of the picket a full mile behind. The picket, concerned for its evening meal, did not protest. A year ago it would have been an officer's command, moving as such. To-day it paid casual allegiance to a Canadian, nominally a sergeant, actually a trooper of Irregular Horse, discovered convalescent in Naauwport Hospital, and forthwith employed on odd jobs. Private Copper crawled up the side of a bluish rock-strewn hill thinly fringed with brush atop, and remembering how he had peered at Sussex conies through the edge of furze-clumps, cautiously parted the dry stems before his face. At the foot of the long slope sat three farmers smoking. To his natural lust for tobacco was added personal wrath because spiky plants were pricking his belly, and Private Copper slid the backsight up to fifteen hundred yards . . .

"Good evening, khaki. Please don't move," said a voice on his left, and as he jerked his head round he saw entirely down the barrel of a well-kept Lee-Metford protruding from an insignificant tuft of thorn. Very few graven images have moved less than did Private Copper through the next ten seconds.

"It's nearer seventeen hundred than fifteen," said a young man in an obviously ready-made suit of grey tweed, possessing himself of Private Copper's rifle. "Thank *you*. We've got a post of thirty-seven men out yonder. You've eleven—eh? We don't want to kill 'em. We have no quarrel with poor uneducated khakis, and we do not want prisoners we do not keep. It is demoralizing to both sides—eh?"

Private Copper did not feel called upon to lay down the conduct of guerrilla warfare. This dark-skinned, dark-haired, and dark-eyed stranger was his first intimate enemy. He spoke, allowing for a clipped cadence that recalled to Copper vague memories of Umballa, in precisely the same offensive accent that the young Squire of Wilmington had used fifteen years ago when he caught and kicked Alf Copper, a rabbit in each pocket, out of the ditches of Cuckmere. The enemy looked Copper up and down, folded and repocketed a copy of an English weekly which he had been reading, and said: "You seem an inarticulate sort of swine—like the rest of them—eh?"

"You," said Copper, thinking, somehow, of the crushing answers he had never given to the young Squire, "are a renegid. Why, you ain't Dutch. You're English, same as me."

"*No*, khaki. If you cannot talk civilly to a gentleman I will blow your head off."

Copper cringed, and the action overbalanced him so that he rolled some six or eight feet downhill, under the lee of a rough rock. His brain was working with a swiftness and clarity strange in all his experience of Alf Copper. While he rolled he spoke, and the voice from his own jaws amazed him: "If you did, 'twouldn't make you any less of a renegid." As a useful afterthought he added, "I've sprained my ankle."

The young man was at his side in a flash. Copper made no motion to rise, but, cross-legged under the rock, grunted, "'Ow much did old Krujer pay you for this? What was you wanted for at 'ome? Where did you desert from?"

"Khaki," said the young man, sitting down in his turn, "you are a shade better than your mates. You did not make much more noise than a yoke of oxen when you tried to come up this hill, but you are an ignorant diseased beast like the rest of your people—eh? When you were at the Ragged Schools did they teach you any history, Tommy—'istory, I mean?"

"Don't need no schoolin' to know a renegid," said Copper. He had made three yards down the hill—out of sight, unless they could see through rocks, of the enemy's smoking-party.

The young man laughed, and tossed the soldier a black sweating stick of "True Affection". (Private Copper had not smoked a pipe for three weeks.)

"*You* don't get this—eh?" said the young man. "*We* do. We take it from the trains as we want it. You can keep the cake—you po-ah Tommee." Copper rammed the good stuff into his long-cold pipe and puffed luxuriously. Two years ago the sister of gunner-guard De Souza, East India Railway, had, at a dance given by the sergeants to the Allahabad Railway Volunteers, informed Copper that she could not think of waltzing with "a poo-ah Tommee". Private Copper wondered why that memory should have returned at this hour.

"I'm going to waste a little trouble on you before I send you back to your picket *quite* naked—eh? Then you can say how you were overpowered by twenty of us and fired off your last round—like the men we picked up at the drift playing cards at Stryden's farm—eh? What's your name—eh?"

Private Copper thought for a moment of a faraway house-maid who might still, if the local postman had not gone too far, be interested in his fate. On the other hand, he was, by temperament, economical of the truth. "Pennycuik," he said, "John Pennycuik."

"Thank you. Well, Mr John Pennycuik, I'm going to teach you a little 'istory, as you'd call it—eh?"

"Ow!" said Copper, stuffing his left hand in his mouth. "So long since I've smoked I've burned my 'and—an' the pipe's dropped too. No objection to my movin' down to fetch it, is there—Sir?"

"I've got you covered," said the young man graciously, and Private Copper, hopping on one leg, because of his sprain, recovered the pipe yet another three yards downhill and squatted under another rock slightly larger than the first. A roundish boulder made a pleasant rest for his captor, who sat cross-legged once more, facing Copper, his rifle across his knee, his hand on the trigger-guard.

"Well, Mr Pennycuik, as I was going to tell you. A little after you were born in your English workhouse, your kind, honourable, brave country, England, sent an English gentle-man, who could not tell a lie, to say that so long as the sun rose and the rivers ran in their courses the Transvaal would belong to England. Did you ever hear that, khaki—eh?"

"Oh no, sir," said Copper. This sentence about the sun and the rivers happened to be a very aged jest of McBride, the professional humorist of D Company, when they discussed the probable length of the war. Copper had thrown beef-tins at McBride in the grey dawn of many wet and dry camps for intoning it.

"*Of* course you would not. Now, mann, I tell you, listen." He spat aside and cleared his throat. "Because of that little promise, my father he moved into the Transvaal and bought a farm—a little place of twenty or thirty thousand acres, don't—you—know."

The tone, in spite of the sing-song cadence fighting with the laboured parody of the English drawl, was unbearably like the young Wilmington Squire's, and Copper found himself saying, "I ought to. I've 'elped burn some."

"Yes, you'll pay for that later. *And* he opened a store."

"Ho! Shopkeeper was he?"

"The kind you call 'sir' and sweep the floor for, Pennycuik
. . . You see, in those days one used to believe in the British
Government. My father did. *Then* the Transvaal wiped thee
earth with the English. They beat them six times running. You
know *thatt*—eh?"

"Isn't what we've come 'ere for."

"*But* my father (he knows better now) kept on believing in
the English. I suppose it was the pretty talk about rivers and
suns that cheated him—eh? Anyhow, he believed in his own
country. Inn his own country. *So*—you see—he was a little
startled when he found himself handed over to the Transvaal
as a prisoner of war. That's what it came to, Tommy—a
prisoner of war. You know what that is—eh? England was
too honourable and too gentlemanly to take trouble. There
were no terms made for my father."

"So 'e made 'em 'imself. Useful old bird." Private Copper
sliced up another pipeful and looked out across the wrinkled
sea of kopjes, through which came the roar of the rushing
Orange River, so unlike quiet Cuckmere.

The young man's face darkened. "I think I shall sjambok
you myself when I've quite done with you. *No*, my father
(he was a fool) made no terms for eight years—ninety-six
months—and for every day of them the Transvaal made his
life hell for my father and—his people."

"I'm glad to hear that," said the impenitent Copper.

"Are you? You can think of it when I'm taking the skin off
your back—eh? . . . My father, he lost everything—everything down to his self-respect. You don't know what *thatt*
means—eh?"

"Why?" said Copper. "I'm smokin' baccy stole by a renegid.
Why wouldn't I know?"

If it came to a flogging on that hillside there might be
a chance of reprisals. Of course, he might be marched
to the Boer camp in the next valley and there operated
upon; but Army life teaches no man to cross bridges unnec-
essarily.

"Yes, after eight years, my father, cheated by your bitch
of a country, he found out who was the upper dog in South
Africa."

"That's me," said Copper valiantly. "If it takes another 'alf-century, it's me an' the likes of me."

"You? Heaven help you! You'll be screaming at a wagon-wheel in an hour . . . Then it struck my father that he'd like to shoot the people who'd betrayed him. You—you—*you*! He told his son all about it. He told him never to trust the English. He told him to do them all the harm he could. Mann, I tell you, I don't want much telling. I was born in the Transvaal—I'm a burgher. If my father didn't love the English, by the Lord, mann, I tell you, I hate them from the bottom of my soul."

The voice quavered and ran high. Once more, for no conceivable reason, Private Copper found his inward eye turned upon Umballa cantonments of a dry dusty afternoon, when the saddle-coloured son of a local hotel-keeper came to the barracks to complain of a theft of fowls. He saw the dark face, the plover's-egg-tinted eyeballs, and the thin excited hands. Above all, he remembered the passionate, queerly-strung words. Slowly he returned to South Africa, using the very sentence his sergeant had used to the poultry-man.

"Go on with your complaint. I'm listenin'."

"Complaint! Complaint about *you*, you ox! We strip and kick your sort by thousands."

The young man rocked to and fro above the rifle, whose muzzle thus deflected itself from the pit of Private Copper's stomach. His face was dusky with rage.

"Yess, I'm a Transvaal burgher. It took us about twenty years to find out how rotten you were. *We* know and you know it now. Your Army—it is the laughing-stock of the Continent." He tapped the newspaper in his pocket. "You think you're going to win, you poor fools! Your people—your own people—your silly rotten fools of people will crawl out of it as they did after Majuba. They are beginning now. Look what your own working-classes, the diseased, lying, drinking white stuff that you come out of, are saying." He thrust the English weekly, doubled at the leading article, on Copper's knee. "See what dirty dogs your masters are. They do not even back you in your dirty work. *We* cleared the country down to Ladysmith—to Estcourt. *We* cleared the country down to Colesberg."

"Yes. We 'ad to clean up be'ind you. Messy, I call it."

"You've had to stop farm-burning because your people daren't do it. They were afraid. You daren't kill a spy. You daren't shoot a spy when you catch him in your own uniform. You daren't touch our loyall people in Cape Town! Your masters won't let you. You will feed our women and children till we are quite ready to take them back. *You* can't put your cowardly noses out of the towns you say you've occupied. *You* daren't move a convoy twenty miles. You think you've done something? You've done nothing, and you've taken a quarter of a million of men to do it! There isn't a nigger in South Africa that doesn't obey us if we lift our finger. You pay the stuff four pounds a month and they lie to you. *We* flog 'em, as I shall flog you."

He clasped his hands together and leaned forward his out-thrust chin within two feet of Copper's left or pipe hand.

"Yuss," said Copper, "it's a fair knock-out." The fist landed to a hair on the chin-point, the neck snicked like a gun-lock, and the back of the head crashed on the boulder behind.

Copper grabbed up both rifles, unshipped the cross-bandoliers, drew forth the English weekly, and picking up the lax hands, looked long and intently at the finger-nails.

"No! Not a sign of it there," he said. "'Is nails are as clean as mine—but 'e talks just like one of 'em though. And 'e's a landlord too! A landed proprietor! Shockin', I call it."

The arms began to flap with returning consciousness. Private Copper rose up and whispered: "If you open your head, I'll bash it." There was no suggestion of sprain in the flung-back left boot. "Now walk in front of me, both arms perpendicularly elevated. I'm only a third-class shot, so, if you don't object, I'll rest the muzzle of my rifle lightly but firmly on your collar-button—coverin' the serviceable vertebree. If your friends see us thus engaged, you pray—'ard."

Private and prisoner staggered downhill. No shots broke the peace of the afternoon, but once the young man checked and was sick.

"There's a lot of things I could say to you," Copper observed, at the close of the paroxysm, "but it doesn't matter. Look 'ere, you call me 'pore Tommy' again."

The prisoner hesitated.

"Oh, I ain't goin' to do anythin' *to* you. I'm reconnoiterin' on my own. Say 'pore Tommy' 'alf-a-dozen times."

The prisoner obeyed.

"*That's* what's been puzzlin' me since I 'ad the pleasure o' meetin' you," said Copper. "You ain't 'alf-caste, but you talk *chee-chee—pukka* bazar *chee-chee. Pro*ceed."

"Hullo," said the sergeant of the picket, twenty minutes later, "where did you round him up?"

"On the top o' yonder craggy mounting. There's a mob of 'em sitting round their Bibles seventeen 'undred yards (you said it was seventeen 'undred?) t'other side—an' I want some coffee." He sat down on the smoke-blackened stones by the fire.

"'Ow did you get 'im?" said McBride, professional humorist, quietly filching the English weekly from under Copper's armpit.

"On the chin—while 'e was waggin' it at me."

"What is 'e? 'Nother Colonial rebel to be 'orribly disenfranchised, or a Cape Minister, or only a loyal farmer with dynamite in both boots? Tell us all about it, Burjer!"

"You leave my prisoner alone," said Private Copper. "'E's 'ad losses an' trouble; an' it's in the family too. 'E thought I never read the papers, so 'e kindly lent me his very own *Ferrold's Weekly*—an' 'e explained it to me as patronizin' as a—as a militia subaltern doin' Railway Staff Officer. 'E's a left-over from Majuba—one of the worst kind, an' 'earin' the evidence as I did, I don't exactly blame 'im. It was this way."

To the picket Private Copper held forth for ten minutes on the life-history of his captive. Allowing for some purple patches, it was an absolutely fair rendering.

"But what I disliked was this baccy-priggin' beggar, 'oo's people, on 'is own showin', couldn't 'ave been more than thirty or forty years in the coun—on this Gawd-forsaken dust-'eap, comin' the squire over me. They're all parsons—we know *that*, but parson *an'* squire is a bit too thick for Alf Copper. Why, I caught 'im in the shameful act of tryin' to start a aristocracy on a gun an' a wagon an' a shambuk! Yes; that's what it was: a bloomin' aristocracy."

"No, it weren't," said McBride, at length, on the dirt, above the purloined weekly. "You're the aristocrat, Alf. Old *Ferrold's* givin' it you 'ot. You're the uneducated 'ireling of a cal-callous aristocracy which 'as sold itself to the 'Ebrew financeer. Meantime, Ducky"—he ran his finger down a column of assorted paragraphs—"you're slakin' your brutal instincks in furious excesses. Shriekin' women an' desolated 'omesteads is what you enjoy, Alf . . . Halloa! What's a smokin' 'ektacomb?"

"'Ere! Let's look. 'Aven't seen a proper spicy paper for a year. Good old *Ferrold's*!" Pinewood and Moppet, reservists, flung themselves on McBride's shoulders, pinning him to the ground.

"Lie over your own bloomin' side of the bed, an' we can all look," he protested.

"They're only po-ah Tommies," said Copper, apologetically, to the prisoner. "Po-ah unedicated khakis. *They* don't know what they're fightin' for. They're lookin' for what the diseased, lying, drinkin' white stuff that they come from is sayin' about 'em!"

The prisoner set down his tin of coffee and stared helplessly round the circle.

"I—I don't understand them."

The Canadian sergeant, picking his teeth with a thorn, nodded sympathetically.

"If it comes to that, *we* don't in my country! . . . Say, boys, when you're through with your English mail you might's well provide an escort for your prisoner. He's waitin'."

"'Arf a mo', sergeant," said McBride, still reading. "'Ere's Old Barbarity on the ramp again with some of 'is lady friends, 'oo don't like concentration camps. Wish they'd visit ours. Pinewood's a married man. 'E'd know how to be'ave!"

"Well, I ain't goin' to amuse my prisoner alone. 'E's gettin' 'omesick," cried Copper. "One of you thieves read out what's vexin' Old Barbarity an' 'is 'arem these days. You'd better listen, Burjer, because, afterwards, I'm goin' to fall out an' perpetrate those nameless barbarities all over you to keep up the reputation of the British Army."

From that English weekly, to bar out which a large and

perspiring staff of Press censors toiled seven days of the week at Cape Town, did Pinewood of the Reserve read unctuously excerpts of the speeches of the accredited leaders of His Majesty's Opposition. The night-picket arrived in the middle of it, but stayed entranced without paying any compliments, till Pinewood had entirely finished the leading article, and several occasional notes.

"Gentlemen of the jury," said Alf Copper hitching up what war had left to him of trousers—"you've 'eard what 'e's been fed with. *Do* you blame the beggar? . . . 'Cause I don't! . . . Leave 'im alone, McBride. 'E's my first and only cap-ture, an' I'm goin' to walk 'ome with 'im, ain't I, Ducky! . . . Fall in, Burjer. It's Bermuda, or Umballa, or Ceylon for you—and I'd give a month's pay to be in your little shoes."

As not infrequently happens, the actual moving off the ground broke the prisoner's nerve. He stared at the tinted hills round him, gasped and began to struggle—kicking, swearing, weeping, and fluttering all together.

"Pore beggar—oh, pore, *pore* beggar!" said Alf, leaning in on one side of him, while Pinewood blocked him on the other.

"Let me go! Let me go! Mann, I tell you, let me go—"

"'E screams like a woman!" said McBride. "They'll 'ear 'im five miles off."

"There's one or two ought to 'ear 'im—in England," said Copper, putting aside a wildly waving arm.

"Married, ain't 'e?" said Pinewood. "I've seen 'em go like this before—just at the last. '*Old* on, old man. No one's goin' to 'urt you."

The last of the sun threw the enormous shadow of a kopje over the little, anxious, wriggling group.

"Quit that," said the sergeant of a sudden. "You're only making him worse. Hands *up*, prisoner! Now you get a holt of yourself, or this'll go off."

And indeed the revolver-barrel square at the man's panting chest seemed to act like a tonic; he choked, recovered himself, and fell in between Copper and Pinewood.

As the picket neared the camp it broke into song that was heard among the officers' tents:—

"'E sent us 'is blessin' from London town
  (The beggar that kep' the cordite down)?
But what do we care if 'e smile or frown,
  The beggar that kep' the cordite down?
The mildly nefarious,
Wildly barbarious
  Beggar that kep' the cordite down!"

Said a captain a mile away: "Why are they singing *that*? We haven't had a mail for a month, have we?"

An hour later the same captain said to his servant: "Jenkins, I understand the picket have got a—got a newspaper off a prisoner to-day. I wish you could lay hands on it, Jenkins. Copy of the *Times*, I think."

"Yes, sir. Copy of the *Times*, sir," said Jenkins, without a quiver, and went forth to make his own arrangements.

"Copy of the *Times*?" said the blameless Alf, from beneath his blanket. "I ain't a member of the Soldiers' Institoot. Go an' look in the Reg'mental Readin'-room—Veldt Row, Kopje Street, second turnin' to the left between 'ere an' Naauwport."

Jenkins summarized briefly in a tense whisper the thing that Alf Cooper need not be.

"But my particular copy of the *Times* is specially pro'ibited by the censor from corruptin' the morals of the Army. Get a written order from K. o' K., properly countersigned, an' I'll think about it."

"I've got all *you* want," said Jenkins. "'Urry up. I want to 'ave a squint myself."

Something gurgled in the darkness, and Private Copper fell back smacking his lips.

"Gawd bless my prisoner, and make me a good boy. Amen. 'Ere you are, Jenkins. It's dirt cheap at a tot."

SIEGFRIED SASSOON
Memoir of an Infantry Officer

The English poet and writer Siegfried Lorraine Sassoon (1886–1967) was born to a wealthy family, and lived the life of a country gentleman before joining the Royal Welch Fusiliers in the trenches of WWI. He reached the rank of Captain and was awarded the Military Cross for heroism. In 1917 he sent a letter to the military authorities openly declaring his refusal to fight. Unexpectedly, he was not courtmartialled, and friends persuaded him to rejoin his regiment.

The following selection is from Sassoon's famous volume of fictionalised war autobiography, Memoirs of an Infantry Officer *(1930), part of his trilogy* The Complete Memoirs of George Sherston *(1937).*

T HERE WASN'T MUCH WIRE IN front of Quadrangle Trench. I entered it at a strong point on the extreme left and found three officers sitting on the fire-step with hunched shoulders and glum unenterprising faces. Two others had gone away wounded. I was told that Edmunds, the Battalion Observation Officer, had gone down to explain the situation to Kinjack; we were in touch with the Northumberland Fusiliers on our left. Nevertheless I felt that there must be something to be done. Exploring to the right I found young Fernby, whose demeanour was a contrast to the apathetic trio in the sand-bagged strong-point. Fernby had only been out from England a few weeks but he appeared quite at home in his new surroundings. His face showed that he was exulting in the fact that he didn't feel afraid. He told me that no one knew what had happened on our right; the Royal Irish were believed to have failed. We went along the trench which was less than waist deep. The Germans had evidently been digging when we attacked, and had left their packs and other equipment ranged along the reverse edge of the trench. I stared about me; the smoke-drifted twilight was alive with intense movement, and there was a wild strangeness in the scene which somehow excited me. Our men seemed a bit out of hand and I couldn't see any of the responsible N.C.O.s; some of the troops were firing excitedly at the Wood; others were rummaging in the German packs. Fernby said that we were being sniped from the trees on both sides. Mametz Wood was a menacing wall of gloom, and now an outburst of rapid thudding explosions began from that direction. There was a sap from the Quadrangle to the Wood, and along this the Germans were bombing. In all this confusion I formed the obvious notion that we ought to be deepening the trench. Daylight would be on us at once, and we were along a slope exposed to enfilade fire from the Wood. I told Fernby to make the men dig for all they were worth, and went to the right with Kendle. The Germans had left a lot of shovels, but we were making no use of them. Two tough-looking privates were disputing the ownership of a pair of field-glasses, so I pulled out my pistol and urged them, with ferocious objurations, to chuck all that fooling and dig. I seemed to be getting pretty handy with my pistol, I thought, for the conditions in Quadrangle Trench were giving me a sort of angry impetus. In some places it was only a foot deep, and already men were lying wounded and killed by sniping. There were high-booted German bodies, too, and in the blear beginning of daylight they seemed as much the victims of a catastrophe as the men who had attacked them. As I stepped over one of the Germans an impulse made me lift him up from the miserable ditch. Propped against the bank, his blond face was undisfigured, except by the mud which I wiped from his eyes and mouth with my coat sleeve. He'd evidently been killed while digging, for his tunic was knotted loosely about his shoulders. He didn't look to be more than eighteen. Hoisting him a little higher, I thought what a gentle face he had, and remembered that this was the first time I'd ever touched one of our enemies with my hands. Perhaps I had some dim sense of the futility which had put an end to this good-looking youth. Anyhow I hadn't expected the Battle of the Somme to be quite like this . . . Kendle, who had been trying to do something for a badly wounded man, now rejoined me, and we continued, mostly on all fours, along the dwindling trench. We passed no one until we came to a bombing post—three serious-minded men who said that no one had been further than that yet. Being in an exploring frame of mind, I took a bag of bombs and crawled another sixty or seventy yards with Kendle close behind me. The trench became a shallow groove and ended where the ground overlooked a little valley along which there was a light railway line. We stared across at the Wood. From the other side of the valley came an occasional rifle-shot, and a helmet bobbed up for a moment. Kendle remarked that from that point anyone could see into the whole of our trench on the slope behind us. I said we must have our strong-post here and told him to go back for the bombers and a Lewis gun. I felt adventurous and it seemed as if Kendle and I were having great fun together. Kendle thought so too. The helmet bobbed up again. "I'll just have a shot at him," he said, wriggling away from the crumbling bank which gave us cover. At this moment Fernby appeared with two men and a Lewis gun. Kendle was half kneeling against some broken ground; I remember seeing him push his tin hat back from his forehead and then raise himself a few inches to take aim. After firing once he looked at us with a lively smile; a second later he fell sideways. A blotchy mark showed where the bullet had hit him just above the eyes.

The circumstances being what they were, I had no justification for feeling either shocked or astonished by the sudden extinction of Lance-Corporal Kendle. But after blank awareness that he was killed, all feelings tightened and contracted to a single intention—to "settle that sniper" on the other side of the valley. If I had stopped to think, I shouldn't have gone at all. As it was, I discarded my tin hat and equipment, slung a bag of bombs across my shoulder, abruptly informed Fernby that I was going to find out who *was* there, and set off at a downhill double. While I was running I pulled the safety-pin out of a Mills' bomb; my right hand being loaded, I did the same for my left. I mention this because I was obliged to extract the second safety-pin with my teeth, and the grating sensation reminded me that I was half way across and not so reckless as I had been when I started. I was even a little out of breath as I trotted up the opposite slope. Just before I arrived at the top I slowed up and threw my two bombs. Then I rushed at the bark, vaguely expecting some sort of scuffle with my imagined enemy. I had lost my temper with the man who had shot Kendle; quite unexpectedly, I found myself looking down into a well-conducted trench with a great many Germans in it. Fortunately for me, they were already retreating. It had not occurred to them that they were being attacked by a single fool; and Fernby, with presence of mind which probably saved me, had covered my advance by traversing the top of the trench with his Lewis gun. I slung a few more bombs, but they fell short of the clumsy field-grey figures, some of whom half turned to fire their rifles over the left shoulder as they ran across the open toward the wood, while a crowd of jostling helmets vanished along the trench. Idiotically elated, I stood there with my finger in my right ear and emitted a series of "view-holloas" (a gesture which ought to win the approval of people who still regard war as a form of outdoor sport). Having thus failed to commit suicide, I proceeded to occupy the trench—that is to say, I sat down on the fire-step, very much out of breath, and hoped to God the Germans wouldn't come back again.

The trench was deep and roomy, with a fine view of our men in the Quadrangle, but I had no idea what to do now I had got possession of it. The word "consolidation" passed through my mind; but I couldn't consolidate by myself. Naturally, I didn't under-estimate the magnitude of my achievement in capturing the trench on which the Royal Irish had made a frontal attack in the dark. Nevertheless, although still unable to see that my success was only a lucky accident, I felt a bit queer in my solitude, so I reinforced my courage by counting the sets of equipment which had been left behind. There were between forty and fifty packs, tidily arranged in a row—a fact which I often mentioned (quite casually) when describing my exploit afterwards. There was the doorway of a dug-out, but I only peered in at it, feeling safer above ground. Then, with apprehensive caution, I explored about half way to the Wood without finding any dead bodies. Apparently no one was any the worse for my little bombing demonstration. Perhaps I was disappointed by this, though the discovery of a dead or wounded enemy might have caused a revival of humane emotion. Returning to the sniping post at the end of the trench I meditated for a few minutes, somewhat like a boy who has caught a fish too big to carry home (if such an improbable event has ever happened). Finally I took a deep breath and ran headlong back by the way I'd come.

Little Fernby's anxious face awaited me, and I flopped down beside him with an outburst of hysterical laughter. When he'd heard my story he asked whether we oughtn't to send a party across to occupy the trench, but I said that the Germans would be bound to come back quite soon. Moreover my rapid return had attracted the attention of a machine-gun which was now firing angrily along the valley from a position in front of the Wood. In my excitement I had forgotten about Kendle. The sight of his body gave me a bit of a shock. His face had gone a bluish colour; I told one of the bombers to cover it with something. Then I put on my web-equipment and its attachments, took a pull at my water-bottle, for my mouth had become suddenly intolerably dry, and set off on my return journey, leaving Fernby to look after the bombing post. It was now six o'clock in the morning, and a weary business it is, to be remembering and writing it down. There was nothing likeable about the Quadrangle, though it was comfortable, from what I have heard, compared with the hell which it became a few days afterwards. Alternately crouching and crawling, I worked my way back. I passed the young German whose body I had rescued from disfigurement a couple of hours before. He was down in the mud again and someone had trodden on his face. It disheartened me to see him, though his body had now lost all touch with life and was part of the wastage of the war. He and Kendle had cancelled one another out in the process called "attrition of man-power." Further along I found one of our men dying slowly with a hole in his forehead. His eyes were open and he breathed with a horrible snoring sound. Close by him knelt two of his former mates; one of them was hacking at the ground with an entrenching tool while the other scooped the earth out of the trench with his hands. They weren't worrying about souvenirs now.

Disregarding a written order from Barton, telling me to return, I remained up in Quadrangle Trench all the morning. The enemy made a few attempts to bomb their way up the sap from the Wood and in that restricted area I continued to expend energy which was a result of strained nerves, I mention this because, as the day went on, I definitely wanted to kill someone at close quarters. If this meant that I was really becoming a good "fighting man," I can only suggest that, as a human being, I was both exhausted and exasperated. My courage was of the cock-fighting kind. Cock-fighting is illegal in England, but in July, 1916 the man who could boast that he'd killed a German in the Battle of the Somme would have been patted on the back by a bishop in a hospital ward.

German stick-bombs were easy to avoid; they took eight seconds to explode, and the throwers didn't hang on to them many seconds after pulling the string. Anyhow, my feverish performances were concluded by a peremptory message from Battalion H.Q. and I went down to Bottom Wood by a half-dug communication trench whose existence I have only this moment remembered (which shows how difficult it is to recover the details of war experience).

It was nearly two o'clock, and the daylight was devoid of mystery when I arrived at Kinjack's headquarters. The circumstances now made it permissible for me to feel tired and hungry, but for the moment I rather expected congratulations. My expectation was an error. Kinjack sat glowering in a surface dug-out in a sand-pit at the edge of Bottom Wood. I went in from the sunlight. The overworked Adjutant eyed me sadly from a corner of an ammunition box table covered with a grey blanket, and the Colonel's face caused me to feel like a newly captured prisoner. Angrily he asked why I hadn't come back with my company bombers in the early morning. I said I'd stayed up there to see what was happening. Why hadn't I consolidated Wood Trench? Why the hell hadn't I sent back a message to let him know that it had been occupied? I made

no attempt to answer these conundrums. Obviously I'd made
a mess of the whole affair. The Corps Artillery bombardment
had been held up for three hours because Kinjack couldn't
report that "my patrol" had returned to Quadrangle Trench,
and altogether he couldn't be blamed for feeling annoyed with
me, especially as he'd been ticked off over the telephone by
the Brigadier (in Morse Code dots and dashes, I suppose). I
looked at him with a sulky grin, and went along to Barton with
a splitting headache and a notion that I ought to be thankful
that I was back at all.

HENRI BARBUSSE
Bombardment

Henri Barbusse (1873–1935) was born in Asnieres, France. Although aged 41 and in poor health, he volunteered at the start of the 1914–18 War, serving on the front line in northern France until 1916. This time was the inspiration for his masterpiece, Le Feu (Under Fire), *published in 1916, one of the most influential war books. It was awarded the* Prix Goncourt. *He later settled in the USSR.*

The extract below is from Under Fire.

W E ARE IN THE FLAT COUNTRY, a vast mistiness, but above it is dark blue. The end of the night is marked by a little falling snow which powders our shoulders and the folds in our sleeves. We are marching in fours, hooded. We seem in the turbid twilight to be the wandering survivors of one Northern district who are trekking to another.

We have followed a road and have crossed the ruins of Ablain-Saint-Nazaire. We have had confused glimpses of its whitish heaps of houses and the dim spider-webs of its suspended roofs. The village is so long that although full night buried us in it we saw its last buildings beginning to pale in the frost of dawn. Through the grating of a cellar on the edge of this petrified ocean's waves, we made out the fire kept going by the custodians of the dead town. We have paddled in swampy fields, lost ourselves in silent places where the mud seized us by the feet, we have dubiously regained our balance and our bearings again on another road, the one which leads from Carency to Souchez. The tall bordering poplars are shivered and their trunks mangled; in one place the road is an enormous colonnade of trees destroyed. Then, marching with us on both sides, we see through the shadows ghostly dwarfs of trees, wide-cloven like spreading palms; botched and jumbled into round blocks or long strips; doubled upon themselves, as if they knelt. From time to time our march is disordered and jostled by the yielding of a swamp. The road becomes a marsh which we cross on our heels, while our feet make the sound of sculling. Planks have been laid in it here and there. Where they have so far sunk in the mud as to proffer their edges to us we slip on them. Sometimes there is enough water to float them, and then under the weight of a man they splash and go under, and the man stumbles or falls, with frenzied imprecations.

It must be five o'clock. The stark and affrighting scene unfolds itself to our eyes, but it is still encircled by a great fantastic ring of mist and of darkness. We go on and on without pause, and come to a place where we can make out a dark hillock, at the foot of which there seems to be some lively movement of human beings.

"Advance by twos," says the leader of the detachment. "Let each team of two take alternately a plank and a hurdle." We load ourselves up. One of the two in each couple assumes the rifle of his partner as well as his own. The other with difficulty shifts and pulls out from the pile a long plank, muddy and slippery, which weighs full eighty pounds, or a hurdle of leafy branches as big as a door, which he can only just keep on his back as he bends forward with his hands aloft and grips its edges.

We resume our march, very slowly and very ponderously, scattered over the now greying road, with complaints and heavy curses which the effort strangles in our throats. After about a hundred yards, the two men of each team exchange loads, so that after two hundred yards, in spite of the bitter blenching breeze of early morning, all but the non-coms. are running with sweat.

Suddenly a vivid star expands down yonder in the uncertain direction that we are taking—a rocket. Widely it lights a part of the sky with its milky nimbus, blots out the stars, and then falls gracefully, fairy-like.

There is a swift light opposite us over there; a flash and a detonation. It is a shell! By the flat reflection that the explosion instantaneously spreads over the lower sky we see a ridge clearly outlined in front of us from east to west, perhaps half a mile away.

That ridge is ours—so much of it as we can see from here and up to the top of it, where our troops are. On the other slope, a hundred yards from our first line, is the first German line. The shell fell on the summit, in our lines; it is the others who are firing. Another shell; another and yet another plant trees of faintly violet light on the top of the rise, and each of them dully illumines the whole of the horizon.

Soon there is a sparkling of brilliant stars and a sudden jungle of fiery plumes on the hill; and a fairy mirage of blue and white hangs lightly before our eyes in the full gulf of night.

Those among us who must devote the whole buttressed power of their arms and legs to prevent their greasy loads from sliding off their backs and to prevent themselves from sliding to the ground, these neither see nor hear anything. The others, sniffing and shivering with cold, wiping their noses with limp and sodden handkerchiefs, watch and remark, cursing the obstacles in the way with fragments of profanity. "It's like watching fireworks," they say.

And to complete the illusion of a great operatic scene, fairy-like but sinister, before which our bent and black party crawls and splashes, behold a red star, and then a green; then a sheaf of red fire, very much tardier. In our ranks, as the available half of our pairs of eyes watch the display, we cannot help murmuring in idle tones of popular admiration, "Ah, a red one!"—"Look, a green one!" It is the Germans who are sending up signals, and our men as well who are asking for artillery support.

Our road turns and climbs again as the day at last decides to appear. Everything looks dirty. A layer of stickiness, pearl-grey and white, covers the road, and around it the real world makes a mournful appearance. Behind us we leave ruined Souchez, whose houses are only flat heaps of rubbish and her trees but humps of bramble-like slivers. We plunge into a hole on our left, the entrance to the communication trench. We let our loads fall in a circular enclosure prepared for them, and both hot and frozen we settle in the trench and wait, our hands abraded, wet, and stiff with cramp.

Buried in our holes up to the chin, our chests heaving against the solid bulk of the ground that protects us, we watch the dazzling and deepening drama develop. The bombardment is redoubled. The trees of light on the ridge have melted into hazy parachutes in the pallor of dawn, sickly heads of Medusæ with points of fire; then, more sharply defined as the day expands, they become bunches of smoke-feathers, ostrich feathers white and grey, which come suddenly to life on the jumbled and melancholy soil of Hill 119, five or six hundred yards in front of us, and then slowly fade away. They are truly the pillar of fire and the pillar of cloud, circling as one and thundering together. On the flank of the hill we see a party of men running to earth. One by one they disappear, swallowed up in the adjoining anthills.

Now, one can better make out the form of our "guests." At each shot a tuft of sulphurous white underlined in black forms sixty yards up in the air, unfolds and mottles itself, and we catch in the explosion the whistling of the charge of bullets that the yellow cloud hurls angrily to the ground. It bursts in sixfold squalls, one after another—bang, bang, bang, bang, bang, bang. It is the 77 mm. gun.

We disdain the 77 mm. shrapnel, in spite of the fact that Blesbois was killed by one of them three days ago. They nearly always burst too high. Barque explains it to us, although we know it well: "Your chamber-pot protects your nut well enough against the bullets. So they can destroy your shoulder and damn well knock you down, but they don't spread you about. Naturally, you've got to be fly, all the same. Got to be careful you don't lift your neb in the air as long as they're buzzing about, nor put your hand out to see if it's raining. Now, our 75 mm.——"

"There aren't only the 77's," Mesnil André broke in, "there's all damned sorts. Spell *those* out for me——" *Those* are shrill and cutting whistles, trembling or rattling; and clouds of all shapes gather on the slopes yonder whose vastness shows through them, slopes where our men are in the depths of the dug-outs. Gigantic plumes of faint fire mingle with huge tassels of steam, tufts that throw out straight filaments, smoky feathers that expand as they fall—quite white or greenish-grey, black or copper with gleams of gold, or as if blotched with ink.

The two last explosions are quite near. Above the battered ground they take shape like vast balls of black and tawny dust; and as they deploy and leisurely depart at the wind's will, having finished their task, they have the outline of fabled dragons.

Our line of faces on the level of the ground turns that way, and we follow them with our eyes from the bottom of the trench in the middle of this country peopled by blazing and ferocious apparitions, these fields that the sky has crushed.

"Those, they're the 150 mm. howitzers."—"They're the 210's, calf-head."—"They're firing percussion, too; the hogs! Look at that one!" It was a shell that burst on the ground and threw up earth and debris in a fan-shaped cloud of darkness. Across the cloven land it looked like the frightful spitting of some volcano, piled up in the bowels of the earth.

A diabolical uproar surrounds us. We are conscious of a sustained crescendo, an incessant multiplication of the universal frenzy. A hurricane of hoarse and hollow banging, of raging clamour, of piercing and beast-like screams, fastens furiously with tatters of smoke upon the earth where we are buried up to our necks, and the wind of the shells seems to set it heaving and pitching.

"Look at that," bawls Barque, "and me that said they were short of munitions!"

"Oh, la, la! We know all about that! That and the other fudge the newspapers squirt all over us!"

A dull crackle makes itself audible amidst the babel of noise. That slow rattle is of all the sounds of war the one that most quickens the heart.

"The coffee-mill! One of ours, listen. The shots come regularly, while the Boches' haven't got the same length of time between the shots; they go crack—crack-crack-crack—crack-crack—crack——"

"Don't cod yourself, crack-pate; it isn't an unsewing-machine at all; it's a motor-cycle on the road to 31 dug-out, away yonder."

"Well, *I* think it's a chap up aloft there, having a look round from his broomstick," chuckles Pépin, as he raises his nose and sweeps the firmament in search of an aeroplane.

A discussion arises, but one cannot say what the noise is,

and that's all. One tries in vain to become familiar with all those diverse disturbances. It even happened the other day in the wood that a whole section mistook for the hoarse howl of a shell the first notes of a neighbouring mule as he began his whinnying bray.

"I say, there's a good show of sausages in the air this morning," says Lamuse. Lifting our eyes, we count them.

"There are eight sausages on our side and eight on the Boches'," says Cocon, who has already counted them.

There are, in fact, at regular intervals along the horizon, opposite the distance-dwindled group of captive enemy ballons, the eight long hovering eyes of the army, buoyant and sensitive, and joined to the various headquarters by living threads.

"They see us as we see them. How the devil can one escape from that row of God Almighties up there?"

There's our reply!

Suddenly, behind our backs, there bursts the sharp and deafening stridor of the 75's. Their increasing crackling thunder arouses and elates us. We shout with our guns, and look at each other without hearing our shouts—except for the curiously piercing voice that comes from Barque's great mouth—amid the rolling of that fantastic drum whose every note is the report of a cannon.

Then we turn our eyes ahead and outstretch our necks, and on the top of the hill we see the still higher silhouette of a row of black infernal trees whose terrible roots are striking down into the invisible slope where the enemy cowers.

While the "75" battery continues its barking a hundred yards behind us—the sharp anvil-blows of a huge hammer, followed by a dizzy scream of force and fury—a gigantic gurgling dominates the devilish oratorio; that, also, is coming from our side. "It's a gran'pa, that one!"

The shell cleaves the air at perhaps a thousand yards above us; the voice of its gun covers all as with a pavilion of resonance. The sound of its travel is sluggish, and one divines a projectile bigger-bowelled, more enormous than the others. We can hear it passing and declining in front with the ponderous and increasing vibration of a train that enters a station under brakes; then, its heavy whine sounds fainter.

We watch the hill opposite, and after several seconds it is covered by a salmon-pink cloud that the wind spreads over one-half of the horizon. "It's a 220 mm."

"One can see them," declares Volpatte, "those shells, when they come out of the gun. If you're in the right line, you can even see them a good long way from the gun."

Another follows: "There! Look, look! Did you see that one? You didn't look quick enough, you missed it. Get a move on! Look, another! Did you see it?"

"I did not see it."—"Ass! Got to be a bedstead for you to see it! Look, quick, that one, there! Did you see it, unlucky good-for-nothing?"—"I saw it; is that all?"

Some have made out a small black object, slender and pointed as a blackbird with folded wings, pricking a wide curve down from the zenith.

"That weighs 240 lb., that one, my old bug," says Volpatte proudly, "and when that drops on a funk-hole it kills everybody inside it. Those that aren't picked off by the explosion are struck dead by the wind of it, or they're gas-poisoned before they can say 'ouf!'"

"The 270 mm. shell can be seen very well, too—talk about a bit of iron—when the howitzer sends it up—hop it, off you go!"

"And the 155 Rimailho, too; but you can't see that one because it goes too straight and too far; the more you look for it the more it vanishes before your eyes."

In a stench of sulphur and black powder, of burned stuffs and calcined earth which roams in sheets about the country, all the menagerie is let loose and gives battle. Bellowings, roarings, growlings, strange and savage; feline caterwaulings that fiercely rend your ears and search your belly, or the long-drawn piercing hoot like the siren of a ship in distress. At times, even, something like shouts cross each other in the air-currents, with curious variation of tone that make the sound human. The country is bodily lifted in places and falls back again. From one end of the horizon to the other it seems to us that the earth itself is raging with storm and tempest.

EDWARD CREBBIN ("SEA-WRACK") Webster

*Edward Horace Crebbin (1889–1964) was
a prolific author of naval fiction, mostly
written under the pseudonym "Sea-Wrack".
His books include* McInnes of the ND
(1941) and the short story collections
Six Bells *(1942) and* Random Soundings *(1945).*

*The short story "Webster" was origi-
nally published as "Seascape: Morning
off Lerwick" in the collection* Sea Trails
(1931).

WHEN PEOPLE TALK ABOUT COURAGE—I always think
of Webster. Yet I shall never forget my complete
bewilderment when first we met, for by some strange chance
Webster was drafted to our destroyer as an officer's steward.

He arrived when we were boiler-cleaning alongside the old
depot-ship, and when I went up on deck to inspect him, hoping
against hope that there would be awaiting me a smart young
steward who could and would stand up to destroyer life, I was
horrified to find myself confronting a distinguished-looking,
elderly gentleman of about fifty.

I groaned. There must have been some mistake. This dear
old boy, whom I should have expected to encounter in Bond
Street, wearing a silk hat, was so very obviously miscast for the
rôle of steward in a destroyer. How on earth the drafting office
had come to make such a mistake was immaterial. Webster
had arrived. Moreover, I soon discovered that he had never
been to sea before—let alone in a destroyer. I groaned again. It

looked to me like pure homicide. Officially, he was R.N.V.R., but, actually, he was a distinguished artist with four pictures in the Paris salon.

I sought out the Captain, and my only consolation was the expression on *his* face when he, himself, sighted Webster.

But we were all wonderfully, marvellously, hopelessly wrong.

For the days passed into weeks, and the weeks into months, and Webster was still with us. Moreover, incredibly and amazingly he had turned out to be the kind of steward that morose first lieutenants of destroyers dream of, and ponder on, at sea, while jammed in between the empty mess-stove and a handy bulkhead, eating ice-cold sardines out of the tin in lieu of a hot breakfast which is not available because the decks are not safe for traffic.

Other boats in the flotilla cast envious and covetous eyes at Webster. Gradually, his fame spread. He performed incredible feats in collaboration with the cook, for he brought to his novel job a first-class intelligence and the enthusiasm of an artist; and, strangely enough, he was as popular with the cook in the galley for'ard as he was with the hands in the fo'c'sle mess decks.

We ourselves, I think, offered up a prayer every time we met that distinguished, spruce figure reeling along the sea-infested upper deck, where the wet corticine offered but precarious foothold. Yet, somehow, when Webster glanced benignly, but with something of disapproval, at the tempestuous waves, the weather seemed to moderate at once. His innocence of all forms of sea-life, and his dignity, were stupendous. And in steady, never-failing stream all the while at sea, hot meals flowed aft, punctual, appetizing, and perfectly served: and they came *via* a ward-room pantry which gleamed and shone in a cleanliness akin to that of the Captain's quarters in a crack battleship.

And the peculiar thing about it all was that Webster, the landsman, who had never been to sea, was never seasick.

As time went on, we found ourselves glancing furtively at one another. Webster was too good to be true. He would blow up. The ship would blow up. Something would happen, and our incomparable steward would disappear, wafted away to some higher plane; for were sea-going mortals ever favoured

July 1996 33

like this without some frightful disaster suddenly shattering
their Utopian comfort?

Then, one day, we were ordered to Lerwick, in the Shetland
Isles. Up there things had been happening: two destroyers had
been lost escorting the Norwegian convoy, but we did several
trips without incident, until . . .

One fine, misty morning we were returning to harbour after
a sticky ten days at sea, when I woke up suddenly in my bunk,
knowing immediately that something was wrong. My head
was buzzing, for I had had the middle watch from twelve to
four, and also, the cabin-flat atmosphere was foul. Glancing
at my watch I saw that we should be close to harbour. The
engines had stopped—it was that that had awakened me.

In a moment I was up on deck, shivering. I glanced for'ard
and then round the mist-laden sea. It was just getting light. A
voice hailed me from the bridge. Quickly I walked out to the
port side. It was the Captain. He said quietly:

"Stay there, No. 1. There's a big mine bumping down the
port side and another one against the starboard hull abreast
the after torpedo-tubes."

My blood ran cold. I peered along the port side.

There it was! A huge, spherical mass, bump, bumping, with
a hollow sound against our frail plates. Unconsciously I noted
the three detonator horns: they looked devilish somehow, and
prehistoric in the half-light, set there like eyes on stalks on that
rusty, bloated body. I didn't trouble to walk over and look at
the starboard mine. I took the "owner's" word for it.

And then a voice, close by, spoke; and I jumped nearly out
of my skin.

"Nasty things, sir," said Webster from the ward-room
hatch; and I think he was carrying in his hands a pot of
tea. But at the moment I was too concerned to reply.

As I stood there on the tiny quarter deck of the destroyer,
not much more than eighteen feet across just there, it struck
me suddenly that the surgeon-probationer was still in his
hammock below.

Webster advanced cautiously from the ward-room hatch
and came towards me. He had a habit of twirling his iron-grey
moustache, and I remember that as he came towards me he
carried the tea-pot in one hand and twirled his moustache

with the other. Silently, I indicated to him the other mine, which was now giving our starboard plates some far too hearty bumps near the third and after funnel. Webster did not drop the teapot, but he stood for a moment tense and still.

"Another, sir?" he breathed to me.

I nodded back, then I whispered to Webster:

"The surgeon-probationer is still below, I believe, Webster. Do you know?"

Webster's answer was to tiptoe back to the ward-room hatch, but first he put down carefully on the quarter deck the small tea-pot he had been carrying, and I remember noting with a kind of wonder that his hand was as steady as a rock. It was one of those ludicrous incidents that sometimes occur—providentially, perhaps—in the midst of some pressing danger, and which ease the strain.

I concentrated on that tea-pot for a moment. It seemed such a homely, friendly object, seated there so primly on the seableached corticine.

Webster only hesitated a moment at the ward-room hatch, then he skirted the canvas shelter above the Captain's quarters, and went forward to the cabin-hatch beyond. Very quietly, he disappeared down the ladder and I heard the murmur of voices; he was warning the surgeon-probationer. By then, the port-side mine was almost abreast of him—not more than fifteen feet away—and it loomed gigantic in the light of dawn, standing quite four feet out of the water.

The whole ship was strangely quiet. Under my feet the propellers were now revolving slowly; the starboard engine going ahead, the port one astern.

I looked forward and up at the bridge. I seemed to have been standing there a long time in a cold grey world filled suddenly with the most ghastly threat. The Captain was leaning over the after bridge rails and his face was set and determined; occasionally, he signalled to the sub and the signalman, standing by the engine-room telegraphs and revolution-indicator, ordering the ship's engines at slow revolutions with a concentrated, fateful caution. Faintly, the tinkle of the telegraph bells came floating aft to me. Suddenly, he called to me again:

"Stay there, No. 1," he said, "I can't get away from

that damned port-side mine—there's a current shoving it up against the hull, and if we roll——" he made a gesture of finality.

Then he added: "I can't see the starboard one very well, it's lower in the water; keep me informed of its position, and stand by because I'm going to try to bump it away—otherwise it's a thousand pounds to a rotten apple that that port-side blighter will foul the propeller-guard.

I said: "Ay, ay, sir," but when I started to move cautiously towards the starboard rail, I found my knees were strangely sagging and my feet seemed to be made of lead—and very cold lead at that. However, I got to the rail and looked over; and there was the mine, nestling under our hull, and bumping, bumping—I've never cared to hear anything bump with quite that deadly sound ever since.

The next few seconds were really unpleasant. I heard the rattle of the steering engine, as the helm went over hard a-starboard, and the deck quivered as the starboard engine-revolutions increased. The Captain was trying out his wheeze. And it worked, but that must have been the most patient, the most long-suffering German mine that ever found its way into Northern waters; for we caught it some really hearty cracks, and the last one cracked it some ten feet out from the ship's side.

I waved my hand for'ard towards the bridge, and a smile of relief came slowly over the "owner's" face. He looked about ten years older than he did the previous day.

Haltingly, I dragged my insubordinate feet back to the port side and there I was joined by Webster. He said: "The surgeon-probationer's gone for'ard, sir; there's no-one else aft."

I said: "Thank you, Webster; that's a great relief. You'd better go for'ard yourself now."

But the old paladin was horrified.

He said: "I must be near my pantry, sir. What are you all going to do for breakfast if the pantry's wrecked?"

It was a ludicrous speech, standing there together as we were literally within a plank's breadth of death, and I'm afraid I giggled weakly.

I said: "Webster, don't you realize that if that damned thing

does an extra bump or fouls the propeller-guard, you and I
and your confounded pantry will go sky-high, and we shan't
want breakfast, no, nor lunch, nor tea either, for a very, very
long time?"

"Ah, sir," said Webster, "I'm afraid you take a pessimistic
view of the situation." Then he said: "Could we not push the
mine away, sir, with a boathook?"

I replied somewhat tersely: "Do you know, Webster, what
these mines are made of? Do you realize that the detonator
underneath that little spur is composed of fulminate of mer-
cury, which patient and brave men test under armour-plate
by tickling the beastly stuff with a feather?"

But Webster had an answer to that too.

He said: "It's a chance, sir. If we can keep our boathook
away from the detonating horns, we might shove it away, don't
you think, sir?"

I thought not, and said so emphatically. But just at that
moment the Captain hailed me quietly again from the bridge.

"It's no go, No. 1," he said. "I can't get away from the
port-side mine and she's too far aft now to risk my coming
astern and letting the mine bump right for'ard. Can you
suggest anything?"

To my amazement, I heard myself answering: "Webster
and I, sir, might try pushing the thing off with a padded boathook—enough, anyhow, to prevent it fouling the
propeller-guard."

The Captain pondered, while the mist gradually dispersed,
and looking ahead, I saw a few miles away, opening up, the
harbour of Lerwick—and, oh, so fair and desirable a harbour
it seemed at that moment!

Then slowly the "owner" said: "I don't like it, but we've got
to do something. I have an idea that that port-side mine is a
nasty customer: I don't like the look of him, so for Heaven's
sake be careful."

I said fervently: "We will, sir!" Then I turned to Webster,
rather sourly, I'm afraid.

"Come on now," I said, "that bearing-out spar over there
is better than a boathook. Bring it over here, then nip
down to your pantry and bring up every dish-cloth and rag
you've got."

Hastily, when he returned, we converted the end of the spar into what looked like an enormous swab. Then, cautiously, we lifted our strange weapon and advanced to the attack; I having impressed upon my enthusiastic helper that he was on no account to push or do anything until I gave the order; and I also warned him of the vital necessity for avoiding any roll of the mine, as it was probably fitted with a rolling detonator as well as an impact one.

I can assure you that those few moments seemed to spin themselves out into years.

We began almost catastrophically, for when, very gingerly, I had placed the head of our spar against the middle of the mine and told Webster to shove, he shoved so heartily that the head of our weapon slipped on the slimy metal of the mine-casing and both he and I almost went over the side on top of it.

In a horrified voice, from the bridge, the Captain urged caution.

Sweat poured off my face as I turned and rent the old artist. Then we had another shot, this time with more success.

The mine was appallingly heavy. It must have weighed nearly a ton, but pushing and shoving with—speaking for myself—our hearts in our mouths, we eventually did manage to shove the thing out a few feet.

Then a frightful thing happened, the memory of which is vivid still. The mine suddenly whirled in, spinning vigorously like a top, towards the ship's side and, after bumping heavily, it made a beeline for the propeller-guard—as if animated by some perverse, impish spirit.

Whether caught in an eddy, or in some way still foul of its moorings, we did not stop to inquire, I yelled at Webster:

"Quick, man! we've got to bear it off before it gets there!"

Rushing aft, we shoved our spar out over the side and braced ourselves up like frantic cavemen awaiting the charge of some fearsome monster, armed only with a spear.

Luck was with us this time; for the mine, rolling in a perfectly horrible manner, thudded right on to the end of our padded spar and jarred us both to the marrow. Then, straining, sweating, we held it off and eased it carefully round the curve of the propeller-guard, which stuck out for two vital feet from the ship's side. Those were a ticklish few seconds, for the mine seemed to be doing its best to slip round the pad and crash into the propeller-guard. It was then I blessed my stars for Webster's thirteen stone or so, which he used to the full.

At last, I croaked in a hoarse voice to the steward: "She's going!" I cried to him, "we've got the darned thing clear. One last heave now!"

We gave that heave: the pad slipped. I let go with one hand and signalled frantically to the Captain. The mine rolled, span, and escaped the pad—all in one breath, but it was just too late. Surging in towards the stern, it grazed the propeller-guard and dashed towards the very curve of the sheer right aft. But, simultaneously, the propellers thrashed madly; the destroyer suddenly gathered way, leaping forward, and Webster and I, losing our balance, came down heavily in a heap on the corticine deck.

I stayed there for a moment, feeling distinctly shaky, but Webster helped me up, and then stared out over the rail astern and to the east'ard, where dawn was breaking.

I watched him, curiously. His face was now pale and his expression still and set; but he wasn't looking at the mine now bobbing twenty-five yards astern in our wake. He looked to me like a man who has seen a vision.

"Jove, sir," he murmured to me, "what a morning, what a sky! If a man painted that, people would not believe; they would laugh; but some time . . . I will try."

Then he turned to me and walked forward and picked up the tea-pot. The routine official Webster, our well-known paragon, had reappeared. "I will make you some fresh tea, sir," he said, saluting; "when you come back from the bridge it will be ready."

Years later, I met Webster again; and, strangely enough, it *was* in Bond Street and he *was* wearing a silk hat, but this time it was I who took off my hat to him.

Later still that same day, I stood in a small picture gallery where Webster had a show of his paintings.

In front of me, dominating the wall, was a large seascape, and, as I looked at it, my breath suddenly caught; for its title was *Morning off Lerwick*.

It was a lovely piece of work: just sea and sky and a wedge

of duck flying low and fast across the foreground. It reminded me of Somerscales' "Dawn". There was about that picture a wonderful sense of space and dignity and harmony.

A hand on my arm recalled me.

"Jove! I was frightened to death that morning," Webster murmured in my ear.

I looked at him in amazement.

"You were, really?" I said. "I thought you were wonderful."

"No!" he smiled at me, "not wonderful; just scared to death! You see, while I was hanging about the naval barracks—an old dodderer of fifty whom nobody knew what to do with—they gave me a three months' course on mines at the Mining School."

RICHARD ALDINGTON
At All Costs

*Richard Aldington (1892–1962) was born
Edward Godfree in Hampshire, Britain.
He joined the infantry in France in 1916,
was wounded and then invalided out of
the service with shell-shock. Out of these
experiences came the bitter, best-selling war
novel,* Death of a Hero, *in 1929. A
collection of short stories in similar vein,*
Roads to Glory, *followed in 1930. In
1939 he moved to the USA, where he
published several military biographies and
volumes of poetry.*

The short story "At All Costs" is from
Roads to Glory.

"**B**LAST!"

Captain Hanley, commanding "B" Company, stumbled
over a broken duckboard and fell forward against the side of
the trench. His tilted helmet shielded his face, but the trench
wall felt oozy and soggy to his naked hand as he tried to steady
himself.

"Mind that hole, Parker."

"Very good, sir."

He felt wet mud soaking through his breeches above the
short gum boots, and his right sleeve was wet to the elbow.
He fumbled in his gas bag, also wet with slimy mud, to see that
the mask goggles were unbroken. O.K., but he swore again
with a sort of exasperated groan over the crashing bruise on
his right knee.

"Are you 'it, sir?"

"No, I only fell in that mucking hole again. I've told the

ser'ant-major umpteen times to get it mended. One of these days the brigadier'll fall into it and then there'll be hell to pay. Help me find my torch. I hope the bloody thing isn't broken."

The two men groped in the darkness, fingering the slimy mud and tilted broken duckboards. Suddenly they crashed helmets.

"Sorry, sir."

"All right, sorry."

"Doesn't seem to be 'ere, sir."

"Never mind, we'll look for it in the morning."

They stumbled on cautiously. The trench was very deep (old German communication), very dark, very shell-smashed, very muddy. A black, heavy-clouded night, about an hour before dawn. Occasionally a strange ghostly glow appeared as a distant Very light was fired, and made for them a near dark horizon of tumbled shell-tormented parapet. The trench swerved, and Hanley dimly made out the shape of three crosses—Canadians. Halfway. Fifty yards farther on was another turn, where a piece of corrugated iron revetment had been flung onto the top of the high parapet, where its jagged outline looked like a grotesque heraldic dragon.

It had been an ideal night for gas and would be an ideal dawn—heavy, windless, foggy—for a surprise attack. Hanley had been up and about the trenches most of the night. Since that rotten gas attack on the Somme, where he lost twenty-three men, he took no risks. Up and down the trenches, warning the N.C.O.'s to look out for gas. Now he was on the way to his advance posts. Be there in case of an attack . . .

Splash, squelch, splodge. Somebody coming towards them.

"Who are you?"

"Mockery."

"Is that the word tonight, Parker?"

"Yessir."

"That you, Hanley?" Voice coming towards them.

"Hullo, Williams. I thought you were in Hurdle Alley?"

"I was, but I thought I'd have a look at these posts. They're a hell of a way from the front line."

"I know. Damn this organization in depth. Are they all right?"

"Yes. He sent over about forty minnies, Ser'ant Cramp said, but no casualties. He was flipping over some of those flying pineapples when I left."

From their own back areas came an irregular but ceaseless crashing of artillery. Heavy shells shrilled high above them as they swooped at enemy communications and night parties.

"Strafing the old Boche a good bit tonight," said Williams.

"Yes, it's been quite heavy. Might almost be a windup at H.Q."

"Boche are very quiet tonight."

"Yes: well, cheerio. Tell Thompson to keep our breakfast hot; and don't stand down until I get back."

"Right you are, cheerio."

Hanley visited his posts. They were established in a ruined and unrepaired German trench at the foot of a long forward slope. This had once been the British front line, but was now held only by scattered observation posts, with the main front line several hundred yards to the rear. The British bombardment increased, and the shrill scream of the passing shells was almost continuous. Very lights and rockets went up from the German lines. Hanley cursed the loss of his torch—damned difficult to get about without it. He came to the first post.

"You there, Ser'ant Tomlinson?"

A figure moved in the darkness.

"Yes, sir."

"Anything to report?"

"No, sir."

"Mr Williams said there were some minnies and pineapples."

"Yes, sir, but it's very quiet, sir."

"Um. Any patrols still out?"

"No, sir, all in."

"Very well. Carry on, ser'ant."

"Very good, sir."

Much the same news at the other posts. Hanley returned to Number 1 post, nearest the communication trench, at dawn. The men were standing to. Hanley got on the fire-step in a shell-smashed abandoned bay, and watched with his glasses slung round his neck. The artillery had died down to a couple of batteries, when the first perceptible lightening of the air came. Hanley felt cold in his mud-soaked breeches and tunic. Very gradually, very slowly, the darkness dissipated, as if thin imperceptible veils were being rolled up in a transformation scene. The British wire became visible. In the trembling misty light No Man's Land seemed alive with strange shapes and movements. Hanley pressed cold hands on his hot eyes, puffy with lack of sleep. He looked again. Yes, yes, surely, they were climbing over the parapet and lying down in front. He seized a rifle leaning against the trench, loaded with an S.O.S. rocket bomb. Funny Sergeant Tomlinson and the men were so silent. Perhaps he was imagining things, the same old dawn-mirage movement which had been responsible for so many false alarms. He waited a couple of minutes with closed eyes, and then looked very carefully through his glasses. Silly ass! The men coming over the parapets were the German wire pickets. He put the rifle down, glad the men had not seen him, and went round the traverse to Sergeant Tomlinson and Parker.

"Stand to for another twenty minutes, ser'ant, and then let two men from Number 2 post and two from Number 4 go and get your breakfasts."

"Very good, sir."

On the way back Hanley found his torch—the glass bulb was smashed; like most things in this bloody war, he reflected. Well, they'd passed another dawn without an attack—that was something. He got on a fire-step in the main line and took another look. A cloudy but rainless morning. Not a sign of life in the enemy trenches, scarcely a sound. He gave the order to stand down, and sent Parker to join his section for breakfast.

The company dugout was a large one, built as the headquarters of a German battalion. It was remarkably lousy. Hanley threw his torch, revolver-belt, and helmet on his wire and sacking bed, and sat down on a box beside a small table laid with four knives and forks on a newspaper. He felt tired, too tired even to enjoy the hot bacon and eggs which formed the infantry officers' best meal of the day. The three subalterns chatted. Hanley pushed away his plate and stood up.

"I'm going to turn in. Tell the signaller to wake me if anything important happens."

"Right-o."

Hanley hung up his revolver and helmet, arranged his pack as a pillow, swung himself still booted and wet onto the bed, and wrapped himself in a blanket. For a few minutes he lay drowsily, listening to the throb of blood in his head and the quiet mutter of the other officers. His eyes still ached even when shut. He drowsed, then half awoke as he remembered that he had not indented for enough ammunition, decided that could wait, and—was dead asleep.

Hanley opened his eyes and lay quite still. Why were they talking so loudly? In a flash he was wide awake and swung up, sitting with his legs over the side of the bed. The colonel. Damn! Being found asleep like that! And, of course, the colonel would not know that he had been up and down the line all night. Damn! Well, never mind. He gave one dab with both hands at his rumpled hair, and stood up.

"Good morning, sir."

"Oh, good morning, Hanley. Williams said you'd been up all night. Sorry to disturb you."

"Quite all right, sir."

A large-scale trench map of their sector was spread on the table, half concealing another smaller-scale artillery map of the whole district.

"Just sit down for a few minutes, Hanley. I've got important news."

The other officers grouped beside them, gazing at the colonel and listening.

"Very important news," the colonel went on in a slow voice, "and not particularly pleasant, I'm afraid."

He pulled a neat bundle of documents from his pocket, opened one labelled "SECRET AND CONFIDENTIAL" and spread it on the table. They all gazed at it—the inexorable decree of Fate—and then again at the colonel, the agent of that Fate, of all their fates.

"That is a confidential document from Corps Headquarters. I'll tell you briefly what it is, and you can look it over afterwards. The night before last the division on our left made an identification raid, and captured a prisoner. From this and other information it seems certain that we shall be attacked—tomorrow morning—about an hour before dawn."

Each of the four company officers drew a short imperceptible breath, glanced at each other and then quickly away. Hanley leaned his elbow on the table.

"Yes, sir?"

"It will be a surprise attack, with a very short but violent preliminary bombardment." The colonel spoke very slowly and deliberately, looking down absently at the map, and gently twisting the lowest button of his tunic with the fingers of his right hand. "All reports confirm our information, and the Air Force report great enemy activity behind the lines. You heard the bombardment of their communications last night."

"Yes, sir."

There was complete silence in the dugout, as the colonel paused. A pile of tin plates fell with a clatter in the servants' compartment. None of the officers moved. Hanley noticed how clean the colonel's gas bag was.

"There will probably be twenty to thirty German divisions in the attack, which will be on a sixteen-mile front. We are about in the middle."

"Yes, sir."

The colonel moved on his box. He stretched out all the fingers of his left hand, and tapped rapidly on the table alternately with the stretched little finger and thumb.

"The Canadian Corps and several reserve divisions are being brought up at once to occupy a position about five miles to our rear. They cannot fully man the whole battle line before three tomorrow afternoon. Our duty is to delay the enemy advance until that time or longer. Our positions must be held at all costs, to the last man."

There was a long silence. The colonel ceased drumming with his fingers and looked at them.

"Have you any questions to ask?"

"Yes, sir. Am I to leave my posts out?"

"Two hours before dawn, you will withdraw them to strengthen your own line. One section, with a sergeant and a subaltern, will remain at the end of the communication trench. The subaltern will be a volunteer. His duty is to fire a green light when the German attacking line reaches him. The artillery barrage will then shorten to defend your line. You, Hanley, will have a Very-light pistol loaded with a red light, and you will fire it when the first German jumps into your trench. The object, of course, is to inform the artillery when they must shorten the defensive barrage."

"Yes, sir."

"Any more questions?"

"No, sir, not for the moment."

"You'll arrange with your officers, Hanley, as to which shall volunteer to fire the green light."

"Very good, sir."

"And I want you to come to a conference of company officers with the brigadier at Battalion Headquarters this afternoon."

"Very good, sir. What time?"

"Oh, make it three o'clock."

"Very well, sir."

The colonel rose.

"You know your battle positions, of course; but we'll discuss that this afternoon. Oh, by the bye, I'm sending up green envelopes for everyone in the company this morning. The letters must be sent down by runner at four. Of course, not a word about the attack must be mentioned either to N.C.O.'s or men until after the letters have gone."

"Of course, sir."

"And—er—naturally you will not mention the matter yourselves."

"No, sir, of course not."

"All right. Good-bye. Will you come along with me, Hanley? I should like to walk round your main defense line with you."

"Very good, sir."

There was silence in the dugout. They could hear the colonel and Hanley scuffling up the low dugout stairs. Williams tapped a cigarette on his case and bent down to light it at the candle burning on the table. He puffed a mouthful of smoke, with a twist to his lips.

"Well, that's that. Napoo, eh?"

"Looks like it."

"What about a drink?"

"Right-o."

Williams shouted:
"Thomp-sooon."
From the distance came a muffled: "Sir?"
A Tommy appeared in the doorway.
"Bring us a bottle of whisky and the mugs."
"Very good, sir."

All that day Hanley was in a state of dazed hebetude, from which he emerged from time to time. He felt vaguely surprised that everything was so much as usual. There were sentries at their posts, runners going along the trenches, an occasional airplane overhead, a little artillery—just the ordinary routine of trench warfare. And yet within twenty-four hours their trenches would be obliterated, he and thousands with him would be dead, obliterated, unless by some chance, some odd freak, he was made prisoner. He heard repeated over and over again in his head the words: "Position must be held at all costs, position must be held at all costs." He felt suddenly angry. Held at all costs! All jolly fine and large to write from the safety of Montreuil, but what about those who had to make good such dramatic sentiments with their lives? The front was ridiculously denuded of men—why, his own under-strength company held very nearly a battalion front, and had a flank to guard as well. If they fought like madmen and stood to the last man, they might hold up three waves—an hour at most. And they were asked to hold out for nearly twelve hours! Ridiculous, good God, ridiculous!

He found the colonel shaking him by the arm.

"What's the matter with you, Hanley? You don't seem to hear what I'm saying."

"I beg your pardon, sir. I——"

"I think you ought to bring a Lewis gun up to this point. You've got an excellent field of fire here."

"Very good, sir."

Hanley noted the change to be made in his field service message book. They walked on, and the colonel made various other suggestions—so many orders—which Hanley duly noted. The colonel paused at the corner of the communication trench leading to Battalion Headquarters. He waved to the orderlies to stand apart.

"We'll discuss the general plan of defense at the conference this afternoon. Make a note of anything that occurs to you, any information you want, and bring it up."

"Right, sir."

The colonel hesitated a moment.

"It's a very difficult position, Hanley, I know, but we must all do our duty."

"Of course, sir."

"I shall lead the counter-attack of the Reserve Company myself."

"Yes, sir."

"A great deal depends on our putting up a good show."

"Yes, sir."

"I suggest you go round to the dugout and speak to all your men this evening. Put a good face on it, you know. Tell them we are all prepared, and shall easily beat off the attack, and that reinforcements are being hurried up to relieve us. And above all impress upon them that these trenches *must* be held at all costs."

"Very good, sir."

The colonel held out his hand.

"I may not have another opportunity to speak to you in private. Good-bye, and the best of luck. I know you'll do your duty."

"Thank you, sir. Good-bye."

"Good-bye."

When Hanley stooped under the low entrance of the dugout chamber, the three subalterns were seated round the table with flushed cheeks, talking loudly. The whisky bottle was more than half-empty. A sudden spurt of anger shot through him. He strode up to the table and knocked the cork level with the top of the bottle neck with one hard smack of his hand. He spoke harshly:

"What's this nonsense?"

Williams, the eldest of the three subalterns, answered, half-defiantly, half-ashamedly:

"We're only having a drink. Where's the harm?"

"Only a drink! Before lunch! Now, look here, you fellows. The whisky that's left in that bottle is all that's going to be drunk in this mess between now and dawn tomorrow. Understand? One of the damned stupidities of this damned war is that every officer thinks it's the thing to be a boozer. It isn't. The men don't drink. They get a tablespoon of rum a day. Why should we make sots of ourselves? We're responsible for their lives. See? And we're responsible for these trenches. We've got to leave 'em on stretchers or stay here and manure 'em. See? We've got a bloody rotten job ahead of us, a stinking rotten job, and I wish those who ordered it were here to carry out their own damned orders. But they're not. Not bloody likely. But the people at home trust us. We're responsible to them, first and foremost. We took on the job, and we've got to carry it out. And carry it out dead bloody sober. Got me?"

The men were silent, looking sheepishly at the newspaper on the table with its wet rings from mug bottoms. Hanley took an empty mug and tossed some of the whisky from William's mug into it.

"Drink up. Here's hell!"

They drank.

Hanley shouted:

"Thomp-soooon!"

Thompson appeared in the door.

"Take those mugs away."

"Very good, sir."

"How many bottles of whisky have you?"

"Three, sir."

"Bring them here, and a sandbag."

"Very good, sir."

Hanley scribbled a few words in his message book, and tore out the slip. He put the bottles in the sandbag.

"Parker!"

Parker in his turn appeared.

"Sir?"

"Take that sandbag down to Battalion H.Q. Give it to one of the officers, and bring back his signed receipt."

"Very good, sir."

The other officers exchanged glances. Williams, who had his back turned to Hanley, made a grimace of derision. The others frowned at him.

*　　*　　*

Hanley was busy throughout the day, making arrangements, giving orders, attending the conference—which lasted a long time—and going round to speak to the men. He only had time to write a very brief letter to his wife, enclosing one still briefer for his father. He wrote calmly, almost coldly in his effort to avoid emotion and self-pity. He even managed to squeeze out a joke for each letter. As soon as they were finished the two letters vanished in the open sandbag containing the company mail, and the runner started at once for Headquarters. Somehow it was a relief to have those letters gone. The last links with England, with life, were broken. Finished, done with, almost forgotten. It was easier to carry on now.

But was it? There was that damned business of the volunteer subaltern. Hanley rubbed his clenched fist against his cheek, and found that he had forgotten to shave. He called his servant and told him to bring some hot water in a cigarette tin. Shaving for the last time. Hardly worth it, really. Still, must be done. Morale, and all that.

He shaved carefully. One of the subalterns went out to relieve the officer on duty. One was asleep. Williams was writing a situation report. Hanley bit the back of his hand hard, then shoved both hands in his breeches pockets, looking at William's bent head.

"Williams!"

Williams looked up.

"Yes?"

"There's this business of the volunteer to——"

"Oh, that's all settled."

"Settled!"

"Yes. I'm going."

"You're going! But you've only been married two months."

"Yes. That's why I thought I'd like to get it over as quickly as possible."

"But I was going to put your platoon at the end of Hurdle Alley. You might just be able to get back to battalion, you know."

"And feel a swine for the rest of my life—which would be about two hours? Thanks. No, I'd rather get it over, if you don't mind, Hanley."

"Oh, all right."

They were silent. Then Hanley said:

"Well, I'll just go and talk to the men . . . er . . . So long."

"So long."

All working parties were cancelled to give the men as much rest as possible, but there was inevitably a lot of extra work, bringing up ammunition, rations, and water. As soon as dusk fell the whole Reserve Company and some pioneers came up to strengthen the wire. The British artillery was ceaselessly active. Hardly a shot came from the German lines—an ominous sign.

After dinner Hanley lay down to sleep for a few hours. Must be as fresh as possible. He wrapped the blanket up to his chin and shut his eyes. The other three off duty were lying down, too. But Hanley could not sleep. It was all so strange, so strange, and yet so ordinary. Just like any other night, and yet the last night. Inevitably the last night? How could they escape, with orders to hold on at all costs? Half of them would go in the bombardment, which would be terrific. Bombs, bullets, and bayonets would finish off the rest. The dugouts would be wrecked with bombs and high explosive charges. A few of the wounded might be picked up later. A few of the men might escape down Hurdle Alley after the officers were gone. But no, the N.C.O.'s could be relied on to hold out to the last. They were done for, napoo. No après la guerre for *them*—bon soir, toodle-oo, goodbyeeee. The silly words repeated and repeated in his brain until he hated them. He opened his eyes and gazed at the familiar dugout. His wire bed was at an angle to the others, and he could see the shapes of Williams and the two other officers muffled up silent in their blankets—as still and silent as they would be in twenty-four hours' time. There was the candle burning in the holder roughly bent from a tin biscuit box. The flame was absolutely steady in the airless, earthy smelling dugout. There were the boxes for seats, the table with its maps, tins of cigarettes, chits, and the five mugs beside the whisky bottle for the last parting drink. The bare, murky walls of chalk were damp and clammy-looking with condensed breath. The revolvers, helmets, and gas bags were hung at the bed-heads.

He listened to the other men breathing, and felt an absurd regret at leaving the dugout to be smashed. After all, that and other dugouts like it were the only home they had known for months and months. Breaking up the happy home! He became aware that he felt a bit sickish, that he had been feeling like that for several hours, and pretending not to.

He gently drew his wrist from under the blanket and looked at his luminous watch. Eleven thirty-five. He had to be up at two—must get some sleep. With almost a start he noticed that Williams was looking at his own watch in the same stealthy way. So he couldn't sleep either. Poor devil. Profoundly, almost insanely in love with that wife of his. Poor devil. But still, for the matter of that, so was Hanley in love with his wife. His heart seemed to turn in his body, and he felt an acute pain in the muscles above it as he suddenly realized fully that it was all over, that he would never see her again, never feel her mouth pressed to his, never again touch her lovely, friendly body. He clutched his hand over his face until it hurt to prevent himself from groaning. God, what bloody agony! O God, he'd be a mass of dead rotting decay, and she'd still be young and beautiful and alert and desirable, O God, and her life would run on, run on, there'd be all the grief and the sorrowing for her and tears in a cold widowed bed, O God, but the years would run on and she'd still be young and desirable, and somebody else would want her, some youngster, some wangler, and youth and her flesh and life would be clamorous, and her bed would no longer be cold and widowed. O God, God. Something wet ran down his cheek. Not a tear, but the cold clammy sweat from his forehead. God, what agony!

Hanley suddenly sat up. If he was suffering like that, Williams must be suffering, too. Better to get up and pretend to talk than lie and agonize like that. He got out of bed. Williams raised his head:

"What's up. It isn't two, is it?"

The other men looked up, too, showing that neither of them had been asleep. Hanley shivered and rubbed his hands to warm them in the chill dugout.

"No, only five to twelve. But I couldn't sleep. Hope I don't disturb you. Benson must be relieved in a few minutes," he added inconsequently.

The other three rolled out of bed and stood stretching and rubbing their hands.

"Too cold to sleep in this damned damp place," said one of them.

"What about a drink?"

"If you have it now, you can't have it later on," said Hanley. "Better wait until two."

Williams put on his equipment and helmet and went up to relieve Benson. The others sat on the boxes trying to talk. Benson came down.

"Anything on?" asked Hanley casually.

"Lots of lights, ordinary strafing on their side. A hell of a bombardment from our side."

"Perhaps if they see we've got wind of it, they'll postpone the attack?" suggested the youngest officer.

"Rot," said Benson. "They know jolly well that all this part of the line has been denuded to feed the Fifth Army. They'll attack, all right."

They were silent. Hanley looked at his watch. Five past twelve. How damnably slowly the time went; and yet these were their last minutes on earth. He felt something had to be done.

"Let's have a hand at bridge."

"What, tonight, now?"

"Well, why not? It's no good sitting here grumping like owls, and you don't suggest a prayer meeting, do you?"

The last suggestion was met with oaths of a forcible nature. Hanley cleared the table and threw down the cards.

"Cut for deal."

Just before two, Hanley slipped into his breeches pocket the ten francs he had won, and stood up. He put on trench coat and muffler, tried his broken torch for about the twentieth time, then threw it down disgustedly and fitted on his equipment. The subaltern who was to relieve Williams on trench duty was already dressed and waiting. Hanley put on his hat and turned to the others.

"I'll come round and see you after you've taken up battle positions; but if by any chance I don't see you again—cheerio."

"Cheerio."

They found Williams, his runner, and a sergeant waiting in the trench outside the dugout entrance.

"Anything doing?"

"Nothing particular. I went on patrol. Their wire's got gaps cut, with knife-rests in the gaps, all the way along."

"Um."

"Lot of signal rockets, too."

"I see. Our artillery seems to have ceased altogether."

"Saving ammunition for the show."

"Be more sensible to strafe now while the Boche is taking up battle positions."

"Oh, well, that's the staff's job, not ours."

Hanley, Williams, the sergeant, two runners, started for the Outpost Line. The trench was drier, the night not so dark, with faint stars mistily gleaming among light clouds. Weather clearing up—just the Boche's luck again. The five men moved along without talking, absorbed partly in a strange anxious preoccupation, partly in keeping upright on the slippery trench. Hanley and Williams, of course, knew the full extent of their danger, had faced the ultimate despair, passed beyond revolt or hope. The sergeant still hoped—that he might be wounded and taken prisoner. The two men only knew they were "in for a show." All were dry-mouthed, a little sickish with apprehension, a little awkward in all their movements; the thought of deserting their posts never even occurred to them.

They passed the three Canadian crosses, distinctly outlined on the quiet sky; then the dragon piece of corrugated iron. At the end of the communication trench they found waiting the men from the four posts, under a sergeant. Hanley spoke in low tones—there might be advance patrols lying just outside their wire.

"All your men present, ser'ant?"

"Yes, sir."

"Right. You know your orders. See that each section joins its own platoon, and then report to your own platoon commander. Don't waste time."

"Very good, sir."

The line of men filed past them in the darkness. For the hundredth time Hanley noticed the curious pathos of fatigue in these silent moving figures—the young bodies somehow tired to age and apathy. When they had gone he took Williams a little aside.

"If I were you, I should see that each of you occupies a separate bay. Get in the first bay yourself, then the runner, then the sergeant. They won't dare try to bolt back past you. Besides—er—there's more chance if you're spread out."

"I was wondering what happens if all three of us are knocked out before the Boche actually gets into the trench, and so no green light is fired?"

"Oh, we must risk that. Besides, there are similar volunteer parties on every company front."

"I see."

"I took a compass bearing from the fire-step outside Company H.Q. yesterday, so I shan't miss your light. I expect they'll be on us ten minutes later. Perhaps we'll beat off the first two or three attacks."

"Yes. Perhaps."

They were silent. Then Hanley made an effort.

"Well, good-bye, old man. Best of luck."

"Best of luck, good-bye."

They were too shy and English even to shake hands.

It was past three when Hanley and Parker got back to their own line and found the whole company standing to in battle positions. Hanley kept his signallers on the first floor of the big dugout. He sent off to Battalion Headquarters the code message which meant they were in battle positions and all ready. He took a candle and went down to the lower dugout, where they had spent so many nights. It looked barer and damper than ever, empty except for the bare sacking beds, the boxes, the table.

Outside in the trench the air was moist and fresh. He took two Very pistols, one loaded with green, one with red, and laid them on either side of him on the parapet. Hanley was at the extreme left of the bay, with two riflemen to his right. Twenty yards to his left was the communication trench leading to the outpost line, now blocked with wire and knife-rests, and guarded by a bombing section.

A signaller came up from the dugout with a message. Hanley went down and read it by the light of a candle. He noticed the bowed back and absorbed look of a signaller tapping out a message on a Fullerphone. The message he had received simply reiterated the order that their positions were to be held at all costs. Hanley felt angry, screwed up the piece of paper and stuffed it in his pocket. Damn them, how many more times did they think that order had to be given? He returned to the trench, and resumed his watch.

3.50 A.M. One battery of German guns languidly firing on back areas—pretense that all was as usual.

3.52 A.M. Signal rockets all along the German line. Then silence.

3.55 A.M. Two miles to his right a fierce bombardment, stretching over several miles. The battle had begun.

3.57 A.M. Two miles to his left another bombardment. The British artillery on their own front opened up a defensive barrage.

4 A.M. With a terrific crash, which immediately blotted out the roar of the other bombardments, the German artillery on their own front came into action. Hanley half-recoiled. He had been in several big bombardments, and thought he had experienced the utmost limit of artillery. But this was more tremendous, more hellish, more appalling than anything he had experienced. The trench of the outpost line was one continuous line of red, crashing trench mortars and shells. The communication trench was plastered with five-nines. Shells were falling all along their own line—he heard the sharp cry "Stretcher-bearer" very faintly from somewhere close at hand.

The confusion and horror of a great battle descended on him. The crash of shells, the roar of the guns, the brilliant flashes, the eerie piercing scream of a wounded man, the rattle of the machine guns, the Lewis guns, the two riflemen beside him madly working the bolts of their rifles and fumbling as with trembling hands they thrust in a fresh clip of cartridges—all somehow perceived, but thrust aside in his intense watch. A green light went up about half a mile to the left, then another a little nearer. Hanley stared more intently in the direction of William's post—and found himself saying over and over again without knowing he was saying it: "O God, help him, O God, help him, O God, help him."

Suddenly two green lights appeared, one fired straight up as a signal—probably Williams—the other almost along the ground, as if fired at somebody—probably the runner, wounded or in a panic. Sergeant dead, no doubt—Williams and his runner dead, too, by now. Hanley fired a green light. Two minutes later the British barrage shortened.

Hanley grasped the Very pistol loaded with red. Their turn now.

"Stretcher-bearer, stretcher-bearer!"

Crash! A shell right on their bay.

Hanley staggered and felt a fearful pain in his right knee where a shell splinter had hit him. In the faint light of dawn he saw vaguely that one of the rifleman lay huddled on the fire-step, leaving his rifle still on the parapet; the other man had been blown backwards into the trench, and lay with his feet grimly and ludicrously caught in a torn piece of revetment. His helmet had been knocked from his head.

Faint pops of bombs to his immediate left—they were coming up the communication trench. He peered into the steel-smashed light of dawn, but saw only smoke and the fierce red flash of explosions.

Suddenly, to his left, he saw German helmets coming up the communication trench—they had passed the wire barrier! He looked to his right—a little knot of Germans had got through the wire—a Lewis gun swept them away like flies. He felt the blood running down his leg.

Somebody was standing beside him. A voice, far off, was speaking:

"Bombing attack beaten off, sir."

"Very good, carry on."

"There's only two of us left, sir."

"Carry on."

"Very good, sir."

More Germans on the right; another, longer row coming up the communication trench. Then, suddenly, Germans seemed to spring up in every direction. Hanley fired six shots from his Webley at those in front. He saw others falling hit, or jumping into the trench on either side.

A red light shot up straight in the air. A second later two bombs fell in the bay. A torn, crumpled figure collapsed sideways. The Germans reorganized, while the moppers-up did their job.

ERICH MARIA REMARQUE
Paul Bäumer Goes on Leave

Erich Maria Remarque (1898–1970) was born in Osnabruck, Germany, and went straight from school into the maelstrom of WWI. His subsequent autobiographical novel, All Quiet on the Western Front *(1929), is arguably the greatest fictional work of the Great War. With the rise of Nazism, Remarque- whose real name was Erich Paul Kramer- left Germany, eventually becoming a naturalised U.S. citizen. His other war fiction includes* The Night in Lisbon *(1962).*

Below is an extract from All Quiet on the Western Front. *The narrator is the novel's hero, Paul Bäumer.*

I LIE DOWN ON MANY A station platform; I stand before many a soup-kitchen; I squat on many a bench;—then at last the landscape becomes disturbing, mysterious, and familiar. It glides past the western windows with its villages, their thatched roofs like caps, pulled over the white-washed, half-timbered houses, its cornfields, gleaming like mother-of-pearl in the slanting light, its orchards, its barns and old lime trees.

The names of the stations begin to take on meaning and my heart trembles. The train stamps and stamps onward. I stand at the window and hold on to the frame. These names mark the boundaries of my youth.

Smooth meadows, fields, farm-yards; a solitary team moves against the sky-line along the road that runs parallel to the horizon—a barrier, before which peasants stand waiting, girls waving, children playing on the embankment, roads, leading into the country, smooth roads without artillery.

It is evening, and if the train did not rattle I should cry out. The plain unfolds itself.

In the distance, the soft, blue silhouette of the mountain ranges begins to appear. I recognize the characteristic out-line of the Dolbenberg, a jagged comb, springing up precipitously from the limits of the forests. Behind it should lie the town.

But now the sun streams through the world, dissolving everything in its golden-red light, the train swings round one curve and then another;—for away, in a long line one behind the other, stand the poplars, unsubstantial, swaying and dark, fashioned out of shadow, light, and desire.

The field swings round as the train encircles it, and the intervals between the trees diminish; the trees become a block and for a moment I see one only—then they reappear from behind the foremost tree and stand out a long line against the sky until they are hidden by the first houses.

A street-crossing. I stand by the window, I cannot drag myself away. The others put their baggage ready for getting out. I repeat to myself the name of the street that we cross over—Bremerstrasse—Bremerstrasse—

Below there are cyclists, lorries, men; it is a grey street and a grey subway;—it affects me as though it were my mother.

Then the train stops, and there is the station with noise and cries and signboards. I pick up my pack and fasten the straps, I take my rifle in my hand and stumble down the steps.

On the platform I look round; I know no one among all the people hurrying to and fro. A red-cross sister offers me something to drink. I turn away, she smiles at me too foolishly, so obsessed with her own importance: "Just look, I am giving a soldier coffee!"—She calls me "Comrade," but I will have none of it.

Outside in front of the station the stream roars alongside the street, it rushes foaming from the sluices of the mill bridge. There stands the old, square watchtower, in front of it the great mottled lime tree and behind it the evening.

Here we have often sat—how long ago it is—; we have passed over this bridge and breathed the cool, acid smell of the stagnant water; we have leaned over the still water on this side of the lock, where the green creepers and weeds hang from the piles of the bridge;—and on hot days we rejoiced in the spouting foam on the other side of the lock and told tales about our school-teachers.

I pass over the bridge, I look right and left; the water is as full of weeds as ever, and it still shoots over in gleaming arches; in the tower-building laundresses still stand with bare arms as they used to over the clean linen, and the heat from the ironing pours out through the open windows. Dogs trot along the narrow street, before the doors of the houses people stand and follow me with their gaze as I pass by, dirty and heavy laden.

In this confectioner's we used to eat ices, and there we learned to smoke cigarettes. Walking down the street I know every shop, the grocer's, the chemist's, the baker's. Then at last I stand before the brown door with its worn latch and my hand grows heavy. I open the door and a strange coolness comes out to meet me, my eyes are dim.

The stairs creak under my boots. Upstairs a door rattles, someone is looking over the railing. It is the kitchen door that was opened, they are cooking potato-cakes, the house reeks of it, and today of course is Saturday; that will be my sister leaning over. For a moment I am shy and lower my head, then I take off my helmet and look up. Yes, it is my eldest sister.

"Paul," she cries, "Paul——"

I nod, my pack bumps against the banisters; my rifle is so heavy.

She pulls a door open and calls: "Mother, mother, Paul is here."

I can go no further—mother, mother, Paul is here.

I lean against the wall and grip my helmet and rifle. I hold them as tight as I can, but I cannot take another step, the staircase fades before my eyes, I support myself with the butt of my rifle against my feet and clench my teeth fiercely, but I cannot speak a word, my sister's call has made me powerless, I can do nothing, I struggle to make myself laugh, to speak, but no word comes, and so I stand on the steps, miserable, helpless, paralysed, and against my will the tears run down my cheeks.

My sister comes back and says: "Why, what is the matter?"

Then I pull myself together and stagger on to the landing. I lean my rifle in a corner, I set my pack against the wall, place my helmet on it and fling down my equipment and baggage. Then I say fiercely, "Bring me a handkerchief."

She gives me one from the cupboard and I dry my face. Above me on the wall hangs the glass case with the coloured butterflies that once I collected.

Now I hear my mother's voice. It comes from the bedroom.

"Is she in bed?" I ask my sister.

"She is ill——" she replies.

I go into her, give her my hands and say as calmly as I can: "Here I am, Mother."

She lies still in the dim light. Then she asks anxiously:

"Are you wounded?" and I feel her searching glance.

"No, I have got leave."

My mother is very pale. I am afraid to make a light.

"Here I lie now," says she, "and cry instead of being glad."

"Are you sick, Mother?" I ask.

"I am going to get up a little today," she says and turns to my sister, who is continually running to the kitchen to watch that the food does not burn: "And put out that jar of preserved whortleberries—you like that, don't you?" she asks me.

"Yes, Mother, I haven't had any for a long time."

"We might almost have known you were coming," laughs my sister, "there is just your favourite dish, potato-cakes, and even whortleberries to go with them too."

"And it is Saturday," I add.

"Sit here beside me," says my mother.

She looks at me. Her hands are white and sickly and frail compared with mine. We say very little and I am thankful that she asks nothing. What ought I to say? Everything I could have wished for has happened. I have come out of it safely and sit here beside her. And in the kitchen stands my sister preparing supper and singing.

"Dear boy," says my mother softly.

We were never very demonstrative in our family; poor folk who toil and are full of cares are not so. It is not their way to

protest what they already know. When my mother says to me
"dear boy," it means much more than when another uses it. I
know well enough that the jar of whortleberries is the only one
they have had for months, and that she has kept it for me; and
the somewhat stale cakes that she gives me too. She must have
got them cheap some time and put them all by for me.

I sit by her bed, and through the window the chestnut trees
in the beer garden opposite glow in brown and gold. I breathe
deeply and say over to myself:—"You are at home, you are at
home." But a sense of strangeness will not leave me, I cannot
feel at home amongst these things. There is my mother, there is
my sister, there my case of butterflies, and there the mahogany
piano—but I am not myself there. There is a distance, a veil
between us.

I go and fetch my pack to the bedside and turn out the things
I have brought—a whole Edamer cheese, that Kat provided me
with, two loaves of army bread, three-quarters of a pound of
butter, two tins of livered sausage, a pound of dripping and a
little bag of rice.

"I suppose you can make some use of that——"

They nod.

"Is it pretty bad for food here?" I enquire.

"Yes, there's not much. Do you get enough out there?"

I smile and point to the things I have brought. "Not always
quite as much as that, of course, but we fare reasonably well."

Erna takes away the food. Suddenly my mother seizes
hold of my hand and asks falteringly: "Was it very bad
out there, Paul?"

Mother, what should I answer to that! You would not
understand, you could never realize it. And you never shall
realize it. Was it bad, you ask.—You, Mother,—I shake my
head and say: "No, Mother, not so very. There are always a
lot of us together so it isn't so bad."

"Yes, but Heinrich Bredemeyer was here just lately and
said it was terrible out there now, with the gas and all the
rest of it."

It is my mother who says that. She says: "With the gas and
all the rest of it." She does not know what she is saying, she is
merely anxious for me. Should I tell her how we once found
three enemy trenches with their garrison all stiff as though

stricken with apoplexy? against the parapet, in the dug-outs, just where they were, the men stood and lay about, with blue faces, dead.

"No Mother, that's only talk," I answer, "there's not very much in what Bredemeyer says. You see for instance, I'm well and fit——"

Before my mother's tremulous anxiety I recover my composure. Now I can walk about and talk and answer questions without fear of having suddenly to lean against the wall because the world turns soft as rubber and my veins become brimstone.

My mother wants to get up. So I go for a while to my sister in the kitchen. "What is the matter with her?" I ask.

She shrugs her shoulders: "She has been in bed some months now, but we did not want to write and tell you. Several doctors have been to see her. One of them said it is probably cancer again."

I go to the district commandant to report myself. Slowly I wander through the streets. Occasionally someone speaks to me. I do not delay long for I have little inclination to talk.

On my way back from the barracks a loud voice calls out to me. Still lost in thought I turn round and find myself confronted by a Major. "Can't you salute?" he blusters.

"Sorry, Major," I say in embarrassment, "I didn't notice you."

"Don't you know how to speak properly?" he roars.

I would like to hit him in the face, but control myself, for my leave depends on it. I click my heels and say: "I did not see you, Herr Major."

"Then keep your eyes open," he snorts. "What is your name?" I give it.

His fat red face is furious. "What regiment?"

I give him full particulars. Even yet he has not had enough. "Where are you quartered?"

But I have had more than enough and say: "Between Langemark and Bixschoote."

"Eh?" he asks, a bit stupefied.

I explain to him that I arrived on leave only an hour or two since, thinking that he would then trot along. But not at all.

He gets even more furious. "You think you can bring your front-line manners here, what? Well, we don't stand for that sort of thing. Thank God, we have discipline here!"

"Twenty paces backwards, double march!" he commands.

I am mad with rage. But I cannot say anything to him; he could put me under arrest if he liked. So I double back, and then march up to him. Six paces from him I spring to a stiff salute and maintain it until I am six paces beyond him.

He calls me back again and affably gives me to understand that for once he is pleased to put mercy before justice. I pretend to be duly grateful. "Now, dismiss!" he says. I turn about smartly and march off.

That ruins the evening for me. I go back home and throw my uniform into a corner; I had intended to change it in any case. Then I take out my civilian clothes from the wardrobe and put them on.

I feel awkward. The suit is rather tight and short, I have grown in the army. Collar and tie give me some trouble. In the end my sister ties the bow for me. But how light the suit is, it feels as though I had nothing on but a shirt and underpants.

I look at myself in the glass. It is a strange sight. A sunburnt, overgrown candidate for confirmation gazes at me in astonishment.

My mother is pleased to see me wearing civilian clothes; it makes me less strange to her. But my father would rather I kept my uniform on so that he could take me to visit his acquaintances.

But I refuse.

It is pleasant to sit quietly somewhere, in the beer garden for example, under the chestnuts by the skittle-alley. The leaves fall down on the table and on the ground, only a few, the first. A glass of beer stands in front of me, I've learned to drink in the army. The glass is half empty, but there are a few good swigs ahead of me, and besides I can always order a second and a third if I wish to. There are no bugles and no bombardments, the children of the house play in the skittle-alley, and the dog rests his head against my knee. The sky is blue, between the leaves of the chestnut rises the green spire of St Margaret's Church.

This is good, I like it. But I cannot get on with the people. My mother is the only one who asks no questions. Not so my father. He wants me to tell him about the front; he is curious in a way that I find stupid and distressing; I no longer have any real contact with him. There is nothing he likes more than just hearing about it. I realize he does not know that a man cannot talk of such things; I would do it willingly, but it is too dangerous for me to put these things into words. I am afraid they might then become gigantic and I be no longer able to master them. What would become of us if everything that happens out there were quite clear to us?

So I confine myself to telling him a few amusing things. But he wants to know whether I have ever had a hand-to-hand fight. I say "No," and get up and go out.

But that does not mend matters. After I have been startled a couple of times in the street by the screaming of the tramcars, which resembles the shriek of a shell coming straight for one, somebody taps me on the shoulder. It is my German-master, and he fastens on me with the usual question: "Well, how are things out there? Terrible, terrible, eh? Yes, it is dreadful, but we must carry on. And after all, you do at least get decent food out there, so I hear. You look well, Paul, and fit. Naturally it's worse here. Naturally. The best for our soldiers every time, that goes without saying."

He drags me along to a table with a lot of others. They welcome me, a head-master shakes hands with me and says: "So you come from the front? What is the spirit like out there? Excellent, eh? excellent?"

I explain that no one would be sorry to be back home.

He laughs uproariously. "I can well believe it! But first you have to give the Froggies a good hiding. Do you smoke? Here, try one. Waiter, bring a beer as well for our young warrior."

Unfortunately I have accepted the cigar, so I have to remain. And they are all so dripping with good will that it is impossible to object. All the same I feel annoyed and smoke like a chimney as hard as I can. In order to make at least some show of appreciation I toss off the beer in one gulp. Immediately a second is ordered; people know how much they are indebted to the soldiers. They argue about what we ought to annex. The head-master with the steel watch-chain wants to have

at least the whole of Belgium, the coal-areas of France, and a
slice of Russia. He produces reasons why we must have them
and is quite inflexible until at last the others give in to him.
Then he begins to expound just whereabouts in France the
break-through must come, and turns to me: "Now, shove ahead
a bit out there with your everlasting trench warfare—Smash
through the johnnies and then there will be peace."

I reply that in our opinion a break-through may not be
possible. The enemy may have too many reserves. Besides,
the war may be rather different from what people think.

He dismisses the idea loftily and informs me I know nothing
about it. "The details, yes," says he, "but this relates to the
whole. And of that you are not able to judge. You see only
your little sector and so cannot have any general survey. You
do your duty, you risk your lives, that deserves the highest
honour—every man of you ought to have the Iron Cross—but
first of all the enemy line must be broken through in Flanders
and then rolled up from the top."

He blows his nose and wipes his beard. "Completely rolled
up they must be, from the top to the bottom. And then
to Paris."

I would like to know just how he pictures it to himself, and
pour the third glass of beer into me. Immediately he orders
another.

But I break away. He stuffs a few more cigars into my pocket
and sends me off with a friendly slap. "All of the best! I hope we
will soon hear something worth while from you."

I imagined leave would be different from this. Indeed, it was
different a year ago. It is I of course that have changed in the
interval. There lies a gulf between that time and today. At
that time I still knew nothing about the war, we had only
been in quiet sectors. But now I see that I have been crushed
without knowing it. I find I do not belong here any more, it
is a foreign world. Some of these people ask questions, some
ask no questions, but one can see that the latter are proud
of themselves for their silence; they often say with a wise
air that these things cannot be talked about. They plume
themselves on it.

I prefer to be alone, so that no one troubles me. For they all come back to the same thing, how badly it goes and how well it goes; one thinks it is this way, another that; and yet they are always absorbed in the things that go to make up their existence. Formerly I lived in just the same way myself, but now I feel no contact here.

They talk too much for me. They have worries, aims, desires, that I cannot comprehend. I often sit with one of them in the little beer garden and try to explain to him that this is really the only thing: just to sit quietly, like this. They understand of course, they agree, they may even feel it so too, but only with words, only with words, yes, that is it—they feel it, but always with only half of themselves, the rest of their being is taken up with other things, they are so divided in themselves that none feels it with his whole essence; I cannot even say myself exactly what I mean.

When I see them here, in their rooms, in their offices, about their occupations, I feel an irresistible attraction in it, I would like to be here too and forget the war; but also it repels me, it is so narrow, how can that fill a man's life, he ought to smash it to bits; how can they do it, while out at the front the splinters are whining over the shell-holes and the star-shells go up, the wounded are carried back on waterproof sheets and comrades crouch in the trenches.—They are different men here, men I cannot properly understand, whom I envy and despise. I must think of Kat and Albert and Müller and Tjaden, what will they be doing? No doubt they are sitting in the canteen, or perhaps swimming—soon they will have to go up to the front-line, again.

In my room behind the table stands a brown leather sofa. I sit down on it.

On the walls are pinned countless pictures that I once used to cut out of the newspapers. In between are drawings and postcards that have pleased me. In the corner is a small iron stove. Against the wall opposite stand the bookshelves with my books.

I used to live in this room before I was a soldier. The books I bought gradually with the money I earned by coaching. Many of them are second-hand, all the classics for example, one volume in blue cloth boards cost one mark twenty pfennig.

I bought them complete because it was thoroughgoing, I did not trust the editors of selections to choose all the best. So I purchased only "collected works." I read most of them with laudable zeal, but few of them really appealed to me. I preferred the other books, the moderns, which were of course much dearer. A few I came by not quite honestly, I borrowed and did not return them because I did not want to part with them.

One shelf is filled with school books. They are not so well cared for, they are badly thumbed, and pages have been torn out for certain purposes. Then below are periodicals, and letters all jammed in together with drawings and rough sketches.

I want to think myself back into that time. It is still in the room, I feel it at once, the walls have preserved it. My hands rest on the arms of the sofa; now I make myself at home and draw up my legs so that I sit comfortably in the corner, in the arms of the sofa. The little window is open, through it I see the familiar picture of the street with the rising spire of the church at the end. There are a couple of flowers on the table. Pen-holders, a shell as a paper-weight, the ink-well—here nothing is changed.

It will be like this too, if I am lucky, when the war is over and I come back here for good. I will sit here just like this and look at my room and wait.

I feel excited; but I do not want to be, for that is not right. I want that quiet rapture again. I want to feel the same powerful, nameless urge that I used to feel when I turned to my books. The breath of desire that then arose from the coloured backs of the books, shall fill me again, melt the heavy, dead lump of lead that lies somewhere in me and waken again the impatience of the future, the quick joy in the world of thought, it shall bring back again the lost eagerness of my youth. I sit and wait.

It occurs to me that I must go and see Kemmerich's mother;—I might visit Mittelstaedt too, he should be at the barracks. I look out of the window;—beyond the picture of the sunlit street appears a range of hills, distant and light; it changes to a clear day in autumn, and I sit by the fire with Kat and Albert and eat potatoes baked in their skins.

But I do not want to think of that, I sweep it away. The room shall speak, it must catch me up and hold me, I want to feel that I belong here, I want to hearken and know when I go back to the front that the war will sink down, be drowned utterly in the great homecoming tide, know that it will then be past for ever, and not gnaw us continually, that it will have none but an outward power over us.

The backs of the books stand in rows. I know them all still, I remember arranging them in order. I implore them with my eyes: Speak to me—take me up—take me, Life of my Youth—you who are care-free, beautiful—receive me again—

I wait, I wait.

Images float through my mind, but they do not grip me, they are mere shadows and memories.

Nothing—nothing—

My disquietude grows.

A terrible feeling of foreignness suddenly rises up in me. I cannot find my way back, I am shut out though I entreat earnestly and put forth all my strength.

Nothing stirs; listless and wretched, like a condemned man, I sit there and the past withdraws itself. And at the same time I fear to importune it too much, because I do not know what might happen then. I am a soldier, I must cling to that.

Wearily I stand up and look out of the window. Then I take one of the books, intending to read, and turn over the leaves. But I put it away and take out another. There are passages in it that have been marked. I look, turn over the pages, take up fresh books. Already they are piled up beside me. Speedily more join the heap, papers, magazines, letters.

I stand there dumb. As before a judge.

Dejected.

Words, Words, Words—they do not reach me.

Slowly I place the books back in the shelves.

Nevermore.

Quietly, I go out of the room.

FREDERIC MANNING
Her Privates We

*Frederic Manning (1887–1935) was born
in Sydney, Australia, the son of the city's
mayor. He joined the British Shropshire
Light Infantry in 1914, and served for the
duration of WWI. His novel of the Western
Front,* The Middle Parts of Fortune
(also known as Her Privates We*), was
published under the pseudonym "Private
19022" in 1929.* Hemingway described
it as "the finest and noblest book of
men in war that I have ever read".

Here is an extract from The Middle
Parts of Fortune. *Bourne is the main
character of the novel, which is set on
the Somme.*

BOURNE ROUSED HIMSELF, AND, AFTER a few minutes
of dubious consciousness, sat up and looked round him,
at his sleeping companions, and then at the rifles stacked
round the tent-pole, and the ring of boots surrounding the
rifle-butts. His right hand finding the opening in his shirt
front, he scratched pleasurably at his chest. He was dirty,
and he was lousy; but at least, and he thanked God for it,
he was not scabby. Half a dozen men from Headquarter
Company, including Shem as a matter of course, had been
sent off yesterday to a casualty clearing station near Acheux,
suffering or rejoicing, according to their diverse temperaments,
with the itch. The day after their arrival at Mailly-Maillet, the
medical officer had held what the men described irreverently
as a prick-inspection. He was looking for definite symptoms
of something he expected to find, and because his inquest

had been narrowed down to a single question, it may have seemed a little cursory. The men stood in a line, their trousers and underpants having been dropped round their ankles, and as the doctor passed them, in the words of the regimental sergeant-major, they "lifted the curtain", that is to say the flap of the shirt, so as to expose their bellies.

Scratching his chest, Bourne considered the boots: if a sword were the symbol of battle, boots were certainly symbols of war; and because by his bedside at home there had always been a copy of the Authorised Version, he remembered now the verse about the warrior's boots that stamped in the tumult, and the mantle drenched with blood being all but for burning, and fuel for the fire. He lit a cigarette. It was, anyway, the method by which he intended to dispose of his own damned kit, if he should survive his present obligations; but the chance of survival seeming to his cooler judgment somewhat thin, he ceased spontaneously to be interested in it. His mind did not dismiss, it ignored, the imminent possibility of its own destruction. He looked again with a little more sympathy on his prone companions, wondering that sleep should make their faces seem so enigmatic and remote; and still scratching and rubbing his chest, he returned to his contemplation of the boots. Then, when he had smoked his cigarette down to his fingers, he rubbed out the glowing end in the earth, slipped out of the blanket, and reached for his trousers. He moved as quickly as a cat in dressing, and now, taking his mess-tin, he opened the flap of the tent, and went out into the cool morning freshness. He could see between the sparse trees to the cookers, drawn up a little off the road. The wood in which they were encamped was just behind Mailly-Maillet, in an angle formed by two roads, one rising over the slope to Mailly-Maillet, and the other skirting the foot of the hill towards Hédauville. It was on a rather steep reverse slope, which gave some protection from shell-fire, and there were a few shelter-trenches, which had been hastily and rather inefficiently dug, as a further protection. It was well screened from observation. The trees were little more than saplings, young beech, birch, and larch, with a few firs, poorly grown, but so far unshattered. Bourne strolled carelessly down to the cookers.

"Good-morning, Corporal; any tea going?"

Williams stretched out his hand for the mess-tin, filled it to the brim, and then, after handing it back to Bourne, went on with his work, without a word. Bourne stayed there, sipping the scalding brew.

"Go up the line, last night?" Williams inquired at last.

"Carrying-party," answered Bourne, who found his dixie so hot he could scarcely hold it, so he was protecting his hands with a dirty handkerchief. "I was out of luck. I was at the end, and when they had loaded me up with the last box of ammunition, they found there was a buckshee box of Verey lights to go, too. The officer said he thought I might carry those as well; and being a young man of rather tedious wit, he added that they were very light. I suppose I am damned clumsy, but one of those bloody boxes is enough for me, and I decided to dump one at the first opportunity. Then Mr Sothern came back along the top of the communication trench, and, finding me weary and heavily laden, said all sorts of indiscreet things about everybody concerned. 'Dump them, you bloody fool, dump them!' he shouted. I rather deprecated any extreme measures. 'Give me that bloody box,' he insisted. As he seemed really angry about it, I handed him up the box of ammunition, as it was the heavier of the two. He streaked off into the darkness to get back to the head of the party, with his stick in one hand, and a box of ammo in the other. I like these conscientious young officers, Corporal."

"'e's a nice chap, Mr Sothern," observed Williams, with a face of immovable melancholy.

"Quite," Bourne agreed. "However, there's a big dug-out in Legend Trench, and between that and the corner of Flag Alley I saw a box of ammunition that had been dumped. It was lying by the duck-boards. It may have been the one I gave Mr Sothern: 'lost owing to the exigencies of active service.' That's what the court of inquiry said about Patsy Pope's false teeth."

Williams went on with his work.

"It won't be long before you lads are for it again," he said in his quiet way.

"No," said Bourne, reluctantly, for there was a note of furtive sympathy in Williams' voice which embarrassed him.

"The whole place is simply lousy with guns," continued the cook.

"Why the hell can't you talk of something else?" exclaimed Bourne, impatiently. "Jerry chased us all the way home last night. Mr Sothern, who knows no more about the bloody map than I do, tried a short cut, and wandered off in the direction of Colin-camps, until we fetched up in front of one of our field batteries, and were challenged. Then an officer came up and remonstrated with him. After that, when we got on the road again and Fritz started sending a few across, you should have seen us! Leaning over like a field of corn in the wind."

"A lot o' them are new to it, yet," said Williams, tolerantly, "You might take a drop o' tea up to the corporal, will you? 'e's a nice chap, Corporal 'amley. I gave 'im some o' your toffees last night, an' we was talkin' about you. I'll fill it, in case you feel like some more."

Bourne took it, thanking him, and lounged off. There was now a little more movement in the camp, and when he got back to his own tent he found all the occupants awake, enjoying a moment of indecision before they elected to dress. He poured some tea into Corporal Hamley's tin, and then gave some to Martlow, and there was about a third left.

"Who wants tea?" he said.

"I do," said Weeper Smart, and in his blue shirt with cuffs unbuttoned and white legs sprawled out behind him, he lunged awkwardly across the tent, holding out his dixie with one hand. Smart was an extraordinary individual, with the clumsy agility of one of the greater apes; though the carriage of his head rather suggested the vulture, for the neck projected from wide, sloping shoulders, rounded to a stoop; the narrow forehead, above arched eyebrows, and the chin, under loose pendulous lips, both receded abruptly, and the large, fleshy beak, jutting forward between protruding blue eyes, seemed to weigh down the whole face. His skin was an unhealthy white, except at the top of the nose and about the nostrils, where it had a shiny redness, as though he suffered from an incurable cold: it was rather pimply. An almost complete beardlessness made the lack of pigmentation more marked, and even the fine, sandy hair of his head grew thinly. It would have been the face of an imbecile, but for the expression of unmitigated misery in it, or it would have been a tragic face if it had possessed any element of nobility; but it was merely abject, a mask of passive suffering, at once pitiful and repulsive. It was inevitable that men, living day by day with such a spectacle of woe, should learn in self-defence to deride it; and it was this sheer necessity which had impelled some cruel wit of the camp to fling at him the name of Weeper, and make that forlorn and cadaverous figure the butt of an endless jest. He gulped his tea, and his watery eyes turned towards Bourne with a cunning malevolence.

"What I say is, that if any o' us'ns tried scrounging round the cookers, we'd be for it."

Bourne looked at him with a slightly contemptuous tolerance, gathered his shaving-tackle together, flung his dirty towel over his shoulder, and set off again in the direction of the cookers to scrounge for some hot water. He could do without the necessaries of life more easily than without some small comforts.

Breakfast over, they cleaned up and aired the tent, and almost immediately were told to fall in on parade with Headquarter Company. Captain Thompson, watching them fall in from the officers' tents, knocked his pipe out against his stick, shoved it in his tunic pocket, and came up the hill, carrying his head at a rather thoughtful angle. He had a rather short, stocky figure, and a round bullet head; his face was always imperturbable, and his eyes quiet but observant. Sergeant-Major Corbett called the company to attention and Captain Thompson acknowledged the salute, and told the men to stand easy. Then he began to talk to them in a quiet unconventional way, as one whose authority was so unquestioned that the friendliness of his manner was not likely to be misunderstood. They had had a good rest, he said (as though he were talking to the same men who had fought their way, slowly and foot by foot, into Guillemont!), and now there was work in front of them: difficult and dangerous work: the business of killing as many superfluous Germans as possible. He would read out to them passages from the letter of instructions regarding the attack, which as fresh and reconditioned troops they would be called on soon to make. He read; and as he read his voice became rather monotonous, it lost the character of the man and seemed to come to them from a remote distance. The plan was handled in too abstract a way for the men to follow it; and their attention, in spite of the gravity with which they listened, was inclined to wander; or perhaps they refused to think of it except from the point of view of their own concrete and individual experience. Above his monotonous voice one could hear, now and again, a little wind stray through the drying leaves of the trees. A leaf or two might flutter down, and scratch against the bark of trunk or boughs with a crackling papery rustle. Here and there he would stress a sentence ever so slightly, as though its significance would not be wasted on their minds, and their eyes would quicken, and lift towards him with a curious, almost an animal expression of patient wonder. It was strange to notice how a slight movement, even a break in the rhythm of their breathing, showed their feelings at certain passages.

". . . men are strictly forbidden to stop for the purpose of assisting wounded . . ."

The slight stiffening of their muscles may have been imperceptible, for the monotonous inflexion did not vary as the reader delivered a passage, in which it was stated, that the Staff considered they had made all the arrangements necessary to effect this humanitarian, but somewhat irrelevant, object.

". . . you may be interested to know," and this was slightly stressed, as though to overbear a doubt, "that it is estimated we shall have one big gun—I suppose that means hows, and heavies—for every hundred square yards of ground we are attacking."

An attack delivered on a front of twenty miles, if completely successful, would mean penetrating to a depth of from six to seven miles, and the men seemed to be impressed by the weight of metal with which it was intended to support them. Then the officer came to the concluding paragraph of the instructional letter.

"It is not expected that the enemy will offer any very serious resistance at this point . . ."

There came a whisper scarcely louder than a sigh.

"What fuckin' 'opes we've got!"

The still small voice was that of Weeper Smart, clearly audible to the rest of the section, and its effect was immediate.

The nervous tension, which had gripped every man, was suddenly snapped, and the swift relief brought with it an almost hysterical desire to laugh, which it was difficult to suppress. Whether Captain Thompson also heard the voice of the Weeper, and what construction he may have placed on the sudden access of emotion in the ranks, it was impossible to say. Abruptly, he called them to attention, and after a few seconds, during which he stared at them impersonally, but with great severity, the men were dismissed. As they moved off, Captain Thompson called Corporal Hamley to him.

"Where will some of us poor buggers be come next Thursday?" demanded Weeper of the crowded tent, as he collapsed into his place; and looking at that caricature of grief, their laughter, high-pitched and sardonic, which had been stifled on parade, found vent.

"Laugh, you silly fuckers!" he cried in vehement rage. "Yes, you laugh now! You'll be laughing the other side o' your bloody mouths when you 'ear all Krupp's fuckin' iron-foundry comin' over! Laugh! One big gun to every bloody 'undred yards, an' don't expect any serious resistance from the enemy! Take us for a lot o' bloody kids, they do! 'aven't we been up the line and . . ."

"You shut your blasted mouth, see!" said the exasperated Corporal Hamley, stooping as he entered the tent, the lift of his head, with chin thrust forward as he stooped, giving him a more desperately aggressive appearance. "An' you let me 'ear you talkin' on parade again with an officer present and you'll be on the bloody mat, quick. See? You miserable bugger, you! A bloody cunt like you's sufficient to demoralize a whole fuckin' Army Corps. Got it? Get those buzzers out, and do some bloody work, for a change."

Exhausted by this unaccustomed eloquence, Corporal Hamley, white-lipped, glared round the tent, on innocent and guilty alike. Weeper gave him one glance of deprecatory grief, and relapsed into a prudent silence. The rest of the squad, all learners, settled themselves with a more deliberate obedience: there was no sense in encouraging Corporal Hamley to throw his weight about, just because he had wind up. They took up their pencils and paper, and looked at him a little coolly. Weeper was one of themselves. With the corporal sending on the buzzer, the class laboriously spelt out his messages. Then he tried two men with two instruments, one sending, and the other answering and repeating, while the rest of the squad recorded.

"You've been at this game before," he said to Weeper.

"I, Corporal?" said Weeper, with an innocence one could see was affected; "I've never touched one o' these things before."

"No?" said the corporal. "Ever worked in a telegraph office? You needn't try to come that game on me. I can tell by your touch."

He was not in a humour to be satisfied, and the men, thinking of the show they were in for, did not work well. A sullen humour spread among them. Bourne was the least satisfactory of all.

"You're just swingin' the lead," said Corporal Hamley. "Those of you who can't use a buzzer will be sent out as linesmen, or to help carry the bloody flapper."

Things went from bad to worse among them. There was a light drizzle of rain outside, and this gradually increased to a steady downpour. Their sullen humour deepened into resentment, fretting hopelessly in their minds; and the corporal's disapproval was expressed now and again with savage brevity. Then the stolid but perfectly cheerful face of Corporal Woods appeared between the flaps of the tent.

"Kin I 'ave six men off you for a fatigue, Corporal?" he asked pleasantly.

"You can take the whole fuckin' issue," said Corporal Hamley, with enthusiasm, throwing the buzzer down on his blankets with the air of a man who has renounced all hope.

Shem returned, wet and smelling of iodine, at dinner time. All that day it rained, and they kept to the tents, but their exasperation wore off, and the spirit of pessimism which had filled them became quiet, reflective, even serene, but without ceasing to be pessimism. Mr Rhys paid them a visit, and said, that, taking into account the interruption of their training by other duties, their progress had been fairly satisfactory. He, too, picked out Weeper Smart as an expert telegraphist, and Martlow as the aptest pupil in the class; as for the other new men, it would be some time before they were fully qualified for their duties. At a quarter to three he told the corporal that they might pack up for the day. If the weather had cleared they would have gone out with flags; but they had been on the buzzer all the morning, and in the monotony of repeating the same practice, hour after hour, men lose interest and learn nothing. From outside came the dense unbroken murmur of the rain, which sometimes dwindled to a whispering rustle, through which one could hear heavy drops falling at curiously regular intervals from the trees on to the tent, or a bough laden with wet would sag slowly downward, to spill all it held in a sudden shower, and then lift up for more. These lulls were only momentary, and then the rain would increase in volume again until it became a low roar in which all lesser sounds were drowned. There was little wind.

Mr Rhys told them they might smoke, and stayed to talk with them for a little while. They all liked him, in spite of the erratic and hasty temper which left them a little uncertain as to what to make of him. From time to time, without putting aside anything of his prestige and authority over them, he would try to get into touch with them, and learn what they were thinking. Only a very great man can talk on equal terms with those in the lower ranks of life. He was neither sufficiently imaginative, nor sufficiently flexible in character, to succeed. He would unpack a mind rich in a curious lumber of chivalrous commonplaces, and give an air of unreality to values which for him, and for them all in varying measure, had the strength, if not altogether the substance, of fact. They did not really pause to weigh the truth or falsity of his opinions, which were simply without meaning for them. They only reflected that gentlefolk lived in circumstances very different from their own, and could afford strange luxuries. Probably only one thing he said interested them; and that was a casual remark, to the effect that, if the bad weather continued, the attack might have to be abandoned. At that, the face of Weeper Smart became suddenly illumined by an ecstasy of hope.

When at last Mr Rhys left them, they relaxed into ease with a sigh. Major Shadwell and Captain Malet they could understand, because each was what every private soldier is, a man in arms against a world, a man fighting desperately for himself, and conscious that, in the last resort, he stood alone; for such self-reliance lies at the very heart of comradeship. In so far as Mr Rhys had something of the same character, they respected him; but when he spoke to them of patriotism, sacrifice, and duty, he merely clouded and confused their vision.

"Chaps," said Weeper, suddenly, "for Christ's sake let's pray for rain!"

"What good would that do?" said Pacey, reasonably. "If they don't send us over the top here, they'll send us over somewhere else. It 'as got to be, an' if it 'as got to be, the sooner it's over an' done wi' the better. If we die, we die, an' it won't trouble nobody, leastways not for long it won't; an' if we don't die now, we'd 'ave to die some other time."

"What d'you want to talk about dyin' for?" said Martlow, resentfully. "I'd rather kill some other fucker first. I want to have my fling before I die, I do."

"If you want to pray, you 'ad better pray for the war to stop," continued Pacey, "so as we can all go back to our own 'omes in peace. I'm a married man wi' two children, an' I don't say I'm any better'n the next man, but I've a bit o' religion in me still, an' I don't hold wi' sayin' such things in jest."

"Aye," said Madeley, bitterly; "an' what good will all your prayin' do you? If there were any truth in religion, would there be a war, would God let it go on?"

"Some on us blame God for our own faults," said Pacey, coolly, "an' it were men what made the war. It's no manner o' use us sittin' 'ere pityin' ourselves, an' blamin' God for our own fault. I've got nowt to say again Mr Rhys. 'e talks about liberty, an' fightin' for your country, an' posterity, an' so on; but what I want to know is what all us 'ns are fightin' for . . ."

"We're fightin' for all we've bloody got," said Madeley, bluntly.

"An' that's sweet fuck all," said Weeper Smart. "A tell thee, that all a want to do is to save me own bloody skin. An' the first thing a do, when a go into t' line, is to find out where t' bloody dressing-stations are; an' if a can get a nice blighty, chaps, when once me face is turned towards home, I'm laughing. You won't see me bloody arse for dust. A'm not proud. A tell thee straight. Them as thinks different can 'ave all the bloody war they want, and me own share of it, too."

"Well, what the 'ell did you come out for?" asked Madeley.

Weeper lifted up a large, spade-like hand with the solemnity of one making an affirmation.

"That's where th'ast got me beat, lad," he admitted. "When a saw all them as didn't know any better'n we did joinin' up, an' a went walkin' out wi' me girl on Sundays, as usual, a just felt ashamed. An' a put it away, an' a put it away, until in th' end it got me down. A knew what it'd be, but it got the better o' me, an' then, like a bloody fool, a went an' joined up too. A were ashamed to be seen walkin' in the streets, a were. But a tell thee, now, that if a were once out o' these togs an' in civvies again, a wouldn't mind all the shame in the world; no, not if I 'ad to slink through all the back streets, an' didn' dare put me nose in t'Old Vaults again. A've no pride left in me now, chaps, an' that's the plain truth a'm tellin'. Let them as made the war come an' fight it, that's what a say."

"That's what I say, too," said Glazier, a man of about Madeley's age, with an air of challenge. Short, stocky, and ruddy like Madeley, he was of coarser grain, with an air of brutality that the other lacked: the kind of man who, when he comes to grips, kills, and grunts with pleasure in killing. "Why should us'ns fight an' be killed for all them bloody slackers at 'ome? It ain't right. No matter what they say, it ain't right. We're doin' our duty, an' they ain't, an' they're coinin' money while we get ten bloody frong a week. They don't care a fuck about us. Once we're in the army, they've got us by the balls. Talk about discipline! They don't try disciplinin' any o' them fuckin' civvies, do they? We want to put some o' them bloody politicians in the front line, an' see 'em shelled to shit. That'd buck their ideas up."

"I'm not fightin' for a lot o' bloody civvies," said Madeley, reasonably. "I'm fightin' for myself an' me own folk. It's all bloody fine sayin' let them as made the war fight it. 'twere Germany made the war."

"A tell thee," said Weeper, positively, "there are thousands o' poor buggers, over there in the German lines, as don' know, no more'n we do ourselves, what it's all about."

"Then what do the silly fuckers come an' fight for?" asked Madeley, indignantly. "Why didn' they stay 't 'ome? Tha'lt be sayin' next that the Frenchies sent 'em an invite."

"What a say is, that it weren't none o' our business. We'd no call to mix ourselves up wi' other folks' quarrels," replied Weeper.

"Well, I don't hold wi' that," said Glazier, judicially. "I'm not fightin' for them bloody slackers an' conchies at 'ome; but what I say is that the Fritzes 'ad to be stopped. If we 'adn't come in, an' they'd got the Frenchies beat, 'twould 'a' been our turn next."

"Too bloody true it would," said Madeley. "An' I'd rather come an' fight Fritz in France than 'ave 'im come over to Blighty an' start bashin' our 'ouses about, same as 'e's done 'ere."

"'e'd never 'ave come to England. The Navy 'd 'ave seen to that," said Pacey.

"Don't you be too bloody sure about the Navy," said Corporal Hamley, entering into the discussion at last. "The Navy 'as got all it can bloody well do, as things are."

"Well, chaps," said Glazier, "maybe I'm right an' maybe I'm wrong, but that's neither here nor there; only I've sometimes thought it would be a bloody good thing for us'ns, if the 'un did land a few troops in England. Show 'em what war's like. Madeley an' I struck it lucky an' went 'ome on leaf together, an' you never seed anything like it. Windy! Like a lot o' bloody kids they was, an' talkin' no more sense; 'pon me word, you'd be surprised at some o' the questions they'd ask, an' you couldn't answer sensible. They'd never believe it, if you did. We jes' kep' our mouths shut, and told 'em the war was all right, and we'd got it won, but not yet. 'twas the only way to keep 'em quiet.

"The boozers in Wes'church was shut most of the day; but Madeley and I would go down to the Greyhound, at seven o'clock, an' it was always chock-a-block wi' chaps lappin' it up as fast as they could, before closin' time. There'd be some old sweats, and some men back from 'ospital into barracks, but not fit, an' a few new recruits; but most o' them were miners, the sort o' buggers who took our job to dodge gettin' into khaki. Bloody fine miners they was. Well, one Saturday night we was in there 'avin' a bit of a booze-up, but peaceable like, when one of them bloody miners came in an' asked us to 'ave a drink in a loud voice. Well, we was peaceable enough, an' I dare say we might 'ave 'ad a drink with 'im, but the swine put 'is fist into 'is trousers' pocket, and pulls out a fistful of Bradburys an' 'arf-crowns, an' plunks 'em down on the bar counter. 'There,' he says, 'there's me bloody wages for a week, an' I ain't done more'n eight hours' work for it, either. I don't care if the bloody war lasts for ever,' 'e says. I looks up an' sees Madeley lookin' white an' dangerous. 'Was you talkin' to me?' says Madeley. 'Aye,' 'e says. 'Well, take that, you fuckin' bastard!' says Madeley, an' sloshes 'im one in the clock. Some of 'is friends interfered first, and then some of our friends interfered, an' in five seconds there was 'ell's delight in the bloody bar, wi' the old bitch be'ind the counter goin' into 'ysterics, an' 'ollerin' for the police.

"Then Madeley got 'old of 'is man, who was blubberin' an' swearin' summat awful, an' near twisted 'is arm off. I were busy keepin' some o' the other buggers off 'im, but 'e didn't pay no attention to nobody else, 'e just lugged 'is man out the back door an' into the yard, wi' the old girl 'ollerin' blue murder; and Madeley lugs 'im into the urinal, an' gets 'im down an' rubs 'is face in it. I'd got out the back door too, be that time, as I seed some red-caps comin' into the bar; an' when 'e'd finished I saw Madeley stand up an' wipe 'is 'ands on the seat of 'is trousers. 'There, you bugger,' 'e says; 'now you go 'ome an' talk to yourself.'—"op it,' I says to 'im, 'there's the fuckin' picket outside'; an' we 'opped it over some palin's at the bottom o' the yard; one of 'em came away, an' I run a bloody great splinter into the palm o' me 'and. Then we just buggered off, by some back streets, to The Crown, an' 'ad a couple o' pints an' went 'ome peaceable."

"Look at ol' tear-gas!" Martlow cried. "Thought you didn't like fightin', Weeper?"

Weeper's whole face was alight with excitement.

"A like a scrap as well as any man, so long as it don't go too far," said Weeper. "a'd 'ave given a lot to see thee go for that miner, Madeley. It's them chaps what are always on the make, an' don't care 'ow they makes it, as causes 'arf the wars. Them's the bloody cowards."

"Is it all true, Madeley?" asked Corporal Hamley.

"It were summat like, but I misremember," said Madeley, modestly. "But it's all true what 'e says about folks at 'ome, most on 'em. They don't care a fuck what 'appens to us'ns, so long as they can keep a 'ole skin. Say they be ready to make any sacrifice; but we're the bloody sacrifice. You never seed such a windy lot; an' bloodthirsty ain't the word for it. They've all gone potty. You'd think your best friends wouldn't be satisfied till they'd seed your name on the roll of honour. I tol' one of 'em 'e knew a bloody sight more'n I did about the war. The only person as 'ad any sense was me mother. She on'y fussed about what I wanted to eat. She didn't want to know anything about the war, an' it were on'y me she were afraid for. She didn't min' about aught else. 'Please God, you'll be home soon,' she'd say. An' please God, I will."

"An' then they give you a bloody party," said Glazier. "Madeley an'' I went to one. You should a seed some o' the pushers. Girls o' seventeen painted worse nor any Gerties I'd ever knowed. One of 'em came on an' sang a lot o' songs wi' dirty meanings to 'em. I remember one she sang wi' another girl, "*I want a Rag.*" She did an' all, too. When this bloody war's over, you'll go back to England an' fin' nought there but a lot o' conchies and bloody prostitutes."

"There's good an' bad," said Pacey, mildly, "an' if there's more bad than good, I don't know but the good don't wear better. But there's nought sure in this world, no more."

"No, an' never 'as been," said Madeley, pessimistically.

"There's nought sure for us'ns, anyway," said Weeper, relapsing. "Didst 'ear what Cap'n Thompson read out this mornin', about stoppin' to 'elp any poor bugger what was wounded? The bloody brass-'at what wrote that letter 'as never been in any big show 'isself, that a dare swear. 'e's one o' them buggers as is never nearer to the real thing than G.H.Q."

"You don't want to talk like that," said Corporal Hamley. "You've 'ad your orders."

"A don't mind tellin' thee, corporal," said Weeper, again lifting a large flat hand, as though by that gesture he stopped the mouths of all the world. "A don't mind tellin' thee, that if a see a chum o' mine down, an' a can do aught to 'elp 'im, all the brass-'ats in the British Army, an' there's a bloody sight too many o' 'em, aren't goin' to stop me. A'll do what's right, an' if a know aught about thee, tha'lt do as I do."

"You don't want to talk about it, anyway," said Corporal Hamley, quietly. "I'm not sayin' you're not right: I'd do what any other man'd do; but there's no need to make a song about it."

"What beats me," said Shem, sniggering, "is that the bloody fool who wrote that instructional letter, doesn't seem to know what any ordinary man would do in the circumstances. We all know that there must be losses, you can't expect to take a trench without some casualties; but they seem to go on from saying that losses are unavoidable, to thinking that they're necessary, and from that, to thinking that they don't matter."

"They don't know what we've got to go through, that's the truth of it," said Weeper. "They measure the distance, an' they count the men, an' the guns, an' think a battle's no' but a sum you can do wi' a pencil an' a bit o' paper."

"I heard Mr Pardew talking to Mr Rhys about a course he'd been on, and he told him a brass-hat had been lecturing them on the lessons of the Somme offensive, and gave them an estimate of the total German losses; and then an officer at the back of the room got up, and asked him if he could give them any information about the British losses, and the brass-hat said: No, and looked at them as though they were a lot of criminals."

"It's a fact," said Glazier; "whether you're talkin' to a civvy or whether you're talkin' to a brass-'at, an' some o' the officers aren't no better, if you tell the truth, they think you're a bloody coward. They've not got our experience, an' they don't face it as us'ns do."

"Give them a chance," said Bourne, reasonably; he hadn't spoken before, he usually sat back and listened quietly to these debates.

"Let 'em take my fuckin' chance!" shouted Weeper, vindictively.

"There's a good deal in what you say," said Bourne, who was a little embarrassed by the way they all looked at him suddenly. "I think there's a good deal of truth in it; but after all, what is a brass-hat's job? He's not thinking of you or of me or of any individual man, or of any particular battalion or division. Men, to him, are only part of the material he has

got to work with; and if he felt as you or I feel, he couldn't
carry on with his job. It's not fair to think he's inhuman. He's
got to draw up a plan, from rather scrappy information, and
it is issued in the form of an order; but he knows very well
something may happen at any moment to throw everything
out of gear. The original plan is no more than a kind of map;
you can't see the country by looking at a map, and you can't
see the fighting by looking at a plan of attack. Once we go
over the top it's the colonel's and the company commander's
job. Once we meet a Hun it's our job . . ."

"Yes, an' our job's a bloody sight worse'n theirs," said
Weeper.

JULES ROMAINS
The Counter-Attack at Mort-Homme

Jules Romains was the pseudonym of the French author, Louis Farigoule (1885–1972). He served in the peacetime French Army and later as an auxiliary during World War I.

The selection that follows is from Verdun *one of the 27 volumes in Romains' great cycle* Les Hommes de bonne volonté. *Mort-Homme is a hill about eight miles from Verdun.*

A T 1 P.M. AN ENCOURAGING RUMOUR began to circulate among the companies in reserve on the slope opposite Mort-Homme, to the west of brigade headquarters:

"The Boche attack has failed."

The bombardment had, in fact, ceased with dramatic suddenness. There was no reason to suppose that this cessation was the prelude to a fresh assault, since at midday, when the German infantry had started to move forward, their guns, so far from being silent, had worked up to a still greater degree of fury, contenting themselves merely with lengthening their range. Wazemmes, who since midnight had run the whole gamut of emotions, was now conscious of an entirely new one. Its elements were a sincere relief, which he did not allow to appear, and a flicker of disappointment, of which he made considerable parade.

"Damn nuisance," he said to his young comrades of the '16 class. "What's the matter with 'em?"

His disappointment was, in fact, perfectly genuine. Since,

obviously, something had got to happen sooner or later, the sooner the better. Wazemmes felt that he was in just the right mood to face a crisis, worked up to a state of unprecedented excitement.

But what a day it had been! About midnight, just when they had all dropped into a sound sleep, had come the fall-in. "It seems the Boches are going to attack tomorrow. Since we're in reserve, you can let your kids sleep a bit longer." (The kids were the members of the '16 class who had been drafted into the regiment a few days earlier.) "But see that they're all ready. The older men, and the NCOs of course, must take over sentry duties." At 7 a.m., just when Wazemmes, his rifle between his legs, was snoozing against an angle of the trench wall, someone had shaken him by the shoulders.

"Hey! Wake up. The lieutenant's asking for you."

The lieutenant commanding the company, who had joined the regiment a few days before Wazemmes, was a very young officer who, in the eyes of the latter, shone with all sorts of reflected glory. His name was Comte Voisenon de Pelleriès. He had been due to start his career at the Military College in 1914, but had been introduced to the school of war before he had known the discipline of that other, more normal school (he and his class-mates had not even had time to sit for their oral entrance examination). Among his companions had been many who had fallen in great numbers during that first winter "advancing in dress uniform". The Comte de Pelleriès was a slim, not very tall young man, who maintained a standard of quiet elegance even in the trenches. He had fine grey eyes, the hint of an auburn moustache, and spoke with so cordial a tone of friendliness that his voice at times took on a warm and tender timbre. Each one of his men felt that he was enveloped in an aura of confidence and affection. He had been wounded three times, once seriously. As a result of his last wound but one, he had been left with a slight limp—quite temporary, he maintained—which he disguised with easy grace.

"My dear Wazemmes," he said, "I understand that you were formerly a corporal. I am pleased to be able to tell you that, as the result of my personal representations, your stripes have been restored to you. Your squad will be composed entirely of young fellows of the '16 class. You will probably have to lead them forward under fire in the course of today. I know that you are brave enough to face any call upon your courage, and that you will give your men an admirable example."

He held out his hand and shook Wazemmes's as though it had been that of an old friend.

At 8 a.m.—"Boom, branranran, bang, bang . . ." Wazemmes, drunk with sleep and with the prospect of glory, spent his time walking up and down among "his men".

"That was a 77 . . . those greeny-yellowish bursts up there are 105 shrapnel . . . That noise? That's probably trench-mortars firing on our front lines."

The poor little devils were both delighted and appalled, now pink with emotion, now green with terror. Since the bombardment, violent though it was, was not falling on their position, they gradually grew in confidence, and more than one was heard to say that the guns' bark was worse than their bite. Without wishing to shatter their illusion on this point, the NCOs repeated various bits of advice about how they should behave in open ground in order to avoid unnecessary risks.

The information given by the Polish prisoners had turned out to be perfectly correct so far as it concerned the preliminary bombardment. It was felt, therefore, that it would probably be no less correct in its other details, and it was expected that the enemy assault would take place at midday.

About half-past eleven, the Comte de Pelleriès assembled his boys of the '16 class and, to the amazement of more than one of them, among whom Wazemmes was certainly numbered, made them a little speech in his kindly, cultivated voice, the gist of which was as follows: "My dear friends, we are probably going to take part in the coming action. We shall not be called upon to receive the first waves of the German assault," (he never let the word "Boche" pass his lips), "but since it is possible that our comrades in the front line may be forced to yield a little ground, we shall be called upon to bar the way to the attacking enemy, or perhaps to counter-attack with the purpose of recapturing the lost trenches. If we have to counter-attack, we shall carry out our duty bravely, shall we not, my friends? We are soldiers of the Republic. We are here to defend Verdun, because the fall of Verdun might mean the defeat of France. We do not want our country, which is a democracy, a republic of free men, to be conquered and enslaved by the men opposite, who are not free men, but live still in feudal conditions. Not far from here, at Valmy, a little over one hundred and twenty years ago, your ancestors drove back the foreigners who had come to crush the Great French Revolution. One of my ancestors, the Comte Voisenon de Pelleriès, was present on that occasion too, with the rank of captain. He was not one of those who had emigrated . . . When, therefore, we move forward, I should like you, my friends, to shout with me: '*Vive la nation! Vive la République!*' as our ancestors shouted at Valmy, and then to advance on the enemy singing the 'Marseillaise'."

In five minutes Wazemmes's political convictions had undergone a radical change. And since the portrait of Mlle Anne de Montbieuze had already been replaced on his heart by that of a charming typist of no marked political views, but probably sympathetic to the Left, whom he had met on the evening of 2 April, he had no difficulty in feeling now that he was a soldier of Valmy and a corporal of the Republic.

Suddenly, a rumour passed down the ranks.

"Seems we've got to counter-attack. The Boches have advanced again. They're going to come down this side of the Mort-Homme . . . The chasseurs have been driven from their trenches . . . We've got to retake them."

There followed a period of intolerable waiting. The bombardment, which had started again, was spreading now on every side. Shells with all the names in the vocabulary, with all the magic, terrifying numbers which served to identify them, with their noises, none of which were really alike but which no ear could distinguish, so overwhelming was the uproar, with their bursts of smoke which looked like different species of poisonous fungus, with their smells which united into a single stench, gave the impression that they were all detonating at one and the same moment in the air, in the earth, in the interior of one's own stomach. The country which one could just glimpse through a breach in the parapet (strictly forbidden to show one's head) looked sad and comfortless. Though the sun was shining, a melancholy exuded from its bare, grey distances, which dwindled away towards the enemy lines in a series of slow undulations. The slope in front was the one to be climbed, there where each moment the earth was torn by some great shell. Smoke came from the ground as though a hook were drawing wool from a mattress with insistent regularity. The attacking line would have to move along the whole length of that slope so torn by shells, so witheringly swept by machine-gun fire. If only it needn't happen! If only the order to advance never came! Things do happen like that sometimes, luck does turn at the very last moment. Perhaps the Boches, too much exhausted by their own efforts, too badly mauled by our artillery (for our guns were hard at it, 75s, 155s, and all the rest) would retire of their own account. Perhaps the chasseurs might have sufficient self-pride to want to retake themselves the trenches they had lost. Perhaps, for some reason or other, the Staff might change its mind . . . It was well known that Pétain did not like sacrificing men's lives.

Lieutenant Voisenon de Pelleriès could be seen putting on his gloves, smoothing his tiny moustache. He drew his sword (for, since this morning, he had taken to wearing it). In a voice of marked politeness he cried:

"My friends, it's our turn now!"

Then he clambered over the parapet, shouting:

"*Vive la nation! Vive la République!*"

The lads behind him shouted too, as men shout in dreams, without being quite sure whether their lips were uttering any audible sound. They leapt forward without, as yet, much difficulty, since the objective was still far away and the machine-guns were not, so far, concentrating on them. The lieutenant began to sing the "Marseillaise". They did their best to sing it too. From time to time, interrupting his singing, the lieutenant shouted to them:

"Do as I do! Lie down!"

But he only half lay down. He watched them from the corner of his eye. They flung themselves down at once.

A few of them began to fall. Sometimes their friends did not notice what had happened; sometimes they saw but could not believe their eyes. They took up a verse of the "Marseillaise", shouting the first words that occurred to them. They had no idea whether it was the same verse as the one the lieutenant was singing, or their pals on either side.

"Careful, boys. We've got to get through an artillery barrage . . . Do as I do . . . Bend as low as you can, and jump to it . . . Don't lie down again until you're fifty yards farther on."

Wazemmes swallowed the scrap of the "Marseillaise" which stuck in his throat, to pass the order back to "his men":

"Do as I do . . . Jump to it!"

He threw himself forward, bending his body as much as he could, and going as fast as he knew how. The noise was staggering.

"Ho!"

It was all over in a second. He had hardly time to realize that he had been hit, that the pain was hideous, that he was done for.

"There you are," said Pétain to Geoffroy, holding out the sheet of manuscript which was still wet. "Have it run off and distributed at once to all units . . . I'd have liked to say something rather special about those lads of the '16 class, but I was afraid it might be too painful for their poor parents . . . Do you know how many of them actually reached the trench lost by the chasseurs? Ten, out of a total of two companies engaged in the counter-attack? Ten, just think of it! I'm told that de Pelleriès was magnificent. He made those boys sing the 'Marseillaise'. He was killed half-way up the slope. I'm going to see that he gets a posthumous award of the Croix de Guerre."

Geoffroy took the paper and read the general's rather large, angular script, to which the shaping of certain letters gave a curiously feminine quality (the ink of the last few lines was not yet dry):

To the Men of the IInd Army

The ninth of April is a glorious day in the annals of our military history.

The furious attacks delivered by the German soldiers under the command of the Crown Prince have been everywhere broken.

Infantry, artillery, engineers, and flying men of the IInd Army vied with one another in heroism.

Honour to them all!

The Germans will undoubtedly attack again. Let every man work and watch to the end that future successes may fall in no way short of yesterday's.

Courage . . . We shall beat them yet!

Ph. Pétain

"Not bad, no, not at all bad," said Geoffroy to himself as he took his way down the staircase. "If only this could be the last order of the day to be issued in connection with the battle of Verdun!"

He crossed the vestibule and stepped out of the front door. There before him the road roared and rumbled, true to itself as ever, with its double line of trucks.

JAROSLAV HAŠEK
The Good Soldier Švejk

Jaroslav Hašek (1883–1923) was born in Prague, the son of a mathematics teacher. He began his working life as a respectable bank clerk, but abandoned this career in favour of drinking, writing and anarchism. He was drafted into the 91st Infantry Regiment of the Austrian Army in 1915 -Czechoslovakia at the time was ruled by Austria- and almost immediately deserted to the Russians.

There follows an excerpt from The Good Soldier Švejk (1923), Hašek's epic satire on army life. The snub-nosed Švejk (pronounced "Svake") is a former Prague dog-dealer, now batman to Lieutenant Lukas.

"**D**ID YOU NOT READ THE advertisement in *Bohemie* and in the *Tagblatt* about the loss of my stable pinscher? You didn't read the advertisement which your superior officer put into the newspaper?"

The colonel clapped his hands.

"Really, these young officers! Where has discipline gone? The colonel puts in advertisements and the lieutenant doesn't read them."

"If only I could give you a few across the jaw, you bloody old dotard," Lieutenant Lukáš thought to himself, looking at the colonel's side whiskers which were reminiscent of an orang-utan.

"Come with me for a moment," said the colonel. And so they walked along and had a very pleasant conversation:

"At the front, lieutenant, a thing like this cannot happen to you again. Promenading with stolen dogs behind the lines is certainly very agreeable. Yes, walking about with your superior officer's dog at a time when every day we are losing a hundred officers on the battlefield. And advertisements are not read! For a hundred years I could insert notices that my dog is lost. Two hundred years! Three hundred years!"

The colonel blew his nose noisily, which with him was always a sign of great fury, and said: "You can go on with your walk." Then he turned round and went away, angrily striking with his riding whip across the ends of his officer's greatcoat.

Lieutenant Lukáš crossed to the opposite pavement and heard once more: "Halt!" The colonel had just stopped an unfortunate infantryman in the reserve, who was thinking about his mother at home and had not noticed him.

The colonel took him in person to the barracks for punishment and swore at him for being a swine and bastard.

"What shall I do with Švejk," thought the lieutenant. "I'll smash his jaw, but that's not enough. Even tearing his skin from his body in little strips would be too good treatment for that blackguard." Disregarding the fact that he was due to meet a lady, he set off home in a fury.

"I'll kill him, the dirty hound," he said to himself as he got into the tram.

Meanwhile the good soldier Švejk was deep in conversation with an orderly from the barracks. The soldier had brought the lieutenant some documents to sign and was now waiting.

Švejk treated him to coffee and they discussed together how Austria would be smashed.

They carried on this conversation as though it could be taken for granted. There was an endless series of utterances which would certainly have been defined in the court as treasonable and for which both of them would have been hanged.

"His Imperial Majesty must be completely off his rocker by this time," declared Švejk. "He was never bright, but this war'll certainly finish him."

"Of course he's off his rocker," the soldier from the barracks asserted with conviction. "He's so gaga he probably doesn't know there's a war on. Perhaps they're ashamed of telling him. If his signature's on the manifesto to his peoples, then it's a fraud. They must have had it printed without his knowledge, because he's not capable of thinking about anything at all."

"He's finished," added Švejk knowingly. "He wets himself and they have to feed him like a little baby. Recently a chap at the pub told us that His Imperial Majesty has two wet nurses and is breast-fed three times a day."

"If only it was all over," sighed the soldier from the barracks, "and they knocked us out, so that Austria at last had peace!"

And both continued the conversation until finally Švejk condemned Austria for ever with the words: "A monarchy as idiotic as this ought not to exist at all," whereupon the other, to complete his utterance by adding something of a practical kind, said: "When I get to the front I'll hop it pretty quick."

And when both continued to interpret the views of the average Czech about the war, the soldier from the barracks repeated what he had heard that day in Prague, that guns could be heard at Náchod and that the Tsar of Russia would soon be in Cracow.

Then they related how our corn was being carted away to Germany and how German soldiers were getting cigarettes and chocolate.

Then they remembered the times of the old wars, and Švejk solemnly argued that when in the olden days they threw stinkpots into a beleaguered castle it was no picnic to have to fight in such a stink. He had read that they had besieged a castle somewhere for three years and the enemy did nothing else except amuse themselves every day in this way with the beleaguered inside.

He would certainly have added something else interesting and informative if their conversation had not been interrupted by the return of Lieutenant Lukáš.

Casting at Švejk a fearful, crushing glance, he signed the documents and after dismissing the soldier motioned Švejk to follow him into his sitting-room.

Frightful lightning shafts darted from the lieutenant's eyes.

Sitting on the chair he looked at Švejk and pondered how he should start the massacre.

"First I'll give him a few across the jaw," he thought. "Then I'll break his nose and tear off his ears. And after that we'll see."

But he was confronted by the honest and kindly gaze of the good and innocent eyes of Švejk who dared to interrupt the calm before the storm with the words: "Humbly report, sir, you've lost your cat. She ate up the boot polish and permitted herself to pass out. I threw her into the cellar—but next door. You won't find again such a good and beautiful Angora cat."

"What shall I do with him?" flashed through the lieutenant's mind. "For Christ's sake, what an idiotic expression he has."

And the kindly innocent eyes of Švejk continued to glow with gentleness and tenderness, combined with an expression of complete composure; everything was in order and nothing had happened, and if something had happened, it was again quite in order that anything at all was happening.

Lieutenant Lukáš jumped up, but did not hit Švejk as he had originally intended to do. He brandished his fist under his nose and roared out. "Švejk, you *stole* the dog!"

"Humbly report, sir, I know of no such case recently and I would like to observe, sir, that you yourself took Max this afternoon out for a walk and so I couldn't have stolen it. I saw at once when you came back without the dog that something must have happened. That's called a situation. In Spálená Street there is a bag-maker named Kuneš and he couldn't take a dog out for a walk without losing it. Usually he left it somewhere at a pub or someone stole it from him or borrowed it and never returned it . . ."

"Švejk, you bastard, you, Himmellaudon, hold your tongue! Either you're a cunning blackguard or else you're a camel and a fat-headed idiot. You're a real object lesson, but I tell you you'd better not try anything on me! Where did you get that dog from? How did you get hold of it? Do you know that it belongs to our colonel, who took it off with him when we happened to meet? Do you realize that this is a colossal world scandal? So speak the truth now! Did you steal it or not?"

"Humbly report, sir, I didn't steal it."

"Did you know that it was a stolen dog?"

"Humbly report, sir, I knew it was stolen."

"Švejk, Jesus Mary, Himmelherrgott, I'll have you shot, you bastard, you cattle, you oaf, you pig. Are you really such a half-wit?"

"Humbly report, sir, I am."

"Why did you bring me a stolen dog? Why did you put that beast into my apartment?"

"To give you a little pleasure, sir."

And Švejk's eyes looked kindly and tenderly into the face of the lieutenant, who sat down and sighed: "Why did God punish me with this bastard?"

The lieutenant sat on the chair in quiet resignation and felt he had not the strength even to roll a cigarette, let alone give Švejk one or two across the jaw, and he had no idea why he sent Švejk to get *Bohemie* and *Tagblatt* so that Švejk could read the colonel's advertisement about the stolen dog.

With the newspaper open on the advertisement pages Švejk returned. He beamed and proclaimed joyfully: "It's there, sir. The colonel describes that stolen stable pinscher so beautifully that it's a pure joy, and into the bargain he offers the finder of it a hundred crowns. That's quite a handsome reward. Generally they only give fifty. A chap called Božetěch from Košíře made a business just out of this. He always stole dogs, then looked in the advertisements to see whether one had run away and at once went there. On one occasion he stole a beautiful black pom, and because the owner didn't advertise it in the newspapers, he tried to put an advertisement in himself. He spent ten crowns on advertisements until finally a gentleman announced that it was his dog, that he had lost it and that he had thought that it would be useless to try and look for it, as he didn't believe any longer in people's honesty. But now he saw that all the same there were honest people to be found, and this gave him tremendous pleasure. He said he was opposed on principle to rewarding honesty, but as a souvenir he would give him his book on indoor and outdoor plant cultivation. The good Božetěch took that black pom by its back legs and hit the gentleman over the head with it and from that time he swore he wouldn't put in any more advertisements. He'd rather sell a dog to a kennel, if no one wanted to advertise for it."

"Go to bed, Švejk," the lieutenant ordered. "You are capable of drivelling on like this till tomorrow morning." And he went to bed too. In the night he dreamt of Švejk, how Švejk had also stolen the horse of the Heir to the Throne and brought it to him, and how the Heir to the Throne had recognized the horse at a review, when the unfortunate Lieutenant Lukáš rode on it at the head of his company.

In the morning the lieutenant felt as if he had gone through a night of debauch during which he had been knocked many times over the head. An unusually oppressive nightmare clung to him. Exhausted by the frightful dream he fell asleep towards the morning, only to be woken by a knocking on the door. The kindly face of Švejk appeared and asked when he should wake the lieutenant.

The lieutenant groaned in bed: "Get out, you monster, this is sheer hell!"

But when he was already up and Švejk brought him his breakfast, the lieutenant was surprised by a new question from Švejk: "Humbly report, sir, would you wish me to look for another nice doggie for you?"

"You know, Švejk, that I feel like having you court-martialled," said the lieutenant with a sigh, "but they'd only acquit you, because they'd never have seen anything so colossally idiotic in all their lives. Do look at yourself in the mirror. Doesn't it make you sick to see your own drivelling expression? You're the most idiotic freak of nature that I've ever seen. Now, tell me the truth, Švejk, do you really like yourself?"

"Humbly report, sir, I don't. In this mirror I am somehow lopsided or something. But the glass is not properly cut. At the Chinaman, Staněk's, they once had a convex mirror and when anybody looked at himself in it he wanted to spew. A mug like this, a head like a slop-pail, a belly like a sozzled canon, in short a complete scarecrow. Then the Governor of Bohemia passed by and saw himself in it and the mirror had to be removed at once."

The lieutenant turned away, sighed and thought it right to pay attention to his coffee rather than to Švejk.

Švejk was already pottering about in the kitchen, and Lieutenant Lukáš heard him singing:

"Grenevil is marching through the Powder Gate.
Swords are flashing, pretty girls are weeping . . ."

And then there came from the kitchen another song:

"We're the boys who make the noise,
Win the hearts of all the tarts,
Draw our pay and then make hay."

"You certainly make hay, you bastard," the lieutenant
thought to himself and spat.

Švejk's head appeared in the doorway: "Humbly report, sir,
they've come here for you from the barracks. You're to go at
once to the colonel. His orderly officer is here."

And he added confidentially: "Perhaps it's because of
that dog."

"I've already heard," said the lieutenant, when the orderly
officer wanted to report to him in the hall.

He said this dejectedly and went out casting an annihilating
glance at Švejk.

This was not regimental report. It was something worse.
When the lieutenant stepped into his office the colonel sat in
his chair frowning frightfully.

"Two years ago, lieutenant," said the colonel, "you asked to
be transferred to the 91st regiment in Budějovice. Do you know
where Budějovice is? It's on the Vltava, yes, on the Vltava,
where the Ohře or something like that flows into it. The town
is big, so to speak, and friendly, and if I'm not mistaken it has
an embankment. Do you know what an embankment is? It is
a wall built over the water. Yes. However, this is not relevant
here. We had manoeuvres there."

The colonel was silent, and looking at the ink pot passed
quickly to another subject: "My dog's ruined after having been
with you. He won't eat anything. Look, there's a fly in the ink
pot. It's very strange that flies should fall into the ink pot in
winter. That's disorderly."

"Well, say your say, you bloody old dodderer," thought the
lieutenant to himself.

The colonel got up and walked once or twice up and down the office.

"I've thought for a long time, lieutenant, what I ought to do with you to prevent this *recurring*, and I remembered that you wanted to be transferred to the 91st regiment. The high command recently informed us that there is a great shortage of officers in the 91st regiment because they have all been *killed by the Serbs*. I give you my word of honour that within three days you will be in the 91st regiment in Budějovice, where they are forming *march battalions for the front*. You don't need to thank me. The army requires officers who . . ."

And not knowing what else to say he looked at his watch and pronounced: "It's half-past ten and high time to go to regimental report."

And with this the agreeable conversation came to an end, and the lieutenant felt very relieved when he left the office and went to the volunteers' school, where he announced that very soon he would be going to the front and was therefore organizing a farewell evening party in Nekázanka.

Returning home he said significantly to Švejk: "Do you know, Švejk, what a march battalion is?"

"Humbly report, sir, a march battalion is a *maršbaťák* and a march company is a *marškumpačka*. We always use abbreviations."

"Very well then, Švejk," said the lieutenant in a solemn voice. "I wish to tell you that you are going with me on the *maršbaťák*, if you like such abbreviations. But don't think that at the front you'll be able to drop such bloody awful clangers as you've done here. Are you happy?"

"Humbly report, sir, I'm awfully happy," replied the good soldier Švejk. "It'll be really marvellous when we both fall dead together for His Imperial Majesty and the Royal Family . . ."

LEWIS RITCHIE ("BARTIMEUS")
The Survivor

Captain Sir Lewis Anselmo Ritchie KCVO (1886–1967) was a career naval officer, later to become the press secretary to the king, 1944–47. He also wrote widely in the genre of naval fiction under the pseudonym "Bartimeus". His books include The Long Trick *(1917),* Naval Occasions *(1936) and* A Ditty Box *(1936).*

The short story "The Survivor" is from Navy Eternal *(1918).*

". . . And regrets to report only one survivor."
Admiralty Announcement

THE GLASS DROPPED ANOTHER POINT, and the captain of the cruiser glanced for the hundredth time from the lowering sky to the two destroyers labouring stubbornly in the teeth of the gale on either beam. Then he gave an order to the yeoman of signals, who barked its repetition to the shelter-deck where the little group of signalmen stamped their feet and blew on their numbed fingers in the lee of the flag-lockers. Two of the group scuffled round the bright-coloured bunting: the clips of the halliards snapped a hoist together, and vivid against the grey sky the signal went bellying and fluttering to the masthead.

The figures on the bridges of the destroyers wiped the stinging spray from their swollen eyelids and read the message of comfort.

"Return to base. Weather conditions threatening."

They surveyed their battered bridges and forecastles, their

stripped, streaming decks and guns crews; they thought of hot food, warm bunks, dry clothing, and all the sordid creature comforts for which soul and body yearn so imperiously after three years of North Sea warfare. Their answering pendants fluttered acknowledgement, and they swung round on the path for home, praising Allah who had planted in the brain of the cruiser captain a consideration for the welfare of his destroyer screen.

"If this is what they call 'threatening'," observed the senior officer of the two boats, as his command clove shuddering through the jade-green belly of a mountainous sea, flinging the white entrails broadcast, "if this is merely threatening I reckon it's about time someone said 'Home, James!'"

His first lieutenant said nothing. He had spent three winters in these grey wastes, and he knew the significance of that unearthly clear visibility and the inky clouds banked ahead to the westward. But presently he looked up from the chart and nodded towards the menace in the western sky. "That's snow," he said. "It ought to catch us about the time we shall make Scaw Dhu light."

"We'll hear the fog buoy all right," said the captain.

"If the pipes ain't frozen," was the reply. "It's perishing cold." He ran a gauntletted hand along the rail and extended a handful of frozen spray. "That's salt—*and* frozen . . ."

The snow came as he had predicted, but rather sooner. It started with great whirling flakes like feathers about a gull's nesting-place, a soundless ethereal vanguard of the storm, growing momentarily denser. The wind, from a temporary lull, reawakened with a roar. The air became a vast witch's cauldron of white and brown specks, seething before the vision in a veritable Bacchanal of Atoms. Sight became a lost sense: time, space, and feeling were overwhelmed by that shrieking fury of snow and frozen spray thrashing pitilessly about the homing grey hulls and the bowed heads of the men who clung to the reeling bridges.

The grey, white-crested seas raced hissing alongside and, as the engine-room telegraphs rang again and again for reduced speed, overtook and passed them. Out of the welter of snow and spray the voices of the leadsmen chanting soundings reached the ears of those inboard as the voice of a doctor reaches a patient in delirium, fruitlessly reassuring . . .

Number Three of the midship gun on board the leading destroyer turned for the comfort of his soul from the contemplation of the pursuing seas to the forebridge, but snow-flakes blotted it from view. Providence, as he was accustomed to visualize it in the guise of a red-cheeked lieutenant-commander, had vanished from his ken. Number Three drew his hands from his pockets, and raising them to his mouth leaned towards the gunlayer. The gunlayer was also staring forward as if his vision had pierced that whirling grey curtain and was contemplating something beyond it, infinitely remote . . . There was a concentrated intensity in his expression not unlike that of a dog when he raises his head from his paws and looks towards a closed door.

"'Ere," bawled Number Three, seeking comradeship in an oppressive, indefinable loneliness. "'Ow about it—eh? . . ." The wind snatched at the meaningless words and beat them back between his chattering teeth.

The wind backed momentarily, sundering the veil of whirling obscurity. Through this rent towered a wall of rock, streaked all about with driven snow, at the foot of which breakers beat themselves into a smoking yeast of fury. Gulls were wailing overhead. Beneath their feet the engine room gongs clanged madly.

Then they struck.

The foremost destroyer checked on the shoulder of a great roller as if incredulous: shuddered: struck again and lurched over. A mountainous sea engulfed her stern and broke thundering against the after-funnel. Steam began to pour in dense hissing clouds from the engine-room hatchways and exhausts. Her consort swept past with screeching syren, helpless in the grip of the backwash for all her thrashing propellers that strove to check her headlong way. She too struck and recoiled: sagged in the trough of two stupendous seas, and plunged forward again . . . Number Three, clinging to the greasy breechblock of his gun, clenched his teeth at the sound of that pitiless grinding which seemed as if it would never end . . .

Of the ensuing horror he missed nothing, yet saw it all with a wondering detachment. A wave swept him off his feet against a funnel-stay, and receding, left him clinging to it like a twist of waterlogged straw. Hand over hand he crawled higher, and finally hung dangling six feet above the highest wave, legs and arms round about the wire stay. He saw the forecastle break off like a stick of canteen chocolate and vanish into the smother. The other destroyer had disappeared. Beneath him, waist deep in boiling eddies, he saw men labouring about a raft, and had a vision of their upturned faces as they were swept away. The thunder of the surf on the beaches close at hand drowned the few shouts and cries that sounded. The wire from which he dangled jarred and twanged like a banjo-string, as the triumphant seas beat the soul out of the wreck beneath him.

A funnel-stay parted, and amid clouds of smoke and steam the funnel slowly began to list over the side. Number Three of the midship gun clung swaying like a wind-tossed branch above the maelstrom of seething water till a wave drove over the already-unrecognizable hull of the destroyer, leaped hungrily at the dangling human figure and tore him from his hold.

Bitterly cold water and a suffocating darkness engulfed him. Something clawed at his face and fastened on to his shoulder; he wrenched himself free from the nerveless clutch without ruth or understanding; his booted heel struck a yielding object as he struggled surfaceward, kicking wildly like a swimming frog . . . the blackness became streaked with grey light and pinpoints of fire. Number Three had a conviction that unless the next few strokes brought him to the surface it would be too late. Then abruptly the clamour of the wind and sea, and the shriek of the circling gulls smote his ears again. He was back on the surface once more, gulping greedy lungfuls of air.

A wave caught him and hurled him forward on its crest, spread-eagled, feebly continuing the motions of a swimmer. It spent itself, and to husband his strength the man turned on his back, moving his head from side to side to take in his surroundings.

He was afloat (he found it surprisingly easy to keep afloat) inside a narrow bay. On both sides the black cliffs rose, all streaked with snow, out of a thunderous welter of foam. The tide sobbed and lamented in the hollows of unseen caverns, or sluiced the length of a ledge to plash in cascades down the face of the cliff.

The snow had abated, and in the gathering dusk the broken

water showed ghostly white. To seaward the gale drove the smoking rollers in successive onslaughts against the reef where the battered remains of the two destroyers lay. All about the distorted plating and tangle of twisted stanchions the surf broke as if in a fury of rapine and destruction . . .

Another wave gripped him and rushed him shoreward again. The thunder of the surf redoubled. "Hi! hi! hi! hi!" screeched the storm-tossed gulls. Number Three of the midship gun abandoned his efforts to swim and covered his face with his soggy sleeve. It was well not to look ahead. The wave seemed to be carrying him towards the cliffs at the speed of an express train. He wondered if the rocks would hurt much, beating out his life . . . He tried desperately to remember a prayer, but all he could recall was a sermon he had once listened to on the quarterdeck, one drowsy summer morning at Malta . . . About coming to Jesus on the face of the waters . . . "And Jesus said 'come' . . ." Fair whizzing along, he was . . .

Again the wave spent itself, and the man was caught in the backwash, drawn under, rolled over and over, spun round and round, gathered up in the watery embrace of another roller and flung up on all fours on a shelving beach. Furiously he clawed at the retreating pebbles, lurched to his feet, staggered forward a couple of paces, and fell on hands and knees on the fringe of a snow-drift. There he lay awhile, panting for breath.

He was conscious of an immense amazement, and, mingled with it, an inexplicable pride. He was still alive! It was an astounding achievement, being the solitary survivor of all those officers and men. But he had always considered himself a bit out of the ordinary . . . Once he had entered for a race at the annual sports at the Naval Barracks, Devonport. He had never run a race before in his life, and he won. It seemed absurdly easy. "Bang!" went the pistol: off they went, helter-skelter, teeth clenched, fists clenched, hearts pounding, spectators a blur, roaring encouragement . . .

He won, and experienced the identical astonished gratification that he felt now.

"You runs like a adjective 'are, Bill," his chum had admitted, plying the hero with beer at the little pub halfway up the cobbled hill by the dockyard.

Then he remembered other chums, shipmates, and one in

particular called Nobby. He rose into a sitting position, staring seaward. Through the gloom the tumult of the seas, breaking over the reef on which they had foundered, glimmered white. The man rose unsteadily to his feet; he was alone on the beach of a tiny cove with his back to forbidding cliffs. Save where his own footsteps showed black, the snow was unmarked, stretching in an unbroken arc from one side of the cove to the other. The solitary figure limped to the edge of the surf and peered through the stinging scud. Then, raising his hands to his mouth, he began to call for his lost mate.

"Nobby!" he shouted, and again and again, "Nobby! Nobby! . . . Nob-bee-e! . . ."

"Nobby," echoed the cliffs behind, disinterestedly.

"Hi! Hi! Hi!" mocked the gulls.

The survivor waded knee-deep into the froth of an incoming sea.

"Ahoy!" he bawled to the driving snow-flakes and spindrift. His voice sounded cracked and feeble. He tried to shout again, but the thunder of the waves beat the sound to nothing.

He retraced his steps and paused to look round at the implacable face of the cliff, at the burden of snow that seemed to overhang the summit, then stared again to seaward. A wave broke hissing about his feet: the tide was coming in.

Up to that moment fear had passed him by. He had been in turn bewildered, incredulous, cold, sick, bruised, but sustained throughout by the furious animal energy which the body summons in a fight for life. Now, however, with the realization of his loneliness in the gathering darkness, fear smote him. In fear he was as purely animal as he had been in his moments of blind courage. He turned from the darkling sea that had claimed chum and shipmates, and floundered through the snow-drifts to the base of the cliff. Then, numbed with cold, and well-nigh spent, he began frantically to scale the shelving surfaces of the rock.

Barnacles tore the flesh from his hands and the nails from his finger-tips as he clawed desperately at the crevices for a hold. Inch by inch, foot by foot he fought his way upwards from the threatening clutch of the hungry tide, leaving a crimson stain at every niche where the snow had gathered. Thrice he slipped and slithered downwards, bruised and torn, to renew his frantic efforts afresh. Finally he reached a broad shelf of rock, halfway up the surface of the cliff, and there rested awhile, whimpering softly to himself at the pain of his flayed hands.

Presently he rose again and continued the dizzy ascent. None but a sailor or an experienced rock-climber would have dreamed of attempting such a feat single-handed, well-nigh in the dark. Even had he reached the top he could not have walked three yards in the dense snow-drifts that had gathered all along the edge of the cliffs. But the climber knew nothing about that; he was in search of *terra firma*, something that was not slippery rock or shifting pebbles, somewhere out of reach of the sea.

He was within six feet of the summit when he lost a foothold, slipped, grabbed at a projecting knob of rock, slipped again, and so slipping and bumping and fighting for every inch, he slid heavily down on to his ledge again.

He lay bruised and breathless where he fell. That tumble came near to finishing matters; it winded him—knocked the fight out of him. But a wave, last and highest of the tide, sluiced over the ledge and immersed his shivering body once more in icy water; the unreasoning terror of the pursuing tide that had driven him up the face of the cliff whipped him to his feet again.

He backed against the rock, staring out through the driving spindrift into the menace of the darkness. There ought to be another wave any moment: then there would be another: and after that perhaps another. The next one then would get him. He was too weak to climb again . . .

The seconds passed and merged into minutes. The wind came at him out of the darkness like invisible knives thrown to pin him to a wall. The cold numbed his intelligence, numbed even his fear. He heard the waves breaking all about him in a wild pandemonium of sound, but it was a long time before he realized that no more had invaded his ledge, and a couple of hours before it struck him that the tide had turned . . .

Towards midnight he crawled down from his ledge and followed the retreating tide across the slippery shale, pausing every few minutes to listen to the uproar of sea and wind. An illusion of hearing human voices calling out of the gale mocked him with strange persistence. Once or twice he stumbled over a dark mass of weed stranded by the retreating tide, and each time bent down to finger it apprehensively.

Dawn found him back in the shelter of his cleft, scraping limpets from their shells for a breakfast. The day came slowly over a grey sea, streaked and smeared like the face of an old woman after a night of weeping. Of the two destroyers nothing broke the surface. It was nearly high water, and whatever remained of their battered hulls was covered by a tumultuous sea. They were swallowed. The sea had taken them—them and a hundred-odd officers and men, old shipmates, messmates, townies, raggies—just swallowed the lot . . . He still owed last month's mess-bill to the caterer of his mess . . . He put his torn hands before his eyes and strove to shut out the awful grey desolation of that hungry sea.

During the forenoon a flotilla of destroyers passed well out to seaward. They were searching the coast for signs of the wrecks, and the spray blotted them intermittently from sight as they wallowed at slow speed through the grey seas.

The survivor watched them and waved his jumper tied to a piece of drift-wood; but they were too far off to see him against the dark rocks. They passed round a headland, and the wan figure, half frozen and famished, crawled back into his cleft like a stricken animal, dumb with cold and suffering. It was not until the succeeding low water, when the twisted ironwork was showing black above the broken water on the reef, that another destroyer hove in sight. She too was searching for her lost sisters, and the castaway watched her alter course and nose cautiously towards the cove. Then she stopped and went astern.

The survivor brandished his extemporized signal of distress and emitted a dull croaking sound between his cracked lips. A puff of white steam appeared above the destroyer's bridge, and a second later the reassuring hoot of a siren floated in from the offing. They had seen him.

A sudden reaction seized his faculties. Almost apathetically he watched a sea-boat being lowered, saw it turn and come towards him, rising and falling on the heavy seas, but always coming nearer . . . he didn't care much whether they came or not—he was that cold. The very marrow of his bones seemed to be frozen. They'd have to come and fetch him if they wanted him. He was too cold to move out of his cleft.

The boat was very near. It was a whaler, and the bowman had boated his oar, and was crouching in the bows with a heaving-line round his forearm. The boat was plunging wildly, and spray was flying from under her. The cliffs threw back the orders of the officer at the tiller as he peered ahead from under his tarpaulin sou'wester with anxiety written on every line of his weatherbeaten face. He didn't fancy the job, that much was plain; and indeed, small blame to him. It was no light undertaking, nursing a small boat close in to a dead lee shore, with the aftermath of such a gale still running.

They came still closer, and the heaving line hissed through the air to fall at the castaway's feet.

"Tie it round your middle," shouted the lieutenant. "You'll have to jump for it—we'll pull you inboard all right."

The survivor obeyed dully, reeled to the edge of his ledge and slid once more into the bitterly cold water.

Half a dozen hands seemed to grasp him simultaneously, and he was hauled over the gunwale of the boat almost before he realized he had left his ledge. A flask was crammed between his chattering teeth; someone wound fold upon fold of blanket round him.

"Any more of you, mate?" said a voice anxiously; and then, "Strike me blind if it ain't old Bill!"

The survivor opened his eyes and saw the face of the bowman contemplating him above his cork lifebelt. It was a vaguely familiar face. They had been shipmates somewhere once. Barracks, Devonport, p'raps it was. He blinked the tears out of his eyes and coughed as the raw spirit ran down his throat.

"Any more of you, Bill, ole lad?"

The survivor shook his head.

"There's no one," he said, "'cept me. I'm the only one what's lef' outer two ships' companies." Again the lost feeling of bewildered pride crept back.

"You always was a one, Bill!" said the bowman in the old familiar accent of hero-worship.

The survivor nodded confirmation. "Not 'arf I ain't," he said appreciatively. "Sole survivor I am!" And held out his hand again for the flask. "Christ! look at my 'ands!"

H.T. DORLING ("TAFFRAIL")
The Night Patrol

Captain Henry Tapprell Dorling (1883–1968) commanded Royal Navy destroyers during WWI, winning a DSO and several mentions in dispatches. He left the navy in 1929 to pursue his career as an author of sea stories, but was recalled at the outbreak of WWII. As well as writing naval fiction under the pseudonym "Taffrail", he was naval correspondent for the Observer *newspaper.*

"The Night Patrol" is abridged from the 1929 novelette of the same name. It is set in the English Channel.

IT MUST HAVE BEEN ABOUT twenty minutes later that M'Call, who was intently watching the horizon through his glasses, grunted with surprise. Was his imagination at fault, or had he really seen something—something vaguely white and indistinct—far away in the darkness?

"Starboard look-out," he asked, lowering his binoculars to wipe the object glasses, "did you see anything fine on the starboard bow just now?"

"Thought I saw a sort o' sudden splash," the man answered. "Thought maybe 'twas a fish jumpin', or a breakin' sea, sir."

"Can't have been a sea," said M'Call, rather puzzled, "it's flat calm."

"That's what it looked like to me, sir," the seaman protested, rather annoyed at being doubted. "There, sir!", after a pause;

"there it is again." He pointed at a glimmer of white with a triumphant forefinger.

The officer's glasses flew to his eyes, and the briefest inspection satisfied him the man was right, for there slowly crept into his field of vision a ghostly looking streak of whitened, splashing water. He did not linger an instant, but shouting, "Action!" pressed the bell-push in front of him.

The time was twelve and a half minutes to two.

The alarm-gongs whirred and jangled throughout the ship, and even as their strident chatter died away he could hear the men be-stirring themselves on deck, and the shuffling of feet as they closed up around their guns.

"Action stations!" roared a voice. "Show a leg, boys! Look lively now."

"What is it?" asked Langlands, already on his feet.

"Bow-waves on the starboard bow, sir!"

"All right," the skipper answered, seemingly quite unmoved by the information, but feeling his heart fluttering with excitement. "I'll take the ship. You look after the gunnery."

"Ay, ay, sir. Hicks!"

"Sir?"

"Pass down. All guns load with lyddite; bearing green, three, five range—one four, double o; deflection—one, five, right."

"That's them all right!" murmured the captain, with his glasses to his eyes, as the dim flicker of a flaming tunnel broke out of the darkness. "Damn bad stoking, too! Is the sub. up here?"

"Yes, sir."

"Warn the tubes to be ready to starboard. Don't fire until you get orders."

"Increasing speed, sir!" sang out a signalman, as the lumped-up water in the wake of the destroyer ahead grew whiter and more distinct. "Leader altering course to starboard, sir!"

Langlands, his glasses still levelled on the approaching enemy, flung an order over his shoulder to the man at the telegraph, and the *Minx*, throbbing to the increased thrust of her turbines, darted forward.

The glimmering bow-waves were now clearly visible to the naked eye, and even as the commanding officer watched them, he saw first the whitened trails of water in the wake of several fast-moving vessels, and then the long, blurred smudges of the ships themselves, dimly silhouetted against a lighter patch on the horizon. They were something over a mile distant.

"How many d'you make out, Number One?"

"Three or four, sir," said M'Call, putting his lips to a voice pipe to press another order to the guns.

"They don't seem to have spotted us," the captain went on. "Perhaps they can't see us against the dark background of the west'ard. Are you all ready?"

"Yes, sir. Quite ready."

The natural sound of his own voice comforted him, for Langlands, though certainly no coward, was not one of those abnormal men who could saunter through the very gates of hell without trepidation in their hearts. In such people heroism and calmness in the face of danger is a natural habit which can cost them little. They actually do not know what fear is, and hence have no difficul in combatting it.

Another species of bravery altogether is shown by those who feel fear, but can manage to stifle it—can make their will triumph over the perfectly natural desire for personal safety.

And Langlands had this quality. He had been in action many times, but always, before the firing began, a sickly feeling of apprehension, and an apparent loss of control of his body and limbs, as if his muscles were suddenly made of jelly. But his mind was ever active in such conditions. His brain worked fast and clearly, and outwardly his demeanour was just the same as usual. The fear he felt in his innermost heart never made itself manifest. He had trained himself to conceal it, and went so far as to smoke a pipe in action to convince others that he was in no way perturbed. Artificiality perhaps, but his men noticed it, and took courage.

It was the suspense that was so intolerable, the awful period of waiting between the time the enemy was sighted and the firing of the first shot. It might be seconds or it might be minutes; but it always seemed hours—hours of mental anguish and nerve-racking anxiety. Once under fire, however, these sensations left him altogether, and all thought of his own personal safety, all terror of the unknown, were brushed aside. He became cool and alert, then followed the period of wild exultation when his chief desire was ever the same—to get to close quarters; to fight, if need be, with his bare fists. Realization, he found, was never quite so bad as anticipation. It was the thinking before hand of what might happen that was maddeningly unnerving.

The orders for the destroyers on patrol were very simple and elastic, and all the commanding officers knew exactly what was expected of them. They knew the exact speed at which the leader intended to fight and that, until they came into close action, they had only to conform to his movements. Complications really began when the engagement became general and the formation was broken, for then it was a case of every ship for herself, her duty to single out an opponent, and, if possible, to stick to him until he was crippled or sunk.

They were at liberty to use their own initiative, taking what chance they were offered of ramming or of using their torpedoes, and utilizing their gun-fire to the best possible advantage. Beyond that, nothing else much mattered; and if, in the *melee* which was almost bound to ensue any friendly vessel had the ill-fortune to be stopped or sunk, it was an understood thing that her crew would have to take their chance until the close of the engagement. Their mates could not break off the action to succour them. The orders were very definite on one point—that while a British ship could steam and a British gun could fire, the raiders were to be pursued, hotly engaged, and reported.

By this time the enemy was at a distance of little more than a thousand yards, and, still steaming quite fast on a roughly parallel and opposite course, seemed oblivious to the presence of the British. It was scarcely possible that he had not sighted them, for even with the naked eye Langlands could clearly see the humped-up, unfamiliar shapes of the German destroyers, with their two squat funnels standing nearly upright, the tall mast aft, and the shortest ones forward. There was no mistaking them.

Perhaps they took the British for friends. Maybe they were merely reserving their fire, or were trusting to their speed to slip past without giving battle, for not a light twinkled down the line, not a gun roared out. They still steamed steadily on, grim, menacing, and silent. There were five of them.

The flotillas must have been drawing together at a combined

speed of fifty knots, possibly more, and if both continued their courses, they would flash by each other at a distance of about four hundred yards. And at fifty knots, one thousand yards is covered in thirty-six seconds, but still the British leader held steadily on his course. The seconds dragged—the enemy came nearer and nearer—the suspense became maddening. Langlands felt his heart thumping like a sledge-hammer. Was the leader missing his opportunity? It seemed as if in another few seconds it would be too late!

But the senior officer was an old hand at the business, and knew what he was about, and at exactly the right moment his helm went over, and Langlands was the leading destroyer swerving abruptly to starboard until she was heading straight for the centre of the hostile line. It was evidently the senior officer's intention to attempt to ram the fourth or fifth ship, leaving those ahead to the other detroyers under his orders. It was the plan agreed upon, the plan they all knew by heart.

There came a blaze of greenish-golden flame and the crash of a ragged salvo as the leader's guns opened the ball. A little cluster of even fountains, white and shimmering, leapt out of the dark sea close to the leading German, and almost before they had tumbled out of sight the guns were flashing all down the hostile line. In another instant every British ship replied and the firing became general.

The time was 1.49.20.

The guns were firing at point blank range, so that careful aiming, even if it had been possible, was unnecessary. The din became deafening as the loading numbers crammed projectile and cartridges home, the breeches of the guns slammed to, and the gun-layers pressed their triggers and fired. The air thudded and shook. Intermingled with the roaring of the heavier weapons came the unmistakable stutter of the two-pounder pom-poms as they fell to work to sweep the opposing bridges and decks, and the shriller stammering of the Lewis guns. Projectiles screeched and whined overhead, burst with a dull, crashing explosion, and sent their fragments humming and hissing through the air to strike funnels, hull and deck fittings with an insistent clatter like pebbles in a can. Machine-gun bullets sprayed around in droves, swishing and crackling as they came like raindrops through foliage.

Langlands, all but blinded by the brilliant flares of the *Minx*'s guns, held steadily on his course. The water round the ship seemed to be spouting and boiling with falling shells, and all he could see of the enemy was the flashes of their guns bursting out redly through a leaping curtain of shell-geysers, and clouds of dense, rolling smoke. The Germans seemed to be altering course a little, for the ship the *Minx* was making for, the third in the line, was drawing slightly across the bows.

"Port ten!" he ordered breathlessly, intent on running her down.

"Port ten it is, sir," came the deep voice of the coxwain, as he twirled the wheel.

"Midships! Steady so, Baker!"

"Steady it is, sir!"

A searchlight from some ship in the German line flickered and brilliance illuminated the scene for an instant in its sickly glare, and was suddenly extinguished.

There came a crash, an explosion, and a momentary blaze of reddish fire from amidships, as a shell drove home by the *Minx*'s after-funnel, but Langlands paid little heed, for the ship still sped on. Another projectile detonated on the water close under the bow, and a signalman on the bridge sat down with a grunt of stupefied astonishment, and began cursing softly to himself. The coxwain, with his right arm broken by a piece of the same shell, groaned audibly as he tried to use the limb and felt the jagged ends of the bone grating horribly together. He suffered excruciating torment, for, unknown to him, another sliver of red-hot steel had penetrated the muscles of his back. He was in agony, but he still watched the captain, waiting for his next order, and casting an occasional glance at the compass before him to keep the ship on her course.

A red Very light, soaring aloft, bathed the scene in a momentary flush of crimson before, curving over, it fell hissing into the water. The crashing, thudding medley still went on, but above the din M'Call could be heard passing orders like an automaton, and without a tremor in his voice. He passed his orders, but he little knew that the man below whose duty it was to transmit them to the guns was stretched out on deck, slowly sobbing his life away.

"Can I fire, sir?" suddenly screamed the sub., hoarse with excitement.

"Yes!" the captain shouted back, without turning his head.

And a moment later, when the boy saw the flame-spouting silhouette of the enemy's leader in line with the sights of his instrument, he pressed an ebonite knob, shouted through a voice-pipe, and looked anxiously aft. He was rewarded, for he saw the dull bluish flash and the silvery streak of a torpedo as it leapt from its tube and plunged with a splash into the water. Where that particular torpedo went he never knew, for there was no resultant explosion.

But an instant or two later, when the second German came in line, he pressed another knob. The range at the time seemed absurdly short, and the enemy flashed by in an instant, but the weapon went home. It seemed to strike her fairly amidships, for there came a lurid blast of flame and a cloud of greyish smoke and spray, followed by the roar of an explosion which for a moment completely drowned the sound of the guns.

"Got her, by George!" the sub. muttered softly to himself, watching her as the turmoil subsided and he caught a glimpse of the dripping bow and stern of the enemy's ship lifting themselves out of the water with the middle portion sagging horribly. "Clean in halves!"

He had never seen the effect of a torpedo before, and could hardly believe his eyes.

Then several things seemed to happen all at once.

A torpedo fired by the enemy, travelling on the surface in a flutter of spray, suddenly shot past within ten feet of the *Minx*'s bows, and almost at the same moment the destroyer astern of the one which had been torpedoed crashed into her helpless consort with a grinding splintering thud which could almost be felt. The firing from both ships ceased abruptly, and a chorus of shouts and screams came out of the darkness.

The collision occurred within about two hundred feet of the *Minx*'s bows, so close and on such a bearing that Langlands could hardly avoid the tangle.

"Hard a-starboard!" he yelled, however, unwilling to risk damaging his own vessel by running down an enemy which must already be helpless through having been collided with by a friend. "Hard a-starboard, Baker!"

The coxswain flung the wheel over with all his strength, but it was too late.

The ship slewed, but a moment later Langlands caught a hasty glimpse of the black hull of his enemy right under the bows.

He found himself looking down on her deck; could see the blurred, white faces of the men as they stared up at him; heard their frightened screams as they saw this new monster bearing down upon them to complete their destruction. It must have been a terrifying sight, the towering, V-shaped bow tearing remorselessly towards them at over twenty knots, with the two bow-waves leaping and playing on each side of the sharp stem.

A gun roared off from somewhere close at hand, and with the orange flash of it Langlands felt his cap whirled off his head and something strike him across the forehead. A warm gush streamed down his face; but in the excitement of the moment he scarcely noticed it.

The next instant the ship struck.

There was a rending, shuddering thud, the shrill, pro-testing sound of riven steel, and then a sudden cessation of speed. The hostile destroyer, struck in the stern, twisted round with the force of the blow, and heeled bodily over until the water poured over the farther edge of her deck. Then the *Minx*'s bows tore their way aft, splintering, grinding and crunching—enlarging the enormous wound, wrenching off the side plating, and allowing the water to pour in. The stern of the enemy slid free, and it could be heard slithering along the starboard side as the *Minx* still drove ahead.

The time was exactly 1.52. Four and a half minutes since the enemy had been sighted; two and a half since the first gun had been fired. It had seemed an eternity.

JOHN W. THOMASON, JR
The Bois de Belleau

*John William Thomason, Jr (1893–1944)
was born in Texas, and was a career
Marine Corps officer, reaching the rank
of colonel. He served in the West Indies,
China, at sea, and in both the World Wars.
He was also a prolific author of stories and
sketches, mostly about the Marines them-
selves. His short story collections include*
Fix Bayonets! *(1926) and* Marines and
Others *(1929).*

"The Bois de Belleau" is an excerpt from
Fix Bayonets! *and is set in 1917.*

THEY TRIED NEW TACTICS TO get the bayonets into the
Bois de Belleau. Platoons—very lean platoons now—
formed in small combat groups, deployed in the wheat, and
set out toward the gloomy wood. Fifty batteries were working
on it, all the field pieces of the 2d Division, and what the French
would lend. The shells ripped overhead, and the wood was full
of leaping flame, and the smoke of H.E. and shrapnel. The
fire from its edge died down. It was late in the afternoon;
the sun was low enough to shine under the edge of your
helmet. The men went forward at a walk, their shoulders
hunched over, their bodies inclined, their eyes on the edge of
the wood, where shrapnel was raising a hell of a dust. Some
of them had been this way before; their faces were set bleakly.
Others were replacements, a month or so from Quantico; they
were terribly anxious to do the right thing, and they watched

zealously the sergeants and the corporals and the lieutenants who led the way with canes.

One such group, over to the left, followed a big young officer, a replacement, too, but a man who had spent a week in Bouresches and was to be considered a veteran, as such things went in those days, when so many chaps were not with the brigade very long. He had not liked Bouresches, which he entered at night, and where he lived obscenely in cellars with the dead, and saw men die in the orange flash of minenwerfer shells, terribly and without the consolation of glory. Here, at last, was attack . . . He thought, absently watching his flank to see that it guided true—guide centre was the word—of the old men who had brought him up to tales of Lee's Army of Northern Virginia, in the War of the Southern Confederacy. Great battles, glamorous attacks, full of the color and the high-hearted élan of chivalry. Jackson at Chancellorsville; Pickett at Gettysburg—that was a charge for you—the red Southern battle-flags, leading like fierce brightwinged birds the locked ranks of fifteen gray brigades, and the screeching Rebel yell, and the field-music, fife and drum, rattling out "The Girl I Left Behind Me":

"Oh, if ever I get through this war,
   And the Lincoln boys don't find me,
I'm goin' to go right back again
   To the girl I left behind me—"

No music here, no flags, no bright swords, no lines of battle charging with a yell. Combat groups of weary men, in drab and dirty uniforms, dressed approximately on a line, spaced "so that one shrapnel-burst cannot include more than one group," laden like mules with gas-masks, bandoleers, grenades, chaut-chaut clips, trudging forward without haste and without excitement, they moved on an untidy wood where shells were breaking, a wood that did not answer back, or show an enemy. In its silence and anonymity it was far more sinister than any flag-crowned rampart, or stone walls topped with crashing volleys from honest old black-powder muskets—he considered these things and noted that the wood was very near, and that the German shells were passing high and breaking in the rear, where the support companies were waiting. His own artillery appeared to have lifted its range; you heard the shells farther in, in the depths of the wood.

The air snapped and crackled all around. The sergeant beside the lieutenant stopped, looked at him with a frozen, foolish smile, and crumpled into a heap of old clothes. Something took the kneecap off the lieutenant's right knee and his leg buckled under him. He noticed, as he fell sideways, that all his men were tumbling over like duck-pins; there was one fellow that spun around twice, and went over backward with his arms up. Then the wheat shut him in, and he heard cries and a moaning. He observed curiously that he was making some of the noise himself. How could anything hurt so? He sat up to look at his knee—it was bleeding like the deuce!—and as he felt for his first-aid packet, a bullet seared his shoulder, knocking him on his back again. For a while he lay quiet and listened to odd, thrashing noises around him, and off to the left a man began to call, very pitifully. At once he heard more machine-gun fire—he hadn't seemed to hear it before—and now the bullets were striking the ground and ricocheting with peculiar whines in every direction. One ripped into the dirt by his cheek and filled his eyes and his mouth with dust. The lamentable crying stopped; most of the crawling, thrashing noises stopped. He himself was hit again and again, up and down his legs, and he lay very still.

Where he lay he could just see a tree-top—he was that near the wood. A few leaves clung to it; he tried to calculate, from the light on them, how low the sun was, and how long it would be until dark. Stretcher-bearers would be along at dark, surely. He heard voices, so close that he could distinguish words:

"*Caput?*"

"*Nein—nicht alles—*"

Later, forgetting those voices, he tried to wriggle backward into a shell-hole that he remembered passing. He was hit again, but somehow he got into a little shell-hole, or got his body into it, head first. He reflected that he had bled so much that a headdownward position wouldn't matter, and he didn't want to be hit again. Men all dead, he supposed. He couldn't hear any of them. He seemed to pass out, and then to have dreamy periods of consciousness. In one of these periods he saw the sky over him was dark, metallic blue; it would be nearly night. He heard somebody coming on heavy feet, and cunningly shut his eyes to a slit . . . playing dead . . . A German officer, a stiff, immaculate fellow, stood over him, looking at him. He lay very still, trying not to breathe. The Boche had out his pistol, a short-barrelled Luger, rested it on his left forearm, and fired deliberately. He felt the bullet range upward through the sole of his foot, and something excruciating happened in his ankle. Then one called, and the German passed from his field of vision, returning his pistol as he went . . .

Later, trying to piece things together, he was in an ambulance, being jolted most infernally. And later he asked a nurse by his bed: "I say, nurse, tell me—did we get the Bois de Belleau?"—"Why, last June!" she said. "It's time you were coming out of it! This is August . . ."

W.E. JOHNS
Biggles to the Rescue

*Captain William Earl Johns (1893–1968)
was born in Hertford, England. During
the Great War he served initially with
the infantry, but transferred to the Royal
Flying Corps on receiving his commission.
He is most famous for his stories featuring
WWI aviator Captain James Bigglesworth
("Biggles"), but wrote many other sorts of
military fiction. These include a cycle of
WWII novels featuring a woman pilot,
Worrals, which are pioneeringly anti-male
chauvinist.*

"Biggles to the Rescue" is from The
Camels are Coming *(1929).*

C APTAIN BIGGLESWORTH OF SQUADRON NO. 266 RFC,
sat shivering in the tiny cockpit of his Camel at rather
less than 1,000 feet above the allied reserve trenches. It was
a bitterly cold afternoon; the icy edge of the February wind
whipped round his face and pierced the thick padding of his
Sidcot suit as he tried to snuggle lower in his "office".

The little salient on his right was being slowly pinched out
by a detachment of infantry; to Biggles it seemed immaterial
whether the line was straightened out or not; a few hundred
yards one way or the other was neither here nor there, he
opined. He was to change his mind before the day was out.
Looking down, he could see the infantry struggling through
the mud from shell-hole to shell-hole, as inch by inch they
drove the enemy back.

Squadron orders for the day had been to help them in every
possible way by strafing back areas with machine-gun fire and

20-lb. Cooper bombs to prevent the enemy from bringing up reinforcements. He had been at it all morning, and as he climbed into his cockpit for the afternoon "show", he anticipated another miserable two hours watching mud-coated men and lumbering tanks crossing no-man's-land, as he dodged to and fro through a venomous fire from small-arms, field-guns and archie batteries.

He was flying a zig-zag course behind the British lines, keeping a watchful eye open for the movements of enemy troops, although the smoke of the barrage, laid down to protect the advancing troops, made the ground difficult to see. It also served to some extent to conceal him from the enemy gunners. From time to time he darted across the line of smoke and raked the German front line with bullets from his twin Vickers guns. It was a highly dangerous, and, to Biggles, an unprofitable pursuit; he derived no sense of victory from the performance, and the increasing number of holes in his wings annoyed him intensely. "I'll have one of those holes in *me* in a minute," he grumbled.

Crash! Something had hit the machine and splashed against his face, smothering his goggles with a sticky substance.

"What's happened now?" he muttered, snatching off the goggles. His first thought was that an oil lead had been cut by a piece of shell, and he instinctively throttled back and headed the Camel nose down, farther behind his own lines.

He wiped his hand across his face and gave a cry of dismay as it came away covered in blood. "My gosh! I'm hit," he thought, and looked anxiously below for a suitable landing-ground. He had little time in which to choose, but fortunately there were many large fields handy, and a few seconds later the machine had run to a standstill in one of them. He stood erect in the cockpit and felt himself all over, looking for the source of the gore. His eye caught a sight of a cluster of feathers stuck on the centre section bracing wires, and he sank down limply, grinning sheepishly.

"Holy mackerel," he muttered, "a bird! So that was it!" Closer investigation revealed more feathers and finally he found a mangled mass of blood and feathers on the floor of the cockpit. "The propeller must have caught it and chucked what was left of it back through the centre section into my face," he mused. "Looks like a pigeon. Oh, well!"

He made to throw it overboard, when something caught his eye. It was a tiny tube attached to the bird's leg.

"A carrier pigeon, eh?" He whistled. "I wonder if it is one of ours or a Boche?"

He knew, of course, that carrier pigeons were used extensively by both sides, but particularly by the Allies for the purpose of conveying messages from spies within the occupied territory.

Sitting on the "hump" of his Camel, he removed the capsule and extracted a small flimsy piece of paper. One glance at the jumbled lines of letters and numbers was sufficient to show him that the message was in code.

"I'd better get this to Intelligence right away," he thought, and looked up to see an officer and several Tommies regarding him curiously from the hedge.

"Are you all right?" called the officer.

"Yes," replied Biggles. "Do you know if there is a field-telephone anywhere near?"

"There's one at Divisional Headquarters—the farmhouse at the end of the road," was the answer.

"Can I get through to 91st Wing from there?"

"I don't know."

"All right; many thanks," called Biggles. "I'll go and find out. Will you keep an eye on my machine? Thanks."

Five minutes later he was speaking to Colonel Raymond at Wing Headquarters, and after explaining what had happened, at the Colonel's invitation read out the message letter by letter. "Shall I hold on?" asked Biggles at the end.

"No; ring off, but don't go away. I'll call you in a minute or two," said the Colonel crisply.

Five minutes passed quickly as Biggles warmed himself by the office fire, and then the phone bell rang shrilly.

"For you, sir," said the orderly, handing him the instrument.

"Is that you, Bigglesworth?" came the Colonel's voice.

"Yes, sir."

"All right; we shan't want you again."

"Hope I brought you good news," said Biggles, preparing to ring off.

"No, you brought bad news. The message is from one of our fellows over the other side. The machine that went to fetch him last night force-landed and killed the pilot. That's all."

"But what about the sp—man?" asked Biggles, aghast.

"I'm afraid he is in a bad case, poor devil. He says he is on the north side of Lagnicourt Wood. The Huns have got a cordon of troops all round him and are hunting him down with dogs. He's heard them."

"How awful!"

"Well, we can't help him; he knows that. It will be dark in an hour and we daren't risk a night landing without looking over the ground. They'll have got him by tomorrow. Well, thanks for the prompt way you got the message to us. By the way, your MC is through; it will be in orders tonight. Goodbye." There was a click as the Colonel rang off.

Biggles sat with the receiver in his hand. He was not thinking about the decoration the Colonel had just mentioned. He was visualizing a different scene from the one that would be enacted in mess that night when his name appeared in orders on the notice-board. In his mind's eye he saw a cold, bleak landscape of leafless trees through which crawled an unkempt, mud-stained, hunted figure, looking upwards to the sky for the help that would never come. He saw a posse of hard-faced, grey-coated Prussians holding the straining hounds on a leash, drawing ever nearer to the fugitive. He saw a grim, blank wall against which stood a blind-folded man—the man who had fought the war his own way, without hope of honour, and had lost.

Biggles, after two years of war, had little of the milk of human kindness left in his being, but the scene brought a lump into his throat. "So they'd leave him there, eh?" he thought. "That's Intelligence, is it?" He slammed the receiver down with a crash.

"What's that, sir? asked the startled orderly.

"Go to blazes," snapped Biggles. "No, I didn't mean that. Sorry," he added, and made for the door.

He was thinking swiftly as he hurried back to the Camel. "North edge of Lagnicourt Wood, the Colonel said; it's nearly a mile long. I wonder if he'd spot me if I got down. He'd have to come back on the wing—it's the only way, but even that's a better chance than the firing party'll give him. We'll try it, anyway; it isn't more than seven or eight miles over the line."

Within five minutes he was in the air heading for the wood, and ten minutes later, after being badly archied, he was circling over it at 5,000 feet.

"They haven't got him yet, anyway," he muttered, for signs of the pursuit were at once apparent. Several groups of soldiers were beating the ditches at the west end of the wood and he saw hounds working along a hedge that ran diagonally into its western end. Sentries were standing at intervals on the northern and southern sides. "Well, there's one thing I can do in case all else fails. I'll lay me eggs first," he decided, thinking of the two Cooper bombs that still hung in their racks. He pushed the stick forward and went tearing down at the bushes where the hounds were working.

He did a vertical turn round the bushes at fifty feet, levelled out, and, as he saw the group just over the junction of his right-hand lower plane and the fuselage, he pulled the bomb-toggle, one—two. Zooming high, he half rolled, and then came down with both Vickers guns spitting viciously. A cloud of smoke prevented him from seeing how much damage had been done by the bombs. He saw a helmeted figure raise a rifle to shoot at him, fall, pick himself up, fall again, and crawl into the undergrowth. One of the hounds was dragging itself away. Biggles pulled the Camel up, turned, and came down again, his tracer making a straight line to the centre of the now clearing smoke. Out of the corner of his eye he saw other groups hurrying towards the scene, and made a mental note that he had at least drawn attention to himself, which might give the spy a chance to make a break.

He levelled out to get his bearings. Left rudder, stick over, and he was racing low over the wood towards the northern edge. At thirty feet from the ground he tore along the side of the wood, hopping the trees and hedges in his path. There was only one field large enough for him to land in; would the spy realize that, he wondered, as he swung round in a steep climbing turn and started to glide down, "blipping" his engine as he came.

He knew that he was taking a desperate chance. A bad landing or a single well-aimed shot from a sentry when he was on the ground would settle the matter. His tail-skid dragged on the rough surface of the field; a dishevelled figure, crouching low, broke from the edge of the wood and ran for dear life towards him. Biggles kicked on rudder and taxied, tail up, to meet him, swinging round while still thirty yards away, ready for the take-off. A bullet smashed through the engine cowling; another struck the machine somewhere behind him.

"Come on!" he yelled frantically, although it was obvious that the man was doing his best. "On the wing—not that—the left one—only chance," he snapped.

The exhausted man made no answer, but flung himself at full length on the plane, close to the fuselage, and gripped the leading edge with his bare fingers.

"Catch!" cried Biggles, and flung his gauntlets on to the wing within reach of the fugitive.

Bullets were flicking up the earth about them, but they suddenly ceased, and Biggles looked up to ascertain the reason. A troop of Uhlans were coming down the field at full gallop, not a hundred yards away. Tight-lipped, Biggles thrust the throttle open and tore across the field towards them. His thumbs sought the Bowden lever of his Vickers guns and two white pencil lines of tracer connected the muzzles with the charging horsemen.

A bullet struck a strut near his face with a crash that he could hear above the noise of his engine, and he winced. Zooming high, he swung round towards the lines.

"I've got him—I've brought it off!" hammered exultantly through his brain. "If the poor fellow doesn't freeze to death and fall off I'll have him home within ten minutes." With his altimeter needle touching 4,000 feet, he pulled the throttle back and, leaning out of the cockpit, yelled at the top of his voice, "Ten minutes!" A quick nod told him the spy had understood.

Biggles pushed the stick forward and dived for the line. He could feel the effect of the "drag" of the man's body, but as it counter-balanced the torque of his engine to some extent it did not seriously interfere with the performance of the machine.

He glanced behind. A group of small black dots stood out boldly against the setting sun. Fokkers!

"You can't catch me, I'm home," jeered Biggles pushing the stick further forward.

He was down to 2,000 feet now, his air-speed indicator showing 150 mph; only another two miles now, he thought with satisfaction.

Whoof! Whoof! Whoof! Three black clouds of smoke blossomed out in front of him, and he swerved. Whoof!—Spang! Something smashed against the engine with a force that made the Camel quiver. The engine raced, vibrating wildly, and then cut out dead. For a split second Biggles was stunned. Mechanically he pushed his stick forward and looked down. The German support trenches lay below.

"My gosh! What luck; I can't do it," he grated bitterly. "I'll be three hundred yards short."

He began a slow glide towards the Allied front line, now in sight. At 500 feet, and fast losing height, the man on the wing twisted his head round, and the expression on his face haunted Biggles for many a day. A sudden thought struck him an any icy hand clutched at his heart.

"By heavens! I'm carrying a professed spy; they'll shoot us both!"

The ground was very close now and he could see that he would strike it just behind the Boche front line. "I should think the crash will kill us both," he muttered grimly, as he eyed the sea of shell-holes below. At five feet he flattened out for a pancake landing; the machine started to sink, slowly, and then with increasing speed. A tearing, ripping crash and the Camel closed up around him; something struck him on the head and everything went dark.

"Here, take a drink of this, young feller—it's rum," said a voice that seemed far away.

Biggles opened his eyes and looked up into the anxious face of an officer in uniform and his late passenger.

"Who are you?" he asked in a dazed voice, struggling into a sitting position and taking the proffered drink.

"Major Mackay of the Royal Scots, the fust of foot, the right of the line and the pride of the British Army," smiled his *vis-à-vis*.

"What are you doing here—where are the Huns?"

"We drove 'em out this afternoon," said the Major, "luckily for you."

"Very luckily for me," agreed Biggles emphatically.

WILLIAM MARCH
To the Rear

*William March (1893–1954) was born
William March Campbell in Mobile,
Alabama. His combat experience during
WWI earned him five decorations for heroism, but left him clinically depressed. His
war fiction, which began with the acclaimed
novel* Company K *(1933), powerfully
reflects this disillusion.*

*The short story "To the Rear" is from
March's collection,* The Little Wife
(1935).

THE COMPANY WAS GOING TO the rear for ten days and
the men were in high spirits. They sat waiting for the
relief troops to arrive, their packs rolled and their equipment
stacked.

Lying flat on one of the wire bunks in the dugout was a
boy with an eager, undeveloped face and weak eyes which
were habitually narrowed against sunlight. His ears crinkled and bent forward like the leaf of a geranium and
his shoulders were high and thin with the sparseness of
immaturity. His name was Ernest Lunham and before his
enlistment he had worked as a soda jerker in a drug store
in Erie, Pa. He was coughing steadily into a soiled handkerchief, his face the color of biscuit dough dusted with
ashes. At intervals he would shiver, as if cold, and then he
would catch his breath with a surprised, wheezing sound.
He had been gassed that afternoon while he and a man
named Overstreet were gathering firewood for the officer's
dugout.

Jimmy Reagan, corporal of the squad, came over to him:

"What did the doctor say, Ernie? Why didn't he send you to the hospital?"

Lunham sat up and stared around him, as if unable to remember exactly where he was. "When I went in the sick bay the doctor looked me over and listened to my heart . . . 'So you claim you got gassed?' he asked in an amused voice. 'Yes, sir.' I said. 'How do you explain that when the Germans haven't thrown over any gas for a week?' . . . 'I don't know,' I said. 'I'll tell you how you got gassed,' said the doctor. 'You dipped a cigarette in iodine and smoked it. Did you think I'd fall for anything like that?' I didn't say anything—it wasn't any use to say anything."

Lunham lay back on the wire bunk as if exhausted and breathed heavily. There were red splotches coming on the backs of his hands and on his forearms. His weak eyes pained him. It was with difficulty that he held them open.

"*That's* a bright son of a bitch for you!" said Joe Birmingham; "why didn't you ask him where you'd get a cigarette to put iodine on?"

"I didn't say anything at all," said Lunham, "I just came on out."

Corporal Reagan called Buckner, LaBella and Davey and they whispered quietly. He conferred with Birmingham and Overstreet. At last he approached the bunk where Lunham lay.

"You don't have to worry about carrying the clip bags or taking your turn on the *chauchat*. You don't have to carry anything but your pack, Ernie."

Max Tolan, the last member of the squad, came off watch and entered the dugout. He was a powerful man with a nose that flattened to a triangle and nostrils that splayed widely. His lips were thick and calm: they seemed made of a substance somewhat harder and somewhat less flexible than flesh. For a moment he stared at Lunham. Then, somehow, his lips managed to open: "He don't have to carry even that. I'll carry his pack for him."

A little later Lloyd Buckner approached the bed, a package in his hand. "Here are some malted milk tablets I've been saving. You'd better eat them, Ernie—they'll do you good."

Lunham nodded his head, but he did not speak. He wanted

more than anything to thank Buckner and Max Tolan and the rest of the men for their kindness, but he was afraid he would start crying and make a fool of himself if he tried to say anything.

At six o'clock the relief troops came and the men moved in single file down the communication trenches that led to the rear.

The trenches widened after a while and became less deep. On either side were the charred remnants of a grove of trees. Many of the trees had been uprooted in past barrages and lay flat on the ground; many, with dead limbs trailing the parent stem, had split asunder in the shelling or snapped halfway up their trunk; but a few of the trees, sapless and black, stood upright in the field, inflexible now in the March wind. The terrain hereabouts was pitted with great shell holes from which the roots of the fallen trees protruded dry and seasoned.

Overstreet became very excited. "That's the place where Ernie got gassed!" he said. The squad stared about them curiously. "That's the very place!" continued Overstreet . . . "I wanted to go farther back, around Mandray Farm, for the wood; but Ernie thought that this would be as good a place as any; so I said all right it suited me, if it suited him."

Overstreet hunched his shoulders and scratched his armpits. He started whistling *La Golondrina* through his teeth. He was a stocky lad, with a neck so short and a chest so thick and rounded that people were surprised, upon regarding him closely, to discover that he was not a hunchback. His teeth were infantile and irregular and they grew together in a V shape. His voice, a countertenor, was high with a quality of tremulous, penetrating sweetness in it.

"How did Lunham happen to get gassed?" asked Buckner.

"Well, it was this way," said Overstreet. "Ernie thought the dry roots in the shell holes would make good firewood so he jumped down and began chopping them off. I sat outside and took the roots that he handed up and cut them small enough for the dugout stove." Overstreet was conscious that the whole squad was listening to him attentively . . . "Well, sir, while we were working there, a French soldier came running toward us. He was waving his arms about and shouting. You know how these Frogs act? . . ." Overstreet turned to his companions.

"Sure!" they said . . . "Well, I put down my axe and I said to Ernie: 'What's wrong with him do you suppose?' and Ernie said: 'He's sore because we're taking this firewood!' . . . "Ain't that right, Ernie?" said Overstreet suddenly. Lunham nodded his head but he did not answer: he was saving his breath for the long march.

"Well," continued Overstreet, "when the Frenchman reached us he began to talk excitedly and make gestures but Ernie and me didn't know what it was all about; so finally this Frenchman catches hold of Ernie's arms and tries to drag him out of the shell hole; but Ernie gives him a shove in the chest and the Frenchman falls backward into a mud puddle. Ernie and me were laughing like everything by that time but the Frog kept staring at us in a peculiar way. Finally he seemed to see the joke because he began laughing too. He made a low bow to Ernie and me and as he turned to go he blew us each a kiss . . ."

The communicating trench was only waist high now and the men could see the barren fields that stretched interminably on either side. It was seven o'clock, but it was not entirely dark. Then, after a time, the trenches ended in a road that was roofed with a framework of wire netting over which burlap sacking, painted brown and green, had been thrown.

"What happened after the Frenchman left?" asked Wilbur Davey.

Overstreet, feeling his importance as a narrator, waited a moment before resuming . . . "Well, Ernie went on cutting roots and I went on chopping them up; but after awhile he said to me: 'Say, Al, did that monkey meat at dinner make you sick?' and I said, 'No, why?' . . . 'Nothing,' said Ernie, 'except I keep tasting it . . .' About five minutes later he said to me: 'Al, I'm beginning to feel funny.' 'What's the matter with you?' I asked. 'I don't know,' said Ernie . . . 'I'm going to heave I think.' I looked down and saw that he had dropped his axe and was leaning against the side of the hole. His face had got gray and his forehead and his lips were sweating like he had a fever . . . 'You better come up here and lay down,' I said; but he didn't answer me . . . 'Listen, Ernie,' I said, 'come on up here with me!'"

Overstreet paused a moment. "When Ernie didn't answer me I jumped down and lifted him out of the hole. He tried to stand up but he couldn't make it. Then he fell down and began to heave . . . Well, as we lay there, who should come back but the French soldier. He had a Frog civilian with him this time who spoke English. He told us that the terrain around Verdun had been shelled so many times that the ground was full of old gas. It was dangerous to dig in shell holes he said because a man could be gassed before he knew what was happening to him."

Overstreet began to laugh in his high, tremulous voice. "The joke sure was on Ernie and me. There he was heaving at the top of his voice and all I could think of to say was: 'We're much obliged to you fellows for telling us.'"

The camouflaged strip ended at last and the troops came out upon the Verdun road. Darkness had settled and the faces of the men were no longer visible. Joe Birmingham was talking about his hoped-for leave. Birmingham was bright-eyed and sudden with an alert, intelligent face. His straight hair, parted in the middle, hung upon his forehead like yellow curtains imperfectly drawn. His teeth were strong and brilliantly white and as he talked he moved his hands with quick, nervous gestures. He could read print which was not too difficult and he could sign his name to the pay roll, but that was about all . . .

"And when I get to Paris the first thing I do will be to round up a dozen of the best-looking ladies in town: four blondes, four brunettes and four red heads."

"I wouldn't be caught short if I were you: I wouldn't cut down on my women that way!"

Joe paid no attention to Overstreet. "One of the blondes is going to be dressed in purple silk and have on violet perfume. The best-looking brunette is going to wear a red dress with pearls sewed down the front of it and be scented up with carnation. The red heads will all wear green dresses and Jockey Club and have lace on their drawers.

"How about a blonde flavored with vanilla?" laughed LaBella.

"I'll take a red head," said Lloyd Buckner, "but she'll have to wash off the Jockey Club, by God!"

Reagan spoke then: "Don't let them kid you, Joe. If there's

anybody in this squad who's particular about his women, it hasn't been brought to my attention."

"Oh, we'll come to your party all right," interposed LaBella; "you can bank on all of us accepting."

Birmingham gave him a friendly shove. "You will like hell come to my party! If one of my girls got a look at you crummy bums they'd—they'd—" Birmingham paused, groping for the appropriate word.

"Swoon?" suggested Buckner helpfully.

Birmingham looked up mildly: "For Christ sake, Buck! . . . Don't you ever get that stuff off your mind?"

Reagan smiled a little but Buckner and LaBella began to shout with laughter. Sergeant Stokes came toward them angrily. "What's going on here?" he demanded; "do you want the Germans to start shelling this road?"

LaBella interrupted him. "All right, Doc; all right," he said quietly.

Lunham walked in silence. He was standing the hike better than he had thought possible. He looked at his pack riding high on Tolan's shoulders and at Tolan walking firmly with no sign of fatigue. It was white of Max to carry the extra pack, particularly since his feet blistered easily as every one knew and long marches were difficult for him . . . "The fellows sure have been white to me," whispered Lunham softly to himself. He began to feel feverish and from time to time he took a mouthful of water from his canteen.

The men continued to laugh and joke, but they were careful not to raise their voices. Then, after a time, when their muscles were cramped and tired with the burdens they carried, they became silent, one by one, and settled down in earnest for the long march.

The road bent again and ran north and east and a late moon rose slowly behind a burned farmhouse. To the west Very lights and colored flares were ascending, hanging motionless for a time and then drifting toward nothingness with a hesitant, languid motion. There came a sound resembling iron wheels jolting over a bridge of unnailed, wooden planks; there was the constant flash of guns along the horizon and the muffled sound of exploding shells.

Birmingham unbuttoned his cartridge belt: "Give 'em hell!" he said excitedly: "I wish I was with you to give the bastards hell!"

"Do you think we're really going back for a rest?" asked Davey.

"That's the dope they're putting out."

Tolan made a gesture of disbelief with his heavy, wooden lips: "That's all bunk about getting a rest."

Eddie LaBella spoke up: "We'll get a rest all right: in a hick burg with a dozen manure piles and one dirty café."

"It might be all right at that," said Birmingham. "Some of these Frog women ain't bad!" He brushed his yellow hair out of his eyes and licked his lips in an exaggerated, sensual way. "Baby! I'll say they're not bad!" Lloyd Buckner stared at him with sudden, unconcealed distaste. He seemed on the point of saying something but changed his mind. He turned his head away.

"The next time they have a war, they'll have to come after me with a machine gun," said Reagan laughingly.

"Some of these Frog women ain't bad," insisted Birmingham; "I'll bet we have just as good a time as we had in Chatillon. I'll bet."

Buckner whispered something to LaBella behind his hand. LaBella laughed and in turn whispered to Reagan; but Reagan shook his head.

"Let him say it!" said Birmingham; "what do I care what he says!"

The early exuberance of the men had disappeared. They were tired now and becoming irritable. Lunham, walking painfully, realized that. He took no part in the conversation. His nausea had returned and he clutched at his belly. "I won't heave again," he kept repeating miserably; "I'll put my mind on something else! I won't heave again!" He hugged his thin ribs with his elbows and rocked back and forth beside the road. He began to retch shrilly. He slipped to the side of the road and pressed his face into a heap of dead leaves that had drifted against a log. When his nausea had passed he felt somewhat stronger. He rose to his feet and stood there swaying. He tried to laugh. "There went Buck's malted milk tablets!" he gasped.

The moon had detached itself from the burned farmhouse and swung now swollen and yellow and low in the sky. The sound of the iron wheels became fainter and at last a turn in the road hid the flashes of the guns from view.

"How long have we been on the road, Jimmy?"

Reagan looked at his watch: "A little better than five hours," he said.

The road rose gradually. The men were feeling the march in earnest now. They shifted their packs and strapped them higher on their shoulders. A rhythmic whirring of motors was heard overhead and then the sound of the motors ceased and across the face of the setting moon the bombing plane floated. Sergeant Stokes came running down the road. "Fall out in the fields and lie down!" He stood there swearing excitedly at the men who were slow in obeying. "Don't bunch up like sheep! . . . Spread out and lie down!"

The men stared up at the plane drifting silently above them. "He's got guts flying so low on a bright night," said LaBella. At that moment there came the sharp, quick bark of an anti-aircraft gun and two flashlights began to play crosswise in the sky. "They'll never get him," said Reagan, "they're firing too high."

Birmingham lifted his quick, excited face. "Shoot hell out of him!" he said. He moved his hands excitedly and bared his white, perfect teeth. "Give the bastard hell!"

The plane with motors whirring again was zigzagging up the sky, the gunners firing impotently. In a moment he was lost in the clouds and the guns became silent again, but the flashlights moved across the sky for a long time, crossing each other and uncrossing with a jerking, mathematical precision.

"They let him get away," wailed Birmingham; "I could shoot that good with a rifle. Christ! They let him get away!"

Buckner could hide his dislike no longer. "You're quite a little fire eater when you're safe behind the lines, aren't you?"

Birmingham looked up resentfully. "I've stood enough of your cracks—who the hell are you, anyway? You act like you were Jesus Christ or somebody!"

Before Buckner could answer, Reagan stopped him. Buckner spat in the road. "I can't help it, Jimmy. I've got a belly full of that common little swine and he might as well know it."

"Who the hell are you?" shouted Birmingham excitedly; "I don't see no bars on your shoulders!"

Overstreet began to laugh in his high, penetrating voice: "That's the idea, Joe. Don't let him get away with that stuff."

"What I said goes for you too!" said Buckner coldly.

LaBella narrowed his eyes and pursed up his lips, as if denying beforehand the malice in his words. "At least Buckner can read and write. He didn't have to get the drill corporal to recite General Orders out loud until he memorized them."

Birmingham's alert little face twisted suddenly. He was eternally conscious of his illiteracy and ashamed of it.

Wilbur Davey, who spoke rarely, spoke now: "That was a dirty crack to make, LaBella."

Reagan turned, his customary good nature gone: "Pipe down, all of you, or I'll report the whole squad when we get in." But the men paid little attention to him. They continued to quarrel for a long time.

Presently the column turned from the main road and took a road to the left. The ground was rising sharply now and the hills of Verdun were imminent and threatening ahead. Lunham raised his canteen and drank the last of his water. As he returned the canteen to its cover and adjusted his belt he noticed that Tolan had begun to limp. A feeling of despair came over him. In terror he leaned forward and touched Tolan's arm. "We'll be paid when we get to the rear, Max, and I got four months' coming." Tolan turned, a slight frown on his primitive features, but he did not answer. "I won't forget about you carrying my pack," he continued, "you can be sure of that." But Tolan continued to limp painfully, giving no sign that he heard. "I won't forget about you being so white, Max. We'll go out pay night and spend every franc of that money." Lunham paused, his face frightened and abject. "What do you say, Max? What do you say to that?" Tolan regarded him in silence, steadily. His round blue eyes were interested and bright. He sighed and shook his head doubtfully.

*   *   *

The company was falling out beside an abandoned village and a young officer on horseback came clattering down the road. "There's running water in the wash house to the left of the square if you want to fill your canteens," he said, as if he were reading from a book. It was apparent that speaking to the men made him nervous and self-conscious. Overstreet made a derisive, sucking sound with his lips and repeated a strong phrase. The young officer's blush could almost be felt. He ignored the remark and a moment later he could be heard delivering his message farther down the line.

Tolan had swung Lunham's pack to the ground and sat regarding it stolidly.

"Honest to God, Max, we'll spend every franc of that money! We'll have a fine time, all right!"

Tolan seemed to be turning the matter over in his mind. His heavy lips opened once or twice but no words came from them. He picked up the pack and laid it regretfully in front of Lunham. "My feet hurt too bad," he said.

The load on Lunham's shoulders was a hand, heavy and insistent, to tug at his breath and draw him gradually backward. His heart began to pump alarmingly and the veins in his neck were taut and swollen . . . "Christ! . . . Christ!" he gasped.

After that he lost all feeling of time, all idea of direction and all sense of his individual identity. He was aware only of feet moving over the surface of the road in an irregular pattern and of men quarreling continuously. He seemed detached and no longer a part of his surroundings and gradually he possessed the power to stand outside his body and to survey himself and his companions impersonally: There was Reagan shuffling doggedly, his dreamy, impractical eyes tired and serious; there was Max Tolan with ankles turned outward, flinching each time his feet touched the road; LaBella, cheap and flashy, his theatrical prettiness caked with dirt and streaked with sweat. He saw Overstreet, his triangular mouth open and his infantile teeth displayed; and Lloyd Buckner's sensitive, deeply curved nose thrust forward, his light eyes cold and sullen. Only Davey walked with dignity and only Birmingham's wiry body seemed impervious to the weight he carried or the steady tug of the miles.

Without warning Lunham staggered and lurched forward. Somebody shoved him into his proper place. He righted himself with difficulty, confused, uncertain. "My mouth tastes salty," he said in a frightened voice. Reagan regarded him closely. "You've started bleeding," he said. Lunham pressed the back of his hand against his mouth and then withdrew it. "You're bleeding, all right," said Buckner . . . The feet of the men were hardly clearing the roadbed. They shuffled in a monotonous rhythm while the moon hung low in the sky, near to setting, and from the west there came the smell of fresh water.

". . . Why can't he take his turn carrying the clip bags?"

"He's sick, Eddie. You wouldn't ask him to do that when he's sick." . . . Reagan's voice seemed to come from a great distance.

Davey made one of his rare speeches. "I guess he's no sicker than anybody else."

". . . If he was gassed why didn't they send him to a hospital?"

The knowledge that his comrades were discussing him gradually penetrated Lunham's consciousness. He realized now that they had been talking about him for a long time . . . Birmingham laughed. "He might fool us, but he didn't fool that doctor at the sick bay none. He's wise to all those old gags."

The road curved to the right and circled the base of a hill. The young liaison officer came galloping down the road again. The moon had set and there was an indefinite feeling of daybreak in the air. "Fall out for fifteen minutes before you start climbing the hill," he said. He repeated the order firmly. If the men tried to razz him this time they'd find out very quickly who he was. But the men remained silent, perversely ignoring him. They fell to the ground gratefully. Tolan took off his shoes and began to pour water on his blistered feet. Davey was already asleep and snoring softly, but Birmingham and Buckner continued their quarrel.

Lunham lay on his back and stared at the sky turning

faintly gray toward the east. An imperative drowsiness was overpowering him but some impulse made him struggle against it. With eyes closed and lips half parted, his thin face and wilting ears seemed unbearably young and pathetic.

The men were talking again, their voices coming from a distance remote and blurred . . . "Why can't Lunham take his turn on the clip bags?" LaBella's voice was flat and toneless . . . And Overstreet, petulant: "By God! he's no sicker than anybody else." There came a thud on the earth beside him and Lunham knew that the clip bags lay before him. He began to laugh. "I never heard of anything so foolish," he thought. "I can't even lift those bags let alone carry them up the hill . . ."

He turned on his face and pressed his body against the cool, damp earth. The feel of the soil against his cheek steadied him and gave him strength and gradually the cloudiness that had obscured his mind disappeared. And he was conscious of his body paining him unbearably. He drew up his arms and pressed his hands against his burning lungs. He began to think, against his will, of many things; of his enlistment, his eagerness, his romantic thoughts concerning noble deaths and imperishable ideas. Then, in justification of himself, he tried to recall one noble thing that he had seen or done since his enlistment, but he could remember nothing except pain, filth and servile degradation . . . "By God, they sold me out!" he thought. "The things they said were all lies!" He lay trembling at his discovery, his eyes closed, his lips opening and shutting silently. An unbearable sense of disgust came over him. He reached for the rifle that lay beside him, surprised to realize that the thought had been in his mind for a long time, and stood bending forward clumsily, his mouth swaying above the barrel as he tried patiently to spring the trigger with his foot.

Joe Birmingham was coming toward him shouting a warning. "Look out! Look out!" he cried. The two men struggling for the rifle stumbled back and forth beside the road. The entire squad was on its feet now, but it was Wilbur Davey who wrenched the rifle from Lunham's weak hands and flung it far into the valley below. He slapped Lunham smartly on both cheeks. He said: "What the hell? What you trying to pull off? Do you want to get court-martialed?"

Lunham had fallen to the road and lay with his face pressed into the dirt, but the men paid no further attention to him. He beat the earth with his fists. "Oh Christ! . . . Oh, Christ almighty! . . ." he cried in a weak, childish voice.

The first light, new and hard, came over the tops of the hills and cast strange shadows on the faces of the men. In a farmyard somewhere a cock crew and below in the valley mist hung above the fields. Word came down the line for the men to fall-in. They rose stiffly and put on their equipment. Lunham did not rise. He lay limp and relaxed, his arms outstretched, and as he lay there he could hear his comrades climbing the hill; he heard their hard breathing and their grumbling voices; he heard the irregular shuffle of their feet, the clink of a canteen and the creaking of a leather strap; but after awhile even these sounds became faint and vanished, and he was alone.

A peasant woman carrying a wicker basket strapped to her back and leading a she-goat with a distended udder paused on her way to market and stood regarding Lunham with uncertainty. The she-goat, feeling the rope slacken, approached cautiously and nibbled his uniform, twitching her sensitive muzzle and baring her yellow teeth, but the woman jerked the cord and the goat moved away. Lunham turned and lifted his head heavily. He was still bleeding, a thin, insistent stream which would not stop, and where his mouth had rested there was a pool of blood which the earth had not entirely absorbed.

From her basket the woman took a metal cup and got down upon her knees, the she-goat spreading her hindquarters obediently. When the cup was full the woman lifted Lunham's head and held it to his lips, but the milk was tepid, with a rank smell, and after he had swallowed a portion of it, he rose to his knees and swayed dizzily from side to side, his face white and dead, his hands splayed like the claws of a hawk. Then he tried to stand upright, but his knees collapsed under him and he fell flat on his face and vomited with a hoarse, screaming voice.

The woman stretched out her arms and raised them slowly sidewise with a gesture singularly frustrate and moving. As she raised her arms the handle of the cup turned on her finger and the milk ran over its edge and spilled into the road . . . But Lunham lay stretched on his back, his face and hands covered with sweat, his thin body trembling.

"Let me alone," he said ... "let me alone, for Christ's sake."

The woman had risen and stood regarding him with compassionate eyes. She shook her head sadly. "*Je ne comprends pas!*" she said.

In the valley a farm-boy shouted to his team, a dog barked on a high, pure note and a flock of rooks, circling slowly, dropped silently into a field.

LIAM O'FLAHERTY
The Alien Skull

*The Irish writer Liam O'Flaherty (1897–
1984) fought in the British Army during
World War I. With the end of hostilities
he wandered America, but returned to
Ireland in 1921 to fight on the Republican side in the Civil War. Later he
settled in London as an author, winning
the James Tait Memorial prize for his
third novel,* The Informer *(1926). Other
novels include* The Assassin *(1928) and*
Land *(1946).*

*The short story "The Alien Skull" is
from 1924.*

W HEN HE WAS WITHIN TEN yards of the enemy outpost,
Private Mulhall lay flat, with his right ear close to the
ground. He listened without drawing breath. He strained his
ear to catch a word, a cough, or the grating sound of a boot
touching the frost-bound earth. There was no sound.

Had they gone?

It was eleven o'clock at night. There was perfect silence
along that section of the battle-front. In the distance there
was the monotonous and melancholy murmur of heavy guns
in action. Here everything was still, as in a tomb. The moon
had not risen. But the sky was not dark. It was an angry blue
colour. There were stars. It was possible to see the ground for
a long distance. It was freezing heavily. Bayonets, lying beside
dead men, gleamed. All the huddled figures scattered about
between the two lines of trenches were dead men. There had
been a battle that day.

They had sent out Mulhall to discover whether the enemy

had retired from his front line. If so, an advance was to be made at midnight into the trenches evacuated by him. If possible, Mulhall was to bring back a live prisoner. A man had been seen a little earlier peering over the top of the advanced post, before which Mulhall was now lying.

Irritated by the silence, Mulhall began to curse under his breath. He had ceased to listen and looked back towards his own line. He had come up a slope. He saw the dim shapes of the newly made scattered posts, the rambling wire fences and the heaps of rooted earth. He cursed and felt a savage hatred against his officers. He had now been three years at the front without leave. He was always doing punishment behind the line for insolence and insubordination. In the line he was chosen for every dangerous duty, because of his ferocious courage. But as soon as he came out he was up again before the adjutant, taken dirty on parade, absent, drunk, or for striking a corporal.

Lying flat on the ground, Mulhall thought savagely of the injustice done to him. He thought with cunning pleasure of crawling back towards his own line and shooting one of the officers or sergeants against whom he had a grudge. With pleasure, he rehearsed, in his mind, this act, until he saw the stricken victim fall, writhe, and lie still. Then terrible disciplinary cries rose up before his mind, his own name shouted by the sergeant, and then the giant figure of the sergeant-major, with his pace stick under his arm, heels together, erect, reading out the documentary evidence. A whole lot of shouting and stamping and awe-inspiring words. An enormous, invisible, inhuman machine, made of terrible words, constituted in his mind the terror that gave power to his superiors over him.

Compared to that it was pleasant out here.

He turned his head and looked towards the enemy outpost again. His hatred was now directed against the enemy. Their words were meaningless. Whenever he heard their words, they sounded like the barking of a dog. He was not afraid of them, and his punishment was remitted when he killed one or two of them.

Now he ceased to think and he thrust upwards his lower lip. His body became rigid. He fondled the breech of his rifle. With his rifle folded in his arms, ready for use, he slowly pushed his body forward, moving on his left side. He propelled himself with his left foot. He was listening intently. He moved like a snail, a few inches at a time. He made no sound. Then he stopped suddenly when he had gone half the distance. He had heard a sound. It was the sound of teeth gnawing a crust of hard bread, an army biscuit or a stale piece of bread, hardened by the frost. An enemy! There was an enemy there in front, five yards away.

He turned over gently on his stomach and brought his rifle to the front. Then he slowly touched various parts of his equipment and of his weapon to see that everything was in order. He settled his steel hat a little farther forward on his head, so that its rim shielded his face. Then he raised his back until he was on his elbows and knees. He then raised his feet and hands. He crawled forward as slowly as before and even more silently, breathing gently through his nose. He reached the post and lay still, behind a little knoll that formed the parapet. The enemy was within a yard of him. The enemy snuffled as he chewed at the crust.

Mulhall slowly raised his right knee. He put his right foot to the ground under him. He balanced his rifle in his right hand. He put his left hand on the ground. Then he jumped. He jumped right on top of the man in the hole beyond. But his foot struck something hard as he fell downwards and he tumbled over the man, losing his rifle. His head struck the side of the hole. He was slightly dazed. Almost immediately, however, he raised himself and held out his hands to grope for the enemy.

The enemy had also been tossed by the impact. Just then he was pulling himself up against the side of the hole, his hands supporting him, his mouth and eyes wide open with fright and wonder. There was a piece of black bread in his right hand. There were crumbs on his lips. His face was within a few inches of Mulhall's face.

Mulhall's hands, which he had thrust forward instinctively to grapple with the enemy, instinctively dropped. With the amazing courage of stupid men, Mulhall saw at a glance that the enemy was much bigger and stronger than himself and that he was almost standing up. Mulhall, on the other hand, was huddled on the ground. Now the enemy was incapable of movement through the paralysis of sudden fear. But if Mulhall touched him the same terror would make him struggle like a madman. Mulhall knew that and lay still. His face imitated the enemy's face. He opened his mouth and dilated his eyes.

They remained motionless, watching one another, like two strange babies. Their rifles lay side by side at the bottom of the hole. The enemy's rifle had been leaning against the side of the hole, and Mulhall had tripped over it, losing his own rifle. Now they were both unarmed. Their faces were so close together that they could hear one another's breathing.

The enemy was a stripling, but fully grown, and of a great size. His cheeks were red and soft. So were his lips. His whole body was covered with good, soft flesh. Mulhall was a squat fellow, thin and hard. His face was pale and marked with scars. He had eyes like a ferret. A drooping, fair moustache covered his lip and curled into his mouth. He looked brutal, ugly, war-worn and humpy compared to the fine young enemy, whose flesh was still soft and fresh on his big limbs.

Although his mouth lay stupidly open, as if with terror, Mulhall's mind remained brutal, calm, and determinedly watching for an opportunity to capture the enemy. If he could only reach his gun or disengage his entrenching tool or release his jack-knife. But he must take the fellow alive and drag him back over the frosty ground by the scruff of the neck, prodding him with his bayonet.

Then the enemy did a curious thing that completely puzzled Mulhall. At first his face broke into a smile. Then he laughed outright, showing his teeth that were sound and white, like the teeth of a negro. He made a low, gurgling sound when he laughed. Then, slowly, with a jerky, spasmodic movement, he raised the hand that held the crust until the bread was in front of Mulhall's face. Then his face became serious again and his expression changed.

The look of fear left his eyes. They became soft and friendly. His lips trembled. Then his whole body trembled. Gesticulating with his hands and shoulders, he offered the bread to Mulhall eagerly. He moved his lips and made guttural sounds which Mulhall did not understand. Every other time that Mulhall heard those words he thought they were like the barking of a dog. But now they had a different sound.

Mulhall became confused and ashamed. His forehead wrinkled. At first, he felt angry with the enemy, because he had aroused a long-buried feeling of softness. Then he became suspicious. Was the bread poisoned? No. The enemy had been eating it himself. Then he suddenly wanted to shed tears. He thought, with maudlin self-pity, of the brutal callousness and cruelty of his own comrades and superiors. Everybody despised Mulhall. Nobody would share blankets with him in the hut. He always got the dregs of the tea. They moved away from him in the canteen. When he was tied to the wheel of the cook-house cart fellows used to jeer at him and cry out: "Are they bitin' ye, Mull?" With tears in his eyes, Mulhall wanted to bite the hand that held out the bread. The action brought to a climax the whole ghastly misery of his existence. It robbed him of his only solace, the power to hate somebody whom he could injure with impunity.

He was on the point of striking away the bread when his instinct of cunning warned him. So he took the bread. He fumbled with it uncertainly. Then he stuffed it into the pocket of his tunic. The enemy became delighted and made fresh gestures, gabbling all the while.

Then the enemy stopped gabbling and both became still, watching one another. Their faces became suspicious again. Their eyes wandered over one another's bodies, each strange to the other. Their features became hostile. Their hands jerked uneasily.

Mulhall, slightly unnerved by the enemy's action, began to feel afraid. He became acutely conscious of the enemy's size. So he also began to make guttural sounds imitating the enemy. He touched the enemy's sleeve and said: "Huh. Yuh. Uh. Uh." Then he put his finger in his mouth and sucked it. Then he nodded his head eagerly. The enemy looked on in wonder, with suspicion in his eyes.

Mulhall took off his steel hat. There was a crumpled cigarette in the hat. He took out the cigarette and gave it to the enemy.

The enemy's face relaxed again. He was overcome with emotion. He took the cigarette and then kissed Mulhall's hand.

Then Mulhall surrendered completely to this extraordinary new feeling of human love and kindness. Were it not for his native sense of reserve, he would return the enemy's kiss. Instead of that he smiled like a happy child and his head swam. He took the enemy's hand and pressed it three times, mumbling something inaudible. They sat in silence for a whole minute, looking at one another in a state of ecstasy. They loved one another for that minute, as saints love God or as lovers love, in the first discovery of their exalted passion. They were carried up from the silent and frightful corpse-strewn battle-field into some God-filled place, into that dream state where life almost reaches the secret of eternal beauty.

They were startled from their ecstasy by the booming of a single cannon, quite near, to the rear of the enemy lines. They heard the whizzing of the shell over their heads, flying afar.

The enemy soldier started. His face grew stern. He sat up on his heels and took Mulhall's hand. He began to make guttural sounds as he pressed Mulhall's hand fervently.

Mulhall also awoke, but slowly. His soul had sunk deeply into the tender reverie of human love so alien to him. Like a sick man awaking from a heavy sleep, he scanned the enemy's face, seeking the meaning of the change that had been caused by the boom and the whizzing passage of the shell. Slowly he became aware of the boom. Then his cunning awoke in him. Was it a signal?

Without changing his features he became cruel again.

Still uttering guttural sounds, the enemy crawled out into the bottom of the hole and picked up his rifle. Mulhall struggled between the desire of his cunning to throttle the enemy while his back was turned, and an almost identical desire to throw his arms around the enemy's neck and beg him to remain. The cunning desire lost in the struggle and he felt very lonely and miserable as if he were on the point of losing somebody he had loved all his life. So he remained motionless, watching the enemy with soft eyes. And yet he felt violently angry at not being able to hate the enemy and throttle him.

Having taken up his rifle, the enemy paused and looked at the crumpled cigarette which he still held in his hand. Then he smiled and began to make effusive gestures. He kissed the cigarette. Then he made curious sounds, his face aglow with joy and friendship. Then he put down his rifle, pointed to Mulhall's helmet and then to his own. He laughed. He took off his own helmet, which was shaped differently from Mulhall's helmet.

Immediately, Mulhall started violently. He became rigid. All his savagery and brutality again returned. The enemy's skull was exposed. As soon as he saw it the lust of blood overwhelmed him, as if he were a beast of prey in sight of his quarry. The enemy's bare skull acted on his senses like a maddening drug. Its shape was alien. It was shaped like a bullet. It had whitish hairs on it. It was hostile, foreign, uncouth, the mark of the beast. The sight of it caused his blood to curdle in him. A singing sound started in his head, at the rear of his forehead. His eyes glittered. He wanted to kill. He again felt exalted, gripped by the fury of despair.

The skull disappeared. The enemy put his helmet back on his head and then peered over the top of the hole in both directions. Then he struck his chest a great blow, murmured something, and crawled out back towards his own line.

As quick as a cat Mulhall pounced on his own rifle and arranged the breech. Then he crouched up against the side of the hole, thrust out his rifle and looked. The enemy was already a few yards away, slouching off in a stooping position. Quickly, taking quick aim, Mulhall fired. The enemy grunted, stopped, and expanded his chest. Then he turned his head towards Mulhall as he sank slowly. Baring his teeth, with glittering eye, Mulhall aimed slowly at the wondering, gaping young face of the enemy. He fired. The enemy's face twitched and lowered to the ground. His whole body lowered to the ground, trembled and lay still. The haunches remained high off the ground. The feet were drawn up. One hand was thrown out. The head was twisted around towards Mulhall. The face, now stained with blood, still seemed to look at Mulhall with awe and wonder.

Mulhall suddenly felt an irresistible desire to run away.

He dashed out of the hole in the direction of his own line, careless of taking cover. He had not gone three yards when he threw up his hands and dropped his gun. He got it right between the shoulder blades. Coughing and cursing, he fell backwards on his buttocks. His head was still erect. With maniacal joy he looked up into the cruel blue sky and laughed out fierce blasphemies.

They got him again, three times, around the shoulders and neck. His head fell forward. In that position he lay still, like a grotesque statue, dead.

At dawn, when the sun began to shine, he was still sitting that way, like a Turk at prayer, stiff and covered with frost.

V.M. YEATES
True Gods

V.M. Yeates (1897–1934) flew 248 hours on Sopwith Camels on the Western Front; and survived two shooting downs. He was invalided out of the RAF in 1918 with tuberculosis, to which he succumbed finally in 1934. His one published book, Winged Victory *(1934), is one of the greatest novels of aerial warfare, the story of RFC pilot Tom Cundall as he falls prey to stress and disenchantment in the summer of 1918.*

In this selection from Winged Victory, *Tom Cundall and his friend Bill Williamson (a character based on Henry Williamson, the real-life author of* Tarka the Otter), *have only two days of active service left.*

HE LAY STILL, BREATHING SLOWLY, deliberately. Two more days. Only two more days. Then they would go to London, celebrate briefly, and go away into the West Country and stay as long as they could on a farm where food might be comparatively plentiful, and they would not have to eat tripe and margarine. They would drink beer and cider, lend a hand with the harvesting, sport with village maidens, climb hills and lie in the sun. They would do no shooting. They would have bicycles and wander carefree from village to remote village, curse dud weather instead of blessing it, swim in the sea, explore old churches, peer into streams. Bill knew well the East Anglian Perpendicular, and the fine beer and cider of Norfolk and Suffolk; the West Country, variation on the same English theme, but hilly, would delight him.

Only two more days; there was infinite relief in the thought. If only it would be dud for those last hours. But the night was fair when they went to bed, sober, talking of what they would do. In the morning there was an open sky above the heat haze.

And on that penultimate day they took off from the dusty aerodrome at 11.15 o'clock and flew unhurryingly to the lines, a journey of thirty miles now. In front of Albert he saw a formation of strange machines above them. Snipes, by God. They were having a look at the lines, and very soon would be taking part in the war. And Mac was coming, and the Fokkers would be driven out of the air. He went alongside Bill, pointed upwards, and waved his fist in an orbit of cheering. Bill nodded and did a thumbs up in reply. Tom dropped back into place.

They split up before Peronne and went to look for targets individually. Tom, as usual, kept near Bill. Only three more jobs at the most after this one. The war was going splendidly. The Huns were on the run, and it was hardly possible they would ever be able to stand against all the tanks that were crawling after them. For a moment his heart was lighter, but then they went down.

Williamson had taken a good look round before crossing the line between Bapaume and St Pierre-Vaast Wood, and there seemed to be no Fokkers about. A patrol of SEs was protecting low fliers. They went east beyond Sailly-Saillisel and zig-zagged southwards behind St Pierre-Vaast Wood. Files and straggles of Huns were retreating out of the wood. A wonderful target. They let their bombs go. Most of the Huns vanished at once, but the bombs must have done damage. Bill was diving and firing. Tom followed him. He supposed he'd better loose off a few rounds, and wished he wasn't shaking so much. Bill did a roll. He did not come out. A double roll. What the devil. He was spinning. Christ, oh Christ. "Come out, Bill!" he shouted. It couldn't be happening to Bill. He followed him down. Oh God, Bill was hit, he would never get out.

"Bill, Bill, for Christ's sake, Bill," he screamed. The Camel spun on. Full engine. It crashed behind the wood. It hit the ground and burst to fragments. It was like a shell exploding.

A cloud of dust and smoke flew up. It did not burn, but Bill was smashed to bits.

He flew right down on the crash. Bullets were holing his planes. He saw flashes of machine guns. There were two in an open pit. They had killed Bill. Damn and blast them. God, he would get them. He was grinding his teeth and drawing back his lips with rage and hatred. God, he'd get them.

He climbed and sideslipped away, watching. They were firing at him. He must be cunning. It would be no use diving straight at a pair of machine guns; he would give them a sitting shot, and they would probably get him first; get him as well as Bill. There seemed to be three men in the pit. He circled about sideslipping and wondering what to do. He dived away from them and fired a short burst at nothing in particular to warm his guns and to make them think he had not seen them.

He could dive vertically on them; they would be unable to reply effectively, but he could not go right down on them vertically. No, he must attack them at an angle that would let him dive right into the pit so that they wouldn't have a chance. He would shoot them from a dozen feet.

What cover had they? There seemed to be a darker patch on the north side that might be a scoop or shallow dugout. He must attack from the south so as to fire into it in case they ran in.

He got in position just in time. One of the guns was not firing. They were doing something to it. It would be out of action some seconds at least. He would take a chance of outshooting one gun with his two.

He dived steeply, pressing his trigger, and eased slowly out, bringing his sights on to his target with his guns already firing. The Huns should not have the advantage of getting in the first burst.

The pit came into the centre of the Aldis. He held it there expertly. Tracers flashed inches away. Chips flew from struts. The engine was hit.

Then it was over. He pulled up out of the pit. There were two dead men in it. He must have riddled them. One man seemed to have got away.

Rage was gone. There was no feeling left in him. He was shaking. Bill was killed. He had avenged him: what was the good? Bill was gone. He did not even know for certain that it was his killers he had killed.

He made for home, engine missing. He was being shot at. They would not get him. He crossed the lines, and flew dazedly westwards, homing by instinct. He landed and walked to the office.

The major and Hollis were both there. "Williamson is killed." Hollis ejaculated "Christ." The major did not at once speak. Tom walked out. His instinctive feeling was to be alone.

"Cundall." It was the major calling him. He turned back. The major came up to him and put his hand on his shoulder.

"I know how you feel. But come and make your report."

Tom went back to the office and told them about it in flat phrases. When he had finished, the major said:

"That was a wonderful effort of yours getting those machine guns."

Tom had nothing to reply.

"You're not to fly any more to-day. You're not fit."

He went to the tent and took off his gear. There was Bill's stuff that he wouldn't want any more. He was dead. Bill of all people; that rock. Ground-strafing, ah! He was not coming back: Bill of all people. Smashed up. Utterly gone.

In the mess people asked him about Bill. Drinking neat whisky, he told them. He had never known the squadron so troubled by a death.

Then lunch. He sat down to it, but found eating impossible, so drank. Hollis told about his avenging of Bill, and people asked Tom details, eyebrows slightly up, solemn before this exploit.

They gave him drink. He went to his tent. He slept, but it was hell to wake up in the desolate tent.

He drank tea. The thing was gaining on him; the glass in his belly was beginning to move and pierce. He couldn't face the night alone. He said to Chadwick, who was P.M.C.:

"Can the mess sell me two bottles of whisky?"

"I'll see you get it, Tom," he replied: and later: "I've put them in your tent. The corks are drawn."

The major said to him: "The wing doctor will be here in the morning, and he'll just run over you."

By dinner he was able to eat something and stop the light-headed feeling produced by alcohol in an empty stomach. He sat about in the mess for a time, but it was impossible to inflict his gloomy presence on fellows trying to make themselves cheery amid all the war.

So he went to his tent, and mourned alone. There was no chance now, that, as once before, Bill would come back. He was gone for ever and for ever. The whisky was on the grassy ledge where the tent overlapped the hole. He filled his tooth mug and drank. God, the way he could swallow whisky nowadays. He could never recover physically or mentally. Body and brain were dull and rotting. He ought to have been killed, not Bill. Better get into bed while he was able. Damned difficult clothes were. "Bill," he was saying, "Bill, old dear." Talking away, tears streaming down his face. Bloody fool. Somehow he got into bed and poured out more whisky, spilling it. He sank into whirling oblivion and then woke up again to the wrongness of the world. The candle had burnt out. Wrongness turned into physical pain. It precipitated out of the darkness and became definite, localizing in his guts. He drank whisky from the neck of the bottle; then he knew he was going to be sick. He groped under the bed for his pot, and spewed into it. He had little to bring up, but went on retching for hours. He lay dully intent on his guts-ache, which at least shut out mental agony.

He heard the pilots for the dawn patrol being called, engines being run, talk in the mess, the take off. He dozed. The batman came in at eight o'clock to see if he wanted anything. He had a cup of tea. Soon afterwards the M.O. arrived.

"Well, how do you feel this morning?" He opened wide the tent flap for more light.

"Rotten. Trying to vomit all night."

"What d'you put that down to?"

"Lobster salad."

"H'm." The M.O. paused for a moment, and then said: "Drinking much?"

"Soaking."

The doctor considered him. "Try to cut down the drink when you get home, or you'll spoil your stomach permanently. You must give up war-flying for a bit. The prescription is a month's leave and Home Establishment. But don't binge. Just go easy for a time. All right?"

"All right, doctor."

"I should think you'd get away to-morrow. Good luck."

Tom got up and wandered about the countryside. The peasants had done most of their reaping. He stood in a stubble field watching a pair of swallows circling, admiring their skill and swiftness. It was marvellous that they could get so much speed with so little effort. He started a hare, and it fled like the spirit of fear. He felt remote from the war. The advance went on; it might have been in a campaign of Marlborough. The squadron was to move forward to Allonville next morning. He would not have to go, as transport from Wing would be ready at eight o'clock to take him to Boulogne. He wrote up his log book finally, and found that he had done altogether one hundred and sixty-three jobs, totalling two hundred and forty eight flying hours.

In the afternoon he packed Bill's stuff, destroying dozens of letters which he thought he would not have wanted his next of kin to possess. He found a photograph of him which he kept. They had been friends, and this eternal parting was bitter. He had become used to thinking of the future as theirs. Now the future was nothing. The desire for life, which had always flowed in him like a strong tide, had ebbed. His life, it seemed, was saved, but the gods that gave back his life into his hands had taken away the value of the gift. They were true gods.

JOHN DOS PASSOS
The Unknown Soldier

The writer and playwright John Rodrigo Dos Passos (1896–1970) was born in Chicago. He served in the US Medical Corps in WWI, but lived most of his life quietly at Cape Cod and at his father's farm in Virginia. One of America's most important writers, his war fiction includes the novels One Man's Inititiation *(1917) and* Three Soldiers *(1921).*

"The Unknown Soldier" is from the novel 1919 *(1932), part of Dos Passos's monumental* USA *trilogy.*

WHEREASTHE CONGRESSOFTHEunitedstates byaconcurrent resolution adopted onthe4thdayofmarch last-authorizedthe Secretaryofwar to cause to be brought to theunitedstatesthe body of an American whowasamemberofthe american expeditionary forcesineurope wholosthislifeduringthe worldwarand whoseidentityhasnotbeenestbalished for burial inthememorialamphitheatre ofthe nationalcemetery atarlingtonvirginia

In the Tarpaper Morgue at Chalons-sur-Marne in the reek of chloride of lime and the dead, they picked out the pine box that held all that was left of

    enie menie minie moe plenty other pine boxes stacked up there containing what they'd scraped up of Richard Roe

    and other person or persons unknown. Only one can go. How did they pick John Doe?

    Make sure he aint a dinge, boys,

    make sure he aint a guinea or a kike,

how can you tell a guy's a hunredpercent when all you've

got's a gunnysack full of bones, bronze buttons stamped with
the screaming eagle and a pair of roll puttees?
. . . and the gagging chloride and the puky dirtstench of the
year-old dead . . .

The day withal was too meaningful and tragic for
applause. Silence, tears, songs and prayer, muffled drums
and soft music were the instrumentalities today of national
approbation.

John Doe was born (thudding din of blood in love into the
shuddering soar of a man and woman alone indeed together
lurching into
and ninemonths sick drowse waking into scared agony and
the pain and blood and mess of birth). John Doe was born
and raised in Brooklyn, in Memphis, near the lakefront in
Cleveland, Ohio, in the stench of the stockyards in Chi, on
Beacon Hill, in an old brick house in Alexandria Virginia, on
Telegraph Hill, in a halftimbered Tudor cottage in Portland
the city of roses,
in the Lying-In Hospital old Morgan endowed on Stuyvesant
Square,
across the railroad tracks, out near the country club, in a
shack cabin tenement apartmenthouse exclusive residential
suburb;
scion of one of the best families in the social register, won
first prize in the baby parade at Coronado Beach, was marbles
champion of the Little Rock grammarschools, crack basketball
player at the Booneville High, quarterback at the State
Reformatory, having saved the sheriff's kid from drowning
in the Little Missouri River was invited to Washington to be
photographed shaking hands with the President on the White
House steps;—

though this was a time of mourning, such an assemblage
necessarily has about it a touch of color. In the boxes are
seen the court uniforms of foreign diplomats, the gold braid
of our own and foreign fleets and armies, the black of the
conventional morning dress of American statesmen, the

varicolored furs and outdoor wrapping garments of mothers and sisters come to mourn, the drab and blue of soldiers and sailors, the glitter of musical instruments, and the white and black of a vested choir.

—busboy harveststiff hogcaller boyscout champeen cornshucker of Western Kansas bellhop at the United States Hotel at Saratoga Springs office boy callboy fruiter telephone lineman longshoreman lumberjack plumber's helper,

worked for an exterminating company in Union City, filled pipes in an opium joint in Trenton, N. J.

Y.M.C.A. secretary, express agent, truckdriver, ford mechanic, sold books in Denver Colorado: Madam would you be willing to help a young man work his way through college?

President Harding, with a reverence seemingly more significant because of his high temporal station, concluded his speech:

We are met today to pay the impersonal tribute;
the name of him whose body lies before us took flight with his imperishable soul . . .
as a typical soldier of this representative democracy he fought and died believing in the indisputable justice of his country's cause . . .

by raising his right hand and asking the thousands within the sound of his voice to join in the prayer:

Our Father which art in heaven hallowed be thy name . . .

Naked he went into the army;

they weighed you, measured you, looked for flat feet, squeezed your penis to see if you had clap, looked up your anus to see if you had piles, counted your teeth, made you cough, listened to your heart and lungs, made you read the letters on the card, charted your urine and your intelligence, gave you a service record for a future (imperishable soul)

and an identification tag stamped with your serial number to hang around your neck, issued O D regulation equipment, a condiment can and a copy of the articles of war.

Atten'SHUN suck in your gut you c—r wipe that smile

off your face eyes right wattja tink dis is a choirch-social?
For-war-D'ARCH.

John Doe
and Richard Roe and other person or persons unknown
drilled hiked, manual of arms, ate slum, learned to salute,
to soldier, to loaf in the latrines, forbidden to smoke on
deck, overseas guard duty, forty men and eight horses,
shortarm inspection and the ping of shrapnel and the shrill
bullets combing the air and the sorehead woodpeckers the
machineguns mud cooties gasmasks and the itch.
Say feller tell me how I can get back to my outfit.

John Doe had a head
for twentyodd years intensely the nerves of the eyes the
ears the palate the tongue the fingers the toes the armpits,
the nerves warmfeeling under the skin charged the coiled
brain with hurt sweet warm cold mine must dont sayings
print headlines:
Thou shalt not the multiplication table long division, Now
is the time for all good men knocks but once at a young man's
door, It's a great life if Ish gebibbel, The first five years'll be
the Safety First, Suppose a hun tried to rape your my country
right or wrong, Catch 'em young, What he dont know wont
treat 'em rough, Tell 'em nothin, He got what was coming
to him he got his, This is a white man's country, Kick the
bucket, Gone west, If you dont like it you can croaked him
Say buddy cant you tell me how I can get back to my outfit?

Cant help jumpin when them things go off, give me the
trots them things do. I lost my identification tag swimmin in
the Marne, roughhousin with a guy while we was waitin to
be deloused, in bed with a girl named Jeanne (Love moving
picture wet French postcard dream began with saltpeter in
the coffee and ended at the propho station);—
*Say soldier for chrissake cant you tell me how I can get back to
my outfit?*

John Doe's
heart pumped blood:

alive thudding silence of blood in your ears

down in the clearing in the Oregon forest where the punkins were punkincolor pouring into the blood through the eyes and the fallcolored trees and the bronze hoopers were hopping through the dry grass, where tiny striped snails hung on the underside of the blades and the flies hummed, wasps droned, bumblebees buzzed, and the woods smelt of wine and mushrooms and apples, homey smell of fall pouring into the blood,

and I dropped the tin hat and the sweaty pack and lay flat with the dogday sun licking my throat and adamsapple and the tight skin over the breastbone.

The shell had his number on it.

The blood ran into the ground.

The service record dropped out of the filing cabinet when the quartermaster sergeant got blotto that time they had to pack up and leave the billets in a hurry.

The identification tag was in the bottom of the Marne.

The blood ran into the ground, the brains oozed out of the cracked skull and were licked up by the trenchrats, the belly swelled and raised a generation of bluebottle flies,

and the incorruptible skeleton,

and the scraps of dried viscera and skin bundled in khaki

they took to Chalons-sur-Marne

and laid it out neat in a pine coffin

and took it home to God's Country on a battleship

and buried it in a sarcophagus in the Memorial Amphitheatre in the Arlington National Cemetery

and draped the Old Glory over it

and the bugler played taps

and Mr Harding prayed to God and the diplomats and the generals and the admirals and the brasshats and the politicians and the handsomely dressed ladies out of the society column of the *Washington Post* stood up solemn

and thought how beautiful sad Old Glory God's Country it was to have the bugler play taps and the three volleys made their ears ring.

*　　*　　*

Where his chest ought to have been they pinned
the Congressional Medal, the D.S.C., the Medaille Militaire,
the Belgian Croix de Guerre, the Italian gold medal, the Vitutea
Militara sent by Queen Marie of Rumania, the Czechoslovak
war cross, the Virtuti Militari of the Poles, a wreath sent by
Hamilton Fish, Jr., of New York, and a little wampum presented
by a deputation of Arizona redskins in warpaint and feathers. All
the Washingtonians brought flowers.

Woodrow Wilson brought a bouquet of poppies.

ANDRÉ MALRAUX
The Prison

The French writer and statesman André Malraux (1901–1976) was born and educated in Paris. In the 1920s he became a Communist and fought in the 1927 Shanghai Uprising—the historical event which forms the setting for his classic novel Man's Estate *(1933). During the Spanish Civil War he organised a volunteer airforce to fight for the Republican side, and was later a leader of the French Resistance. With the end of WWII, he joined the Gaullist movement, eventually becoming France's Minister of State.*

"The Prison" is an excerpt from Man's Estate. *The Shanghai Uprising has been defeated, and the Communists have been captured by the Nationalists under Chang Kai-shek. The Communists, including the novel's hero, Katow, await their death.*

6 P.M.

IN THE GREAT HALL OF the prison—once a school courtyard, covered in—two hundred wounded Communists waited for some one to come and finish them off. Katow, who had been brought along with the last batch, looked around him, leaning on his elbow. They all lay flat on the floor. Many groaned, and there was an extraordinary regularity about their groaning. Some, like the wounded at the Depôt, were smoking and the swirls of smoke were lost in the roof, dark already despite the large European windows showing the fog and the failing evening light outside. It seemed a long way off, high above all these reclining men. Although daylight had not yet entirely faded, in the hall it seemed as though night had fallen. "Is that because every one's wounded," Katow wondered, "or because we're all lying down, like in a railway-station? A railway-station—that's what this place really is; we shall leave it and yet go nowhere, but that's what it is . . ."

Four Chinese regulars marched up and down among the wounded with bayonets fixed; sticking up hard and distinct above so many indeterminate bodies, their bayonets weirdly reflected the failing daylight. Outside, pale yellow flares gleaming in the depths of the fog—no doubt they were gas-lamps—seemed also to keep watch over them. And, as if it came from them (because it, too, issued from the further depths of the fog), a whistle shrilled, drowning the whispers and the groans: the whistle of a locomotive. They were close to Chapei station. There was in the room some hideous sense of strain, which was not expectancy of death. His own throat told Katow what it was: thirst—and hunger. Propped against the wall, he looked to right and left: a good number of the faces were known to him, for many of the wounded had fought in the *tchons*. All along one of the two narrower sides of the hall, an open space had been kept, three yards broad. "Why," he asked out loud, "do the wounded lie one on top of the other instead of moving over into that space?" He was among the last arrivals. Clinging to the wall he helped himself on to his feet; although his wounds hurt terribly he believed he could stand—but he paused, bent double; for, although no word had been spoken, he felt a wave of such complete terror surge up all round him that he stopped short. Was it in the way eyes looked at him? No, he could hardly make them out. Was it their gestures? Their gestures were, above all else, the gestures of wounded men occupied with their own sufferings. Yet, whatever its means of communication to him, the fear was there—not fright, but terror, the terror of dumb animals, of men face to face with something unhuman. Still supporting himself against the wall, Katow stepped over the prone body of his next door neighbour.

"Are you mad?" asked a voice from the ground.

"Why?"

His question was peremptory. But no one answered. And

one of the guards, five yards away, instead of hurling him back into his place, gazed at him in stupefaction.

"Why?" he asked again, even more roughly.

"He doesn't know why," declared another voice, again from floor-level, and at the same time still another voice, in a lower tone, said:

"It'll come in time . . ."

He had asked his second question in a very loud voice. There was something of itself essentially horrible in the hesitancy of this crowd, furthermore, since he was known to most of these men, the threat that hung on the wall opposite weighed on them all and on him in particular.

"Lie down," some one said.

Why did not a single one of them call him by his name? And why didn't the guard step in and intervene? Only a few minutes before he had seen him fell a man, who had wanted to change places, with the butt of his rifle . . . He stooped over towards the man who had spoken last, and lay down by his side.

"That's where they put the ones who are going to be tortured," the man explained under his breath.

Now Katow understood. They were all of them aware of it, but they hadn't dared tell him; either because they were too frightened to speak of it, or because they were afraid to tell *him*—no, they couldn't tell him. A voice had said: "It'll come . . ."

The door opened. Soldiers with torches entered, wheeling in trolleys on which wounded men lay like luggage, and tipped them off quite close to Katow. Night came in with them, came up from the floor—amid the most appalling stench: the sound of groaning was like the scurrying of rats. Most of the men could not move. The door closed.

Time passed. Only the sentinels paced to and fro; overhead the last gleam of light glinted on their bayonets; below seethed the myriad sounds of anguish. Suddenly, as though the darkness had added to the impenetrability of the fog, from afar came the deadened shriek of the locomotive's whistle. One of the last batch of prisoners, lying on his face, pressed his hands over his ears, and screamed. None of the others cried out, but again the terror was in their midst, low on the ground.

The man lifted up his head, raised himself on his elbows. "The swine!" he yelled. "The murderers!"

One of the sentries came across and turned him over with a jab of his boot. The man shut his mouth. The sentry moved away. The wounded man began to mumble and rave. It was too dark for Katow to see how he looked, but he could hear the sound of his voice; soon, no doubt, he would become coherent. Sure enough: "They don't shoot them, they fling them alive into the furnace of the locomotive," he was saying. "Then that's that—they blow the whistle . . ." The sentry was coming back. Silence, except for the sounds of the suffering.

The door again opened. More bayonets—this time lit from below by the torch-flares; but no wounded. A Kuomintang officer came in alone. Although now he could distinguish nothing in all this mass of bodies, Katow was aware that each man stiffened. The officer, over in the distance, a shadow thrown up dimly by the torchlight against a background of the dying day, was giving orders to a sentry. The sentry came over in Katow's direction, looked for him; found him. Without laying hands on him, respectfully and without a word, he merely signed to him to get up. Katow with difficulty followed him, to where, by the door, the officer was still busy issuing orders. The soldier, with rifle in one hand, torch in the other, took up his position on his left. On his right there was nothing but the open space and the white wall. The soldier jerked his rifle to indicate the open space. Bitterly Katow smiled, with desperate pride, but no one saw his face: the sentry was careful not to look at it, and all the wounded who were not on the point of death raised on an arm, a leg, or rested heads on chins, to watch his shadow, still faint, loom larger on the wall reserved for those awaiting torture.

The officer went out. The door remained open . . .

Soldiers were among the crowd picking out two of the prisoners unable to stand up. Evidently to be burned alive entitled one to special, though limited, privileges: they were trundled along on a single trolly, one on top, or almost on top, of the other and then tipped off on Katow's left; Kyo, dead, lay to his right. In the empty space separating these men from those condemned merely to death, the soldiers squatted down

beside their torches. Little by little heads and watching eyes
sank back into the gloom, glancing only rarely now at this light
which, at the end of the hall, marked where the condemned
men lay.

After Kyo's death—he had lain gasping for at least a
minute—Katow had felt himself again thrown back into a
loneliness all the deeper and more desperate because he was
surrounded by men he knew. He could not get the Chinaman
whom they had had to carry to his death, struggling and
screaming, out of his mind. And yet he was discovering in his
total abandonment a certain sense of peace, as if for years he
had been waiting for just this: a restfulness stumbled upon and
encountered anew at all the darkest moments of his life. Where
had he read: "It was not the discoveries explorers made, but
the tribulations they endured, that caused my envy . . ."? As
if in answer to his thought, for the third time a distant whistle
made itself heard in the hall. The two men on his left gave a
start. They were very young Chinese; one was Souen, whom he
knew only because he had fought beside him at headquarters;
the other he did not know—it wasn't Pei. Why were they here,
aside from the others?

"Organizing groups for armed resistance?" he asked.

"Attempt on the life of Chang Kai Shek," answered the one
who wasn't Pei.

"Was Chen with you?"

"No. He wanted to throw his bomb alone. Chang wasn't in
the car. I was waiting for it farther along. I was taken with
the bomb on me."

So strangled was the voice that had answered his question
that Katow peered into both their faces: the young men were
weeping, soundlessly. "There's not much help in words,"
thought Katow. Souen tried to shift his shoulder and his face
contorted with pain—he was wounded in the arm.

"Burned," he said. "To be burned alive! One's eyes too,
even one's eyes—can you realize . . ."

The other man, his friend, was sobbing now.

"It could happen in an accident, a fire . . ." Katow said.

It was as though they were talking not to each other, but
to some invisible third person.

"That's not the same."

"No. It is less good."

"Even one's eyes." The young man spoke, lower still. "Eyes as well . . . Every finger and then one's stomach . . . the stomach . . ."

"Shut up!" the other said; his voice was broken.

He would have cried out, but he couldn't. His hands gripped tight on Souen's wounded arm; Souen went rigid with pain.

"Human dignity," Katow murmured, thinking of Kyo's interview with König. Neither of the young men spoke now. Beyond the torch, in the now complete darkness, the voices of pain still mumbled . . . He edged over closer to Souen and his companion. One of the guards was telling the others a story; all their heads were together, they crouched between the torch and the condemned men, who could now no longer see each other. Despite the sound of voices, despite the presence of all these men who had fought side by side with him, Katow was alone, alone between the body of his dead friend and his two frightened comrades, lost between this wall at his back and the locomotive-whistle far away in the darkness. But a man could rise superior to this solitude, possibly even superior to that ghastly screech of the whistle. Within him fear battled against the most terrible temptation he had ever known. He, in his turn, unclasped his belt. Finally:

"You there, listen," he said, in what was barely a whisper. "Souen, put your hand on my chest and shut your fingers when I touch them: I'm going to give you my cyanide. There's just—only just—enough for two."

He was renouncing, giving up everything, save this admission that there was only enough for two. Lying on his side, he broke the cyanide in half. The guards screened the light, which cast a hazy aureole about them—but wouldn't they be sure to move? However, it was far too dark to see. Katow was making this gift of more than his life to a warm hand upturned on his chest—not even to an actual body, not even to a voice. As if it were an animal, the hand snatched and was immediately withdrawn. He waited, his whole body tense. Then suddenly he heard one of the voices say:

"I've dropped it. It's lost."

It was a voice in which there was almost no trace of horror, as if so vast, so tragic a catastrophe could not have happened, as if everything would have to be all right. For Katow, too, the thing was beyond possibility. A boundless fury mounted within him, then subsided, powerless in the face of this impossibility. And yet—! To have given *that*, and then for this blundering maniac to lose it!

"Where?" he asked.

"By me. Couldn't hold it when Souen passed it to me: I'm wounded in the hand."

"He's dropped both pieces," Souen said.

They were, of course, searching the space between them. Then they felt between Katow and Souen—on whom, probably, the other man was almost lying, for Katow, unable to see anything, was conscious that both the bodies were at his elbow. He searched, too, forcing himself to control his nerves, making sure to place his hand flat on the ground, moving it sideways its own width, groping to the full length of his arm. Their hands brushed against his. Then suddenly one of these hands seized his hand, clutched it, held it fast.

"Even if we don't find anything," said one of the voices, "still . . ."

He, Katow, too, pressed the hand—he was beyond the meaning of tears, overcome by the sadness of this unseen and barely heard gratitude (all murmurings here were alike) that was being offered to him, blindly, in the surrounding darkness, in return for the greatest gift he had ever made—made, perhaps, in vain. Although Souen went on searching, the hand that held his stayed where it was. Its grip, all of a sudden, tightened madly

"Here it is!"

Oh, triumphant release! But—

"You sure it's not just a pebble?" the other asked. The ground was covered with fallen plaster.

"Give it me!" said Katow.

With the tips of his fingers he recognized the shape of the pieces.

He gave them back—gave them back!—more fiercely held the hand that again sought his, and waited, his shoulders shuddering, teeth rattling in his head. "If only the cyanide hasn't spoiled, even through its silver paper," he thought. The hand he held suddenly wrenched at his and, as if he were joined by it to this other body lost in the darkness, he felt the body stiffen. This convulsion of asphyxia filled him with envy. Almost in the same moment, there broke from the other a strangled cry which no one heeded. Then silence.

Katow felt himself alone, deserted. He rolled over on to his stomach and waited. The quaking in his shoulders would not stop.

In the middle of the night, the officer returned. Amid a clatter of unslung rifles, a squad of six soldiers marched up to the condemned men. All the prisoners were awake. The new torch, too, lit up only dimly a few long vague shapes—graves in the loose earth already—and the reflection of here and there a pair of eyes. Katow had managed to scramble to his feet. The sergeant in command of the squad seized Kyo's arm, found it rigid, then immediately took hold of Souen: he, too, was stiff. The first rows of prisoners began to mutter, and the muttering spread through the hall. The sergeant picked up first one leg, then the next: they fell back, stiff. He called the officer. The officer did likewise. The rumour among the prisoners grew louder. The officer stared at Katow.

"Dead?"

Why answer?

"Isolate the six prisoners nearest to them."

"No point in that," Katow remarked. "It was I who gave them the cyanide."

The officer hesitated.

"How about yourself?" he asked at last.

Exultant, overjoyed, "There was only enough for two," said Katow. "I'll get a rifle-butt in my face," he thought.

The murmuring among the prisoners was now almost a clamour.

"Quick march." The officer said no more.

Katow had not forgotten that he had already been condemned to death, that he had seen machine-guns pointing at him, had heard them fire . . . "As soon as I get outside, I shall try to strangle one of them, and I'll manage to keep my hands on his throat long enough for them to be forced to kill me. They may burn me, but I'll die first." At that same second, one of the escort flung his arm round him, while another dragged Katow's arms behind his back and tied them. "The other boys are well out of this," he thought. "Hell! Let's suppose that a fire broke out and I was among the casualties . . ." He started to walk. Despite the groans, again there was silence. Just as a little while before it had cast his shadow on the white-washed wall, the torch-flare now showed him in even blacker silhouette against the windows that looked out on to the night. He walked heavily, slumping first on one leg, then the other, hampered by his wounds; as he staggered towards the glare of the torch, the shadowed outline of his head merged into the roof. The entire darkness of the hall had come to life and watched him step by step. The silence now was such that the ground rang at each heavy tread of his foot. Nodding up and down, every head followed the rhythm of his walk, tenderly, in terror, in resignation, as if, although all the movements were the same, each man would himself have struggled to follow these faltering footsteps. No head fell back as the door closed.

A sound of deep breathing, like the sound of sleep, came up from the ground; breathing through the nose, jaws clenched in anguish, not stirring now, quite still, all those who were not yet dead waited to hear the shriek of a distant whistle . . .

ERNEST HEMINGWAY
The Trick of El Sordo on the Hilltop

Ernest Miller Hemingway (1899–1961) was born in Oak Park, Chicago, the son of a doctor. In 1917 he joined the Kansas City Star, *and in the following year volunteered as an ambulance driver on the Italian Front. He was twice decorated for bravery. In 1929, already a successful author and poet, he published* A Farewell to Arms, *one of the great novels of WWI. He later went as a journalist to the Spanish Civil War, a time dealt with in his most popular novel* For Whom the Bell Tolls *(1940). He took his own life in 1961. He was awarded the Nobel Prize for Literature in 1954.*

The following extract from For Whom the Bell Tolls *begins with El Sordo, a leftist guerrilla chief based in the Spanish Sierra, surrounded on a hilltop by Fascist forces.*

E L SORDO LAY NOW ON his good side and looked up at the sky. He was lying on a heap of empty cartridge hulls but his head was protected by the rock and his body lay in the lee of the horse. His wounds had stiffened badly and he had much pain and he felt too tired to move.

"What passes with thee, old one?" the man next to him asked.

"Nothing. I am taking a little rest."

"Sleep," the other said. "*They* will wake us when they come."

Just then someone shouted from down the slope.

"Listen, bandits!" the voice came from behind the rocks where the closest automatic rifle was placed. "Surrender now before the planes blow you to pieces."

"What is it he says?" Sordo asked.

Joaquin told him. Sordo rolled to one side and pulled himself up so that he was crouched behind the gun again.

"Maybe the planes aren't coming," he said. "Don't answer them and do not fire. Maybe we can get them to attack again."

"If we should insult them a little?" the man who had spoken to Joaquin about La Pasionaria's son in Russia asked.

"No," Sordo said. "Give me thy big pistol. Who has a big pistol?"

"Here."

"Give it to me." Crouched on his knees he took the big 9 mm Star and fired one shot into the ground beside the dead horse, waited, then fired again four times at irregular intervals. Then he waited while he counted sixty and then fired a final shot directly into the body of the dead horse. He grinned and handed back the pistol.

"Reload it," he whispered, "and that everyone should keep his mouth shut and no one shoot."

"*Bandidos*!" the voice shouted from behind the rocks.

No one spoke on the hill.

"*Bandidos*! Surrender now before we blow thee to little pieces."

"They're biting," Sordo whispered happily.

As he watched, a man showed his head over the top of the rocks. There was no shot from the hilltop and the head went down again. El Sordo waited, watching, but nothing more happened. He turned his head and looked at the others who were all watching down their sectors of the slope. As he looked at them the others shook their heads.

"Let no one move," he whispered.

"Sons of the great whore," the voice came now from behind the rocks again.

"Red swine. Mother rapers. Eaters of the milk of thy fathers."

Sordo grinned. He could just hear the bellowed insults by turning his good ear. This is better than the aspirin, he thought. How many will we get? Can they be that foolish?

The voice had stopped again and for three minutes they heard nothing and saw no movement. Then the sniper behind the boulder a hundred yards down the slope exposed himself and fired. The bullet hit a rock and ricocheted with a sharp whine. Then Sordo saw a man, bent double, run from the shelter of the rocks where the automatic rifle was across the open ground to the big boulder behind which the sniper was hidden. He almost dove behind the boulder.

Sordo looked around. They signalled to him that there was no movement on the other slopes. El Sordo grinned happily and shook his head. This is ten times better than the aspirin, he thought, and he waited, as happy as only a hunter can be happy.

Below on the slope the man who had run from the pile of stones to the shelter of the boulder was speaking to the sniper.

"Do you believe it?"

"I don't know," the sniper said.

"It would be logical," the man, who was the officer in command, said. "They are surrounded. They have nothing to expect but to die."

The sniper said nothing.

"What do you think?" the officer asked.

"Nothing," the sniper said.

"Have you seen any movement since the shots?"

"None at all."

The officer looked at his wrist watch. It was ten minutes to three o'clock.

"The planes should have come an hour ago," he said. Just then another officer flopped in behind the boulder. The sniper moved over to make room for him.

"Thou, Paco," the first officer said. "How does it seem to thee?"

The second officer was breathing heavily from his sprint up and across the hillside from the automatic rifle position.

"For me it is a trick," he said.

"But if it is not? What a ridicule we make waiting here and laying siege to dead men."

"We have done something worse than ridiculous already," the second officer said. "Look at that slope."

He looked up the slope to where the dead were scattered close to the top. From where he looked the line of the hilltop showed the scattered rocks, the belly, projecting legs, shod hooves jutting out, of Sordo's horse, and the fresh dirt thrown up by the digging.

"What about the mortars?" asked the second officer.

"They should be here in an hour. If not before."

"Then wait for them. There has been enough stupidity already."

"*Bandidos!*" the first officer shouted suddenly, getting to his feet and putting his head well up above the boulder so that the crest of the hill looked much closer as he stood upright. "Red swine! Cowards!"

The second officer looked at the sniper and shook his head. The sniper looked away but his lips tightened.

The first officer stood there, his head all clear of the rock and with his hand on his pistol butt. He cursed and vilified the hilltop. Nothing happened. Then he stepped clear of the boulder and stood there looking up the hill.

"Fire, cowards, if you are alive," he shouted. "Fire on one who has no fear of any Red that ever came out of the belly of the great whore."

This last was quite a long sentence to shout and the officer's face was red and congested as he finished.

The second officer, who was a thin sunburned man with quiet eyes, a thin, long-lipped mouth and a stubble of beard over his hollow cheeks, shook his head again. It was this officer who was shouting who had ordered the first assault. The young lieutenant who was dead up the slope had been the best friend of this other lieutenant who was named Paco Berrendo and who was listening to the shouting of the captain, who was obviously in a state of exaltation.

"Those are the swine who shot my sister and my mother," the captain said. He had a red face and a blond, British-looking moustache and there was something wrong about his eyes.

They were a light blue and the lashes were light, too. As you looked at them they seemed to focus slowly. Then "Reds!" he shouted. "Cowards!" and commenced cursing again.

He stood absolutely clear now and, sighting carefully, fired his pistol at the only target that the hilltop presented: the dead horse that had belonged to Sordo. The bullet threw up a puff of dirt fifteen yards below the horse. The captain fired again. The bullet hit a rock and sung off.

The captain stood there looking at the hilltop. The Lieutenant Berrendo was looking at the body of the other lieutenant just below the summit. The sniper was looking at the ground under his eyes. Then he looked up at the captain.

"There is no one alive up there," the captain said. "Thou," he said to the sniper, "go up there and see."

The sniper looked down. He said nothing.

"Don't you hear me?" the captain shouted at him.

"Yes, my captain," the sniper said, not looking at him.

"Then get up and go." The captain still had his pistol out. "Do you hear me?"

"Yes, my captain."

"Why don't you go, then?"

"I don't want to, my captain."

"You don't *want* to?" The captain pushed the pistol against the small of the man's back. "You don't *want* to?"

"I am afraid, my captain," the soldier said with dignity.

Lieutenant Berrendo, watching the captain's face and his odd eyes, thought he was going to shoot the man then.

"Captain Mora," he said.

"Lieutenant Berrendo?"

"It is possible the soldier is right."

"That he is right to say he is afraid? That he is right to say he does not *want* to obey an order?"

"No. That he is right that it is a trick."

"They are all dead," the captain said. "Don't you hear me say they are all dead?"

"You mean our comrades on the slope?" Berrendo asked him. "I agree with you."

"Paco," the captain said, "don't be a fool. Do you think you are the only one who cared for Julián? I tell you the Reds are dead. Look!"

He stood up, then put both hands on top of the boulder and pulled himself up, kneeing-up awkwardly, then getting on his feet.

"Shoot," he shouted, standing on the gray granite boulder and waved both his arms. "Shoot me! Kill me!"

On the hilltop El Sordo lay behind the dead horse and grinned.

What a people, he thought. He laughed, trying to hold it in because the shaking hurt his arm.

"Reds," came the shout from below. "Red canaille. Shoot me! Kill me!"

Sordo, his chest shaking, barely peeped past the horse's crupper and saw the captain on top of the boulder waving his arms. Another officer stood by the boulder. The sniper was standing at the other side. Sordo kept his eye where it was and shook his head happily.

"Shoot me," he said softly to himself. "Kill me!" Then his shoulders shook again. The laughing hurt his arm and each time he laughed his head felt as though it would burst. But the laughter shook him again like a spasm.

Captain Mora got down from the boulder.

"Now do you believe me, Paco?" he questioned Lieutenant Berrendo.

"No," said Lieutenant Berrendo.

"*Cojones!*" the captain said. "Here there is nothing but idiots and cowards."

The sniper had gotten carefully behind the boulder again and Lieutenant Berrendo was squatting beside him.

The captain, standing in the open beside the boulder, commenced to shout filth at the hilltop. There is no language so filthy as Spanish. There are words for all the vile words in English and there are other words and expressions that are used only in countries where blasphemy keeps pace with the austerity of religion. Lieutenant Berrendo was a very devout Catholic. So was the sniper. They were Carlists from Navarra and while both of them cursed and blasphemed when they were angry they regarded it as a sin which they regularly confessed.

As they crouched now behind the boulder watching the captain and listening to what he was shouting, they both disassociated themselves from him and what he was saying. They did not want to have that sort of talk on their consciences on a day in which they might die. Talking thus will not bring luck, the sniper thought. Speaking thus of the *Virgen* is bad luck. This one speaks worse than the Reds.

Julián is dead, Lieutenant Berrendo was thinking. Dead there on the slope on such a day as this is. And this foul mouth stands there bringing more ill fortune with his blasphemies.

Now the captain stopped shouting and turned to Lieutenant Berrendo. His eyes looked stranger than ever.

"Paco," he said, happily, "you and I will go up there."

"Not me."

"What?" The captain had his pistol out again.

I hate these pistol brandishers, Berrendo was thinking. They cannot give an order without jerking a gun out. They probably pull out their pistols then they go to the toilet and order the move they will make.

"I will go if you order me to. But under protest," Lieutenant Berrendo told the captain.

"Then I will go alone," the captain said. "The smell of cowardice is too strong here."

Holding his pistol in his right hand, he strode steadily up the slope. Berrendo and the sniper watched him. He was making no attempt to take any cover and he was looking straight ahead of him at the rocks, the dead horse, and the fresh-dug dirt of the hilltop.

El Sordo lay behind the horse at the corner of the rock, watching the captain come striding up the hill.

Only one, he thought. We get only one. But from his manner of speaking he is *caza mayor*. Look at him walking. Look what an animal. Look at him stride forward. This one is for me. This one I take with me on the trip. This one coming now makes the same voyage I do. Come on, Comrade Voyager. Come striding. Come right along. Come along to meet it. Come on. Keep on walking. Don't slow up. Come right along. Come as thou art coming. Don't stop and look at those. That's right. Don't even look down. Keep on coming with your eyes forward. Look, he has a moustache. What do you think of that? He runs to a moustache, the Comrade Voyager. He is a captain. Look at his sleeves. I said he was *caza major*. He has the face of an *Inglés*. Look. With a red face and blond hair and blue eyes. With no cap on and his moustache is yellow. With blue eyes. With pale blue eyes. With pale blue eyes with something wrong with them. With pale blue eyes that don't focus. Close enough. Too close. Yes, Comrade Voyager. Take it, Comrade Voyager.

He squeezed the trigger of the automatic rifle gently and it pounded back three times against his shoulder with the slippery jolt the recoil of a tripoded automatic weapon gives.

The captain lay on his face on the hillside. His left arm was under him. His right arm that had held the pistol was stretched forward of his head. From all down the slope they were firing on the hill crest again.

Crouched behind the boulder, thinking that now he would have to sprint across that open space under fire, Lieutenant Berrendo heard the deep hoarse voice of Sordo from the hilltop.

"*Bandidos!*" the voice came. "*Bandidos!* Shoot me! Kill me!"

On the top of the hill El Sordo lay behind the automatic rifle laughing so that his chest ached, so that he thought the top of his head would burst.

"*Bandidos,*" he shouted again happily. "Kill me, *bandidos!*" Then he shook his head happily. We have lots of company for the Voyage, he thought.

He was going to try for the other officer with the automatic rifle when he would leave the shelter of the boulder. Sooner or later he would have to leave it. Sordo knew that he could never command from there and he thought he had a very good chance to get him.

Just then the others on the hill heard the first sound of the coming of the planes.

ERIC JENS PETERSEN
Who Called You Here?

Eric Jens Petersen. No biographical details
about the author are available.
The following WWII story was origi-
nally published in Story Magazine *in*
the early 1940s.

T HE HALDER FARM LAY IN the northern part of the Tyrol, more than three thousand feet above the German frontier. It was not a big farm; only one hired man was needed to help run it. As long as he was able to do it, old Vincent Halder had done most of the work alone, from cow-milking to hay-making. But at seventy-five years of age he had become irritable and cranky.

"I won't eat the stuff!" he had growled when, in October 1939, his son had sent him the first packages of sausages and eggs from Poland. The family were on the verge of starvation in the Tyrol and his daughter-in-law was delighted with the parcels. "Take them away!" the old farmer added angrily.

Halder was a good Austrian and had been glad to go to war in 1915, against Italy. As a Tyrolean crack marksman he had defended his mountains. "What are you doing here? Who called you here?" he had bellowed at the enemy before he fired. Later, when the peace treaty divided the Tyrol and the southern part fell to the Italians he had protested to the government in Vienna which allowed such things. Why did no one in Austria stand up to the robbers of the South Tyrol? When the German agents came through the land telling about the Fuehrer Adolf Hitler, they said that South Tyrol would be freed if Austria joined Germany. Old man Halder believed them. And actually Hitler did march in and take North Tyrol. After waiting for six months old Vincent asked the village

innkeeper when the Italians were going to get out of South
Tyrol, whereupon the new constable, who wore a swastika
on his arm, told him that if he did not shut his mouth and
do it quickly, he would bash in his skull, for Hitler was on
the friendliest terms with Italy.

Halder's son, whose face was tanned and whose beard
was black—like Andreas Hofer's a hundred years before
him—protected his father from more serious trouble. This
son was clever. Already in the autumn of 1938 he saw war
and famine looming. "I shan't join up," he had said to his
wife. "I think they need people in the civil service too." So
he found a job in Kufstein to do secret errands and make
reports to the Gestapo. Then in September 1939, when the
war broke, he disappeared for four weeks. Suddenly he sent his
address—from Poland—"Balthasar Halder, Gestapo Lodz."
And at the same time came a shipment of parcels with lard
and sausages, flour, bacon and eggs.

"I won't eat it," said old Vincent sullenly. "It was stolen
from Poles and Jews!"

"Poles and Jews are all criminals!" said Agatha, his
daughter-in-law. "Didn't you read in the newspaper? They
murdered German children!"

German children? A wide-eyed German boy stood beside
them. The boy was Hans Halder, the old man's grandson.
He was sixteen years old.

"Now I shall soon be a soldier, just like grandfather,"
thought Hans and he took the Austrian military medals out
of the cupboard. But his grandfather snatched them out of his
hands. "You are a German!" he said angrily. Then he wept
a little.

When Hans turned seventeen—in November 1939—he
entered the barracks at Kufstein. There he found Alois
Ortner, the Ebeseder boy, and others. It was only a little
while before that they were playing childish games or skiing
together.

Their senior, a boy of twenty, was a student from Wörgl,
the son of the village pharmacist.

They all cursed England and Poland. (Hardly any mention
was made of the French, they had just been misled by England
and would lose their land anyhow.) At the mountain barracks,

they learned to shoot—but above all they learned how to ski expertly. None of them had ever dreamed that being in the army would be such good sport. Only the food was bad; but that was the same everywhere. "You mark my words," the student from Wörgl whispered. "One fine day we'll head for Switzerland! Adolf Hitler will take Switzerland! Why else should we be learning to ski?"

Nevertheless some of them still clung to the thought that they would march against Italy. "Quit talking!" was the instant response to that idea, or "Quit thinking!" At Christmas, when they had leave, they were told by Captain Rengger, "Say good-bye to your folks! We'll be off soon now!" Yet Easter came and still they had not gone.

But in April came a sudden mustering. The young soldiers were called to report with their overcoats, packs, rifles, skis and minimum rations. Where were they going skiing? The train was already whistling. Good-bye Tyrol! An hour later they were in Munich. The countryside grew warmer.

No snow anywhere. How *flat* was Germany! They traveled all one night over a lowland plain dotted with desolated dwarf trees, with not a hill in sight. Were they being taken to the Western Front? The air was misty but mild. Another night passed. At a great distance huge lights rose from the earth. They still had no idea where they were going; but in war, of course, it was necessary to be secretive. The train stopped; Prussian voices were heard.

"This must be Hamburg or Bremen!" said the son of the pharmacist. He was educated and was familiar with maps. "Perhaps we shall go to sea!"

"Why must we travel by sea?" was the astonished reaction of the Austrians.

"Everybody out! Change trains!" called the captain.

They were moved into another train. The bright lights disappeared again. This train moved cautiously, haltingly, through the dark. Now and then a searchlight flared across the night sky. A tepid breeze wafted the smell of coal and fog toward them. A black surface glinted. Was this the sea? They climbed out of the train.

The captain went through the battalion whispering, "Quiet! Spies around! We are going aboard . . ."

"Aboard a ship?" Their hearts dropped a beat.

The captain shrugged his shoulders. "Destination unknown!" He looked serious. The youngsters liked him.

By companies they crossed quickly over wet planks and sand. It was pitch dark. Far off in the distance two lighthouses swung their rays in a circle. "Bremerhaven!" whispered the pharmacist's son who was next to Hans.

Suddenly it was as light as day. A searchlight was fixed on the marching men. To right and left of them stood long rows of marines with drawn bayonets. Through them marched the Austrians. "Are they to keep us from running away?" thought Hans Halder.

Soon they reached a huge companionway, which was dazzling bright in the beams of the searchlight; beyond it and thrown into sharp relief against the dark towered two smoke stacks. The ship emitted a howl, like that of an animal, and outlying vessels responded.

Bewildered, laden with skis, helmets, and rifles, the companies climbed up the gangway. The last of one company was crowded by the first of the next. Cabins? There were no cabins. They tramped into the cargo hold.

It was a Polish freighter and reeked of mice, sacking and rotting vegetables. Someone came across the name of the ship-owners. "The filthy Poles! The swine!" They cursed. "Can't someone open a window? Where are we going anyhow?"

"To Africa!" sighed the pharmacist. "We are going out to conquer some colonies!"

"But why the skis?"

That was a logical question. But logic did not make them any happier. The sides of the boat began to sway. They were under way. The floor rose and fell.

All night they traveled. Through the cracks the youths could see it was morning outside. The student from Wörgl saw by his pocket compass that they were moving steadily northward. "Later on," he sighed, because he was still fearful of the possibility of going to Africa. "We shall probably turn west or south."

No life belts were seen. The ship's cooks brought them their usual rations: lentil mash and stale zwieback. They played cards by candlelight. Many of them smoked. The air became unbearable; but there was no porthole down in the hold of the ship. They had to climb up ladders and push through a trap door to get out on deck, and that was forbidden. This was because, as the ship's cooks explained to them, no light nor sound must be allowed to be observed from the ship.

But why they were not allowed on deck even during the daytime was not said.

Once in the night following the second day a quarrel broke out below deck.

"They should at least have showed us," grumbled Ebeseder, "how to get into a lifeboat."

"We don't need any lifeboats," another growled sarcastically, "we'll ski across the water!"

"It's because there aren't enough lifeboats. The ones they have are for the crew!"

"Are these dumb sailors better than we are?"

"I'd say so. And why not? There are fewer of them. They are a technical troop. Dolts like us just fill up the ranks."

With that Alois Ortner slapped the speaker. He didn't understand that the lad was only trying to be funny. A brawl resulted in which old scores between Kufstein and Wörgl had to be settled all over again. The pounding and wrangling grew to such proportions that some officers came down. They were officers from a Prussian detachment. They wore small gold daggers at their sides, were slim in body, smooth-shaven. They looked like beings from another world.

The officers expressed delighted surprise that the five hundred Tyrolean youngsters were punching each other's heads, were "threshing each other" as one of the officers, a tall first lieutenant, put it. It was quite natural that they should be doing this down here in the dark, foul air. "When German men are bored they fall naturally to fighting," a lieutenant of artillery concluded. "However, tomorrow everything will be different—tomorrow we'll be there!"

"There? Where?" Before the astonished eyes of the men the strangers disappeared and the trap door slammed before any answer was given them.

The youngsters lay down, all packed together like fish, squirming and steaming. There were five or six men to every straw mattress. If any one wanted more room he was free to lie on the bare floor.

Four hours later the hold was wakened. Several of the youths thought the ship had been struck. The trap door was yanked open and a yelled order came, "Every man on deck."

Eyes blurred with sweat, bewildered, dizzy after the foul atmosphere of their caged existence, the battalion came up. Nipping cold greeted them as they emerged through the trap door.

It was daylight but none could see more than ten paces ahead. The ship's huge smokestacks (they couldn't really be that big), were distorted and ghostly in the fog. The sea was calm, the waves hardly rippled. The men lined up, their hearts thumping. Their breath steamed as they coughed the bad air out of their lungs. A biting cold went through their sweat-soaked underwear.

"Are we at the North Pole?" thought Hans.

Suddenly he drew in his breath. He smelled something. It was not the sea, nor the smell of oysters and fish that came to him through the cold air. It was mountains! High mountains! As a Tyrolean he could sense the granite even though he might not see the mountains. Mountains give off a smell for the people who live on them, as the sea does for sailors.

And joy welled high in Hans Halder's heart. So he was back in the Tyrol! And they hadn't gone to Africa, as they had half-jokingly, half-seriously feared! Here was the old land smell of the Tyrol. The country's steep black cliffs towered like the pipes of a church organ—and perhaps there were green upland meadows among them where cows grazed and tinkled. There was no sweeter music on earth.

"Bazi, where do you think we are?"

"I should think we're in Scotland!" said his neighbor. "That's where the men run around in short skirts and bare knees . . . like women, the Scots are!"

"It can't be as cold as this in Scotland," said the pharmacist's son.

"Stand still there! Ten men go down to get the skis and packs! Nothing else! You have your rifles with you!" At last a familiar voice. It was that of their Tyrolean captain, Rengger.

But the unfamiliar Prussian, with his elongated face, soon came along. "Men!" he said, and his voice was so high that it cracked, "We have landed in Norway! We have outwitted the English fleet. Since early yesterday all points along the coast are firmly in German control. The Norwegian government has called our army over to help defend this friendly neutral country from an English invasion. Heil Hitler!"

"Halitlaa!" reverberated along the deck. And as though summoned by the power of that name the fog rose and was dissipated. To every eye was revealed the magnificent majesty of Norway. Black, chiseled iron mountains stretched out to the north and to the south, scrawling their jagged peaks against the sky as far as the eye could reach. And on their tops lay great heavy masses of snow.

The coast—the Tyrolean peasant boys after all had a keen eye for distances—lay some five miles away. Clouds of smoke and puffing noises began to come from the port side: these were the longboats. The transfer into them was quickly made.

Hans Halder's company was the first.

"Overcoats on!"

With their rifles between their knees, their helmets on, their skis and packs behind, they sat down. But they did not strap their packs on. That was surprising. But it was even more surprising when life belts were suddenly handed out. Now? After they were already in Norway? After a three-day sea journey during which time the British fleet had not fired a single torpedo at them?

The longboat captain was at the helm. His face was sharp and uneasily tense. They moved slowly, in a zigzag course. Once they moved in a curve, describing a wide arc away from the harbor town which lay inland up a river. It lay like a mountain village beside a river . . . In Hans Halder's company no one knew a *fjord* when he saw it.

The atmosphere turned misty again. The longboats passed jagged islands around which a light surf foamed; they went through veils of wet mist. No one understood the Prussian speech which the captain of the longboat used in talking to his boatswain. But they somehow got the idea that he was calling the Norwegians swine. "The whole harbor is dead! They didn't send us any pilot. If the fog had been thicker we should have been obliged to be out here until noon!"

The boat slowed down. A few rowboats came out from the shore and signaled. The mist blew away. Three and then four other longboats, which had left the steamer a quarter of an hour later than the first, now caught up with Hans Halder's boat. They steamed into the narrows.

Suddenly there was a thundering explosion. The rocky sides of the near-lying islands quadrupled the reverberations.

"They must be blasting rock," thought Hans.

That was the sound one heard when they used dynamite to make a hole in a mountainside. But not a stone budged on the stone cliff along which they were passing. Then the man next to him, his face chalk-white, pointed out that the fourth longboat had stopped. A black column of water and smoke had risen to the starboard and now crashed across it. For a moment the black mass obscured the sight of the whole boat. Then the sea opened, the boat staggered like a drunken animal, and plunged with a twisting motion into the depths.

Hans followed this drama of water and wood with horrified eyes. As yet he had not seen a single man but when he heard the boatswain yell, "Mines to the starboard! Four points to the right," he suddenly caught sight of clusters of drowning Tyroleans, like bees in a swarm. Several dozen of them were swimming and calling with sharp, far-away voices. Why did no one pick them up?

Hans hardly dared to turn his head. The danger must be terrible. But there was no more thunder. The seven boats, the eighth being lost, hastened up the river, which—now that they were in it they could see—was really an inlet from the sea.

"Narvik!" said the captain and that was a name none of them had ever heard before.

Land again at last! It looked like a village with its cobblestones among which the melting snow trickled. At least they had reached here alive! They even cracked a few feeble jokes with the comrades who had landed the day before and who now appeared on the shore with cups of steaming hot coffee.

"Boys, this is *real* coffee!" was the astonished ejaculation which broke from the battalion from the Tyrol. For since the Tyrol had become part of Germany none of the Tyroleans had tasted anything but *Ersatz* or coffee substitute.

In the bay lay several half-sunken hulls with long protruding cannon muzzles. "Norwegian battleships!" said the earlier arrivals proudly as though they had sent the Norwegians to the bottom with their own bare hands.

The pharmacist's son from Wörgl would have liked to ask why it was necessary to sink the Norwegian cruisers since the Norwegian government had called the Germans in. But he thought it safer not to ask any questions and, besides, dinner was more important.

There was, to be sure, no hurry about that. First they had to stand around for three or four hours before they were marched to their quarters. "I bet we get meat today!" said Karl Leittner to the Ebeseder boy. "The neutrals do have meat." But the few steaming pots that seemed to be coming their way went off in another direction. As none of them had had any breakfast, their necks grew longer and their bellies flatter.

Finally the Tyrolean boys were told off and a few Prussian officers began to take the individual battalions into the town. The streets were narrow, as narrow as the streets of Innsbruck. The town was small, and built out on spurs from the hills crowned with hospitable-looking white villas. And how high the clouds were! They were cold as winter, like tufts of cotton being spun in the bright light and blue wind. That's just the way they looked at home. And how the snow smelled! No, the sea was not for Tyroleans and they were happy as they marched along. They had forgotten the wrecked boat, the mine, the drowned men. They swung along in good order, with their fifes and drums ahead making the street resound. And yet it was not quite like that in the Tyrol: not a soul came out of the houses when the drums rolled. Not even a woman appeared at the windows.

Hans Halder's battalion, the first, marched up a hill. So the schoolhouse was to be their billet! What could be finer than a school? The soldiers laughingly tried to squeeze into the little seats. Everything was so doll-like. The little boys' and girls' copybooks and schoolbags lay scattered around. Too bad there was no one there. The Tyroleans would have loved to have some fun with the children and learn some Norwegian. But they must have left in a great hurry, almost a panic. Under the benches there were apples and sandwiches, and in the round hand of a child there was written in chalk on the blackboard: *Gud Bevare Faedrelandet.*

Hans Halder spelled it out. The pharmacist's son from Wörgl said it sounded like something about fatherland: "God protect our Fatherland!" Hans Halder was uncomfortable. It made him thoughtful to realize that the Germans were not the only ones with a fatherland.

But were they hungry! At four o'clock in the afternoon their food finally arrived; it was bread soup. They were also given canned fish in oil, little fish as big as your thumb. A hubbub arose: weren't they after all abroad, in a neutral country, with butcher shops? Or was it the same here as in Germany where all the meat was commandeered for "higher purposes?" They were furious. It was only when their own Captain Rengger talked to them in their familiar dialect and told them that things would soon be better, that their good humor was restored and they began to settle down.

Mattresses and pillows were brought up from the houses at the foot of the hill. There was plenty of opportunity to wash (the Norwegians, it seemed, were a clean people). A few sentries were detailed, then they stripped to the waist, hummed and laughed a little—and soon all the seventeen-year-old youngsters were snoring. Exhausted from the excitement of the last three days, they fell asleep.

About midnight they jumped out of their beds, with terror in their hearts, their hands clenched. At exactly midnight the world seemed to be crashing and thundering to an end. It sounded as though great chunks of stones were being dropped on the city. The boys ran out in their barefeet into the snow. There they stood in their shirttails, like a herd of sheep, and put their heads together. What was up?

The cursed sea had opened, a wall of fiery lightning storms had risen from the water, a colossal vessel which they couldn't see, and which out of the all-powerful darkness was raining flames and iron on them.

"The English!" said Ortner, and turned pale and the shock was so great to him, in his half-somnolent state, that he laid his hands together on his bare stomach under his shirt. He gagged as though he were going to be ill.

Hell had yawned. Under the grisly rain of flaming stars the harbor and the town began to fill with fires. Sirens shrieked. The harbor guns of the Germans barked helplessly in the direction of the invisible sea, whence the enemy hurled their shells in devastating parabolas. When several houses at the foot of the hill began to burn, the Tyroleans remembered their prayers. Some of them ran back into the classroom and mumbled on their knees to the Virgin Mary. What sort of heathen place was this? On the walls of a schoolroom there should be pictures, pictures of the Sacred Heart, of Jesus, and of the saints. But Protestants lived here. How horrible, and they had never thought of this when they left Kufstein! What had they thought about? How would all this end?

Meantime the yelling outside continued. An automobile, filled with Prussian officers, had roared up the hill. Several long-faced men in green had jumped out and bellowed, "You blasted idiots! Get to cover! Wait for orders inside!" The men crowded back into the building. "Lights out!" They stumbled over each other and cursed the children's benches.

In front of the school the automobile was preparing to turn around. The snow crunched under the tires. Then—sixty feet off to the left came a shell! It struck into the school garden. Snow, earth, branches of trees were hurled in the air. The officer at the wheel of the car threw up his hands: a mysterious force tore him from his seat. The others jumped out quickly and laid him in the snow. Immediately afterward, in through the windows of the schoolhouse, came a cry like nothing human. The Tyroleans held their ears so as not to listen to this uninterrupted screaming sound, which rose and rose—then stopped abruptly as though it had never begun. With pocket flashlights they went out and found the door of a shed, they carried the now silent body in, then the motor drove off again.

"A splinter from a grenade," whispered Ebeseder, "can be as sharp as a razor blade."

"Shut up," was the hushed command.

They sat in a huddle, with their packs strapped on their backs, and trembled. "If only it were daylight!" they prayed.

By dawn the bombardment would stop, wouldn't it? Because the English would themselves become targets as soon as day broke. No one believed that with so much anguish and distress they could go to sleep again. And yet nearly all of them dropped off, with their coats and helmets on, their rifles in their hands, overcome by the healthy compulsion of their seventeen years.

Hans Halder slept, too, and he dreamed of his Grandfather Vincent. He had been a soldier; in his youth he had gone out to meet the Italians. "What are you doing here? Who called you here?" he had bellowed, and shaken his rifle at them. His voice rang out so loud that, in the middle of the dream the boy woke up.

The bombardment had not let up although it was getting light outside. Again a car drove up. "Companies, fall in! Double-quick march to the station!" Where was the station? They hurried down the hill so fast they made the snow fly. They ran through a few streets littered with broken glass, charred beams, an occasional corpse, looking like a doll and very unreal. No one knew how far they ran. Some of them declared they went around twice in a circle. In a neighboring street two houses were still burning. The crackling and crashing seemed so pointless, it made one think of circuses at country fairs. As usual there was no one around to put it out. "Haven't they any fire engines here?" thought Hans Halder. It was the most foolish thought which had yet come into his mind—and yet the very foolishness of not understanding what was going on was the one thing to which he could cling for support.

There, at last, was the railroad station! Now they could get out of this mantrap, out of Narvik, this cursed city on a cursed sea! It was to be hoped there were enough cars . . . It was pleasant for Hans Halder to realize that he was marching with the first detachment. They would be sure to get away. But quickly, quickly!

As they hurried across the square in front of the station they saw flames licking the vaulted roof, way up on the left side. So they had struck this building too! And probably only a few seconds before—but the air was so full of noise that they had not heard it. By all the saints in the calendar, what did one burning station more or less matter in this world!

Into the train! Things were done in double-quick time and before another shell struck the remaining wall of the station, the train pulled out and puffed off into the mountains. Mountain air! This was different from travelling in the belly of a ship! The Tyroleans opened every window. Since no one had forbidden them to do this it was probably allowed. With a magnificent wind streaming around them they rode into a snowy valley, between gleaming mountain slopes.

"This looks like Kufstein and Wörgl!" someone exclaimed jubilantly. From a neighboring train came yodeling, and the long signal calls which the shepherds send across the great distances from valley to valley back home. Hans Halder, in relief, pulled his mouth organ out of his pocket. They had brought along the apples and cakes of chocolate they had found in the schoolhouse—these were great delicacies for German soldiers since the war had begun. "If we only had some post cards we could write home to Tyrol!"

A sudden jolt; they were thrown on top of each other, their skis and poles fell down on them. The train had stopped. What was the matter now?

They heard doors slam, then Captain Rengger came running along outside. "Everyone get out."

They jumped out into the soft snow. "What does this mean? Are we going to camp here?"

Near the railroad tracks were two farmhouses with great hoods of snow on their heads, standing like two outposts of the mountain village which lay beyond under the pale blue blazing sky.

"The tunnel has been blown up! Companies form and go through the village. Forward march! We're going over the mountain on foot . . ."

Who had blown up the tunnel? Had the English been here? They tramped through the village. Captain Rengger forbade them to sing.

All the houses were closed but from the fresh footprints they could tell that people had just been there. Only two women with long skirts and black hoods came their way. They tripped along the high road. Their gait was artificial, they picked their way stiffly like birds. They looked like strange nuns.

"Our girls are better looking!" said Hans Halder.

They were leaving the village and the road began to rise when they came to a post office. "I'll take a chance," said Ortner to Ebeseder.

He and four others dashed into the building. It was a post office, a Norwegian post office. It looked like any other post office, except that there was no picture of Adolf Hitler. On the wall hung a large timetable; to the left there was a desk and over it hung a calendar. But the official at the window! They had never seen such a frightened face or two such pale blue eyes. Hans Halder was the bold one. He stepped up and asked for five stamped postal cards to go to the Tyrol. They all had money—no Norwegian money but some German—and the man at the window could reckon the rate of exchange.

Then something astonishing happened. The post-office official pulled his window shut with a bang! The five mountaineer boys from the Tyrol saw quite clearly that this foreign postal official would not sell them anything.

"And yet it is in office hours," thought Hans Halder, and shook his head.

"Norway has shut up shop!" said the man standing beside him and glowered at the closed window.

"The post office is mad at us, comrades!" An obstacle had arisen to prevent them from writing to their faraway homes. "All right. We won't send any of their post cards then!" The five boys straggled out with their helmets on their heads, their rifles and their skis on their backs.

The rest of the battalion was five hundred paces ahead of them up the mountainside by now. In the brilliant winter sunshine the five could see the others distinctly raise their feet as they marched. Should they get in a sweat by going after them in double-quick time? "We have run enough for one day! We'll catch up with them on top of the mountain!"

All were eagerly waiting for the moment when they could buckle on their skis. On the crest they would be sure to get that order and then they would go down the other side in great style. That much the regiment had learned.

"Halloo-daridariiii!" yodeled Ortner.

Above them on the winding road the tail end of the battalion disappeared. Now the boys would have to hurry if they were to catch up with them.

Then down a white slope to the right of them they noticed some low-flying birds, sweeping down over the dazzling snow. No, they were not birds: they were skiers, perhaps a dozen of them. They were looming bigger and bigger. "Gee, but they know their stuff!" said the pharmacist's son and stood still, clicking his tongue. Hans, too, looked up with admiration. From a distance they heard a whistle which sounded like some sporting signal.

Were they holding some championship event here?

Down from the snow field, facing them, some thirty blue-black figures were now racing. With a graceful movement they encircled the five Tyroleans. When Hans Halder recognized the small, black caps with dark ear muffs as belonging to Norwegians he was relieved. His neighbors and he had all used caps like that at home, before they had ever gone into the army. This was sport and it occurred to him that of course it was the Norwegians who had invented his beloved skis. Didn't he know a few words of Norwegian too—for instance the expression *telemark*?

His lips began to form it but he did not have time to say it.

One of the Norwegians came forward. His face was tanned by the sun, his eyes were sad but unflinching. He opened his mouth several times, then he said in a strange rhythmic German, "What are you doing here? Who called you here?"—and emptied a four-barreled revolver in Hans Halder's breast. Hans fell, amazed beyond all measure. And when the other Tyroleans saw the snow turn red they slowly raised their arms above their heads.

OLIVIA MANNING
The Journey

Olivia Manning (1908–80) was born in Portsmouth, England, the daughter of a naval officer. Her first novel, The Wind Changes, *was published in 1937. In 1939 she married a British Council lecturer and moved with him to Romania, then Greece, before being evacuated to Egypt when the Nazis occupied. The war years were the subject of much of her best fiction, including the* Balkan *and* Levant *trilogies of novels (televised as* The Fortunes of War).

The short story "The Journey" is from Manning's collection Growing Up *(1948).*

MARY MARTIN, SETTING OUT TO report the Hungarian occupation of Transylvania, believed that journalists were magically immune from danger. Another woman, a journalist, had asked her to go to Cluj, while she herself remained to see how things went in Bucharest. "I wouldn't do anything for her if I were you," said one of the newspaper men in the Athenee Palace bar. "It's pretty risky and you'll get no thanks." Mary's husband, an oil engineer, was even less enthusiastic. "The plane service has stopped. You'll have to go by train. It'll be a grim journey." But she had made up her mind to go and it was too late to start the process of altering it.

The train was crowded. The peasants stood tightly packed in the corridors gazing out with their solemn faces at the wildly-moving crowds on the platforms. They would stand so, gazing for hours as though they saw no difference between stations and the varying countryside. Mary found a seat in the restaurant-car. Here the sun poured through hotly on to dishevelled business men sleeping with their heads on the tables among crumbs and spilt wine. The train stood another two hours before moving out. As the shadows slid across the tables and things began to shake and rattle, the men roused themselves. The majority of them were Hungarian. Mary could not understand what they said, but from the malicious pleasure of their tone and gestures she guessed they were imagining the discomfort of the Rumanians running from Cluj.

The sun slowly moved off the tables. The atmosphere remained stifling. It was heavy with tobacco smoke. They were soon off the Bucharest plain where the oil derricks stood in hundreds, spidery in the hard light, and climbing the foothills into the mountains. At the first skiing village Mary took a walk on the platform. Outside the air sang past her face with a startling freshness. Among the dark peaked pines that covered the hills were trees already turning yellow, patching the green like lion-skins. She had to get back inside the train, where the heat carried up from the summer-hot capital was stupefying.

More people crowded into the carriage at every station, but the restaurant-car, where no one dared enter who could not pay for a meal, remained half-empty. Twilight fell. At stations faces came against the window, seemed to stick a moment as though blown there like leaves, and then whisked away again. Dinner was served; meat that a few months before would have been thrown back at the waiters, was accepted without comment. Everyone knew the best meat now had to go as a bribe to Germany.

By dark they were on the great Transylvanian plateau. The train was very late. The men fell asleep one by one, collars undone, coats off, hair tousled. Mary began to feel anxious about arriving so late. She had wired a hotel, but received no reply. She did not know if a room were booked for her or not. She knew only one person in Cluj—an English governess whom she had met once in Bucharest. Now that the carriage was quiet she could hear two Rumanian Jews talking in half-whispers at the table behind her. They were, she gathered, going to settle some business in Cluj before the

barrier of a new frontier came down. One was apparently of
Austrian origin; the other from the Bukhovina. One of them
said: "Much use it is now, a Rumanian passport." The other
said: "The sooner one changes it, the better."

At last some time in the middle of the night they reached
Cluj. The station was deserted and glossy-looking in the
meagre electric light. Half a dozen soldiers with rifles stood
at the station entrance. Some of the businessmen forced their
way out first, as though in a panic. Outside, Mary realized
their eagerness had been to get one of the half-dozen rickety
horse-carriages that had been waiting for the train. There were
no taxis. All petrol had been requisitioned by the Rumanian
army, so the Hungarians could get none of it. Mary changed
her suitcase into her right hand and set out to walk the two
miles from the station to the main square. A line of lights in
frosted globes stretched down the centre of the road. People
hurried darkly on the pavements as though to get out of sight,
to get under cover.

A dim light came from the hotel in the square. Some people
were leaving as Mary entered. The clerk shook his head at
her before she spoke. She was near to tears from anxiety and
tiredness.

"But I sent a wire," she said.

"We have had many wires. There is not a bed to be found
in the town."

She sat down on her suitcase as though broken at the waist.
After some moments, she said in a small voice: "Can you
suggest anything?"

"Shall I telephone the British consul for you?"

"It's too late. He'd be asleep."

"No matter," said the clerk. "It is his business. But if you
prefer I could telephone the sanatorium. They don't like it—but
perhaps as a concession for a young foreign lady." He dialled
a number and Mary, as though through the haze of a drug,
listened to one side of a conversation in German. "They
agree," said the clerk. "Now if you will come to the door I
will show you the road you must take. I regret I cannot come
with you."

He refused to accept any reward and Mary, startled, said:
"You must be a Saxon."

"I'm a German. I come from Coblenz. Good night."

She found the sanatorium at last. An elderly night nurse opened the door and put out a hand as though she needed to be helped in. She followed the nurse down a white passage lit with red buttons. The door of one of the rooms opened and another nurse hurried out. From within came the sound of a deep, harsh voice rambling in Hungarian. There was, Mary felt, something peculiarly horrible about delirium in a foreign language.

"He is very ill," said the nurse. "Dying, we fear."

Mary could still hear the man's voice in the distance as she sat down on her iron bedstead with its thin, sterilized covers. A temperature chart hung on the wall. Dimly lit, in one corner of the room, stood a chromium-plated surgical machine of some sort. A little black-shaded reading-lamp lit the pillow. She thought of her own bed that she shared with her kindly, comfortable husband and wondered why she had ever come here.

Next morning her mood had changed. The strange town was full of the movement of a break-up. There was a tenseness and suspicion in the atmosphere. The shop windows had their shutters up against riots. Some were shut, others had their doors half open on the chance of somebody at such a time giving thought to purchase of furniture, shoes and books. Women crowded round the grocery stores asking one another when life would be organized again and bread, milk and meat reappear for sale. Only the large café on the square, that baked its own rolls, was open. A waiter stood at the door holding the handle and only opening for those whose faces he knew. Curiosity persuaded him to let Mary in. When she had eaten her rolls and drunk a pint of strong, sweet coffee, she felt life regaining its charm. Through the large café window, in the centre of the square, stood the cathedral, new and uninteresting, rebuilt after fire. Around the cathedral went the traffic—the only petrol-driven vehicles were the military cars filled with the dressy, anxious, little Rumanian officers. Everything else—carriages, motor-cars, tractors, buses, carts—was being pulled by men or horses. They were laden with Rumanian goods being hastily got out of the way of the coming Hungarians. Mary had nothing definite to do—only wander around and notice things and get people talking. She wanted first to find the English governess, Ellie Cox, who might be able to tell her a great deal.

The Hungarian Jewish family with which Ellie had worked were delighted when Mary telephoned. One female voice after another came to the telephone and chatted delightedly in English—but Ellie was not there. No, she had not gone to Bucharest. She had married. She had married a Hungarian, a doctor, and now lived at the hotel in the square with her husband. Mary, making excuses to the family that would have had her come to luncheon, went to the hotel in the square. The German clerk was not on duty, but another told her that the English lady had gone out. They were sure she had gone to visit her new flat, which was in Strada Romano. Mary found the flat—one floor of an enormous eighteenth-century Hungarian mansion. Ellie was measuring the windows in the main room. She gave a friendly squeal when she saw Mary.

"You lucky woman," said Mary at the door.

Ellie's eyes followed Mary's round the big white room. "Not what you'd call homey," she said. "Not what I'd have chosen myself."

"It's wonderful. We've had to live in such awful places. We'd have given anything to find a place like this."

"My hubby found it."

They stood together by one of the big windows watching the flight of the Rumanians. A farm motor-tractor went past laden with bedding and pulled by an old horse. Ellie gave a giggle.

"Look at that," she said. "You can't help laughing—but it's an awful nuisance all this happening just now when we want to get our flat ready. We've got a lot of stuff waiting to come here and we can't get a furniture van for love nor money."

"It doesn't worry you—the idea of being left alone here in the centre of Europe?"

"Well, I won't be exactly alone. I've got my husband. And the people I used to work for are ever so decent."

"Are there any other English people here?"

"Only the consul. He's a nice little chap. He's been ever so kind and he told me to keep my British passport in case I want to leave—but why should I? I'm all right here. But he'll have to go soon. You know, we'll probably have the Germans here."

"I see the shops are boarded up."

"Oh it's been awful. Shocking, it's been. Crowds rushing about the streets and fighting and throwing stones. It really wasn't safe to go out. What's the good of their behaving like that? And of course the Rumanian army—army! I ask you!—just stood and grinned. Anybody could take anything for all they cared. Then the Germans said they'd come in to restore order and that pulled them up with a jerk. They got busy taking the stuff out before someone stopped them. And it's all Hungarian stuff, too—all left after the last war. Yesterday they dismantled the telephone exchange."

"Can't I telephone Bucharest?"

"Doubt it." Ellie started laughing again as another ridiculous conveyance went past. She was a tall, large-boned, blonde girl. Her face was very English. Mary suddenly felt a deep affection for her.

"What made you come here in the first place?" she asked her. "It's such a long way from home."

"I don't quite know. I was doing some classes at the Polytechnic, just for fun, and these people wrote wanting a young lady who'd go and live with them and teach them all English. The letter was put up on the board and I read it. I didn't give it a thought. My friend Addie Clay said just for a joke: "Why don't you go, Ellie, you're always wanting to see the world." "What, me!" I said, "out in the wilds. Not likely." Then I began to think about it and it began to get me—and here I am."

"The English are like that," said Mary, thinking of a memorial she had seen in the English port where she had been born—erected to ships' crews, to ordinary Englishmen who might have stayed comfortably at home and instead had gone to the ends of the earth to die of yellow fever or cholera or at the hands of enemies about whom they knew nothing.

There were footsteps echoing up the empty stairway. A handsome, middle-aged man entered the room. Ellie's confidential seriousness of manner dissolved into playfulness.

"What do you think of my hubby?" she asked.

"Perhaps he can give me the latest news," said Mary.

"News," the Hungarian looked her up and down, and laughed. "What about? The fashion in hats?"

Ellie put on a severe look: "Don't you be so silly. You always think women can't understand anything. Mary's come here for a newspaper. She's a reporter."

The Hungarian became serious, as was required of him. He had been taking lessons from Ellie and spoke English with a stiff precision. The latest news was that Manu, the Transylvanian leader, had arrived—but he had arrived too late. Two days before, when the riots were at their height, the peasants had held the post office for a short time and had telephoned Manu in Bucharest: "Come and save us from the Germans," they begged. He had answered: "Don't be foolish. Go back to your work and I will come later." For a day they had hung round the station expecting him by every train. What a welcome he would have received! What a hero he would have been! But now, enthusiasm had died; the riots were suppressed. There had been no one at his house when he arrived by car, and no one had cared. A small crowd had gathered outside when his arrival became known and he had gone out and said: "Have patience. Now we can do nothing, but our time will come. I return now to Bucharest to work for our cause." Then he had gone inside to pack his goods.

"I'll have to go," said Mary. "I must try and see Manu. Perhaps I can send a telegram."

"It will be delayed for days," said Ellie's husband.

She walked through the bare-looking, comfortless town to the post office that was still the centre of activity. It was crowded; the telephone boxes were being dismantled and the Rumanian police were holding back groups of indignant Hungarians. Mary waved her British passport and was allowed to enter. Inside people were fighting for telegraph forms. She struggled through to the counter and asked how long it would take a telegram to get to Bucharest. "Two, three, four days," said the clerk. She decided to go back with her news that night.

She hurried to police headquarters to report her entry into the town and to get permission to leave it. All doors lay wide open and men hurried past her too busy to notice her. She wandered in and out of empty rooms and up to the iron gallery running round the central court yard. Here the police were throwing down bundles of papers to the lorries below. Furniture, typewriters, the glass from the windows, the handles from the doors, the radiators, the shutters were all stacked up awaiting transport. Only the shell of a building remained.

A clerk leaning against a doorway patted Mary on the shoulder. "This time it does not matter," he said. "Everyone is coming and going without permits."

Mary set out to find Manu's house. None of the carriages would leave the centre of the town, so she walked to the outskirts to which she had been directed. The town thinned out quickly into the rich, flat countryside. Manu's house looked to her like the setting for a Russian play. It stood back in its garden, square and naked-looking with a small porch flanked by nineteenth-century stone nymphs. The door of the house lay open. Within the wide hallway the furniture was covered with sheets, and crowded around it were ornaments, mirrors, oil paintings in heavy oval frames, and suitcases. Two busy young men were in the old-fashioned depths of the house. Mary called to them. They gazed at her without understanding. "Manu," she insisted. "Journal Londres." They grasped it at last and one sped up the great curve of the staircase. At once Manu appeared on the upper landing, made a little gesture of pleasure as though Mary were an old friend, and fixing her with a steady glare of pleasure, surprise and questioning, descended the long flight of stairs with the competent grace of an actor. At the bottom he flung out a hand, then hurrying to her, took hers and held it.

"Journal? London?" he enquired eagerly.

"Yes," Mary nodded.

"Ah!" he smiled with great charm.

Mary knew only that he was notable in Bucharest as the one, the only, honest Rumanian politician. He was a short, sturdy, middle-aged man with a long nose and a bright, empty stare. He wore an outdoor cape and carried a wide-brimmed hat which he put on as he stepped into the air.

"Do you speak French or English?" asked Mary.

No, he spoke only Rumanian, Hungarian and German. And

she? Only French and a little Rumanian. They looked at one another, silenced, but smiling. Mary watched a large, silvery butterfly that had settled on his shoulder. A smell of apples came from the trees.

"What now?" she asked in Rumanian.

Ah! He lifted a hand and replied rapidly: "We must have patience. Now we can do nothing, but our time will come. I return now to Bucharest to work for our cause." She nodded her recognition of the sentence. He took her hand again and patted it, then bowed very low over it. She went down the flight of steps from the porch and looked back. He took off his hat and waved it a little towards her. His smile was brilliant.

She was relieved the interview was safely over, but she felt a little dazzled, as though she had come for a moment within the aura of a distinguished actor.

The Istanbul Express was said to be arriving at Cluj at eight o'clock. She went down to the station in the afternoon to get her ticket stamped. The offices, waiting-rooms and buffets were all shut and padlocked. A telephone was ringing urgently within. She found an official who told her that the Istanbul Express would not stop there that evening because it had been besieged the evening before. She said she would come to the station nevertheless, and asked him to stamp her ticket. He took it, stared at it as though he did not know what it was, then pushed it back into her hand and walked away.

Under the brilliant sunlight stood half a dozen trucks laden with rich furniture. In one truck was a gilded French suite upholstered in red satin. There was nothing else but the naked rails, the grit heaps and the shut, dusty, dispirited-looking station. The peasants who had been cleared off the station lay in heaps around the square outside.

Back in the town Mary saw Ellie rushing towards her: "What a life!" Ellie cried and rushed past, beaming and excited by something. At Cook's Agency Mary found that not only was the train expected to stop at Cluj, but an extra wagon-lit was being put on. People were snatching over each other's shoulders to get berths. Mary got the last and feeling like someone who has just taken out an insurance policy against life, faced the rest of the day. She found a large bookshop modelled on German lines. Inside she discovered it was kept by the family that had employed Ellie. The mother questioned her when she was leaving and how? Who was looking after her? Who would take her to the station? She said she supposed she would go alone.

"Ah!" she said. "We would take you were we not forced to an engagement tonight. But I will give you this boy," she called to a small messenger-boy, "he will carry the trunk."

"But I can carry it; it is only a light suitcase."

"No, he will take it. He can go now and get it for you and when you come he will be waiting for you."

This kindness lessened a little for Mary the star of anxiety that was burning in her solar plexus.

By twilight crowds of incipient rioters had collected again, but they had no leader. Manu had left Cluj and now people did not know what they wanted. They moved about in shadowy groups, rushing suddenly this way and that in pursuit of a rumour. They seemed harmless. No one took much notice of them. A tremendous rose-and-violet sunset stretched up from behind the cathedral. Clouds were flung in semicircles as though by a sower. The streets were fading in a misty, greenish light through which groups of youths drifted out of side-streets and round corners and were lost in the distance. The lorries were still dragging past with their loads of furniture. The Hungarians were gathered on the pavements to watch the flight of the Rumanians. Sometimes a military car went past at important speed, hooting unceasingly. Only a few street lamps were coming on. The electricity plant was being disabled. People were saying that the water was cut off. Some of the grocery shops had opened and women were queuing outside them. A Rumanian aeroplane sped at an angle round the square a few feet above the house-tops.

Mary had arranged to see Ellie at the hotel and found her sitting crocheting in a comfortless little private sitting-room; her husband was lying down in the bedroom beyond.

"Did you hear the latest?" she asked. "No water and they're drawing water from the old well. Not very nice, I don't think. Not very safe."

At that moment there was a rapid knock on the door. A man entered without waiting to be called and asked for Ellie's husband. Ellie motioned him into the inner room. The two men began talking furiously while Ellie's husband put on his outdoor shoes.

"Did you ever!" said Ellie, with a shocked, excited gasp.

"What is the matter?" asked Mary.

"Those Rumanians! They're taking away all the instruments and things from the hospital. And in 1918, when it was handed over—everything was there complete to the last needle. My hubby says the doctors stood like soldiers and handed over everything complete to the last needle . . . There! You don't understand, do you? He's just saying that they're taking the beds and bedding from under the patients; they're even taking the chromium handles off the doors . . . My hubby says perhaps if all the doctors go and reason with them, it may shame them. What a hope!"

The two men hurried out. Ellie clicked her tongue as the door shut and started a new row of her crochet. She was about thirty, but looked much younger.

Mary said: "I wonder how long it will be before we meet again? It looks as though we may have to make a getaway soon."

"Yes," Ellie shook her head over her work. "Things don't look too good. It's all right for me now, being married to a Hungarian—but it's awful for you being cut off from England like this. Where will you go?"

"We don't know. Perhaps we can get to Egypt."

"Bit of a journey."

"Yes." Mary could only think of Ellie left alone here in all her Englishness as the English retreated out of Europe. "Where is your family?"

"Highgate. My pop's got a shop there. I've written them that I'm married and won't be leaving like the other people. The consul put it in the bag for me. Very decent he's been. I hope they won't worry about me. They'll know I'll be all right."

It was time for Mary to go to the station.

"I wish I could go with you. But I've got my in-laws coming to dinner. They're nice old things, but they don't know a word of English."

"You've been very kind." There was a strong sympathy

between them there in the foreign hotel-room in the centre of Europe as the time came to separate.

"I haven't got my Hungarian passport yet," said Ellie. "They don't half make a fuss about giving you one."

"They won't touch you—a young woman alone here. If you were a man . . ." Mary, thinking of her husband, caught her breath and said quickly: "We must get away soon."

Ellie said nothing for a moment, then: "You're English. That means a lot."

"After France fell, they made us realize it meant a lot less."

Ellie came down to the hotel door. The bat-black plane was still swooping above the square. The little boy with the suitcase was waiting for Mary. She set out with him down the long, wide road to the station. There were crowds of other people carrying bags and parcels. Mary, half in panic, began hurrying and the small boy, changing the bag from one hand to the other, manfully hurried too. When she wanted to take a turn in carrying the bag he would not give it up. In the distance there was a dark wavering movement of people packed round the station. She began to feel sick with apprehension. At the third-class entrance the peasants were fighting to get in.

Rumanians and Jews were moving steadily through the first and second-class entrances. The half-lit station was a desolate place in spite of the crowds. The peasants were settling down prepared for a long wait. Some were cooking their messes of maize over spirit-stoves. They remembered the cruelty with which they had driven out the Hungarians and they were not waiting to give them revenge. The parents-in-law of some who had married into the enemy were trying to persuade them to remain, but their instincts advised them more soundly. Groups of women were weeping together. Furniture heaped across the platform formed a barricade over which people climbed to get from one end to the other.

Mary tried to make enquiries of a porter. She spoke in Rumanian, then French. He brushed past her roughly, saying: "Speak Hungarian." She spoke to one of the Rumanians in the crowd. He told her they were all expecting the express, which had now been signalled two hours late. It should be in at ten. She found some seats among the heaped furniture and settled down like the peasants to wait. She tried to persuade the small boy who had carried the bag to go home to bed, but he refused. She gave him a hundred lei piece, thinking he might then go more willingly, but he remained. Every few moments he opened his small, dirty hand, took a glimpse at the coin, then quickly closed his fingers over it. Suddenly, amazingly, a train came in. It was a wooden, third-class local train. The peasants flung themselves to their feet and ran madly, from carriage to carriage. The doors were locked. They climbed in through the glassless windows hauling one another up by arms and legs until the carriages were choked. Then they climbed on to the roof. While some were still only half in and half on, the train suddenly moved out. Bunches of people fell off like lice. Others ran along the line yelling madly. From one of the bridges came the crackle of rifle fire. The peasants panicked back to the platform and huddled against the wall.

It was now half past ten. Mary again tried to persuade the boy to go. He shook his head. She showed him by pantomime that he should be asleep—he smiled with a thin, tired cynicism.

Some time after eleven a second local train came in. The peasants rushed at it. A few minutes later there was the sound of another train coming in on the line behind. People shouted to one another that this was the express, but for some moments they stood uncertainly, expecting the local train to move away. Then someone shouted that the express was leaving. People began to run to the end of the platform to get round the local train to the rail behind. Mary ran too, and the small boy who would not give up the suitcase came after her. When they rounded the engine of the local train they were in complete darkness. Tripping over slag-heaps and rails they got into the space between the two trains. The doors of the express were locked. People climbed up the steps and thumped on the windows, but no one attempted to open for them. The express engine had been uncoupled. Suddenly it spurted forward. Mary and the boy threw themselves back against the local train and felt the heat of the passing engine. She caught the boy's hand and ran round to the other side of the express carriages. At the end there was an open door from which a light fell across the line. She ran madly for it and leapt up the steps. The boy handed up her bag and, as she took it, the train moved, pulling away his hand, and she did not see him again.

She was, she found, at the kitchen door of the restaurant-car. Trembling, nearly sobbing, she leant for some moments staring into the kitchen, stunned as though she had come in out of a storm. Inside, the cook, a remote, dark little man, was sharpening his knives. He was absorbed, as though by a work of creation. When he glanced at her she gave him a smile that was almost affectionate. Gentle and humble with relief at her escape, she asked if she could pass through to the dining-car. He made way for her at once. Inside the car the tables were occupied, mostly by men, dissociated like the whole train from the chaos outside. In a few moments Mary had adjusted herself and was as dissociated as they. The train shunted back to the station. She lifted the blind and glanced out at the faces lifted a moment to the patch of light. There was a sound of shots, some cries and a heavy pelting of feet. The train started again. A stone struck the window glass and she lifted the blind. People were running beside the train, waving their hands, shouting unheard, trying to jump on the steps to the kitchen door. As the train gathered speed they fell back one by one. A waiter started serving the third dinner.

GEOFFREY COTTERELL
Then a Soldier

Geoffrey Cotterell (1920–) was born in England, and served in infantry during WWII. His books include This is the Way *(1947) and* Westward the Sun *(1952).*

The following is an extract from his 1944 novel, Then A Soldier.

ABOUT TEN O'CLOCK ONE MORNING towards the end of April, 1940, Jackie Kraus, a young swing pianist, was drying himself after a hot bath. He was not at his best in the nude. His long, thin body did not seem to fit his face, which was big and square and Jewish. He rubbed himself very energetically. Outside a competition was going on between the sun and half a dozen shower clouds, so that the back garden of the Wembley house where he rented two rooms was in turn dark and brightly lit. Jackie whistled discordantly the arrangement of Rhapsody in Blue, which the Band, Eddie Trent and His Bad Boys, were presenting when they went on tour next week.

He was looking forward to this tour, although normally he preferred to stay in London as much as possible. But this was the first time he had been billed on the posters as a star feature of the band, along with Alex Lion, and Elsa Dalby, their crooners. Apart from playing the piano, he was to provide some comedy, for which he had a special flair; and there was to be a special big moment when immediately on concluding a very short, very heavy classical piece he was to be lifted out of his trousers and left to dangle in the air, wearing some chosen pants and sock suspenders. Eddie was confident that it would be a great success and he was usually right. "It's a chance in a lifetime for you, Jackie," he had said.

Moderately dry, he used his towel to wipe over the shaving mirror and then inspected his chin. Yes, he would have to shave. He noted that his eyes looked heavy, which was not surprising for they had been rehearsing until early in the morning, five hours before. He had curious eyes, large and narrow, so that at a quick glance you were not sure if he were a Jew or a Chinaman. He might ring up Eddie in a few minutes and arrange to have lunch at some nice place, he thought. It was a happy idea. He continued whistling as he started to lather his face.

There was a knock on the bathroom door.

"Letter for you, Mr Kraus. Shall I leave it in the hall or push it under your door?"

He stopped whistling. It was the housemaid, who didn't like him, and he knew from the tone of her voice what this was.

"Under the door," he said airily. But he felt terrible. The envelope appeared between the bottom of the door and the lino. He stared at it as if it were a snake. He had been waiting for it ever since the medical exam, rationalising, planning, making himself forget—but now it had come and his heart thumped like a mill.

He picked it up, sat down on the edge of the bath and opened it. The note inside was headed in large black letters "National Service (Armed Forces) Act, 1939," and beneath a stamped warning, "You should take this notice with you when you report," there was the fatal message.

He was to report to the 653rd Searchlight Training Regiment, Canderbridge. Nearest railway station: Canderbridge. "A travelling warrant for your journey is enclosed. Before starting your journey you must exchange the warrant for a ticket at the booking office named on the warrant. If possible this should be done a day or two before you are due to travel. A Postal Order for 4s. in respect of advance of service pay is also enclosed. Uniform and personal kit will be issued to you after joining H.M. Forces. Any kit that you take with you should not exceed an overcoat, a change of clothes, stout pair of boots, and personal kit, such as razor, hair brush, tooth brush, soap and towel. Immediately on receipt of this notice, you should inform your employers of the date upon which you are required to report for service. Yours faithfully."

He obeyed the letter unconsciously as soon as he was dressed. He rang up Eddie. "I've had wonderful news," he said. "Bloody wonderful. I'm bloody well called up."

Eddie said, "Aw that's too bad. After all we tried. Hell, what do they think of?"

"The bastards," Jackie Kraus said, and saying it caused a tightness at his throat, a helpless feeling that he hadn't known since he was a small child. "They might have overlooked me."

"Poor Jackie. When d'you go?"

"Next Tuesday. Twenty pounds a week to two shillings a day."

"Too bad," Eddie said again. "Too bad, Jackie. What are you doing this morning? Let's have a party to cheer you up."

"And to say good-bye," Jackie said bitterly. "Okay, Eddie, I'd like it. Get the boys together and we'll have a big weep."

It was a good party, they all drank too much, except Eddie, who was always careful. Eddie made a speech. "I made this boy," he said. "I've made him famous and successful. He's done as much as any of us—yes, including me—to make our name. And now he's going to do his bit. Good luck, Jackie! Come and see us whenever you get leave. I don't know what we'll do without him, do you, boys?" Then they all sang that he was a jolly good fellow. Elsa Dalby, their crooner, said to him, "I expect you'll like it really." He wanted to say something bitter in return. In fact he wanted to get up and make a speech telling them that they were all rats, but all he could do was smile weakly. He was already out of them. Some other pianist would have to fit in with Eddie's latest arrangements. He heard Fred Killenbaum and Johnny Brodsky discussing who it would be in one corner, and then they stopped dead when they saw he was listening. Easy come, easy go. But he felt better for the party, and Eddie said to him quietly, "Don't let it get you down, Jackie. I know what it means, but don't let the bastards beat you. Beat them."

"Okay, Eddie."

"Cheerio, pal," they all said in their American accents.

On the Tuesday he arrived at Victoria in his Teddy Bear coat and there, thronging gloomily or with false gaiety on the platform, were his comrades to be. Almost all of them wore macs and carried small suitcases. "You're in the army now!" they were saying to each other, smiling, trying to keep their spirits up. Here and there was a little group where a family was saying good-bye, tearlessly and pathetically. He looked them up and down with a sinking feeling and found himself a seat in a first-class compartment. When the ticket collector came round he paid the difference. He was frightened. By himself he was afraid of no one, but in this mass he felt all wrong, lost. He listened to them all through the long journey across the south of England, to their unashamed vulgarity, to the amateur funny men who were raising their voices in the corridors. He swore to himself bitterly, and then remembered Eddie. He got up and walked down the corridor towards the third class. He'd start talking to them. But it was no use. As he passed them, they winked and said, "Wotcher, mate!" and "Cheer up, Charlie!" He couldn't do it; he ignored them and went back to his seat. When they all got out somewhere in Somerset, a big mechanical voice began to intone, "Army Class, Army Class form up in threes on the platform and stay where you are." He stayed in the carriage as long as he could, then bowing to the inevitable he staggered out, crept along the platform as inconspicuously as he could to the end of the long queue.

It was about half-past three, mid afternoon. The weather was overcast, though it had been sunny in London. All at once it started to rain, for a moment in hesitant drips, and then in a downpour. A huge, comic groan went up. "It 'ad to do this, mate!" the man next to Jackie said. "Bloody rain wouldn't let us alone, don't you worry!" Jackie said nothing, he felt like hell. "La di da!" the man added. He was a big, fat fellow, with an expression of ironical gloom on his face, as if he took considerable satisfaction in the worst.

The rain grew worse. At the end of the queue they had no cover at all. Macs became sodden, little cases dripped, collars soaked, spirits dropped to the bottom. The megaphone voice went on, "Army Class, Army Class form up in threes on the platform and stay where you are." Suddenly a corporal appeared and walked down the length of them. There was a shiver of interest. He was a thin, light-haired man, who entirely disregarded the rain. This was the first time they had really seen an N.C.O., one, that is, who would actually order them about. He had power over them, a new kind of power. Jackie hated him, but tried to catch his eye familiarly, in an instinctive commercial effort to get in his good books. But the corporal went by without saying anything.

Suddenly they began to move forward. From now on there was no escape. The next man to him said, "On we go, chum. Into the fiery burning bloody furnace, eh!" Jackie said, "That's the way it goes." They were the first words he had spoken to anyone. "You said it," the man said feelingly. "Cor, what a game, eh?" And he spat, just missing Jackie's suède shoes. The microphone voice had stopped. The procession was filing out of the station. It was still raining hard.

When they got outside into the station yard, there was nothing there but four lorries. Then some more Army N.C.O.'s appeared and began to arrange the wet mass into groups of thirty each. Jackie counted fourteen groups. The four first ones suddenly advanced to the lorries and climbed into the back of them. Everybody watched them with bated breath, it was like looking on at your fellow Christians being led into the Roman arena and knowing that your turn was coming soon. When the lorries drove off, with rows of white faces looking back through the back opening, a cheer was raised by the funny men. Then the rumour went through every group that the camp was miles away and they would have to wait here till the lorries returned empty to pick them up each in turn, four groups at a time. The rumour was confirmed by the N.C.O.'s. The one who seemed to be in charge of Jackie's group told them, "Ah, there'll be a nice long wait for us, it seems. We've got a hot meal waiting for you when you arrive, though. It's only three or four miles away." He spoke with the pride of a housekeeper. He sounded quite kind. The group looked at him, then at each other, with a certain amount of relief. At least he had spoken to them quite civilly. Perhaps it might not be so bad. Half of them indulged in an orgy of wishful thinking. But the rain kept on and they got wetter and wetter. Gloom settled again.

Jackie, seeing that a long wait was inevitable, for his group was the last one, settled down a little. Already Eddie and the boys and Wembley seemed a long way behind him. He took a look round at his fellow recruits. They were a pretty depressed-looking lot. The man who had been next to him on the station platform seemed to have disappeared. He must be in another group. Most of these people looked white-faced, round-shouldered young men with spotty skins and no confidence. Half a dozen wore labourers' clothes, and there were one or two smart alecs with cheap waisted suits. Jackie felt better. Why, if he couldn't rise above this set, well . . . he smiled to himself. It was just a case of keeping himself under control. What these people could do he could do better and no fooling. When the N.C.O. stood near him, Jackie smiled at him. The N.C.O., who had been instructed to be gentle, smiled back.

"Well, is it wet enough for you?" he enquired genially.

"Just about, corporal!" Jackie laughed.

"Ah," said the N.C.O., glad of the opportunity to speak one of his mechanical pieces, "now that's one thing you've all got to learn. You're in the Artillery now and there aren't any corporals. Bombardiers is what we are called."

"Oh, really?" said Jackie.

"That's right. One stripe is a lance-bombardier, two stripes is a full bombardier. You call them both Bombardier, see?"

"Oh, yes, I see, Bombardier," Jackie said smartly.

"Crikey, you're starting soon enough, aren't you?" somebody murmured.

"Ah, well you can't start too soon," the N.C.O. pointed out reprovingly. "There's plenty for you to learn."

"I bet there is," said Jackie.

"But don't let it worry you," said the N.C.O. "Just do as you're told and you'll have the time of your lives, believe me."

The group listened to him respectfully. Jackie felt pleased. He had definitely made the right kind of impression. Keen and intelligent. Already he was a stride ahead of the other suckers. He only hoped that they would see plenty of this N.C.O.

"You can smoke if you like," the N.C.O. announced.

In a flash Jackie had his silver case out and was offering him one. "Well, thanks, don't mind if I do," said the N.C.O. They all began to puff away. Not that there was much pleasure in it. They were becoming so wet that none of them cared any more. The lorries suddenly came back to pick up the second four groups. Now they were all looking forward to barrack life. Anything dry would do. Half an hour later the lorries came back again.

It was a dark, jolting, huddled journey in the back of the lorry. Those on the end could watch the small country town vanish behind them, with its over-cheerful women and old men, and then give way to rolling, wet, discouraged-looking fields on either side. Jackie stood in the middle, unable to see a thing, owing to his shortness. There was no difficulty about standing up, however, for they were so packed in that it was impossible even to lean over. Quite suddenly the lorry stopped with a jerk.

"Right, out you get," a voice commanded.

They got out. They found themselves surrounded by a town of wooden huts, which bordered long, well made roads. It was a militia camp.

"Doesn't look too bad," somebody said. It was at once the prevailing opinion, which Jackie shared. The huts looked quite nice really.

"I wish they'd get us out of this bloody rain," someone else said, and everyone agreed with that, too, though not loudly.

After they had stood there for a few minutes they were shepherded into the nearest hut. It was a bare, empty room inside, except for a table at one end on which an N.C.O. with ginger hair was sitting, swinging his long legs. The rain kept on, making a loud noise on the roof, and there was a cold draught coming through the open door. But it was heaven to be out of the rain.

"Right, stop talking," said the ginger-haired N.C.O. They all prefaced every remark with the word "right". "Now all we want you to do is everyone with surname beginning from A to K to fall out along this wall, and everyone with surname L to Z along this wall. Got it? Right, move."

When they had been sorted out, another N.C.O. appeared and took away the L to Z's.

"Right. Now all of you, you're in the right half of Camp

Battery. The right half of Camp Battery. Got it? Right. Now you're going to have a meal. Fall in outside on the road and form up in threes, facing this way. Got it?" He looked them up and down critically. "Right, move."

They shambled out hurriedly, once more into the rain.

"Get a move on, now, get a move on. Longer you take the wetter you'll get. Sort yourselves out. Move, come on, move! When I say 'shun' you come to attention. Party, party, shun! Right turn. Come on, move, there's only one right. Quick march! Get the step now. Left, left, left right left. Left, left, left right left."

They did their best to march properly, swinging their arms in a self-conscious way. This was their first dose of real army discipline. Strangely enough they were rather happy about it. It was in a way comforting to be really ordered about so that you had no time to feel uncomfortable. It was interesting to see all the music-hall jokes about the army come to life. From the windows of the huts as they marched along soldiers in battle dress, who had been called up the month before and were now experiencing their first feeling of superiority, yelled cheerful insults at them. The recruits grinned back. Jackie Kraus held himself unnaturally erect and marched, he thought, like a guardsman. Every few minutes he found that he had drooped back to his normal gait and he had to jerk himself together again. He was thinking of himself heroically, like an aristo at the guillotine.

They right-wheeled at the end of the road, where he noticed that the roads were all called by the names of well-known generals. The one they had just marched down was called Gort Road. Now they were in Ironside Road. And here was the mess hut, the cookhouse. "Party, 'alt!" cried the N.C.O. "Wake up there, do as you're told, face the front."

He went inside the hut, which was much larger than the others. Some people started to murmur, "The bastard!" in low voices, but they did not mean it very strongly. "Proper ginger 'ead, ain't he?" others remarked, in the semi-affectionate tone which is often reserved for strong disciplinarians. The N.C.O. was now nicknamed "Ginger". It pleased everyone to mention this, it gave them all a bond, a feeling that they were "in".

Ginger appeared again. "Left 'and rank file in, come on, move—wake up, left 'and I said, there's only one left!"

After the meal, which made Jackie almost vomit to see, but was surprisingly eatable, they were marched up Gort Road again, but at the end turned into Haig Road. The warm food certainly had a bracing effect on them, but it also released them from the numbed wetness which had been their principal feeling up to now, and they became more conscious of the general discomfort they had come into. They started quite suddenly to remember home again. The conscript's misery, passing on from Caesar's levies and the uncountable hundreds of thousands who had been pressed into service under the Tsars and the Prussians and the Hapsburgs, reached them too. The little town of army huts now showed itself as lying in a valley, with a sloping hill on either side. One of these was at the end of Haig Road. Jackie was just rationalising to himself the idea of life in a communal hut, when he noticed that there were some tents on the hill.

He was not alone in this observation.

"Holy Mother!" groaned the man next to him, who from the way he marched obviously suffered from corns and was going through hell. "Look at them ruddy things!"

"They might not be for us," Jackie ventured, but he felt chillingly certain that they were.

"Don't you worry yourself, mate. It's just a little surprise for us. Bit of icing to the ruddy cake, like."

They put Jackie in Tent number 12. George, Fred, John, Stan and Syd were in it too. When Jackie arrived they were all there, standing round the tent pole, except for Fred, who was sitting on his suitcase and making a low, concentrated speech. He wore the clothes of a labourer and shoes that were eaten through with wear and cheapness.

"Cor, suffering cats, what a bleedin' perishin' 'ole!" he was saying. He had a thin, tinny, screechlike voice, like a parrot. "Cor, what the ole woman'd say if she saw! She'd have a fit! Better off in the work'ouse—let me tell you you're a bloody sight better off in the bloody work'ouse! Cor! 'Ullo, come to join us, mate? Welcome to the 'appy 'ome!"

"Very tasty, very sweet," George said. He was a thin,

gloomy looking young man with horn-rimmed glasses and a white, pimply complexion.

Jackie said nothing. There was nothing he could think of to say. Had he really got to live with people like these?

"La di da," George said.

Jackie still said nothing. He had stepped inside and he was still standing in front of the flap, his Teddy Bear coat like an old piece of drenched rag.

"Cheer up, mate!" Fred croaked ecstatically. "What's the bloody matter? It's got a wooden floor. Might be the bloody earth, you know."

"Got to make the best of it, I suppose," Syd said. He was a fat little Jew, very young and cheerful, who was fated to be disliked. "It may not be so bad. It's all in a day's work." It was making maddening remarks like these that was to get him disliked, but he did not realise it and he never would.

"If this is your idea of a day's work, then I should bloody well try for another job," Fred said.

The others just stood around. Stan was young-looking, with crinkly hair and glasses like Henry Hall. He was eating an apple his mother had given him at the station. He was thinking that if Mum could see this she just wouldn't believe it, and when she did she would demand to see the manager to get him changed to a room of his own. John, who stood next to him, was a solid-looking labourer, rather better off than Fred in appearance. His face was expressionless and inside him not a great deal was going on other than digestion. He was a fatalist.

Stan said, "We'll have to go and draw our kit soon."

"Can't be too soon for me," Fred said. "Sooner I get out o' this bloody clobber the better."

Syd followed his example and sat down with a gay sigh on his own case.

"We had better make up our minds where we're going to sleep," he remarked brightly.

"Oh, shut up," said Fred.

"All right, all right, keep your hair on!" Syd at once became a cheerful martyr, a heckled salvationist. "I'll sleep by the door if nobody objects. Quicker to get up in the morning."

"If this ruddy rain goes on I shan't sleep at all," Fred

observed hoarsely. "Cor, listen to it: harder than ever! Makes a noise on the ruddy tent, don't it?"

Jackie conquered his desperation and made an effort to be sociable.

"By the way my name is Kraus," he said smoothly, "Jackie Kraus. You may know it. I've broadcasted quite a lot with Eddie Trent's outfit."

"Lucky for you, mate," said Fred calmly.

Jackie opened his mouth and shut it again, feeling crushed.

Suddenly Ginger's voice was heard, penetrating the storm with ease. Stan said, "Ah, that's for the kit. He wants everybody with names beginning A, B, or C. Me for one. Any buyers?"

Fred Batley, John Caldwell and Syd Cohen accompanied him gloomily out of the tent. George, whose name was Felstead, remained with Jackie.

The rain seemed to beat down harder.

"It's fine, isn't it?" Jackie said grimly.

"Very tasty, very sweet," George said again.

"I don't know how I'm going to get through it. I'm used to everything that money can buy."

"La di da," said George. "Makes you want to give birth, don't it?"

JULIAN MACLAREN-ROSS
They Put Me in Charge of a Squad

The English writer Julian Maclaren-Ross (1921-) was educated in Paris and the south of France. He served in the British army during WWII, a time captured in his books Memoirs of the Forties *(1965) and* The Stuff to Give the Troops *(1944).*

The short story "They Put Me in Charge of a Squad" is from Modern Reading, *1944.*

W E WERE SHORT OF N.C.O.s at the time. One of our corporals had scabies, two were away on escort, and another was at B.H.Q. being court-martialled for slackness.

So one morning as I was walking past Company, Office, trying not to slip on the frozen pavement, Corporal Dexter yelled down at me from upstairs: "Hey, you! Come on up, Gillo! I got a job for you."

Corporal Dexter was the orderly sergeant. He didn't like me because he thought I'd threatened to do him in the black-out. It was really another bloke who'd threatened to do him, and I was only repeating the story when he heard me, but Dexter wouldn't believe that. So he had his knife in me.

I went upstairs and stood to attention in front of his desk. "Right!" he said. "You got to take a fatigue squad up the town this morning 0930 hours. There's some furniture wants shifting from out them billets D Company had. You parade 'em out front 0920 sharp. All right? Any questions?"

"You want me to take a squad up the town, Corporal?"

"Ain't I just said so? Don't I speak plain bloody English?"

"Yes, Corporal. But I'm not an N.C.O. How can I take a squad."

"You're an O.C.T.U. wallah, aincher? In for a pip? Well then, how the hell you going to lead men if you don't never have charge of nothing? Now's your chance to learn."

"Very good, Corporal," I said.

"Right! Now I got to rustle up the bastard sick."

Corporal Dexter buckled on his belt and bayonet and left the room. He could be heard dowstairs getting the sick together, threatening them with thickuns. I went over to the fire and tried to thaw out my fingers. They were frozen stiff. It was December.

The orderly corporal sat writing, surrounded by stacks of sick reports. There was a big route march on tha morning and nearly the whole company had gone sick as a result. The orderly corporal looked up.

"O.C.T.U. candidate, are you?" he asked in a cultured voice.

"Yes," I said.

"Had your board yet?"

"Which board? I've had two."

"That's nothing, I've had three. And another fellow I know's had four and *he's* still waiting."

"God!"

"It takes some time."

He borrowed ten bob off me and I went down the stairs into the street where Corporal Dexter had the sick lined up at last.

"Don't forget—0920," he yelled after me. "And get a crease in them slacks 'fore you come on parade, see?"

"Very good, Corporal," I said.

At 0920 hours I reported back to the company office. A squad of men shivered sullenly on the kerb outside. Their denim suits, buttonless, flapped open in the bitter wind. My heart sank when I saw them. Dexter must have got them together on purpose. All the worst janker wallahs were there, mixed with a few well-known malingerers and a man just back

from detention barracks who had no top teeth. Behind them
was the frozen grass plot facing the office and beyond that
again the sea. Against this background they looked terrible.
But their faces, covered with pimples and blue with the cold,
brightened when they saw me.

"Squad! Squad, 'shun!" shouted out a bloke at the back.
They all clicked to attention while the man with no top teeth
gave a wavering salute.

"What you a-doing of?" Corporal Dexter roared out,
appearing from nowhere. Grins vanished immediately and
all stood at ease. "Shun!" Dexter shouted. They shunned.
Dexter came across to me and shouted: "That how you keep
discipline? Letting 'em salute you? Ain't got your bleeding
pip yet, y'know!"

"No, Corporal," I said.
"Now let's see them slacks." He inspected the crease in
my trousers minutely but couldn't find anything wrong: I'd
just pressed the bloody things. "Right. Got to look after you
O.C.T.U. blokes, y'know," and: "What you got to laugh
about?" he bawled at a recruit in the rear rank, who'd got
on gym shoes. "Where's your boots?"
"Excused boots, Corp."
"Excused marching?"
"No, boots."
"Right." Dexter turned to me. "Get cracking now. They're
all yours."
"Dressing," I told them in a weak voice. "Get your dressing."
They shuffled about shooting out their arms. They were in
two ranks by the time they'd finished, and had to be sorted
out in threes again.
"Come on, come on," Corporal Dexter shouted. "You're
wasting time."
Meanwhile heads had appeared at the office window,
watching us. The company clerk and two of the runners
and behind them the C.Q.M.S. They were all having the
time of their lives.
"Good as a play," the C.Q.M.S. was heard to say. "Beats
cockfighting."

At last they were properly fallen in and I tried to shout "Shun." Nobody moved. "Louder!" Corporal Dexter shouted. "Louder! They can't hear you."

"I can't shout any louder. I've got a cold."

The Company Commander came on the scene. The heads at the window withdrew. Corporal Dexter shouted "Shun!" They heard him all right.

"What're all these men standing about for, Corporal?"

"Fatigue party, sir. That there furniture."

"Well, for God's sake get them marched off before they bloody well take root. Who's in charge?"

I stepped forward and saluted. "Short of N.C.O.s, sir," Corporal Dexter explained.

"Right. Well, get moving, you should've been there by now."

"Right—turn," I managed to get out. They all turned left.

"Oh God," the Company Commander said, and he went in.

"As you were. Right turn. By the left."

The heads at the window appeared again to watch us march off. The man in gym shoes was limping.

"Pick up the step," I told him.

"You ain't in step yourself," called back the man with no top teeth. It was true; I'd slipped on the pavement again. "Stop talking," I said.

"Barlocks," they said.

I gave it up. They were all chatting merrily as we came round the Pavilion and the empty bandstand, enclosed now by Dannert wire. "Left wheel," I gave them. They broke into a trot. The P.T. instructor, on the steps of the pavilion, stood astounded.

"Stop!" I shouted. "Stop!"

No use; they only slowed down when they were all out of breath. "Nice little run," remarked a man who'd gone sick with blisters the day before.

Now there was the hill to get up. They embarked on the climb with enthusiasm. One fell down half-way up. "I've broke me bloody leg," he said. Everyone halted to examine it.

"Fall in!" I shouted. "March!"

"*I* can't march. Broke me bleeding leg."

"Fall in the rear, then."

I didn't dare take them up the town, so getting them to the house took some time. A small man in civvy clothes, from the Garrison Engineer's office, awaited us outside.

"Thought you was never coming," he said. He led the way into the house and pointed at various pieces of furniture piled up in the hall. "Start on this first," he said.

There was an immediate scramble for the less heavy articles; they staggered about laden with chairs; one had hold of a leather poufé.

"Where we take 'em to?"

"Out back, round the corner. First house on the left."

They disappeared out with the load, all except the man who'd fallen down on the hill. He'd changed his broken leg to a sprained ankle now, and sat on a wooden chest nursing it.

The blokes came back again and looked about them in despair. All the chairs had been taken and the heavier pieces now confronted them. Three fellows, seeing there was nothing for it, tried to tackle a table. They got it wedged in a doorway.

"Careful," the man from the Garrison Engineer's shouted, "you'll scratch the paint."

"Sod the paint," they said.

Eventually the table was manœuvred out sideways. I lent a hand with it myself, resisting an attempt on their part to drop the table on my foot.

"Now this chest."

The man with the sprained ankle was dislodged from on top of it after a lot of talk, during which I threatened him with jankers.

"You can't get me jankers. I'm on 'em already."

"Well, you can have another lot."

That shook him, and four chaps got hold of the chest. The man from the Garrison Engineer's watched their struggles in disgust.

"Last war we had to handle double that lot, and with full kit on," he said.

At last the hall was empty.

"That the lot?" the man in gym shoes, asked wiping an icicle of snot from his nose.

"Not by no means. Look in the next room."

"Ah, sod it," they said.

More chairs were shifted out by the back door. But this time the men didn't return. After they'd been gone ten minutes, I went to have a look. They weren't in the other house. I couldn't see them anywhere. They'd all vanished.

"Having a tea, likely," the man with the sprained ankle said. "Don't blame 'em, poor sods."

The Y.M. was not far off. I rushed up the steps and looked inside. They weren't there. I turned into the next street. A wireless was blaring in one of the houses. I looked up at the window. There sat a sailor, waving a pack of cards at me and grinning. Two more sailors sat with him, and one of my fatigue party dodged out of sight just as I looked up.

"Come out!" I shouted. "Come out at once. I'll have you all on a——" I couldn't remember the number of the form you wrote out charges on, so I finished: "I'll have you all on thickuns."

That fetched them. One by one they filed out, swearing; the sailors grinned from the window. I thought I saw a woman in a brassière lurking in the background, but I'm not sure: it may have been a mirage.

"Come on," I said. "Back to work."

"Ah hell. What about a break first. We're bleeding froze."

"All right," I said; it was break-time. But then it turned out they couldn't have a break because none of them had any money and no fags.

"Lend me half a dollar," the man with no top teeth said, coming up with his fist clenched.

"I'll be damned if I do," I said. Lending the orderly corporal ten bob had left me short myself. So he unclenched his fist and said "F——."

The man in gym shoes produced twopence and disappeared into the Y.M. "Bleeding capitalist," they said.

Finally I got them back to work. Slowly the furniture changed its abode. The men blew on their fingers and swore.

"That the lot?"

"That's the lot."

"Thank Christ."

"Fall in on the road," I said. This time they obeyed

promptly: they wanted to get back. "Wait a minute," I said. "What about that man in the Y.M."

"Oh, *he's* gone. You won't find *him*."

They were right. I looked all over the Y.M., but he wasn't there. He must have dodged out the back door.

They'd started off already when I got back: I had to run to catch up with them. The man with the sprained ankle ran, too. A small crowd collected in front of the company office to watch us dismiss. Corporal Dexter was there, of course. They broke off before I'd time to finish the word of command. All of them ran straight for their billets, including the man with the sprained ankle. I stood there watching them run.

"Well, me old cocker," Corporal Dexter said, coming up. "How d'you like being in charge of a squad?"

"F——the squad," I said.

I thought he'd put me on a charge for insolence, but he didn't. He only burst out laughing. I walked away.

Somehow I don't think I'll ever make an officer.

JACK LUSBY
A Flying Fragment

*Jack Lusby (1913–80) was an RAF pilot
during World War II.*
  *The short story "A Flying Fragment"
was originally published in* Bulletin *in
1944.*

IT WAS HARD ON MICK MOONEY that, near the end of his
tether, he had to break in the rustiest bunch of pilots he'd
encountered. Being the oldest, rustiest, and one of the slowest
to get going, I was able to study him at uncomfortably close
quarters.

It was said that his long and colourful Hurricane career
included a Battle of Britain bullet in the head. This was
hearsay.

Perhaps because planes and ships were scarce, or front-line
losses temporarily few, odd times saw groups of aircrew
mouldering in reserve or transit camps dotted round the
world and, it seemed to them, forgotten. Via the back lanes
of the East our small party moved slowly and spasmodically
to Egypt.

There, after only three months to get acclimatized and say
hello to old friends, who'd trekked round the globe the other
way, we were told to fly.

"Hurricanes or Kitties—whichever they have when you get
there. Be ready in half an hour."

We reached our 'drome at midnight, packed like pigs in the
back of a truck, dog-tired and stiff with cold.

"Out, bods!" cried a sing-song English voice.

It was a hard, white night. Scattered pagoda-like EPI tents
squatted moon-hazed in the sand. The "Out, bods" voice said
"Three to a tent, chums, wakey-wakey 0430 hours."

I chucked two blankets on the ground and passed out.

Waking grunts and snarls revealed that the other numbed hip bones in the tent belonged to Steve and Hawkeye. The new boys comprised Australians, Englishmen, and Canadians, plus one, Rafe, who'd made his way to this RAF 'drome from Texas. Most were sergeant-pilots, and in age retired schoolboys.

The 'drome was a big claypan. Sustained by what passed for tea at an ME RAF station we gathered flying-gear and started walking to the Flight tent nearly a mile away. The ground was spread with thick white fog and its surface was treacherously greasy.

A prairie voice said "After all, when you get right down to it, in what way is this any different from Miami?"

Someone said "The things they don't tell you in books!"

We heard on either side the reluctant stuttering of cold Merlins. Occasionally, silhouetted against the fog, we saw the ghostly, humpbacked shapes of sleeping Hurricanes.

"Easy, easy," said Rafe, "or we trip on an erk in the dark."

The English fitters and riggers *did* seem jockey sized. They could be heard rumbling batteries about, shocking their winged charges into a fury of wakefulness. Exhaust flames lit figures clinging limpet-like to cockpits in icy, fog-swirling prop-blasts. You felt the brittle pre-dawn tension of any wartime 'drome.

A blot ahead became the Flight tent. It was formed by three joined EPIs. Inside some Irving-jacketed fellows turned and looked us over. They were young, quiet, and looked tired. Operational men, instructing for a "rest".

There was a muttered "Your turn, Kim."

One of them hooked his elbows on the 'chute-bench and kept looking at our faces, harsh-lit by a hanging globe. He threw his cap back on the bench. Lank, bleached hair topped a healthy brown face; a horse-kick scar circled one of his amber eyes, which had the round, unblinking look seen in some "old" fighter-pilots. Medium build, a policeman would have said. Outside it was still dark. A soft Canadian voice ruffled the silence.

"I'm Kimber. Here we teach you to fight and shoot; to use an airplane as a weapon, not an airborne automobile. I guess you all know by now if you hold it wrong it kills *you*. We've got about a week to teach you all we can. No time for horse-dung on your part or ours. Out there," thumbing the west, "it's really grim. The tougher we make it here the longer, maybe, you'll last. I hear most of you haven't flown in a long time. Here's where you catch up. You'll find it's like riding a bike; you just don't forget. In a week you'll be flying rings round *us*; and that's the way it should be." But he seemed humbly aware of the gap he had to bridge between our knowledge and his.

From outside came the fog-muffled but sustained and unmistakable sound of an aircraft committed to flight. A glance ricocheted among the instructors. They straightened and strode out and we followed. The noise churned around in the distance and we heard a groaned "Not again, Mick, not again!"

Cat's-eyes head-high in the fog grew to twin moons, and, when we uncrouched, the tent still breathed in the turbulence. Again the Hurricane's landing-lights spread at us rocking as wing-tips were lifted over ill-seen obstacles.

"Urrrr, Mick, ye don't have to do it," burred a voice near by.

Soon we heard him taxi-ing.

"Who was it?" asked Hawkeye.

Kimber sighed "The Squadron Leader, seeing if the fog's cleared for flying."

As the fog thinned, a couple of circuits in two-seater Harvards gave us a bit of the feel back. I heard a heart-warming Australian voice in the earphones: "Give her a burst for luck on the home turn—go for a fast-wheeler—tell Flight next gent., please."

After breakfast a languid, droopy-moustached and fashionably unkempt type was nursing a dachshund near a Hurricane. He beckoned and indicated the cockpit, assuring the animal that this would only take a minute. Sitting among the unfamiliar gadgets, I listened to the cockpit drill. It wasn't much trouble, eyes shut, to put a hand on this and that. Then the dachshund-fancier said "Don't be more than an hour, old boy. Oh, and the Squadron Leader's watching." Then he went away.

Gear on and back in the aircraft, the situation still seemed unreal. A battery was trundled under the nose. A voice in the cockpit screeched the "All clear, contact" routine and I saw gloved fingers press the maggie buttons. The thing started without the slightest hesitation, and off went the erks and battery. Looking around I saw other props spinning and ground-crews trotting on to wreak more havoc among the atrophied pilots. Hell, it *must* be fair dinkum. And "the Squadron Leader's watching".

Brakes off, my machine gambolled along to take-off point like a cocker promised a walk. Round the forty-four gallon marker drums and into wind. Nothing for it but to push the throttle and hope.

Taking over from the Hurricane a few minutes later I rediscovered the Suez Canal by some masterly pin-point navigation and sneaked furtively along it wondering if there were any way of landing invisibly. Unable to move the lever, I'd been beetling around the sky wheels-down. And since the same handle worked flaps, I could only look forward to a slightly spectacular, highspeed, flapless arrival. With no gatecrashing on my part, a meeting with the fog-dispersing Squadron Leader seemed imminent.

As the Hurri. slowed to about sixty, a utility overhauled it. The driver's face seemed mottled with rage; his mouth was opening and shutting. Unable to hear him, I waved in "See you later" fashion and parked.

Carrying the 'chute over the sand to the Flight tent I could hear someone screaming as if in unbearable pain. It was Squadron Leader Mick Mooney. He was screaming at me.

I walked up to him and stood still, wincing.

He was slightly built, dark, and a thin Hollywood moustache writhed like a snake along the violent contortions of his upper lip. The nose was small, sharp and hooked; the eyes opal-black in wrinkled slits of skin. He was perhaps thirty. That's all I saw the first time. Suddenly his voice dropped to a comparatively soothing level.

"How long since you *flew*?"

"Getting on for a year, sir."

"No excuse for assuming the Hurricane has a fixed under-cart. Overheats the motor. Looks bloody awful . . . *Do you expect every——in the RAF to fly wheels-down so* YOU *can stay in formation?*"

"No, sir."

"What did you fly?"

"Wirraways, sir."

"Wirraway? Wirraway? What is it? Some half-feathered marsupial?"

With that Mooney turned and walked into the tent.

Shortly my dog-nursing adviser came out looking somewhat unsettled. He made quite a speech.

"It's all right, you know. I've just lost a strip, too. 'Careless instruction.' Please don't do it again. At least you did bring the plane back; somebody's vanished with one. Probably hocked it in Cairo. The Squadron Leader is taking five of you up now; formation take-off. Do remember that release-tit on the undercart lever."

He made for the nearest sandbag and sat on it.

It was nine o'clock.

In the tent Mooney said to us "We fly Hurricanes hood open and goggles off. Better vision. We also like your *eyes open*! Wing-tip clear of the next man's, able to move forward or back and level with his roundel. Form up at take-off point in the order you get there. Now *get cracking*!"

When we faced up at the barrier Mooney was waiting with all the patience of a fire-engine at traffic-lights. I found myself next to him, and he stared at me with what could only have been recognition. Up went the thumbs and we were racing. Some gremlin got in front of the throttle lever and risked a hernia. I trailed lengths behind on take-off.

The rest of the flight was uneventful. Pansy, practice stuff; it steadied the flying a lot. Mooney swept the formation gracefully round to land like a matador spreading a cape.

I heard it as my feet hit the sand.

"Put that bloody parachute *back*!" Mooney was standing near his plane fifty yards away aiming the words like bullets.

Signing at the Flight he spat out, "You can't overtake

the leader on take-off; he's watching you and progressively opening the throttle. This time open *yours!* Aeroplanes *want* to fly, *but you've got to help a little bit!*"

At the last moment I had to switch to another machine, the heaviest, faster four-cannon job. It had a lot more power for take-off. There were just the two of us. Determined not to be left behind again, I shoved the throttle lever forward with commendable enthusiasm. The look on Mooney's face as I sailed past him and soared alone into the dust-haze will live with me for ever. Back there no doubt he was "progressively opening the throttle" until it came out by the roots.

I waited in a gentle turn. He came sliding up on the inside like a wide-finned, sand-coloured fish and led. Just above a low, thin cloud-layer Mooney signalled "Line astern". In this position, behind and a shade below, you look as though the leader were pulling you on a short string. The still air caused not even the usual gentle lift and sway of one plane in relation to another. We were as if fixed in space for ever.

In a flash he was upside-down. He hung there for a moment studying my reaction, then plummeted from sight. As he screwed down, my heavier plane seemed to be catching up. The thin cloudscreen whipped away, the canal twirled up, streamed by my shoulder, flecked with felucca sails and went. Dust-haze, white flicker of cloud, blue sky and, thank God, Mooney. I came to heel like a guilty pup who'd almost lost its master.

Again he rolled, dived, pulled out and rocketed into the face of the sun. His black silhouette dissolved in the furnace. I found him right beneath me like a shark under a fishing-boat. We must have looked like a biplane. Then he skidded to one side and did a brace of beautiful rolls. Struth, I thought, the man must be happy! He'd damn near led me into the ground.

Mooney darted for home. As I was closing up for landing he shied violently sideways like a startled horse. I edged back alongside and we landed. On the ground he shouted "Blast you! Out here *never* join up from astern—come in from the beam so we know what you are! You'd better get some lunch."

*　　*　　*

Rafe was standing in the sun, hand-talking excitedly to Steve and some Canadians. The pilots' universal pantomime, infuriating when abused, can describe almost anything that happens in the air. Rafe's hands converged with a smack and separated, fluttering groundwards. The inevitable "who was it?" brought "Couple English fellers in a practice dog-fight—man, you shoulder seen it. One baled out."

The 'drome was now hot and dry. Walking to lunch Hawkeye said "This time yesterday we were busy swatting flies at Almaza."

Wacker said "Yes, flat out trying to fill in time!"

Some of the lunch-time babble: "They found the type who disappeared this morning, about thirty miles away."

"OK?"

"Dead as a doornail—force-landed wheels down in soft sand."

"Oh, bloody bad luck!"

"Bloody clueless!"

"Been up with friend Mooney?"

"Not yet and not anxious. Believe he put an Aussie through it this morning."

"Don't worry. Puts everyone through it in turn."

"Yes—if you don't stick in like a dart you're OK."

About sundown a group of us, feeling justifiably weary, stood watching the last formations washing off speed before landing. Hurricanes came shoaling in shark-like over the sand; sank into the dusk and lost shape.

The beer tasted good. Even the food seemed palatable. The tension was off.

In the dark next morning Mooney performed his tent-high fogchurning chore and stepped into the Flight tent.

"Start with you again," he said. "Individual attacks with film. Come in from five hundred yards out and a thousand feet above. And for God's sake *fly!*"

We climbed, levelled, separated, and I turned to wait for him. The day exploded over Egypt in a kaleidoscopic broken-egg vastness of cloud and air. A black speck raced towards me along the rim of a mile-high blood-red cliff of cumulus. The world pitched on its side, streaked past the cowling, steadied, and there was Mooney far too small in the ringsight. I fired the camera-gun, broke away and climbed. Must be quicker next time.

After half an hour of this we dived to breakfast.

Armourers took the film, and I rather hoped they'd lose it. Mooney shouted "Out of range and no deflection! *Get in close*! You don't hit 'em when you're pointing *at* 'em. Be here after breakfast and *bloody well get it right!*"

Rafe said "Jeez, you must hate that guy."

"No, strangely enough," I said.

"Strangely enough, I *do*!" said an Englishman, with curious intensity. He was a tall bloke standing, bare-headed, in open battlejacket and shorts. His long, thin face was expressionless; and the reddish colour of his tight-kinked hair showed in the skin and flecked his eyes. He said no more.

Later Mooney was squatting, head bowed, on a sandbag. Faded cap, bulky fleece-lined jacket, spindly drab-clad legs. A white pup sat between his shoes and he was patting it. Suddenly, he twisted and shouted back into the Flight tent, "Where's my bloody utility?" The pup scuttled away.

A sergeant came out and said "Transport's fixin' it, sir."

"Fixing it or mucking it?" He raced into the tent and grabbed the telephone. "Transport? Bring back that bloody truck or I'll drive a Hurricane tail-up where I want to go! Get your bloody fingers out. *I've had you, Transport!*"

He crashed the phone to the table and ran to the nearest plane. The motor burst into life and the tail swung and lifted as he raced down the mile-long road to the administrative section. I sat and waited.

A plane had landed and taxied to a stop near by. I recognized the pilot as the red-haired Mooney-hater. He was said to be eccentric. Some fitters gathered expectantly. The pilot rose in the cockpit, stood rigid and announced at the top of his voice, "Once again man has defied Nature." The show was over.

Some of the erks were staring upward. A plane was spinning high in the sky. A sergeant growled "Now then, lads, ain't y' seen 'em doin' that before?" They still looked up. Kimber, inside, sensed something and came out. "Goddam it man, pull *out!*"

Mooney, who had returned unnoticed, said "He can't, or he would," and went into the tent.

Black smoke rose a couple of miles out in the sand and Mooney was saying on the phone "I'll tell you, sir, when we know who it was," when a Hurricane came in and landed very fast. When it taxied we saw a third of one wing was missing. It was Steve who climbed out. He was sweating and shivering.

He said "Me and Wacker—did he get *out*, Freddie?"

I said "No."

Mooney said "No; you seem to have won. See the MO, then see me."

To me he said "Up, Jackson—let's get some dung off our livers. *And this time come in close!*"

I found myself shouting "I'm doing my best! I'll show you 'coming in close!'"

Mooney's smile was like the Mona Lisa's.

A Canadian sergeant-instructor waiting near my plane said "Take it easy; makin' guys mad's his technique."

The first attack was far too close. The other plane suddenly overflowed ringsight, windscreen, and filled most of the view ahead. I wallowed in Mooney's wash before striking solid air and breaking away. My plane got the bit in its teeth and bored in each time as though bent on gnawing Mooney's tail off. When the cinegun ran out of film we landed.

Mooney screamed "You came to within *seven feet*! Are you trying to *mate 'em?*"

"Anything for variety," I said.

No comment.

After lunch Mooney flew with the Eccentric; the postmortem was a delight to hear.

"I propose to cite you as listless, slow, consistent only in unreliability, and without a vestige of natural ability."

"But, sir, nothing detrimental, I hope!"

That night in the crowded film hut there was some beautiful demonstration stuff by Kimber—bead stuck like glue ahead of the target's spinning prop while the cloudy backdrop whirled and raced. My own film was frightening to watch. The target turned its tail into the camera and hurtled at us, filling the screen with belly and tail before it flicked from sight.

The film interpreter said "God! You could count the rivets!"

There was another exclamation and someone said "That was the Squadron Leader. He's gone." Each pilot's films were run off to expert comment such as "Deflection about right—slightly out of range—that's better—bad button-stabbing—longer squirts, please."

The Eccentric's reel, after showing the usual whirling emptiness of sky with occasional views of aircraft, concluded with a screen-filling close-up of the stolid face of an armourer.

After a moment of stunned silence the interpreter said "Surprise ending!"

Back in the sergeants' mess the senior WO answered a knock on the door and returned with the Squadron Leader, dapper and polished, black hair close-brushed and shining.

Tombstone asked "Like a beer, sir?" Mooney dragged up a stick-and-canvas chair and sat down.

The Eccentric rose gracefully and carried his drink to the trestle bar. There, feet crossed, and comfortably hooked by his elbows, he stared back at us. A hanging bar-light glowed on the fiery hair, narrow forehead, high nose and cheekbones. The rest was shadow.

Mooney, sitting low in the chair, looked steadily at him, dead pan and rigid. I had a curious feeling that the Eccentric stood, remote, to better *concentrate* on Mooney. His attitude had a bone-pointing quality.

Tombstone came back and whacked beer on the table; and the honest sound was welcome.

Mooney said smoothly "Ah! Quick work, Tomson—looks a nice drop. Luck!"

Turning my way, he said "That was extremely dangerous today. Strike the happy medium. Smoke?"

More instructors came in and joined the growing circle. Flying reverted to its proper status—"a piece of cake"; child's play.

An Englishman tossed in a suggestion for a list of fineable offences to be posted in the Flight. From fifty-ackers for a landing-or taxi-ing-prang to ten for "goddam" or "son-of-a-bitch".

Rafe said "Yeah, and fifty for 'a-a-actualleh!'"

"What price breaking a neck?" shot from the figure under the barlight.

There was a noticeable sprinkling of DFCs and a couple of DFMs on the instructors' khaki tunics. Affecting eye-trouble, Rafe jumped in with "so many goddam gongs here a guy could hammer out the Anvil Chorus!"

Steve's laugh startled me—he'd been unnaturally quiet for a kid who laughed easily.

Mooney turned on him. "Hear you've some damned good songs, Hampton. What about it?"

The usual all-in sing-song developed from tentative "da-de-das" among the more cautious to full-throated competition, ending in husky good-nights and sleep.

One morning was cloudless and perfect for shadow-shooting. We did this in pairs using the four-cannon machines. You dived at the other man's shadow, and the spurts of sand showed where your shells were hitting. Burton, an English pupil, went with Hawkeye. Hawkeye returned alone and reported Burton crashed while shooting.

Mooney, writing at a trestle-table, grunted, "Probably selected his own shadow and pressed home the attack."

Thwaites, of the dachshund, picked up a piece of cloth, walked to the roster-board and looked inquiringly at Hawkeye, who nodded. Thwaites erased Burton's name and went to the telephone.

About an hour later, Lofty, who did everything with a flourish, turned an ordinary run-of-the-mill forced landing into an arrival to write home about. When the engine cut he dropped the wheels and tried to reach the 'drome. Skimming a distant sandhill, he hit a nearer one and bounced two hundred yards on to the runway. No damage. Lofty had already established a formidable reputation for luck at poker, crap, and the Gezira races; so, naturally, Mooney was flying and not available for immediate comment.

He was giving the Eccentric a last-chance test in individual combat. On the joystick were two buttons, one camera and the other guns; and it was important not to confuse exercises. After this one Mooney treated his languid opponent to a brilliant, if vitriolic, discourse on deflection.

He was saying "Well, what the bloody hell *were* you aiming at? Certainly couldn't have been me!" when he noticed a rigger at attention beside him. "Well, what do you want?"

"Sergeant Smithers, sir; he just found a bullet hole in your tailplane, sir."

Mooney swung back to face the Eccentric, who didn't miss the trick. "Certainly couldn't have been me," he said.

Mooney knew when to be silent.

In the mess afterwards I heard a whisper that the Eccentric a-a-actually was really rather hot. Just didn't want to be in it. Someone had seen him doing things when he thought no one was looking. And that a few days ago he'd forgotten himself and pulled off a wizard bit of flying, then deliberately mucked it up. Rafe voiced a wish that in his own case this process could be occasionally reversed. The man from Texas provided the following morning's chai-time entertainment:

"Ambitioning" to ultimately join a Yank unit, he'd "organized" a Kittyhawk. Landing the first time, he was travelling so fast that when he tried to put the flaps down nothing happened. He touched down at some extravagant speed, hurtled across the 'drome with fire-tender in pursuit, saw a sandbank and date-palms coming at him, took off again and barely cleared them. He went round again and this time got in nicely.

As we picked up our tea-mugs again Kimber said "God send me back to the war where I'm safe."

"Touching on that," said Thwaites, "Mick intends to give the hundred-and-nine a whizz round after lunch."

The captured Messerschmitt 109 was a neat little job; and half the fuselage seemed engine. It heated quickly on the ground and started up at take-off point. Mooney got in and went. The cooling system blew up and an oil-pipe burst. With cockpit full of fumes and oil, the ME came over at about a hundred and fifty feet, leaving a snowy trail of glycol.

Mooney, half-blinded, and with little control, was a trier. He skidded round and reached the runaway via a gap between some tents and a parked Tomahawk. The Messerschmitt crouched steaming with fury; and Lofty said "Must be a one-man dog".

Mooney drove to the mess.

*   *   *

Before breakfast on our second-last day the Eccentric stood facing Mooney on the sand between their planes. We could hear Mooney's voice, pitched high.

"That was a bloody stinking gutless imitation of an attack! Your breakaway perfect example of straight and level flying! Aren't you *game to do it?*"

What the Eccentric said we don't know. Mooney seemed about to spring; then turned and came toward the tent. The Eccentric just stood out there staring after him.

During that afternoon vapour trails marked the high, blue ceiling of the sky; and, looking up, we saw a pin-point star of fire.

Mooney burst out "*Burn, you bastard, burn!*" and watched it down the long air-lane to the horizon. Some Arab workmen also watched; and one asked "Inglezi?"

Mooney blasted them. "How the bloody hell should *we* know? *Escut! Yallahimshi!*"

He strode off, his small black shoes jabbing the sand.

Thwaites said to Kimber "Saw him cannon-firing at a camel today, all directions. Wog chappie scuttling around seeking safe side of the beast."

An Australian instructor laughed. "Believe he'd spend his last leave with a saucer of milk and a waddy—killing cats."

I said "Oh, I dunno—saw him one day patting a pup."

"Probably interrupted him," said the Eccentric. "Anyway, he shan't kill *me!*"

There were curious glances at the speaker; the chatter had ended on a wrong note.

Trudging over a sandhill in the dark next morning, pilots saw a plane, wing-lights ablaze, rolling along the surface of the low fog.

"Aha! The act's improving!" exclaimed someone unseen.

This was the day of the ultimate demonstration.

The crew of the Nazi JU88, briefed to scan the port, had no thought of meeting Mooney in the final frenzy. The 88's four-Messerschmitt escort, too, must have been surprised. Mooney had attained the suicidal recklessness which sometimes accompanies the limit of fatigue.

In a bloodshot mackerel sky the four school Hurricanes

weaved in loose patrol formation at 15,000 feet, Mooney and his three charges—Lofty, the Eccentric, and myself. It was the hour when "Lo! The hunter in the East has caught the sultan's turret in a noose of light."

At the sight of a simple, stupid minor accident Mooney had led us off downward in silent fury. In the bracing upper air the camouflaged, light-bellied planes performed a wobbegong quadrille. I was singing with the engine "First lady forward; second lady back."

Our leader, just ahead, rolled violently, and, wings vertical, skidded high above. Beneath him streaked a three-pronged, black-crossed shape and a Hurricane shrank in vertical pursuit. They faded chameleon-like into the emptiness below.

My head almost whanged the cockpit edge; it surprised me that the plane was diving and dodging.

A Hurri. was plunging abreast of me, barrelling. Beyond it another was simply standing on its nose. And hurtling past us dived the four Messerschmitts. Sleek darts with a flash of sun on them.

Intent on removing the threat that was Mooney, they'd left their run too late. As my controls glued stiff with speed I saw an orange-coloured shooting-star below.

The radio crackled in my ears, and this time I got some words "—get 'em on the way up."

The Eccentric turned away; he was pulling out. With the anticipation of a veteran he cut the corner of the Germans' dive and zoom. I followed, with a momentary impression that he'd done this thing before; and sand, sea, and sky all misted into blackness.

With vision clearing and face back in position, I saw one of the gnats, rocketing after Mooney, trailing smoke. As the Hurricane behind it pulled away an ME followed with the inevitability of a shadow. I heard myself screech something on the radio.

We all winged over in a curve of flight that seemed as preordained as the path of planets.

A Hurricane like a humpbacked projectile came firing on a tangent, and I hastily took thumb off cannon-button. The Eccentric's German shadow staggered, flipped over, shedding

pieces from a wing-root and vanished. Something struck my
plane with a terrifying "Crack!"

Desperate shove on rudder-pedal, stick in corner, and I
spiralled in a maelstrom of confusion. I lifted hard against
the safety-harness and slammed back with a spine-buckling
jar. The goggles dropped down over my eyes and I snatched
left hand from throttle and pushed them off.

There was a taste of bile, smell of petrol, black-out, sight
again: Going straight up.

Comparative calm, and an even keel restored, with no
apparent damage, I did some overdue looking around.

To my left an ME nosed shell-like from the depths, turned,
levelled. Above, a Hurricane poised, falcon-like, careening,
whirled, and with split-second fury struck.

A black-crossed wing spun feather-light in a dust of smaller
fragments. Flame blossomed in the air below; then the sky
was empty.

I flew home feeling that I'd sat out an exhausting film.

On the 'drome:

"Freddie! Were you in that do? Here, have a smoke!"

"Light it for me. I was there—and that's about all."

"Lofty's back—boy, you should see his kite!"

"They reckon Mooney got an eighty-eight, and an ME went
off smoking."

"On a training flight!"

"Probably arranged the whole thing."

"Oh, fair go!"

Kimber came into the circle with Lofty. He said "OK? Well,
what did *you* see of it?"

"A bloody awful collision—Hurricane rammed an ME."

"So the ack-ack says on the phone. See who it was?"

"No."

"The long red guy—pounds to ackers," said Rafe.

I said "Well, he shot one down, I think."

With the phone filling in the gaps, the picture fell together:
the JU88 skimming the desert, burning like a torch; the
doomed reargunner still firing point-blank back at Mooney. In
the vengeful skyward chase two ME's hit, and the collision.

Someone suggested that whoever rammed the German had been hit mortally; nothing to lose. A German had baled out OK.

My plane seemed to have been struck by a bit off another aircraft.

A Hurricane screamed low across the 'drome, flashed over us, zoomed, and circled to land.

A dozen voices: "*Mooney!*"

The prop stopped spinning and the pilot shed his headgear. We saw the red thatch of the Eccentric. It was the first time we'd seen him laughing.

H.E. BATES
No Trouble At All

Herbert Ernest Bates (1905–74) was born in Rushden, England. At the start of WWII, already a well-known author, he was commissioned into the RAF to write short stories about the service in wartime. These stories, which were intended to raise public awareness and morale, were later published under the pseudonym "Flying Officer X" as The Greatest People in the World *(1942) and* How Sleep the Brave *(1943). Among his many other books are the war novel,* Fair Stood the Wind for France *(1944), and the enduring story of English country life,* The Darling Buds of May *(1958).*

The short story "No Trouble At All" is from the collection, The Greatest People in the World.

T HE DAY WAS TO BE GREAT in the history of the Station; it was just my luck that I didn't come back from leave until late afternoon. All day the sunlight had been a soft orange colour and the sky a clear wintry blue, without mist or cloud. There was no one in the mess ante-room except a few of the night-staff dozing before the fire, and no one I could talk to except the little W.A.A.F. who sits by the telephone.

So I asked her about the show. "Do you know how many have gone?" I said.

"Ten, sir," she said.

"Any back yet?"

"Seven were back a little while ago," she said. "They should all be back very soon."

"When did they go? This morning?"

"Yes, sir. About ten o'clock." She was not young; but her face was pleasant and eager and, as at the moment, could become alight. "They looked marvellous as they went, sir," she said. "You should have seen them, sir. Shining in the sun."

"Who isn't back? You don't know?"

But she did know.

"K for Kitty and L for London aren't back," she said. "But I don't know the other."

"It must be Brest again?" I said.

"Yes, sir," she said. "I think it's Brest."

I didn't say anything, and she said, "They are putting you in Room 20 this time, sir."

"Thank you. I'll go up," I said.

As I went upstairs and as I bathed and changed I made calculations. It was half-past three in the afternoon and the winter sun was already growing crimson above the blue edges of flat ploughed land beyond the Station buildings. I reckoned up how far it was to Brest. If you allowed half an hour over the target and a little trouble getting away, even the stragglers should be back by four. It seemed, too, as if fog might come down very suddenly; the sun was too red and the rim of the earth too blue. I realised that if they were not back soon they wouldn't be back at all. They always looked very beautiful in the sun, as the little W.A.A.F. said, but they looked still more beautiful on the ground. I didn't know who the pilot of L for London was; but I knew, and was remembering, that K for Kitty was my friend.

By the time I went downstairs again the lights were burning in the ante-room but the curtains were not drawn and the evening, sunless now, was a vivid electric blue beyond the windows. The little W.A.A.F. still sat by the telephone and as I went past she looked up and said:

"L for London is back, sir."

I went into the ante-room. The fire was bright and the first crews, back from interrogation, were warming their hands. Their faces looked raw and cold. They still wore sweaters and flying boots and their eyes were glassy.

"Hallo," they said. "You're back. Good leave?" They spoke as if it was I, not they, who had been 300 miles away.

"Hallo, Max," I said. "Hallo, Ed. Hallo, J.B."

I had been away for five days. For a minute I felt remote; I couldn't touch them.

I was glad when someone else came in.

"Hallo. Good trip?"

"Quite a picnic."

"Good. See anything?"

"Everything."

"Good show, good show. Prang them?"

"Think so. Fires burning when we got there."

"Good show."

I looked at their faces. They were tired and hollow. In their eyes neither relief nor exhilaration had begun to filter through the glassiness of long strain. They talked laconically, reluctantly, as if their lips were frozen.

"Many fighters?"

"Hordes."

"Any trouble?"

"The whole bloody crew was yelling fighters. Came up from everywhere."

"Any Spits?"

"Plenty. Had five Me.'s on my tail. Then suddenly wham! Three Spits came up from nowhere. Never saw anything like those Me.'s going home to tea."

"Good show. Good show."

The evening was darkening rapidly and the mess-steward came in to draw the curtains. I remembered K for Kitty and suddenly I went out of the ante-room and stood for a moment in the blue damp twilight, listening and looking at the sky. The first few evening stars were shining and I could feel that later the night would be frosty. But there was no sound of a 'plane.

I went back into the ante-room at last and for a moment, in the bright and now crowded room, I could not believe my eyes. Rubbing his cold hands together, his eyes remote and chilled, his sweater hanging loose below his battle-dress, the pilot of K for Kitty was standing by the fireplace. There was a cross of flesh-pink plastic bandage on his forehead and I knew that something had happened.

"Hallo," I said.

"Hallo," he said. "You're back."

For a minute I didn't say anything else. I wanted to shake his hand and tell him I was glad he was back. I knew that if he had been in a train-wreck or a car crash I should have shaken his hand and told him I was glad. Now somebody had shot him up and all I said was:

"When did you get in?"

"About an hour ago."

"Everything O.K.?"

"Wrapped her up."

"Well," I said. "Just like that?"

"Just like that," he said.

I looked at his eyes. They were bleared and wet and excited. He had made a crash landing; he was safe; he was almost the best pilot in the outfit.

"Anyone see me come in?" he said.

"Saw you from Control," someone said.

"How did it look?"

"Perfect until the bloody airscrew fell off."

Everyone laughed: as if airscrews falling off were a great joke. Nobody said anything about anybody being lucky to be back, but only:

"Have an argument?"

"Flak blew bloody great bit out of the wing. The inter-comm. went and then both turrets."

"Many fighters?"

"Ten at a time."

"Get one?"

"One certain. Just dissolved. One probable."

"Good show. What about the ships?"

"I think we pranged them."

"Good show," we said. "Good show."

We went on talking for a little longer about the trip: beautiful weather, sea very blue, landscape very green in the sun. And then he came back to the old subject.

"How did I land? What did it look like?"

"Beautiful."

"I couldn't get the tail down. Both tyres were punctured."

"Perfect all the same."

He looked quite happy. It was his point of pride, the good landing; all he cared about now. With turrets gone, fuselage like a colander, wings holed, and one airscrew fallen off, he had nevertheless brought her down. And though we all knew it must have been hell no one said a word.

Presently his second dicky came into the ante-room. He was very young, about nineteen, with a smooth aristocratic face and smooth aristocratic hair. He looked too young to be part of a war and he was very excited.

"Went through my sleeve."

He held up a cannon shell. Then he held up his arm. There was a neat tear in the sleeve of his battle-dress. He was very proud.

"And look at this."

Across the knuckles of his right hand there was a thread line of dried blood, neat, fine, barely visible. He wetted his other forefinger and rubbed across it, as if to be sure it wouldn't wash away.

"Came in on the starboard side and out the other."

"Good show," said somebody quite automatically. "Good show."

"Anybody hurt?" I asked.

"Engineer."

"Very bad?"

"Very bad. I bandaged him and gave him a shot coming home."

As he went on talking I looked down at his knees. There were dark patches on them, where blood had soaked through his flying-suit. But all that anyone said was:

"Think you pranged them?"

"Oh! sure enough. They've had it this time."

"Good show," we said. "Good show."

Now and then, as we talked, the little W.A.A.F. would come in from the telephone to tell someone he was wanted. With her quiet voice she would break for a moment the rhythm of excitement that was now rising through outbursts of laughter to exhilaration. She would hear for a second or two a snatch of the now boisterous but still laconic jargon of flight, "Think we may have pranged in, old boy. Good show. Piece of cake. No trouble at all," but there would be no sign on her calm and rather ordinary face that it conveyed anything to her at all. Nor did the crews, excited by the afternoon, the warmth and the relief of return, take any notice of her. She was an automaton, negative, outside of them, coming and going and doing her duty.

Outside of them, too, I listened and gathered together and finally pieced together the picture of the raid; and then soon afterwards the first real pictures of operations were brought in for the Wing Commander to see, and for a moment there was a flare of excitement. We could see the bomb-bursts across the battleships and the quays and then smoke over the area of town and docks. "You think we pranged them, sir?" we said.

"Pranged them? Like hell we did."

"Good show. Bloody good show."

"Slap across the Gluckstein."

"No doubt this time?"

"No doubt."

"Good show," we said. "Good show."

At, last, when the photographs had been taken away again, I went out of the ante-room into the hall. As I walked across it the little W.A.A.F., sitting by the telephone, looked up at me.

"A wonderful show, sir," she said.

I paused and looked at her in astonishment. I wondered for a moment how she could possibly know. There had been no time for her to hear the stories of the crews; she had not seen the photographs; she did not know that K for Kitty had been wrapped up and that it must have been hell to land on two dud tyres and with a broken airscrew; she did not know that the ships had been hit or that over Brest, on that bright calm afternoon, it had been partly magnificent and partly hell.

"How did you know?" I said.

She smiled a little and lifted her face and looked through the glass door of the ante-room.

"You can tell by their faces, sir," she said.

I turned and looked too. In the morning we should read about it in the papers; we should hear the flat bulletins; we should see the pictures. But now we were looking at something that could be read nowhere except in their eyes and expressed in no language but their own.

"Pretty good show," I said.

"Yes, sir," she said. "No trouble at all."

ALUN LEWIS
They Came

Alun Lewis (1915–44) was born in Cwmaman, South Wales. He enlisted in 1940 and later served as an officer with the South Wales Borderers. He was killed in a military accident in Burma. Although best known for his poetry, Lewis is increasingly regarded as one of the finest British prose writers of World War II.

The short story "They Came" is from his collection, The Last Inspection *(1942).*

THE EVENING WAS SLOWLY CURDLING the sky as the soldier trudged the last mile along the lane leading from the station to the Hampshire village where he was billeted. The hedgerows drew together in the dusk and the distance, bending their waving heads to each other as the fawn bird and the black bird sang among the green hollies. The village lay merged in the soft seaward slope of the South Downs; the soldier shifted his rifle from left to right shoulder and rubbed his matted eyelashes with his knuckles. He was a young chap but, hampered by his heavy greatcoat and equipment, he dragged his legs like an old clerk going home late. He cleared his throat of all that the train journey, cigarettes and chocolate and tea and waiting, had secreted in his mouth. He spat the thick saliva out. It hung on a twig.

Someone was following him. When he heard the footsteps first he had hurried, annoyed by the interfering sound. But his kit was too clumsy to hurry in and he was too tired. So he dawdled, giving his pursuer a chance to pass him. But the footsteps stayed behind, keeping a mocking interval. He couldn't stop himself listening to them, but he refused to look back. He became slowly angry with himself for letting them occupy his mind and possess his attention. After a while they seemed to come trotting out of the past in him, out of the Welsh mining village, the colliers gambling in the quarry, the county school where he learned of sex and of knowledge, and college where he had swotted and slacked in poverty, and boozed, and quarreled in love. They were the footsteps of the heavy-jawed deacon of Zion, with his white grocer's apron and his hairy nostrils sniffing out corruption.

But that was silly, he knew. Too tired to control his mind, that's what it was. These footsteps were natural and English, the postman's perhaps . . . But still they followed him, and the dark gods wrestling in him in the mining valley pricked their goaty ears at the sound of the pimping feet.

He turned the corner into the village and went down the narrow street past the post office and the smithy, turned the corner under the A.A. sign and crossed the cobbled yard of the hotel where the officers' and business men's cars were parked. A shaggy old dog came frisking out of its straw-filled barrel in the corner, jumping and barking. He spoke to it and at once it grovelled on its belly. He always played with the dog in the mornings, between parades. The unit did its squad drill in the hotel yard, kitchen maids watching flirtatiously through the windows, giggling, and the lavatory smelling either of disinfectant or urine.

He pushed open the little door in the big sliding doors of the garage which had been converted into a barrack room for the duration. Thin electric bulbs high in the cold roof dangled a weak light from the end of the twisted, wavering flex. Grey blankets folded over biscuits or straw palliasses down both sides of the room. Equipment hanging from nails on the whitewashed wall—in one corner a crucifix, over the thin, chaste, taciturn Irish boy's bed. He was the only one in the room, sitting on his bed in the cold dark corner writing in his diary. He looked up and smiled politely, self-effacingly, said "Hallo. Had a good leave?" and bent his narrow head again to read what he'd written.

"Yes, thanks," said the soldier, "except for raids. The first night I was home he raided us for three hours, the sod," he said, unbuckling his bayonet belt and slipping his whole kit off his shoulders.

Last time he returned from leave, four months back, he had sat down on his bed and written to his wife. They had married on the first day of that leave and slept together for six nights. This time he didn't ferret in his kitbag for notepaper and pencil. He went straight out.

The hotel management had set a room aside for the soldiers to booze in. It was a good class hotel, richly and vulgarly furnished with plush and mirrors and dwarf palms in green boxes. The auctioneers and lawyers and city men, the fishermen and golfers and bank managers, most of whom had week-end cottages or villas of retirement in commanding positions at the local beauty spots, spent the evening in the saloon bar and lounge, soaking and joking. So the soldiers were given a bare little bar parlour at the back, with a fire and a dartboard and two sawdust spitoons. The soldiers were glad of it. It was their own. They invited some of their pals from the village to play darts with them—the cobbler, the old dad who lived by himself in the church cottage and never shaved or washed, the poacher who brought them a plucked pheasant under his old coat sometimes—all the ones the soldiers liked popped in for an evening. A few girls, too, before the dance in the church hall, on Tuesdays.

Fred Garstang, from Portsmouth, and Ben Bryant, from Coventry, the two eldest soldiers in the unit—regulars who had never earned a stripe—were playing darts, two empty pint glasses on the mantelpiece by the chalk and duster.

"'Owdee, Taffy?" they said in unison. "'Ave a good leave, lad?"

"Yes thanks," he said automatically, "except for raids. The sod raided us for three hours the first night I was home."

"Damn. Just the wrong side of it," said Fred, examining the quivering dart. "I deserve to lose this bloody game, Ben. I 'xpect you're same as me, Taff; glad to get back to a bit of peace and quiet and a good sleep. My seven days in Pompey's the worst I've ever spent in India, China, the Rhineland, Gallygurchy or anywhere. But we're nice and cosy here, thank God. They can keep their leave. *I* don't want seven nights in an Anderson. I'd rather stay here, I would."

Old Fred never stopped talking once he started. The soldier tapped the counter with a shilling and leaned over to see whether the barmaid was on the other side of the partition. He saw her silky legs and the flutter of her skirt. He hit the counter harder, then, while he waited, wondered at his impatience. His body wasn't thirsty; it was too damned tired to bother, too worn-out. It was something else in him that wanted to get drunk, dead, dead drunk.

The barmaid came along, smiling. She was natural with the soldiers. She smiled when she saw who it was and held her pretty clenched fist to him across the counter. He should have taken it and forced it gently open, of course. Instead, he just put his flat palm underneath it. She looked at him with a hurt-faun reproach in her sailing eyes, and opening her hand let a toffee fall into his.

"One from the wood, Madge," he said.

"I'll have to charge you for *that*," she said.

"That's all right," he replied. "You always pay in this life."

"Why don't you take the girl, Taffy?" said old Fred as he came and sat by them, their darts over. "If I was your age—"

He had been in the army since he was fifteen. Now he was past soldiering, wandering in the head sometimes, doing odd jobs; in peacetime he kept the lawns trimmed at the depot, now he was tin-man in the cooking-shed, cleaning with Vim the pots and pans Ben Bryant used for cooking. "Vermicelli tastes all right," he said. "Better than anything you can pick up in the streets. Yellow or black or white, German or Irish. I've never had a Russian though, never. It's not bad when you're young, like a new crane when the jib runs out nice and smooth; it's better than sitting in the trenches like an old monkey, scratching yourself and not knowing whose leg it is or whose arm it is, looking in his pockets to see if there's anything worth taking, and not knowing who'll win the race, the bullet with your number on it or the leaky rod you're nursing. But I like it here. It's nice and peaceful up here, in the cookhouse all day. We ought to try some vermicelli, Ben, one day."

"Don't you get impatient now, Freddy," Ben said with the calmness of a father of many children. "We'll stuff your pillow full of it next Christmas and put a sprig of it on your chest. Don't you worry, boy."

But old Fred went on talking like an old prophet in a volcanic world, about and about. "There's no knowing when you've got to fight for your king and country," he said. "No matter who you are, Russian or Frenchy or Jerry—and the Yankee, too. He'll be in it, boy. I've seen him die. It's only natural, to my way of thinking. I wore a pair of gloves the Queen knitted herself, she did, last time. The Unknown Soldier I was, last time."

None of us are ourselves now, the Welsh boy sat thinking: neither what we were, nor what we will be. He drained his pint glass and crossed to the counter, to Madge smiling there.

"You never looked round all the way up from the station," she said, pulling her shoulder-straps up under her grey jumper and exposing the white rich flesh above her breasts.

"So it was you followed me, eh?" he said, sardonic.

"Why didn't you turn round?" she asked. "Did you know it was me? You knew someone was behind you, I could tell."

"I didn't turn round because I didn't want to look *back*," he said.

"And you mean to say you don't know how the Hebrew puts out the eyes of a goldfinch?" Freddy's aggrieved voice swirled up.

"Afraid of being homesick for your wife, eh?" she jeered.

He covered his eyes with his hand, tired out, and looked up at the vague sensual woman playing upon his instincts there like a gipsy on a zither.

"Not homesick," he said drily. "Death-sick."

"What d'you mean?" she said.

"Well, she was killed in a raid," he shouted.

He went up to the orderly room then, having forgotten to hand in his leave pass to the orderly corporal. The room was in the corner of an old warehouse. The building also housed the kitchen and the quartermaster's stores. About the high bare rooms with their rotten dry floors and musty walls rats galloped in the darkness; in the morning their dirt lay fresh on the mildewed sacks and the unit's cat stretched her white paws and got a weak and lazy thrill from sniffing it.

The orderly corporal was dozing over a Western novelette

from Woolworth's, hunched up in a pool of lamp-and-fire-light.

"Hallo, Taffy," he said. "Had a good leave?"

"Yes thanks," he replied. "Except for raids. Am I on duty to-morrow?"

"You're on duty to-night, I'm afraid," the orderly corporal replied with the unctuous mock-regret of one who enjoys detailing tired or refractory men for unexpected jobs. "Dave Finley had a cold on his chest this morning and didn't get out of bed. So they fetched him out on a stretcher and the M.O. gave him pneumonia pills before Dave could stop him; so he's got pneumonia now. You'll go on guard duty at midnight and at six hours."

"O.K."

He turned to go.

"Better get some sleep," said the orderly corporal, yawning noisily. "Hell! I'm browned off with this war."

The soldier yawned too, and laughed, and returned to the barrack room to lie down for a couple of hours. He rolled his blankets down on the floor and stretched out.

Old Ben and Fred were back, also, Ben fixing bachelor buttons into his best trousers and singing Nelly Dean comfortably to himself, Fred muttering by the stove. "There's some mean and hungry lads in this room," he said; "very hungry and mean. It's an awful nature, that. They'll borrow off you all right, but they won't lend you the turd off their soles. And always swanking in the mirror, and talking all the time, saying Yes, they can do the job easy. The fools! Whip 'em! Whip 'em!"

Ben was toasting bread on the point of his bayonet and boiling water in his billy. A tin of pilchards left over from tea was for them all.

"Come on, Taffy. Have a bellyful while you can," he said.

"No thanks," said the soldier, restless on his blankets. "I don't feel like food to-night, Ben, thanks."

"Ain't you never bin hungry?" Fred shouted angrily. "You don't know what food is, you youngsters don't."

"I've been without food," the soldier said, thinking of the '26 strike; and going without peas and chips in the chip shop by the town clock in college when a new book must be bought. But not now, when everything is free but freedom, and the doctor and dentist and cobbler send you no bills.

What survives I don't know, the soldier thought, rubbing his hot eyelids and shifting his legs on the spread-out blankets. What is it that survives?

He got up and buckled his battle order together, adjusting his straps, slipping the pull-through through his Enfield, polishing boots and buttons, tightening his helmet strap under his chin.

"There was a religious woman used to come to our house," Ben was saying, "and one day she said to me, sociable like, 'You're a Guinness drinker, aren't you, Mr Bryant?' and I says 'I am, mum,' and she says 'Well, can you tell me what's wrong with the ostrich on them advertisements?'"

The soldier went out to relieve the guard.

They were only twenty soldiers altogether, sent up here to guard a transmitting station hidden in the slopes of the Downs. A cushy job, safe as houses. There was a little stone shed, once used for sheep that were sick after lambing, in a chalky hollow on the forehead of the hill, which the guard used for sleeping in when they were off duty. Two hours on, four hours off, rain and sun and snow and stars. As the soldier toiled up the lane and across the high meadow to the shed, the milky moon came out from grey clouds and touched with lucid fingers the chopped branches piled in precise lengths at the foot of the wood. The pine trees moved softly as the moon touched their grey-green leaves, giving them a veil that looked like rainy snow, grey-white.

The lane running up through the wood shortened alarmingly in perspective. A star fell. So surprising, so swift and delicate, the sudden short curved fall and extinction of the tiny lit world. But over it the Plough still stayed, like something imperishable in man. He leant against the gate, dizzy and light-headed, waves of soft heat running into his head. He swallowed something warm and thick; spitting it out, he saw it was blood. He stayed there a little, resting, and then went on.

He went along the sandy lane, noticing as he always did the antique sculptures of sea and ice and rain, the smooth twisted flints, yellow and blue and mottled, lying in the white sand down which the water of winter scooped its way.

At the top of the lane was the lambing shed—guard room. He slipped quickly through the door to prevent any light escaping. There was gun-fire and the sound of bombs along the coast.

The sergeant of the guard was lying on a palliasse in front of the stove. He got up slowly, groaning lazily. "So you're back again, Taffy, are you?" he said, a grudge in his too hearty welcome. "Relieving Dave Finley, eh? He's swinging the lead, Dave is. I've a good mind to report him to the O.C. It's tough on you, going on night guard after a day's journey. Have a good leave, Taff?"

"Not bad," the soldier replied, "except for the raids. Raided us the first night I was home."

"It's a sod, everybody's getting it," the sergeant replied, yawning. "They dropped two dozen incendiaries in our fields in Lincs. last week."

He was drinking a billy can of cocoa which he had boiled on the fire, but he didn't offer any. He had weak blue eyes, a receding chin, fresh features of characterless good-looks, wavy hair carefully combed and brilliantined. He was always on edge against Taffy, distrusting him, perhaps envying him. He lived in terror of losing a stripe and in constant hunger to gain another promotion. He sucked and scraped the officers for this, zealously carrying out their orders with the finnicky short temper of a weak house-proud woman. He polished the barrack room floor and blackleaded the stove himself because the boys refused to do more than give the place a regulation lick. And he leaped at the chance of putting a man on the peg, he was always waiting to catch somebody cutting a church parade or nipping out of camp to meet a girl when he should be on duty. Yet he was mortally afraid of a quarrel, of unpopularity, and he was always jovial, glassily jovial, even to the Welsh boy whom he knew he couldn't deceive.

"Who am I to relieve on guard?" the soldier asked.

"Nobby Sherraton. He's patrolling the ridge."

"O.K." He slipped his rifle sling over his shoulder and put his helmet on. "You marching me out? Or shall I just go and see Nobby in?"

For once laziness overcame discretion.

"There's nobody about. Just go yourself," the sergeant said, smiling, posing now as the informal honest soldier. "I'll be seeing yer."

"Some day."

He left the hut and crossed the dry dead-white grass to the ridge where Nobby was on guard.

Nobby was his mate.

He had only been in the unit about a month. Before that he had been stationed just outside London and had done a lot of demolition and rescue work. He was from Mile End, and had roughed it. His hands and face showed that, his rough blackened hands, cigarette-stained, his red blotchy face with the bulbous nose, and the good blue eyes under tiny lids, and short scraggy lashes and brows. His hair was mousy and thin. He had been on the dole most of the time. He had been an unsuccessful boxer; he cleared out of that game when his brother, also a boxer, became punchdrunk and blind. He had plenty of tales of the Mosley faction. He was sometimes paid five bob to break up their meetings. He always took his five bob but he let the others do the breaking up. Who wants a black eye and a cut face for five bob? 'Tain't worth it. He rarely said anything about women. He didn't think much of lots of them; though like all Cockney youths he loved the "old lady," his mother. He wasn't married. No, sir.

He was a conscript. Naturally. He didn't believe in volunteering. And he didn't like the Army, its drills and orders and its insistence on a smart appearance. Smartness he disliked. Appearances he distrusted. Orders he resented. He was "wise" to things. No sucker.

Taffy felt a warm little feeling under his skin, relief more than anything else, to see Nobby again. He hadn't to pretend with Nobby. Fundamentally they shared the same humanity, the unspoken humanity of comradeship, of living together, sharing what they had, not afraid to borrow or talk or shut up. Or to leave each other and stroll off to satisfy the need for loneliness.

Nobby was surprised so much that he flung out his delight in a shout and a laugh and a wave of his arms. "Taffy, lad!" he said. "Back already, eh? Boy!" Then he became normal.

"Can't keep away from this bloody sannytorium for long, can we?" he grumbled.

Taffy stood looking at him, then at the ground, then he turned away and looked nowhere.

"What's wrong, kid?" Nobby said, his voice urgent and frightened, guessing. "Anything bad? Caught a packet, did you?" He said the last two phrases slowly, his voice afraid to ask.

"*I* didn't," Taffy said, his voice thin and unsteady. "*I* didn't. *I'm* all right. *I'm* healthy."

Nobby put his hand on his shoulder and turned him round. He looked at the white sucked-in face and the eyes looking nowhere.

"Did *she* get it?" and he too turned his head a little and swallowed. "She did," he said, neither asking a question nor making a statement. Something absolute, the two words he said.

Taffy sat down, stretched out. The grass was dead; white, wispy long grass; Nobby sat down, too.

"They came over about eight o'clock the first night," Taffy said. "The town hadn't had a real one before. I've told you we've only got apartments, the top rooms in an old couple's house. The old ones got hysterics, see, Nobby. And then they wouldn't do what I told them, get down the road to a shelter. They wouldn't go out into the street and they wouldn't stay where they were. 'My chickens,' the old man was blubbering all the time. He's got an allotment up on the voel, see? Gwyneth made them some tea. She was fine, she calmed them down. That was at the beginning, before the heavy stuff began. I went out the back to tackle the incendiaries. The boy next door was out there, too. He had a shovel and I fetched a saucepan. But it was freezing, and we couldn't dig the earth up quick enough. There were too many incendiaries. One fell on the roof and stuck in the troughing. The kid shinned up the pipe. It exploded in his face and he fell down. Twenty odd feet. I picked him up and both his eyes were out, see?"

He had gone back to the sing-song rhythm and the broad accent of his home, the back lanes and the back gardens. He was shuddering a little, and sick-white, sallow.

Nobby waited.

"I took him into his own house," he said, controlling his voice now, almost reflective. "I left him to his sister, poor kid. Then I went in to see if Gwyneth was all right. She was going to take the old couple down the road to the shelter. She had a mack on over her dressing gown. We'd intended going to bed early, see? So I said she was to stay in the shelter. But she wanted to come back. We could lie under the bed together.

"I wanted her back, too, somehow. Then some more incendiaries fell, so I said 'Do as you like' and went at them with a saucepan. I thought sure one would blow my eyes out. Well, she took them down. Carried their cat for them. Soon as she'd gone the heavy stuff came. Oh Christ!"

Nobby let him go on; better let him go on.

"It knocked me flat, dazed me for a bit. Then I got up and another one flattened me. It was trying to stop me, see, Nobby. I crawled out of the garden, but it was dark as hell and buildings all down, dust and piles of masonry. Then he dropped some more incendiaries and the fires started. I knew she must be somewhere, see? I knew she must be somewhere. I began pulling the masonry away with my hands, climbed on to the pile of it in the fire. I couldn't see with the smoke and I knew it wasn't any use, only I had to do it, see?

"Then suddenly the masonry fell downwards. The road was clear on the other side. I thought it was all right after all, then I thought she'd have reached the shelter . . . But she hadn't.

"I found her about twenty yards down the road.

"She wasn't dead. Her clothes were gone. And her hands. She put them over her face, I reckon.

"She couldn't speak, but I knew she knew it was me.

"I carried her back in my arms. Over the fallen house. The fire wasn't bad by then. Took her home, see, Nobby. Only the home was on fire. I wanted her to die all the time. I carried her over a mile through the streets. Fires and hoses and water. And she wouldn't die. When I got her to the clearing station I began to think she'd live.

"But they were only playing a game with me, see?"

He stood up and made himself calm.

"Well there it is." He rubbed his face with the palm of his hand, wiping the cold sweat off.

"I knew she was going to die. When they told me she was—I didn't feel anything, Nobby."

"But she died while they were messing her body about with their hands, see?

"And she never said anything. Never said anything to me.

"Not that it makes any difference, I suppose. We never did speak about those things much. Only, you know how it is, you want a word somehow. You want it to keep."

"Sure. I know," Nobby said.

"What's it all for, Nobby?" he said in a while. He looked so tired and beat. "I used to know what it was all about, but I can't understand it now."

"Aw, forget all about that," Nobby said. "You're here, aincher, now?"

He put his hands on his mate's shoulders and let him lean against him for a bit.

"I reckon you belong to each other for keeps, now," Nobby said.

"You believe that, Nobby?" he asked, slow and puzzled, but with a gathering force as his uncertainty came together.

"Yes. For you and 'er, I do. It wouldn't be true for me, or the sergeant in there, but for you two it is."

Taffy was still against his shoulder. Then slowly he straightened himself, moved back onto himself, and lifting his face he looked at the milky-white fields and the sentinel pines and the stars.

"I knew it was so, really," he said. "Only I was afraid I was fooling myself."

He smiled, and moved his feet, pressing on them with his whole weight as if testing them after an illness.

"I'm all right now, Nobby. Thank you, boy."

"I'll go, then," Nobby said. He slipped his rifle over his shoulder and as he moved off he hesitated, turned back, and touched his mate's arm lightly.

"Two's company, three's none," he said, and stumped off slowly to the lambing shed through the dead straw-grass.

And the soldier was left alone on the flat upland ridge.

Below him the valleys widened into rich arable lakes on which the moonlight and the mist lay like the skeins which spiders spin round their eggs. Beyond the pools another chain of downland lay across the valleys, and beyond those hills the coast. Over him, over the valleys, over the pinewoods, blue fingers came out of the earth and moved slanting across their quarters as the bombers droned in the stars over his head and swung round to attack the coastal city from inland. The sky over the coast was inflamed and violent, a soft blood-red.

The soldier was thinking of the day he received his calling up papers, just a year ago. Sitting on the dry-stone wall of his father's back garden with Gwyneth by him; his ragged little brother kneeling by the chicken-run, stuffing cabbage stumps through the netting for the hens to peck, and laughing and pulling the stumps out as the old hen made an angry jab; his father riddling the ashes and the ramshackle garden falling to bits, broken trellis and tottering fence; his mother washing her husband's flannel vest and drovers in the tub, white and vexed. He had taken Gwyneth's hand, and her hand had said, "In coming and in going you are mine; now, and for a little while longer; and then for ever."

But it was not her footsteps that followed him down the lane from the station.

Now over his head the darkness was in full leaf, drifted with the purity of pines, the calm and infinite darkness of an English night, with the stars moving in slow declension down the sky. And the warm scent of resin about him and of birds and of all small creatures moving in the loose mould in the ferns like fingers in velvet.

And the soldier stood under the pines, watching the night move down the valleys and lift itself seawards, hearing the sheep cough and farm-dogs restlessly barking in the farms. And farther still the violence growing in the sky till the coast was a turbulent thunder of fire and sickening explosions, and there was no darkness there at all, no sleep.

"My life belongs to the world," he said. "I will do what I can."

He moved along the spur and looked down at the snow-grey ever-green woods and the glinting roofs scattered over the rich land.

And down in the valleys the church bells began pealing, pealing, and he laughed like a lover, seeing his beloved.

ELIZABETH BOWEN
Careless Talk

*Elizabeth Bowen (1888–1973) was born
in Dublin, Ireland, and is one of the most
distinguished of modern writers. Her novel*
The Heat of the Day *(1949) and the
short pieces collected in* The Demon Lover
*(1945) are perhaps the best fictional record
we have of London during the Blitz.*

*The short story "Careless Talk", a rather
pointed piece about the war-experience of
the rich, was originally published in 1941.*

"**H**OW GOOD, HOW KIND, *HOW* thoughtful!" said Mary
Dash. "I can't tell you what a difference they will
make! And you brought them like this all the way from
Shepton Mallet in the train?" She looked helpless. "Where
do you think I had better put them?" This table's going to
be terribly small for four, and *think*, if one of Eric Farnham's
sweeping gesticulations . . ." She signalled a waiter. "I want
these put somewhere for me till the end of lunch. *Carefully*," she
added. "They are three eggs." The waiter bowed and took the
parcel away. "I do hope they will be all right," said Mrs Dash,
looking suspiciously after him. "But at least they'll be quieter
with the hats or something. I expect you see how crowded
everywhere is?"

Joanna looked round the restaurant and saw. The waiters
had to melt to get past the backs of the chairs; between the
net-curtained windows, drowsy with August rain, mirrors
reflected heads in smoke and electric light and the glitter
of buttons on uniforms. Every European tongue struck its
own note, with exclamatory English on top of all. As fast as
people went wading out people came wading in and so many

greeted each other that Joanna might easily have felt out of it. She had not lunched in London for four months and could not resist saying so to her friend.

"Honestly, you haven't deteriorated," said Mary. Herself, she was looking much as ever, with orchids pinned on to her last year's black. "Then how lucky I caught you just today! And I'm glad the others will be late. The only men one likes now are always late. While it's still just you and me, there's so much to say. I don't know what I've done without you, Joanna." She fixed enraptured eyes on Joanna's face. "For instance, can *you* tell me what's become of the Stones?"

"No, I'm afraid I can't. I . . ."

"And Edward and I were wondering if you could tell us about the Hickneys. I know they are somewhere in Dorset or Somerset. They're not by any chance anywhere near you? . . . Well, never mind. Tell me about yourself."

But at this point Eric Farnham joined them. "You don't know how sorry I am," he said. "I was kept. But you found the table all right. Well, Joanna, this couldn't be nicer, could it?"

"Isn't she looking radiant?" said Mary Dash. "We have been having the most tremendous talk."

Eric was now at the War Office, and Joanna, who had not seen him in uniform before, looked at him naïvely, twice. He reminded her of one of the pictures arrived at in that paper game when, by drawing on folded-over paper, you add to one kind of body an intriguingly wrong kind of head. He met her second look kindly through his shell-rimmed glasses. "How do you think the war is going?" she said.

"Oh, we mustn't ask him things" said Mary quickly. "He's doing most frightfully secret work." But this was lost on Eric, who was consulting his wristwatch. "As Ponsonby's later than I am," he said, "that probably means he'll be pretty late. Though God knows what they do at that Ministry. I propose not waiting for Ponsonby. First of all, what will you two drink?"

"Ponsonby?" Joanna said.

"No, I don't expect you'd know him. He's only been about lately," said Mary. "He's an expert; he's very interesting."

"He could be," said Eric. "He was at one time. But he's not

supposed to be interesting just now." The drinks came; then they got together over the *cartes du jour*. Ponsonby did not arrive till just after the potted shrimps. "This is dreadful," he said. "I do hope you'll forgive me. But things keep on happening, you know." He nodded rapidly round to several tables, then dropped exhausted into his place. "Eat?" he said. "Oh, really, anything—shrimps. After that, whatever you're all doing."

"Well, Mary's for grouse," said Eric. Ponsonby, after an instant of concentration, said, "In that case, grouse will do me fine."

"Now you must talk to Joanna," said Mary Dash. "She's just brought me three eggs from the country and she's longing to know about everything."

Ponsonby gave Joanna a keen, considering look. "Is it true," he said, "that in the country there are no cigarettes at all?"

"I believe there are sometimes some. But I don't—"

"There are. Then that alters everything," said Ponsonby. "How lucky you are!"

"I got my hundred this morning," said Eric, "from my regular man. But those will have to last me to Saturday. I can't seem to cut down, somehow. Mary, have you cut down?"

"I've got my own, if that's what you mean," said she. "I just got twenty out of my hairdresser." She raised her shilling-size portion of butter from its large bed of ice and spread it tenderly over her piece of toast. "Now, what is your news?" she said. "Not that I'm asking anything, of course."

"I don't think anything's happened to me," said Eric, "or that anything else has happened that you wouldn't know about. When I say happened I mean *happened*, of course. I went out of London for one night; everywhere outside London seemed to me very full. I must say I was glad to be home again." He unlocked his chair from the chair behind him, looked at the grouse on his plate, then took up his knife and fork.

"Eric," said Mary, after a minute, "the waiter's trying to tell you there's no more of that wine *en carafe*."

"Bring it in a bottle then. I wonder how much longer—"

"Oh, my dear, so do *I*," said Mary. "One daren't think about that. Where we were dining last night they already had several numbers scratched off the wine list. Which reminds me. Edward sent you his love."

"Oh, how *is* Edward?" Joanna said. "What is he doing?"

"Well, I'm not strictly supposed to say. By the way, Eric, I asked Joanna, and she doesn't know where the Stones *or* the Hickneys are."

"In the case of the Hickneys, I don't know that it matters."

"Oh, don't be inhuman. You know you're not!"

"I must say," said Eric, raising his voice firmly, "I do like London now a lot of those people have gone. Not *you*, Joanna; we all miss you very much. Why don't you come back? You've no idea how nice it is."

Joanna, colouring slightly, said, "I've got no place left to come back to. Belmont Square—"

"Oh, my Lord, yes," he said. "I did hear about your house. I was so sorry. Completely? . . . Still, you don't want a house, you know. None of us live in houses. You could move in on someone. Sylvia has moved in on Mona—"

"That's not a good example," said Mary quickly. "Mona moved out almost at once and moved in on Isobel, but the worst of that is that now Isobel wants her husband back, and meanwhile Sylvia's taken up with a young man, so Mona can't move back to her own flat. But what would make it difficult for Joanna is having taken on all those hens. Haven't you?"

"Yes, and I have evacuees—"

"But we won't talk about those, will we?" said Mary quickly. "Any more than you would want to hear about bombs. I think one great rule is never to bore each other. Eric, *what's* that you are saying to Ponsonby?"

Eric and Ponsonby had seized the occasion to exchange a few rapid remarks. They stopped immediately. "It was quite boring," Ponsonby explained.

"I don't believe you," said Mary. "These days everything's frightfully interesting. Joanna, you must be feeling completely dazed. Will everyone ask you things when you get home?"

"The worst of the country these days," said Joanna, "is everyone gets so wrapped up in their own affairs."

"Still, surely they must want to know about us? I suppose London is too much the opposite," said Mary. "One lives in a perfect whirl of ideas. Ponsonby, who was that man I saw you with at the Meunière? I was certain I knew his face."

"That was a chap called Odgers. Perhaps he reminded you of somebody else? We were talking shop. I think that's a nice place, don't you? I always think they do veal well. That reminds me, Eric. Was your friend the other evening a Pole, or what?"

"The fact is I hardly know him," said Eric. "I'm never quite sure of his name myself. He's a Pole all right, but Poles aren't really my thing. He was quite interesting, as a matter of fact; he had quite a line of his own on various things. Oh, well, it was nothing particular . . . No, I can't do you Poles, Mary. Warrington's really the man for Poles."

"I know he is, but he keeps them all up his sleeve. You do know about Edward and the Free French? I hope it didn't matter my having told you that, but Edward took it for granted that you already knew."

Ponsonby recoiled from his wristwatch. "Good heavens," he said, "it *can't* be as late as this? If it is, there's someone waiting for me."

"Look," said Eric, "I'll hurry on coffee."

"You know," Mary added anxiously, "you really can't concentrate without your coffee. Though I know we mustn't be difficult. It's like this all the time," she said to Joanna. "Have *you* got to hurry, Eric?"

"I needn't exactly hurry. I just ought to keep an eye on the time."

"I'll do that for you," Mary said. "I'd love to. You see you've hardly had a word with Joanna, and she's wanting so much to catch up with life. I tell you one thing that *is* worrying me: that waiter I gave Joanna's lovely eggs to hasn't been near this table again. Do you think I put temptation right in his way? Because, do you know, all the time we've been talking I've been thinking up a new omelette I want to make. One's mind gets like that these days," she said to Joanna. "One seems able to think of twenty things at one time. Eric, do you think you could flag the *maître d'hôtel*? I don't know how I'd feel if I lost three eggs."

C.S. FORESTER
An Egg for the Major

*The British writer Cecil Scott Forester
(1899–1966) was born in Cairo and studied
medicine before turning to full-time writing
after the success of his first novel* Payment
Deferred *(1926). Although most famous
for his Napoleonic sea-sagas featuring Captain Horatio Hornblower, he wrote many
types of military and adventure fiction.
Among his best known novels are* The
Ship *(1943) and* The African Queen
*(1935), which was later made into a classic
film by John Huston.*

"An Egg for the Major" is from 1944.

T HE MAJOR COMMANDING THE SQUADRON of light tanks
was just as uncomfortable as he had been for a number
of days. For the officer commanding a light tank there is a
seat provided, a sort of steel piano stool, but, in the opinion
of the major, it had been designed for men of a physique that
has no counterpart on earth. If one sat on it in the normal
way, with the part of one which Nature provides for sitting
on on the stool, one's knees bumped most uncomfortably on
the steel wall in front. And contrariwise, if one hitched oneself
back and sat on one's thighs, not only was the circulation
interfered with to an extent which led to cramps but also
the back of one's head was sore with being bumped against
the wall of the turret behind. Especially when the tank was
rolling over the desert, lurching and bumping from ridge to
ridge; on a road one could look after oneself, but it was weeks
and weeks since the major had set eyes on a road.

He left off thinking about the sort of shape a man should be who has to pass his days in a light tank, and gave the order for the tank to stop. He climbed out through the steel door with his compass to take a fresh bearing. Out in the desert here an army had to navigate like a ship at sea, with the additional difficulty that inside the steel walls, with the spark coils to complicate matters, a compass was no use at all. The only thing to do was to get out of the tank, carry one's compass well away from its influence, and look over the featureless landscape and mark some patch of scrub, some minor rise in the ground, on which one could direct one's course. He walked stiffly away from the tank, laid the compass level and stared forward. This was perhaps the five-hundredth time he had done this, and he had learned by long experience the difficulties to be anticipated. There was never anything satisfactory directly ahead on which he could direct his course. There would be fine landmarks out to the right or left where they were no use to him, but nothing straight ahead. He would have to be content with some second best, the edge of that yellow patch on the brown, and he knew quite well that it would appear quite different when he got back into the tank again. Furthermore, it would appear more different still when they had traveled a little way toward it—there had been times long ago, when the desert was new to him, when he had found at a halt that he was more than ninety degrees off his course. He was far more experienced now; five months of desultory warfare and now this last tremendous march across the desert had accustomed him to the difficulties.

Experience taught him to empty his mind of the hundreds of previous landscapes which he had memorized, to concentrate on this one, to note that yellow patch whose edge would be his guiding mark for the next ten miles, and to look back and absorb the appearance of the country in that direction as well. Then he went back to the tank, decided against the piano stool, slammed the door shut, and climbed up onto the roof before giving the word to start. On the roof he could lie on the unyielding steel to the detriment of hip and elbow, anchoring himself into position by locking his toe round the muzzle of the machine gun below him. After a time his leg would go to sleep at about the same time that his hip could bear it no longer; then he would have to change over; three changes—two turns with each foot and hip—would be as much as he could stand, and then it would be time to take a fresh bearing and go back to the piano stool and the other problem of which part to sit on.

He lounged on the steel roof while the tank pitched and rolled under him; it was as well to keep that foot firmly locked below the gun muzzle to save himself from being pitched off. It had happened to him sometimes; everything had happened to him at one time or another. The wind today was from ahead, which was a mercy; a gentle following wind meant that the dust of their progress kept pace with them and suffocated him. He looked away to the left and the right, and he could see a long line of great plumes of dust keeping pace with him as the other tanks of the squadron plowed their way across the desert. The major was an unimaginative man, but that spectacle never failed to move him. That long line of dust plumes sweeping across the desert had menace and sinister beauty about it. There were the high yellow clouds, and at the base of each a little dot, a nucleus, as it were, sometimes concealed from view by the inequalities of the ground, and every cloud indicated the presence of one of the tanks of his squadron. There were other clouds behind, when the major turned his gaze that way; they showed where the stragglers were trying to regain their places in the line after some necessary halt. The ones farthest back were the ones who had had track trouble or engine trouble. There could be no waiting for them, not in the face of the orders which the wireless brought in, insisting on the utmost speed in this dash across the desert.

Already in the major's mind the total of days already consumed in the march was a little vague. If he set his mind to it, he could have worked it out, but he felt as if he had done nothing all his life except lead this squadron across the desert. Something enormous and of vital importance was happening to the north, he knew—Sidi Barrani and Tobruk had fallen, but his command had been plucked out of that attack and sent off on this wide flanking sweep, and were already a little in the dark about the situation. These Italian maps were of no use at all. They showed things which simply did not exist—he could swear to that from bitter experience—and in consequence, the major did not know within twenty miles where he was. But somewhere ahead of him there was the sea, across the great hump of Northern Africa which he was traversing, and beside the sea ran the great road which Mussolini had built, and he knew he had only to arrive on that road to start making things unpleasant for the Italians. What the situation would be when he did arrive he could not imagine in the least, but the major had absorbed the philosophy of the desert, and left that problem to be solved when it arose, wasting no mental effort on hypothetical cases which probably would have no resemblance to the reality he would encounter sooner or later.

The squadron was moving on a wide front, impressive on account of the distant plumes of dust, but even so, the width of the front was nothing compared with the immensity of the desert. They had marched five hundred miles so far, and a thousand miles to the south of them the desert extended as far as the plains of the Sudan. Sometimes the major would allow his imagination to think about these distances, but more often he thought about eggs. Tinned beef and biscuits, day after day, for more days than he could count, had had their effect. Nearly every idle thought that passed through his mind was busy with food. Sometimes he thought about kippers and haddock, sometimes about the green vegetables he had refused to eat as a little boy, but mostly he thought about eggs—boiled eggs, fried eggs, scrambled eggs—mostly boiled eggs. The lucky devils who were doing the fighting in the north were in among the villages now which Mussolini had peopled with so much effort; they would have a hen or two for certain, and a hen meant an egg. A boiled egg. For a day or two, eggs had formed a staple topic of conversation when he squatted at mealtimes with the gunner and the driver, until the major had detected a certain forbearing weariness mingled with the politeness with which his crew had received his remarks about eggs. Then he had left off talking about them; in this new kind of war, majors had to be careful not to become old bores in the eyes of the privates with whom they lived. But not being able to talk about them made him think about them all the more. The major swallowed hard in choking dust.

The sun was now right ahead of him, and low toward the horizon; the sky around it was already taking up the colors of the desert sunset, and the brassy blue overhead was miraculously blending into red and orange. To the major that only meant that the day's march was drawing to a close. Sunsets came every day, and eggs came only once a year, seemingly.

When darkness came, they halted; each tank where it happened to find itself, save for the outposts pushed forward in case the Italians should, incredibly, be somewhere near and should have the hardihood to attempt operations in the dark. The driver and the gunner came crawling out of the tank, dizzy with petrol fumes and stiff with fatigue, still a little deaf with the insensate din which had assailed their ears for the whole day. The most immediate duty was to service the tank and have it all ready for prolonged action again, but before they did that they washed their mouths round with a little of the precious water taken from the can which had ridden with them in the tank all day. It was at blood heat, and it tasted of the inside of a tank—indescribably, that is to say. But it was precious, all the same. There was always the possibility that their ration of water would not come up from the rear; and if it did, there was also the chance that there had been so much loss in the radiators during the day that no water could be spared for the men.

Once, long back, there had been a heavenly time when the day's ration had been a gallon a head a day. That had been marvelous, for a man could do simply anything with a gallon a day; he could shave, wash his face, sometimes even spare a little to wash off the irritating dust from his body. But the ration, now that they were so far from the base, was half a gallon, and a man, after a day in a tank, could drink half a gallon at a single draught if he were foolish enough to do so. Half a gallon meant only just enough water to keep thirst from coming to close quarters; only the most fussy among the men would spare a cupful for shaving, and the days when the radiators had been extra thirsty, so that the men's rations were cut in half, were days of torment.

The major and the gunner and the driver settled down in the desert for their supper. Long habit had blunted the surprise the major had once felt at finding himself, a field officer, squatting in the dust with a couple of privates, and, fortunately, long habit had done the same for the privates. Before this campaign opened they would have been tongue-tied and awkward at his presence. It had not been easy to reach adjustment, but they had succeeded—as witness the way in which, without saying a word, they had caused him to leave off talking about eggs. He was still "sir" to them, but almost the only other way in which his rank was noticeable in their personal relationships was that the two privates both suspected the major of being the guilty party in the matter of the loss of one of their three enameled mugs. They had not ventured openly to accuse him, and he remained in ignorance of their suspicions, taking it for granted that the gunner—a scatterbrained fellow—had been at fault in the matter.

It was an infernal nuisance, being short of a mug; two mugs among three of them called for a whole lot of organization, especially in the morning, when they had to clean their teeth, and sometimes to shave and sometimes to make tea—and the gunner liked his strong, and the driver liked his weak, and the major was the only one who did not want sugar in it. If ever the three of them were to quarrel, the major knew it would be over some difficulty arising out of the loss of the mug. Yet he did not see nowadays anything odd about a major worrying over the prospect of a disagreement with a couple of privates over an enameled mug.

And tonight he was additionally unlucky, because the rations for the day were a tinned meat and vegetable concoction that he particularly disliked. But the gunner and the driver were loud in their delight when they discovered what fate had brought them tonight. They ate noisily and appreciatively, while the major squatting beside them made only the merest pretense of eating and allowed his thoughts to stray back to memories of dinner at the Berkeley and the Gargantuan lunches at Simpson's in the Strand. And also of eggs.

It was dark now, and cold—before supper was over the major had to reach out for a blanket and wrap it round his shoulders as the treacherous desert wind blew chilly. The stars were out, but there was no moon yet and the darkness was impenetrable. There was nothing to do now except sleep. The major chose himself a spot where the scrub grew not too thickly, and where the rock did not jut entirely through the thin skin of earth which overlaid it. He spread his blankets over his fleabag and crawled in with the dexterity of long practice without disturbing the arrangement. The bit of tarpaulin stretched from the side of the tank to the earth kept off the dew, if there should be any, and the joints that had suffered on the steel piano stool and on the steel roof snuggled gratefully against the more kindly contact of the earth. And long habit was a help.

He awoke in the middle of the night with a shattering roar in his very ear. The driver had his own system of keeping his beloved motor warm enough to start. He slept only under two blankets, and when the cold awoke him he knew that it was necessary to warm up the motor. He would crawl out of bed, start it up, allow it to run for five minutes, and then switch it off. That meant that the light tank was always ready for instant action, but the major had never been able to acquire the habit of sleeping through the din of the motor. The only habit he had been able to form was that of cursing to himself at the driver, feebly, half awake, and then of turning over and completing his night's sleep. The gunner, on the other hand, slept stolidly through the whole racket, snoring away stubbornly—the major suspected him of dreaming about eggs.

Before dawn they were up and doing. Two inches of sand in the bottom of a petrol tin made an admirable wick; petrol soaked into it burned with an almost clear flame and heated the water for their tea in a flash. They had grown cunning lately and brushed their teeth after breakfast, using the remains of the tea for the purpose; that gave them an additional two swallows of water apiece to drink at the midmorning halt for filling up. The motor started, shatteringly noisy as usual. Then they were off, the long line of tanks heaving and rolling over the desert, the familiar plumes of dust trailing behind them, the familiar weary ache beginning to grow in the joints of the major as he settled himself on the piano stool.

*　　　*　　　*

The major's calculation of his position was a hazy one, and through no fault of his own. Erratic compasses, ridiculous Italian maps and strict wireless silence combined, after a march hundreds of miles long, to make it very doubtful where they were. But the major was philosophic about it. British light tanks were capable of fighting almost anything in Africa, and what they could not fight they could run away from; they had learned that lesson in innumerable untold skirmishes in the old days of the beginning of the war. The major felt ready for anything that might happen, as he stared out through the slit of the conning tower across the yellowish brown plain.

Yet all the same it is doubtful if he was really ready for the sight that met his eyes. The tank came lurching and rolling up a sharp slope. It heaved itself over the crest—the note of the motor changing ever so little as the gradient altered—and a new landscape was presented to the major's eyes.

First of all he saw the sea, the blue sea, the wonderful blue sea, flecked with white. The major wriggled on the piano stool and yelled involuntarily at the top of his voice when he saw it. That marvelous horizon, that beautiful color, that new-found sense of achievement and freedom—they were simply intoxicating. The driver and the gunner were as intoxicated as he was, screwing their necks round to grin at him, the fluffy immature beard of the gunner wagging on his chin.

And then they cleared the next curve of the crest, and the major saw the road, that long coastal road for the construction of which Mussolini had poured out so much treasure. The major had expected to see it from the moment when he had seen the sea—in fact, he was craning his neck for a sight of it. But he was not ready for the rest of what he saw. For twenty miles the road was black with the fleeing Italian army—an enormous column of men and vehicles, jamming the road from side to side, hastening westward—Bergenzoli's army escaping from Bengasi and from the wrath of the English behind them. From a point nearly ahead of them away off to the right stretched that hurrying column. From his point of vantage the major could see it looping like some monstrous water snake along the curves of the road. Now he knew why his squadron had been hurled across the desert at such a frantic speed. It had been planned to cut off Bergenzoli's retreat, and the object had been achieved, with no more than ten minutes to spare.

Those ten minutes were only to spare if the major did the right thing on the instant. But twenty years of training had prepared the major for that very purpose. He was still a hussar, even though his squadron's horses had long ago been replaced by light tanks. His mental reactions were instantaneous; there was no need to stop and ponder the situation. The trained tactical eye took in the lie of the land even while he was shouting into the wireless transmitter the vital information that he was ahead of the Italians. He saw the road and the ridge beside it, and the moment that the information had been acknowledged he was speaking again, quietly already, giving his orders to the squadron. The long line of tanks wheeled and swooped down upon the road.

So close was the race that they were barely in position before the head of the column was up to them. An hour later and the Italians would have been able to post a flank guard behind whose shelter most of them would have been able to slip away. As it was, the major just had time to give his orders to his two troops as the head of the Italian column came down upon them.

The tanks bucked themselves into position and the machine guns spoke out, pouring their fire into the trucks packed with infantry which were so recklessly coming down upon them. It was slaughter, the dire punishment of a harebrained attack. The major watched the trucks swerve off the road, saw the startled infantry come tumbling out while the machine-gun fire cut swaths through them. Truck piled upon truck. The poor devils in them were deserving of pity. At one moment they had thought themselves safe, rolling along a good road back to Tripoli, and then the next these gray monsters had come darting out of the desert across their path, spraying death.

With the checking of the head of the column, confusion spread up the road. The major could see movement dying away as each successive section bumped up against the one ahead; the sudden outburst of firing, taking everyone by surprise, was rousing panic among the weaker individuals.

So much the better. From the major's point of view, there could not be too much panic. Somewhere up that column there were field guns and there were heavy tanks, and to neither of them could he offer any real resistance. The more confusion there was in the column, the longer would it take to extricate these, the only weapons that could clear its path. Time was of the utmost importance; he turned and looked back over his shoulder at where the sun was dipping toward the horizon and the blue sea. This time, by some curious chance, his mind was in a condition to take in the fact that the approaching sunset would be red and lurid. He was smiling grimly as he turned back to his work.

Someone over there was trying to urge the unarmored infantry to the attack—to certain death, in other words, in the face of the two grim little groups of tanks that opposed them. Some of them came forward to the certain death too. And the sun was nearer the horizon.

Farther back down the column frantic officers were clearing a path for the artillery. There were eddies and swirls in the mass. Trucks were being heaved off the road as the guns came through. The major took his glasses from his eyes and gave another order. The tanks curvetted and wheeled, and next moment they had a ridge of solid earth between them and the guns. There was a dreary wait—the major had time for another glance at the sun sinking in a reddened sky—before the shells began to come over. Then the major could smile; they were shrieking over the crest and a good two yards above his head before they buried themselves in the ridge behind him. But there was infantry creeping forward again; there was still the chance that he might be forced sideways out of his position and have to leave a gap through which the mob might escape. He looked at the sun again, and then out to his right, the direction from which he had come, and he felt a glow of relief. The rest of the advance guard was coming—a battalion of motorized infantry with their battery of antitank guns. Now they had a chance. But where were the cruiser tanks, the only weapons in Africa that could stop the heavy tanks when they should be able to make their way out of the column?

It had been touch and go in the first place, when the light

tanks had cut off the retreat of the column. It was touch and go now, when the light tanks and five hundred British soldiers were trying to stop the advance of fifty thousand Italians. But night was close at hand. Darkness blinded the Italian gunners and paralyzed the efforts being made to clear the road for the heavy tanks. The major neatly withdrew his tanks over one more ridge, in case of a night attack—in all his extensive experience with the Italians they had never ventured a single operation in darkness—and went round his squadron to see that they were as well prepared as might be for a battle on the morrow.

The major always remembers that night as one when there was nothing he found it necessary to do. The British soldier was on the offensive. The veriest fool could see victory just ahead, victory of a crushing type, nothing less than annihilation of the enemy, if only the force of which the squadron formed a part could hold back Bergenzoli until pressure on his rear and the arrival of help to themselves should convince Bergenzoli of the hopelessness of his position. With victory depending on the proper lubrication of their tanks, on their precautions against surprise, they needed no telling, no inspection, to make them do their duty. The major was not an imaginative man, but something in his imagination was touched that night when he talked to his men. The final destruction of the Italians was what they had in mind; the fact that they would be opposed tomorrow by odds of a hundred to one, and that there was more chance of their being dead by evening than alive, did not alter their attitude in the least.

The major walked from one little group to another; the once khaki overalls worn by everyone, even himself, had been bleached almost white by exposure, and the oil stains somehow did not darken them in a bad light, so that the men he spoke to showed up as ghostly figures in the darkness. There was laughter in the voices of the ghosts he spoke to—laughter and delight in the imminent prospect of victory. And in the stillness of the desert night they could hear, across two valleys, the din of the heavy Italian tanks roaring up to take up positions for the charge that would try to clear the way for the Italians next day. That was the lullaby the major heard as he stretched out in the desert to try to snatch a couple of hours' sleep, side by side with the driver and the gunner. Only in the grave did officers and men sleep side by side until this war came.

Dawn—the first faint light that precedes dawn—showed, looming over the farther crest, the big Italian tanks which had been somehow forced forward during the night along the tangled column. They came forward ponderously, with fifty thousand men behind them, and in front of them there was only a thread of infantry, a single battery, a squadron of light tanks whose armor was only fit to keep out rifle bullets. It was as if the picadors and the matadors in the bull ring had to fight, not a single bull but a whole herd of bulls, all charging in the madness of desperation.

There is an art in the playing of a charging bull, even in the handling of a whole herd. Through a long and weary day, that was just what the major's squadron and the rest of the British force succeeded in doing. Since time immemorial—from Alexander to Hitler—it has been the fate of advance guards to be sacrificed to gain time for the maneuver of the main body, to be used to pin the enemy to the ground, so that his flank can be safely assailed. Only troops of the highest discipline and training can be trusted to fulfill such a mission, however. The Italian tanks which were recklessly handled were lured into the fire of the battery; the timid ones were prevailed upon to procrastinate. The slow retreat of the British force was over ground marked with crippled tanks and littered with Italian dead; and there were British dead there, too, and knocked-out British guns, and burned-out British tanks.

It was an exhausted British force that still confronted the Italians. The line had shrunk, so that on its left flank, toward the sea, there was an open gap through which, among the sand dunes, some of the Italians were beginning to dribble on foot, creeping along the edge of the sea in the wild hope of escaping captivity. And then, at that last moment, came the decisive blow. At least to us here it seemed the last moment. That can only be a guess—no one can dare say that the British had reached the end of their resistance. But it was at that moment, when British riflemen were fighting hard to protect their headquarters, when two thirds of the British guns were out of action, when the major's squadron was reduced to three tanks, that help arrived. From out of the desert there came a sweeping line of huge British cruiser tanks. They came charging down on the Italian flank, enormous, invulnerable and terrifying. It is impossible to guess at the miracle of organization, at the prodigy of hard work, which had brought these monstrous things across sands which had scarcely even been trodden by camels.

From out of the desert they came, wreathed in dust, spouting fire, charging down upon the tangled mass of the Italian army pent back behind the thin dam of the British line. The Italian tanks wheeled to meet them, and then and there the battle was fought out, tank to tank, under the brazen sky, over the sand where the dead already lay. The dust clouds wrapped them round, dimming the bright flames—visible even in the sunshine—which streamed from the wrecked tanks, the Viking pyres of their slain crews.

When it was over, the whole battle was finished. There was no fight left in the Italians. The desert had already vomited out three fierce attacks—first the major's light tanks, then the infantry, and last the cruiser tanks, and no one could guess what next would come forth. And from the rear came the news that the pursuing British were pressing on the rear guard; at any moment the sea might bring its quota of death, should the British ships find a channel through the sandbanks which would bring their guns within range of the huddled army. Front, rear and both flanks were open to attack, and overhead the air force was about to strike. Nor was that all. Thirst was assailing them, those unhappy fifty thousand men massed without a single well within reach. There was nothing for it but surrender.

The major watched the fifty thousand men yield up their arms; he knew that he was witness to one of the great victories of history, and he was pleased about it. Through the dreadful fatigue that was overwhelming him he also was aware that he had played a vital part in the gaining of that victory, and that somewhere in the future there would be mentions in dispatches and decorations. But his eyelids were heavy and his shoulders drooping.

Then came the gunner; his faded, oil-stained overalls made more shocking than ever by the stains of the blood of the wounded driver, and that horribly fluffy yellow beard of his, like the down on a baby chick, offending the sunlight. Now that they had reached the sea, the distillation plants would supply them with a sufficiency of water and that beard could be shaved off. But the gunner was grinning all over his face, his blue eyes nearly lost in the wrinkles round them, lines carved by the blinding light of the desert. The gunner had heard a cock crowing down beside the solitary white farmhouse toward the sea on the edge of the battlefield, and he had walked there and back on stiff legs. The gunner held out a big fist before the major, and opened the fingers like a man doing a conjuring trick. In his hand was an egg.

LOTHAR-GÜNTHER BUCHHEIM
The Boat

Lothar-Günther Buchheim (1921–) was born in Weimar, Germany. When World War II broke out he joined the Kriegsmarine, and served on destroyers, minesweepers and U-boats.

Below is an excerpt from U-Boat *(1974), Buchheim's novel about the long patrol of U-A, a VIIC-type submarine, in the North Atlantic in 1943. The book was turned into a cult film* The Boat *(Das Boot) by Wolfgang Petersen.*

A MAST, NO DOUBT ABOUT IT, but a mast without an accompanying plume of smoke. Just a single hairline of a mast? Strain my eyes as I would, nothing showed but this pig's bristle which seemed to climb above the skyline as I watched.

Every merchantman trailed a plume of smoke which betrayed her presence long before her masts showed above the horizon. Ergo, this was no merchantman.

A minute went by. I kept my eyes glued to the pig's bristle and felt my throat throb with mounting excitement.

All doubt had vanished. The mast was growing steadily taller, so the destroyer must be heading our way. There was no possibility of evasion on the surface, not with our engines.

"They must have spotted us—damn and blast!" The Captain hardly raised his voice as he gave the alarm.

I reached the upper lid in a single bound. My boots hit the deck-plates with a metallic thud. The Captain gave the order to open all main vents even before he had fully secured the upper lid.

"Periscope depth," he called down to the control-room. The Chief restored trim. The needle of the depth-gauge halted, then travelled slowly back across the dial. Dufte stood panting beside me in his wet oilskins. Zeitler and Böckstiegel, the two planesmen, were seated at their push-button controls, intently watching the water-level in the Papenberg. The first lieutenant inclined his head and let the rainwater drip off the brim of his sou'wester.

Nobody spoke. The only sound was a gentle electric hum which seemed to come from behind padded doors.

The silence was eventually broken by the Captain's voice. "Depth?"

"Twenty metres," reported the Chief.

"Periscope depth."

The water in the Papenberg slowly sank. The submarine rose until the periscope broke surface.

We were not levelled off yet, so the Chief pumped aft from the forward trimming tank. *U-A* gradually returned to the horizontal but did not lie still. The waves nudged her in all directions, heaving, pulling, shoving. Periscope observation would be difficult.

I was listening for the Captain's voice when the hydrophone operator reported propeller noises on the starboard beam.

I passed the report to the conning-tower.

"Very good," replied the Captain. Then, just as drily: "Action stations."

The hydrophone operator was leaning out of his cubby-hole into the passage. His unseeing eyes were dilated. Seen from the front, his face was a flat mask with two holes for a nose. Apart from the Captain, he was the only man aboard whose senses extended to the world outside our steel shell: the Captain could see the enemy, the hydrophone operator could hear him. The rest of us were blind and deaf. "Propeller noises increasing," he reported. "Drawing slowly aft."

The Captain's voice was muted. "Flood tubes 1 to 4."

I thought so. The Old Man planned to take on the destroyer—he had his sights on a red pennant. He needed a destroyer to complete his collection, I knew it as soon as I heard him order us to periscope depth.

Another order from the conning-tower: "Captain to control-room—Chief, accurate depth, please."

A tall order, in this sea. The muscles in the Chief's lean face tautened and relaxed spasmodically as though his jaws were busy with chewing-gum. Woe to him if the boat rose too far, if she broke surface and betrayed us to the enemy . . .

The Captain was sitting astride his saddle in the cramped space between the periscope shaft and the conning-tower casing, head clamped to the rubber eyepieces and splayed thighs gripping the massive shaft. His feet rested on the pedals which enabled him to rotate the shaft swiftly and silently through 360 degrees, saddle and all. His right hand gripped the lever which extended and retracted it.

The periscope motor hummed. He had slightly withdrawn the periscope head so as to keep it as close to the surface as he possibly could.

The Chief was standing utterly motionless behind the two look-outs, who were now operating the hydroplanes. His eyes, too, were fixed on the Papenberg. The column of water slowly rose and fell, each rise and fall corresponding to the height of the waves on the surface.

Subdued murmurs. The hum of the periscope motor sounded as if it had been passed through a fine filter. It started, stopped, started again. The Captain was extending the look-stick for seconds at a time, then letting the sea wash over it. The destroyer must be quite close now.

"Flood No. 5 tube," came a whisper from above.

The order was quietly passed to the stern torpedo compartment. We were in action.

I sat down on the sill of the bulkhead door. A whispered report from aft: "No. 5 tube ready, bow-cap shut."

It was extremely difficult to hit a destroyer, with its shallow draught and high degree of manoeuvrability. Once hit, however, it vanished like a puff of thistledown. An explosion, a geyser of water and fragmented steel, and finis—nothing remained.

The Captain's steady voice came from above. "Open bow-caps, tubes 1 and 2. Enemy speed fifteen. Angle on the bow, four zero left. Range one thousand."

The second lieutenant set the values on the calculator. The fore-ends reported bow-caps open. The first lieutenant passed the word, quietly but distinctly: "Tubes 1 and 2 ready, sir."

With his hand on the firing-lever, the Captain waited for the enemy to cross the hairline.

I longed to see.

Silence lent wings to my imagination. Baneful pictures took shape: a British destroyer bearing down on us at point-blank range. A ship's bow with its creaming bow-wave—a bird of prey with a white bone in its beak—loomed over us, about to ram. Dilated eyes, a rending of metal, jagged steel plates, a torrent of green water pouring into our torn hull.

The Captain's voice rang out, sharp as a whiplash. "Flood Q. Sixty metres. Shut all bow-caps."

The Chief, a fraction of a second later: "Planes hard-a-dive, full ahead both. All hands forward!"

A babble of voices. I flung myself to one side, feet scrabbling the deck-plates. The first man dived through the after bulkhead, tripped, regained his footing and hurried on forward past the wireless office at a crouching run.

I caught a series of wide-eyed inquiring looks as more men passed me, slipping and stumbling. Two bottles of fruit-juice rolled down the passage from the POs' mess and smashed against the control-room bulkhead.

All hydroplanes were still hard-a-dive. The submarine was already at a steep bow-down angle, but still the men kept coming. They slid through the tilted control-room like skiers. One of them swore sibilantly as he fell headlong.

Only the engine-room watch remained aft now. I lost my footing but managed to grab the shaft of the search periscope just in time. The sausages seemed to be almost parallel with the deckhead. I heard the Captain's voice superimposed on a slither and thud of boots: "Any time now." It sounded quite casual, like a passing remark.

He climbed slowly down the ladder with the exaggerated

deliberation of someone demonstrating a drill movement, ascended the incline and propped one buttock on the chart-stowage. His right hand encircled a pipe for support.

The Chief brought us slowly up by the head and ordered all hands back to diving stations. The men who had hurried forward worked their way aft again, hand over hand.

Using the sausages as a rough-and-ready inclinometer, I estimated that we were still thirty degrees bow-down.

RRABUMM! RRUMM! RRUMM!

I was jolted by three resounding blows like axe-strokes. Half-stunned, I heard a muffled roar. Icy fingers palpated my heart. What was the roaring sound? Then I realized: it was water rushing back into the submarine cavities created by the explosions.

Two more colossal thuds.

The control-room PO had retracted his head like a tortoise. The new control-room hand, the Vicar, swayed and clung to the chart-table.

Another detonation, louder than the rest.

The lights went out, leaving us in Stygian gloom.

"Secondary lighting's failed!" I heard someone shout.

The Chief's orders seemed to come from far away. Cones of torch light drilled yellowish holes in the darkness. A voice demanded fuses. The captains of stations made their reports by voice-pipe: "Fore-ends well."—"Motor-room well."—"Engine-room well."

"No leaks reported, sir," said the quartermaster. His voice sounded quite as unemotional as the Captain's.

A moment later the deck-plates danced to the impact of two double detonations.

"Blow Q." The pump started up with an incisive noise. As soon as the sound of the detonations had died away, it was stopped again to prevent the enemy's hydrophone from getting a bearing.

"Bring up the bow," the Chief ordered his planesmen. Then, to the Captain: "Boat trimmed, sir."

"There'll be more to come," the Captain said. "They actually spotted the periscope, damn them. Almost incredible, in a sea like that."

He looked round without a trace of dismay. I even detected

a note of mockery in his voice. "Psychological warfare, gentlemen, that's all."

Nothing happened for the next ten minutes. Then a violent detonation shook the hull. More thuds followed in quick succession. The U-boat quaked and groaned.

"Fifteen," counted the quartermaster, "sixteen, seventeen. Eighteen, nineteen."

The Chief was staring at the needle of the depth-gauge, which jumped a line or two at every concussion. His eyes were wide and looked even darker than usual. The Captain's eyes were shut in concentration: own course, enemy course, avoiding course. His reactions had to be instantaneous. Alone of us all, he was fighting a battle. Our lives depended on the accuracy of his decisions.

The hydrophone operator murmured: "Getting louder."

The Captain detached himself from the periscope shaft and walked over to me on tiptoe. "Bearing?"

"Bearing steady at two-six-zero, sir."

Four explosions in quick succession. Before the roar and gurgle of their aftermath had died away the Captain said in an undertone: "She was handsomely painted. An oldish ship with a heavily red raked forecastle, but otherwise flush-decked."

I was jolted by another explosion. The deck-plates rattled.

"Twenty-seven, twenty-eight," counted the quartermaster, emulating the Captain's studiously offhand tone.

A bucket rolled across the deck.

"Quiet, blast it!"

This time it sounded as if someone had put the gravel in a tin can and shaken it to and fro, once in each direction. The Asdic was overlaid by a brisk, intermittent chirping of a different kind: the throb of the corvette's propellers. They were clearly audible. I froze again as though the slightest movement, the smallest sound, would bring the propeller-beats nearer. Not a blink, not a flicker of the eye, not a breath, not a nervous twitch, not a change of expression, not a goose pimple.

Another five depth-charges for the quartermaster's tally. My face remained a frozen mask. The Captain raised his head. Articulating the words clearly, he dropped them into the dying echoes of the last explosion: "Easy, everyone. It could be a lot worse."

The calm in his voice was good to hear. It settled on my jangling nerves likes balm.

Then we lurched under a single shattering blow which sounded like a gigantic club thrashing a sheet of iron. Two or three men staggered.

Wisps of blue smoke hung in the air. And again: BRUMM! BRUMM! RRABUMM!

"Thirty-five, thirty-six, thirty-seven." This time the words came in a whisper.

The Captain said firmly: "Never mind the noise—a few bangs never hurt anyone." Then he reinterred himself in his course calculations. A deathly silence fell. After a while he murmured: "How does she bear now?"

"Two-six-zero, sir, growing louder."

The Captain's head lifted. He had reached a decision. "Hard-a-starboard," he ordered, then: "Hydrophone operator, we're turning to starboard."

He leant forward and addressed Herrmann. "Check if she's going away." Impatiently, he added: "Well, any change?"

"Constant, sir," Herrmann replied. After a while: "Growing louder."

"Bearing?"

"Bearing study at two-two-zero, sir."

At once the Captain went hard-a-starboard. We were doubling back on our tracks.

Both motors were ordered slow ahead.

Drops of condensation punctured the almost tangible silence at regular intervals: Plink, plonk—tip, tap—plip, plop.

A new series of concussions made the deck-plates dance and rattle. "Forty-seven, forty-eight," Kriechbaum counted. "Forty-nine, fifty, fifty-one."

I glanced at my wrist-watch: 1430. When had we dived? It must have been shortly after midday, so we had been under counter-attack for two hours.

"Propeller noises drawing aft," reported Herrmann. Two more depth-charges exploded almost simultaneously, but the detonations were fainter and more muffled than their predecessors.

"Miles away," said the Captain.

RRUMM, RRABUMM!

Still more muffled. The Captain reached for his cap. "Dummy runs. They might as well go home and practise."

Isenberg had already substituted some new glass tubes for the broken gauge-glasses, as though he realized that the sight of their shattered remains was bad for morale.

I stood up. My legs were stiff and numb. I extended a bloodless foot and felt as if I had stepped into a void. Grabbing the table for support, I looked down at the chart.

There was the pencil-line representing U-A's route, and there was the pencilled cross which marked our last fix. The line ended abruptly. I resolved to make a note of the grid reference if we got out alive.

Herrmann made a sweep through the full 360 degrees.

"Well?" asked the Captain, looking bored. His left cheek bulged as he rammed his tongue against it from the inside.

"Going away," Herrmann replied.

The Captain looked round with an air of satisfaction. He even grinned. "Well, that seems to be that."

He stretched and shook himself. "Quite instructive, really. In line for a red pennant one minute, clobbered the next." He ducked stiffly through the bulkhead and vanished into his cubby-hole, calling for a piece of paper.

I wondered what he was drafting—something pithy for his patrol report or a signal to base. If I knew anything about him, it would be a handful of bone-dry words like "Surprised by corvette in rainstorm. Counter-attacked three hours."

Five minutes later he reappeared in the control-room. He exchanged a glance with the Chief, ordered us to periscope depth and climbed leisurely into the conning-tower.

The Chief gave a series of plane orders.

"Depth?" came the Captain's voice from above.

"Forty metres," the Chief reported, then: "Twenty metres, fifteen metres—periscope depth."

I heard the periscope motor hum, stop, hum again. A minute went by. No word from above. We waited in vain for a sign of life.

"Something must be up . . ." murmured the control-room PO.

At last the Captain spoke. "Take her down quick! 50 metres all—hands forward."

I repeated the order and the hydrophone operator passed it on. The words travelled aft like a multiple echo. Men began to hurry forward through the control-room, grim-faced once more.

"Bloody hell," muttered the Chief. The needle of the depth-gauge resumed its slow progress: 20 metres, 30, 40 . . .

The Captain's sea-boots appeared. He clambered slowly down the ladder. All eyes were fixed on his face, but he only gave a derisive grin. "Slow ahead both. Steer zero-six-zero." At last he enlightened us: "The corvette's lying a thousand metres away. Stopped, by the look of her. The crafty sods were planning to jump us." He bent over the chart. After a while he turned to me. "Cunning bastards—you can't be too careful. We may as well dawdle west for a bit."

"When's dusk?" he asked the quartermaster.

"1830, sir."

"Good. We'll stay deep for the time being."

NICHOLAS MONSARRAT
The Blooding of HMS Compass Rose

Nicholas John Turney Monsarrat (1910–79) was born in Liverpool. During WWII he served as an officer in the Royal Navy, spending most of his time on convoy duty in the North Atlantic. Out of this experience emerged his best-selling novel, The Cruel Sea, *(1951), later filmed by Leslie Norman. Monsarrat's other novels include* The Story of Esther Costello *(1953) and* The Pillow Fight *(1965).*

An extract from The Cruel Sea *follows. The action takes place aboard HMS Compass Rose, a corvette commanded by the novel's central character, Lieutenant-Commander George Ericson. It is 1940.*

W HEN THE ALARM BELL WENT, just before midnight, Ferraby left the bridge where he had been keeping the first watch with Baker, and made his way aft towards his depth-charges. It was he who had rung the bell, as soon as the noise of aircraft and a burst of tracer bullets from the far side of the convoy indicated an attack; but though he had been prepared for the violent clanging and the drumming of feet that followed it, he could not control a feeling of sick surprise at the urgency which now possessed the ship, in its first alarm for action. The night was calm, with a bright three-quarter moon which bathed the upper deck in a cold glow, and showed them the nearest ships of the convoy in hard revealing outline; it was a perfect night for what he *knew* was coming, and to hurry down the length of *Compass Rose* was like going swiftly to the scaffold. He knew that if he spoke now there would be a tremble in his voice, he knew that full daylight would have shown his face pale and his lips shaking; he knew that he was not really ready for this moment, in spite of the months of training and the gradually sharpening tension. But the moment was here, and somehow it had to be faced.

Wainwright, the young torpedo-man, was already on the quarter-deck, clearing away the release-gear on the depth-charges, and as soon as Wainwright spoke—even though it was only the three words "Closed up, sir,"—Ferraby knew that he also was consumed by nervousness . . . He found the fact heartening, in a way he had not expected: if his own fear of action were the common lot, and not just a personal and shameful weakness, it might be easier to cure in company. He took a grip of his voice, said: "Get the first pattern ready to drop," and then, as he turned to check up on the depth-charge crews, his eye was caught by a brilliant firework display on their beam. The attacking aircraft was now flying low over the centre of the convoy, pursued and harried by gun-fire from scores of ships at once. The plane could not be seen, but her swift progress could be followed by the glowing arcs of tracer-bullets which swept like a huge fan across the top of the convoy. The uproar was prodigious—the plane screaming through the darkness, hundreds of guns going at once, one or two ships sounding the alarm on their sirens: the centre of the convoy, with everyone blazing away at the low-flying plane and not worrying about what else was in the line of fire, must have been an inferno. Standing in their groups aft, close to the hurrying water, they watched and waited, wondering which way the plane would turn at the end of her run: on the platform above them the two-pounder gun's crew, motionless and helmeted against the night sky, were keyed ready for their chance to fire. But the chance never came, the waiting belts of ammunition remained idle: something else forestalled them.

It was as if the monstrous noise from the convoy must have a climax, and the climax could only be violent. At the top of the centre column, near the end of her run, the aircraft dropped two bombs: one of them fell wide, raising a huge pluming spout of water which glittered in the moonlight, and the other found its mark. It dropped with an iron clang on some ship which they could not see—and they knew that now they would never see her: for after the first explosion there was a second one, a huge orange flash which lit the whole convoy and the whole sky at one ghastly stroke. The ship—whatever size she was—must have disintegrated on the instant; they were left with the evidence—the sickening succession of splashes as the torn pieces of the ship fell back into the sea, covering and fouling a mile-wide circle, and the noise of the aircraft disappearing into the darkness, a receding tail of sound to underline this fearful destruction.

"Must have been ammunition," said someone in the darkness, breaking the awed and compassionate silence. "Poor bastards."

"Didn't know much about it. Best way to die."

You fool, thought Ferraby, trembling uncontrollably: you fool, you fool, no one wants to die . . .

From the higher vantage-point of the bridge, Ericson had watched everything; he had seen the ship hit, the shower of sparks where the bomb fell, and then, a moment afterwards, the huge explosion that blew her to pieces. In the shocked silence that followed, his voice giving a routine helm-order was cool and normal: no one could have guessed the sadness and the anger that filled him, to see a whole crew of men like himself wiped out at one stroke. There was nothing to be done: the aircraft was gone, with this frightful credit, and if there were any men left alive—which was hardly conceivable—*Sorrel*, the stern escort, would do her best for them. It was so quick, it was so brutal . . . He might have thought more about it, he might have mourned a little longer, if a second stroke had not followed swiftly; but even as he raised his binoculars to look at the convoy again, the ship they were stationed on, a hundred yards away, rocked to a sudden explosion and then, on the instant, heeled over at a desperate angle.

This time, a torpedo . . . Ericson heard it: and even as he jumped to the voice-pipe to increase their speed and start zig-zagging, he thought: if that one came from outside the convoy, it must have missed us by a few feet. Inside the asdic-hut, Lockhart heard it, and started hunting on the danger-side, without further orders: that was a routine, and even at this moment of surprise and crisis, the routine still ruled them all. Morell, on the fo'c'sle, heard it, and closed up his gun's crew again and loaded with star-shell: down in the wheel-house, Tallow heard it, and gripped the wheel tighter and called out to his quartermasters: "Watch that telegraph, now!" and waited for the swift orders that might follow. Right aft, by the depth-charges, Ferraby heard it, and shivered: he glanced downwards at the black water rushing past them, and then at the stricken ship which he could see quite clearly, and he longed for some action in which he could lose himself and his fear. Deep down in the engine-room, Chief E.R.A. Watts heard it best of all: it came like a hammer-blow, hitting the ship's side a great splitting crack, and when, a few seconds afterwards, the telegraph rang for an increase of speed, his hand was on the steam-valve already. He knew what had happened, he knew what might happen next. But it was better not to think of what was going on outside: down here, encased below the water-line, they must wait, and hope, and keep their nerve.

Ericson took *Compass Rose* in a wide half-circle to starboard, away from the convoy, hunting for the U-boat down what he presumed had been the track of the torpedo; but they found nothing that looked like a contact, and presently he circled back again, towards the ship that had been hit. She had fallen out of line, like one winged bird in a flight of duck, letting the rest of the convoy go by: she was sinking fast, and already her screws were out of water and she was poised for the long plunge. The cries of men in fear came from her, and a thick smell of oil: at one moment, when they had her outlined against the moon, they could see a mass of men packed high in the towering stern, waving and shouting as they felt the ship under them begin to slide down to her grave. Ericson, trying for a cool decision in this moment of pity, was faced with a dilemma: if he stopped to pick up survivors, he would become a sitting target himself, and he would also lose all chance of hunting for the U-boat: if he went on with the hunt, he would, with *Sorrel* busy elsewhere, be leaving these men to their death. He decided on a compromise, a not too dangerous compromise: they would drop a boat, and leave it to collect what survivors it could while *Compass Rose* took another cast away to star-board. But it must be done quickly.

Ferraby, summoned to the quarter-deck voice-pipe, put every effort he knew into controlling his voice.

"Ferraby, sir."

"We're going to drop a boat, sub. Who's your leading hand?"

"Leading-Seaman Tonbridge, sir."

"Tell him to pick a small crew—not more than four—and row over towards the ship. Tell him to keep well clear until she goes down. They may be able to get some boats away themselves, but if not, he'll have to do the best he can. We'll come back for him when we've had another look for the submarine."

"Right, sir."

"Quick as you can, sub. I don't want to stop too long."

Ferraby threw himself into the job with an energy which was a drug for all other feeling: the boat was lowered so swiftly that when *Compass Rose* drew away from it and left it to its critical errand the torpedoed ship was still afloat. But she was only just afloat, balanced between sea and sky before her last dive; and as Tonbridge took the tiller and glanced in her direction to get his bearings, there was a rending sound which carried clearly over the water, and she started to go down. Tonbridge watched, in awe and fear: he had never seen anything like this, and never had a job of this sort before, and it was an effort to meet it properly. It had been bad enough to be lowered into the darkness from *Compass Rose*, and to watch her fade away and be left alone in a small boat under the stars with the convoy also fading and a vast unfriendly sea all round them; but now, with the torpedoed ship disappearing before their eyes, and the men shouting and crying as they splashed about in the water, and the smell of oil coming across to them thick and choking, it was more like a nightmare than anything else. Tonbridge was twenty-three years of age, a product of the London slums conditioned by seven years' naval training; faced by this ordeal, the fact that he did not run away from it, the fact that he remained effective, was beyond all normal credit.

They did what they could: rowing about in the darkness,

guided by the shouting, appalled by the choking cries of men who drowned before they could be reached, they tried their utmost to rescue and to succour. They collected fourteen men: one was dead, one was dying, eight were wounded, and the rest were shocked and prostrated to a pitiful degree. It was very nearly fifteen men: Tonbridge actually had hold of the fifteenth, who was gasping in the last stages of terror and exhaustion, but the film of oil on his naked body made him impossible to grasp, and he slipped away and sank before a rope could be got round him. When there were no more shadows on the water, and no more cries to follow, they rested on their oars, and waited; alone on the enormous black waste of the Atlantic, alone with the settling wreckage and the reek of oil; and so, presently, *Compass Rose* found them.

Ferraby, standing in the waist of the ship as the boat was hooked on, wondered what he would see when the survivors came over the side: he was not prepared for the pity and horror of their appearance. First came the ones who could climb aboard themselves—half a dozen shivering, black-faced men, dressed in the filthy oil-soaked clothes which they had snatched up when the ship was struck: one of them with his scalp streaming with blood, another nursing an arm flayed from wrist to shoulder by scalding steam. They looked about them in wonder, dazed by the swiftness of disaster, by their rescue, by the solid deck beneath their feet. Then, while they were led to the warmth of the mess-deck, a sling was rigged for the seriously wounded, and they were lifted over the side on stretchers: some silent, some moaning, some coughing up the fuel oil which was burning and poisoning their intestines: laid side by side in the waist, they made a carpet of pain and distress so naked in suffering that it seemed cruel to watch them. And then, with the boat still bumping alongside in the eerie darkness, came Tonbridge's voice: "Go easy—there's a dead man down here." Ferraby had never seen a dead man before, and he had to force himself to look at this pitiful relic of the sea—stone-cold, stiffening already, its grey head jerking as it was bundled over the side: an old sailor, unseamanlike and disgusting in death. He wanted to run away, he wanted to be sick: he watched with shocked amazement the two ratings who were carrying the corpse: how can you bear what you are doing, he thought, how can you touch—it . . .? Behind him he heard Lockhart's voice saying: "Bring the whole lot into the fo'c'sle—I can't see anything here," and then he turned away and busied himself with the hoisting of the boat, not looking behind him as the procession of wrecked and brutalized men was borne off. When the boat was in-board, and secure, he turned back again, glad to have escaped some part of the horror. There was nothing left now but the acrid smell of oil, and the patches of blood and water on the deck: nothing, he saw with a gasp of fear and revulsion, but the dead man lying lashed against the rail, a yard from him, rolling as the ship rolled, waiting for daylight and burial. He turned and ran towards the stern, pursued by terror.

In the big seamen's mess-deck, under the shaded lamps, Lockhart was doing things he had never imagined possible. Now and again he recalled, with a spark of pleasure, his previous doubts: there was plenty of blood here to faint at, but that wasn't the way things were working out . . . He had stitched up a gash in a man's head, from the nose to the line of the hair—as he took the catgut from its envelope he had thought: I wish they'd include some directions with this stuff. He had set a broken leg, using part of a bench as a splint. He bound up other cuts and gashes, he did what he could for the man with the burnt arm, who was now insensible with pain: he watched, doing nothing with a curious hurt detachment, as a man who had drenched his intestines and perhaps his lungs with fuel oil slowly died. Some of *Compass Rose's* crew made a ring round him, looking at him, helping him when he asked for help: the two stewards brought tea for the cold and shocked survivors, other men offered dry clothing, and Tallow, after an hour or two, came down and gave him the largest tot of rum he had ever seen. It was not too large . . . Once, from outside, there was the sound of an explosion, and he looked up: by chance, across the smoky fo'c'sle, the bandaged rows of wounded, the other men still shivering, the twisted corpse, the whole squalid confusion of the night, he met the eye of Leading-Seaman Phillips. Involuntarily, both of them smiled, to mark a thought which could only be smiled at: if a torpedo hit them now, there would be little chance for any of them, and all this bandaging would be wasted.

Then he bent down again, and went on probing a wound for the splinter of steel which must still be there, if the scream of pain which the movement produced was anything to go by. This was a moment to think only of the essentials, and they were all here with him, and in his care.

It was nearly daylight before he finished; and he went up to the bridge to report what he had done at a slow dragging walk, completely played out. He met Ericson at the top of the ladder: they had both been working throughout the night, and the two exhausted men looked at each other in silence, unable to put any expression into their stiff drawn faces, yet somehow acknowledging each other's competence. There was blood on Lockhart's hands, and on the sleeves of his duffle-coat: in the cold light it had a curious metallic sheen, and Ericson looked at it for some time before he realized what it was.

"You must have been busy, Number One," he said quietly. "What's the score down there?"

"Two dead, sir," answered Lockhart. His voice was very hoarse, and he cleared his throat. "One more to go, I think—he's been swimming and walking about with a badly-burned arm, and the shock is too much. Eleven others. They ought to be all right."

"Fourteen . . . The crew was thirty-six altogether."

Lockhart shrugged. There was no answer to that one, and if there had been he could not have found it, in his present mood: the past few hours, spent watching and touching pain, seemed to have deadened all normal feeling. He looked round at the ships on their beam, just emerging as the light grew.

"How about things up here?" he asked.

"We lost another ship, over the other side of the convoy. That made three."

"More than one submarine?"

"I shouldn't think so. She probably crossed over."

"Good night's work." Lockhart still could not express more than a formal regret. "Do you want to turn in, sir? I can finish this watch."

"No—you get some sleep. I'll wait for Ferraby and Baker."

"Tonbridge did well."

"Yes . . . So did you, Number One."

Lockhart shook his head. "It was pretty rough, most of it. I must get a little book on wounds. It's going to come in handy, if this sort of thing goes on."

"There's no reason why it shouldn't," said Ericson. "No reason at all, that I can see. Three ships in three hours: probably a hundred men all told. Easy."

"Yes," said Lockhart, nodding. "A very promising start. After the war, we must ask them how they do it."

"After the war," said Ericson levelly, "I hope they'll be asking us."

ALISTAIR MACLEAN
The Storm

Alistair Maclean (1922–87) was born in Glasgow, and educated at the city's university. He served in the Royal Navy from 1941–46, mostly on patrol in the Atlantic. In 1954, while working as a schoolteacher, he won a short story competition held by the Glasgow Herald. *At the encouragement of the publisher William Collins, he followed up this success with a full-length novel:* HMS Ulysses *(1956), a best-seller around the world.* The Guns of Navarone *(1957) and* Where Eagles Dare *(1967) are among his other famous war stories.*

"The Storm" is an excerpt from HMS Ulysses, *and a reminder that the elements can also be the enemy of those at war.*

IT WAS THE WORST STORM of the war. Beyond all doubt, had the records been preserved for Admiralty inspection, that would have proved to be incomparably the greatest storm, the most tremendous convulsion of nature since these recordings began. Living memory aboard the *Ulysses* that night, a vast accumulation of experience in every corner of the globe, could certainly recall nothing even remotely like it, nothing that would even begin to bear comparison as a parallel or precedent.

At ten o'clock, with all doors and hatches battened shut, with all traffic prohibited on the upper deck, with all crews withdrawn from gun-turrets and magazines and all normal deck watchkeeping stopped for the first time since her commissioning, even the taciturn Carrington admitted that the Caribbean hurricanes of the autumns of '34 and '37—when he'd run out of sea-room, been forced to heave-to in the dangerous right-hand quadrant of both these murderous cyclones—had been no worse than this. But the two ships he had taken through these—a 3,000-ton tramp and a super-annuated tanker on the New York asphalt run—had not been in the same class for seaworthiness as the *Ulysses*. He had little doubt as to her ability to survive. But what the First Lieutenant did not know, what nobody had any means of guessing, was that this howling gale was still only the deadly overture. Like some mindless and dreadful beast from an ancient and other world, the Polar monster crouched on its own doorstep, waiting. At 2230, the *Ulysses* crossed the Arctic Circle. The monster struck.

It struck with a feral ferocity, with an appalling savagery that smashed minds and bodies into a stunned unknowingness. Its claws were hurtling rapiers of ice that slashed across a man's face and left it welling red: its teeth were that subzero wind, gusting over 120 knots, that ripped and tore through the tissue paper of Arctic clothing and sunk home to the bone: its voice was the devil's orchestra, the roar of a great wind mingled with the banshee shrieking of tortured rigging, a requiem for fiends: its weight was the crushing power of the hurricane wind that pinned a man helplessly to a bulkhead, fighting for breath, or flung him off his feet to crash in some distant corner, broken-limbed and senseless. Baulked of prey in its 500-mile sweep across the frozen wastes of the Greenland ice-cap, it goaded the cruel sea into homicidal alliance and flung itself, titanic in its energy, ravenous in its howling, upon the cockleshell that was the *Ulysses*.

The *Ulysses* should have died then. Nothing built by man could ever have hoped to survive. She should have been pressed under to destruction, or turned turtle, or had her back broken, or disintegrated under those mighty hammer-blows of wind and sea. But she did none of these things.

How she ever survived the insensate fury of that first attack, God only knew. The great wind caught her on the bow and flung her round in a 45° arc and pressed her far over on her side as she fell—literally fell—forty heart-stopping feet over and down the precipitous walls of a giant trough. She crashed into the valley with a tremendous concussion that jarred every plate, every Clydebuilt rivet in her hull. The vibration lasted an eternity as overstressed metal fought to re-adjust itself, as steel compressed and stretched far beyond specified breaking loads. Miraculously she held, but the sands were running out. She lay far over on her starboard side, the gunwales dipping: half a mile away, towering high above the mast-top, a great wall of water was roaring down on the helpless ship.

The "Dude" saved the day. The "Dude", alternatively known as "Persil" but officially known as Engineer-Commander Dodson, immaculately clad as usual in overalls of the most dazzling white, had been at his control position in the engine-room when that tremendous gust had struck. He had no means of knowing what had happened. He had no means of knowing that the ship was not under command, that no one on the bridge had as yet recovered from that first shattering impact: he had no means of knowing that the quartermaster had been thrown unconscious into a corner of the wheelhouse, that his mate, almost a child in years, was too panic-stricken to dive for the madly-spinning wheel. But he did know that the *Ulysses* was listing crazily, almost broadside on, and he suspected the cause.

His shouts on the bridge tube brought no reply. He pointed to the port controls, roared "Slow" in the ear of the Engineer WO—then leapt quickly for the starboard wheel.

Fifteen seconds later and it would have been too late. As it was, the accelerating starboard screw brought her round just far enough to take that roaring mountain of water under her bows, to dig her stern in to the level of the depth-charge rails, till forty feet of her airborne keel lay poised above the abyss below. When she plunged down, again that same shuddering vibration enveloped the entire hull. The fo'c'sle disappeared far below the surface, the sea flowing over and past the armoured side of "A" turret. But she was bows on again. At once the "Dude" signalled his WO for more revolutions, cut back the starboard engine.

Below decks, everything was an unspeakable shambles. On the mess-decks, steel lockers in their scores had broken adrift, been thrown in a dozen different directions, bursting hasps and locks, spilling their contents everywhere. Hammocks had been catapulted from their racks, smashed crockery littered the decks: tables were twisted and smashed, broken stools stuck up at crazy angles, books, papers, teapots, kettles and crockery were scattered in insane profusion. And amidst this jumbled, sliding wreckage, hundreds of shouting, cursing, frightened and exhausted men struggling to their feet, or knelt, or sat or just lay still.

Surgeon-Commander Brooks and Lieutenant Nicholls, with an inspired, untiring padre as good as a third doctor, were worked off their feet. The veteran Leading SBA Johnson, oddly enough, was almost useless—he was violently sick much of the time, seemed to have lost all heart: no one knew why—it was just one of these things and he had taken all he could.

Men were brought in to the Sick Bay in their dozens, in their scores, a constant trek that continued all night long as the *Ulysses* fought for her life, a trek that soon overcrowded the meagre space available and turned the wardroom into an emergency hospital. Bruises, cuts, dislocations, concussion, fractures—the exhausted doctor experienced everything that night. Serious injuries were fortunately rare, and inside three hours there were only nine bed-patients in the Sick Bay, including AB Ferry, his already mangled arm smashed in two places—a bitterly protesting Riley and his fellow-mutineers had been unceremoniously turfed out to make room for the more seriously injured.

The *Ulysses* did not die. Time and again that night, hove to with the wind fine on her starboard bow, as her bows crashed into and under the far shoulder of a trough, it seemed that she could never shake free from the great press of water. But time and again she did just that, shuddering, quivering under the fantastic strain. A thousand times before dawn officers and men blessed the genius of the Clyde shipyard that had made her: a thousand times they cursed the blind malevolence of that great storm that put the *Ulysses* on the rack.

Perhaps "blind" was not the right word. The storm wielded its wild hate with an almost human cunning. Shortly after the first onslaught, the wind had veered quickly, incredibly so and in defiance of all the laws, back almost to the north again. The *Ulysses* was on a lee shore, forced to keep pounding into gigantic seas.

Gigantic—and cunning also. Roaring by the *Ulysses*, a huge comber would suddenly whip round and crash on deck, smashing a boat to smithereens. Inside an hour, the barge, motor-boat and two whalers were gone, their shattered timbers swept away in the boiling caudron. Carley rafts were broken off by the sudden hammer-blows of the same cunning waves, swept over the side and gone for ever: four of the Balsa floats went the same way.

It was dawn now, a wild and terrible dawn, fit epilogue for a nightmare. Strange, trailing bands of misty-white vapour swept by barely at mast-top level, but high above the sky was clear. The seas, still gigantic, were shorter now, much shorter, and even steeper: the *Ulysses* was slowed right down, with barely enough steerage way to keep her head up—and even then, taking severe punishment in the precipitous head seas. The wind had dropped to a steady fifty knots—gale force: even at that, it seared like fire in Nicholls's lungs as he stepped out on the flag-deck, blinded him with ice and cold. Hastily he wrapped scarves over his entire face, clambered up to the bridge by touch and instinct. The Kapok Kid followed with the glass. As they climbed, they heard the loudspeakers crackling some unintelligible message.

Turner and Carrington were alone on the twilit bridge, swathed like mummies. Not even their eyes were visible—they wore goggles.

"Morning, Nicholls," boomed the Commander. "It *is* Nicholls, isn't? "He pulled off his goggles, his back turned to the bitter wind, threw them away in disgust. "Can't see damn all through these bloody things . . . Ah, Number One, he's got the glass."

Nicholls crouched in the for'ard lee of the compass platform. In a corner, the duckboards were littered with goggles, eye-shields and gas-masks. He jerked his head towards them.

"What's this—a clearance sale?"

"We're turning round, Doc." It was Carrington who answered, his voice calm and precise as ever, without a trace of exhaustion. "But we've got to see where we're going, and as the Commander says all these damn' things there are useless—mist up immediately they're put on—it's too cold. If you'll just hold it—so—and if you would wipe it, Andy?"

Nicholls looked at the great seas. He shuddered.

"Excuse my ignorance, but why turn round at all?"

"Because it will be impossible very shortly," Carrington answered briefly. Then he chuckled. "This is going to make me the most unpopular man in the ship. We've just broadcast a warning. Ready, sir?"

"Stand by, engine-room: stand by, wheelhouse. Ready, Number One."

For thirty seconds, forty-five, a whole minute, Carrington stared steadily, unblinkingly through the glass. Nicholls's hands froze. The Kapok Kid rubbed industriously. Then:

"Half-ahead, port!"

"Half-ahead, port!" Turner echoed.

"Starboard 20!"

"Starboard 20!"

Nicholls risked a glance over his shoulder. In the split second before his eyes blinded, filled with tears, he saw a huge wave bearing down on them, the bows already swinging diagonally away from it. Good God! Why hadn't Carrington waited until that was past?

The great wave flung the bows up, pushed the *Ulysses* far over to starboard, then passed under. The *Ulysses* staggered over the top, corkscrewed wickedly down the other side, her masts, great gleaming tree trunks thick and heavy with ice, swinging in a great arc as she rolled over, burying her port rails in the rising shoulder of the next sea.

"Full ahead port!"

"Full ahead port!"

"Starboard 30!"

"Starboard 30!"

The next sea, passing beneath, merely straightened the *Ulysses* up. And then, at last, Nicholls understood. Incredibly, because it had been impossible to see so far ahead, Carrington had known that two opposing wave systems were due to interlock in an area of comparative calm: how he had sensed it, no one knew, would ever know, not even Carrington himself: but he was a great seaman, and he had known. For fifteen, twenty seconds, the sea was a seething white mass of violently disturbed, conflicting waves of the type usually found, on a small scale, in tidal races and overfalls—and the *Ulysses* curved gratefully through. And then another great sea, towering almost to bridge height, caught her on the far turn of the quarter circle. It struck the entire length of the *Ulysses*—for the first time that night—with tremendous weight. It threw her far over on her side, the lee rails vanishing. Nicholls was flung off his feet, crashed heavily in the side of the bridge, the glass shattering. He could have sworn he heard Carrington laughing. He clawed his way back to the middle of the compass platform.

And still the great wave had not passed. It towered high above the trough into which the *Ulysses*, now heeled far over to 40°, had been so contemptuously flung, bore down remorselessly from above and sought, in a lethal silence and with an almost animistic savagery, to press her under. The inclinometer swung relentlessly over—45°, 50°, 53°, and hung there an eternity, while men stood on the side of the ship, braced with their hands on the deck, numbed minds barely grasping the inevitable. This was the end. The *Ulysses* could never come back.

A lifetime ticked agonizingly by. Nicholls and Carpenter looked at each other, blank-faced, expressionless. Tilted at that crazy angle, the bridge was sheltered from the wind. Carrington's voice, calm, conversational, carried with amazing clarity.

"She'd go to 65° and still come back," he said matter-of-factly. "Hang on to your hats, gentlemen. This is going to be interesting."

Just as he finished, the *Ulysses* shuddered, then imperceptibly, then slowly, then with vicious speed lurched back and whipped through an arc of 90°, then back again. Once more Nicholls found himself in the corner of the bridge. But the *Ulysses* was almost round.

The Kapok Kid, grinning with relief, picked himself up and tapped Carrington on the shoulder.

"Don't look now, sir, but we have lost our mainmast."

It was a slight exaggeration, but the top fifteen feet, which had carried the after radar scanner, were undoubtedly gone. That wicked, double ship-lash, with the weight of the ice, had been too much.

"Slow ahead both! Midships!"

"Slow ahead both! Midships!"

"Steady as she goes!"

The *Ulysses* was round.

The Kapok Kid caught Nicholls's eye, nodded at the First Lieutenant.

"See what I mean, Johnny?"

"Yes." Nicholls was very quiet. "Yes, I see what you mean." Then he grinned suddenly. "Next time you make a statement, I'll just take your word for it, if you don't mind. These demonstrations of proof take too damn' much out of a person!"

Running straight before the heavy stern sea, the *Ulysses* was amazingly steady. The wind, too, was dead astern now, the bridge in magical shelter. The scudding mist overhead had thinned out, was almost gone. Far away to the south-east a dazzling white sun climbed up above a cloudless horizon. The long night was over.

EVELYN WAUGH
Leaving Crete

*Evelyn Arthur St John Waugh (1903–66)
was born in Hampstead, London. He published numerous successful novels in the 1930s,
including* Scoop *(1938), before serving as
a junior officer in the Royal Marines from
1941–45. His* Sword of Honour *trilogy
of novels—*Men at Arms *(1952),* Officers
and Gentlemen *(1955) and* Uncondi-
tional Surrender *(1961)—featuring the
travails of Guy Crouchback is based on this
time. Waugh's other books include the classic
of Oxford undergraduate life,* Brideshead
Revisited *(1945).*

"Leaving Crete" is an extract from
Officers and Gentlemen.

O N THE 31ST OF MAY Guy sat in a cave overhanging
the beach of Sphakia where the final embarkation was
shortly to begin. By his watch it was not yet ten o'clock but
it seemed the dead of night. Nothing stirred in the moonlight.
In the crowded ravine below the Second Halberdiers stood
in column of companies, every man in full marching order,
waiting for the boats. Hookforce was deployed on the ridge
above, holding the perimeter against an enemy who since
sunset had fallen silent. Guy had brought his section here
late that afternoon. They had marched all the previous night
and most of that day, up the pass, down to Imbros, down a
gully to this last position. They dropped asleep where they
halted. Guy had sought out and found Creforce headquarters
and brought from them to the Hookforce commanders the last
grim orders.

He dozed and woke for seconds at a time, barely thinking.

There were footsteps outside. Guy had not troubled to post a lookout. Ivor Claire's troop was a few hundred yards distant. He went to the mouth of the cave and in the moonlight saw a familiar figure and heard a familiar voice: "Guy? Ivor."

Ivor entered and sat beside him.

They sat together, speaking between long pauses in the listless drawl of extreme fatigue.

"This is damn fool business, Guy."

"It will all be over to-morrow."

"Just beginning. You're sure Tony Luxmore hasn't got the wrong end of the stick? I was at Dunkirk, you know. Not much fuss about priorities there. No inquiries afterwards. It doesn't make any sense, leaving the fighting troops behind and taking off the rabble. Tony's all in. I bet he muddled his orders."

"I've got them in writing from the G.O.C. Surrender at dawn. The men aren't supposed to know yet."

"They know all right."

"The General's off in a flying-boat to-night."

"No staying with the sinking ship."

"Napoleon didn't stay with his army after Moscow."

Presently Ivor said: "What does one *do* in prison?"

"I imagine a ghastly series of concert parties—perhaps for years. I've a nephew who was captured at Calais. D'you imagine one can do anything about getting posted where one wants?"

"I presume so. One usually can."

Another pause.

"There would be no sense in the G.O.C. sitting here to be captured."

"None at all. No sense in any of us staying."

Another pause.

"Poor Freda," said Ivor. "Poor Freda. She'll be an old dog by the time I see her again."

Guy briefly fell asleep. Then Ivor said: "Guy, what would you do if you were challenged to a duel?"

"Laugh."

"Yes, of course."

"What made you think of that now?"

"I was thinking about honor. It's a thing that changes, doesn't it? I mean, a hundred and fifty years ago we would have had to fight if challenged. Now we'd laugh. There must have been a time a hundred years ago when it was rather an awkward question."

"Yes. Moral theologians were never able to stop dueling—it took democracy to do that."

"And in the next war, when we are completely democratic, I expect it will be quite honorable for officers to leave their men behind. It'll be laid down in King's Regulations as their duty—to keep a *cadre* going to train new men to take the place of prisoners."

"Perhaps men wouldn't take kindly to being trained by deserters."

"Don't you think in a really modern army they'd respect them the more for being fly? I reckon our trouble is that we're at the awkward stage—like a man challenged to a duel a hundred years ago."

Guy could see him clearly in the moonlight, the austere face, haggard now but calm and recollected as he had first seen it in the Borghese gardens. It was his last sight of him. Ivor stood up saying: "Well, the path of honor lies up the hill," and he strolled away.

And Guy fell asleep.

He dreamed continuously, it seemed to him, and most prosaically. All night in the cave he marched, took down orders, passed them on, marked his map, marched again, while the moon set and the ships came into the bay and the boats went back and forth between them and the beach, and the ships sailed away leaving Hookforce and five or six thousand other men behind them. In Guy's dreams there were no exotic visitants among the shades of Creforce, no absurdity, no escape. Everything was as it had been the preceding day, the preceding night, night and day since he had landed at Suda, and when he awoke at dawn it was to the same half-world; sleeping and waking were like two airfields, identical in aspect though continents apart. He had no clear apprehension that this was a fatal morning, that he was that day to resign an immeasurable piece of his manhood. He saw himself dimly at a great distance. Weariness was all.

"They say the ships left food on the beach," said Sergeant Smiley.

"We'd better have a meal before we go to prison."

"It's true then, sir, what they're saying, that there's no more ships coming?"

"Quite true, Sergeant."

"And we're to surrender?"

"Quite true."

"It don't seem right."

The golden dawn was changing to unclouded blue. Guy led his section down the rough path to the harbor. The quay was littered with abandoned equipment and the wreckage of bombardment. Among the scrap and waste stood a pile of rations—bully beef and biscuit—and a slow-moving concourse of soldiers foraging. Sergeant Smiley pushed his way through them and passed back half a dozen tins. There was a tap of fresh water running to waste in the wall of a ruined building. Guy and his section filled their bottles, drank deep, refilled them, turned off the tap; then breakfasted. The little town was burned, battered and deserted by its inhabitants. The ghosts of an army teemed everywhere. Some were quite apathetic, too weary to eat; others were smashing their rifles on the stones, taking a fierce relish in this symbolic farewell to their arms; an officer stamped on his binoculars; a motor bicycle was burning; there was a small group under command of a sapper Captain doing something to a seedy-looking fishing-boat that lay on its side, out of the water, on the beach. One man sat on the sea-wall methodically stripping down his Bren and throwing the parts separately far into the scum. A very short man was moving from group to group saying: "Me surrender? Not bloody likely. I'm for the hills. Who's coming with me?" like a preacher exhorting a doomed congregation to flee from the wrath to come.

"Is there anything in that, sir?" asked Sergeant Smiley.

"Our orders are to surrender," said Guy. "If we go into hiding the Cretans will have to look after us. If the Germans found us we should only be marched off as prisoners of war—our friends would be shot."

"Put like that, sir, it doesn't seem right."

Nothing seemed right that morning, nothing seemed real.

"I imagine a party of senior officers have gone forward already to find the right person to surrender to."

An hour passed.

The short man filled his haversack with food, slung three water-bottles from his shoulders, changed his rifle for the pistol which an Australian gunner was about to throw away, and bowed under his load, sturdily strutted off out of their sight. Out to sea, beyond the mouth of the harbor, the open sea calmly glittered. Flies everywhere buzzed and settled. Guy had not taken off his clothes since he left the destroyer. He said: "I'll tell you what I'm going to do, Sergeant. I'm going to bathe."

"Not in *that*, sir?"

"No. There'll be clean water round the point."

Sergeant Smiley and two men went with him. There was no giving of orders that day. They found a cleft in the rocky spur that enclosed the harbor. They strolled through and came to a little cover, a rocky foreshore, deep clear water. Guy stripped and dived and swam out in a sudden access of euphoria; he turned on his back and floated, his eyes closed to the sun, his ears sealed to every sound, oblivious of everything except physical ease, solitary and exultant. He turned and swam and floated again and swam; then he struck out for the shore, making for the opposite side. The cliffs here ran down into deep water. He stretched up and found a hand hold in a shelf of rock. It was already warm with the sun. He pulled up, rested luxuriously on his forearms with his legs dangling knee deep in water, paused, for he was feebler than a week ago, then raised his head and found himself staring into the eyes of another, a man who was seated above him on the black ledge and gazing down at him; a strangely clean and sleek man for Creforce; his eyes in the brilliant sunshine were the color of oysters.

"Can I give you a hand, sir?" asked Corporal-Major Ludovic. He stood and stooped and drew Guy out of the sea. "A smoke, sir?"

He offered a neat, highly pictorial packet of Greek cigarettes. He struck a light. Guy sat beside him, naked and wet and smoking.

"Where on earth have you been, Corporal-Major?"

"At my post, sir. With rear headquarters. With Major Hound."

"I thought you'd deserted us?"

"Did you, sir? Perhaps we both made a miscalculation."

"You mean you couldn't make the ships? Did Major Hound get away?"

"No, sir. I fear not. He miscalculated too."

"Where is he now? Why have you left him?"

"Need we go into that, sir? Wouldn't you say it was rather too early or too late for inquiries of that sort?"

"What are you doing here?"

"To be quite frank, sir, I was considering drowning myself. I am a weak swimmer and the sea is most inviting. You know something of theology, I believe, sir, I've seen some of your books. Would moralists hold it was suicide if one were just to swim out to sea, sir, in the fanciful hope of reaching Egypt? I haven't the gift of faith myself, but I have always been intrigued by theological speculation."

"You had better rejoin Sergeant Smiley and the remains of headquarters."

"You speak as an officer, sir, or as a theologian?"

"Neither really," said Guy.

He stood up.

"If you aren't going to finish that cigarette, may I have it back?" Corporal Ludovic carefully pinched off the glowing end and returned the half to its packet. "Gold-dust," he said, relapsing into the language of the barracks. "I'll follow you round, sir."

Guy dived and swam back. By the time he was dressed, Corporal-Major Ludovic was among them. Sergeant Smiley nodded dully. Without speaking, they strolled together into Sphakia. The crowd of soldiers had grown and was growing as unsteady files shuffled from their hiding-places in the hills. Nothing remained of the ration dump. Men were sitting about with their backs against the ruined walls eating. The point of interest now was the boating party who were pushing their craft towards the water. The sapper Captain was directing them in a stronger voice than Guy had heard for some days.

"Easy . . . All together, now, heave . . . steady . . . keep her moving . . ." The men were enfeebled but the boat moved. The

beach was steep and slippery with weed. ". . . Now then, once
more all together . . . she's off . . . let her run . . . What ho,
she floats . . ."

Guy pushed forward in the crowd.

"They're barmy," said a man next to him. "They haven't
a hope in hell."

The boat was afloat. Three men, waist deep, held her; the
Captain and the rest of his party climbed and began bailing
out and working on the engine. Guy watched them.

"Anyone else coming?" the sapper called.

Guy waded to him.

"What are your chances?" he asked.

"One in ten, I reckon, of being picked up. One in five
of making it on our own. We're not exactly well found.
Coming?"

Guy made no calculation. Nothing was measurable that
morning. He was aware only of the wide welcome of the open
sea, of the satisfaction of finding someone else to take control
of things.

"Yes. I'll just talk to my men."

The engine gave out a puff of oily smoke and a series of
small explosions.

"Tell them to make up their minds. We'll be off as soon as
that thing starts up."

Guy said to his section: "There's one chance in five of getting
away. I'm going. Decide for yourselves."

"Not for me, sir, thank you," said Sergeant Smiley. "I'll
stick to dry land."

The other men of his Intelligence section shook their
heads.

"How about you, Corporal-Major? You can be confident
that no moral theologian would condemn this as suicide."

Corporal-Major Ludovic turned his pale eyes out to sea and
said nothing.

The sapper shouted: "Liberty boat just leaving. Anyone else
want to come?"

"I'm coming," Guy shouted.

He was at the side of the boat when he noticed that Ludovic
was close behind him. The engine started up, drowning the
sound which Ludovic had heard. They climbed on board

together. One of the watching crowd called, "Good luck, chums," and his words were taken up by a few others, but did not carry above the noise of the engine.

The sapper steered. They moved quite fast across the water, out of the oil and floating refuse. As they watched they saw the crowd on shore had all turned their faces skyward.

"Stukas again," said the sapper.

"Well, it's all over now. I supposed they've just come to have a look at their spoils."

The men on shore seemed to be of this opinion. Few of them took cover. The match was over, stumps drawn. Then the bombs began to fall among them.

"Bastards," said the sapper.

From the boat they saw havoc. One of the airplanes dipped over their heads, fired its machine-gun, missed and turned away. Nothing further was done to molest them. Guy saw more bombs burst on the now-deserted waterfront. His last thoughts were of X Commando, of Bertie and Eddie, most of all of Ivor Claire, waiting at their posts to be made prisoner. At the moment there was nothing in the boat for any of them to do. They had merely to sit still in the sunshine and the fresh breeze.

So they sailed out of the picture.

DOUGLAS REEMAN
Winged Escort

*Douglas Edward Reeman (1924–) served
as a Lieutenant in the RNVR in WWII.
He is Britain's foremost author of naval
stories. As the pseudonymous Alexander
Kent he writes historical tales featuring
midshipman Richard Bolitho; under his
own name he writes novels of modern sea
warfare, the first of which was* A Prayer
for a Ship, *published in 1958.*

*"Winged Escort" is an extract from the
1975 novel of the same title. The setting is
the North Atlantic, where HMS* Growler,
*a converted aircraft carrier, is on patrol.
Tim Rowan is a Seafire pilot.*

THE SIX AIR CREWS SAT in the Ready Room, not looking
at each other, their breathing reduced almost to the gentle
throb of *Growler's* main engine.

The lights were dimmed to ease the strain on their eyes.
It was like sitting and waiting for the world to end, Rowan
thought. His emotions were in turmoil, so that he was
surprised to find that his hands and feet were quite still,
his breathing slow and regular.

He let his eyes move around the others. Six aircraft. Twelve
men. Ready to move. *Expendable.*

Bill Ellis, legs out-thrust, eyes closed, his blond hair ruffling
slightly from a deckhead fan.

Creswell his face even more youthful in the orange glow.

The Swordfish crews, pilots, observers, and air gunners. It
was odd to realise that Troup, the ex-actor, had an orchid
grower as his observer. And young Cotter had come from the

opposite end of the world to meet this moment.

True to Bray's calculations, *Growler* had arrived at the pencilled cross, some one hundred nautical miles north-west of the Lofoten Islands. They had not sighted a single ship or aircraft since they had left the convoy, and with their four rust-streaked escorts they had had the Arctic to themselves.

From the babble of W/T signals it seemed that the convoy had been stalked twice by U-boats. No ships had been sunk or damaged, and the escorts had not reported any kills. A probing exercise perhaps. *Flexing muscles.* Either way, the enemy knew about the convoy, its strength and its value. The destination was obvious. Over the last days Rowan had often thought about the thirty-five ships steaming in their long, straight lines. Not crews or human beings. Just the ships. Unflinching. Unstoppable.

The door opened and Lieutenant Commander Miller walked below the one central light.

He said quietly, "Time to go, lads." He smiled, his devil's beard jutting above his leather jacket.

They all stood, picking up their helmets and goggles, mentally stripping and readjusting their minds. The plans and charts, Broderick's sketches of islands and landmarks were now real and stark.

Rowan walked with him towards the passageway. How quiet the ship was. She had been at action stations for four hours. Every gun manned, all air crews mustered and ready just in case the enemy knew about Chadwick's private war.

They had been briefed and briefed again, until their minds had refused to accept another titbit of information. *There was a ship at anchor close inshore of an island. It had to be sunk.*

Miller said, "If you can't hit the bloody thing, forget it and come back." He sounded grim. "There'll be other targets."

Out on to the flight deck, empty but for the six aircraft. Below in the hangar deck the rest of *Growler*'s planes and crews waited and listened.

Rowan shivered and tightened the scarf around his neck. He had never got used to this strange copper light. But it was five in the morning, and the wind across his face was quite raw.

He saw Petty Officer Thorpe crouching by the aircraft. He

looked towards him and gave a brief wave. He would know what Rowan was thinking.

Just a few hours ago he had said worriedly, "You could have had Jonah tomorrow, sir. But in all honesty I can't let you take her on a caper like this one. Not after the hammering she had."

Chitty, the Air Engineer Officer, had confirmed it. "You'll have to be content with Dusty Miller's." He had tried to dispel Rowan's apprehension. "Good as gold."

He was right of course. This stupid preference, this superstition and folk-lore were absurd. Things were bad enough without ... He stopped his racing thoughts as the first Swordfish roared into life.

Miller shouted. "Give van Roijen his head, Tim. You just watch for fighters and flak."

Rowan nodded, feeling his pockets, adjusting his leather helmet. He could see it in his mind as if he were there. The low, sleeping hump of an island, the swirling water and the long, boxlike hull of the tanker. He tried to remember all the other details. The Germans had plenty of fighters at Tromso and Bardufoss. There were probably some local fields as well.

He looked at the shadowy figures around the aircraft and on the nearest walkway. Some were friends. All were part of him. It was dangerous to think that in twenty minutes he would be over the target.

He dragged on his gloves and strode quickly to the waiting Seafire, and climbed into the cockpit with barely another glance. *When you started to think of what you were leaving behind.* Again he had to check himself.

Rowan slammed the canopy over his head and settled himself on his parachute, his hands and eyes moving over the instruments, checking, trusting nothing.

How loud the Merlin sounded as he tightened his harness and eased the throttle very slightly.

He watched the darting flames from the Swordfish exhausts, the shaded blink of a lamp from the bridge. He saw the twin wings of van Roijen's plane like black lines against the strange sky, the sudden tilt as it began to move forward, the others pivoting clumsily to follow. He could just make out the pencil-like shape of a torpedo slung below the nearest plane. That would be young Cotter's.

He turned his head to look for Bill's plane, seeing only a wingtip shivering violently as its engine shattered the dawn air. In his mirror he could see the third fighter more clearly. Creswell's cockpit hidden by the uplifted nose and racing prop.

A crackling voice said into his earphones. "All Swordfish airborne. Stand by, *Jonah*."

Rowan gripped the stick and tried not to think about his real Jonah, down there in a corner of the hangar deck. Like a patient in a hospital. On the sidelines.

The lamp blinked again and he opened the throttle with slow deliberation. It was always a difficult time, with so much to see and do that it was rarely possible to contemplate what would happen if the plane stalled as it left the deck and plunged over the bows. *Growler* would not even notice.

He felt the cockpit quivering violently as he swung the Seafire to one side, searching for the white centre line, oblivious to the pale faces and scarlet fire-fighting gear, yet noting it all the same.

A voice crackled "Good luck" in his ears, but he forgot everything but the final moments of take-off.

He saw the sea rushing beneath him, like black silk, touched here and there by metallic reflections. He swallowed hard checking his compass, the undercarriage light, the boost, as with joyful roar he lifted higher and higher from the carrier.

He said after a few moments, "This is *Jonah*. Take station on me."

R/T would be unused from now on, until the fun-and-games started. It was dangerous even to test the guns. There could be a patrol boat below, an outgoing U-boat.

He smiled despite his taut nerves. If they had any sort of sense they would all be asleep.

He felt as if he were flying at ten times his usual speed, the sea flashing beneath him in an unending panorama, broken occasionally by small white-horses or darker patches of deep troughs.

Rowan checked either quarter, seeing Bill and Creswell spread out like the other two prongs of a deadly trident.

He wondered what van Roijen and his companions were doing. Slower, and flying even lower than the three fighters, they were quite invisible.

Something small and dark and ringed with white spray leapt out of the gloom. A fishing boat by the look of it. Rowan felt sweat under his helmet. He should have seen it much earlier. He saw the single mast and tiny wheelhouse vanish beneath him, half expecting to feel the flak slamming into the Seafire's belly. Just a fishing boat. But he should have seen it. It could have been anything.

It was getting much brighter already. He could see the camouflage paint on the port wing, the red and blue roundel at the end of it. And there, through the throbbing prop, the low-lying hump of land.

He checked his instruments, his mind taking one thing at a time. He was at two thousand feet. He moved the stick gently, knowing the others were watching him, waiting to follow. Fifteen hundred. A thousand.

Another boat was end-on across the starboard bow, and he thought he saw smoke rising from it. But not flak. Either its engine or an early breakfast. He grinned, feeling his jaw ache with the effort.

Then all at once the land was right there underneath, hills, tiny streams and barren looking crags leaping towards him as he swept across the island from west to east. Two little houses, like white cubes, a tiny, fast moving dot. A dog probably.

A wide arrowhead of glittering water to starboard, and more houses far beyond. That would be Svolvaer.

He pulled the aircraft to port in a wide turn, losing height, his eyes straining across a smoother patch of sheltered water. There was the little church, the one he had memorised from the files.

He stared, his thumb on the firing button, his brain unwilling to accept that the anchorage was empty.

There was a puff of smoke to starboard and he felt a shell exploding, well clear, unreal.

He snapped on his microphone. "This is *Jonah*. We'll steer north."

He heard Bill reply just as tersely, "Roger."

Rowan was sweating badly. This was no good at all. The islands seemed to be all round him, and there was more flak rising from the top of a bald hill. A line of scarlet jewels, lifting so slowly and then whipping past the fighter with the speed of light.

He pushed up his goggles and wiped his eyes with his glove. Ten more minutes. No *longer*. He saw the three Swordfish for the first time, flying in line ahead between two islands. Very slow and sedate, as if they were seeking a place to perch.

More flak. This time it was from a battery inland. He saw the dirty brown explosions like cotton wool against the sky, catching the first real sunlight above a small village.

All hell would be breaking loose now. Phones ringing. Pilots and ack-ack crews leaping out of bed. Serve 'em right, he thought vaguely.

He thrust the stick forward and watched the water dashing to meet him as a tall headland screened the shellbursts and the torpedo bombers from view.

And there she is. Larger than he had expected, making just a small wash as she turned slightly towards the main channel.

He shouted, "Tanker dead ahead! I'm attacking!"

Unblinking he watched the rounded poop and squat bridge structure blocking his way, a flag hanging limp above her taffrail. Some men were tearing a canvas canopy from a machine gun mounting abaft her single funnel.

He riveted his full attention on the sight, his hand almost numb while he controlled stick and firing button in one unit.

She was full to the gills with fuel. Beyond the bridge he could see the small shadow her hull was making on the water. She was so deep-laden he could almost feel the frantic efforts of her captain to take her closer inshore.

He pressed the button, feeling the wings jerk violently while he watched the tracers smoking towards the stern and the limp flag. With a great roar he was climbing diagonally across the ship, seeing his shadow on the water being joined, first by that of Bill's Seafire and then young Creswell's. He levelled off, taking precious seconds to watch the tracers raking across the hull. The machine guns pointed at the sky, the canvas cover still in place. One body lay nearby, of the others there was no sign.

He heard van Roijen's thick voice, "Hello, *Jonah*! *I see her*! Am attacking now, by God!"

Rowan tried to imagine the scene below. For days the tanker's captain had been moving and hiding. Dodging the R.A.F., keeping close inshore to avoid submarine attack. Then, when he was moving into safe waters, and at a time of day when few felt at their best, enemy fighters had appeared. Where from, how many, no longer mattered. They were attacking his ship, while he and his men were standing on one giant bomb.

"Close on me!"

Rowan tore his eyes from the tanker and the moth-like wings of the first Swordfish as it flew straight down the channel towards her.

Flak interlaced between two islands, but it was haphazard, blind.

All caution was gone now. He heard the Swordfish pilots yelling to one another, van Roijen's great bellow as he took his plane even lower, so that it seemed to be straddling its racing reflection on the swirling current.

There was a brief white splash as the torpedo hit the water. Rowan wiped his face, tilting over to watch, holding his breath. But the torpedo ran true. It did not porpoise and break its back as so many did when the moment came.

As the Swordfish lifted away he saw the rear gunner pouring a long burst across the tanker's steel deck.

Here was the next one. That was Troup. What a perfect name for an actor. He tore his eyes away, veering from side to side as some bright tracer floated past him. Some shellbursts, too. From between two islands, so there was probably an anchored warship here. The tanker's escort maybe.

He saw a vivid flash, and imagined he could hear the torpedo explode as it struck the tanker's hull just forward of her bridge. Spray and smoke erupted skyward, and he saw Troup's plane fly directly through it, reeling violently as it was caught in the shock-wave.

The second torpedo also truck home, and with it came the biggest explosion so far. When the smoke drifted to the nearest island the whole of the tanker's foredeck was belching flames, the catwalk and forward mast pitching down into a great, glowing crater.

The ship's wake was curving, the wash dropping away, as a boat was swayed out from some derricks, and several splashes showed that rafts were being jettisoned. The crew were abandoning her.

Creswell's frantic voice seemed to scrape the inside of his skull.

"*Fighters! Twelve o'clock high!*"

Then Bill's voice, harsh and angry. "You bloody fool! You should have seen them!"

Rowan said, "This is *Jonah*. Break off the attack."

Van Roijen sounded far away, almost drowned in static. "Roger." A pause. "Pull away, damn you!"

His last comment was addressed to the third Swordfish. It was circling round the blazing tanker, and Cotter obviously intended to fire his torpedo, having been driven from his original attempt by the explosion and great gouts of burning fuel.

"Tallyho!" That was Cotter. He was yelling aloud, his voice that of a jubilant schoolboy.

Rowan forgot Cotter as he opened the throttle and went into a steep climb. He had seen the German fighters coming out of the pale sunlight. Two of them, with another one just lifting over the nearest island.

Bill was right. Creswell should have done his job and watched over his leader. Now it was all too late. The thing to do was to wing one of them and then get away after the Swordfish.

A shadow flashed across his sight and he hurled the Seafire into a steep turn, the other plane's silhouette twisting away and then starting another climb. Rowan tried to steady his breathing, to stop himself from peering into his mirror. It was an ME 109, with yellow stripes on its wings, inboard from the stark black crosses.

He pressed the button and swore as the tracers fanned harmlessly above the German's tail.

Round again, the cannon and machine guns hammering while the other pilot tried to shake him off.

Thoughts scurried through his mind, while his eyes, hands and feet moved in oiled unison. The German pilot was handling his machine as if going through the training manual.

He was probably brand new, sent to Norway to get in some training before going to the Eastern Front.

He pressed the button again and saw the shells ripping across the black crosses, the tell-tale plume of smoke twisting and writhing as the Messerschmitt went plunging out of control.

Rowan sucked in his breath, willing the man to bale out. But he did not, and he knew he must have been hit in the last burst.

He levelled off, his eyes watering as he swept round into the sun's path.

He heard the muffled rattle of machine guns, and twisted his head to see Bill and another ME 109 tearing across the empty sky, through a pall of smoke which must have reached this far from the torpedoed tanker.

"Hello, *Jonah*!" It was Creswell. "Derek's under attack!"

Rowan did not bother to acknowledge, but put the Seafire into a steep dive, the engine's note rising to a whistling whine.

He called, "Hello, Derek, this is *Jonah*. Drop that bloody fish and get the hell out of it!"

From a corner of his eye he saw the first ME 109 explode on a hillside, and the shadow of Bill's plane as he roared above, all guns firing as he went after his quarry.

Creswell was close on Rowan's tail now, his lesson learned.

Cotter shouted, "*Here we go!*"

Rowan gritted his teeth as the low-flying ME 109 swept round the jutting headland to meet the Swordfish almost head-on. It was finished before Cotter even knew what was happening.

The darting tongues of flame from the German's guns, the familiar sight of fragments hurled across the water, and then the Swordfish drove on to explode against the sinking tanker in a great ball of orange fire.

Bill's ME 109 was trailing smoke, and without stopping for more was already heading towards the mainland.

Creswell was almost sobbing. "Let me go for him!"

"Denied! Return to base!" Rowan peered at his clock, his eyes stinging with sweat. They had been far too long already.

Creswell was saying, "He killed Derek!"

Bill called, "Shut your mouth and do as you're told!"

The two Seafires swam out like sharks and formed up on Rowan's quarter.

Van Roijen called, "Returning to base. Over and out."

The islands vanished under the curved wings, and ahead stretched the great desert of empty, glittering water.

Compass, clock, height and fuel. He found that he wanted to blow his nose.

Beneath him the two Swordfish, unhampered by their torpedoes, were working up to their full speed of one hundred and thirty plus, and he could see van Roijen's red scarf whipping over his cockpit like a banner on a field of battle.

Three young men dead in exchange for a shipload of desperately needed fuel. It made sense, he thought bitterly. It had to.

He craned his head round, the sun following him in his mirror. *Watch for the Hun who comes out of the sun.* And they were not home and dry yet. Not by a long shot.

IRWIN SHAW
The Priest

*The novelist and playwright Irwin Shaw
(1913–84) was born in New York. He
served in the US Army from 1942–45,
reaching the rank of warrant officer. The
war inspired many of his best works, including the novel* The Young Lions *(1945)
and such short stories as "Retreat", "Act
of Faith", "Gunner's Passage" and "The
Priest". He is perhaps most famous, however, as the author of the blockbuster,* Rich
Man, Poor Man *(1970).*

*The short story "The Priest" is from
1946.*

T HE PRIEST WALKED LEISURELY ACROSS the Besançon
Bridge. The Doubs flowed swiftly past, springlike and
ruffled and green, carrying with it a bright mountain breeze
through the sunny valley. The priest was round and small
and his dark, tanned face was rosy and cheerful in the
pleasant morning as he walked with little steps next to
the stone balustrade, keeping off the side as a tank marked
with the black cross rumbled past a wagonload of cabbages
into town. Two young blond paratroopers, with their caps
off, were leaning on the balustrade, staring quietly into the
rushing water, their hair blowing in the wind, and the priest
stopped next to them and stood by their side looking east to
the mountains.

"Very pretty morning," the priest said, smiling.

"Excuse us, Father," one of the paratroopers said, haltingly,
"we do not speak French. We speak only German."

The priest shrugged, smiled, patted one of the boys in

a fatherly gesture on the shoulder. "*Guten tag*," he said, moving off.

"*Auf Wiedersehen*, Father," the boy said, standing up straight. He was almost a foot taller than the priest and he seemed very young, seventeen, eighteen perhaps, standing there with his hair blowing over his unlined, rather pale face.

The priest moved on, his small, scuffed, dusty shoes making a little mincing pattern under the swinging, worn folds of his cassock. He walked slowly along the busy street, pleased with the morning traffic, nodding agreeably at the housewives with their net shopping bags stuffed with vegetables. He stopped in front of one of the shops which was used as an art gallery, and looked at a local painter's water-colour of the Besançon cathedral, his dark, round face grave with judgment.

In the same window, by the same artist, there were three plump, long-legged nudes lying in abandoned positions on rugs and sofas, and the priest glanced rather hastily at the pink and fleshy confections. A little grin played around the corners of his mouth as he turned away from the window and continued up the street.

He crossed the cobbled square at the end of the street, and, holding the skirts of his cassock, skipped nimbly and good-naturedly to dodge a large German Army truck that was rumbling through. A little out of breath, and smiling, he walked to a table on the open terrace of the large café that stood under the new foliage of the trees along one side of the square. The man sitting at the table stood up as he approached.

"Good morning, Father," he said, holding a chair for the priest, and smiling with pleasure.

"Good morning, my son." The priest sat down, smiling at him, but sighing, too, as a fat man does at sudden changes of position.

The man seated himself beside the priest, so that they both could look out over the square and enjoy the fresh bustle of the spring morning. He was a large, slender man, with weary, dark eyes and a sharp mouth, and he was dressed in faded workman's clothes, with old, washed oil and grease stains evident here and there in the worn cloth.

"I hope," said the priest, "I didn't keep you waiting long."

"I just arrived," the man said.

The waiter trotted to their table. "Messieurs," he said.

"White wine for me," said the priest.

"Two," said the other man.

The waiter trotted off.

The man in workman's clothes surveyed the priest fondly, but with amusement. "Solomon," he said, "you're getting fatter every week."

The priest sighed. "Flesh is the curse of man. I live on cabbage and skimmed milk and I walk a hundred kilometres a week up and down mountain roads and I grow more and more like a pincushion. Still, Maurice, in a way, it has its points. Everyone expects a priest to be fat."

"That's true," said Maurice.

The waiter came back with the two glasses of white wine and the saucers. "Messieurs," he said, serving them. He trotted off.

The priest looked after him absently, noticing that there was no one at the nearby tables. "All right, Maurice," he said.

Maurice sipped his wine. "In Marcel Artois' barn, in the hayloft . . ."

"Yes," said the priest.

"On the road to Epinal."

"I know the house." The priest sipped his drink, nodding absently, his eyes squinted a little, looking out over the square.

"Two Sten guns with a thousand rounds of ammunition . . ."

"Well," said the priest.

"Three Enfield rifles with two hundred and fifty rounds of ammunition. A Luger and six grenades. How many men does Philip have with him?"

"Ten."

"Does that include you?"

"That includes me." The priest nodded.

"The difficulty with the child," Maurice said loudly, as two German lieutenants passed, "is that he refuses to recognize the authority of his mother."

"I will come by Wednesday afternoon," the priest said clearly, "and attempt to reason with him."

"There will be a gasoline convoy passing the crossroad two

miles north of Epinal around eleven o'clock to-morrow night,"
said Maurice. "Ordinarily, the convoys are lightly guarded in
this area, and there is brush right down to the roadside, and
they stop at the crossroads for a minute or two to wait for
stragglers. Tell Philip I suggest that that is the most profitable
place . . ."

"I'll tell him," said the priest.

"However, he understands," Maurice said, "that it is his
business and I am merely offering suggestions."

"I'll tell him," said the priest.

"Messieurs?" The waiter was standing over them, questioning.

"Nothing more for me, thank you," said the priest.

Maurice put down the money for the drinks and the waiter
cleared away the glasses and the saucers.

"Gasoline trucks," said Maurice, "make a very satisfactory
target. They have a tendency to blow up."

"Philip will be pleased." The priest nodded again, with a
trace of amusement in his dark eyes.

"Tell Philip I pray that God smiles upon your enterprise,"
said Maurice, very seriously.

The priest smiled a little. "I will pass on yours and God's
good wishes . . ."

Maurice turned and stared soberly at the priest for the first
time. "Solomon," he said softly, "I think you are taking too
much of a risk."

The priest grinned. "Again," he said, "the old song . . ."

"But to pretend to be a priest!" Maurice shook his head.
You're always on the verge of being discovered. Any *curé*
with his eyes half-open . . . Any sudden or unexpected
situation . . ."

The priest looked around him, his eyes crinkled. "I know
this will offend your deep religious sensibilities, Maurice,"
he said, "but it is amazing how little people expect of
the servants of the Church. And priests're always rambling
around, poking their noses into other people's business. They
make perfect messengers for the Underground. If we could
really get the holy men of France into the movement, we
would have a system of intelligence better than any telephone
network . . ."

"The Church has its own spiritual problems," Maurice said bleakly.

"Forgive me." The priest stretched out his hand and touched Maurice's arm. "I mean no offence."

"It still strikes me as dangerous," Maurice said.

The priest shook his head. "Look at me," he said.

Maurice stared at him. "Well?"

"In every magazine," the priest said, "on every wall, there are pictures of criminals against Germany who look just like me—Jews, swarthy, with thick lips, and hooked noses . . . Why, Maurice," the priest said, grinning, "I could make a fortune as a photographer's model in Berlin."

Maurice chuckled. "I must admit . . ."

"But dressed like this . . ." The priest shrugged. "A priest is expected to look like anything at all in the world. Anyway, I've got away with it for three years now. I couldn't conduct Mass, but I tell my beads in public, and I carry a breviary and read a little Latin, and I got a smattering of the sacraments from Farther Morand before they killed him, and my papers look more authentic than a monastery full of Benedictine brothers, and the cassock is very handy when it comes to hiding my pistol."

Maurice stood up, smiling. "You always win this argument. Still, it gives me a chill every time I see you pass a church."

"I promise to defrock myself," the priest said, "ten minutes after the Germans're out of France."

"Well," said Maurice, "I must get back to work." They shook hands. "Goodbye, Father."

"I promise," Solomon said gravely, "to do nothing to disgrace the cloth. God be with you, my son."

Solomon sat at the table in the playful, sunny wind, watching Maurice cross the square. Maurice had a square, upright way of walking, and, knowing him, Solomon felt that by his walk Maurice betrayed himself to all the world—honest, righteous, devoid of subservience or fear. Each time, after their meetings, when they said goodbye, Solomon was moved by worriment and sorrow for his friend, and a bitter sense that they would not meet again. The trick was, in their business, to feel nothing, no affection, no sympathy, no regrets for the dead and dying. But fighting beside men in this obscure war, with your lives on the tips of each other's tongues a hundred times a day, with your life dependent every moment on their rectitude and sacrifice, you found yourself loving the good ones better than a wife or a son, and then the trick, of course, did not work . . .

Maurice disappeared around a corner and Solomon sighed and stood up heavily, pulling his cassock down.

He stared back across the terrace, but at that moment a canvas-covered Army truck drove up and the soldiers jumped out and the young lieutenant said loudly, "Nobody will move, if you please. All the patrons of this establishment will come with me, if you please . . ."

Solomon looked at the corner to make sure that Maurice had disappeared and then sat down, sighing like a fat man, waiting for the Germans to reach him.

The interior of the truck was dark and crowded with some twenty patrons of the café. An odour of fear hung over the twenty heads and people attempted to remain frigid and remote from neighbours pressing on all sides.

"This is a formidable nuisance," one gentleman said in a loud voice, looking angrily at the impassive guard at the rear of the truck. "I have a very important business engagement at one o'clock. And I have a pass signed personally by General Meister himself, who is a personal acquaintance of mine."

"I have a personal request," a voice cut into the semi-gloom under the canvas from near the front of the truck. "Please keep personally quiet."

"I will remember that voice," said the personal acquaintance of General Meister threateningly.

The priest wriggled a little on his bench and his two neighbours looked at him sourly.

"Excuse me," he said apologetically. "A fat man finds it difficult to be comfortable in his clothes . . ." He put his hands under his cassock, through the side slits and pulled at his belt.

"What's the matter?" a man across the aisle muttered. "The priest wearing a corset?"

Two or three of the men tittered a little sourly.

"Excuse me again," the priest said, lifting himself a little from the narrow wooden bench, under which there were some tow chains loosely stowed.

"Only the priests," said his neighbour loudly, "still remain uncomfortably fat in France."

Solomon sat back once more, sighing, a tiny smile on his lips in the darkness. Below him, hidden by the chains, lay the small pistol he had contrived to loosen from his belt and drop there.

"What did you have for dinner last night, Father?" his neighbour asked unpleasantly. "A whole stuffed duck?"

"God be with you, my son," Solomon said serenely as the truck rattled into the courtyard of Gestapo headquarters.

Solomon was sleeping when they came to his cell and opened the door. It was near dawn and dark and cold, and he woke shivering when the two S.S. men drew back the bolt and shone the beam of the electric lantern in his face, where he lay on the wooden bench that served the cell as a bed.

"You," one of the jailers said. "Get up."

Solomon sat up, rubbing the ruffled thin hair on the top of his head, still half-caught in the sharp darkness in the vague, delicious dream he'd been having in which he had been eating a large dinner in a warm, sunny café in Marseilles. A warm, peppery soup and lobster with a tomato sauce . . .

"Well," he said, blinking, struggling with the old, familiar cold knot of fear at the sight of the black uniforms, "well, gentlemen . . ."

"Get up."

Solomon stood up.

"Are you dressed?" The man with the lantern played it up and down the ragged cassock.

"Yes." Solomon swallowed and he felt himself shiver, thin waves of cold trembling from his groin upwards, finally tightening the skin on his forehead and around his ears in little spasms.

"This way," said the man with the flashlight.

Between the two S.S. men, Solomon walked out of the cell and down the stone corridor, his knees hurting as though the act of walking was a shocking and unnatural activity. Too bad, too bad, Solomon thought, licking the corner of his lips dryly, as he followed the dark figure along the dim stone. He had thought that he was going to get away with it. His papers had been in perfect order, excellently forged, and they had searched him only perfunctorily and questioned him hardly at all, and had even been slightly apologetic, or as apologetic as you could ever expect a German to be. When he had dropped off to his cold sleep he had really thought they would release him in the morning. Well, he thought wryly, there are several different kinds of release.

The S.S. men stopped in front of a door.

"There's a man in there," the German with the lantern said, "who's going to be shot in a few minutes. He wants the last rites of the Church. Ordinarily, we are not so agreeable, but"—with a small grin in the weak light—"since we had the Church so handy this evening, we saw no harm in letting him make his soul comfortable. I, myself, am a Catholic, and I understand that a man, before he . . . At any rate, you have fifteen minutes."

He swung the door open and put his lantern down on the floor inside the cell. Solomon walked slowly in and stood still as the door closed behind him.

The lantern diffused a thin pale light along the floor, leaving the corners and walls of the cell in heavy darkness. A man was standing with his back to the door, his head lost in the shadows in the bare room. He turned when the sound of the Germans at the door had ceased.

"Father," he said softly, but mechanically, as though he had rehearsed the speech, "I am very glad you came. I have lived by the Church all my life and I believe in the life everlasting and I wish to make my peace with God in accordance with the sacraments before facing judgment . . ." The voice was bruised and muffled in the shadowy room, as though it came from a throat and lips that had been sorely torn and battered, but Solomon recognized it.

"We have fifteen minutes, my son," he said, trying to control the sorrow in his throat. He stepped forward so that Maurice could see his face.

Maurice slowly lifted his eyes to look at Solomon. His lips were puffed and cut and three teeth were missing, with the blood still coming from the sockets. He held his hands stiffly in front of him. They were torn and swollen and covered with blood from the places at the fingertips where his nails had been torn out.

"The Germans told me," Maurice said evenly, "that I was lucky to be killed on just this night, being a good Catholic. They happened to have a priest here and they were releasing him in the morning. Shall we begin, Father?"

"Are you sure . . ." Solomon could not keep his voice from trembling.

"Yes, Father," said Maurice, staring at the door of the cell, behind which the Germans might or might not be listening.

Solomon sat on the small three-legged stool in the centre of the room and, stiffly, with the pale light making his ruined face look clotted and grotesque, Maurice kneeled before him.

The jail was absolutely quiet and Solomon could hear the breath whistling brokenly through Maurice's smashed nose. Solomon closed his eyes, trying to remember some scraps of what Father Morand had taught him before the Germans killed him.

"Son, I will hear your confession now," he said, surprised at the clarity and steadiness of his own voice.

Maurice bowed his head at Solomon's knee. "Forgive me, Father," he said evenly, "for my sins . . ." Then, in the quiet night, he confessed. He confessed to the sin of doubt, the sins of anger and murder, the sins of envy and desire, the sin of despair. Kneeling rigidly, his wounded hands-resting for support on Solomon's knees, staining the old cloth with the slow, dark blood, he spoke soberly and clearly, his voice swelling occasionally in the stone room, loud enough to be heard through the open grating of the oak door, if anyone were listening there . . .

As the voice went on, Solomon remembered another man he had talked with, played another game with, before death. It was when he was a boy of fourteen and a neighbour was dying and too weak to leave the house, and Solomon had gone every afternoon and played chess with the dying man in the sick-room. The man had once been fat and red of face, but now his skin was yellow and old and hung in loose folds from his bones. He was an avid player and loved to win, and occasionally cheated, moving pieces surreptitiously and taking back moves, falling back to his pillows in exhausted triumph after the game was over. Solomon had played with him on the day of his death, and at the funeral had watched with dry eyes as the coffin was lowered, the mourners and the cold earth, and stone crosses of the cemetery somehow mixed in his mind with bishops taking pawns and black wooden knights held in a yellow hand advancing over red squares. Ever since then, death and chess had lain in troubled confusion in his mind, funerals and ivory, flowers and squares, tears and pawns tumbled in a box mingling in obscure, painful symbols in his brain. As he regarded his friend, kneeling before him, he felt as though he were betraying him in this double game of priest and chessman, and he wrenched at his will to focus all his pity and affection on the dying man. He put his hand out humbly and touched the bloody fingers of his friend. The Jews did it differently, he thought. They went into death hot and guilty, as to a roaring battle in a dark, bloody, doubtful abyss, with intercession to their wrathy, fitful God not to be hoped for. He thought of the times he had seen Maurice coldly skirt death, and the times he had seen him wash his child's face, and of the times he had seen Maurice kill, with a rather abstracted, calm, regretful air, and of the times he had seen him walk side by side with his wife, dressed for Sunday, on the road to church.

As the voice went on in the cold stone room, Solomon thought of the times he had looked at Maurice's slender, strained face, and known deep in his heart that he was going to die before their business came to an end. You felt that about yourself from time to time, and often about others, and you took a drink, or you got into an argument, and tried to forget it, but he had been sure of Maurice. Solomon was not a religious man, and he doubted that God would condemn Maurice because he had been shriven by a Jew, but he looked closely at Maurice to see if the orthodox Catholic soul, so obedient to the ordered sacraments and hierarchy, was suffering at the deception. But Maurice's face and voice were calm and clear, as though he were being granted absolution for all his earthly deeds by the Bishop of Rome, himself.

Finally, the droning, broken voice stopped in the cold cell. Somewhere down the corridor there was the chilly clank of steel and a young German voice singing the mournful words of "Lili Marlene", the sorrowing, sentimental melody hanging cloyingly on the stale, condemned, frozen air. Solomon stared at the austere, destroyed face of his friend. If there were only some way of giving him one word to carry with him to the final wall, one word to tell him, you are loved, you will not be forgotten, we do not believe the shallow coffin and the quick lime-pit are the end, we will mention your name later in the century . . . His hands groped in a small, lost gesture before him, but there was the sound of steps outside the door, and the fiddling with the lock.

He blindly ruffled the pages of his breviary and read a scrap of Latin for the absolution, and as the door swung open, made vague, wandering motions with his hands, from some dim memory of another deathbed.

Maurice stood up as the Germans came in. "I am very happy, Father," he said courteously as the Germans bound his hands, "that you were here to-night. I hope it has not interfered too much with your business in these parts."

Solomon stared at the Germans, knowing that Maurice was telling him he had not broken, that he had told the Germans nothing, that no plans were invalidated by his death.

"It has not interfered, son," he said. He stood up and followed them out to the corridor and watched Maurice walk away between the Germans, the familiar walk unchanged by the prison, or the cords on his wrist, or the knowledge that the wall was waiting. Maurice walked away, as he had walked away from the terrace of the café, the lean shoulders set square and upright, betraying himself to all the world.

A third guard came up to Solomon, touched his elbow. "This way, Father," he said, and led him back to his cell. He was sitting there, waiting for his deliverance, when he heard the small muffled sound, like a door closing sharply far away, from the other side of the prison.

JAMES JONES
The Big Day

James Jones (1921–77) was born in Robinson, Illinois, the son of a dentist. He served as a sergeant in the US army during WWII, and later wrote one of the most famous novels of the conflict, From Here to Eternity *(1951). It won a National Book Award, and was made into a Hollywood film by Fred Zinnemann. Jones's other war novels include* The Thin Red Line *(1962).*

The following is an excerpt from From Here to Eternity. *The setting is Pearl Harbor, December 1941.*

MILT WARDEN DID NOT REALLY get up early the morning of the big day. He just had not been to bed.

He had gone around to the Blue Chancre, after Karen had gone home at 9:30, on a vague hunch that Prewitt might be there. Karen had asked him about him again and they had discussed him a long time. Prewitt hadn't been there, but he ran into Old Pete and the Chief; Pete was helping the Chief to celebrate his last night in town before going back into his garrison headquarters at Choy's. They had already made their bomb run on the whorehouse and dropped their load on Mrs Kipfer's New Congress. After Charlie Chan closed up the Blue Chancre, the four of them had sat out in the back room and played stud poker for a penny a chip while drinking Charlie's bar whiskey.

It was always a dull game; Charlie could not play poker for peanuts; but he always let them have the whiskey at regular wholesale prices and if they complained loud enough he would even go in on it and pay a full share, although he drank very little. So they were always willing to suffer his poker playing. They would always overplay a hand to him now and then to keep him from finding out how lousy he was.

When they had drunk as much as they could hold without passing out, it was so late the Schofield cabs had stopped running. They had hired a city cab to take them back because there was nowhere else to go at 6:30 on Sunday morning.

Besides, Stark always had hotcakes-and-eggs and fresh milk on Sundays. There is nothing as good for a hangover as a big meal of hotcakes-and-eggs and fresh milk just before going to bed.

They were too late to eat early chow in the kitchen, and the chow line was already moving slowly past the two griddles. Happily drunkenly undismayed, the three of them bucked the line amid the ripple of curses from the privates, and carried their plates in to eat at the First-Three-Graders' table at the head of the room.

It was almost like a family party. All the platoon sergeants were there, and Stark was there in his sweated undershirt after getting the cooks started, and Malleaux the supply sergeant. Even Baldy Dhom was there, having been run out by his wife for getting drunk last night at the NCO Club. All of this in itself did not happen often, and today being Sunday nobody was less than half tight and since there had been a big shindig dance at the Officers' Club last night none of the officers had shown up, so that they did not have to be polite.

The conversation was mostly about Mrs Kipfer's. That was where Pete and the Chief had wound up last night, and most of the others had gone there. Mrs Kipfer had just got in a shipment of four new beaves, to help take care of the influx of draftees that was raising Company strengths all over Schofield. One was a shy dark-haired little thing who was apparently appearing professionally for the first time, and who showed promise of someday stepping into Lorene's shoes when Lorene went back home. Her name was Jeanette and she was variously recommended back and forth across the table.

At least one officer was always required to eat the men's food in the messhall, either Lt Ross, or Chicken Culpepper, or else one of the three new ROTC boys the Company had been issued during the last week; the five of them passed the detail around them; but whichever one got it, it was still always the same and put a damper over the noncoms' table. But today it was just like a big family party. Minus the mother-in-law.

Stark was the only one, outside of Warden and Baldy, who had not been around to Mrs Kipfer's last night. But he was drunk, too. Stark had picked himself off a shackjob down at the Wailupe Naval Radio Station while they had had the CP out at Hanauma Bay. Some of them had seen her, and she was a hot-looking, wild, I'll-go-as-far-as-you-will wahine, but Stark would not talk about her. So he did not enter the conversation much at the table; but he listened. He had not spoken to Warden since the night at Hickam Field except in the line of duty, and at the table he ignored Warden and Warden ignored him.

It was a typical Sunday morning breakfast, for the first weekend after payday. At least a third of the Company was not home. Another third was still in bed asleep. But the last third more than made up for the absences in the loudness of their drunken laughter and horseplay and the clashing of cutlery and halfpint milk bottles.

Warden was just going back for seconds on both hotcakes and eggs, with that voracious appetite he always had when he was drunk, when this blast shuddered by under the floor and rattled the cups on the tables and then rolled on off across the quad like a high wave at sea in a storm.

He stopped in the doorway of the KP room and looked back at the messhall. He remembered the picture the rest of his life. It had become very quiet and everybody had stopped eating and looked at each other.

"Must be doin some dynamitin down to Wheeler Field," somebody said tentatively.

"I heard they was clearin some ground for a new fighter strip," somebody else agreed.

That seemed to satisfy everybody. They went back to their eating. Warden heard a laugh ring out above the hungry gnashings of cutlery on china, as he turned back into the KP room. The tail of the chow line was still moving past the two griddles, and he made a mental note to go behind the cooks' serving table when he bucked the line this time, so as not to make it so obvious.

That was when the second blast came. He could hear it a long way off coming toward them under the ground; then it was there before he could move, rattling the cups and plates in the KP sinks and the rinsing racks; then it was gone and he could hear it going away northeast toward the 21st Infantry's football field. Both the KPs were looking at him.

He reached out to put his plate on the nearest flat surface, holding it carefully in both hands so it would not get broken while he congratulated himself on his presence of mind, and then turned back to the messhall, the KPs still watching him.

As there was nothing under the plate, it fell on the floor and crashed in the silence, but nobody heard it because the third groundswell of blast had already reached the PX and was just about to reach them. It passed under, rattling everything, just as he got it back to the NCOs' table.

"This is it," somebody said quite simply.

Warden found that his eyes and Stark's eyes were looking into each other. There was nothing on Stark's face, except the slack relaxed peaceful look of drunkenness, and Warden felt there must not be anything on his either. He pulled his mouth up and showed his teeth in a grin, and Stark's face pulled up his mouth in an identical grin. Their eyes were still looking into each other.

Warden grabbed his coffee cup in one hand and his halfpint of milk in the other and ran out through the messhall screendoor onto the porch. The far door, into the dayroom, was already so crowded he could not have pushed through. He ran down the porch and turned into the corridor that ran through to the street and beat them all outside but for one or two. When he stopped and looked back he saw Pete Karelsen and Chief Choate and Stark were all right behind him. Chief Choate had his plate of hotcakes-and-eggs in his left hand and his fork in the other. He took a big bite. Warden turned back and swallowed some coffee.

Down the street over the trees a big column of black smoke was mushrooming up into the sky. The men behind were crowding out the door and pushing those in front out into the street. Almost everybody had brought his bottle of milk to keep from getting it stolen, and a few had brought their coffee too. From the middle of the street Warden could not see any more than he had seen from the edge, just the same big column of black smoke mushrooming up into the sky from down around Wheeler Field. He took a drink of his coffee and pulled the cap off his milk bottle.

"Gimme some of that coffee," Stark said in a dead voice behind him, and held up his own cup. "Mine was empty."

He turned around to hand him the cup and when he turned back a big tall thin red-headed boy who had not been there before was running down the street toward them, his red hair flapping in his self-induced breeze, and his knees coming up to his chin with every step. He looked like he was about to fall over backwards.

"Whats up, Red?" Warden hollered at him. "Whats happening? Wait a minute! Whats going on?"

The red-headed boy went on running down the street concentratedly, his eyes glaring whitely wildly at them.

"The Japs is bombing Wheeler Field!" he hollered over his shoulder. "The Japs is bombing Wheeler Field! I seen the red circles on the wings!"

He went on running down the middle of the street, and quite suddenly right behind him came a big roaring, getting bigger and bigger; behind the roaring came an airplane, leaping out suddenly over the trees.

Warden, along with the rest of them, watched it coming with his milk bottle still at his lips and the twin red flashes winking out from the nose. It came over and down and up and away and was gone, and the stones in the asphalt pavement at his feet popped up in a long curving line that led up the curb and puffs of dust came up from the grass and a line of cement popped out of the wall to the roof, then back down the wall to the grass and off out across the street again in a big S-shaped curve.

With a belated reflex, the crowd of men swept back in a wave toward the door, after the plane was already gone, and then swept right back out again pushing the ones in front into the street again.

Above the street between the trees Warden could see other planes down near the smoke column. They flashed silver like mirrors. Some of them began suddenly to grow larger. His shin hurt where a stone out of the pavement had popped him.

"All right, you stupid fucks!" he bellowed. "Get back inside! You want to get your ass shot off?"

Down the street the red-haired boy lay sprawled out floppy-haired, wild-eyed, and silent, in the middle of the pavement. The etched line on the asphalt came up to him and continued on on the other side of him and then stopped.

"See that?" Warden bawled. "This aint jawbone, this is for record. Thems real bullets that guy was usin."

The crowd moved reluctantly back toward the dayroom door. But one man ran to the wall and started probing with his pocketknife in one of the holes and came out with a bullet. It was a .50 caliber. Then another man ran out into the street and picked up something which turned out to be three open-end metal links. The middle one still had a .50 caliber casing in it. The general movement toward the dayroom had stopped.

"Say! Thats pretty clever," somebody said. "Our planes is still usin web machinegun belts that they got to carry back home!" The two men started showing their finds to the men around them. A couple of other men ran out into the street hurriedly.

"This'll make me a good souvenir," the man with the bullet said contentedly. "A bullet from a Jap plane on the day the war started."

"Give me back my goddam coffee!" Warden hollered at Stark. "And help me shoo these dumb bastards back inside!"

"What you want me to do?" Chief Choate asked. He was still holding his plate and fork and chewing excitedly on a big bite.

"Help me get em inside," Warden hollered.

Another plane, on which they could clearly see the red discs, came skidding over the trees firing and saved him the trouble. The two men hunting for metal links in the street sprinted breathlessly. The crowd moved back in a wave to the door, and stayed there. The plane flashed past, the helmeted head with the square goggles over the slant eyes and the long scarf rippling out behind it and the grin on the face as he waved, all clearly visible for the space of a wink, like a traveltalk slide flashed on and then off of a screen.

Warden, Stark, Pete and the Chief descended on them as the crowd started to wave outward again, blocking them off and forcing the whole bunch inside the dayroom.

The crowd milled indignantly in the small dayroom, everybody talking excitedly. Stark posted himself huskily in the doorway with Pete and the Chief flanking him. Warden gulped off the rest of his coffee and set the cup on the magazine rack and pushed his way down to the other end and climbed up on the pingpong table.

"All right, all right, you men. Quiet down. Quiet down. Its only a war. Aint you ever been in a war before?"

JAMES A. MICHENER
Wine for the Mess at Segi

James Albert Michener (1917–) was a Harvard professor before being appointed Naval historian in the South Pacific, 1944–46. Tales of the South Pacific *(1947), his collection of short stories based on this time, won a Pulitzer prize. It also formed the basis for the Broadway musical* South Pacific *by Rodgers and Hammerstein. Michener's other best-selling fiction includes the novels* Hawaii *(1959) and* Caravan *(1963).*

The short story "Wine for the Mess at Segi" is from Tales of the South Pacific.

I THINK THAT SEGI POINT, at the southern end of New Georgia, is my favorite spot in the South Pacific. Opposite the brutal island of Vangunu and across Blanche Channel from Rendova, lies Segi promontory. Behind the point hills rise, laden with jungle. The bay is clear and blue. The sands of Segi are white. Fish abound in the near-by channel. To the north runs the deadly Slot.

I cannot tell you what the charm of Segi was. Partly it was the natives, who made lovely canes of ebony and pearl. Partly it was the mission boys, who, as you will see, sang in Latin. It was the limes, too, best in the Solomons, the fishing, the great air battles where your friends died, and the blue-green coral water. But mostly, I guess, it was Tony Fry.

On my trips up and down The Slot I made it a point to stop off at Segi whenever I could. Tony had a small hut on the hillside overlooking the tiny fighter strip. There I was sure

of a welcome, a hot bath, some good food, and a native boy to
do my laundry. I think the Roman emperors made war the
way Tony Fry did. No man worked less than he, and few
accomplished more.

An unkind critic would have called the indolent fellow a
cheap Tammany politician. A friendly admirer would have
termed him an expediter, such as they have in big plants to
see that other people work fast. I, who was Tony's stanchest
admirer, call him a Yale man. Since I am from Harvard, you
can tell what I mean.

Tony would never have died for Yale. Don't misunderstand
me. I doubt if he even contributed much money to the college's
incessant alumni drives. But when he pulled out the cork of
a whiskey bottle, draped a long leg over a chair, pointed a
long finger at you, and asked, "How about those planes?" you
could tell at once that his combination of laziness, insolence,
competence and good breeding could have been concocted
only at Yale.

For example, it was Tony's job to run the Wine Mess at Segi
Point. Officers who drank more than I never missed Segi, even
if they had to wreck their planes to justify a landing. Admiral
Kester might be low on whiskey; Tony Fry, no. Where he got
the stuff I never knew until one Christmas. And that's quite
a story.

Word seeped out that there would soon be a strike at Kuralei
or Truk. There was pretty good authority for the belief that the
crowd at Segi Point would be in on it! Therefore the skipper
said, "This will be our last Christmas here. We'll make it the
best there ever was!" He appointed the chaplain to look after
the sacred aspects of the holiday. Tony Fry was given the
profane.

It was the third week in December when Tony discovered
that he could get no more whiskey from his regular sources. I
was his guest at the time. He was a mighty glum man. "Damn
it all!" he moaned. "How can a man celebrate Christmas with
no Wine Mess?"

Now nothing prettier than the phrase "Wine Mess" has
ever been devised in the armed forces. It is said that an
ensign fresh out of divinity school once went into a Wine
Mess and asked for wine. The man behind the bar dropped

dead. A Wine Mess exists for the sole purpose of buying and selling beer, whiskey, rum, gin, brandy, bitters, cordials, and at rare intervals champagne. It is called a Wine Mess to fool somebody, and if the gag works, so much the better.

Well, Tony Fry's Wine Mess was in a sad state! He decided to do something about it. With nebulous permission from his skipper he told Bus Adams to get old *Bouncing Belch* stripped for action. The *Belch* was a condemned TBF which Fry and Adams had patched together for the purpose of carrying beer back from Guadalcanal. If you had your beer sent up by surface craft, you lost about half of it. Solicitous deck hands sampled it hourly to see if it was getting too hot.

The *Belch* had crashed twice and seemed to be held together by piano wire. Everything that could be jettisoned had been tossed overboard, so that about the only things you could definitely rely upon when you got up in the air were gas tanks, stick and wings.

Four pilots had taxied the *Belch* around the South Pacific. Each loved it as a child, but none had been able to finagle a deal whereby it got very far from Tony Fry. It was his plane. When ComAirSoPac objected, he just sat tight, and finally Admiral Kester said, "Well, a certain number of damned fools are killed in every war. You can't prevent it. But Fry has got to stop painting beer bottles on his fuselage!"

For every mission to Guadalcanal Tony had his crewmen paint a rosy beer bottle on the starboard fuselage. The painter took pride in his work, and until Admiral Kester saw the display one afternoon at Guadal, the *Bouncing Belch* was one trim sight as it taxied in after a rough landing. Tony always rode in the bombing compartment and was one of the first out. He would pat the beer bottles lovingly and congratulate the pilot on his smooth landing, no matter how rough it had been. His present pilot, Bus Adams, was just slap-happy enough for Tony. Fry was mighty pleased with *Bouncing Belch*. It was some ship, even if he did have to scrape the beer bottles off. "I suppose," he philosophized, "that when you got braid you have to sling it around. Sort of keep in practice so that if you ever meet a Jap . . ." His analogy, whatever it was, dribbled off into a yawn.

We started out from Segi one stinking hot December

morning at 0900. We had with us $350 in mess funds, four dynamotors, a radio that would pick up Tokyo Rose, and an electric iron. We proposed to hop about and horsetrade until we got refreshments for Christmas.

Since we knew there was no whiskey in the warehouses at Guadal, we decided to try the Russells, the secondary liquor port in the Solomons. At Wimpy's, the jungle hot-dog stand where pilots came for a thousand miles to wink at the Red Cross girl, we learned that the Russells were dry. "But there's some up on Bougainville!" a Marine SCAT pilot assured us. "Got two bottles there the other night. Off'n a chaplain. For a Jap uniform. He was sendin' it home to his two kids."

We revved old *Bouncing Belch* for about a minute and roared northward up The Slot. When we approached Segi I prayed that Bus wouldn't buzz the field. But of course he did. I pulled my shoulders together, tightened my stomach, and waited for the whining howl that told me we had reached the bottom of our dive. At such times I prayed that TBF's were better planes than the little blue book said.

Then we were off again, past Rendova, Munda, Kolombangara, Vella and up to the Treasuries, those minute islands lying in the mouth of Jap positions on Bougainville. Aloft we saw the tiny airfield on Stirling Island, the famous one at which the young pilot asked, "Do you tie her down in a heavy sea?" And ten miles away four thousand Japs studied every plane that landed. In this manner a few Americans, fighting and bombing by day, guarding the beaches in the tropic night, by-passed the Japs and left them not to wither but to whimper.

Now we were over Bougainville! A dark and brooding island, most difficult of all our conquests after Guadal. Its natives were the meanest; its rains the hardest, its Japs the most resourceful. We skimmed the southwestern coastline, searching for Empress Augusta Bay. Then, heading for the gaunt volcano's white clouds of steam, we put the *Belch* down at Piva North. It was growing dark. There was the sound of shell fire near the airstrip. It was raining. It was Bougainville.

We found a jeep whose driver took us to a transient camp. That night, amid the rain, we met a group of F4U pilots who were fighting daily over Rabaul. We talked till nearly morning, so next day it was useless to try to do any business. Tony and Bus arranged to go out on a bombing hop over Rabaul. They rode in a Liberator and were very silent when they got back. Rabaul was a flowery hell of flak in those days.

Early next morning at about 0930 Tony set out in a borrowed jeep. Late that day he returned with no whiskey but two ice-making machines. By some queer accident the two valuable articles had been sent to Bougainville in excess of need. Tony traded our radio for them.

"What will we do with them?" I asked. They filled the jeep.

"They tell me there's some whiskey at Ondonga!" he replied. "Fellow flew up here yesterday."

We decided at once to fly to Ondonga to see what trades we could make. Before we took off a long-faced lieutenant from the tower came out to see us. He carried a map.

"Got to brief all pilots. Stay clear of the Professor," he said.

"Who's the Professor?" Tony asked.

"Best Jap gunner in the islands. Hangs out on a point . . . Right here. Shortland Islands. Knocked down three of our planes so far."

"What's his game?"

"Has a radio beam like the one at Treasury. If the sky covers up, he goes on the air. Sucks the damn planes right over him and then lets go!"

"Any tricks in clear weather?" Bus asked. Our sky looked fine.

"If you get Treasury and Shortland mixed up, he lets you get close and then pops you down. Intelligence says he's phenomenal. Stay clear of the guy."

"Let me see that aerial view of Treasury again," Bus asked. "Yeah, I was right. Two small islands with cliffs. I got it OK."

"Brother," the sad lieutenant warned. "You keep 'er OK! We bomb the Professor once in a while, but he's death on bombers. Come back all shot up! Boy, if all Jap shooters had eyes like him, this war would be plenty tough."

"You bet!" Bus agreed. "It would be plenty tough!"

With some apprehension we stowed our ice machines and started south. We circled the volcano and watched plumes of smoke rise high into the air. Behind the jagged cone, among tall mountain ranges, lay an extinct crater filled with clear blue water. Billy Mitchell Lake it was named, a strange monument to a strange man.

Beyond the lake we saw smoke from Jap encampments. There was the jungle line on Bougainville, the roughest fighting in the Pacific. There the great Fiji Scouts, Americals, and our only Pacific Negro battalion slugged it out in swamps, jungle heat, and perpetual gloom. We dipped low over the Jap lines, a gesture Bus could never forswear. Then we sped southeast for Ondonga.

We found no whiskey there. Just enough for their own Christmas celebration. But they thought a shipment had come in at Munda. Try the Marines on top of the hill. It was a fifteen-minute hop from Ondonga to Munda, but it was the longest fifteen minutes of my trip to the South Pacific.

We took off without difficulty and flew over Kula Gulf, where our Navy had smashed the last big Jap attempt to retake Guadal. We could see ships beached and gutted, and one deep in the water. But as we turned to fly down the channel to Munda, we started to lose altitude. The engine gradually slowed down.

Bus elected not to tell us anything, but when he started crabbing down the channel both Tony and I knew something was seriously wrong. From time to time Bus would pull the nose up sharply and try to climb, but after he nearly stalled her out, he gave that up.

"Prepare for ditching!" he said quietly over the interphone. "She'll take water easy. But protect your faces! Tony, sit on the deck and brace yourself."

I took my parachute off and wedged it over the instruments facing me. If we crashed badly my face would crack into something soft. I was sweating profusely, but the words don't mean much in recollection. Even my lungs were sweating, and my feet.

We were about two hundred feet over the water. The engine was coughing a bit. We were near Munda. Then we heard

Tony calling over the interphone: "Take her in and land on Munda. You can do it, Bus!" His voice was quiet and encouraging.

"It's the carburetor, Tony!" Bus called back. "She may cut out at any minute!"

"So might a wing drop off. Take her in, I tell you. You can make it easy, Bus. Call the airfield!"

Bus started talking with Munda again. "Permission to stagger in," he said. "Got to land any way I can get in. Even cross field. I'll crash her in. Permission to stagger in!"

"Munda to 21 Baker 73. Munda calling. Come in. Field cleared!"

"Will try to make it from channel approach. Is that one ball?"

"Channel approach one ball. Wind favorable."

"Well, guys!" Bus called. "Stop squinchin your toes up. Here we go!"

He tried to maintain altitude with the heavy TBF and swing her down channel for a turn onto the field. Before he had gone far he realized that to bank the plane in either direction meant a sure stall. That was out. He then had to make an instant decision whether to try a down-wind, no-bank, full-run landing or to set her down in the ocean and lose the plane.

"Coming in down wind. Clear everything!"

From my perch in the radio seat I could see Bus' flashing approach. The airplane seemed to roar along the tops of the trees. I could not imagine its stopping in less than two miles. Then, straight ahead gleamed Munda airfield! It was a heavenly sight. Longest of the Pacific strips, it had been started by the Japs and finished by us. In twelve days we built as much as they did in almost twelve months. To port the mountain marking the airfield rose. At the far end of the field the ocean shone green above the coral. I breathed deeply. If any field could take a roaring TBF, this one could.

But at that moment a scraper, unwarned of our approach, started across the near end of the strip. I screamed. I don't know what Bus did, but he must have done the right thing, for the old *Belch* vaulted over the scraper and slammed heavily onto the coral. Two tires exploded in a loud report. The *Belch* limped and squealed and ground to a stop.

As usual, Tony was the first out. He looked at the burred wheel hubs and the slashed rubber. He looked back at the scraper, whose driver had passed out cold, grazed by a TBF tail wheel. Then he grinned at Bus. "Best landing you ever made," he said.

It would take two days to put new wheels, tires, and carburetor in the *Belch*. Meanwhile, Munda had no whiskey. That is, they had none to sell. But as hosts, well. They could help us out. We stayed in the camp formerly occupied by the Jap imperial staff. It was on a hilltop, magnificent in proportions. A bunch of Marines had it now, fliers and aviation experts. They were glorious hosts, and after telling us how wonderful they and the F4U's were, they showed us to a vacant hut. We were glad to get some sleep, for Marine entertainment is not child's play.

But there was no sleep for us! Around our tent metal stripping had been laid to drain away excess water. Two days before a pig had died somewhere in the bush. All that night huge land crabs crawled back and forth across the tin.

"What the hell is that noise?" Tony shouted when he first heard the unholy rasping of crab claws dragging across corrugations.

"Sounds like land crabs!" Bus said with a slight shiver in his voice.

"Oh, my God!" Tony cried and put his pillow over his ears.

But the slow, grisly sound of land crabs cannot be erased in that manner. They are gruesome creatures, with ugly purple and red bodies as big as small dinner plates. Two bluish eyes protrude on sticks and pop in angular directions. Eight or nine feet carry the monstrous creatures sideways at either a slow crawl or a surprising gallop. A big, forbidding claw dangles in front below the eyes. This they sometimes drag, making a clacking noise. Upon tin their hollow, deathly clatter is unbearable.

Finally it became so for Tony. With loud curses he grabbed a flashlight and a broom. Thus armed he dashed out and started killing crabs wherever he could see them. A sound wallop from a broom crushed the ungainly creatures. Before long the tin was strewn with dead crabs.

"What the hell goes on?" a Marine pilot yelled from another hut.

"Killing these damned crabs!" Tony replied.

"You'll be sorry!" the Marine cried mournfully.

But we weren't. We all went to sleep and had a good night's rest. It was not until nine o'clock next morning that we were sorry.

"My God!" Tony groaned. "What's that smell?"

"Do you smell it, too?" I asked.

"Smell it?" Tony shouted. "I thought I was lying in it!"

"You'll be sorry!" Bus whined, mimicking the Marine.

"It's the crabs," Tony cried. "Holy cow! Smell those crabs!"

How could we help smelling them! All around us, on hot tin strips, they were toasting in the tropical sun. And as they toasted, they gained terrific revenge on their tormentor. We suffered as well as Tony. Our clothes would reek of dead crabs for days. As soon as we could dress, we left the stinking hut. Outside, a group of Marines who had learned the hard way were waiting for us.

"You'll be sorry!" they chanted. The garbage detail, waiting with shovels, creosote, and quicklime, grinned and grinned at Tony as he tiptoed over the mess he had made.

Next morning we shoved off for home. We were disappointed. Christmas was only five days away, and we had no whiskey. In disgust Tony gave one of the ice machines to the Marines for a hot-water heater. "You can never tell what might be just the thing to get some whiskey," he explained. Dismally we flew our disappointing cargo south along the jagged shoreline of New Georgia. We were about to head into Segi Channel when Bus zoomed the *Belch* high into the air and lit out for Guadal.

"I'm ashamed to go back!" he shouted into the interphone.

"Where we going?" Tony asked languidly.

"Anywhere there's some whiskey."

"There's some in New Zealand," Tony drawled.

"If we have to go there, that's where we'll go!" Bus roared.

At the Hotel De Gink on Guadal we heard there were ample stores on Espiritu Santo. That was five hundred miles south.

And we had no satisfactory compass on the *Belch*. "We'll trail a C-47 down," Bus said. "And we'll pray there's no clouds!"

I arranged a deal with a New Zealand pilot. He would wait aloft for us next morning and let us follow his navigation. It would be a clear day, he was sure.

Since we had to leave at 0430 there was not much reason to sleep, so we killed that night playing Baseball, a poker game invented by six idiots. You get three cards down. Then you bet on three cards, face up. Lucky sevens are wild. Fours are a base on balls, so you get an extra card. On threes, of course, you strike out and have to leave the game. Unless you want to stay in, whereupon you bribe the umpire by matching all the money in the kitty. You get your last card face down. Then one card is flipped in the middle. If it's a one-eyed jack, a blind umpire calls the game and you start over with a new deal and the old kitty! If a nine appears, it's a tie game, and you all get an extra card, face up. By this time it's pretty risky to bet on anything less than five nines. So the pot is split between the best hand and the poorest. Trouble is, you can't tell what the man next you is bidding on, the three queens that show or the complete bust that doesn't. It's a man's game.

At 0345 we trailed out into the tropic night. Orion was in the west. Far to the south Canopus and the Southern Cross appeared. It was a lonely and beautiful night.

Guadalcanal was silent as we left the De Gink. But as we approached Henderson Field the strip was alive with activity. Liberators were going out to photograph Kuralei at dawn. Medium bombers were getting ready for a strike. And two C-47's were warming up. The *Bouncing Belch* was out of place among those nobler craft. We wheeled the tired old lady into position and waited for the New Zealand C-47 to take the air. We followed, and before the transport had cleared Guadal, we were on its tail. There we stayed, grimly, during the tedious overwater flight. It was daylight long before we reached Espiritu. Eventually we saw the long northwestern finger of that strange island.

As soon as Bus was satisfied that it was Espiritu we dipped twice to the C-47. Its pilots waved to us. We zoomed off through the bitter cold morning air. We were on our own. Bus gunned the engine, which had been idling to stay back with the C-47. Now the *Belch* tore along, and at the same time we lost altitude. The old girl became liveable once more. The intense cold was gone.

We hurried past the great bay at the northern end of Santo, down the eastern side of the island, well clear of its gaunt, still unexplored mountains. The morning sun was low when we passed the central part of Santo, and I can still recall the eerie effect of horizontal shadows upon the thickest jungle in the South Pacific. A hard, forbidding green mat hid every feature of the island, but from time to time solitary trees, burdened with parasites, thrust their tops high above the mat. It was these trees, catching the early sunlight, that made the island grotesque, crawling, and infinitely lonely. Planes had crashed into this green sea of Espiritu and had never been seen again. Ten minutes after the smoke cleared, a burnt plane was invisible.

As if in contrast, the southern part of the island was a bustling military concentration. The *Bouncing Belch* sidled along the channel and sought out Luganville strip. Bus eased his adventuresome plane down, and before we were fairly stopped, Tony had wangled a jeep. How he did it one never knew. He came back much excited. He had not found any whiskey, that was true. But he was certain that at Noumea the Army had more than a thousand cases. All we had to do was get there.

It was over six hundred miles, due south, and Bus had never flown the route before. He studied the map a minute and said, "We'll hop down to Efate. That's easy. Then we'll pick up some big plane flying the rest of the way. OK?" Who could object? At five that afternoon we were in Noumea!

This time Tony was right! There was whiskey in Noumea. Barrels of it. Using our official permit, we bought $350 worth and then tossed in all the spare cash we had. We traded our dynamotors, ice machine, electric iron, and hot-water heater for more. If we could have traded the rear end of the *Belch* we would have done so. We wound up with twenty-two cases of Christmas cheer. We locked it in a warehouse, gave the mechanics at Magenta two bottles for checking the engine, and set out to find some fun in Noumea.

Next morning Bus and Tony looked at one another, each

waiting for the other to make the suggestion. Finally Bus gave in. "Tony," he drawled, "what do you say we fly up to Luana Pori and look around?" Fry, as if his heart were not thumping for such a trip, yawned and said casually, "Why don't we?" And I, who had never seen either Luana Pori or the Frenchman's daughter, made patterns with my toe and wondered, "Why don't they get started? They're both dying to go."

We flew north over the hundred islands of New Caledonia, down the valleys between massive mountains, and over to Luana Pori. Bus lowered the *Belch* for a wild buzzing of the plantation. The Frenchman's daughter ran out into the garden and waved. I could see her standing on tiptoe, a handsome, black-haired Javanese girl. She turned gracefully with her arms up and watched us.

"Hey?" Bus cried through the interphone. "Does that look like home?"

"You get the plane down," Tony replied. At the airfield he gave the mechanics a quart of whiskey for a jeep. As we drew near the plantation, I could see that he was excited. Then I saw why. At the white fence the Frenchman's daughter was waiting for us. She was like an ancient statuette, carved of gold.

"This is Madame Latouche De Becque Barzan," Bus began. But she ignored me. She rushed to Tony, caught him in her arms, and pulled his face down for a shower of kisses. Every gesture she made was like the exquisite posing of a jeweled statue.

"Tony!" she whispered. "I dream you coming back. I see you so plain." She led him to a small white house near the edge of her garden. Bus watched them go and shrugged his shoulders.

"To hell with it," he said. "Let's go into the bar. Hey, Noé!" he shouted. "Get some ice!"

Bus led me to the salon at Luana Pori. I had heard much of this place, of the way in which American officers used it as a kind of club. But I was unprepared for the shock I got that afternoon. On the edge of jungle Latouche had a grand salon, soft lights, a long bar, pictures in bamboo frames, magazines from New York, and a piano. Bus laughed when he saw the latter. He sat down and picked out "The last time I saw Paris" with two fingers. He tried a few chords.

"The ice, Monsieur Bus!" a tinkling voice behind me announced. I whirled around. A young Javanese girl more delicate even than her sister, stood in the doorway. Bus leaped from the piano and caught her by the waist, kissing her across the bowl of ice. "This is Laurencin De Becque," he cried delightedly. "And your sisters?"

"They coming," Laurencin said softly. In a moment they, too, appeared.

"Marthe," Bus said gravely, "and Josephine." He kissed each one lightly.

"Not so many Americans here now," Laurencin said to me. "They all up north. I think they try to take Kuralei next." I gasped at the easy way she discussed what to me was a top secret.

"Of course," Josephine said, fixing Bus a drink. "If there are many wounded, we get a lot of them back here later on. Rest cure."

"What goes on here?" I asked Bus in a whisper.

"Sssh! Don't ask questions," he replied. Before he had finished his drink two Army majors drove up with a case of frozen chicken.

"Noé!" they called.

"He not here today, major," Josephine cried.

"Show me where to put this frozen chicken. We'll have it for dinner tomorrow." The major disappeared with Josephine.

"Boy," the other major said. "This Major Kenderdine is a caution. He just went up to the commissary and said, 'Calling for that case of frozen fowl.' He got it, too. I don't know whose name he signed."

When Kenderdine reappeared he smiled at Bus. "Goin' to fly in the big push?" he asked.

"You know how it is," Adams replied.

The major nodded toward the white house on the edge of the garden. "Fry come along?" he asked.

"Yep," Bus said.

"You ever hear about Fry and Adams down here, commander?" the major asked.

"Not exactly," I replied.

"Ask them to tell you sometime. Quite a tale." He poured himself a drink and held his hands out to Marthe, the smallest of the three wonderful girls. She dropped her head sideways and smiled at him, making no move. I noticed that she wore a ring.

"Is that child married?" I whispered to Bus.

"Sssh!" Bus said, but Laurencin heard my question.

"Oui, commander," she said. "We all married." Josephine blushed. "All 'cept Josephine. She be married pretty soon. You watch!" Laurencin patted her sister on the arm. Marthe disappeared and soon returned with some sandwiches. As I ate mine I studied this fabulous place. Two more Army officers arrived at the entrance to the garden. "Hello, Bus!" they cried. "Tony here?" They nodded toward the house.

At that moment Tony and Latouche appeared. The lovely girl was sad. She walked toward us, leaning slightly on Fry. He was grinning at the Army officers. "Looks as if the Navy is goin' to make the next push, too," he said.

"Like Guadal!" a captain joked. "You guys get a toehold. Then yell for us to take the island."

We looked up. A two-engined plane came in for a landing. It would be our pilot to Espiritu.

"We better be shoving!" Bus said. "It's a long hop to Santo. That C-47 won't wait for us."

Bus kissed the three younger girls but did not even shake hands with Latouche. She was lost in a world of her own, telling Tony to take care of himself, giving him a handkerchief she had lately bought from an Australian trader. She stayed behind in the salon when we went to the jeep escorted by the Army men and the three sisters. We buzzed the garden while waiting for the C-47 to take to the air. The younger girls ran out and threw kisses to us. But not Latouche. Goodbyes for her were terrible, whether one said them to human beings or to airplanes.

The C-47 landed right behind us at Luganville. "We'll be going north at 0400," the pilot said. "You can tag along if you want." We felt so good, what with our cargo of liquor, that we decided to hold a premature holiday. Tony had friends everywhere. That night we decided to visit some on the other side of the island. In driving over to Pallikulo we came upon a weird phenomenon of the islands. The crabs of Espiritu were going to the sea! We met them by the coral pits, more than eight hundred in a slimy, crackling trek across the road. Nothing could stop them. At uncertain times land crabs are drawn to the sea. In endless waves they cross whatever comes between them and the water. We stopped the jeep, aghast at their relentless, sideways heaving bodies.

"You mean we drive right through them?" Tony asked.

"That's right," I answered. Reluctantly, Tony put the car in second and forged ahead. As our tires struck the frantic crabs, we could hear crunching sounds in the night. It was sickening. Crabs increased in number as we bore through them. From the opposite direction a large truck came upon them. The driver, accustomed to the experience, ignored them, and killed thirty or forty as he speeded through their grisly ranks.

Tony swallowed, jammed the car into high, and hurried on. After about two hundred yards, the avalanche ended. We were through the crabs! Those that lived pushed on toward the ocean.

At 0400 we were in the air again, climbing to 12,000 feet, where the temperature felt like Christmas. From the bomb bay Tony whistled "Jingle Bells" into the mike. Bus had told us he didn't like the performance of the *Belch* and hoped she would make it all right. I had broken out new life jackets at the time, and Tony, thinking of his cargo, had shuddered.

But we made it into Guadal! As we landed a groundcrewman hurried up and told us we were spitting oil. It was hydraulic fluid. So that was it! Bus laughed and said all the old girl needed was another drink. But even as he spoke the port wheel slowly folded up until the knuckle touched coral. Then even Bus' eyes grew big.

"Can you fix it by 1400?" he asked.

"Can't do it, sir!" the mechanic replied.

"If you knew what we had in there, you'd be able to," Bus said.

"What's in her?" the mech asked.

"Tomorrow's Christmas, ain't it?" Bus countered.

"You ain't foolin' there, sir!" the mech grinned.

"Well, maybe you fix that hydraulic system, maybe tomorrow really will be Christmas!"

The mech hunched his shoulders up and tried not to appear too happy. "You can take her up at 1400. But I ain't sayin' you can get her down later."

"You see to it that she gets up, pal," Bus said. "I'll get her down!"

When Bus and I looked around, Tony was gone. We didn't see him for several hours, and then at 1400 an ambulance clanged furiously across the field.

"Where's the *Bouncing Belch?*" the driver cried in some agitation.

"My God!" I shouted. "What's up! What's happened?"

"Nothin'," the ambulance driver replied. "I just want to get rid of this damned washing machine and get back to the hospital." He jumped out of the ambulance and threw the doors open. There was Tony Fry, riding in comfort, with the prettiest white washing machine you ever saw!

"Don't ask me where I got it!" he yelled. "Give the driver two cases of whiskey!" We broke out the whiskey and turned it over to the sweating driver. He shook Tony's hand warmly and drove off as we loaded the washing machine, priceless above opals, in the *Belch*.

"I better warn you fellows," Bus said, "that we may have some trouble getting back to Segi. OK by you?"

We nodded. Any thought that *Bouncing Belch* might conceivably give trouble was so difficult to accept that we would have flown her to Yokohama. Especially if Bus were pilot.

We knew that take-off time was critical. Would the wheels hold up? We held our breath as the old girl wheezed into position. The propeller whirred coral into the bushes. Slowly Bus released the brake. With terrifying momentum, for we must get up fast, we roared down the strip. We were airborne. "Oh boy!" I sighed.

"Are the wheels up?" Bus asked.

There was a long silence and then Tony's languid voice: "All but the starboard!" he said. "And the port is dragging, too!"

"Well, anyway, we're up!" Bus said. "Even if the wheels aren't."

"Now all we got to do is get down!" Tony replied.

We were over Iron Bottom Bay, off Guadal, where many Jap ships lay rotting, and where American ships, too, had found their grave. Along the shore several Jap cargo vessels, gutted and half-sunk, stuck their blunt snouts into the sandy beach. We were on our way. Home for Christmas!

Somewhere north of the Russells Bus said to us, "It's a tough decision, fellows. If we try to snap those damned wheels into position, we'll probably spring the bomb-bay doors and lose our whiskey. If we belly land, we'll break every damned bottle anyway."

There was a grim silence. I had no suggestions, but slowly, from the bottom of the plane, Tony's voice came over the interphone. "I thought of that," he said. "All the whiskey's out of the bomb bays. Moved inside. I'm sitting on it!"

"You wonderful man!" Bus shouted. "Shall we snap 'em down?"

He rose to 9,000 feet and went into a steep dive. I pressed my feet and hands against the bulkhead, but even so felt the blood rushing into my head. Suddenly, we snapped up violently. My head jerked back and the blood started down to my feet.

"Any luck?" Bus asked.

"Didn't do the wheels any good," Tony reported. "Damn near killed me. Whiskey cases everywhere."

"Get 'em squared away!" Bus ordered. "We'll belly land her!"

"Good old *Bouncing Belch*!" Tony said.

At the moment we were over the islands south of Segi. Although I was considerably frightened at the prospect of a belly landing, I remember studying the unequaled loveliness of that view. Below us lay hundreds of coral islands, some large, some pinpoints with no more than a tree or two. From the air they formed a fairyland.

For the coral which pushed them above the water also grew sideways under the water, so that the area was one vast sheet of rock. From above it looked like a mammoth gray-green quilt, with tufts of islands sticking through. Here and there along the quilt deep patterns of darkest blue ran helter-skelter. They were the places where coral broke off, and the ocean dropped to five or six thousand feet! It was over this vast sea of islands south of Segi that we sweated and crossed our fingers and made preparations for landing.

We padded our heads, and braced ourselves. Tony wedged

the dangerous whiskey cases against the washing machine. I wondered how he would sit? He was the one would take a fearful beating if we bounced.

Bus cleared with the tower. Word sped through the men of Segi. To heighten their apprehension and relieve his own, Bus announced, "I've got a washing machine, nineteen cases of whiskey, and Tony Fry in the bomb compartment." Then, with nerve and know-how, he brought *Bouncing Belch* in for her last landing.

Bus did his job well. He used neither a full stall, which would crush the plane and Tony, too, nor a straight three-point landing which might nose the old girl over. Instead he skimmed the strip for perhaps a thousand feet, feeling for the coral with his tail wheel. Slowly, slowly, while we ate up the safe space on the runway, *Bouncing Belch* reached for the coral. Then, with a grinding crunch, she felt it.

We skidded along for two hundred feet on our tail assembly, and Bus let her go! The old *Belch* pancaked in and screamed ahead, cutting herself to death upon the coral!

This time Tony was the last man out. In fact, we had to cut him out, and then he handed us first the nineteen cases of whiskey, next the washing machine, and finally himself. He grinned at Bus and reached for his hand. "Best landing you ever made!" he said. He was sweating.

That night we celebrated on Segi Point! Many toasts were drunk to the *Bouncing Belch*. There would never be another like her! Our beer ship was gone! Tony, in honor of the occasion, set up his washing machine and ran through a preliminary laundry of six khaki shirts and some underwear. Already the washer was supplanting the *Belch* in his affections.

At 2300 the chaplain held Christmas Eve services. Even men already drunk attended. In simple manner the chaplain reminded us of Christmas. He read in slow voice the glorious passage from St Luke: "*And it came to pass . . . to be taxed with Mary his espoused wife . . . And there were in the same country . . . I bring you good tidings of great joy . . . lying in a manager . . . and on earth peace, good will toward men.*" Then a choir of mission boys, dressed only in khaki shorts, rose and sang five Christmas carols. They sang "Adeste Fideles" in Latin, and "Silent Night" in German. Their voices were majestic.

Between numbers they grinned and grinned at the little sailor who had taught them the carols.

Finally the skipper took over. He said only a few words. "I see from the glassy stares of some of you men that you have already received certain presents." A roar went up! "I have a Christmas present of another kind for you!" He paused and unfolded a small piece of yellow paper. "The news is in, men! It came this afternoon!" The excitement was unbearable. "You have been selected to hit the next beachhead!"

There was a moment of silence, and then somebody started to cheer. The long waiting was over! Another voice took up the shout, and for more than two minutes Segi Point echoed with hoarse cheers. These men had their Christmas present, a grim and bloody one. Yet their shout of thanks could be heard half a mile away along the shore.

ROBERT LOWRY
Layover in El Paso

James Collas Robert Lowry (1919–) was
born in Cincinnati, Ohio. He served in
the US Army Air Forces, 1942–5, seeing
combat in Africa and Europe. He received
six battle stars for valour. His many books
include The Wolf That Fed Us *(1949)*
and The Big Cage *(1949).*
   "Layover in El Paso" is from The Wolf
That Fed Us.

T HE COACHES ARE CRAMMED AND JAMMED, and by the
     time that the Los Angeles-Chicago train gets to Douglas,
Arizona, there's no more room anywhere, and a whole pack of
eager disappointed soldiers are left behind, waiting with their
little furlough-bags at the station. Inside the train everybody
has gone mad with the fury of the war. Who cares! says the
soldier going back to his tent from a furlough. Who cares!
says the girl whose boy friend is far away. Who cares! says
the lonely wife returning from visiting her husband for the last
time before overseas duty. She holds hands with two soldiers
she never saw before, and she has starry eyes and a short skirt,
and helps kill a pint on the platform.
   The train moves slowly through the desert—everyone is
bored looking out the window at the thirsty, burnt-out flatland.
The people go in upon themselves to pass the time. A fat lady
with two kids dozes off to sleep, her head rocking back and
her mouth opening with a soprano snore. A girl named Edna
with mascaraed green eyes looks hard at a soldier passing; on
his next trip through the cars he sits down and talks with her
and wonders what he'll get around to when the coach is dark
tonight. A thin effeminate fellow about thirty-five in a snappy

blue suit explains to two soldiers sitting across from him that he's traveling for the government on very important business; otherwise he'd be in uniform too. He'd like nothing better, of course! The two soldiers just listen to him for a while, then get up and leave. Loud shouts and laughter come from the men's washroom—thirty GIs who couldn't find seats have gotten around to telling all the dirty jokes they can think of.

Red couldn't keep his eyes open. He was coming from Indio, California, and he'd already been on the train one rocky, cold night. In Indio he was on kitchen detail to an air force unit; he washed their trays for them. But nobody looking at him would have suspected this; he wore a uniform like anybody else and might have been a pilot for all some girls knew. It was the one good thing about being a soldier: everybody dressed pretty much alike.

Across from him sat an old lady with faded blue eyes, wearing a dilapidated straw hat held on with a stickpin. She carried all her stuff in a shopping bag and a paper box tied up with soiled Christmas-package ribbon. She was very eager to talk and chose Red as the one to listen. It was all about her son who'd been killed in the last war. The kind of pie he'd liked, and some of his sayings as a child. She leaned forward eagerly as she spoke, looking like a bird that hears a worm in the ground, and every time Red started dozing off she talked still louder and higher, and put her hand on his arm. Finally, he remembered someplace he had to go up the car a ways, and mumbled something in apology and beat it.

Out on the platform a sailor offered him a drink. He took a long one and coughed. "Thanks, pal," he said.

The sailor was a short stocky fellow, with button eyes set wide apart under thick eyebrows. "Hey, there's a couple quail I been talking to up in the next car," the sailor said. "You wanta try out on one of them?"

"Sure," Red said.

So they shoved into the next car—went right on through, with Red looking anxiously at every face to see what kind of babe it would be.

The two of them were sitting in the last seats. "Jesus," Red said, "they're kinda old, ain't they?"

"This is Red," the sailor was saying. "I don't know either of yer names but I guess you know em yerself so it's all right."

So the two babes laughed, and since the seats opposite were empty Red and the sailor sat down.

Both the babes wore pants and both of them, judging by the little lines around their eyes, were thirty-five years old anyhow. The one had a tilted-up nose and large eyes, but when she smiled the whole coach was filled up with big teeth. The other kept looking at Red. She was smaller, had shrewd bright eyes and short black hair with just a few strands of gray in it. She wore a blue pants suit with an orange polka-dot kerchief around her neck. Her sandaled feet she kept tucked up under her. Red just looked at her. He'd spent nine months out on the California desert and he couldn't help it.

"Where you coming from, Red?" she asked in a voice that reminded him of somebody like Katharine Hepburn.

"Oh, I'm comin from Indio," he said.

"Furlough?" she asked.

"Yeah," Red said. He found he was holding on pretty hard to the arm of the seat. She was smiling at him all the time; there were little crinkles around her sharp eyes and her manicured hand played with the kerchief. She's kind of tight, Red thought.

"Your first furlough?" she asked.

"Yeah," Red said. "I waited a heck of a time for it. Ten months. Seemed like a heck of a time, anyhow."

"Where you going?"

"I'm goin home—back to Elder, Tennessee."

"Wife and kids?"

Red blushed and looked down at this hands. "Ah, I haven't got any wife and kids," he said. "Just mom and pop and a couple brothers and sisters."

"Well, you *might* have a wife and kids," she said, looking at him sidewise. "I mean, you're *capable* of it, aren't you?"

"Yeah, I guess I'm capable of it," Red said. The blush still hadn't faded.

"Come on, let's go out on the platform and have a drink," the sailor said.

Before long they all had their arms around one another and were singing "What a Friend We Have in Jesus." It didn't feel to Red like she had anything on under that costume. The whiskey and her made him feel faint. She kept laughing and saying clever things. Her name was Kay, and the bigtoothed woman she called Boots. They had a standing joke between them about somebody named Harry, but Red couldn't figure out exactly who he was. Kay was always saying, "Oh, *Harry* doesn't know the half of it!" And then a little later Boots would say, "If Harry could see you now!" And Kay would say, "But sweet, he's such a *bore*. I can't *bear* boring people. I'm out for a good *time*," and pull Red's head down to her and bite his ear. Once she put her tongue in his ear, which sobered him for a minute—it was such a surprise.

About seven o'clock they got hungry and went and stood in the chow line.

"This is one of the reasons I just *hate* the war," Kay said. "You've got to *wait* and *wait* and *wait*." She looked mad for a second, but then she began to laugh. She took Red's cap off and put it on her own head; it sure made her look funny. Then they were all giggling and laughing and Boots said, "Did you ever hear about the lady moron who went to bed naked with a fellow and nine months later she woke up with a little more on?" and Kay pinched her fat rear and said, "*That's* what you get for telling *that*." Red saw other soldiers in line looking at him and he knew they were wondering. He felt pretty swell. He'd thought for ten months about something like this happening when he went home on the train.

It was sort of funny in the diner, though. There were just two dinners advertised on the menu because of the food rationing, and she got in a big argument with the colored waiter about a shrimp cocktail. She *must* have a shrimp cocktail. "Just what's on the menu, ma'am," he said. "You could at least find out if they *have* a shrimp cocktail," she said. "Yes, ma'am," he said. He went away and came back and said, "They got some shrimp back there, but it ain't for servin in no cocktail."

"Why, I never *heard* of such a thing," she said, looking from the waiter to Red and then back to the waiter. "Go get me the steward."

"Yes'm," the tall Negro said.

In a minute the steward come, a frowning fellow in a navy-blue suit with menus in his hand. She explained the whole situation to him very slowly, as if to a child, and he didn't say anything till she was all finished. Then he just said, "No," and walked away.

It took about fifteen minutes more to get the waiter back and meanwhile Red was trying to pick out his choices on the two meals. He wanted to choose the same things she chose, but everything he said he liked she disagreed with. "Are you *really* going to order milk?" she asked. "I simply can't *stand* milk." So he ordered coffee.

The sailor and Boots had had to take a table at the other end of the car, but the four of them finished about the same time and went out on the platform for another drink. Kay kept her arms around Red's neck most of the time; she was about a foot shorter than him and he had to stay bent over so she could reach him. He kissed her a lot, and she took to that all right. He got in some good feels too. Only once did she object and then she said, "Oh *don't*, darling," and kissed him again. Red didn't know what to make of her.

They all went back to their seats and there were only two available so the women sat on the men's laps. They made so much noise everybody looked at them, and Red felt kind of embarrassed. He tried to pass it off by winking at one pimply faced Pfc across the aisle, but the Pfc just stared through his tortoise-shell glasses for a minute, then turned around and went on reading *A Critique of Pure Reason.*

The women weren't embarrassed at all, though; they kept shouting and laughing at each other, and Boots reached over and pulled Red's ear and said, "Hey, Red, I bet you never heard about the little moron who thought a mushroom was someplace to pitch woo in," then filled up the car with those teeth again. Kay's arm was around Red's head, and her hair was up under his chin. She kept buttoning and unbuttoning one of his shirt buttons. "*Oh* but I'm tired—simply *dead.* I think I'll just go to sleep right here. *Red* doesn't mind if I sleep on top of him tonight, do you, Red?"

Red didn't know what to say to that; he looked over at the kid reading the book and then back at the sailor. "Naw," he said.

He could feel himself blushing but it was okay too, only he'd never met any woman like Kay before, except maybe in the movies. These women really live fast, he thought.

Red halfway dozed off, and woke up to see the big creased face of the conductor over hem.

"Better get your luggage together," the conductor was saying to Kay. "Next stop is El Paso."

"Oh, my *God*," Kay was saying, "my luggage is all over the *train*." So Red had to help her go round it up; it was pretty swell stuff, all yellow leather and heavy as hell.

The four of them were still half asleep when they got off the train. Red carried luggage under his arms and in both hands, and sweated as bad as he did back in Indio.

When they arrived in the station, Kay suddenly stopped and turned around to him, the way some movie actress like Bette Davis would, and said "Darling, are you taking *another* train out right away or spending the night in El Paso?"

The question hit Red like a ton of bricks, and he glanced over to the sailor and Boots for an answer, but the sailor was whispering in Boots's ear and they were laughing to beat the band. Then he looked back at Kay—her shrewd eyes with the little crinkles around them were regarding him in a kind of funny way. What the devil did she mean?

"I hadn't thought about it," Red said.

"We-ell, you'll have a *horrible* time if you try to find a place to stay in *this* ole town." She studied a ring on her right hand for a minute, then looked up at him. "But I was thinking: Boots and I have an apartment and you can sleep over there if you *want* to."

Red still just stared at her. His blood pressure was up about twenty points and a big lump had settled in his throat. She'd taken off her jacket and he noticed all of a sudden how her two little breasts pushed through the thin white blouse.

". . . if you'll promise to be real *good*," she was saying, and she laughed at him again.

Jesus, Red thought, I'll never get back to Elder now, and I told Mom, and they're all going to be there looking for that train.

But there didn't seem to be anything else to do, what with her looking at him that way, like a challenge or something, so he just mumbled, "I guess I'll stay here tonight," and Kay laughed at him, and went on gazing into his eyes for almost a minute. Then she ran over to Boots and said, "Red wants to get some sleep in El Paso tonight and I told him he could stay over at our place," and Boots looked at Red and then back to Kay. "Why, that's swell," she said, "Georgie's going to stay too." Red and Georgie caught each other's eye for a second—they were in complete understanding. They went back together for their bags, but neither said anything.

With themselves and all the luggage bundled into a taxi, they drove out through town a long ways before they finally stopped on some dark street. The others waited for Red while he paid the driver, and then there was the business of opening the front door.

The apartment was on the second floor and it was a pretty swell place with real low, plain furniture like nothing Red had ever seen before. He was almost afraid to move, it was all so nice, and he only sat down after Kay had told him to a couple times.

"Wait, I'll go out and fix us all a drink," Kay said, and Red saw how small and nicely built she was from the rear.

Red and Georgie sat on the couch and the two babes sat in separate chairs. They drank the whiskey-and-sodas and Kay talked about how *horrible* trains were, and how she always *swore* she'd never take another trip, but then when the time came she always *did* anyhow. She had a scratch on her suntanned leg and while leaning over to examine it, she explained how she'd got it when she'd slipped on the train step in Los Angeles. Red felt like getting down and examining it too.

But as she was talking, Red suddenly had a funny feeling: he thought of those little five- or six-line notes his mom always wrote him and that last one was plain as day right there in front of him: *Well son were sure glad all about youre furlo* . . . Twenty one-dollar bills had been enclosed—he'd already spent four of them on the dinner and a couple more on the cab. He thought of his old man too, a tall skinny fellow who never said much, just worked hard all day in the field. He remembered that funny look, as if he were going to cry, on his old man's face the day he'd left, ten months go. Now look at me, Red thought.

Kay was standing up, pushing her arms above her head and yawning—a position that sure made her figure stand out. "I'm *dead,*" she was saying, "simply *dead*. I think I'll get in the tub and just *soak* for a while—I've *never* felt so filthy before . . . That couch opens up, darlings. You two can sleep there snug as bugs."

Red just sat and looked at her. She looked down at him and smiled. "And remember what I said to *you*, Mr Red, about being *good*." She came over and kissed him on the cheek and smoothed his hair. "Hmmmm?"

Red couldn't get up enough nerve to reach out and pull her down to him. He didn't know what to make of her. What kind of a woman was she, anyhow, and where'd she get all the dough to keep this big apartment? . . . He watched which of the two bedrooms she went into, though.

He and the sailor lay on the couch in the dark.

"I never did get home on a leave yet," the sailor said. "I tried about three other times, but I never make it; I always get into something like this. It ain't bad though, they got a good set-up. Boots says she works in an office and yours lives off some rich guy she's divorced from. Ain't a bad set-up for us, is it?"

"Looks pretty good," Red said.

They lay there a while longer, then the sailor said, "Well, I know what I'm gonna do," and jumped out of bed.

"Where you goin?" Red asked, straining his eyes, but not able to make out anything.

"I ain't goin to play tiddly-winks, soldier," the sailor's voice came back from halfway across the room.

Red heard the door open and close, and Boots's voice saying, "Oh don't, Georgie—" There was a little scuffle and then he heard her giggling.

Well, I'll be damn, Red thought. He didn't move for a minute, his heart was raising so much Cain.

Then he got out of bed and went in his bare feet across the room to Kay's door.

He listened for a while outside—couldn't hear a sound above the pounding of his heart, He reached out, turned the knob and pushed. The door opened!

He stood flatfooted. His heart was making twenty-foot leaps trying to get out of his throat.

Then he heard her stir. He took three steps into the room. "Is that *you*, Red?" she asked.

He went on over to the bed.

"Yeah?"

He got into the bed and knelt above her.

"But *Red*, you promised you'd be *good*," she said.

He couldn't think of anything to say, so he grabbed her and kissed her. For a minute she tried to push him away and talk with his mouth on hers, but then she gave up and put her arms around him. This is the part they always leave out of the movies, Red thought. It was such a damn thing to think, he felt like laughing right there.

When he woke up, nobody was in the bed with him and he lay for a moment trying to remember everything that had happened, and not feeling very good about anything. I ought to be on the train, he thought. I ought to be on the train going back home to Elder right this minute.

She came into the room without looking at him and began combing her hair in front of the mirror. It made his heart stop dead to see her like that, stark naked.

Pretty soon she turned around and for a minute gave him a blank early morning stare, like she didn't even know him. Then her face came all together and got that quick crinkle-eyed smile. "Sleep well?" she asked, coming over to the bed.

My God, she was beautiful and put together, Red thought. She was little, but she was sure put together. It made him want to cry almost, looking at a woman like her.

She was smiling down at him and kind of mysteriously and he realized all of a sudden, he hadn't answered her question. Did he sleep well? "I slept pretty good," he said.

"You *know* you're going to the bullfight with me this afternoon, don't you, darling?" She sat down on the bed. "Now don't muss my hair!"

So Red got dressed and they went out in the kitchen and she sure looked swell, sitting across the breakfast table from him in that flowered kimono, her little sharp face sort of turned to one side, smiling and talking to him. He couldn't take his eyes off her.

"You know . . . I like you a lot," Red said.

"Want some more toast, darling?" she answered.

"I never thought I had a chance with you on the train."

"I *told* you to be good last night," she said. "And you just *wouldn't.*"

"I think you're really . . . really a swell girl."

She didn't seem so old to him now. Everything he was saying just slipped out; he just listened to it and it didn't sound like him speaking at all.

"I guess you got lots of guys crazy about you," he said. "But I could really go for you."

"Oh, you'll go home to that little girl in Tennessee and forget *all* about me," she said. "You won't even be able to remember the color of my *eyes*, darling."

"They're blue," Red said automatically. He hadn't really noticed the color before and he felt a little ashamed.

Watching her over there at the sink rinsing the dishes, he couldn't help it—he went over and grabbed her clumsily and tried to kiss her. But the look that came over her face made him let go quick. "Go *away*," she said, really mad. "Can't you see I'm busy?"

"I'm sorry," Red said, and got the towel and began drying.

He was just finishing up when Georgie and Boots came out; they were both all dressed and feeling pretty good about something. While they ate, he sat in the front room and read the funnies, and Kay filed her nails and talked about how terribly *boring* she found Sundays. If it weren't for the bullfights, she didn't know *what* she'd do—she got so tired of movies. That was the reason she traveled so much, she said.

Red couldn't keep from stealing glances at her all the time; she looked so pretty, sitting over there. And he got that sick, lonely feeling inside and he didn't know what to do about it.

Walking along beside her in Juarez he felt very proud of himself, and kept looking at her out of the corner of his eye. He still couldn't believe a woman like her would really have a guy like him—she was sure something, prancing along down there in her oxfords and her green plaid suit. When he looked at the couple ahead he thought, Georgie got the short end of the bargain this time, all right, even if Boots does keep throwing her arms around his neck and laughing at him with her big teeth every other minute.

"There's the bull ring!" Kay said, and Red looked and there it was: the dirty white curved front of the bull ring. He felt desperate.

"Let's not go to the bullfight, Kay," he said.

That crease was between her eyes when she looked up at him.

"Why, darling, whatever do you *mean*?" she asked.

For a couple steps he couldn't say anything; he felt all hot and there was a tightness in his head.

"It's just"—he swallowed—"it's just that I'm pretty crazy about you, that's all. I don't think you know how crazy I am about you, Kay." He was looking straight ahead with a blank scared expression; his mind was running wild and he didn't know what he was saying, but he was going to let it all come out anyhow—the way it all felt like coming out. "I wish we could ditch Georgie and Boots and go somewhere and be all alone together, even a restaurant, and just talk. God Almighty, Kay," he swallowed again, "I'm crazier about you than I ever—"

"Why, *Harry*!" Kay screamed.

It scared Red so he jumped and turned white. She was running wildly across the street toward a dapper middle-aged fellow in a pepper-and-salt suit. Red watched them embrace, then stand there holding hands while they talked and smiled.

In a minute she came rushing back across the street. Georgie and Boots had stopped: they were watching to see what was up.

"Do you mind *awfully*, Red?" Kay asked.

"Mind what?" Red said.

"But I haven't seen Harry in such a long time and he wants me to have a drink with him. Do you *mind*?"

"No," Red said.

"You go on to the fight with Georgie and Boots and we'll see you there."

"Okay," Red said.

He watched her run across the street away from him. He felt rotten all the way down to his shoe soles.

Georgie and Boots came on over.

"She's just that way, Red, don't pay any attention to her,"
Boots said.

"Yeah," Red said.

"Come on along, Red," Boots said, taking his arm.

He looked at her and suddenly he liked her. He hadn't liked
her much before, but she didn't seem so ugly and loud now.
He went along with them to wait in line and get the tickets.
Afterward they stopped in a cafe and had a drink—it would
be an hour till the bullfight started.

Boots tried to be gay, but pretty soon even she got quiet
and the three of them just stared at the rest of the people.
There was a little excitement over in the corner where a
Mexican kid was trying to sell a banderilla—dried blood,
hair, and all—to a drunken GI. The kid was giving his sales
talk plenty of punch by using the table top for the bull's hump
and pretending he was inserting the banderilla. After gazing
dreamily at the performance for a while, the GI finally jerked
off the tablecloth and started acting like a bullfighter and a
bull both at once. He ran all around the room, making faces
and waving the cloth and imitating the bull with snorts and
stomps.

"You think we'll see Kay at the fight?" Red asked.

"Sure," Boots said. "We'll look for her. You'll probably get
to sit with her."

"Yeah," Red said. He finished off the tequila with one gulp,
feeling at that moment like running out of the cafe and taking
the first train east. But somehow he went on sitting there: he
couldn't pull himself together. How could Kay be so swell to
him one minute and then just turn around and leave him like
that the next?

They went to the bullfight and Red kept looking all around,
but he didn't see her. There were a lot of Americans at the
fight and they were all pulling for the bull—everybody yelled
and screamed when the bullfighter got scared and hid behind
a kind of wooden backstop down there. Then when he tried
to sneak up behind the bull and jab him with a knife, people
went hog-wild, standing up and throwing stuff and booing.
Red didn't want to look at the fight. He felt lousy. He wanted
to get out of there.

The three of them ate supper together in an El Paso

restaurant. Red couldn't eat all of his steak; he just sat looking out of the window. The little big-eyed waitress took a shine to him and acted hurt that he didn't eat, but he was feeling too rotten even to pay any attention to her. All he wanted to do was stare out the window at the sign across the street. It went off and on and off and on forever, saying: LOANS.

"I guess I oughta be movin on," he said, when they got back to the apartment and Kay wasn't there.

"Hell, you can't shove off without tellin Kay good-bye," Georgie said.

"I oughta be goin soon, though," Red said. "I let my folks know I was comin."

They sat in the living room. Georgie and Boots were over on the couch together; he was fooling around with two pieces of string, trying to show her how to tie the different kinds of knots. But when he'd get one made for her, she'd giggle and look at his face instead of at the knot.

Red got the idea and said, "Think I'll go out and walk around a bit."

He walked around the dark streets. A dog barked at him and he didn't even tell it to shut up. When he got back to the apartment, Georgie and Boots were gone.

He lay down on the couch and closed his eyes. He didn't know how long he'd been sleeping, when he woke up and there she was standing over him.

"Hello, darling," Kay said.

He sat up and rubbed his eyes like a little kid.

"But you've been *sleeping* and you've forgotten all *about* me, darling," she said. Her hair was mussed—he could see she was tight.

"Naw," he said.

She sat down on his knee and ran her fingers through his hair. "You've forgotten all *about* little ole me."

He started to say something, but she was kissing his mouth so he couldn't. He kissed her too. He tightened his hold on her. "Oh, Red," she said, lying back in his arms and giggling up at him, "you sure do things to me."

He didn't know what to say. All of a sudden, looking down

at her like that, he began to bawl. He tried to stop himself but
couldn't.

"Now, now, Red baby," she said, smiling, and dug his
handkerchief out of his pocket and dabbed at the tears. He
felt ashamed of crying.

"I never did that before," he said when he got himself in
gear again.

She grinned at him, making a *tck-tck* noise with her tongue
and moved her head from side to side. "Red baby," she said.
"Tck-tck-tck."

"Your hands are cold," he said, "Are you cold?"

She went on grinning, raising her eyebrows and narrowing
her eyes. "You're sweet . . . and you're a Red baby," she
murmured, shoving her cold hand inside his shirt so that he
jumped a little.

God, she was nice when she was like this. He'd never
known a girl as nice as her. He forgave her for running
off—forgave her for everything. There was just one thing:
he wanted to ask her who Harry was, but he couldn't
bring himself to. She's pretty pie-eyed, he thought. God,
she's nice.

She jumped up. "Oh come *on*, you old Red," she said,
swaying a little. "I thought you were a great big *strong* man.
Come on, let's see you *catch* me!"

And she took off into the kitchen, with him after her. She
ran first one way around the table, then the other, laughing
shrilly when she knocked over a chair. He heard a lamp crash
a minute after she'd dodged into the living room again, and
he went bounding in there just in time to see the door to her
room slam closed. He heard the key turn in the lock and he
heard her giggling softly.

Breathing hard, feeling all excited, he stood up close to the
door. "Let me in, Kay."

She didn't answer.

"Please let me in."

He couldn't hear her at all now. He waited maybe five
minutes, then he knocked timidly. She didn't make any sound.
He knocked louder. Still no answer.

He waited a long while outside her door. Gradually his heart
calmed down and he went over and sat on the couch.

He sat there for half the night, just looking at the design in the rug. He didn't think of anything at all.

She woke him next morning.

"Is it late?" he asked.

She was wearing her flowered kimono. She gave him her smile. "Did you *sleep* well, darling?"

She even buttered his toast for him at the breakfast table. Why in hell was she so kind to him now, he wondered, after the funny way she'd acted last night? He kept looking at her, trying to find the answer in her face.

"I was a little high last night, wasn't I," she said. "I hope I didn't seem *too* silly."

"That was okay," he said. "I thought you were swell. I don't mind anything you do."

She was studying him, looking so nice and pert-like with that smile lingering around her mouth. "You don't?" she asked.

"Ah, Kay."

But even as his insides dissolved at the contact her hand made with his, it flashed across his mind that he was really supposed to be getting home about this time. He reached in his pants pocket and felt the thirty-thirty shell he was bringing for his brother Jack.

"What have you got there? Secrets?"

He brought out the shell. "I was just bringing it home for my brother; he wrote and said to."

"You have a *brother*?" she asked. "Redhead like you?"

"Yeah," he said. "He's only fifteen, crazy about guns and huntin. I used to hunt some too."

Her fingers slipped in against the palm of his hand; she leaned a little toward him. "What'd *you* hunt, baby?"

"Oh . . . like rabbits . . . squirrels . . ." But his voice trailed off—she was smiling at him in such a peculiar way and squeezing his hand.

"Love to see you shoot your gun sometime, honey," she murmured, and her fingers slipped in under his shirtcuff, pulled at the hairs on his wrist. Then suddenly she jumped up and made him get up too and put his arm around her. Like that she led him into the bedroom and closed the door.

"Undress me, baby," she whispered, standing close against him. "Do *everything* for me."

He didn't say a word. He did what she said.

In the afternoon they went to a movie that had Cary Grant, and Kay said she just *loved* Cary Grant. When they got back to the apartment, Georgie and Boots were leaving. Georgie looked pretty worn out, but Boots was still wearing her big toothy smile.

"I feel almost ashamed of myself going out for breakfast this time of day," she said to Kay, and Kay said, "Well, I'd *think* so."

Alone with him in the living room she said, "I've just *got* to leave you by yourself tonight, darling. You don't *mind*, do you?"

"No," Red said.

She gave his hand a squeeze, ran off to take a shower, and came out in a plain black dress with a high collar that made her look like a queen or something.

He read magazines all evening, looking up vacantly every now and then to wonder where she was. He felt angry, but at the same time he didn't know what to do about it. Once he went into her room and stood there in the darkness wishing she'd come back and be with him.

He'd never felt this way before. He felt helpless, like a dog that's been run over.

He read more magazines. Read the jokes in *Esquire* and finally got into an article about Errol Flynn's latest yachting trip with a girl who on the first page was fifteen but who grew to be nineteen farther back in the magazine.

Yet he was always finding himself staring off at the wall.

He heard himself saying, "I oughta go home. I really oughta go home. My old man would be mad as hell if he knew I was here like this."

He didn't have but $5.95 left.

I'll never get to Elder if I don't watch out, he thought. I got to start now, beat it out of here now or I'll never get there.

He stood up. For a single moment he was going.

Then he thought of Kay and sat back down again.

When he woke up it was morning. Georgie and Boots were eating breakfast in the kitchen, and Boots told him that Kay had gone out early. "She had to meet somebody," Boots said. "She didn't know exactly when she'd be back."

He drank some orange juice. Those two were all interested in themselves—he felt glad he didn't have to think of anything to contribute to the conversation.

He went into the living room and stared at the wall. If I started home now, he thought, I could still make it. I could stay for a couple days and still have time to get back.

He went out at noon. Went across the line and took in the row of bars down the main street. He got so drunk he wanted to fight, and in the Chicago Club he struck out wildly at a big soldier with two girls standing next to him. Without even being hit he flopped full length on the floor, and when he came to he was in the gutter out on the street and it was night. He got up and made his way to the International Bridge. The side of his face was covered with blood, but the MP at the soldiers' gate didn't say anything.

He had to ring the apartment bell for fifteen minutes before Georgie came and let him in. Georgie had on one of Boots's kimonos. It was dark in the room so Georgie didn't see what a hell of a shape Red was in. Georgie was mad at having had to get out of bed anyhow—he beat it back into the bedroom.

Red tried to wash the blood off. But finally he settled for just getting rid of his shirt and going to sleep on the couch.

When he woke up next morning his mouth was swollen big and he noticed he had one tooth missing. He stared at his face in the mirror for a while, before he realized what was different: it was all on one side. He couldn't even laugh at himself.

After a shower he felt better . . . till he reached in his pocket and found that he had no money at all. But there was his furlough-rate train ticket—and some woman's handkerchief, with lipstick on it. He tried to remember who'd given it to him but he couldn't remember anything.

I'm no good at all, he thought, looking straight ahead. I'm not worth anything. I don't even deserve to get home.

He was hungry, but there was nothing in the kitchen except some bread.

I hope to hell I never get home now, he thought. He went over and looked out the window. Nothing down there to look at.

When he went back into the living room, he noticed that Kay's door was a little ajar. He looked in—the bed hadn't been slept in.

So he got his grip and put on his cap and went out the door.

I don't deserve to get home, he thought again. I'm just about the lowest kind of heel that ever lived. They've got the kids up at the station every day, watching for me.

Out on the street, walking fast, he realized for the first time that he was free of that apartment, and he felt good. He hadn't realized how wonderful it would feel, being free of that apartment. He began to run, he felt so good, and after a ride on a bus he was at the railroad station.

By God, I'm going to make it, he thought. By God, I'll get home after all.

He ran up to the first train official he saw and asked: "Where's the New Orleans train?"

The paunchy official took out his watch and considered it a long time before he answered. "It's just now leaving. If you run maybe you can still make it. Got your ticket?"

Red ran out on the platform and saw the train all set to go. One door was still open so he leaped on and then the train started. I'm on the damn thing! he told himself. By God, I'm really on the damn thing!

He pushed up into the car, shoved his grip on the rack, and sat down puffing. Next to him was a man with a detective-story magazine. The man said something to Red, but Red didn't want to talk to anybody; all he wanted to do was sit here and let this old train take him home. He didn't want to meet anybody or look at anybody till he got there.

He dozed off finally. The conductor had to wake him to get his ticket.

The conductor looked at Red's ticket, then looked at Red. I must look funny, Red thought, with this swollen jaw.

"Where you going, soldier?" the conductor asked.

"I'm goin to Elder, Tennessee," Red said.

The conductor's smile was sarcastic; he glanced around at several other passengers to bring them in on the joke.

"Well, you're sure going a funny way to get to New

Orleans," the conductor said. "This train is bound for Los Angeles."

Red just looked at the conductor. The conductor meanwhile was punching the detective-story fan's ticket.

"I can fix it for you to get off at the next stop and catch the train going the other way," the conductor said.

"When is the next train?"

The conductor looked at his watch. "Next train at . . . twelve-thirty-two A.M. tomorrow.

Red began to figure quickly. If this was the right train, he thought, I'd have one day at home. But this ain't the right train and I won't have any days at home so there's no sense going on.

"I'll just stay on this way," Red said.

The conductor punched his ticket, gave him part of it back, and went on up the aisle.

He sat for a long time looking out of the train window without seeing anything. He felt the thirty-thirty shell in his pocket. I can mail it to him, he thought.

After a while he went out on the platform. There was a bunch of other soldiers out there and they gave him a drink from their bottle.

"Just gettin back from a furlough?" one fat soldier with a great mop of black hair asked.

"Yeah," Red said. He turned his face away so they wouldn't see it.

JOSEPH HELLER
Yossarian and the Psychiatrist

Joseph Heller (1923–) was born in Brooklyn, New York. He served as a bombadier with the US Air Force during World War II, drawing on the experience for his black comic novel, Catch-22 *(1961). Set on the fictitious Mediterranean island of Pianosa, the novel tells of an absurd air force bomber base ruled by Colonel Cathcart, who continually increases the quota of missions his pilots must fly in an effort to impress his superiors. Any pilot who wants to be excused combat duty need only ask. However, there is a catch—Catch 22: any pilot who asks to be relieved of his duty proves that he is sane by so asking. And is therefore fit to fly.*

In the excerpt below, the tireless efforts of Captain Yossarian to avoid combat duty have succeeded in securing him another stay in hospital. Alongside him are the similarly recalcitrant Dunbar and Dobbs, the latter hatching a plot to assassinate Colonel Cathcart. Yossarian's sojourn is being somewhat spoilt by the attention of the base psychiatrist, Major Sanderson.

"THAT'S A HORRIBLE DREAM!" Major Sanderson cried. "It's filled with pain and mutilation and death. I'm sure you had it just to spite me. You know, I'm not even sure you belong in the Army, with a disgusting dream like that."

Yossarian thought he spied a ray of hope. "Perhaps you're right, sir," he suggested slyly. "Perhaps I ought to be grounded and returned to the States."

"Hasn't it ever occurred to you that in your promiscuous pursuit of women you are merely trying to assuage your subconscious fears of sexual impotence?"

"Yes, sir, it has."

"Then why do you do it?"

"To assuage my fears of sexual impotence."

"Why don't you get yourself a good hobby instead?" Major Sanderson inquired with friendly interest. "Like fishing. Do you really find Nurse Duckett so attractive? I should think she was rather bony. Rather bland and bony, you know. Like a fish."

"I hardly know Nurse Duckett."

"Then why did you grab her by the bosom? Merely because she has one?"

"Dunbar did that."

"Oh, don't start that again," Major Sanderson exclaimed with vitriolic scorn, and hurled down his pencil disgustedly. "Do you really think that you can absolve yourself of guilt by pretending to be someone else? I don't like you, Fortiori. Do you know that? I don't like you at all."

Yossarian felt a cold, damp wind of apprehension blow over him. "I'm not Fortiori, sir," he said timidly. "I'm Yossarian."

"You're who?"

"My name is Yossarian, sir. And I'm in the hospital with a wounded leg."

"Your name is Fortiori," Major Sanderson contradicted him belligerently. "And you're in the hospital for a stone in your salivary gland."

"Oh, come on, Major!" Yossarian exploded. "I ought to know who I am."

"And I've got an official Army record here to prove it," Major Sanderson retorted. "You'd better get a grip on yourself before it's too late. First you're Dunbar. Now you're Yossarian. The next thing you know you'll be claiming you're Washington Irving. Do you know what's wrong with you? You've got a split personality, that's what's wrong with you."

"Perhaps you're right, sir." Yossarian agreed diplomatically.

"I know I'm right. You've got a bad persecution complex. You think people are trying to harm you."

"People *are* trying to harm me."

"You see? You have no respect for excessive authority or obsolete traditions. You're dangerous and depraved, and you ought to be taken outside and shot!"

"Are you serious?"

"You're an enemy of the people!"

"Are you nuts?" Yossarian shouted.

"No, I'm not nuts," Dobbs roared furiously back in the ward, in what he imagined was a furtive whisper. "Hungry Joe saw them, I tell you. He saw them yesterday when he flew to Naples to pick up some black-market air conditioners for Colonel Cathcart's farm. They've got a big replacement center there and it's filled with hundreds of pilots, bombardiers and gunners on the way home. They've got forty-five missions, that's all. A few with Purple Hearts have even less. Replacement crews are pouring in from the States into the other bomber groups. They want everyone to serve overseas at least once, even administrative personnel. Don't you read the papers? We've got to kill him now!"

"You've got only two more missions to fly," Yossarian reasoned with him in a low voice. "Why take a chance?"

"I can get killed flying them, too," Dobbs answered pugnaciously in his rough, quavering, overwrought voice. "We can kill him the first thing tomorrow morning when he drives back from his farm. I've got the gun right here."

Yossarian goggled with amazement as Dobbs pulled a gun out of his pocket and displayed it high in the air. "Are you crazy?" he hissed frantically. "Put it away. And keep your idiot voice down."

"What are you worried about?" Dobbs asked with offended innocence. "No one can hear us."

"Hey, knock it off down there," a voice rang out from the far end of the ward. "Can't you see we're trying to nap?"

"What the hell are you, a wise guy?" Dobbs yelled back and spun around with clenched fists, ready to fight. He whirled back to Yossarian and, before he could speak, sneezed thunderously six times, staggering sideways on rubbery legs in the intervals and raising his elbows ineffectively to fend each seizure off. The lids of his watery eyes were puffy and inflamed. "Who does he think," he demanded, sniffing, spasmodically and wiping his nose with the back of his sturdy wrist, "he is, a cop or something?"

"He's a C.I.D. man," Yossarian notified him tranquilly. "We've got three here now and more on the way. Oh, don't be scared. They're after a forger named Washington Irving. They're not interested in murderers."

"Murderers?" Dobbs was affronted. "Why do you call us murderers? Just because we're going to murder Colonel Cathcart?"

"Be quiet, damn you!" directed Yossarian. "Can't you whisper?"

"I am whispering. I—"

"You're still shouting."

"No, I'm not. I—"

"Hey, shut up down there, will you?" patients all over the ward began hollering at Dobbs.

"I'll fight you all!" Dobbs screamed back at them, and stood up on a rickety wooden chair, waving the gun wildly. Yossarian caught his arm and yanked him down. Dobbs began sneezing again. "I have an allergy," he apologized when he had finished, his nostrils running and his eyes streaming with tears.

"That's too bad. You'd make a great leader of men without it."

"Colonel Cathcart's the murderer," Dobbs complained hoarsely when he had shoved away a soiled, crumpled khaki handkerchief. "Colonel Cathcart's the one who's going to murder us all if we don't do something to stop him."

"Maybe he won't raise the missions any more. Maybe sixty is as high as he'll go."

"He always raises the missions. You know that better than I do." Dunbar swallowed and bent his intense face very close to Yossarian's, the muscles in his bronze, rocklike jaw bunching up into quivering knots. "Just say it's okay and I'll do the whole thing tomorrow morning. Do you understand what I'm telling you? I'm whispering now, ain't I?"

Yossarian tore his eyes away from the gaze of burning entreaty Dobbs had fastened on him. "Why the goddam hell don't you just go out and do it?" he protested. "Why don't you stop talking to me about it and do it alone?"

"I'm afraid to do it alone. I'm afraid to do anything alone."

"Then leave me out of it. I'd have to be crazy to get mixed up in something like this now. I've got a million-dollar leg wound here. They're going to send me home."

"Are you crazy?" Dobbs exclaimed in disbelief. "All you've got there is a scratch. He'll have you back flying combat missions the day you come out, Purple Heart and all."

"Then I really will kill him," Yossarian vowed. "I'll come looking for you and we'll do it together."

"Then let's do it tomorrow while we've still got the chance," Dobbs pleaded. "The chaplain says he's volunteered the group for Avignon again. I may be killed before you get out. Look how these hands of mine shake. I can't fly a plane. I'm not good enough."

Yossarian was afraid to say yes. "I want to wait and see what happens first."

"The trouble with you is that you just won't do anything." Dobbs complained in a thick infuriated voice.

"I'm doing everything I possibly can," the chaplain explained softly to Yossarian after Dobbs had departed. "I even went to the medical tent to speak to Doc Daneeka about helping you."

"Yes, I can see." Yossarian suppressed a smile. "What happened?"

"They painted my gums purple," the chaplain replied sheepishly.

"They painted his toes purple, too," Nately added in outrage. "And then they gave him a laxative."

"But I went back again this morning to see him."

"And they painted his gums purple again," said Nately.

"But I did get to speak to him," the chaplain argued in a plaintive tone of self-justification. "Doctor Daneeka seems like such an unhappy man. He suspects that someone is plotting to transfer him to the Pacific Ocean. All this time he's been thinking of coming to *me* for help. When I told him I needed *his* help, he wondered if there wasn't a chaplain *I* couldn't go see." The chaplain waited in patient dejection when Yossarian and Dunbar both broke into laughter. "I used to think it was immoral to be unhappy," he continued, as though keening aloud in solitude. "Now I don't know what to think any more. I'd like to make the subject of immorality the basis of my sermon this Sunday, but I'm not sure I ought to give any sermon at all with these purple gums. Colonel Korn was very displeased with them."

"Chaplain, why don't you come into the hospital with us for a while and take it easy?" Yossarian invited. "You could be very comfortable here."

The brash iniquity of the proposal tempted and amused the chaplain for a second or two. "No, I don't think so," he decided reluctantly. "I want to arrange for a trip to the mainland to see a mail clerk named Wintergreen. Doctor Daneeka told me he could help."

"Wintergreen is probably the most influential man in the whole theater of operations. He's not only a mail clerk, but he has access to a mimeograph machine. But he won't help anybody. That's one of the reasons he'll go far."

"I'd like to speak to him anyway. There must be somebody who will help you."

"Do it for Dunbar, Chaplain," Yossarian corrected with a superior air. "I've got this million-dollar leg wound that will take me out of combat. If that doesn't do it, there's a psychiatrist who thinks I'm not good enough to be in the Army."

"I'm the one who isn't good enough to be in the Army," Dunbar whined jealously. "It was my dream."

"It's not the dream, Dunbar," Yossarian explained. "He likes your dream. It's my personality. He thinks it's split."

"It's split right down the middle," said Major Sanderson, who had laced his lumpy GI shoes for the occasion and had slicked his charcoal-dull hair down with some stiffening and redolent tonic. He smiled ostentatiously to show himself reasonable and nice. "I'm not saying that to be cruel and insulting," he continued with cruel and insulting delight.

"I'm not saying it because I hate you and want revenge. I'm not saying it because you rejected me and hurt my feelings terribly. No, I'm a man of medicine and I'm being coldly objective. I have very bad news for you. Are you man enough to take it?"

"God, no!" screamed Yossarian. "I'll go right to pieces."

Major Sanderson flew instantly into a rage. "Can't you even do one thing right?" he pleaded, turning beet-red with vexation and crashing the sides of both fists down upon his desk together. "The trouble with you is that you think you're too good for all the conventions of society. You probably think you're too good for me too, just because I arrived at puberty late. Well, do you know what you are? You're a frustrated, unhappy, disillusioned, undisciplined, maladjusted young man!" Major Sanderson's disposition seemed to mellow as he reeled off the uncomplimentary adjectives.

"Yes, sir," Yossarian agreed carefully. "I guess you're right."

"Of course I'm right. You're immature. You've been unable to adjust to the idea of war."

"Yes, sir."

"You have a morbid aversion to dying. You probably resent the fact that you're at war and might get your head blown off any second."

"I more than resent it, sir. I'm absolutely incensed."

"You have deep-seated survival anxieties. And you don't like bigots, bullies, snobs or hypocrites. Subconsciously there are many people you hate."

"Consciously, sir, consciously," Yossarian corrected in an effort to help. "I hate them consciously."

"You're antagonistic to the idea of being robbed, exploited, degraded, humiliated or deceived. Misery depresses you. Ignorance depresses you. Persecution depresses you. Violence depresses you. Slums depress you. Greed depresses you. Crime depresses you. Corruption depresses you. You know, it wouldn't surprise me if you're a manic-depressive!"

"Yes, sir. Perhaps I am."

"Don't try to deny it."

"I'm not denying it, sir," said Yossarian, pleased with the

miraculous rapport that finally existed between them. "I agree with all you've said."

"Then you admit you're crazy, do you?"

"Crazy?" Yossarian was shocked. "What are you talking about? Why am I crazy? You're the one who's crazy!"

Major Sanderson turned red with indignation crashed both fists down upon his thighs. "Calling me crazy," he shouted in a sputtering rage, "is a typically sadistic and vindictive paranoiac reaction! You really are crazy!"

"Then why don't you send me home?"

"And I'm going to send you home!"

"They're going to send me home!" Yossarian announced jubilantly, as he hobbled back into the ward.

"Me too!" A. Fortiori rejoiced. "They just came to my ward and told me."

"What about me?" Dunbar demanded petulantly of the doctors.

"You?" they replied with asperity. "You're going with Yossarian. Right back into combat!"

And back into combat they both went. Yossarian was enraged when the ambulance returned him to the squadron, and he went limping for justice to Doc Daneeka, who glared at him glumly with misery and disdain.

"You!" Doc Daneeka exclaimed mournfully with accusing disgust, the egg-shaped pouches under both eyes firm and censurous. "All you ever think of is yourself. Go take a look at the bomb line if you want to see what's been happening since you went to the hospital."

Yossarian was startled. "Are we losing?"

"Losing?" Doc Daneeka cried. "The whole military situation has been going to hell ever since we captured Paris. I knew it would happen." He paused, his sulking ire turning to melancholy, and frowned irritably as though it were all Yossarian's fault. "American troops are pushing into German soil. The Russians have captured back all of Romania. Only yesterday the Greeks in the Eighth Army captured Rimini. The Germans are on the defensive everywhere!" Doc Daneeka paused again and fortified himself with a huge breath for a piercing ejaculation of grief. "There's no more Luftwaffe left!" he wailed. He seemed ready to burst into tears. "The whole Gothic line is in danger of collapsing!"

"So?" asked Yossarian. "What's wrong?"

"What's wrong?" Doc Daneeka cried. "If something doesn't happen soon, Germany may surrender. And then we'll all be sent to the Pacific!"

Yossarian gawked at Doc Daneeka in grotesque dismay. "Are you crazy? Do you know what you're saying?"

"Yeah, it's easy for you to laugh," Doc Daneeka sneered.

"Who the hell is laughing?"

"At least you've got a chance. You're in combat and might get killed. But what about me? I've got nothing to hope for."

"You're out of your goddam head!" Yossarian shouted at him emphatically, seizing him by the shirt front. "Do you know that? Now keep your stupid mouth shut and listen to me."

Doc Daneeka wrenched himself away. "Don't you dare talk to me like that. I'm a licensed physician."

"Then keep your stupid licensed physician's mouth shut and listen to what they told me up at the hospital. I'm crazy. Did you know that?"

"So?"

"Really crazy."

"So?"

"I'm nuts. Cuckoo. Don't you understand? I'm off my rocker. They sent someone else home in my place by mistake. They've got a licensed psychiatrist up at the hospital who examined me, and that was his verdict. I'm really insane."

"So?"

"So?" Yossarian was puzzled by Doc Daneeka's inability to comprehend. "Don't you see what that means? Now you can take me off combat duty and send me home. They're not going to send a crazy man out to be killed, are they?"

"Who else will go?"

CHESTER HIMES
Two Soldiers

*The black American writer Chester Himes
(1909-1984) was born in Missouri, and
first began writing while serving a prison
sentence for jewel theft. He is most famous
for his cycle of Harlem detective novels
featuring Coffin Ed Johnson and Grave
Digger Jones, but wrote in many genres,
including war. In the early 1950s he left
the USA for Europe, eventually settling
in Spain.*

*The short story "Two Soldiers" was first
published in* Crisis *in 1943.*

MOMENTS BEFORE, as the six of them, a sergeant and five
first class privates, had crawled over the desert sand, a
Nazi machine gunner had spotted them, and had cut loose.
And the six of them, as one, had taken a running dive head-first
into a shallow bomb crater and burrowed like gophers into the
hot sand.

Now the gunner kept popping away, kicking sand over them,
and locking them up for execution.

They were mad, just plain mad—and hating. They hated
the Nazi tanks, specking the desert terrain for miles, darting
about like vicious, fire-spitting bugs, grinding indifferently
over their own dead soldiers as they fell. They hated the
Stukas, piloted by mad-men; they hated the hidden gunners,
the slave-driven infantry. They hated the arrogance of the Nazi
officers, the vicious, underhandedness of the whole dirty Axis
war machine and everything it stood for.

But it was sight of the seventh soldier whom they discovered
in the bomb crater when they raised their heads, spitting sand,

and looked about, that caused Private Joshua Crabtree's eyes
to get small and bitter mean. The seventh soldier was a very
black American Negro, and Private Crabtree was from Elmira,
Georgia. The sight of a Negro in a uniform similar to his was
enough to make him go berserk.

Here, when he was just in a mind to do some really
serious fighting, he finds himself in a bomb gully beside a
nig—enough to make him take out his gun and shoot out
the coon's brains. Ridges rolled down his jaws and his hand
trembled on his gun.

The sergeant in command greeted the colored soldier
pleasantly, "Hello there, soldier, how'd you find this hole?"

"Ah was chasin' a fly," the colored soldier grinned. "Kinda
rough outside, ain't it?"

Private Crabtree turned to the colored soldier and asked
gratingly, "Whuss yo' name, George?"

Flatly, the colored soldier replied, "George'll do."

The sergeant said, "If we had some tea we could talk
better—"

"Ef'n Ah had a quart of gin—" George began.

". . . but since we ain't got any," the sergeant continued,
slipping back into authority, "we got to get outa here."

It hit them, hard and heavy, cutting conversation and
bringing back the battle. Tanks were now moving somewhere
close, the flat, steady flack of automatic cannons topping motor
roar; and overhead could be seen the Stukas, coming down one
at a time in their crazy intricate dives with Spitfires on their
tails and F.W. 190's trying to fight them off.

They had to get out of there; they had to go somewhere.

"If bullets were made of butter—" a soldier began facetiously,
and caught a face full of sand from another burst of machine
gun fire cutting away the lip of the crater.

"Well, it ain't like we could choose the Ritz instead," the
sergeant pointed out. "That gunner is digging close."

White-faced and taut, the men looked at each other. They
could make a break for it, all in opposite directions, and hope
that some would get away. It wasn't so far back to where their
lines had been, but judging from the closeness of the tanks it
was highly probable that this flexible front had warped a mile
since they had set out on their mission twenty minutes before.

But the reality of desert warfare had taught them that a man going away was as big as a battleship, and even the Italians could hit soldiers in the back.

Or they could lie there and pray for rain, as the saying goes.

Private Crabtree tamped chewing tobacco into his jaw, spat in the sand. "Who'll jine me for the jubilee?" he asked. He got it off all right; not a quaver.

"We'll all go," the sergeant hung up the tentative suggestion, giving all choice of a hero's death.

"Naw, two can do it better," Private Crabtree vetoed. "If we get the jaybird, the rest of you make a break for the lines. And if we don't—well, put out the light and go to bed. Now who's the man?"

"Me!" five voices chimed in unison, but the colored soldier, George, halfway over the far edge, came suddenly to his feet, caught in the blinding glare, gun slanted at a rabbit hunter's angle. He pressed his elbows to his hips, hitched up his pants, said, "Well, ef'n it ain't Basin Street," and took off, running a zigzag course toward the slight elevation where the machine gun lay. Slugs picked up puffs about his feet.

Cursing a blue streak, Private Crabtree jumped erect in the crater and ran straight up over the edge like a mountain-climbing goat, his tall, angular, cotton-chopping frame looking like a scarecrow chasing birds. Out of the corners of his eyes he saw George churning up a grotesque pattern of sand, and he thought evilly, "Goldurned coon, thinks he's good as a white man in that uniform." But the main funnel of his vision was focused on the machine gunner whom he could see quite plainly now.

For an instant the gunner ceased firing to level his sights on George. Private Crabtree dug in, plowing to a stop, caught a quick balance and drew a bead on the gunner's neck, just below the ear. Used to knocking squirrels out of pine trees with a twenty-two rifle, he hadn't missed anything as big as the head of a man he had shot at since he was twelve years old.

But he hesitated—let the smart-alecky coon get it first, he thought. So occupied was he with this private hatred in his soul, he forgot the winning of the war; and he did not even hear the shrill, piercing stab of the Stuka's whistle, doing a vertical dive on top of his head, until he saw George turn and begin firing at it, disregarding the machine gun blasting away at him.

It all blew in at once, happening on Private Crabtree's brain, but it did not rationalize. The machine gun burst and George went down like a chopped tree. Private Crabtree knocked the top off the Nazi gunner's head; and at two hundred feet the Stuka dug a three-foot hole with machine gun slugs right in front of his face. Private Crabtree jumped backwards six feet, as if dodging the bullets; and the Stuka climbed and started down again.

That Nazi pilot must be blowing his top, Private Crabtree thought. If Adolf could see him now, wasting his ammunition and risking, not only the precious dive bomber, but himself, a precious dive pilot, as well, trying to get one lone soldier in a battle that ran for miles, he'd throw another epileptic fit. But as these thoughts cut their slightly amusing trajectory across the surface of his brain, he was already running toward George.

Reaching him, he swung his own rifle across his back and hoisted him in his arms. It seemed as if suddenly the whole war came to a head at that spot. Crazily, insanely, peppering the sand with machine gun slugs, the Stuka pilot let go a bomb like a drugged maniac, and riding so close on top of it, blew himself out of the sky.

Seeing the bomb coming, Private Crabtree had dived with George, hitting the sand and rolling over, feet up. The blast flung him an even dozen feet, buried him in the sand; but for the heel of his shoe which had been neatly hewn off, the bomb fragments had gone just above.

From a short distance, the Nazi tankers, thinking surely the Stuka pilot had spotted the United Nations' camouflaged headquarters, turned towards them, cutting loose. But the British and American tanks (those General Grants) came out to meet them, and caught them in a bag.

Resurrecting himself and spitting sand, Private Crabtree crawled back to George, picked him up again and started running, squinting half-blindedly through the dirt in his eyes.

"Set me down, white brother, and save yo'self," George whispered through blood-flecked lips. "Ah hear de chariot comin'."

But Private Crabtree kept running on, through the ankle-deep sand, hot enough to broil a pheasant, through the tanks and the bombers and the bullets and the whole, roaring, screaming, bloody war, hanging on to George.

And even after George was dead, in his heart Private Crabtree still carried him, for days, for weeks, for years, back to home, back to Georgia.

NORMAN MAILER
The Education of Samuel Croft

*The American novelist Norman Mailer
(1923–) was born in New Jersey, and
educated at Harvard. During World War
II he served in the Pacific as an infantryman
with the 112th Cavalry from Texas. His
first novel,* The Naked and the Dead
*(1948). a classic of realistic war fiction,
draws heavily on this time. The novel tells
the story of a platoon of diverse American
GIs as they invade and later undertake a
long-range patrol on the fictitious Japanese-
held island of Anopopei. Mailer's other
books include* Barbary Shore *(1951),*
An American Dream *(1965), and the
Pulitzer Prize-winning* The Armies of
the Night *(1969). He was gaoled in
1967 for his part in the Vietnam anti-war
movement.*

The selection that follows is from The
Naked and the Dead. *Sergeant Croft,
the platoon's leader, has just taken up a
position opposite the Japanese line. The
"Time Machine" mentioned in the story is
the technique Mailer uses to transport the
reader back to the character's life before they
joined up.*

HE SAT DOWN ON THE edge of the hole and peered
through the bushes at the river. The jungle completely
surrounded him, and now that he was no longer active, he felt

very weary and a little depressed. To counteract this mood, he began to feel the various objects in the hole. There were three boxes of belt ammunition and a row of seven grenades lined up neatly at the base of the machine-gun. At his feet were a box of flares and a flare gun. He picked it up and broke open the breech quietly, loaded it, and cocked it. Then he set it down beside him.

A few shells murmured overhead and began to fall. He was a little surprised at how near they landed to the other side of the river. Not more than a few hundred yards away, the noise of their explosion was extremely loud; a few pieces of shrapnel lashed the leaves on the trees above him. He broke off a stalk from a plant and put it in his mouth, chewing slowly and reflectively. He guessed that the weapons platoon of A Company had fired, and he tried to determine which trail at the fork would lead to them in case he had to pull back his men. Now he was patient and at ease; the danger of their position neutralized the anticipation for some combat he had felt earlier, and he was left cool and calm and very tired.

The mortar shells were falling perhaps fifty yards in front of the platoon at his left, and Croft spat quietly. It was too close to be merely harassing fire; someone had heard something in the jungle on the other side of the river or they would never have called for mortars so close to their own position. His hand explored the hole again and discovered a field telephone. Croft picked up the receiver, listened quietly. It was an open line, and probably confined to the platoons of A Company. Two men were talking in voices so low that he strained to hear them.

"Walk it up another fifty and then bring it back."

"You sure they're Japs?"

"I swear I heard them talking."

Croft stared tensely across the river. The moon had come out, and the strands of beach on either side of the stream were shining with a silver glow. The jungle wall on the other side looked impenetrable.

The mortars fired again behind him with a cruel flat sound. He watched the shells land in the jungle, and then creep nearer to the river in successive volleys. A mortar answered from the

Japanese side of the river, and about a quarter of a mile to the left Croft could hear several machine-guns spattering at each other, the uproar deep and irregular. Croft picked up the phone and whistled into it. "Wilson," he whispered. "*Wilson!*" There was no answer and he debated whether to walk over to Wilson's hole. Silently Croft cursed him for not noticing the phone, and then berated himself for not having discovered it before he briefed the others. He looked out across the river. Fine sergeant I am, he told himself.

His ears were keyed to all the sounds of the night, and from long experience he sifted out the ones that were meaningless. If an animal rustled in its hole, he paid no attention; if some crickets chirped, his ear disregarded them. Now he picked a muffled slithering sound which he knew could be made only by men moving through a thin patch of jungle. He peered across the river, trying to determine where the foliage was least dense. At a point between his gun and Wilson's there was a grove of a few coconut trees sparse enough to allow men to assemble; as he stared into that patch of wood, he was certain he heard a man move. Croft's mouth tightened. His hand felt for the bolt of the machine-gun, and he slowly brought it to bear on the coconut grove. The rustling grew louder; it seemed as if men were creeping through the brush on the other side of the river to a point opposite his gun. Croft swallowed once. Tiny charges seemed to pulse through his limbs and his head was as empty and shockingly aware as if it had been plunged into a pail of freezing water. He wet his lips and shifted his position slightly, feeling as though he could hear the flexing of his muscles.

The Jap mortar fired again and he started. The shells were falling by the next platoon, the sound painful and jarring to him. He stared out on the moonlit river until his eyes deceived him; he began to think he could see the heads of men in the dark swirls of the current. Croft gazed down at his knees for an instant and then across the river again. He looked a little to the left or right of where he thought the Japanese might be; from long experience he had learned a man could not look directly at an object and see it in the darkness. Something seemed to move in the grove, and a new trickle of sweat formed and rolled down his back. He twisted uncomfortably. Croft was unbearably tense, but the sensation was not wholly unpleasant.

He wondered if Wilson had noticed the sounds, and then in answer to his question, there was the unmistakable clicking of a machine-gun bolt. To Croft's keyed senses, the sound echoed up and down the river, and he was furious that Wilson should have revealed his position. The rustling in the brush became louder and Croft was convinced he could hear voices whispering on the other side of the river. He fumbled for a grenade and placed it at his feet.

Then he heard a sound which pierced his flesh. Someone called from across the river, "Yank, Yank!" Croft sat numb. The voice was thin and high-pitched, hideous in a whisper. "That's a Jap," Croft told himself. He was incapable of moving for that instant.

"Yank!" It was calling to him. "Yank. We you coming-to-get, Yank."

The night lay like a heavy stifling mat over the river. Croft tried to breathe.

"We you coming-to-get, Yank."

Croft felt as if a hand had suddenly clapped against his back, traveled up his spine over his skull to clutch at the hair on his forehead. "Coming to get you, Yank," he heard himself whisper. He had the agonizing frustration of a man in a nightmare who wants to scream and cannot utter a sound. "We you *coming-to-get*, Yank."

He shivered terribly for a moment, and his hands seemed congealed on the machine-gun. He could not bear the intense pressure in his head.

"We you coming-to-get, Yank," the voice screamed.

"COME AND GET ME, YOU SONSOFBITCHES," Croft roared. He shouted with every fiber of his body as though he plunged at an oaken door.

There was no sound at all for perhaps ten seconds, nothing but the moonlight on the river and the taut rapt buzzing of the crickets. Then the voice spoke again. "Oh, we come, Yank, we come."

Croft pulled back the bolt on his machine-gun, and rammed it home. His heart was still beating with frenzy. "Recon . . .

RECON, UP ON THE LINE," he shouted with all his strength.

A machine-gun lashed at him from across the river, and he ducked in his hole. In the darkness, it spat a vindictive white light like an acetylene torch, and its sound was terrifying. Croft was holding himself together by the force of his will. He pressed the trigger of his gun and it leapt and bucked under his hand. The tracers spewed wildly into the jungle on the other side of the river.

But the noise, the vibration of his gun, calmed him. He directed it to where he had seen the Japanese gunfire and loosed a volley. The handle pounded against his fist, and he had to steady it with both hands. The hot metallic smell of the barrel eddied back to him, made what he was doing real again. He ducked in his hole waiting for the reply and winced involuntarily as the bullets whipped past.

BEE-YOWWWW! ... BEE-YOOWWWW! Some dirt snapped at his face from the ricochets. Croft was not conscious of feeling it. He had the surface numbness a man has in a fight. He flinched at sounds, his mouth tightened and loosened, his eyes stared, but he was oblivious to his body.

Croft fired the gun again, held it for a long vicious burst, and then ducked in his hole. An awful scream singed the night, and for an instant Croft grinned weakly. Got him he thought. He saw the metal burning through flesh, shattering the bones in its path. "AIIYOHHHH." The scream froze him again, and for an odd disconnected instant he experienced again the whole complex of sounds and smells and sighs when a calf was branded. "RECON, UP ... UP!" he shouted furiously and fired steadily for ten seconds to cover their advance. As he paused he could hear some men crawling behind him, and he whispered, "Recon?"

"Yeah." Gallagher dropped into the hole with him. "Mother of Mary," he muttered. Croft could feel him shaking beside him.

"Stop it!" He gripped his arm tensely. "The other men up?"

"Yeah."

Croft looked across the river again. Everything was silent, and the disconnected abrupt spurts of fire were forgotten like vanished sparks from a grindstone. Now that he was no longer alone, Croft was able to plan. The fact that men were up with him, were scattered in the brush along the bank between their two machine-guns, recovered his sense of command. "They're going to attack soon," he whispered hoarsely in Gallagher's ear.

Gallagher trembled again. "Ohh. No way to wake up," he tried to say, but his voice kept lapsing.

"Look," Croft whispered. "Creep along the line and tell them to hold fire until the Japs start to cross the river."

"I can't, I can't," Gallagher whispered.

Croft felt like striking him. "Go!" he whispered.

"I can't."

The Jap machine-gun lashed at them from across the river. The bullets went singing into the jungle behind them, ripping at leaves. The tracers looked like red splints of lightning as they flattened into the jungle. A thousand rifles seemed to be firing at them from across the river, and the two men pressed themselves against the bottom of the hole. The sounds cracked against their eardrums. Croft's head ached. Firing the machine-gun had partially deafened him. BEE-YOWWWW! A ricochet slapped some more dirt on top of them. Croft felt it pattering on his back this time. He was trying to sense the moment when he would have to raise his head and fire the gun. The firing seemed to slacken, and he lifted up his eyes cautiously. BEE-YOWWWW, BEE-YOWWWW! He dropped in the hole again. The Japanese machine-gun raked through the brush at them.

There was a shrill screaming sound, and the men covered their heads with their arms. BAA-ROWWMM, BAA-ROWWMM, ROWWMM, ROWWMM. The mortars exploded all about them, and something picked Gallagher up, shook him, and then released him. "O God," he cried. A clod of dirt stung his neck. BAA-ROWWMM, BAA-ROWWMM.

"Jesus, I'm hit," someone screamed, "I'm hit. Something hit me."

BAA-ROWWMM.

Gallagher rebelled against the force of the explosions. "Stop, I give up," he screamed. "STOP! . . . I give up! I give up!" At that instant he no longer knew what made him cry out.

BAA-ROWWMM, BAA-ROWWMM.

"I'm hit, I'm hit," someone was screaming. The Japanese rifles were firing again. Croft lay on the floor of the hole with his hands against the ground and every muscle poised in its place.

BAA-ROWWMM, TEEEEEEE! The shrapnel was singing as it scattered through the foliage.

Croft picked up his flare gun. The firing had not abated, but through it he heard someone shouting in Japanese. He pointed the gun in the air.

"Here they come," Croft said.

He fired the flare and shouted, "STOP 'EM!"

A shrill cry came out of the jungle across the river. It was the scream a man might utter if his foot was being crushed. "AAAIIIIII, AAAIIIIII."

The flare burst at the moment the Japanese started their charge. Croft had a split perception of the Japanese machine-gun firing from a flank, and then began to fire automatically, not looking where he fired, but holding his gun low, swinging it from side to side. He could not hear the other guns fire, but saw their muzzle blasts like exhausts.

He had a startling frozen picture of the Japanese running toward him across the narrow river. "AAAAIIIIIIIIIIH," he heard again. In the light of the flare the Japanese had the stark frozen quality of men revealed by a shaft of lightning. Croft no longer saw anything clearly, he could not have said at that moment where his hands ended and the machine-gun began; he was lost in a vast moil of noise out of which individual screams and shouts etched in his mind for an instant. He could never have counted the Japanese who charged across the river; he knew only that his finger was rigid on the trigger bar. He could not have loosened it. In those few moments he felt no sense of danger. He just kept firing.

The line of men who charged across the river began to fall. In the water they were slowed considerably and the concentrated fire from recon's side raged at them like a wind across an open field. They began to stumble over the bodies ahead of them. Croft saw one soldier reach into the air behind another's body as though trying to clutch something in the sky and Croft fired at him for what seemed many seconds before the arm collapsed.

He looked to his right and saw three men trying to cross the river where it turned and ran parallel to the bluff. He swung the gun about and lashed them with it. One man fell, and the other two paused uncertainly and began to run back toward their own bank of the river. Croft had no time to follow them; some soldiers had reached the beach on his side and were charging the gun. He fired point blank at them, and they collapsed about five yards from his hole.

Croft fired and fired, switching targets with the quick reflexes of an athlete shifting for a ball. As soon as he saw men falling he would attack another group. The line of Japanese broke into little bunches of men who wavered, began to retreat.

The light of the flare went out and Croft was blinded for a moment. There was no sound again in the darkness and he fumbled for another flare, feeling an almost desperate urgency. "Where is it?" he whispered to Gallagher.

"What?"

"Shit." Croft's hand found the flare box, and he loaded the gun again. He was beginning to see in the darkness, and he hesitated. But something moved on the river and he fired the flare. As it burst, a few Japanese soldiers were caught motionless in the water. Croft pivoted his gun on them and fired. One of the soldiers remained standing for an incredible time. There was no expression on his face; he looked vacant and surprised even as the bullets struck him in the chest.

Nothing was moving now on the river. In the light of the flare, the bodies looked as limp and unhuman as bags of grain. One soldier began to float downstream, his face in the water. On the beach near the gun, another Japanese soldier was lying on his back. A wide stain of blood was spreading out from his body, and his stomach, ripped open gaped like the swollen entrails of a fowl. On an impulse Croft fired a burst into him, and felt the twitch of pleasure as he saw the body quiver.

A wounded man was groaning in Japanese. Every few seconds he would scream, the sound terrifying in the cruel blue light of the flare. Croft picked up a grenade. "That sonofabitch is makin' too much noise," he said. He pulled the pin and lobbed the grenade over to the opposite bank. It dropped like a beanbag on one of the bodies, and Croft pulled Gallagher down with him. The explosion was powerful and yet empty like a blast that collapses window-panes. After a moment, the echoes ceased.

Croft tensed himself and listened to the sounds from across the river. There was the quiet furtive noise of men retreating into the jungle. "GIVE 'EM A VOLLEY!" he shouted.

All the men in recon began to fire again, and Croft raked the jungle for a minute in short bursts. He could hear Wilson's machine-gun pounding steadily. "I guess we gave 'em something," Croft told Gallagher. The flare was going out, and Croft stood up. "Who was hit?" he shouted.

"Toglio."

"Bad?" Croft asked.

"I'm okay," Toglio whispered. "I got a bullet in my elbow."

"Can you wait till morning?"

There was silence for a moment, then Toglio answered weakly, "Yeah, I'll be okay."

Croft got out of his hole. "I'm coming down," he announced. "Hold your fire." He walked along the path until he reached Toglio. Red and Goldstein were kneeling beside him, and Croft spoke to them in a low voice. "Pass this on," he said. "We're all gonna stay in our holes until mornin'. I don't think they'll be back tonight but you cain't tell. And no one is gonna fall asleep. They's only about an hour till dawn, so you ain't got nothin' to piss about."

"I wouldn't go to sleep anyway," Goldstein breathed. "What a way to wake up." It was the same thing Gallagher had said.

"Yeah, well I just wasn't ridin' on my ass either, waitin' for them to come," Croft said. He shivered for a moment in the early morning air and realized with a pang of shame that for the first time in his life he had been really afraid. "The sonsofbitch Japs," he said. His legs were tired and he turned to go back to his gun. I hate the bastards, he said to himself, a terrible rage working through his weary body.

"One of these days I'm gonna really get me a Jap," he

whispered aloud. The river was slowly carrying the bodies downstream.

"At least," Gallagher said, "if we got to stay here a couple of days, the fuggers won't be stinkin' up the joint."

The Time Machine:
SAM CROFT THE HUNTER

A lean man of medium height but he held himself so erectly he appeared tall. His narrow triangular face was utterly without expression. There seemed nothing wasted in his hard small jaw, gaunt firm cheeks and straight short nose. His gelid eyes were very blue . . . he was efficient and strong and usually empty and his main cast of mind was a superior contempt toward nearly all other men. He hated weakness and he loved practically nothing. There was a crude unformed vision in his soul but he was rarely conscious of it.

No, but why *is* Croft that way?

Oh, there are answers. He is that way because of the corruption-of-the-society. He is that way because the devil has claimed him for one of his own. It is because he is a Texan; it is because he has renounced God.

He is that kind of man because the only woman he ever loved cheated on him, or he was born that way, or he was having problems of adjustment.

Croft's father, Jesse Croft, liked to say, "Well, now, my Sam is a mean boy. I reckon he was whelped mean." And then Jesse Croft, thinking of his wife who was ailing, a weak woman sweet and mild, might add, "'Course Sam got mother's milk if ever a one did, but Ah figger it turned sour on him 'cause that was the only way his stomach would take it." Then he would cackle and blow his nose into his hand and wipe it on the back of pale-blue dungarees. (Standing before his dirty wood barn, the red dry soil of western Texas under his feet.) "Why, Ah 'member once Ah took Sam huntin', he was only an itty-bitty runt, not big enough to hold up the gun hardly . . . but he was a mean shot from the beginning. And Ah'll tell ya, he just didn't like to have a man interfere with him. That was one thing could always rile him, even when he was an itty-bitty bastard.

"Couldn't stand to have anyone beat him in anythin'.

"Never could lick him. Ah'd beat the piss out o' him and he'd never make a sound. Jus' stand there lookin' at me as if he was fixin' to wallop me back, or maybe put a bullet in mah head."

Croft hunted early. In the winter, in the chill Texas desert, it used to be a cold numbing ride across twenty miles of rutted hard-baked road with the dust blowing like emery into the open battered Ford. The two big men in the front would say little, and the one who was not driving would blow on his fingers. When they reached the forest, the sun would still be straining to rise above the brown-red line of ridge.

Now, look, boy, see that trail, that's a deer run. They ain't hardly a man is smart enough to track down a deer. You set and wait for 'em, and you set where the wind is blowin' down from the deer to you. You got to wait a long time.

The boy sits shivering in the wood. Ah'm fugged if Ah'll wait for any old deer. Ah'm gonna track 'em. He stalks through the forest with the wind on his face dark, and the trees are silver-brown, and the ground is a deep-olive velvet. Where is that ole deer? He kicks a twig out of his way, and stiffens as a buck goes clattering through the brush. Goddam! Ole deer is fast.

Next time he is more cautious. He finds a deer track, kneels down and traces the hoofprint tenderly, feeling a thrill. Ah'm gonna track this old deer.

For two hours he creeps through the forest, watching where he places his feet, putting his heel down first, then his toes before he shifts his weight. When the dried thorny branches catch in his clothing, he pulls them free quietly, one by one.

In a little clearing he sees a deer and freezes. The wind is blowing gently against his face, and he thinks he can smell the animal. Goddam, he whispers to himself. What a big ole bastard. The stag turns slowly, looks past him from a hundred yards. Sonofabitch cain't see me.

The boy raises his gun, and trembles so badly the sights waver. He lowers it, and curses himself. Jus' a little ole woman. He brings it up again, holding it steadily, moving the front sight over until it points a few inches below the muscle of the foreleg. Ah'm goin' to git him through the heart.

BAA-WOWW!

It is someone else's gun, and the deer drops. The boy runs forward almost weeping. Who shot him? That was mah deer. I'll kill the sonofabitch who shot him.

Jesse Croft is laughing at him. Ah tole you, boy, to set where ah put you.

Ah tracked that deer.

You scared that deer into me. Ah heard ya footing it from a mile away.

You're a liar. You're a goddam liar. The boy throws himself at his father, and tries to strike him.

Jesse Croft gives him a blow across the mouth, and he sits down. You ole sonofabitch, he screams, and flings himself at his father again.

Jesse holds him off, laughing. Little ole wildcat, ain't ya? Well, you got to wait ten years 'fore you can whop your pa.

That deer was mine.

One that wins is the one that gits it.

The tears freeze in the boy's eyes and wither. He is thinking that if he hadn't trembled he would have shot the deer first.

"Yes, sir," Jesse Croft said, "they wa'n a thing my Sam could stand to have ya beat him in. When he was 'bout twelve, they was a fool kid down at Harper who used to give Sam a lickin'." (Scratching the back of his gray scraggly hair, his hat in his hand.) "That kid would lick Sam every day, and Sam would go back and pick a fight the next day. Ah'll tell ya, he ended up by whoppin' the piss out of that kid.

"And then when he was older, about seventeen maybe, he used to be bustin' horses down to the fair in August, and he was known to be 'bout the best rider in the county. Then one time a fella all the way from Denison came down and beat him in a reg'lar competition with judges and all. I 'member Sam so mad he wouldn't talk to no one for two days.

"He got good stock in him," Jesse Croft declared to his neighbors. "We was one of the first folks to push in here, must be sixty years ago, and they was Crofts in Texas over a hunnered years ago. Ah'd guess some of them had that same meanness that Sam's got. Maybe it was what made 'em push down here."

Deer hunting and fighting and busting horses at the fair make up in hours a total of perhaps ten days a year. There are other things, the long flat sweeps of the terrain, the hills in the distance, the endless meals in the big kitchen with his parents and brothers and the ranch foreman.

There are the conversations in the bunkhouse. The soft reflective voices.

Ah tell ya that little girl is gonna remember me unless she was too goddam drunk.

Ah jus' looked at that nigger after that, an' Ah said, Boy, you no-good black bastard, an' Ah jus' picked up that hatchet an' let him have it right across the head. But the sonofabitch didn't even bleed much. You can kill an elephant about as fast as you can kill a nigger in the head.

A whoor is no damn good for a man, Ah gotta have it at least five six times 'fore Ah'm satisfied, and that ole business of stickin' it in once an' then reachin' for your hat jus' leaves me more fussed than it's worth.

Ah been keepin' an eye on that south herd leader, the red one with the spot 'hind his ear, and he's gonna be gittin' mean when the hot weather comes.

The education of Samuel Croft.

ERIC LAMBERT
Creatures of the Mud

*Eric Lambert (1918–1966) was born in
England, but grew up in Australia. During
WWII he served with the Australian army
in the Middle East, New Guinea and
Singapore. His war novels include* The
Twenty Thousand Thieves *(1951) and*
The Veterans *(1954).*

The following extract from The Veterans *is set in the New Guinea jungle in
late 1943. Lieutenant Davey Bruce, who
commits virtual suicide at the end of the
story, has earlier killed four Australian soldiers whom he had mistaken for Japanese.*

I T WAS THREE WEEKS BEFORE we took that ridge. Three
weeks twisting along the trails, through the great grey
curtain of rain. Creatures of the mud, with an appearance
of being half human, threaded among the rainforests four
thousand feet up, in pursuit of an elusive and unpredictable
foe, whom we found at times in a clearing, an abandoned
village, round a bend of a trail; sometimes in the depths of the
jungle, in ravines, along the steep banks of hurtling streams.
We shot them down out of the tops of trees. We trapped them
in isolated pits and filled in the pits over their riddled corpses.
We found them in ones and twos, sometimes in dozens and
scores. If the dense green roof of the jungle could have been
lifted, a man looking down from an aeroplane would have
seen a fantastic spectacle. Thousands of them and thousands
of us, divided up into thin writhing columns, scurrying in and
out and around each other; at times cutting across each other
and clashing amid a sudden clatter of gunfire; he would have

seen the trails scattered with bodies numbering all told many, many thousands. A silent, wary, merciless system of mutual annihilation, whose outcome depended alone on who would lose the most men first. I only say how I became because everyone became like me. I was a man without a past and without a future, only a present in which he toiled upward to some grim Everest, that he might take his part in a final act of mass murder. Not a human being who pursued other human beings, but a creature with the means to murder who pitted his cunning and endurance against a similarly equipped creature—each striving for the total extinction of the other, driven forward by a compulsion both inhuman and infinite, which our minds were no longer able to recognise or understand. Our bodies obeyed a necessity to kill in order to live; we had reduced ourselves to the same necessity as that which had governed those monsters who had occupied slime, such as that through which we now struggled, æons ago, in the time before our kind of creature began.

We became like skeletons. We all looked similar in years—old; only the faces of some seemed older and more ravaged than others, and these were sometimes the men who, to tell the truth, were young in years. I think of the faces of my comrades as thin, pale masks crushed and cut to evince the misery of their spirit. I think of the face of that good man Hal Farley, who learnt that the spirit of any one man is not indestructible; for daily he saw souls destroyed. There was only humanity left to believe in. But what had humanity to do with us?

We were each the same, because we were all doing the same terrible thing; and in the end, I believe, we each forgot, or only recalled at odd times, our personal reasons for being there, for doing what we were doing. Lucky the brute, feeling power and exultation as he killed, for the first time in his life . . . Lasher, killing calmly and without mercy but without joy, avenging his headless friend . . . Davey with that look in his eyes of seeing beyond you, expiating the murder of four of his comrades; hoping for death but not finding it . . . Big Robbie and Silent Lew in their instinctive courage and goodness, their inarticulate beliefs . . . Tully, who thought ill of no man, who was gentle all through, yet killed because he knew that his land and his loved ones must be made safe

... I, who thought as Tully did, but more articulately, in whom passion and terror were stronger; afraid above all of cowardice ... No, it could not be imagined that these things were sharp, painful, and clear in our minds as we saw in each sodden dawn, and rose to seek out more of our enemy. It is said that each man has thoughts of which he is not aware, and if this is so, what thoughts, hates, fears, and visions were our minds creating then. And now, afterwards, those things have grown and swollen in the mind, become fantastic or contorted, degenerating or noble, as the case may be; years after, even, they may drive a man to cowardice, or self-destruction, or to try and tell the world about it.

To see the sun shining was an occasion for surprise, for the roof of the jungle was nearly impenetrable, and light coming through the walls was transformed into a creeping green ghost. Always the trees thrust upwards straight to where they could find light and air. Each tree carried its burden of fungus and staghorn, its festoons of vines. Always in our nostrils was the flat, hot, deathly smell of the jungle, of its decay and its over-abundance of fleshy green life. Always the mud, oozing up like black pus from the corruption of ages beneath our feet. In the green gloom through which we strove our skins turned white and puffy like the fungus. In our pallid faces the eyes of each of us were like black pools.

Malaria began to rack our skinny frames. When it was blackwater, the man lay next to death, emitting black urine; when it was cerebral he lay in the mud out of his mind, muttering, wailing, writhing. They went back on stretchers down the winding trails through the Jap-infested jungle to the coast, to the cool, airy plantations, to the hospitals, to the graveyard. They were borne by the men we called the Fuzzies, the black men in whose abandoned huts we sometimes found the Japs. Barefoot, in their flimsy lap-laps, they followed behind us and gently, patiently, their kind, dark faces shiny with the strain, they bore the sick, the wounded, the dead down the mountains to safety. When the Japs cut one of these to pieces or beheaded him, he never became a name on a casualty list, nobody sought out his relatives and gave them comfort, for we never knew who his relatives were. But any man who saw them in those mountains remembers them as his brothers, and many a sick or wounded man came to remember them as his saviours.

On the twenty-third day after we had left the plantation the jungle began suddenly to thin; it became a series of little clearings dotted with huts. Our scouts reported the huts as abandoned. A little farther ahead the jungle ended entirely, and before us rose a steep, smooth ridge on which grew nothing but shoulder-high kunai. We had reached our objective.

Davey, Tully and I went forward to the very edge of the kunai, and climbing a small knoll, we each examined the ridge in different directions. We all discerned through our glasses the same thing: seemingly endless earthworks and fortifications; wide swathes cut through the kunai for fire lanes; pits reinforced by coconut logs. And the place seethed with Japs. We could see their heads above the parapets, bobbing in the kunai. Then we went back to tell Tuttle.

His long death's-head of a face was ghastly with the common pallor. Only in his strange eyes could you discern the savagery of his determination to keep on and fulfil the destiny he had made out for himself. But his harsh voice no longer demanded of you; it besought. Tuttle was a sick man, wasted with malaria.

"Well, what did you see?"

"There are three or four hundred Japs," Davey said tonelessly. "Well dug in. They've had time to cut coconut logs. They've got a trench system." He turned to Tully and me and asked indifferently: "Agreed?"

We nodded. Tuttle nodded back.

"What was expected. The main force of what we struck back on the beach. We have two courses, which I'll discuss with the platoon commanders at once. We can get a phone line back down to the first village and ask for an air strike. That may take days. If we get a line back tonight to the second village and give them map references, we can get an area shoot tomorrow morning from the artillery and attack on that!"

"Get the artillery," Davey broke in. "Attack tomorrow, I say. The Japs may pull out any day and get down into the Markham Valley. Attack as soon as possible!"

It was as good as an order.

"We're outnumbered five to one if there are as many Japs as you think."

"Attack tomorrow!" repeated Davey.

Tuttle turned to his runner. "Get the other platoon commanders."

Tully and I went back to the platoon, who crouched along the fringe of the kunai. Big Robbie lay there on the ground, shivering, teeth rattling, eyes alight with fever.

"J-Jesus, I'm cold!" Suddenly he gave a horrible grin. "N-no I'm n-not . . . I'm hot!" He laughed and his voice cracked.

"Quiet!" growled Lasher. "Do you want the foggin' Samurai down on us?"

"Fog the S-samurai!"

Tully looked down grimly at Big Robbie, his mind made up.

"You're going back down tonight. You're getting the bug every second day."

"I'm not g-g-going b-back! B-Bill gets it . . . as often as m-me."

"Your're a bloody liar," I said.

"I'm not going back! I'll be OK tomorrow."

He lay back and closed his eyes, body alive with tremors.

"What's the caper? What's Tuttle say?" Lucky asked broodingly.

"Looks like we go in tomorrow, but it's not certain."

Lucky turned and gazed moodily up the ridge. Something strange and unwholesome kindled in his eyes.

"We'll know soon enough," said old Tully

By sunset it had been decided. There would be an area shoot by the artillery and we would attack the next morning. Then we dug in and lay watchfully through the night.

Early the next morning we moved five hundred yards back down the mountain. Maps of those parts were inaccurate, and since the artillery would be trying to blast an area we had a chance of being trapped under our own shellfire if we got too close to the ridge. In the middle of the morning the guns opened up. We could hear the shells moaning in the air above us, their crash and roar as they burst on the ridge and echoed along the mountain, to be muffled finally by the jungle.

As we sheltered among the trees a strange, muted excitement came over us, as if we were actually looking forward to the attack up the slopes ahead of us. Perhaps our minds, after the three weeks behind us, felt it as some ghastly sort of alleviation. I only know that as Tuttle gave the order to advance I sprang forward and thrust my way through the undergrowth as if impelled from behind: that I was filled with a savage eagerness. It seemed that the moment in which we should come upon the Japs in their numbers above us, the slow, grinding misery of the last three weeks would be justified; their memory would erupt from our minds like pollution from an abscess. We would be cleansed, purged and made at peace.

The trees began to thin and we were running now. We burst out of the jungle with a sudden great cry.

Into the sunlight, into the open, free of the trees, surrounded by space in which we could see our enemies. Clatter-clatter in the sunlight and bullets sweeping the grass, setting it afire. Clatter-clatter-clatter ... Pek-pek-pek ... The kunai flattened and laid aside by the bullets ... Men falling and still crying as they fell ... Pek-pek-pek.

At first the slope was gentle and only few fell. But as the ground became steeper our cries became more frenzied, the racket of the guns so sharp and continuing that we were maddened by it. The kunai threw up smoke and burst into flame. Men lay in it darkening it with their blood. The noise of the guns became like a gigantic cackle, beating in our brains and sending us forward, devoid of fear or thought. Cackle-cackle—we are mad, we are ageless, we are indestructible. Tuttle wailed and arched backwards, hands groping for the great splotchy yawning at his waist, flinging blood across the kunai—then he was behind us and forgotten. Now we were halfway up the ridge on to a false crest where the bullets could not reach us, but shrilled above our heads. We lay there breathing in huge croaks. Silent Lew crawled up beside me, blood and air coming liquidly between his lips. His chest was bathed in blood. I turned him on his back, fumbled at his pocket, and got his field-dressing. I tore it from its cover with my teeth, and ripping his sodden shirt apart, I laid the field-dressing upon it. A long, soft sigh came out of him; the life began to run from his eyes. He smiled once gently, shook his head, then died as he had lived—quietly and without complaint.

Now we were on our feet again, clawing our way upwards, screaming and cursing. We were safe from the bullets; we were just beneath the nearest guns, and they could not shoot us at the angle. One final, supreme convulsion and we were over the crest, right upon them. Lasher next to me suddenly dropped his gun; he turned and looked at me from a scarlet mask; he shrieked and fumbled at his face; his brains came bubbling through hair; he fell and his head dropped apart. For a second I knelt beside him, but then I was on my feet again and crazy to kill, to see blood flow. "Lasher! Lasher!" I was calling it like a battle cry.

A Jap leant back in a pit to shoot me. I leapt across and put my boot on his neck, crushing it. He wriggled and thrashed like a snake. I blew his brains out an inch from my boot. I went down into the trench and a Jap ran away from me, firing as he fled. Lucky appeared at its end and the Jap turned again, uttering a shrill and child-like cry, and I cut him in two with bullets. The cries of men and the din of shots was like the sound of a great sea in my ears. I passed a dugout and threw a grenade into it; blood splashed along the logs at its entrance. Men shot and ran, staggered, stumbled, clutched, knelt, lay, bled, wriggled, thrashed in pain and terror. "Lasher!" I cried. "Lasher!"

"Lasher!" They came from their pits and faced us with bayonets, firing, mouthing at us. We mowed them and blew them aside with grenades. Their wounded on the ground crawled about and tried to kill our wounded. We shot and stabbed them as they crawled. In my ears the sound of that sea was thinning; between the shouts and the shots the ears could discern odd silences, broken again by a sudden cry or shot. We sought them out as they scrambled around in ones and twos, pursuing each movement, until nothing moved but ourselves.

"Lasher!" I was shouting. "Lasher!" But now the battle cry was useless. We had taken the ridge.

"Lasher!" I said. Suddenly I sank to the ground. "Lasher!" I repeated softly. Then a blackness came over my eyes.

When I opened them I saw Tully. He was kneeling in front of me. His face seemed to be all broken and trembling.

"Bill," he said softly.

"Tully," I said. "Lasher . . . Lasher's gone."

He nodded. "I know." He was silent for a while; then he said: "I've cleaned him and laid him out."

I leant forward, grown all cold and weak, and laid my head against him, crying quietly. Inside his chest I thought I heard a long sigh.

Presently we rose and went together to look at our friend . . .

The ridge was like a great carcass fallen on the top of the mountains. After we had looked long and without words at the face of Lasher, flushed of its blood, the flesh already sinking closer to the bone, all subdued but his nose which defied the sky it pointed at, nostrils bitter and severe; a proud, unforgiving nose contemptuous of the world of men and what it had done to him—after this we came away in the dream-like way of men for the time overwhelmed.

The top of the ridge was like a long, shiny saddle on the body of the kunai now scared by fire, pecked at by shells, and disarrayed by the strange attitudes of corpses. That summit was a remote battleground, from which its survivors looked down on the green velvety folds of the jungle below. It was scored and carved by pits and trenches in which the dead huddled and seemed at times in their last agony to have struck a terrible pose. Those who huddled had little meaning, but those who had been agonised in their death, whose faces turned upwards, seemed to be uttering some silent and furious message.

"Here," said Tully, stooping, "this is poor Sims."

Beneath the corpse of a fat Jap an arm reached out and a leg was bent with the boot biting the mud, as if its owner had died in an effort to thrust himself from beneath the oppression of his enemy. We grasped the Jap by his ankles and flung him away from Sims, who was revealed with a dark face on which the lips were crushed and tattered. As we arranged his body one leg flopped languidly as if merely attached by string, for his loins had been cloven by a bayonet.

Among the heaped corpses and the scattered weapons and

pieces of equipment men walked past and around each other. Some had purpose; intent and remote as they sought a friend among the dead; others, it seemed, walked aimlessly as though there was nothing else in the world to do, faces empty with shock. And about the heads and shoulders of those who moved or stood, blue, acrid tendrils of smoke curled and wandered as if to bind the actors for ever to the scene they occupied. These filmy blue ghosts of the gunfire stabbed at the nostrils, mingling with the briny smell of blood and the sweet, close stench of innards.

Hal Farley was bending over Sims now, like a statue of tragic futility. Seeing us, he became upright and approached.

"Lasher—" he said.

"We know."

He nodded gravely. "He was a fine man," he said, "fine and very generous. He was afraid of nothing."

"Only himself," I said. "But now he is past everything, and I had often been angry at him—and now I can't imagine myself without him."

"He was a fine soldier," said Hal. "But I know that has little meaning. In a place like this my kind means nothing." He swept his arm about him. "This is a denial of God."

"I know nothing of God," I answered. "To me it seems a denial of man."

Looking helpless, he left us to continue doing what he could.

In the shade of a little clump of bamboo we found Big Robbie on a stretcher. He lay back smoking a cigarette with his left hand. On the right side his shirt was gone entirely and his arm and shoulder had been trussed with several bulky bandages. He grinned as we reached him. His bloodshot eye was like a big red marble and yet a gleam shone through it, a fantastic sort of gleam.

"I copped one!" he exulted. "I copped a beauty."

"Where, Robbie?"

"Elbow! Fogged! Hangin' by a bit of gristle." He regarded us amiably. "I'll never deal another poker hand with this!"

"Good luck, Robbie," we said.

"Thanks!" Then he seemed to forget us. "Home! Home to Mum! Good old Aussie!"

We left him, still smiling excitedly.

Davey came up without greeting us, hardly looking at us, and thrust Lasher's Bren into my hands.

"Hand your Owen in and take this," he told me. "You're a two-man section now, you and Lucky."

So we were! Lasher, Silent Lew, Big Robbie, all gone.

"Tuttle's gone," Davey said, as if he were telling us the time.

"We know."

He turned away and just for an instant I caught his eye and saw desolation.

By the afternoon we had cleared the place of Japs by flinging their bodies down the steepest slope of the ridge. At its southern end, where the kunai grew high on a gentle rise, we saw Don Company in the distance advancing to occupy that extremity; a procession of heads and shoulders jogging through the kunai.

Without warning one or two of the heads fell aside and vanished, and in the next instant the chatter of a wood-pecker reached our ears. The Don Company men sank into the kunai. The Jap was firing on a fixed line, for from our eminence we saw how the bullets threw the kunai flat in a level path, as if it had been mown. A little below us the lane of singing missiles spent themselves in the depths of the jungle.

Davey came running along the ridge.

"Go down a bit and give them a burst of Bren!"

I scrambled down the slope with Tully behind me, until we were only a few feet from the lane of shrill steel. Behind a hummock we lay down and I commenced to fire short bursts down the lane in the kunai. There was a noise and Davey appeared next to us. He lay down and began to pump shots from his Owen at the distant gun. It ceased firing for a second, then began again. "Keep at 'em!" muttered Tully. "Don Company's coming up around them." Suddenly he exclaimed, and looked about. "Where's Davey?"

As if in reply. Davey's head and shoulder rose just ahead of us in the kunai, advancing on the fire-lane, Owen pulsing at his hip. Then, quite deliberately, he stepped into that belt of screeching bullets and advanced along it. He faltered as the first bullets hit him; he pulled himself upright and broke into a drunken run, still firing; he bent forward, almost on his knees but still moving. Petrified, we saw him reach the end of that lane. His gun ceased and then began again. It gave one shot, then was silent. Everything was silent. It seemed our hearts had stopped. The next thing I remembered I was running along that lane, and when I reached the end of it I already knew what I should see. Four Japs dead over the gun, another wounded behind them and by their side the torn body of Davey.

SVEN HASSEL
Wheels of Terror

Sven Hassel (1917–) is the pseudonym of Sven Pedersen, born in Fredriksborg, Denmark. He joined the German Wehrmacht in 1936 to escape unemployment, and served with the Panzer Corps until 1945, reaching the rank of Lieutenant. His decorations include the Iron Cross First Class. His best-selling books featuring a platoon of the 27th (Penal) Panzer Regiment began with *Legion of the Damned in 1957, and include* Wheels of Terror *(1960) and* March Battalion *(1963). The novels, according to Hassel, are loosely based on fact, and most of the characters actually existed.*

The following selection comes from Wheels of Terror.

I T STARTED SNOWING, a porridgy ice-cold snow. Everything was turned into a bottomless mess.

It was shortly before midnight. We were sitting half-asleep in our tanks. We had not had one moment's peace for five days. Many of the regiment's vehicles lay scattered—burnt out wrecks—across the enormous area where the fighting had taken place. But we kept getting new reserves of men and material in a steady stream so somewhere behind the lines we knew there must be a great concentration of supplies . . .

We are getting unbelievably dirty with gun-powder, mud, oil and slime. Our eyes are red with lack of sleep. We have not seen any water apart from what we collect in muddy ditches. Food supplies have broken down and that

bombastic nonsense—the iron-ration—is long since eaten.
Porta is famished. The Little Legionnaire several times goes
out in search of something to eat, but where we advance
seems to be vacuum-cleaned of edibles. The only supplies
behind the lines are ammunition, tanks and crews. As The
Old Un says:

"They seem to have found out they can earn money by
trading the rations of the coolies."

Now somewhere in the town some distance from where we
sit we hear the rattling of tank chains.

"Hope it isn't Ivan," says Pluto and stretches his neck to
look into the rumbling darkness which surrounds us.

Many of the tank crews are getting nervous. All ears strain
to identify the goose-flesh pregnant chain-rattling coming from
behind the silent buildings.

The engines are revved. The gears growl. The dynamos
sing.

Nervousness is spreading. We cannot make out whose tanks
they are. Porta who is a specialist in detecting tank noises
is hanging half-way out of his driver's hatch in the front
of the tank. He listens tensely. Suddenly he pops back and
categorically says:

"It's healthier to withdraw with clean noses. They're Ivan's
tanks in there, T34s."

"Not on your nelly," comes from Pluto. "It's our Mark
VI tank. Sounds like an army of Dutchmen in clogs. Anybody can hear that. You need to gargle those cardboard
ears!"

"Why the hell are you so careful then?" snaps Porta with a
jeer. "But we'll soon see, lads."

He bends back and looks up at me:

"See that you have your pop gun ready!"

"If that's Ivan," says Tiny, "call me Adolf. It's either the
Mark IV or heavy artillery."

Colonel Hinka is coming down the long columns of tanks,
talking quietly to the company commander.

A little later von Barring reaches our tank and says to The
Old Un who is sitting in the turret:

"Unteroffizier Beier, make ready for a reconnaissance patrol.
We have to find out who's in front of us. If it's Ivan, hell's

breaking loose. He's liable to get behind us, the way we're sitting."

"Yes, sir, No. 2 Section is ready to patrol." The Old Un took out his map and went on: "The section will move—"

Then a few shells come whistling down and burst into a house.

"Ivan—Ivan . . ." the cry goes up.

Everybody is rushing about. Machine-pistol and rifle-shots split the air. Panic spreads. Some jump out of their tanks. The fear of burning to death in a tank is deep-seated in all tank-crews.

A pack of the dreaded T34 tanks is coming down the street rumbling menacingly, spreading fire from all guns. A couple of flame-throwers stick out their blood-red tongues at a flock of panzer grenadiers squeezed up against the walls of a house. At once they are changed into living torches.

Several of our tanks are burning and illuminate the streets with their deep-red blaze. Explosions come from petrol-tanks and ammunition going up. Everywhere is chaos.

Tanks collide in their attempt to escape. Nobody knows who is friend or enemy.

Two Russian tanks smash together with a rain of sparks. They fire simultaneously and in a second are swallowed by flames. The crew of one appears from the turret, but a burst from a machine-gun mows them down. They grill there, hanging half-out of the red-hot hull.

Four 10.5-cm. field-guns start ragged firing directly at the T34s. Red and white balls of fire fly skywards. The Russian tank-guns blaze incessantly. The whole battle is completely without plan or direction. All leadership has ceased.

Several of our tanks firing furiously with all guns swing out and seek desperately for shelter.

Tiny, our loader, is standing with a couple of tank-shells under each arm and bellows:

"Fire, you fool, fire!"

I bid him shut up and take care of his own job.

"Muck-heap," says Tiny.

Porta sitting at the steering-rods grins.

"You're trembling round the gob, what, lads? Well, that's

how it is when you don't believe Porta. Lovely tanks, T34s, eh?"

He backs the tank into a wall which collapses on top of us in a cloud of dust. Quickly he gets the huge tank free, makes full speed ahead and crashes thunderously into a T34.

I just manage to see part of its turret in my periscope before I fire. The fire from the muzzle and the shell-explosion merge at this short distance. The breech shoots back. A hot shell-casing rattles down to the bottom of the tank. Tiny flings high-explosive S-shells into the gun.

The Old Un roars.

"Back! Hell! Porta, you idiot, back! Another one is coming down the street. Turret at eleven. Got it? Fire, for God's sake!"

... I stared wildly through the periscope, but could see nothing but a river of tracers rushing through the street.

"You imbecile cow, the turret's at 9, not 11. Turn to 7 minus 36. Got it? Fire, man!"

A shell whistled past the turret. And another. The next moment our 60-ton Tiger tank nearly overturned as Porta backed. Scarcely five inches from our bows a T34 trundled past. It swung round flinging water and mud sky-high, then slid a dozen yards, but Porta was just as quick as the Russian driver. His tank spun two or three times round on its axis with Porta sitting at the huge steering-rods grinning genially.

I pressed the pedal. The turret swung round. The triangles met in the sighting mechanism. A shell sped out, and another. Then it seemed as if the tank capsized.

Our ears were ringing and clanging with the din of steel meeting steel.

Pluto was half-way out of his hatch, when it dawned on him that we'd been hit by a T34 at full speed. For a moment the Russian tank rocked in its tracks. Then the engine roared as the driver speeded it up to its full stretch. Like a ram running wild it bashed into our left flank. Our tank rose in a forty-five degree lurch.

Porta was flung on top of Pluto, tearing out all the radio-wires in the fall. I was sent flying and landed in Porta's seat. Luckily I had my steel-helmet on. My head crashed with terrific force against the steering-rods. Only Tiny remained standing as if welded to the tank-floor.

The Old Un hit his head on a steel edge and fell unconscious with blood spurting from a deep wound in the head.

"Bastards, swine, bloody Stalin-droppings!" shouted Tiny out of the hatch which in his fury he had opened.

A couple of stray shells hissed past the turret and he hurriedly banged the hatch to. He shovelled shells out of the lockers till they lay in wild confusion on the deck of the turret. It did not seem to disturb him that the heavy 8-cm. shells time and time again landed on his feet. He slapped oil-saturated rags on The Old Un's head, tore a piece off his shirt to bandage him, and then pushed him into an empty ammunition locker.

"I'm the biggest and strongest here," roared Tiny. "I'll take over command!"

He pointed at me:

"And you, you miserable pimp, all you have to do is fire. That's why we were sent to Russia."

He stumbled over The Old Un's protruding legs. It was a miracle that his head was not shattered as the gun-breech banged back. Speechless he glared at me, then full of rage burst out:

"You little devil, you'll kill your commander! What in flaming hell is the good of firing that pop-gun? I refuse to take command. I won't be shot at!"

Porta and Pluto collapsed with laughter at Tiny's ranting. For a moment we forgot the deadly danger we were in. We were surrounded by confused masses of guns, tanks and infantry. The whole scene was lit by the furious waves of machine-gun bullets. Two 8.8-cm. flak-guns were in position a little way from us. They sent off shell after shell into the darkness. But the muzzle-flashes betrayed them and they were soon ground down by a T34.

. . . This night is an apocalypse when everything is cleansed by the annihilating fire. The cry for medical orderlies from hundreds of wounded German and Russian soldiers is the accompaniment of the death-dance in the inferno of darkness.

The only helpful thing is to press your nose to the dirt and flatten yourself to escape the whistling bullets.

Our tank is hit, and in a second becomes a roaring ocean of fire. Tiny looks like a satyr standing bathed in flames as he throws The Old Un out of the side-hatch before he jumps away himself in a shower of sparks. He rolls on the ground in his oil-saturated uniform to extinguish the leaping flames.

Exhausted we lie, gasping for air, coughing painfully with smoke-filled lungs. Only Porta is indifferent. He lifts up the mangy cat he had adopted and now carries in the breast of his tunic and shouts:

"We got away by the skin of our teeth again, old pussy-lad. Only a few hairs on your backside singed!"

Panic everywhere. Grenadiers, pioneers, tank-gunners, home-guards, infantrymen, artillerymen, officers, NCOs and privates, all in a disorderly mob. Sharp pings from the snipers sound round us. Porta clutches a magnetic fuse. We get hold of some T-mines. Like snakes we crawl towards the huge T34s.

I see Porta jump at one. The fuse is placed where it ought to be. An explosion. Sharp flames lick out of the turret.

Tiny crawls up to another tank. Carefully he places the big T-mine beneath the turret, pulls out the stick and lets himself drop from the bucking tank. A thundering boom, and another T34 is finished. Tiny is going mad.

"I've finished one. Blimey, I've sent a whole tank to the gods."

That such a clumsy oaf as he is not hit is a miracle, but evidently he is bullet-proof.

I unlock a T-mine, but I can't get it up on the tank crashing by. It explodes a little behind it, and the air-pressure sends me several yards along the gutted street.

The roaring steel monsters turn and twist like sledges when they brake. Shell after shell thunders from their guns.

Slowly it dawns on us that these are not just a few stray tanks which have broken through our defences. Fortunately it is only a fraction of their left flank we have contact with. We flatten ourselves against the ground, pretend we are dead. The soil tastes sweet. Our friend affording us shelter! Lovely, dirty churned-up earth! Never have you tasted so delicious, although your porridgy mud and slush penetrate our ears, mouths, noses and eyes.

You blood-saturated lovely earth, you hold us in your

embrace and hide us in your bottomless mire. The water running in at our collars feels like a caress from a gentle woman's hand.

The dirt on our equipment and uniforms makes us look like animated clods of mud.

At eight o'clock in the morning all is over. But near the eastern part of Cherkassy town we can still hear heavy firing and the rattling of tank-tracks.

Nobody suggests they might be Mark IVs. Never again will we make that mistake when we listen to that rattling, banging sound.

GRIGORY BAKLANOV
The Foothold

Grigory Baklanov (1921–) was born in the USSR and served as an artillery officer in the Red Army during WWII.
The following is an extract from his third novel. The Foothold *(1959), and is set in the Dnieper bridgehead, 1944.*

L IFE IN THE BRIDGEHEAD BEGAN at night: at night we would crawl out of our holes and dugouts, stretch ourselves, and loosen our creaking joints. We would walk on the earth drawn up to our full height, as people had walked before the war, and as they will walk again when the war is over. We would lie down on the ground and fill our lungs with air. With the dew already settled, the night air smelled of wet grass. I am convinced that only in war does grass have such a peacetime smell.

Above would be a black sky and large southern stars – somebody else's suns. When I had fought in the north, the stars had been bluish and small, but here they were all bright, as though they were nearer. When the wind blew the stars twinkled and their lights flickered. Perhaps there was life on one of them?

The moon, that night, was not yet up. It would rise later from behind the German lines, and once in the sky, would light up everything on our side: our dew-covered meadow and the wood stretching to the bank of the Dniester – silent and hazy in the moonlight. But the slopes occupied by the Germans would remain in darkness for some time yet; the moon would light them up before daybreak. It was just before it rose that our observers from the other side of the Dniester used to cross over to us each night, bringing with them hot

mutton in earthenware pots and flasks of cold Moldavian
wine as dark as ink. In most cases, too, they brought us
barley bread, bluish in colour, and extremely tasty if eaten
on the day it was baked. A day later, it would be stale and
crumbly. Sometimes they would bring us maize bread, and
amber-yellow briquettes of this would lie untouched on the
parapets of our trenches. This was such a common sight that
a joke had been going around:

"When the Germans push us out of here, they will say:
'There's no doubt about it, the Russians thrive on horse-
fodder'."

We would eat our mutton and wash it down with the ice-cold
wine which hurt our teeth. At first we would not be able to
recover our breath; our eyes would water, and our throats and
tongues burn – such was the effect of Partsvaniya's cooking.
He put his soul into his cooking, and his soul was an ardent
one. It did not admit of food without pepper. To argue with
him was hopeless. He would only look reproachfully at you
with his kind, liquid round eyes, which were as black as the
eyes of a Greek, and say: "Ay, Comrade Lieutenant, tomatoes
and young sheep – how can you cook them without pepper?
Young sheep love pepper."

While we ate, Partsvaniya used to sit next to us on the
ground, his legs tucked up under him in Oriental fashion.
His hair was closely cropped. Beads of sweat glistened on
his round, sunburnt head through the tufts of hair which
had grown since his last haircut. He was rather small and
pleasantly plump – almost an unbelievable sight in the
front-line. Even in peacetime it was reckoned that a thin
man joining the army was bound to put on weight, while a fat
man was bound to get thinner. But not Partsvaniya, however.
The soldiers called him 'batono Partsvaniya', although few of
us knew that in Georgian 'batono' means 'mister'.

Until the outbreak of the war, Partsvaniya had been the
manager of a department store somewhere in Zugdili. Now he
was a linesman and a most conscientious one at that. When
laying a line, he would load himself up with three reels and,
sweating under their weight, his round eyes popping out of
his head, he would set about the job without complaining.
But when on duty, he would fall asleep and this made him

unreliable. He would fall asleep without realizing it, and then he would snore and wake up with a start. Alarmed, he would look around with sleepy eyes, and in less time than it took the other linesman to roll himself a cigarette, Partsvaniya would doze off again.

We would eat his mutton and praise it. Pleasantly embarrassed, Partsvaniya would all but melt under our praise. One had to praise him, as otherwise he felt offended. He betrayed the same attractive embarrassment when he spoke of women. From his cautious stories one could conclude that the women of Zugdili did not admit that his wife enjoyed exclusive rights to his person.

For some reason Partsvaniya and the observers were late in arriving that night. We lay on the earth and looked at the stars: Sayenko, Vasin, and I. The sun had bleached Vasin's hair, eyebrows, and eyelashes, as though he were a village urchin. Sayenko called him 'Kid' and acted in a patronising manner towards him. Sayenko was the laziest of my observers. He had a round face, thick lips, and fat calves.

At present his large body was stretched out next to mine on the ground. I was looking at the stars. I wondered whether I had realized before the war how satisfying it could be to lie like this, my mind blank, gazing at the stars? A mortar was fired from the German side. We heard the bomb screaming over us in the darkness, and then the sound of its explosion somewhere in the direction of the river. We were between the battery and the river. If one pictured the trajectory of the bomb, we lay beneath its highest point. It was astonishing how enjoyable it was to be able to stretch oneself, to be idle after a whole day spent in a trench, and to feel each muscle tingle pleasantly with soreness.

Sayenko shaded his eyes with his hand and looked at his watch. His watch was large, full of luminous green hands and figures, so that even I, from my position, could see what time it was.

"They should be here by now, the devils," he said in his drawling voice. "I am so hungry it hurts." And Sayenko spat into the dusty grass.

The moon would rise soon; it was already getting perceptibly lighter behind the ridge on the German side. And in the meantime the mortar continued to fire, and the bombs to fall on the road which the observers and Partsvaniya would presently have to take on their way to our positions. In our mind's eye we saw it in all its length. It began at the river-bank, at the spot where we had first landed to establish this bridgehead. It also began with the grave of one of us, Lieutenant Griva. I remember how, hoarse with shouting, with a light machine-gun in his hands, he ran up the bank, his boots sinking in the shifting sand. At the very top, beneath a pine-tree, where he was killed by a mortar bomb, was his grave. From there the sandy road turned towards the wood, where it became safe. It wound its way around shellcraters; these were not caused by shells fired at sighted targets, for the Germans fired quite blindly at that stretch of the road, without being able to register the shell-bursts, even in daytime.

At one point the road passed close to an unexploded shell. As tall as a man and with a huge round head, it had been fired by one of our *Andryushas*, and had landed on this spot whilst we had still been on the other side of the Dniester. It was now getting rusty and overgrown with grass, and each time one passed it one became tense and anxious.

Our men usually stopped to have a smoke in the wood before negotiating the remaining six hundred yards of open ground. Our observers were probably sitting smoking there now, with Partsvaniya hurrying them on. He would be worrying lest the mutton in the earthenware pots, which he had wrapped up in blankets and tied up with string, should get cold. There was no need for him to accompany the food in person, but he had no confidence in any of the observers and therefore always escorted the mutton himself. Moreover, he had to see how it was received.

The rim of the moon had risen above the ridge. The wood was now a place of black tree-shadows and shafts of hazy moonlight. The dew-drops sparkled as they caught the light and the wood smelled of wet flowers and mist. The mist would soon rise from the bushes. This was a good time for strolling about in the wood, cutting through the shadows and the shafts of moonlight.

Sayenko raised himself on one elbow. Three people were making their way towards us. My observers? They were about a hundred yards away, but we did not hail them; at night nobody was hailed from a distance in the bridgehead. The three reached the bend in the road, and almost immediately a covey of red bullets passed very, very low over their heads. We had a perfect view of the scene from where we were lying.

Sayenko again lay down on his back.

"Infantry," he said.

The day before yesterday an infantry driver in a jeep had tried to cross the same place in daytime. Under a hail of bullets, he had swerved violently at the bend in the road and had catapulted his colonel out of the jeep. Infantrymen rushed up to help him; the Germans opened up with their mortars, our divisional artillery replied, and for half an hour the firing went on; eventually all became confused, and on the other side of the Dniester a rumour flew round that the Germans were attacking. It was of course impossible to recover the jeep in daytime, and the Germans used it as a target for their machine-guns until nightfall, firing one burst after another until they finally set it on fire.

The moon had now risen above the ridge, but there was no sign of our observers. We were beginning to get cross when Panchenko, my batman, appeared. From the distance we saw that he was alone and that he was carrying something unidentifiable in one hand. He came nearer. We saw a cheerless face and the neck of an earthenware pot hanging on a string from his hand. We suddenly felt so wronged that we did not say a word, and only looked at Panchenko and all that remained of the pot.

"Partsvaniya has been killed," he said gloomily, in self-justification. But his words somehow did not reach us at first.

Panchenko stood downcast before us, and we sat on the ground, the three of us, and were silent. We had had no hot food during the day and now would not be brought any until the following night; we only had one proper meal every twenty-four hours. And again tomorrow, all the day long, there would be firing, blinding sun in the lenses of my periscope, heat. And I would be smoking and smoking in my dugout until I felt dazed, but never forgetting to fan away the tobacco smoke with my hand, because the

Germans fired even at the sight of smoke in the bridge-head.

Panchenko put a round barley loaf on the ground, detached flasks of wine from his belt and sat down by himself, away from us, chewing a blade of grass. We ate the still warm bread and drank the wine, which hurt our teeth. Because we had had little to eat during the day, the wine went straight to our heads. We munched our bread and thought of Partsvaniya. He was killed bringing us his pots of mutton, specially wrapped so that, the Lord forbid, they should not get cold on the way. He used to sit just there, his fat legs tucked under him in Oriental fashion, looking at us with his kind, liquid round eyes which were as black as the eyes of a Greek, and now and then wiping his sunburnt head, which would be sweating heavily after the long march. He would wait for us to offer praise.

"You're not wounded?" I asked Panchenko.

Delighted, he moved over to us.

"Look," he said, and he pointed at his trouser leg which had been pierced beneath the pocket by a shell-fragment, and, to be more convincing, he pushed his finger through the two holes. And suddenly, remembering something, he hurriedly pulled out of his pocket some yellow leaf tobacco wrapped up in a piece of linen. "I almost forgot it."

We crushed the brittle, weightless leaves between our palms, taking care not to drop any of the tobacco. Suddenly I noticed that the powdered tobacco in my palm was stained with blood. Where did it come from? I was not wounded, I had only been cutting bread. There was also some blood on the bottom crust of the loaf. And we guessed that it was Partsvaniya's blood.

"Where did you cop it?" Sayenko asked after a time. As he spoke, tobacco smoke came out of his mouth; he always inhaled deeply.

"In the wood. Just by the *Andryusha* shell. That's where we were at the time and this is where he fell." Panchenko drew it all on the ground. "That's where the bomb landed. And Partsvaniya happened to be walking on that side."

I spent the night lying in the same slit-trench as Vasin, after sending back Sayenko and Panchenko. They would have to carry Partsvaniya to their boat and then row him across the river. Our slit-trench was narrow, but we widened it a little at the bottom, so that there was enough room for two people to lie down. The nights were cold, but by sleeping together, we felt warm even under a single ground-sheet. The only difficulty was turning over. While one was doing this, the other had to crouch on all fours. But we could not widen our trench any more, for a shell landing anywhere near might cause it to cave in. A heavy German battery fired at regular intervals and our own guns replied over our heads from the other side of the Dniester. For some reason shells always seem to explode very close when one is below ground. This was so-called "harassing fire", and it went on all through the night until daybreak. How curious that before the war people used to complain of insomnia, that they would tell you: "I could not sleep a wink last night. There was a mouse scurrying about under the floor-boards." And if there was a cricket in the room, well, that was a real calamity. As for us, we slept every night under artillery fire and woke up only when there was an unexpected lull.

I lay thinking of Partsvaniya, and of the bread on which a little of his blood had remained. I recalled a party when I was in the tenth form at school, at which we were given free bread rolls with sausage. The rolls were crisp and round and cut in two down through the top, and thick slices of pink, choice sausage were inserted between the two halves. While the rolls and sausage were being distributed to us, the headmaster stood next to the buffet-attendant, full of pride, for it was his idea.

We ate the sausage, but the rolls could be found later in all sorts of odd places, behind flower pots and under the staircase. I recalled it now as a crime.

Vasin was asleep, snoring through his nose. I should have loved to have a smoke, but the tobacco was in my right-hand pocket and I was lying on my right side. Each time a German rocket flared up, I saw Vasin's hairy neck and one of his little ears flushed in sleep. Strange that I should feel almost like a father towards him.

ALEXANDER BARON
Shannon ain't so Tough

*The English writer Alexander Baron
(1920–) served in the British Army
from 1940, and went through the Sicilian
campaign and the Normandy landings. He
attained the rank of corporal before being
invalided out of the service. His* From
the City, From the Plough *(1948)
is probably the finest novel about the
ordinary British infantryman to come out
of WWII.*

The story below is excerpted from From
the City, From the Plough, *and takes
place on D-Day, 1944. The soldiers belong
to the fictitious 5th Wessex Battalion.*

T HE DAVITS ON THE BOAT deck groaned and the
men lining the railings on the deck below saw the
landing craft come jerkily down to their level. It hung motionless for a moment, then descended slowly until it was bobbing
on the grey swell below, with the scummy white foam swirling
round it.

Charlie Venable shivered. "Bleed'n cold," he complained.
"Lousy mornin' for a battle. We oughta complain to the
union."

"You should ha' worked in t'mills," said Sergeant Shannon.
"Fourteen year old, up at five on a raw mornin' an' off
to work."

"We're too wide for that in London, Sarge," grinned Charlie
Venable.

Mister Paterson, the platoon officer, came up and began to
talk quietly to the sergeant. They checked their watches. It

was growing lighter; the strip of white light across the eastern horizon had spread like a sliding roof across the sky, and now it was daylight.

The sergeant turned again to Charlie Venable. He asked: "Sorry you come back to the battalion, Charlie?"

"Nah," said Charlie. "Wouldn'a missed this for a million quid." He looked out across the grey waters to the mist that hid the shore. "Ever been down the East End, Sarge?"

"Not since the war.".

"They done it up proper in the blitz," he said, "the—ers." He hawked, and spat down into the water. "Ev'ry night down under the stairs, my ol' lady was. Fifty-six the ol' gal is. Never done 'er no good. They want showin' a lesson, them—ers."

"Think a lot of yer ma, don't yer, Charlie?" said the sergeant.

"The only gal in the world for me," said Charlie. "Your mum's dead, ain't she?"

"Aye," said Sergeant Shannon, "me dad were killed in t'last war. 'E were Irish. Mum died when I were a kid. I lived wi' relations till I were sixteen, workin' in t'mills. Then I left 'ome an' come down t'London."

"Where'd yer live in London?"

"Battersea, in lodgin's. I worked in a fact'ry, in a pickle fact'ry. Lab'rer. It were all right in London, but I were always pretty lonely. It's not a good place for a stranger. Anyway, I lost me Lancashire accent there."

"Well," grinned Charlie, "you don' exactly talk like a Cockney now."

"You're a lucky lad," said Sergeant Shannon, "'avin' a mother like yours."

"Tellin' me!" Charlie answered him. "It must a' been a dog's life for you."

"Aye," said the sergeant, "I were pretty sick of it. This is t'best life I've known, in t'Army."

"Strewth!" said Charlie Venable. "Never mind. I'll take yer to see the ol' lady when we get back. She won' arf go to town. She'll cook yer a meal you'll never forget."

The sergeant laughed. "That's a date."

"Talkin' o' meals," said Charlie, "that was a lousy—in'"

breakfast they give us. Three biscuits an' a mug o' char. A
sparrer couldn' fight on it, never mind a swaddy."

"Never mind," said Sergeant Shannon, "they've got champagne where we're going," and moved away.

"—me drunk," exclaimed Baldy, who had been listening
quietly all the time. "Never 'eard 'im talk so much since 'e
joined the battalion. 'E ain't so tough, is 'e?"

"Shut your jaw," said Charlie Venable.

Sailors pulled at cords and the wet scramble nets thumped
over the sides.

Mister Paterson pulled himself up on to the bulwarks and
looked at his watch again.

"Off you go, laddie," said the bearded naval officer who was
in charge.

Paterson disappeared over the side. The men swarmed over
after him and down the scramble nets.

The landing craft was wallowing on a wicked swell, riding
high and falling away again. As it came up, Mister Paterson
and two of the men leaped clear of the net and crashed on to
the steel deck. "Wait for her to come up," Paterson shouted up
at the men on the net. Each time the landing craft rose, three
or four men dropped clear of the nets, while above more came
clambering down like spiders hurrying across a great web.

Now they were all in place, crouching along the steel sides
of the craft, settling their weapons across their knees and
fumbling with cigarette tins. They had a long trip ahead,
four miles to the shore.

The sailors were shouting.

"All gone forrard."

"All gone aft."

The engines throbbed more loudly and they could feel the
tug of power beneath them. The landing craft began to sidle
away from the troopship; the waste of foam and heaving water
between the two vessels widened. The engine note became
deeper and more powerful and the squat craft began to move
forward, butting into the waves, painfully climbing them and
slithering down into the troughs to attack the next hillock of
grey-green water. Paterson stood up and looked around him.
As far as he could see other little craft were bobbing towards

the shore. Somewhere ahead of them the first flights of assault craft must be piling in now.

"Make yourselves comfortable, lads," he told the men. "There's plenty of time yet."

Some of the men were talking, some smoking, some vomiting quietly into brown bags of greaseproof paper. The wind was bringing to them now the sound of shells bursting ashore. Each man could feel each thudding detonation somewhere inside him. The talking stopped. Men took up their rifles and machine carbines; there was the clack of bolts being drawn and rammed home. The slow, wallowing motion of the craft eased; they were coming into shallower water. Orders were being shouted in the stern and a marine heaved himself up over the side and began to take soundings. There was smoke sprawling across the beach ahead, and the black plumes of explosions, each with a cherry-red flicker of flame at its heart, were leaping up in front of the high bows.

The landing craft nosed inshore through a mass of floating rubbish. A dead sailor came floating out to sea, face and legs under water, rump poking upwards; then a dead soldier, his waxen face turned up to the sky, his hands floating palm upwards on the water; he was kept afloat by his inflated lifebelt. Ahead of them lay beached landing craft, some wrecked, scattered untidily along the waterline.

There was a jarring explosion beneath the bows and the whole craft lurched forward. Men toppled forward in a heap, clambered to their feet as the ramps crashed down, and ran splashing down into the water. They had no time to stop for the two men who had been caught by the mine exploding beneath the bows and whose blood stained the dirty seawater as the boat began to submerge. They were all away now, and wading with weapons held above their heads towards the wet sand ahead.

A dirty tape wriggled across the beach and the riflemen came stumbling along it, shedding water from their sodden trousers. Mister Paterson flopped beneath a wrecked landing craft that lay broadside on and waited for his platoon to come up. One by one they dropped to the sand behind him. There were German shells falling a little inland, where the first assault troops had already passed, and somewhere among the yellowed, battered houses scattered along the waterfront and the smashed rubble of wrecked pillboxes a machine gun was rapping remotely.

"All right, my lads," said Paterson breathlessly. He ducked under the bows of the beached craft and ran heavily along the tape. There was a tangle of wire ahead, with German mine warnings poking up everywhere and a few British dead lying with their faces in the sand. They followed the tape along a path torn through the wire and came on to a narrow track running laterally. In front of them now were gentle, dreary dunes rising from pools and runnels of water, with grass growing scantily on their upper flanks. On each side of them sappers were rooting up mines as hastily as potatoes, and a little away to the right a beach dressing station had just been established, with a row of loaded stretchers waiting on one side and a row of corpses laid out on the other, each a still mound under a grey blanket, with big boots protruding at the end. Some pioneers were trying to dig in along the far side of the road, in the wet sand.

They moved on. There was the sudden *wheep-wheep* of bullets. Paterson could not see where they were coming from; then the grating, shrieking descent of their first shell. They flopped, pressing themselves frantically into the sand, then staggered to their feet and went lumbering after Paterson.

Someone was whimpering loudly; it was like the crying of a spoilt child. Sergeant Shannon stopped and looked round. Little Alfie Bradley was lurching about in a wide circle, well away from the tape, pressing his hands to his face. The sergeant raced after him and pulled him down to the ground.

As the boy felt the pressure of the sergeant's hands on his shoulders he tried to stifle his crying; he kept on sniffling jerkily. There was a red pit where one of his eyes had been. Blood welled darkly from the other.

"I can't see," he whispered, "I can't see."

The sergeant comforted him.

"All right, lad, there's nowt t'worry about. Yer eyes are full of blood. You'll be all right when they've washed them." He whipped out the boy's field dressing, his hands already bright with fresh blood. He knew the boy would never see again. He bound the dressing tightly over the boy's face. It began to stain red at once.

"There, lad," he said soothingly, "that'll do just t'keep dirt out." He steered the blind boy back to the tape, forced him down to his knees and put the tape between his fingers.

"Foller this back, lad," he said gently. "When yer get on t' that road again you'll be by the dressing station. They'll take you in."

He stood for a moment watching Little Alfie crawling back towards the beach on all fours, the tape between his fingers. Then he stooped, wiped his bloody hands in the sand and doubled after the platoon.

Most of the Fifth Battalion were across the beach. As the last of them clambered up a steep bank of sand, sticking close to the tape for fear of mines, they moved aside cautiously to pass Corporal Shuttleworth.

He was sitting, dazed, on his pack by the tape. Where his right boot had been there was a raw, red stump. "Mind the mines," he muttered dreamily to the men passing him, "or you'll get what I got."

No one had time to stop for him. One after another the riflemen looked curiously at him, as if they had never known him, and hurried on. The blood was draining away from him fast. There was no pain and he was becoming sleepy. Some of the men trudging past him were his friends; sometimes one of them would stoop over him and tell him apologetically that the stretcher-bearers would be along in a moment to look after him. He would shake his head drunkenly, and once he giggled. One of his old comrades from the Green Howards, bending over him, heard him snigger, "Half a man, half a bloody man. The cow, she'll get my pension." The blood was running away from him into the thirsty sand. He shook, as if enjoying some great secret joke. He mumbled something and toppled forward across the tape. The last riflemen of the Fifth Wessex stepped over the body and plodded on.

Lieutenant Paterson walked lightly at the head of his platoon. The first numb, obsessed rush was over. He was beginning to enjoy himself. For months he had wondered what his first day in battle would be like. There would be fear to conquer, he had thought; there would be sickness and disgust at the sight of death and mutilation. But the time had come and there were none of these things. Instead he felt free, triumphant, detached somehow from all that was happening around him; as if he were seeing it on a cinema screen, as if all the noises were on a sound-track and there were no fleet bullets or whanging steel splinters to harm him. And everything—he puzzled about it—everything was so familiar. He had seen it all before, on newsreels, in war films, in the war books on which he had grown up. There was nothing new here, nothing to shock. He had grown up in the aftermath of one war, with the shadow of another already over him.

The first corpses and the first wounded aroused only curiosity in him, and a strange craving to look more closely and note every detail. Only once was he shaken. He was marching with Sergeant Shannon close behind him when he heard a shell coming. He shouted, "Get down, there!" and flopped. As he lay with his head between his arms, quailing under the explosion, he heard something thump into the ground in front of him. He looked up and saw, lying only a yard ahead of him, a human trunk with a head but no limbs. He spewed over his tunic as he rose to his feet and lurched forward, white-faced and overcome with sudden nausea. He looked over his shoulder. Sergeant Shannon was quite unmoved.

The platoon moved in open file along a sunken road running inland, weapons ready. There were broad ploughlands on both sides, with *Achtung, Minen* boards every few yards. Far away on the left there was a wood. A machine gun opened fire from the wood and they dropped into the shelter of the road's steep bank. "Keep moving, chaps," called Mister Paterson, and they moved forward on hands and knees with the bullets squealing overhead.

Charlie Venable swore bitterly; he was finding it hard going and his hands and knees were raw already. There were the first houses of a village ahead of them now, and shelter; behind them the German machine gun stopped its fruitless probing; then they heard it firing again at another party coming up behind them. The village was captured and the cottages were swarming with British infantrymen searching for German stragglers. There was some looting. A mob of German prisoners squatted at the foot of a long wall, listless, furtive, uninterested in the army that was streaming past them. Paterson and his platoon trudged past the prisoners. Charlie Venable swore again, this time at the top of his voice. "You—ers," he shouted at the prisoners, "you're lucky I never got 'ere first."

D-Night. The Fifth Battalion were dug in beyond the village, waiting to be counter-attacked. The men lay in their holes listening to the German bombers which had been prowling about the sky since the coming of darkness. The night was lurid with flares and tracers. Guns were booming. The Germans were shelling the beach. Colonel Pothecary, standing at the foot of the steps leading down to the cellar which was his headquarters, brooded over the casualty return he had just signed; the first. He watched the gun-flashes over the dark silhouettes of the treetops, and wondered where his boy was, whether he was alive or floating in some grey waste of water like the corpses of the morning's assault. There was a party of his men still out doing an ammunition fatigue. He worried for them. Colonel Pothecary could not forget his boy, or the parents of the men he led; his burden was heavy upon him.

As they heard the shell rushing down at them through the night the file of men who were moving across the dunes dropped the boxes they were carrying and flung themselves to the ground.

They pressed their bodies into the wet sand, cowering from the blast which buffeted them. They heard the clang of splinters striking the sides of wrecked landing craft and felt the upflung sand raining on to their clothes.

"On your feet," called Mister Challis, the platoon officer, "Everyone all right?"

"The Swedebasher's stopped one," somebody answered in the darkness.

The lieutenant recognised the voice. "That you, Martin?" he asked, moving towards the speaker. Martin was kneeling beside a dark bundle on the sand.

"All right . . ." This time it was the strong, dark voice of Sergeant Ferrissey. ". . . Hit the trail. Golly, you an' Martin look after the Swedebasher."

The men heaved the boxes on to their shoulders and moved off towards the anti-aircraft guns whose intermittent flashes were stabbing the night.

"He's all right," said Corporal Gonigle, "it's a head wound. He's breathing." The wounded man was breathing hard; each time he expelled his breath he made a little snoring noise. Martin had already pulled a field dressing from the wounded man's thigh pocket, and he applied the bandage with quick and expert movements.

The corporal straightened up after his scrutiny of the wound. "Looks like a splinter. Opened up the side of his head; messed his face up a bit, too. It's knocked him cold for a bit. I reckon he won't take long to come round, though."

They lifted the Swedebasher carefully between them and bore him to the beach dressing station.

When they handed him over to the orderlies and were walking back to rejoin the platoon, Martin spoke again. "That'll just suit that bastard," he said, "the miserable sod. He's got a Blighty one there."

The corporal laughed. "The Swede's all right," he replied. "He just can't keep his troubles to himself."

"I'd've given 'im trouble if 'e'd kept on much longer," said Martin savagely, "moanin' all the time. Give me the sick, that bastard did."

Martin was right, and the corporal did not answer. Two months ago the sergeant had brought a new man into the platoon's Nissen hut. "Golly," he had said, "here's Private Gotham. He's fresh from the farm. Find him a bed." They had found him a bed and humped his kitbag up from the gate for him, had poured him a mug of tea from the can that was boiling on the stove and had squeezed together on the benches on which they were sitting round the stove to make room for him. They were offering him his place in their community. But Gotham—after ten minutes of his Gloucestershire accent they named him Swedebasher—had refused their kindnesses, without thanks, and had crawled into bed with his face to the wall. The next day he had started grumbling: about his farm, about the money he was losing, about the injustice of dragging him away into the Army, about his wife, about his three children, about the food and the beds. The rest of the platoon were preparing for an invasion; they were trained to the limit and impatient to go. They had no time for Gotham and his grumbling. At any other time he would have been accepted as a character and tolerated; but now they turned their backs on him and let him sulk in solitude. His loneliness, his bitterness against this strange and hostile world, his longing for his farm and family had grown every day. He had gone aboard the troopship like a convict to the hulks.

"You know," said the corporal, as they fell in again with the platoon, "he was pretty quiet all through the day."

"Know why?" growled Martin. "Before we went down the nets I told him I'd put a bullet in him if I heard him moan once, just once."

They were back at the dump now, each lifting one of the boxes of ammunition that were stacked there. "He said his wife and kids came first," said Martin. "I've got a wife and kids, too. The bastard."

They delivered their loads and plodded back towards the dump. There was no time for rest.

Somewhere in the darkness they could hear the throb of aero-engines. Red, dotted lines of tracer were sailing slowly up into the sky; more and more of them until they criss-crossed in pyrotechnic patterns. Bombs were falling in the distance, and the men watched with fascination as they exploded, first seeing the second's incandescent glare of white flame, then hearing the noise, as if all about them giant furnace doors were swinging open and slamming shut again.

The ground shook with the thudding reply of distant batteries. Guns on a nearby beach joined in, the heavies with a dull booming, the Bofors with their insistent banging, the little quick-firing Oerlikons, noisiest of all, with their incessant crack-crack-crack. The ships out in the anchorage were firing now with all their armament, and the noise rose to a hysterical crescendo.

The droning of engines grew louder, challenging the din of the barrage. The ammunition carriers heard the battery ahead of them open fire and each man, as he walked, looked about him for cover.

There was the sudden drumming roar of an engine, low over their heads. The corporal, leaping into an abandoned slit trench, thought he saw the shadow of wings flitting past. He landed heavily on top of someone else who was already crouching in the narrow pit and gasped instinctively, "Sorry."

They did not even hear the explosion; the sides of the trench closed in on them like clapping hands; the weight of sand and splintering timbers pressed the corporal down into suffocating darkness. He heaved and struggled, and felt the man beneath him fighting to move. He forced one hand up through the wet, scratching sand and felt it moving free. There was movement above him, and voices strangely muffled; the timbers were being lifted from his back and he was out, gasping, into the sweet, fresh air.

He gulped and raised himself on all fours. Everyone was safe. The platoon trailed off again for more ammunition, the corporal, breathing painfully, in the rear. Mister Challis watched his men plod by, and counted them. One, two, three—the fourth man's head was a strange and shapeless blob of white against the box on his shoulder.

"Gotham?" exclaimed the lieutenant. "What the *hell* are you doing here?"

The Swedebasher looked sheepish in the gloom.

Corporal Gonigle came up to him. "Look," he said, coming close to the Swedebasher, "he's still got an evacuation label tied to him."

He took the Swedebasher by the shoulders. "Swede," he shouted, "Swede, did you walk out on them? Did you come back here on your own?"

The Swede nodded his bandaged head violently in the darkness. He managed to speak at last. "I felt a fool in there," he said. "There were some terrible bad cases there, Corp."

"You silly old bastard," the corporal chuckled, and punched the Swede affectionately in the ribs.

"Here, Corp," said Private Gotham suddenly, taking his handkerchief from his pocket and unfolding it, "the doctor gave me this. It's what he took out of my head."

"Wait till I show the missus," he said with gloomy pride. He wrapped the splinter of steel carefully in his handkerchief, replaced it in his pocket, shouldered his box again and stumbled away in pursuit of his comrades.

In the sweet, summer orchards the men of the Fifth Battalion crouched in their slit trenches listening to the guns and watching the gun-flashes tearing the darkness apart. Sometimes men dozed off, no longer kept awake by the ceaseless rumbling of artillery; but the faintest rapping of machine carbines in the distant woods brought them trembling to their feet.

Sergeant Shannon peered into the darkness, consumed with terror. His day in battle was catching up on him, and living in retrospect the hours through which he had shown no sign of fear, he huddled shivering against the earth wall of the trench, feeling his stomach muscles contract and his lungs freeze with the physical sensation of fear until the pain became unbearable. He had known this in Africa and Sicily, in the secret moments of the night; there was no escaping it. He looked at the rifleman who was slumped sleeping in the bottom of the trench, and wondered that the mad chattering of his teeth did not awaken the man. The darkness was alive with shadows and strange shapes. He saw again, against the flares and the gay rockets that were dancing over the treetops, little Bradley crawling on all fours back along the tape, his own hands bright with blood, the limbless trunk in the roadway in front of him. He heaved himself up on to the parapet and leaned forward, supporting himself with one hand on the ground while he vomited loudly and violently.

Charlie Venable and Baldy, who were on duty behind a Bren in a heap of rubble that commanded the roadway nearby, lay silently watching the sergeant retching. They were close enough to see his dreadful shivering, the shivering of his whole body—limbs and trunk and flaccid cheeks.

"See," whispered Baldy, "what did I tell yer? Shannon ain't so tough."

"Quiet, you cowson," hissed Charlie Venable. "Keep your eyes on the road."

PAUL GALLICO
Bombardier

Paul William Gallico (1897–1976) was born in New York, the son of a concert pianist. He served as a US Navy gunner in 1918. and was the European war correspondent for Cosmopolitan *during WWII. His many books include the novel about the evacuation from Dunkirk* The Snow Goose (1941).
"Bombardier" is from 1942.

SECOND LIEUTENANT SALVO JENKINS crouched on his knees in the greenhouse of the big B-31 bomber as the ship, shaking, trembling, and complaining, swiveled into the wind and thundered down the runway for the take-off. This, then, was it at last. The practice days were over. The hunt was on. And he was miserable.

The concrete strip, streaked like scratchy film, reeled interminably beneath the glass nose of the bombardier's bay. Lumbering Annie, wing and belly heavy with her load of gasoline, demolition bombs, and depth charges, took her own sweet time about getting into the air. Of the dangers that might be encountered on the mission, this was the worst moment, the leap into the sky. The B-31 had a reputation for crankiness at the end of the runway.

But Bombardier Salvo Jenkins—aged twenty-two, blue-eyed, slight; his face, beneath the short-cut tawny hair, the face of a child; quick and nervous as a cat in his movements—was not entertaining visions of what would befall Lumbering Annie if she failed to shake loose at the end of the field—the crashing green of stripped trees, the red bricks of the barracks, white faces staring upward, and the final holocaust of flame. His fears and doubts reached far ahead to that moment which might come upon him out over the blue wastes of water, when the success or failure of the mission and all that it meant to his crew would depend upon him alone.

What if he should let them down? He fought off the sickish feeling his thoughts brought on and swallowed to get the dryness out of his throat. This was for keeps. The pilot and navigator would bring him to the target. They could do no more. He was the bombardier. It would be he who must make the kill. Must make it . . . must make it . . . must make it . . . The words throbbed to the engines beating slightly out of synchronization.

Runway, fence, trees, barracks, and sand waste fell away beneath them. They crossed the white edge of the Atlantic as they climbed into the sky. In ten minutes the target area would begin. To ease his nerves, Salvo Jenkins reached in his data kit for his computer. Pilot Captain Strame had given him his bombing instructions before the take-off. "We'll bomb at X feet altitude and zero-zero-zed speed."

You bombed at low altitude and in a hurry on those sub hunts. You had just so many seconds to lay your eggs from the moment the tin shark was sighted until it vanished to safety beneath the sea. Salvo made his computations, ground speed, temperature, true altitude, checked and rechecked them and set his Rube Goldberg, the Flanick hand sight used for low-level bombing. He loved the Flanick. It was like pointing and sighting a fine gun. If your computations were right, steady eye, steady hand, finger ready on the solenoid switch for firing, you couldn't miss. You dared not miss.

He knew that his figures were correct, but it gave him no feeling of ease or relaxation. If and when the emergency came, he might have to discard them in an instant, and in the trembling space of ticking seconds recalculate entirely for different height and speed. No one could instruct or help him. A fractional error, and chance and prey would be gone. The men upstairs trusted him. If he failed, he could never face them. So this was what it meant to be a bombardier.

But fearful and anguished of nerves as he was, Salvo would not have traded places with any of those above in the ship. The thought of his name in the crew list, chalked up on the blackboard in the squad room, filled him with pride: "Bombardier. Sec. Lt. Horace Jenkins."

He had found excuses to go in there more often than was necessary, so that he could glance up at it. He would catch himself sneaking those glances and would say to himself, "Dawgone it, Jenkins; you're actin' just like a kid. Ain't you evah goin' tuh grow up?"

But the line kept bringing a glow to his heart. There it was, up with the finest crew on the field—Pilot Captain: John (Cappy) Strame; Navigator: Lt. Carl Jorgens; Co-pilot: Lt. Ed Hammond; Engineer: Sgt. James Bradley; the radioman and the gunners. But how his own name stood out—"Bombardier: Sec. Lt. Horace Jenkins." Why, that was himself. That line was the end of a long-ago dream come true—or at least almost the end.

The altimeter needle settled at 1000 feet and stayed there. Automatically, Salvo checked the centigrade thermometer and inspected the green lights glowing on his bomb-indicator panel. Below him rolled the Atlantic, calm, capless, and shimmering in the afternoon sunlight.

The earphones of the intercommunication system crackled and he heard, "Navigator from pilot: What is the course?"

When the navigator gave it, Salvo checked it with his own compass.

He heard the pilot's brief acknowledgment, "Roger."

"Roger." Salvo savored the word. It was the airman's response and meant "Received order." Jenkins used it whenever he could in his everyday talk. It was one of the things that set you apart, like the title "Bombardier" in front of your name. Instead of saying "Okay," or "That's right," or "You're darn tootin'," you said "Roger." It was air forces.

They were ten minutes out and flying south over the water, paralleling the yellow-and-green strip of shore in the starboard haze. The mission was yet young and there was a moment's kidding on the interphone.

"What'll you bet the lunch is ham sandwiches again?"

"Co-pilot from navigator: You'd holler if it was caviar."

"Shut up! You'll wake the bombardier."

Something seemed to choke the throat of Salvo Jenkins. He was so proud to be kidded by them.

Yes, that was his gang up above. He belonged to them and they to him. He had become a member of the greatest team in the world. In school, at the outbreak of the war in Europe, he had dreamed of someday become a bombardier. But he had not imagined that it would be like this.

As a boy, back on his father's farm in the Greak Smokies of North Carolina, he had yearned for the day when he would go to college and play on a team—when he would belong. But he had been far too slight for football at State University. He could run and play a little ball, but he had never made anything. He had been a wistful wanderer on the fringes of the great who belonged. He admired the football men who had their own talk and fellowship of play and strategy and bruises. Young Jenkins thought the finest thing in the world was the friendship between the star halfback, Swifty Morgan, Ted Jones, who ran interference for him, and Sparky Slade, the quarterback. They did everything together. It was all for one and one for all, and everything for the team.

The pilot called for a crew check-in over the intercommunication, and in his turn Salvo barked, "Bomber, Roger!" and listened to the others, "Navigator, Roger! . . . Co-pilot, Roger! . . . Radio, Roger! . . . Engineer, Roger!"

This was a real team. How they worked together! Each trusting in and dependent on the other. Only this was such a game as none of them had ever played before. And, at the thought, the old pang returned to the bombardier and his nerves quivered again. He was the only member of the crew as yet untried. He was still Salvo Jenkins.

His mind turned back to that awful moment during a patrol flight over the California coast two months ago, when, in one sickening moment of error, confusion and a momentarily jammed lever, he had gone to "Salvo" instead of "Selective," and had dumped two thousand, five hundred pounds of expensive demolition bombs into the Pacific Ocean. And he had picked the time to do it when the general was on board and at the controls of the ship. There had been a truly magnificent explosion, but outside of killing all the fish in the vicinity, it had accomplished nothing but to pin a nickname on him. From that moment on, he was known as "Salvo" Jenkins.

It had gotten around, this really Gargantuan blunder. They

knew of it in Texas the same night, in Louisiana, New Mexico, and the Atlantic seaboard the next day, and in Australia, India, and Java the following week; in the primary and advanced schools, the flying fields, the bombing grounds, and the fighting squadrons. News moved swiftly in the air forces. The radio would talk, a transfer would carry the story, or an outward-bound pilot of the Ferry Command, hot with the latest home news, would squat down in Africa, or South America, or the Near East, and say to the gang, "Did you hear about that kid Jenkins from the Eighteenth? Salvoed a ton on a turtle. Had the general riding with him."

The earphones came alive. "Target at ten o'clock. Eight miles."

The left wing dropped slightly and Lumbering Annie turned and then slid downhill a little. Salvo crouched and strained his eyes in the direction indicated. The sparkling water rushed beneath them. "Target" to the Army Air Forces Bomber Command was anything that floated above or beneath the waves. Only after it identified itself did it become a ship. They were still hours away from the area designated by Intelligence as possibly harboring a U-boat, but Salvo's fingers were itching for his levers.

The intercommunication clicked, "Subchaser!"

"Roger!"

She looked like a greyhound, long, lean, slim of flank, blue-gray in color, and flecked with the white hats of her crew. A curving white wake boiled out behind her. The racing ship changed course and charged on as the lumbering bomber dipped her left wing and staggered around her in a wide circle. The hairs at the back of Salvo's neck bristled. The navy was on the hunt too. Was she following a scent with her instruments? If so, there might be work for him to do. In a heap, he tried to remember everything he had been taught.

He saw the subchaser's blinker light flash, and read the code. Up above, Cappy Strame was talking to her with his blinker, too, probably querying whether they were following a trail of sinister submerged engines, distantly beating.

The firefly light from below winked, "N-O."

"Huh," said Salvo Jenkins to himself. "They probably wouldn't tell us if they had one treed," and then, in an

onrush of loyalty, corrected himself with, "Jenkins, ain't
you ever a-goin'tuh grow up? You know the navy's been
co-operatin' a hundred percent. But I sure wish she was on
a sub."

The black ball of the compass jogged around until they
were on their course again, southward. *Just one sub*, prayed
Salvo Jenkins; *just a conning tower.* How he'd like to lay an
egg right alongside. In his mind he saw the upheaval of the
depth charge, the crushed U-boat lurching to the bottom. His
imagination took him further. Now he stood on the field, his
head cocked a little to one side, and watched the technical
sergeant in charge of the ground crew proudly painting a tiny
submarine on the fuselage of Lumbering Annie near the tail.
One for the team. One for Cappy Strame, the best pilot and
the greatest guy who ever lived. One for—The dream broke.
What if Salvo Jenkins lost his head and missed?

Again the imagining of failure brought that cold horror
to his stomach. So terribly much was at stake. He was just
Salvo Jenkins, the kid who had gummed things up the day
the general was aboard.

He thought back to the third day after his arrival at
Humphrey Field, from the West, discouraged and miserable,
and his summons to the office of the commanding officer. The
C.O. was a great lanky stalk of a man, six foot six, with a
craggy face, beak nose, and an abrupt manner that covered
his absorbing passion for his command.

He said, "Lieutenant Jenkins, there is a vacancy for a
bombardier in the crew of Captain Strame. I am assigning
you to that crew."

"Yes, sir. Did you say 'Captain Strame'?" It was no wonder
he had asked. Strame's was the crack bombing crew of the
squadron. It had been together for more than a year. It was
like the coach calling up a third-string substitute and saying,
"Okay, son. You're on the varsity. Go in there and score."

The C.O. sucked at a pipe carved in the shape of a skull,
and said: "Captain Strame asked for you, Lieutenant Jenkins.
I don't mind telling you that I questioned his judgment. He
could have had any man he wanted. I made that plain. I am
going to repeat to you his exact words. He said, 'I'll take the
kid, if you don't mind, sir. He's a bombardier. I know all about

that Salvo stuff, but it doesn't cut any ice. He's got hunting blood. He signed up for bombardier from way back. He's no washed-out pilot or flop navigator. Ever since he's come into the air forces he's done nothing but eat, sleep, live, and dream bombing. He just wants to bomb. When we get over a target, that's the kind of kid I want at the sights.'"

The C.O. blew a wisp of smoke, studied Jenkins a moment and then concluded, "That's all, Lieutenant."

The big bomber droned along on its mission. The men in her watched their instruments and the surface of the sea. Thinking back over what the C.O. had said, Salvo Jenkins knew that he would never want to succeed for anyone as much as he wanted to succeed for John Strame, not even for Mary Lou Allen, who was pledged to him back at State University ar Raleigh. And he loved Mary Lou with all his youth and yearning and imagination.

Strame was a pink-cheeked, black-haired, black-eyed boy from Alabama who was a born pilot the way Jenkins felt he was a born bombardier. He radiated love for his work, his ship, and his crew. He was as trim and fiery as a Derby race horse. His specialty was flying. The other specialties he left to the various members of his crew. But he expected and accepted nothing short of perfection.

It wasn't the job Jenkins worshiped, but the man, his spirit, and his friendship. It seemed as if Strame was the first person who had ever understood him and had faith in him. Jenkins's fear of letting Strame down became a sweating nightmare that never wholly left him.

He remembered that not even Mary Lou had quite understood him when he explained his great ambition to her. They had sat one night in the rear booth of Mason's drugstore. She wore a muslin dress that was soft and inexplicably thrilling to touch. It smelled of a mixture of warm cloth and flowers. Her presence brought pangs of sweetness to his heart that were nearly unbearable. When he put his fingers beneath her chin and turned her head to him, she gave him her mouth without restraint. It was that night that he told her that he had passed his preliminary examinations and was going to try for a commission as a bombardier.

She looked at him with her wide, serious eyes, contemplating what he had told her. She was not a lion hunter, but, womanlike, she wanted her man to have the best. She said, "It sounds teh'bly exciting, honey." But it was not exciting the way she said it. Then she added, "Swifty and Ted and Sparky are going to be pilots. I mean—"

"Let 'em." Jenkins leaned forward on the table top wet with the circles of their glasses, his face flushing, his young blue eyes shining with enthusiasm. "Anybody can fly a plane. But when they get where they're agoin' to, the bombardier pulls the trigger. That's me."

She had continued to stare at him strangely. He could not decide whether it was because she did not quite understand what a big job the bombardier had, or because she was surprised at him for wanting to be one. He hadn't meant to boast, but the ambition had burned so long inside him, unexpressed, that he had to talk about it.

"It's the most wonderful job in the war, Mary Lou. You've got to have a good bombardier. And it ain't as though anybody can do it. Why, if you know how, you can knock out a battleship from over twenty thousand feet in the air. It's the shooting part, Mary Lou. That's why I know I can do it better'n anybody else. I'm goin' to be the best bombardier they evah had. I'm goin' to sink a battleship."

Of course, he was only a kid of twenty then, or he wouldn't have talked like that. He knew a lot more now. Well, if Mary Lou had not quite grasped the significance of his ambition, she had divined the enthusiasm and the yearning behind it. Her loyal attitude was that if he said so, it must be all right. She had taken his hand and said, "I know you will, honey, a big one."

What children they had been, and how different it all was, now that he was no longer a boy, but a second lieutenant and a bombardier. It was one thing sitting with your girl in a booth and telling her what a big shot you were going to be, and another to be squatting in the nose of a flying ice wagon, out over the Atlantic Ocean, desperately afraid of making a botch of dropping a bomb on an enemy submarine, if you ever saw one.

The heavy ship hit a bump in the air and jarred Jenkins back to reality. Somebody clicked a microphone and said, "Oh-oh!"

which wasn't regulations, but got over the idea. Ahead and slightly to the east, a pillar of black smoke boiled up into the sky, a furious, volcanic, writhing thing, as though the ocean were erupting at that point.

Talk crackled on the intercommunication. "Tanker! Got it last night!"

"Roger!"

"Engineer from pilot: Get a picture of her."

"Engineer, Roger!"

They came down to within fifty feet of the surface of the water to let Bradley, the engineer, who doubled as photographer, get a shot. Only the stern of the tanker was visible. The rest was smoke threaded with orange flames. She was already down by the bow and the water around her was burning too. Salvo Jenkins stared hard. It was the first torpedoed ship he had ever seen. Somewhere beneath the surface of the sea, miles away by now, crept the enemy that had done this. And he, Horace Jenkins, was hunting him now, to wipe him out if he could. Somehow it was like being back on the farm when a wildcat would come down from the mountains and get into the chickens. Then you would go out with dog and gun and track him down and kill him.

He remembered suddenly what his father had told him when he taught him to shoot.

"Yuh got to be able to hit what you aimin' at, son," his father had said, "or it ain't no use goin' out with a gun. The dogs kin git you tuh where the cat's at, an' yore legs cain carry yuh there, but it don't do yuh no good if yuh miss."

Here in this strange element, the air, out over the endless wastes of water, the same held true. Pilot, navigator, and radioman would find the quarry if it was humanly possible, and would carry him to it. But once there, they were helpless. Their work was done. He must aim the deadly charge and send it straight to the target.

He remembered the day he had decided to be a bombardier. It was when a British bomber pilot had come to State University to lecture. There had been questions permitted after the talk, and everybody stared when young Jenkins asked, "Who pushes the button that lets the bomb go, sir? I mean is there anyone special who has to—"

"Rather! That's the bombardier. He's the top card in the deck. I fancy we've got the keenest chap in the whole push in our crew. We caught a Nazi supply ship off the coast of Norway once, a big one. He put one right down her funnel from ten thousand. That's bombing, you know. He got a medal for it, and dashed well deserved it. We called him Dead-Eye Dick."

Jenkins' heart beat faster. Dead-Eye Dick! Right down the funnel from ten thousand! Top card in the deck! "That's for me," said young Horace Jenkins under his breath, and from that moment on had hardly thought of anything else.

And all the time these thoughts were racing through his head he was crouching on his knees in the glass nose, straining his eyes onto the glittering surface of the sea to catch the first glimpse of a rising periscope, fingering his instruments, rechecking his calculatons, mentally making his selection of depth charges from the indicator panel, working, studying, fretting, worrying, thinking of Strame and his crew mates and the wonderful team of which they were all a part, and how terribly he wanted to make good for them, to make them as proud of him as he was of them.

They passed over a convoy escorted by a busy destroyer. Abeam of the lighthouse, the navigator set a new course and they wheeled left and headed out to sea, away from the sheltering land.

They saw nothing for a hundred miles but a broad oil slick from sunken tankers, and then they came upon a stubby freighter, all gray under war paint, terribly lonely and nervous, pushing her way eastward. She changed her course as they circled her, and then changed it twice more, rapidly.

Salvo recognized the symptoms of her jitters. Those lone freighters got to thinking, whenever they saw a bomber hovering about them, that there must be a submarine in the vicinity, and immediately began cutting semipanicky patterns to avoid possible torpedoes.

He felt a sudden pity for the solitary vessel. He wanted to call down to her, "It's all right. Don't you worry. We're here." The big bomber spread her wings protectingly over the hysterical ship. Salvo's heart went out to her; she seemed so helpless. That was why they were flying around out there, to watch over wanderers like her, to blast to the bottom of the sea the steel sharks that lay in wait.

Then the ship was gone from beneath them as Lumbering Annie clattered on, sniffing the sea lanes. Salvo understood better now the whys and wherefores of the long training grind that aimed only at perfection. Ground school, long sieges of physics, mathematics, navigation, meteorology, sighting and theory of bombing, the arithmetic of falling bodies, followed by the long weeks of practice with hundreds upon hundreds of missiles dropped from every altitude. He thought of all the mil errors made, never to be recovered, of the fractions miscalculated in the mind, the hundredth part of an infinitesimal error that magnified itself to a hundred yards off the target below and failure. Inevitably his mind returned once more to the culmination of his frailty—the day he had salvoed and wasted his whole load.

Again close to panic at the awesome picture of responsibility that had opened itself out, he reviewed his time from student to bombardier, and wished desperately that he had applied himself even more to his studies.

Legs appeared at the hatchway and descended the short iron ladder, bringing after them Hammond, the co-pilot. He carried a cup of grapefruit juice and a sandwich wrapped in wax paper.

"It's ham again," he said. "I thought we'd plowed all those pigs under years ago." He made himself comfortable in the narrow bay crammed with instruments, levers, tubing, cable leads, petcocks, wiring, and aluminum. "Nice place you have here, provided you've got a can opener to get out of it with," he commented. "Best view in the house."

Salvo munched on his sandwich. The fruit juice felt good in his dry throat. He was glad to have company for a moment.

The co-pilot retailed the gossip from above. "Carl's going to have a fine shiner in the morning. He was taking drift when we hit that bump away back. Good old navigator's drift-meter eye. Cappy's fidgety as all hell. He thinks he smells a sub. Say, I wish I had your job. Why didn't I think of putting in for bombardier? Ride around like an air-line passenger all day and when a target pops up, push a button and Bloo-o-o-ey! Pretty soft."

Salvo said, "Oh, it is, is it?" Of course Hammond was kidding, but through his mind there flashed all the other myriad duties of a bombardier besides hitting his target—the loading of bombs, repair and cleaning of guns, repair of his equipment in the air, knowledge of Morse code, blinker code, flag code, flare code, hydraulic, fuel, and fire-extinguisher system of the ship, as well as a working knowledge of how to fly and land her in emergency.

As he looked at Hammond, Salvo had an instant's temptation to unburden himself of all the doubts and fears and worries that had assailed him since the take-off, to rid his mind somehow of the nightmare of failure that haunted him. But he held it back. That was kid stuff, spilling your guts. The air forces didn't care about what you thought or how you felt. There was only one thing you could do for it—deliver.

"Guess I'll be getting back upstairs to the club," said the co-pilot. "The carburetors want to ice up. In June! So long, kid. If we flush something, don't miss."

Don't miss! Don't miss! That awful refrain. Earlier in the flight, Salvo had prayed for a target, had asked to be allowed to see just one sub. Now his jangled nerves cried for a reprieve. If they would only complete this mission without sighting a target, it would give him another chance—for more study, more practice. Just two hours, just an hour more on the training tower. The next time he would be ready.

He looked at his watch. Four hours under way. They would be turning back soon. He heard Cappy Strame on the interphone, "Navigator from pilot: Turning back. What is the new course?"

"New course, two-nine-zero, turn now."

"Roger!" Then, informally, "We'll have another look at that freighter on the way in."

"Roger!"

Salvo saw the big starboard wing dip. The sun, already low on the horizon, floated in an arc around them as they made their turn. The wind had freshened and occasional whitecaps frothed on the sea below.

He was glad, in a way, that they were going to pay another

visit to the lonely freighter pushing its way eastward. It might make it cut those frantic circles again, but it would be a comfort to it, too, when those friendly wings flew overhead, watching over it.

An hour passed, and another. Salvo's eyes ached from straining to the sea. The white patches of froth made observation more difficult. His duty was never to take his eyes from the sea below.

The impersonal, colorless, metallic voice of the interphone said, "Ship at one o'clock. Ten miles."

Salvo crouched low in his bay to see ahead out from under the glass nose. She was ahead and a little to starboard, a tiny speck on the darkening sea, growing larger as the thundering motors ate up the misty miles. She looked lonelier than ever. One tiny ship, an endless waste of water and sky, a tiring sun swelling and yellow as it neared the horizon and—

"Bomber from pilot: Open bomb-bay doors!"

"Roger!"

"Submarine three o'clock five miles."

With what seemed like a single lightning movement, Salvo hit the three steel levers to his left, one after the other, but faster than the eye could follow. Doors open! Selective! Depth charges armed!

"Pilot from bomber: Bomb-bay doors open. Hey! We've got something!"

He did not even know he had yelled the last into the interphone. The surface of the sea was rising up to meet him with incredible speed as the big bomber descended, her air-speed indicator leaping forward.

There she lurked, the sub's black form, barely at surface. Already she was tilting forward for the crash dive. A matter of seconds and she would be gone. Salvo Jenkins was as cold as a glacier. His fingers had already pressed the selector switch—depth charges Two and Five, one from each side, two in reserve. He crouched like a cat waiting to spring, his nostrils spread, eyes staring, his rear end waggling catlike as he got himself set.

There were only seconds, but his mind was so clear and keyed and ready that he seemed to know everything that was needed to be known at the same instant, as though there were different compartments in his head, and all of them were functioning independently. He knew altitude, air speed, ground speed, temperature, and time. And he knew at once—had known it from the first instant he had sighted the diving sub and while his fingers were pressing the selector switch—that they would not be able to bomb at the predetermined level. By the time they got there the target would be gone.

He had eyes in the back of his head, in his knees and elbows, and in the seat of his pants. Inside his brain a computer worked like a machine. In the time that the swooping ship drooped fifty feet he knew at what level Strame would make the run, and recalculated. The figures popped up and leaped into place as though he were seeing them on a gigantic screen.

"Bombardier from pilot: On course! Level!"

No time for a verbal answer. Salvo double-clicked his mike. His right hand held the hand sight, swung from its steel shaft, the ring and bead centered on the vanishing conning tower. The fingers of his left hand quivered over the firing switch, hovering, barely touching, moving slightly to keep the barest contact.

Half the conning tower and periscope was still visible, tilting forward . . . Breath held . . . Steady aim! Like shooting a gun at a treed wildcat.

The bead lifted inexorably from the sea to the black steel poised there, held—

Just a tightening of the fingers on the solenoid firing switch

"Bomb away! Okay to turn!"

Two legless gray pigs appeared beneath the glass nose of the ship and drifted downward lazily, shrinking in size like deflating toy balloons. They kept forward pace with the hurtling ship as it raced across the line straight to the sub. The wing had already dipped for turning.

At the precise moment that the bombs met water, the nose of the ship passed over the target and Salvo's vision was cut off.

"Engineer from pilot: Prepare to take picture left side!"

"Engineer, Roger!"

Then the intercommunication seemed to go haywire for

an instant as somebody up above yelled "Yahooo!" into it.

Salvo had already selected two more depth charges.

He was a split second ahead of Strame with a new set of calculations when the order came, "Bombardier from pilot: Stand by for second run! We've got him!"

"Bomber, Roger!"

Lumbering Annie swung heavily into a diving turn. The freighter hove into sight again, veering frantically away, black smoke belching from her single funnel. Then into Salvo's view came an expanse of tumbled white froth, as though there had been a sub-sea eruption. In the center of it bubbled a thick yellowish slick from which something black was upthrust. It was the bow of the stricken submarine, poised there for an instant.

Salvo felt no elation. He was too busy. Computations checked, bombs armed, fingers gentling the firing switch, bead drifting onto target, steady—

"Bomb away!"

"Pilot from engineer: Picture taken okay! Oh, baby!"

Salvo Jenkins tried to remember what had happened, what he had done, what his calculations had been, whether he had left anything out. He couldn't. He remembered nothing. Lumbering Annie circled and circled. The yellow oil patch grew in size and length, bits and pieces of unidentifiable things appeared in the center. The freighter was stuttering hysterical cheers with her blinker.

Someone came down through the hatch from above and began to beat Salvo on the back, yelling, "Wow! Wow! Wow! Wow" in tune with the thrumming motors.

Salvo Jenkins went back to the orderly room of the squadron to pick up his data kit, which he had left there in the excitement. He felt very tired and a little queer in his insides.

Voices came drifting through from the partitioned office of the C.O. The door was shut, but he recognized the speech of Ed Hammond, the co-pilot. "Say, Cappy. We've got a bombardier, haven't we?"

The hard, crackling voice of the C.O. broke in. "He's your man, John. I was wrong. And glad of it."

Salvo Jenkins wanted to get his brief case and get out of there. But his hands were trembling so, he fumbled it.

Captain Strame said, "That kid's a honey. Say, Ed, that 'Salvo' stuff is gonna be out. From now on we're calling him 'Bull's-eye.'"

Bull's-eye Jenkins got his brief case, but found suddenly that he could not see his way clearly to the door until he stopped and brushed the tears away from his eyes.

"Dawgone it, Jenkins," he said to himself. "There you go, actin' just like a kid again. Ain't you evah goin' tuh grow up?"

DAN DAVIN
Not Substantial Things

Dan Davin (1913–) is one of New Zealand's leading writers. During World War II he served with the New Zealand Division, reaching the rank of major. He fought in Greece, Crete, North Africa and Italy. Between 1946 and 1953 he wrote the volume on the battle of Crete for the New Zealand official war history.

The short story "Not Substantial Things" is from his collection, The Gorse Blooms Pale *(1947).*

A FEW MILES BEYOND THE VILLAGE we came to a blown bridge the way Amedeo had said we would. So we began to have some confidence in him. Perhaps he did know a way through the minefields and round the demolitions after all.

But it was well after midday by now and we thought we might as well stop here as anywhere else and have something to eat. So Terry and I helped Ned get out the scran-box and then we left him to master the Primus and brew up while we took another look at the map. Amedeo skipped round helpfully at first. But we'd worked out a technique of putting a feed together in the past few years which didn't allow for spare parts like Amedeo and so in the end there was nothing to do for Amedeo but sit sadly on a stone while Ned brought the billy to the boil.

I still didn't really feel as if my heart was in the business. When Terry drove into HQ that morning and suggested a day's liberating I'd jumped at the idea, thinking it would be a change from just hanging round and chafing at the bit. Jerry had pulled out a couple of days before and was going North hell for leather to shape up on his new line above Rome. But the Div. wasn't being allowed to follow. The big shots were cooking up some new job for us and according to current latrino-gram we were going to be given a rest and then put in to crack a hole in the next line. Whatever it was we were all pretty browned off. We weren't allowed to follow up now we had him on the run, there was nothing much to do and there was no leave yet to Rome.

In fact, liberating in the territory old Jerry had vacated was about the only diversion there was and everyone who could lay his hands on a vehicle was cruising round looking for some village that hadn't been spoiled by other liberators getting in first. That would have been enough by itself to make Terry welcome when he and Ned turned up in the Brigadier's car.

But there was another reason. I'd thrown a farewell party the night before for my batman, Bandy Grimm. He and I had been together a long time. And now he was off to New Zealand on his three months' leave. With the Jerries rocking on their heels the way they were the odds were they'd have taken the count before he got back. Somehow it wasn't the way you expected to see the last of a bloke in this war. You got used to them pushing off for a while to Base or a hospital, but you knew they'd turn up again. And you got used to them setting out on some offensive when you knew there was a good chance they wouldn't turn up again. But somehow to realise all of a sudden that a chap you'd got as used to as Bandy was going for keeps, and going home at that, was different. It meant times were changing. Change and decay, in fact. You had to face up to it that you were probably going to survive after all All these years you'd been thinking that as long as you hung on and didn't let your cobbers down and took the rough with the smooth, it didn't make much odds what else you did because there was no guarantee you wouldn't go back to the battalion any time, and then you'd soon reach the end of your ration of tomorrows. You'd have had your firkin, in fact.

But if blokes like Bandy were getting out of it alive, going home and all, then the chances were you would yourself. And then what the hell would you do?

So when we saw Bandy off in the jeep for Rear Div., all his traps along with him, and he leaned out and shook hands and the jeep roared out with Bandy looking at the HQ sign and the serial number for the last time, and raising a last crack for the Provost on point duty, I turned back to the Mess tent feeling pretty low. And breakfast didn't help any. It just reminded me I had a hang-over as well and that I'd been pretty offensive to the G2 at the party, calling him a bank clerk in battle-dress. Which he was, but that's another story.

So Terry's arrival couldn't have been better timed.

All the same, the hang-over, or whatever it was, wasn't as easy to shake off as all that. And Avezzano, our first stop, didn't help. There were a couple of armoured cars in the main square and the Div. Cav. had roped off a section for themselves. A few blokes were sitting on top of the cars reading the NZEF *Times* and a few more were brewing up alongside. The Ites were crowded round the ropes, gaping. The usual kids had got to close quarters and were cadging biscuits. Wally Riddell was in charge.

"Hallo," he said, "you bloody base-wallopers. Is the war over? Or are you doing an advance guard for AMGOT?"

"No, Wally," Terry said, "just showing ourselves to keep up the morale of the forward troops. AMGOT'll be along when the mines are lifted."

"Poor old Ites," said Wally. "They've had everything. Ostrogoths, Visigoths, and all the rest. And now AMGOTS."

"Don't blame us, Wally," Terry said. "We're just a couple of liberators like yourself."

Wally gave us a bit of a look, as if to say: Not so like as all that, you come along afterwards. But he didn't need Terry's MC ribbon to remind him we'd had our share and he said nothing. Besides, a hell of an uproar broke out in a side street just then and so we all strolled over to have a look.

A crowd of Ites was struggling down the middle of the road. In the centre we got a glimpse of a woman they were dragging along and she was certainly getting a rough spin. She must have been quite good-looking, but her face was all scratched now and one old dame in particular kept grabbing her by the hair, peroxided it was with the peroxide beginning to fade, and trying to yank it out by the handful. The equivalent number of Gyppos could hardly have made more noise than this crowd.

"You speak Itie, don't you, Mick?" Wally said. "What the hell's it all about?"

One of those bright kids you always find on the edge of a crowd explained.

"Well, what's he say?"

"Seems she and the local Jerry commandant went in for a bit of horizontal collaboration. He dropped her in the getaway and she's been hiding out. The general idea is to tear her to bits."

"Oh, Jesus, here we go again. That's the second today. Where the hell's that Field Security bloke? I have to do all his dirty work."

"Well, you'd better get cracking, Wally, on your errand of mercy," Terry said. "Remember her only sin is that she has loved too much."

Wally glowered at him and shouldered his way into the mob, a couple of his men after him.

There was no point in hanging around and so we went back to the car where Ned was waiting for us.

"Popular as a bag of measles, poor bitch," Ned said as we watched Wally's boys escorting her towards the Field Security place and the Ites trailing after like wolves.

In the next village we came to we were still a novelty and the wine was shoved through the windows at us in vast quantities. The usual Ite who'd been to the USA came and demonstrated his English and we pretended to understand him till all his cobbers were convinced he hadn't been lying all these years and really could speak English.

"He'd have been a top-sergeant if he'd stayed in the States," said Ned.

"Why top-sergeant?" I asked.

"All Yanks are top-sergeants," said Ned.

Just then I picked out what seemed to me a bright-looking youth and he turned out to be this joker Amedeo. According to him all the roads out of the village were blown. But he reckoned he could find a way through to his own village which was a few miles north-east of us.

"The only thing is," Terry said then, "I feel the call of Uncle Spam."

I wasn't sure whether it was hang-over or hunger with me
but I felt pretty hollow myself. And, anyhow, I was keen to
get away from one particularly unpleasant bloke in a blue suit
who kept telling us he was a bank manager and inviting us
to lunch. I've always maintained there must be something
wrong with people who can look after all that money without
spending it and it was pretty clear Blue-suit was no exception
because the rest of the crowd kept their eyes on him the way
a horse does when there's a fly he doesn't like hanging about.
In fact, it was obvious he was one of the local Fascist johnnies
and the crowd were still scared of him and wanted to see if he
could make his marble good with us.

"This joker's a bit of *non buono*," said Terry, who'd smelt
him too. "Let's get out of here into the fresh air."

So we put Amedeo in the back with the plonk we hadn't
been able to drink and driving East we came to the blown
bridge.

But the plonk hadn't had time to take much effect yet and
my mind kept running over the day's bad marks: a hang-over,
old Bandy's face when we shook hands, that crack of Wally's
about base-wallopers, the poor scragged whore, the Ite from
the USA and the bloody business man. A poor catch so far.

"You know, Terry," I said, "what say we call it a day and
go home?"

"Don't be a piker, Mick," he said. "I know it's not been
much chop so far but we're only getting started. Come on,
take a pull of this plonk."

So I knocked back a bottle and sure enough what with that
and the smell of some eggs frying that Ned had scrounged, and
the sun shining on the nice colours of the 1/200,000 map with
the roads marked in yellow and red, I began to feel better.

On the broken bridge someone had splashed up in tar: Viva
Stalin, Viva Churchill.

"Wonder why there aren't any Viva Roosevelts?" said
Terry.

"Too hard to spell," Ned said, looking up from the pan.

"Suit them better to defend their bloody bridge rather than
paint it after it's down," I said. But I didn't really mean it
any more. And I'd just realised from looking at the map that
the drained swamp on our right was the setting of Silone's

Fontamara. The wonder was that they still had the heart to splash up even the names of hope.

After that pretty nearly every bridge and culvert was blown. And we weren't very anxious to go near the ones that weren't. Even as it was, creeping down into the gullies and skirting along the faces or tacking up them, we always stood a reasonable chance of going up on a Teller.

Once we came on a mule with its guts blown out but still alive. Terry got out and finished it off.

"Jesus," he said as he put away his pistol. "And to think we're doing this for pleasure." So I could tell he was feeling the way I was. And I remembered he and his truck had gone up in one of the Ruweisat battles when he was an LO. He still had a bit of metal in his bum.

It wasn't so bad for Ned. He had all he could do keeping the car going and right side up. She was one of the few vehicles left in the Div. with the old desert camouflage and she had a mileage behind her that was nobody's business. Ned was very attached to her.

"One thing," Ned remarked some time after we'd passed the mule, "if we do go up I can always blame you jokers."

Of course it soon turned out that Amedeo had no idea where the mines were. But he was quite happy and like most Ites he put all his brains into finding reasons for staying that way. He sat on the roof and dangled his legs in front of the windscreen. He had confidence in us, he explained.

Eventually we struck a good bit of road and were able to hit her up, keeping well clear of the verges. Every time we passed one of those little Ite farms the kids dropped everything and rushed out after us. But the old people just waved and went on with whatever they'd been doing as if they'd got to the stage of not caring who drove by in fast military cars. Germans or anyone else. They knew they'd never do any riding themselves, by this time.

Well, it all took time and it was late afternoon when I poked my head out the trap in the roof to see what Amedeo was screeching about.

"Ecco, ecco," he was shouting. "Castel di Goriano."

And sure enough, a couple of miles away you could see a village perched up on top of a knoll. And very nice it looked too, so old it was the colour of the ground and sitting up there soaking the sun into itself the way a lizard does.

"He says it's Castel di Goriano," I said, pulling inside again. "It's really in 5 Corps territory, I should think."

We checked up on the map and sure enough it was.

"First come, first served," says Terry. "The poor old pongos are probably still indenting in triplicate for mine-detectors."

By this time we were climbing up the last slopes and had had to slow down. There were swarms of partisans all round us, banging off those Itie tommy-guns. The roof was covered in kids and Amedeo had moved to the bonnet. At the main gate we found the whole town had turned out to meet us and there wasn't a dog's chance of getting the car through. There was nothing for it but to abandon ship.

The next thing I knew was that I was being hoisted shoulder high and carried up the main street. I got my head round long enough to see that Terry and Ned were aloft too and even young Amedeo for good measure. So I didn't feel quite such a fool. Besides, I was tickled at Ned's face. You could see he was worrying his head off about the car. But I wasn't going to worry, because I'd seen a hefty partisan with a carbine sitting on top of it and it was obvious that it would have been high treason for anyone to start monkeying with it that day.

Well, as we go up the street we're pretty busy what with keeping our balance and catching the wreaths of flowers tossed up by the girls and taking a swig from every bottle that was pushed at us and kissing all the babies their mothers kept holding up to us. And there was an old woman who kept kissing me on the boot. But the other two didn't notice, thank God. They had troubles enough of their own.

As a matter of fact, once you got used to it, it wasn't at all unpleasant. Of course, we knew we were pretty phoney heroes but the Ites wouldn't have believed us if we told them and, anyhow, it's amazing how quickly you get to take this sort of thing for granted. In fact, if you had enough of it you'd always want more. That's the way old Musso went, I expect, and a good many others before him.

At the town hall things were slightly easier. All the big shots were there and they weren't bad blokes for big shots. They seemed to be under the impression one of us was General

Montgomery but they weren't at all upset when we explained
it was only us. They weren't weeping tears of joy like most of
the people outside and they had a tendency to keep the thing
rather dignified and ceremonial. But that suited us all right
because we weren't very tight. And the glasses kept coming
overhead in a continuous chain, which was the main thing.
I haven't seen the booze flow so freely since the old days at
Wallacetown pub after a Southland-Otago match.

In fact, all was as merry as a marriage bell until Terry got
the notion into his head I ought to make a speech, since I had a
smattering of the tongue. The idea took on like a house on fire
and I must say I didn't put up as much opposition as I might
have done what with the plonk and the feeling I had at the
time that there was a good deal to be said for the human race.
It almost seemed worth it that day, all the good cobbers that
were gone, the hard backward fighting in Greece and Crete,
the boredom and sweat of Maadi, and all the scares a man
had had in the desert.

So the next thing I find myself out on a balcony with a great
red carpet over it and the mayor holding forth explaining what
was going to happen the way mayors always do. Then he bows
to me and I go forward and put my hands on the balcony.
And below me in the piazza is the whole population, man,
woman and child, all absolutely crammed, with their faces
turned up and waiting. When I saw them my heart jumped
into my mouth and in spite of all the plonk I was so dry I
could scarcely move my tongue.

"Give her the gun, boy," says Terry by my side.

So I lift up my hand.

"Popolo di Castel di Goriano," I paused and I could feel
the silence go shuddering over them like the sun on a hill side
and over me too and I knew I had them.

"Popolo," I began again, "popolo questo giorno libero."
A simple trick, after all. But it worked and I thought that
one word "free" had sent them mad. The applause went
roaring up out of that narrow square and past my ear like
a rocket.

Meanwhile Terry spots I've shot my bolt for the moment
and am working out my next sentence and so he starts up a yell
in the background: Viva il Maggiore Michele. Of course, that

was all they needed—a handle for me and away they went. They like things personal.

When he saw I was ready Terry leans forward and lifts his hand: "Silenzio per il Maggiore," he says.

And then there was the sort of silence Shakespeare must have heard waiting for him over the centuries when he wrote the first line of one of his best spellbinders.

"Siamo venuti," I said, "noi, il terrore del mondo, i novozelandesi, i diavoli e cannibali, i rubatori, i negri—come vedete." And I threw my hands out wide like Abraham and smiled my sweetest smile.

Well, give me the Ites for speed at picking up irony. They jumped to that one all the faster because the Jerries had been doing a special line for months on what scoundrels, cannibals and niggers the Kiwis were. And since Terry and Ned and I were only just a bit off white the "negri" part underlined the nonsense of the rest.

By that time, I'd got properly into my stride and what with Terry leading the cheers whenever I stopped to think I had plenty of time to think the thing out into Latin and then work out what the Italian words must be.

"Siamo venuti," I repeated, "soltanto tre; perciò possete vedere come forti sono i tedeschi."

At that there was a terrific burst of booing which had me puzzled till I saw it was the mention of Jerries that had started them off. But then I thought of a further refinement. You see, they were a bit narked because only three of us had turned up and not a battalion or so and it was a bit delicate to explain.

"E perciò possete vedere," I went on, "che il vostro futuro è per voi stessi."

Of course they jumped to this immediately, too. We didn't want to overawe them but just to suggest by our fewness that now they were their own masters.

"Siete liberati dei tedeschi," I began to develop the idea, "si deve adesso liberarvi di voi stessi, del tyrannismo ancora rimasta, dei fascisti, e si deve fare per voi stessi uno governo di libertà, di giustizia, di ugualità, di fraternità." By this time I was well away and that little man who sits on your shoulder and sneers when you're talking English was completely out of it. Danton had nothing on me.

"Restono cose difficili per il popolo Italiano." That hushed them a bit. They didn't like the sound of difficult things ahead much. So I came in again with a swing.

"Ma, senza dubbio, questo popolo Italiano col suo corragio, colla sua onestà, la sua fortezza, va fare una vita piu bella, una vita chi saro conforme colle tradizioni splendidissime di questa patria, questa patria piena della grandezza passata e in questo momento gravida d'una grandezza piu magnifica, uno futuro digno del madre della civilizzazione."

I'd got pretty tangled in my nouns, what with all those genitives, but it didn't seem to matter. The older people were all weeping and the younger all cheering. The vivas were deafening and above them came sharply the crackling of enthusiastic carbines where the partisans were grouped on the fringes of the square.

"Siamo soldati, uffiziali forse, ma ciònonostante soldati, soldati semplici, come i vostri eroici partigiani." I had to stop there again. The partisans were not at all modest and joined more vociferously than anyone in the vivas for themselves. I made a mental note of that as another useful motif to use when things got dull. Meantime I wasn't going to be cheered away from my joke.

"Non siamo oratori," I went on, "non piu duci."

The allusion got them. "Abbasso il Duce, abbasso il fascismo, abbasso Mussolini." The roar was deep and angry. The was the first time I'd ever roused and heard the anger of a crowd.

Well, it went on in that fashion. I'd worked out the keynotes. The Jerries and Musso when you wanted rage, the glorious partisans when you wanted to cheer them up a bit, the glorious allies for terrific applause, the distant past of Italy for sentiment and the difficult future for sobriety. My difficulty now was to find some way of stopping.

Then during one particularly prolonged bit of cheering I leaned over the balcony and was watching them. As a matter of fact, I was thinking to myself that I could understand old Musso's point of view a bit better now. There was something that got you about having all those people below you there in the piazza and feeling your mind one jump ahead of your voice all the time and your voice being able to produce whatever emotion you wanted out of them. It was very exciting. And you felt it was dangerous, too. Something like taking risks with a very powerful car at top speed. At the same time you felt a certain phoneyness in your power, the way when you're shickered you know in the back of your mind things aren't really as good as they seem.

As I was staring down at them like that and trying to think of how the hell to finish without an anti-climax, I suddenly spotted the parish priest in front of the crowd and immediately I saw my end all cut and dried. I started into a peroration about the magnificence of the alliance of which Italy had now proved herself worthy, drew them into a series of vivas for Roosevelt, Churchill and Stalin and then when I'd got them at the top of their pitch, pointed suddenly at the priest and said: "Now the time has come when the lion can lie down with the Lamb of God, the Te Deum can be sung in Moscow, and here in Castel di Goriano, as a symbol of the glorious alliance which is winning us freedom and the future, the parish priest can join with us in singing 'The Red Flag'."

And so out it comes in those magnificent Italian voices: "Bandiera Rossa trionferà," and I must admit I was so moved myself that I forgot to look to see whether the priest was singing with us. And it was a good moment to make my getaway.

"You didn't say which got up again," said Terry, "the lion and the lamb. Or just the lion."

"Where's the plonk?" I said. I needn't have troubled to ask.

And that was the programme for the next hour or two except that from time to time one of us had to show himself on the balcony just so that the crowd wouldn't feel they were out of it. Then when we thought it was time we got going, the mayor wouldn't hear of it because they'd jacked up a special liberation dinner for us and the widows of all the partisans the Jerries had shot before they left were invited as well.

Well, by the time that dinner was over, and a pretty queer dinner it was, with lovely girls waiting on us and the widows bursting into tears from time to time and a stream of people coming in and out all the time to shake our hands, and gallons of plonk and more speeches, I was just about done. I had just enough sense to stop Ned abandoning his seat of honour towards the end and sneaking out with one of the women. Not one of the widows, though.

Anyhow, that settled it and in spite of all the protests we decided to get cracking. So we had a last round of speeches, nobbled Ned and made for the car.

The cold air must have got me then because the last thing I remember was thinking it was midnight and wondering how the hell Ned was going to get us first of all through the crowd and then through the minefields and wishing the partisans escorting us wouldn't fire off their carbines so much. Then I must have passed out.

The next thing I knew it was bloody cold and there was a rooster crowing somewhere and I had an iron throat. I tried to pull up my sleeping bag and it wasn't there. That brought me to and I saw we were still in the car and it was just cracking dawn.

I felt so depressed I didn't care where we were or how we'd got there. I reckon that most of the time we've got ourselves so organised that we only see as much truth as is good for us. Just the way our bodies only get as much air as is good for them. But all the time all sorts of muscles are probably at work stopping the atmosphere from closing in and squashing us. And that's the way with truth. The muscles of a man's mind are constantly engaged in keeping it back and only letting in a trickle at a time. But when he's exhausted or got a hangover, which is the same thing, he can't keep the truth out and it all bursts in. And that's what we call being depressed.

Well, that's the state I was in. The bloody truth came pouring in like water into a diver's suit. I saw that what we'd thought was good fun was deadly serious for the poor old Ites. They really believed the things I told them. And of course in theory they were true. But they weren't true, all the same.

Nothing is as simple as that. And nobody can risk being as simple as those Ites. Even after all these years they hadn't guessed what was coming to them, the steady disappointments, the gradual realisation that nothing had really changed, because they were still men and women and so still vulnerable. Only it would be less easy for them now because they were rid of the enemy outside themselves, the scapegoat.

They'd been reckless enough to hope and they'd have the rest of their lives for a hang-over.

But it wasn't only that. I could see what was coming to me as well. I'd got a glimpse of it the day before when old Bandy went. The fact was that chaps like me had got older without noticing it. We'd never give anything again what we'd given the Div. We'd never bring the same energy to anything that we'd brought to things like the break-through at Minqar Qaim or the assault on Cassino. And we'd never be able to make friends again the same way or drink and laugh and die the same way. We'd used up what we had and we'd spend the rest of our lives looking over our shoulders.

Yes, that was it. The best was over with the worst. There was nothing left now except the dragging of some wretched whore through the streets in Avezzano yesterday, in Castel di Goriano today perhaps, and in the rest of the world tomorrow. Now that we knew the war was won, it was just a question of a lot more people dying for another year or two. The real excitement when you might lose was gone. And the peace everyone had felt while the war was really on was going too. A man'd soon have to start up again all the old fights with himself that used to go on in the days when there was no danger to his skin.

Terry stirred beside me and woke up.

"What the bloody hell are we doing here and where the hell are we?" I asked.

"Jesus, it's cold," he said, "listen to those bloody frogs. Petrol, we're out of petrol. We missed Avezzano in the dark and then when the petrol ran out we had to stop here." He looked out the window. "A mist, frogs, and it's pretty flat. We must be in that Fucine Swamp of theirs."

"We're in the bloody cactus, in fact," I said. Not that I cared much but it was a pleasure to think of something else.

"We'll be jake," he said. "We'll rustle up some breakfast and then make tracks up to the main road. If there's an armoured car about or a boy with a bicycle we can easily get a message back for petrol."

"Yes," I said.

But we didn't stir. Neither of us cared much for the thought of Wally's jokes when we passed through again.

"I could do with a drink," I said. The muscles of my mind were doing so much work I could hear them creaking. But there was still too much truth getting by.

Ned opened his eyes. "I saved a couple of bottles," he said. And he pulled them out of the front pocket.

We sat there drinking in the early morning and the cold seeped into us like reality.

"Never mind, Ned," Terry said. "It was all that third gear work that used up the petrol."

"Shouldn't have happened all the same," said Ned.

"Anyhow, it was a great day," Terry said. "She's been a bonny war."

"She's been a bonny war," I said, and took another swig at the bottle.

MILES NOONAN
Reunion

*The English writer Miles Noonan (1921–)
is the author of several volumes of military short stories and sketches. "Reunion"
is from his 1983 collection,* Tales from
the Mess.

T HE INTRODUCTION OF COMPUTERS MIGHT by now have
made a difference and the contraction of British overseas
commitments has certainly reduced the scope, but it was not
unknown for the War Office to post the wrong man to the
wrong place at the wrong time.

An example of this occurred in 1951 during the Korean
War. It became evident to a brigade headquarters that an
improvement in the coordination of their arrangements with
their allies would be achieved if they were to be given an
additional officer, charged with looking after liaison with the
South Koreans on a fulltime basis.

Realism dictated that the finding of an ideal candidate for
the job, a speaker of Korean, would be unlikely. An acceptable
second-best, it was suggested, would be somebody with Far
Eastern experience.

The War Office found somebody with Far Eastern experience. He was an able officer who had served in Hong Kong
in the late 1930s and had been captured by the Japanese
in Singapore in 1942. His time as a prisoner-of-war had, of
course, deprived him of the operational opportunities that
had been open to luckier contemporaries. It was felt that an
active appointment in Korea would help him to catch up in
this respect.

He was flown out immediately. He reported himself eager
for work, at the brigade headquarters housed in a requisitioned

school. The brigade major welcomed him hospitably and said the brigade commander would see him as soon as he could. At the moment the brigadier was talking to his Korean liaison officer, whose English was none too good and who was inclined to verbosity. There might be quite a wait. Have a cup of tea.

Over the tea the brigade major, who had himself drafted the job specification, put some tactful research into the newcomer's Asian background. It was impressive. Among other things he was an enthusiastic linguist who had qualified in Cantonese and Malay. He would start on Korean at once.

Had he come across any Koreans before?

Only on the railway.

The railway?

The Burma–Siam railway. Prisoners-of-war of the Japanese had been put to work building the bloody thing. It had been unpleasant. For obvious reasons, nobody at the time had been able to keep an overall count of casualties, but he'd seen the figures recently. Sixty-one thousand POWs had been sent there. Sixteen thousand had died. All the guards had been bastards. The biggest bastards of the lot had been Koreans.

The brigade major was beginning to wonder whether there might not be a touch of reserve in the new man's attitude to his allied opposite numbers, when the brigadier's door opened and the Korean liaison officer came out.

The brigade major rose to his feet to make the introductions. "This is . . ." he started.

The newly joined member of the brigade staff drew his pistol and shot the Korean dead.

"Recognized him at once," he explained later. "He was one of the bastards on the railway."

His replacement matched exactly the requirements redrafted jointly by the brigadier and the brigade major. He was a qualified Finnish speaker who had never before set foot out of Europe.

LESLIE THOMAS
Virgin Soldiers on Parade

*Leslie Thomas (1931–) did his National
Service in Malaya during the time of the
Communist Emergency. This conflict forms
the setting for his best-known novel, the
serio-comic* The Virgin Soldiers *(1966),
later filmed with Hywel Bennett as the
novel's 19-year old hero, Brigg. Like many
young conscripts in dangerous times, the
dilemma of Brigg and his companions is
whether they will achieve sex before death.
The adventures of Brigg and his fellow
conscripts were continued in* Onward Virgin Soldiers *and* Stand Up Virgin
Soldiers.*

This selection is from The Virgin
Soldiers. *The parade takes place at the
Panglin military barracks.*

BY EIGHT O'CLOCK THE FOUR companies were on the
parade ground. It was hard and sharp white, curiously
like ice, because the sun had cleared the buildings and was
now directly on the concrete. Brigg came out of the shower
behind the barrack room, knotted a towel around him, and
went to stand in a slice of sunlight on the balcony.

He heard Driscoll laughing and saw that he had come
from his room at the end and was leaning on the door-
frame, naked except for his beret and socks. The Sergeant
moved forward and leaned on the piperail of the balcony, considering, with disgust, the parade ground and the
soldiers.

"The echelons of power," he breathed. "See the might of

Britain's Army in foreign parts. For King and Country. With men like this, how can we fail?"

Brigg shuffled to the rail and bent over it. Directly below, the mad Corporal Brook was squeaking his wan and sickly section to attention.

Brigg said, "Well, it's not supposed to be the Coldstream Guards, is it?"

Driscoll turned and suddenly shouted at him: "It's the Royal Army Crap Corps! Look at it! For God's sake, look! Kids who can't get home to Mum quick enough, and misfits—sick and stupid bastards, hanging on because it's all they have and they haven't got anywhere else to live. "Go on, look! You don't see an army, do you? They're not soldiers. They're a freak show."

He calmed quickly and turned his naked belly to the parapet again. Quietly he said: "Just take a look at the Corporal we all love. Do you know why Corporal Brook is mouthing like that and nothing's coming out? D'you know? Well, I'll tell you why. It's because he's got a blockage. Up here, in his nut." Driscoll tapped his own head spitefully. "Yes, no kidding. Up here. The poor sod is incapable of getting the next order out. He knows what it should be—he *knows* all right—but he can't say it. So he's stuck there. Like a bleeding goldfish."

Deliberately Driscoll leaned over the rail. The wordless, panicked, white Corporal Brook was immediately below. "Stand aaart ease!" bellowed Driscoll.

The section stood at ease. Brook gave a jump of terror as though the message had come from the sky. He looked and saw Driscoll, and with relief, shame and anger, mumbled: "Yes, that's right. Stand at ease."

Brigg, laughing without sound, backed away from the rail so that Brook would not see him.

Once, at night, the Corporal had sidled to his bed like an old aunt and sublimely detailed how he was an illegitimate son of the peerage, but that he did not tell everyone because it was not the sort of thing he wanted to get around.

Driscoll continued his commentary, the complaints drifting towards Brigg, but only casually, as though the Sergeant did not care whether he was getting them or not.

"Now, *who* would do that?" he whispered in disbelief. Then louder: "Who in God's name would *do* that? Put Cutler behind Forsyth? But they *can't*. Surely even they must realise how it looks. I mean, they know Cutler's got a diseased thigh and he hangs over to the right. But if that's not bad enough, they have to put Forsyth in the rank behind him, and he's got amnesia or dreaded pox or something nasty in his left hip, and he's leaning the other way! It's horrible. Horrible. Don't they know? Can't they see. It's a carnival, not a parade." He swore viciously but quietly to himself.

Brigg looked up from examining Cutler and Forsyth, their opposite arms hanging limply as they marched, like men fishing from two sides of a boat.

"Observe Sinclair," said Driscoll. "See the damp look on his face? He is dreaming about trains. Trains? He's drilling, and his mind's on railway engines. I wouldn't mind, I wouldn't complain a bit, if he had incest or something that mattered on his mind, but it's not. It's bloody engine numbers and which chuff-chuff has the biggest and the littlest wheels."

Brigg knew the analysis was sound. Sinclair hated the army even more than most of them, and flew away from it often by closing his eyes and arriving at platform nine, Euston, with the steam and the grinding wheels, and the handsome engines. They were the things, the real stuff, he said, that counted. He could also do it with his eyes open, as he was now.

On his own, Brigg began playing Driscoll's game. He counted first the men who wore glasses. There were fifty-two out of one hundred and sixty, including two pairs with yellow lenses. Seven of the NCOs wore them and all of the officers but three. In addition there were minor psychiatric cases, men with fingers or toes missing, men with ruptures, bald men, one of them aged twenty-two, those who were visited by deafness, and many who had curses, the details of which they preferred to keep to themselves. There were also two members of the unit who were each only capable of vision in one eye. One of these was the Commanding officer, Colonel Wilfred Bromley Pickering, and the other a regular lance-corporal called Hackett.

In the dull, hot, everyday life of the garrison, there were few more stimulating experiences than witnessing Hackett march to his commander, each salute, and, in a stretched moment of aching suspense, each try to focus the other with his active eye.

Walking out of the sun, Brigg felt the shadows flow cold across his shoulders and neck. He sat on the side of his bed, by the double door, and began to polish his boots with no enthusiasm. Being on guard meant he was excused the morning muster, but he still had to be in the office at eight-thirty. He could see Driscoll on the balcony rail, and Driscoll could see him cleaning his boots.

"In Private Longley," said Driscoll, unhurried, like a medical lecturer, "we have a unique physical oddity. Even for this place. Unique. He is the very opposite to a hunchback. He is a hunchfront! Just see that pigeon chest. It's forcing his head back. And here . . . oh, now this is really it . . . Here they are, top of the circus bill."

Brigg got up and with his left boot still over his hand walked into the streak of sun again. He saw what Driscoll meant. Rolling along, now directly beneath him, like two benign, green elephants, were Sergeant Organ and Sergeant Fisher.

"At last night's weigh-in," recited Driscoll, "it was twenty-two stone to Herbie Fisher, and Fred Organ—he can't help his name, poor bastard—was twenty-one. I know. I'm not kidding, because I was there when they were talking about it like a couple of poncing chorus girls. 'You know, Herbie, I think I'm losing a little bit.' 'I reckon you are, too, Fred, and I am too, I'm sure of it.' God, you should have heard them.

"I mean—look! Look—Great pounding slobs. You'd think the army would have enough pride to pension them off, wouldn't you? But no, they send them abroad where all the bongos can laugh at them too. And they keep providing great bales of cloth for special uniforms for them, and no shorts, because that would be too hilarious, and on top of that size eighteen boots and reinforced beds. Jesus help us! How can men get like that and keep their self-respect? And they quarrel like a pair of fashion models. I heard Fred call Herbie 'Fatty' once. Fatty!"

Brigg turned and went back to his bed. He sat down, his towel hung across his knees, and spat on the toecaps of his boots. Driscoll, who somehow did not look ridiculous even if he was wearing only his socks and his beret, half turned.

As he looked down intently at the dull black toecap gradually coming to a reluctant shine, Brigg guessed what was coming next. He did not raise his head, and Driscoll said: "And then there's your little bunch."

Still looking down, Brigg said tonelessly: "We don't want to be here."

"What sort of an answer is that?" rasped Driscoll. He mimicked: "'We don't want to be here.' I don't suppose the poor buggers who built the Burma Railway for the Japs wanted to be there either."

Nor all the dead men we left lying around outside Caen, he thought, but he didn't say it because he'd killed three of them by mistake with his own bren gun.

Instead he said: "Pale little ninnies, bleating and moaning and crossing off the dates on your going-home calendars, and getting that Chink in the village to make you swank suits. You can't wait to get home to Mum, can you? You get out here and the first thing you want to do is to go home."

Brigg thought he had finished, but he hadn't. "But when you *do* get home," he said. "Then it will be different. On Saturdays with the girls. 'I was out in Malaya. Murder out there. Stinking hot and those Communist bandits . . .' I can hear all you little bastards now."

Driscoll was riling him, so he got up and went through the barrack room to the lavatory. He sat down and thought how true it was. When they got home he knew just how it would be. They would go around like proud little fighters, armed to the teeth with lies. Their stories would be as good as the next man's, even if he had spent his National Service with swamps and fear and true death waiting every day and night.

Some of Panglin's clerks, whose conscript years had been scratched and blotted away on wooden desks, had gone to the village tailor and been fitted with splendid uniforms for the day when they arrived home. They were of smooth, lime, slime green, and they had fancy flashes and impressive insignia, and MALAYA in yellow letters across the shoulder. The fragile, sere, rickety virgin soldiers of the hopeless garrison became stern, strong, eye-catching warriors, once they had reached dear old

England and safety. The uniforms cost forty dollars and they could only be worn for the two weeks of terminal leave. But what glory.

Driscoll heard him pull the chain and turned and waited for him to come out. But the Sergeant changed his mind about talking and returned to watching the parade. Brigg walked through the rows of beds, got to his own, and began to dress. He put on his socks and boots first and then his drawers cellular. He caught a sudden appearance of himself in the full mirror at the end of the barrack room and confirmed that he looked long, white and ridiculous.

He had never had sex, and one of his most virulent fears was that he might, by some military mischance, get killed before he had known the experience. It was of huge importance, bigger, much bigger, than any of the other things he could think of living for, or, at least, that he would miss if he died. Not to know about it would be the ultimate, awful tragedy, far worse, for instance, than never knowing who your mother was.

Now, at nineteen, he did not know, and could not imagine, although he tried hard enough, what it actually felt like. When you did it, was it hard or easy, inspiring or merely perspiring, comforting or exhausting? Did it drift into boredom, as so many things did with use, or was it new and tremendous every time. Did it hurt first time? How quick or how slow was it? Was it HOT?

Once he had thought this was a private obsession. It seemed unreal and unreasonable that you could miss something so much when you did not even know what it was. Miss it more than you knew you would miss ordinary happiness. But he had come to realise that it was the same with the others.

Sometimes in the evenings, particularly on a Tuesday or a Wednesday when they did not have any money to go out, Tasker and Lantry would lie on their beds and see who could think the dirtiest thoughts and get the biggest and best erection.

They pursued this activity with fetid enthusiasm, sometimes beneath the sheets and sometimes above them, and viewed their finished achievements with academic, even medical, pride.

"That blue vein seems to be getting bigger," Tasker would

announce with concern. "Perhaps I'd better show it to the medical officer."

"Well, you've shown it to everyone else," said Lantry amiably. "Why miss him out?"

"No birds, though," grumbled Tasker. "There's never a woman seen this, except my Mum. I wonder if I'll ever get around to using it at all." He turned over and regarded Lantry with ashen seriousness. "I might get killed first. I mean it's possible, isn't it?"

Brigg, sitting on his bed writing to Joan, his girl, glanced up.

Lantry looked drawn, fully sharing the concern. They lay there with their sheets propped up like a small Arctic encampment.

"You could, you know," said Lantry. "Get killed, I mean. There's blokes getting killed out here regularly—well, upcountry, anyway, and it's no distance, is it? Those three last week. I saw their papers today and their numbers were all 2234-something, younger than us. It's a bit worrying."

Panglin's only casualty of the Malaya Emergency had been a drunken cook-corporal who was decisively struck by a truck while staggering across the garrison road by moonlight and who was buried with solemnity and honours the following day. So the chances of Brigg, Tasker or Lantry being killed, as things were then, were remote. But only as remote, Brigg considered, as his chances of opening his sexual life.

There were the obvious ways, but he was reluctant to pay for it at the very start, because it might spoil it for good and it might become a habit. Besides which, it was expensive and unhealthy.

At Panglin there was a small unselect stable of WRAC girls, who could have been winners of a whole series of reverse beauty contests. They were the ugliest girls in the world, and even the humidity and the scarcity of the commodity could do nothing to make them un-ugly. Apart from this there was a downright jinx on some of them. A thirsting lance-corporal, a wine steward, was still doing three months after being apprehended while screwing one of them on the top table at the officers' mess.

A few nights later a harmless mechanic, while quietly

furgling another WRAC in the long elephant grass at the side of the garrison road, was accidently soaked when a passing Hussar paused to relieve himself.

Brigg considered the WRACs out of the running for his virginity anyway. There remained the everyday Malay and Chinese girls, some of whom looked very soft and gentle, but these were very hard even to talk to. There were the officers' wives, grey and timid or rosy and exuberant, but all out of the question; and the NCOs' wives, who were not really made for loving, even had they been willing.

There was also Phillipa, the twenty-year-old daughter of Regimental Sergeant-Major Raskin. Brigg did not dare think of her because when he did he had fiery, uncomfortable dreams, and had to take a walk on the balcony in the dark to cool off. Sometimes it took an hour or more.

CHINUA ACHEBE
Girls at War

Chinua Achebe (1930–) was born Albert Chinualumogo in Ogidi, Nigeria. Educated at the University College of Ibadan, he is one of Africa's most important novelists. His books include Things Fall Apart *(1958) and* A Man of the People *(1966).*

The short story "Girls at War" is set during the Nigerian Civil War of 1967–70, and is from Achebe's 1977 collection, Girls at War.

THE FIRST TIME THEIR PATHS crossed nothing happened. That was in the first heady days of warlike preparation when thousands of young men (and sometimes women too) were daily turned away from enlistment centres because far too many of them were coming forward burning with readiness to bear arms in defence of the exciting new nation.

The second time they met was at a check-point at Awka. Then the war had started and was slowly moving southwards from the distant northern sector. He was driving from Onitsha to Enugu and was in a hurry. Although intellectually he approved of thorough searches at road-blocks, emotionally he was always offended whenever he had to submit to them. He would probably not admit it but the feeling people got was that if you were put through a search then you could not really be one of the big people. Generally he got away without a search by pronouncing in his deep, authoritative voice: "Reginald Nwankwo, Ministry of Justice." That almost always did it. But sometimes either through ignorance or sheer cussedness the crowd at the odd check-point would refuse to be impressed. As happened now at Awka. Two constables carrying heavy Mark 4 rifles were watching distantly from the roadside leaving the actual searching to local vigilantes.

"I am in a hurry," he said to the girl who now came up to his car. "My name is Reginald Nwankwo, Ministry of Justice."

"Good afternoon, sir. I want to see your boot."

"Oh Christ! What do you think is in the boot?"

"I don't know, sir."

He got out of the car in suppressed rage, stalked to the back, opened the boot and holding the lid up with his left hand he motioned with the right as if to say: After you!

"Are you satisfied?" he demanded.

"Yes, sir. Can I see your pigeon-hole?"

"Christ Almighty!"

"Sorry to delay you, sir. But you people gave us this job to do."

"Never mind. You are damn right. It's just that I happen to be in a hurry. But never mind. That's the glove-box. Nothing there as you can see."

"All right sir, close it." Then she opened the rear door and bent down to inspect under the seats. It was then he took the first real look at her, starting from behind. She was a beautiful girl in a breasty blue jersey, khaki jeans and canvas shoes with the new-style hair-plait which gave a girl a defiant look and which they called—for reasons of their own—"air force base"; and she looked vaguely familiar.

"I am all right, sir," she said at last meaning she was through with her task. "You don't recognize me?"

"No. Should I?"

"You gave me a lift to Enugu that time I left my school to go and join the militia."

"Ah, yes, you were the girl. I told you, didn't I, to go back to school because girls were not required in the militia. What happened?"

"They told me to go back to my school or join the Red Cross."

"You see I was right. So, what are you doing now?"

"Just patching up with Civil Defence."

"Well, good luck to you. Believe me you are a great girl."

That was the day he finally believed there might be

something in this talk about revolution. He had seen plenty of girls and women marching and demonstrating before now. But somehow he had never been able to give it much thought. He didn't doubt that the girls and the women took themselves seriously, they obviously did. But so did the little kids who marched up and down the streets at the time drilling with sticks and wearing their mothers' soup bowls for steel helmets. The prime joke of the time among his friends was the contingent of girls from a local secondary school marching behind a banner: WE ARE IMPREGNABLE!

But after that encounter at the Awka check-point he simply could not sneer at the girls again, nor at the talk of revolution, for he had seen it in action in that young woman whose devotion has simply and without self-righteousness convicted him of gross levity. What were her words? We are doing the work you asked us to do. She wasn't going to make an exception even for one who once did her a favour. He was sure she would have searched her own father just as rigorously.

When their paths crossed a third time, at least eighteen months later, things had got very bad. Death and starvation having long chased out the headiness of the early days, now left in some places blank resignation, in others a rock-like, even suicidal, defiance. But surprisingly enough there were many at this time who had no other desire than to corner whatever good things were still going and to enjoy themselves to the limit. For such people a strange normalcy had returned to the world. All those nervous check-points disappeared. Girls became girls once more and boys boys. It was a tight, blockaded and desperate world but none the less a world—with some goodness and some badness and plenty of heroism which, however, happened most times far, far below the eye-level of the people in this story—in out-of-the-way refugee camps, in the damp tatters, in the hungry and bare-handed courage of the first line of fire.

Reginald Nwankwo lived in Owerri then. But that day he had gone to Nkwerri in search of relief. He had got from Caritas in Owerri a few heads of stock-fish, some tinned meat, and the dreadful American stuff called Formula Two which he felt certain was some kind of animal feed. But he always had a vague suspicion that not being a Catholic put one at a disadvantage with Caritas. So he went now to see an old friend who ran the WCC depot at Nkwerri to get other items like rice, beans and that excellent cereal commonly called Gabon gari.

He left Owerri at six in the morning so as to catch his friend at the depot where he was known never to linger beyond 8.30 for fear of air-raids. Nwankwo was very fortunate that day. The depot had received on the previous day large supplies of new stock as a result of an unusual number of plane landings a few nights earlier. As his driver loaded tins and bags and cartons into his car the starved crowds that perpetually hung around relief centres made crude, ungracious remarks like "War Can Continue!" meaning the WCC! Somebody else shouted "Irevolu!" and his friends replied "shum!" "Irevolu!" "shum!" "Isofeli?" "shum!" "Isofeli?" "Mba!"

Nwankwo was deeply embarrassed not by the jeers of this scarecrow crowd of rags and floating ribs but by the independent accusation of their wasted bodies and sunken eyes. Indeed he would probably have felt much worse had they said nothing, simply looked on in silence, as his boot was loaded with milk, and powdered egg and oats and tinned meat and stock-fish. By nature such singular good fortune in the midst of a general desolation was certain to embarrass him. But what could a man do? He had a wife and four children living in the remote village of Ogbu and completely dependent on what relief he could find and send them. He couldn't abandon them to kwashiokor. The best he could do—and did do as a matter of fact—was to make sure that whenever he got sizeable supplies like now he made over some of it to his driver, Johnson, with a wife and six, or was it seven?, children and a salary of ten pounds a month when gari in the market was climbing to one pound per cigarette cup. In such a situation one could do nothing at all for crowds; at best one could try to be of some use to one's immediate neighbours. That was all.

On his way back to Owerri a very attractive girl by the roadside waved for a lift. He ordered the driver to stop. Scores of pedestrians, dusty and exhausted, some military, some civil, swooped down on the car from all directions.

"No, no, no," said Nwankwo firmly. "It's the young woman I stopped for. I have a bad tyre and can only take one person. Sorry."

"My son, please," cried one old woman in despair, gripping the door-handle.

"Old woman, you want to be killed?" shouted the driver as he pulled away, shaking her off. Nwankwo had already opened a book and sunk his eyes there. For at least a mile after that he did not even look at the girl until she finding, perhaps, the silence too heavy said:

"You've saved me today. Thank you."

"Not at all. Where are you going?"

"To Owerri. You don't recognize me?"

"Oh yes, of course. What a fool I am . . . You are . . ."

"Gladys."

"That's right, the militia girl. You've changed, Gladys. You were always beautiful of course, but now you are a beauty queen. What do you do these days?"

"I am in the Fuel Directorate."

"That's wonderful."

It was wonderful, he thought, but even more it was tragic. She wore a high-tinted wig and a very expensive skirt and low-cut blouse. Her shoes, obviously from Gabon, must have cost a fortune. In short, thought Nwankwo, she had to be in the keep of some well-placed gentleman, one of those piling up money out of the war.

"I broke my rule today to give you a lift. I never give lifts these days."

"Why?"

"How many people can you carry? It is better not to try at all. Look at that old woman."

"I thought you would carry her."

He said nothing to that and after another spell of silence Gladys thought maybe he was offended and so added: "Thank you for breaking your rule for me." She was scanning his face, turned slightly away. He smiled, turned, and tapped her on the lap.

"What are you going to Owerri to do?"

"I am going to visit my girl friend."

"Girl friend? You sure?"

"Why not? . . . If you drop me at her house you can see her. Only I pray God she hasn't gone on weekend today; it will be serious."

"Why?"

"Because if she is not at home I will sleep on the road today."

"I pray to God that she is not at home."

"Why?"

"Because if she is not at home I will offer you bed and breakfast . . . What is that?" he asked the driver who had brought the car to an abrupt stop. There was no need for an answer. The small crowd ahead was looking upwards. The three scrambled out of the car and stumbled for the bush, necks twisted in a backward search of the sky. But the alarm was false. The sky was silent and clear except for two high-flying vultures. A humorist in the crowd called them Fighter and Bomber and everyone laughed in relief. The three climbed into their car again and continued their journey.

"It is much too early for raids," he said to Gladys, who had both her palms on her breast as though to still a thumping heart. "They rarely come before ten o'clock."

But she remained tongue-tied from her recent fright. Nwankwo saw an opportunity there and took it at once.

"Where does your friend live?"

"250 Douglas Road."

"Ah! that's the very centre of town—a terrible place. No bunkers, nothing. I won't advise you to go there before 6 p.m.; it's not safe. If you don't mind I will take you to my place where there is a good bunker and then as soon as it is safe, around six, I shall drive you to your friend. How's that?"

"It's all right," she said lifelessly. "I am so frightened of this thing. That's why I refused to work in Owerri. I don't even know who asked me to come out today."

"You'll be all right. We are used to it."

"But your family is not there with you?"

"No," he said. "Nobody has his family there. We like to say it is because of air-raids but I can assure you there is more to it. Owerri is a real swinging town and we live the life of gay bachelors."

"That is what I have heard."

"You will not just hear it; you will see it today. I shall take you to a real swinging party. A friend of mine, a Lieutenant-Colonel, is having a birthday party. He's hired the Sound Smashers to play. I'm sure you'll enjoy it."

He was immediately and thoroughly ashamed of himself. He hated the parties and frivolities to which his friends clung like drowning men. And to talk so approvingly of them because he wanted to take a girl home! And this particular girl too, who had once had such beautiful faith in the struggle and was betrayed (no doubt about it) by some man like him out for a good time. He shook his head sadly.

"What is it?" asked Gladys.

"Nothing. Just my thoughts."

They made the rest of the journey to Owerri practically in silence.

She made herself at home very quickly as if she was a regular girl friend of his. She changed into a house dress and put away her auburn wig.

"That is a lovely hair-do. Why do you hide it with a wig?"

"Thank you," she said leaving his question unanswered for a while. Then she said: "Men are funny."

"Why do you say that?"

"You are now a beauty queen," she mimicked.

"Oh, that! I mean every word of it." He pulled her to him and kissed her. She neither refused nor yielded fully, which he liked for a start. Too many girls were simply too easy those days. War sickness, some called it.

He drove off a little later to look in at the office and she busied herself in the kitchen helping his boy with lunch. It must have been literally a look-in, for he was back within half an hour, rubbing his hands and saying he could not stay away too long from his beauty queen.

As they sat down to lunch she said: "You have nothing in your fridge."

"Like what?" he asked, half-offended.

"Like meat," she replied undaunted.

"Do you still eat meat?" he challenged.

"Who am I? But other big men like you eat."

"I don't know which big men you have in mind. But they

are not like me. I don't make money trading with the enemy
or selling relief or . . ."

"Augusta's boy friend doesn't do that. He just gets foreign
exchange."

"How does he get it? He swindles the government—that's
how he gets foreign exchange, whoever he is. Who is Augusta,
by the way?"

"My girl friend."

"I see."

"She gave me three dollars last time which I changed to
forty-five pounds. The man gave her fifty dollars."

"Well, my dear girl, I don't traffic in foreign exchange and
I don't have meat in my fridge. We are fighting a war and I
happen to know that some young boys at the front drink gari
and water once in three days."

"It is true," she said simply. "Monkey de work, baboon
de chop."

"It is not even that; it is worse," he said, his voice
beginning to shake. "People are dying every day. As we
talk now somebody is dying."

"It is true," she said again.

"Plane!" screamed his boy from the kitchen.

"My mother!" screamed Gladys. As they scuttled towards
the bunker of palm stems and red earth, covering their heads
with their hands and stooping slightly in their flight, the entire
sky was exploding with the clamour of jets and the huge noise
of home-made anti-aircraft rockets.

Inside the bunker she clung to him even after the plane
had gone and the guns, late to start and also to end, had all
died down again.

"It was only passing," he told her, his voice a little shaky.
"It didn't drop anything. From its direction I should say it
was going to the war front. Perhaps our people are pressing
them. That's what they always do. Whenever our boys press
them, they send an SOS to the Russians and Egyptians to
bring the planes." He drew a long breath.

She said nothing, just clung to him. They could hear his boy
telling the servant from the next house that there were two of
them and one dived like this and the other dived like that.

"I see dem well well," said the other with equal excitement.

"If no to say de ting de kill porson e for sweet for eye. To God."

"Imagine!" said Gladys, finding her voice at last. She had a way, he thought, of conveying with a few words or even a single word whole layers of meaning. Now it was at once her astonishment as well as reproof, tinged perhaps with grudging admiration for people who could be so light-hearted about these bringers of death.

"Don't be so scared," he said. She moved closer and he began to kiss her and squeeze her breasts. She yielded more and more and then fully. The bunker was dark and unswept and might harbour crawling things. He thought of bringing a mat from the main house but reluctantly decided against it. Another plane might pass and send a neighbour or simply a chance passer-by crashing into them. That would be only slightly better than a certain gentleman in another air-raid who was seen in broad daylight fleeing his bedroom for his bunker stark-naked pursued by a woman in a similar state!

Just as Gladys had feared, her friend was not in town. It would seem her powerful boyfriend had wangled for her a flight to Libreville to shop. So her neighbours thought anyway.

"Great!" said Nwankwo as they drove away. "She will come back on an arms plane loaded with shoes, wigs, pants, bras, cosmetics and what have you, which she will then sell and make thousands of pounds. You girls are really at war, aren't you?"

She said nothing and he thought he had got through at last to her. Then suddenly she said, "That is what you men want us to do."

"Well," he said, "here is one man who doesn't want you to do that. Do you remember that girl in khaki jeans who searched me without mercy at the check-point?"

She began to laugh.

"That is the girl I want you to become again. Do you remember her? No wig. I don't even think she had any earrings . . ."

"Ah, na lie-o. I had earrings."

"All right. But you know what I mean."

"That time done pass. Now everybody want survival. They call it number six. You put your number six; I put my number six. Everything all right."

The Lieutenant-Colonel's party turned into something quite unexpected. But before it did things had been going well enough. There was goat-meat, some chicken and rice and plenty of home-made spirits. There was one fiery brand nicknamed "tracer" which indeed sent a flame down your gullet. The funny thing was looking at it in the bottle it had the innocent appearance of an orange drink. But the thing that caused the greatest stir was the bread—one little roll for each person! It was the size of a golf-ball and about the same consistency too! But it was real bread. The band was good too and there were many girls. And to improve matters even further two white Red Cross people soon arrived with a bottle of Courvoisier and a bottle of Scotch! The party gave them a standing ovation and then scrambled to get a drop. It soon turned out from his general behaviour, however, that one of the white men had probably drunk too much already. And the reason it would seem was that a pilot he knew well had been killed in a crash at the airport last night, flying in relief in awful weather.

Few people at the party had heard of the crash by then. So there was an immediate damping of the air. Some dancing couples went back to their seats and the band stopped. Then for some strange reason the drunken Red Cross man just exploded.

"Why should a man, a decent man, throw away his life. For nothing! Charley didn't need to die. Not for this stinking place. Yes, everything stinks here. Even these girls who come here all dolled up and smiling, what are they worth? Don't I know? A head of stockfish, that's all, or one American dollar and they are ready to tumble into bed."

In the threatening silence following the explosion one of the young officers walked up to him and gave him three thundering slaps—right! left! right!—pulled him up from his seat and (there were things like tears in his eyes) shoved him outside. His friend, who had tried in vain to shut him up, followed him out and the silenced party heard them drive off. The officer who did the job returned dusting his palms.

"Fucking beast!" said he with an impressive coolness. And all the girls showed with their eyes that they rated him a man and a hero.

"Do you know him?" Gladys asked Nwankwo.

He didn't answer her. Instead he spoke generally to the party:

"The fellow was clearly drunk," he said.

"I don't care," said the officer. "It is when a man is drunk that he speaks what is on his mind."

"So you beat him for what was on his mind," said the host, "that is the spirit, Joe."

"Thank you, sir," said Joe, saluting.

"His name is Joe," Gladys and the girl on her left said in unison, turning to each other.

At the same time Nwankwo and a friend on the other side of him were saying quietly, very quietly, that although the man had been rude and offensive what he had said about the girls was unfortunately the bitter truth, only he was the wrong man to say it.

When the dancing resumed Captain Joe came to Gladys for a dance. She sprang to her feet even before the word was out of his mouth. Then she remembered immediately and turned round to take permission from Nwankwo. At the same time the Captain also turned to him and said, "Excuse me."

"Go ahead," said Nwankwo, looking somewhere between the two.

It was a long dance and he followed them with his eyes without appearing to do so. Occasionally a relief plane passed overhead and somebody immediately switched off the lights saying it might be the Intruder. But it was only an excuse to dance in the dark and make the girls giggle, for the sound of the Intruder was well known.

Gladys came back feeling very self-conscious and asked Nwankwo to dance with her. But he wouldn't. "Don't bother about me," he said, "I am enjoying myself perfectly sitting here and watching those of you who dance."

"Then let's go," she said, "if you won't dance."

"But I never dance, believe me. So please enjoy yourself."

She danced next with the Lieutenant-Colonel and again with Captain Joe, and then Nwankwo agreed to take her home.

"I am sorry I didn't dance," he said as they drove away. "But I swore never to dance as long as this war lasts."

She said nothing.

"When I think of somebody like that pilot who got killed last night. And he had no hand whatever in the quarrel. All his concern was to bring us food . . ."

"I hope that his friend is not like him," said Gladys.

"The man was just upset by his friend's death. But what I am saying is that with people like that getting killed and our own boys suffering and dying at the war fronts I don't see why we should sit around throwing parties and dancing."

"You took me there," said she in final revolt. "They are your friends. I don't know them before."

"Look, my dear, I am not blaming you. I am merely telling you why I personally refuse to dance. Anyway, let's change the subject . . . Do you still say you want to go back tomorrow? My driver can take you early enough on Monday morning for you to go to work. No? All right, just as you wish. You are the boss."

She gave him a shock by the readiness with which she followed him to bed and by her language.

"You want to shell?" she asked. And without waiting for an answer said, "Go ahead but don't pour in troops!"

He didn't want to pour in troops either and so it was all right. But she wanted visual assurance and so he showed her.

One of the ingenious economies taught by the war was that a rubber condom could be used over and over again. All you had to do was wash it out, dry it and shake a lot of talcum powder over it to prevent its sticking; and it was as good as new. It had to be the real British thing, though, not some of the cheap stuff they brought in from Lisbon which was about as strong as a dry cocoyam leaf in the harmattan.

He had his pleasure but wrote the girl off. He might just as well have slept with a prostitute, he thought. It was clear as daylight to him now that she was kept by some army officer. What a terrible transformation in the short period of less than two years! Wasn't it a miracle that she still had memories of the other life, that she even remembered her name? If the affair of the drunken Red Cross man should happen again now, he said to himself, he would stand up beside the fellow and tell the party that here was a man of truth. What a terrible fate to befall a whole generation! The mothers of tomorrow!

By morning he was feeling a little better and more generous in his judgements. Gladys, he thought, was just a mirror reflecting a society that had gone completely rotten and maggotty at the centre. The mirror itself was intact; a lot of smudge but no more. All that was needed was a clean duster. "I have a duty to her," he told himself, "the little girl that once revealed to me our situation. Now she is in danger, under some terrible influence."

He wanted to get to the bottom of this deadly influence. It was clearly not just her good-time girl friend, Augusta, or whatever her name was. There must be some man at the centre of it, perhaps one of these heartless attack-traders who traffic in foreign currencies and make their hundreds of thousands by sending young men to hazard their lives bartering looted goods for cigarettes behind enemy lines, or one of those contractors who receive piles of money daily for food they never deliver to the army. Or perhaps some vulgar and cowardly army officer full of filthy barrack talk and fictitious stories of heroism. He decided he had to find out. Last night he had thought of sending his driver alone to take her home. But no, he must go and see for himself where she lived. Something was bound to reveal itself there. Something on which he could anchor his saving operation. As he prepared for the trip his feeling towards her softened with every passing minute. He assembled for her half of the food he had received at the relief centre the day before. Difficult as things were, he thought, a girl who had something to eat would be spared, not all, but some of the temptation. He would arrange with his friend at the WCC to deliver something to her every fortnight.

Tears came to Gladys's eyes when she saw the gifts. Nwankwo didn't have too much cash on him but he got together twenty pounds and handed it over to her.

"I don't have foreign exchange, and I know this won't go far at all, but . . ."

She just came and threw herself at him, sobbing. He kissed her lips and eyes and mumbled something about victims of circumstance, which went over her head. In deference to him, he thought with exultation, she had put away her high-tinted wig in her bag.

"I want you to promise me something," he said.

"What?"

"Never use that expression about shelling again."

She smiled with tears in her eyes. "You don't like it? That's what all the girls call it."

"Well, you are different from all the girls. Will you promise?"

"O.K."

Naturally their departure had become a little delayed. And when they got into the car it refused to start. After poking around the engine the driver decided that the battery was flat. Nwankwo was aghast. He had that very week paid thirty-four pounds to change two of the cells and the mechanic who performed it had promised him six months' service. A new battery, which was then running at two hundred and fifty pounds was simply out of the question. The driver must have been careless with something, he thought.

"It must be because of last night," said the driver.

"What happened last night?" asked Nwankwo sharply, wondering what insolence was on the way. But none was intended.

"Because we use the head light."

"Am I supposed not to use my light then? Go and get some people and try pushing it." He got out again with Gladys and returned to the house while the driver went over to neighbouring houses to seek the help of other servants.

After at least half an hour of pushing it up and down the street, and a lot of noisy advice from the pushers, the car finally spluttered to life shooting out enormous clouds of black smoke from the exhaust.

It was eight-thirty by his watch when they set out. A few miles away a disabled soldier waved for a lift.

"Stop!" screamed Nwankwo. The driver jammed his foot

on the brakes and then turned his head towards his master in bewilderment.

"Don't you see the soldier waving? Reverse and pick him up!"

"Sorry, sir," said the driver. "I don't know Master wan to pick him."

"If you don't know you should ask. Reverse back."

The soldier, a mere boy, in filthy khaki drenched in sweat lacked his right leg from the knee down. He seemed not only grateful that a car should stop for him but greatly surprised. He first handed in his crude wooden crutches which the driver arranged between the two front seats, then painfully he levered himself in.

"Thank sir," he said turning his neck to look at the back and completely out of breath.

"I am very grateful. Madame, thank you."

"The pleasure is ours," said Nwankwo. "Where did you get your wound?"

"At Azumini, sir. On tenth of January."

"Never mind. Everything will be all right. We are proud of you boys and will make sure you receive your due reward when it is all over."

"I pray God, sir."

They drove on in silence for the next half-hour or so. Then as the car sped down a slope towards a bridge somebody screamed—perhaps the driver, perhaps the soldier—"They have come!" The screech of the brakes merged into the scream and the shattering of the sky overhead. The doors flew open even before the car had come to a stop and they were fleeing blindly to the bush. Gladys was a little ahead of Nwankwo when they heard through the drowning tumult the soldier's voice crying: "Please come and open for me!" Vaguely he saw Gladys stop; he pushed past her shouting to her at the same time to come on. Then a high whistle descended like a spear through the chaos and exploded in a vast noise and motion that smashed up everything. A tree he had embraced flung him away through the bush. Then another terrible whistle starting high up and ending again in a monumental crash of the world; and then another, and Nwankwo heard no more.

He woke up to human noises and weeping and the smell

and smoke of a charred world. He dragged himself up and staggered towards the source of the sounds.

From afar he saw his driver running towards him in tears and blood. He saw the remains of his car smoking and the entangled remains of the girl and the soldier. And he let out a piercing cry and fell down again.

GUSTAV HASFORD
Spirit of the Bayonet

*Gustav Hasford (1952-) served as com-
bat correspondent with the First Marine
Division in Vietnam. His best-selling novel
based on the conflict,* The Short-Timers
*(1979), was turned into the Hollywood
movie,* Full Metal Jacket, *directed by
Stanley Kubrick.*

The following excerpt from The Short-
Timers *takes place at Parris Island, the
basic training facility for the Marine Corps.
The new recruits of the novel, particularly
the hapless Leonard "Pyle" Pratt, are being
terrorised by the sadistic Sergeant Gerheim.
The character of Private "Joker" is based
on Hasford himself.*

DURING OUR SIXTH WEEK, Sergeant Gerheim orders us
to double-time around the squad bay with our penises in
our left hands and our weapons in our right hands, singing:
This is my rifle, this is my gun: one is for fighting and one is for fun.
And: *I don't want no teen-aged queen; all I want is my M-14.*

Sergeant Gerheim orders us to name our rifles. This is
the only pussy you people are going to get. Your days of
finger-banging ol' Mary Jane Rottencrotch through her pretty
pink panties are over. You're married to *this* piece, this weapon
of iron and wood, and you *will* be faithful.

We run. And we sing:

> Well, I don't know
> But I been told
> Eskimo pussy
> Is mighty cold . . .

Before chow, Sergeant Gerheim tells us that during World War I Blackjack Pershing said, "The deadliest weapon in the world is a Marine and his rifle." At Belleau Wood the Marines were so vicious that the German infantry called them *Teufel-Hunden*—"devil dogs."

Sergeant Gerheim explains that it is important for us to understand that it is our killer instinct which must be harnessed if we expect to survive in combat. Our rifle is only a tool; it is a hard heart that kills.

Our will to kill must be focused the way our rifle focuses a firing pressure of fifty thousand pounds per square inch to propel a piece of lead. If our rifles are not properly cleaned the explosion will be improperly focused and our rifles will shatter. If our killer instincts are not clean and strong, we will hesitate at the moment of truth. We will not kill. We will become dead Marines. And then we will be in a world of shit because Marines are not allowed to die without permission; we are government property.

The Confidence Course: We go hand over hand down a rope strung at a forty-five-degree angle across a pond—the slide-for-life. We hang upside down like monkeys and crawl headfirst down the rope.

Leonard falls off the slide-for-life eighteen times. He almost drowns. He cries. He climbs the tower. He tries again. He falls off again. This time he sinks.

Cowboy and I dive into the pond. We pull Leonard out of the muddy water. He's unconscious. When he comes to, he cries.

Back at the squad bay Sergeant Gerheim fits a Trojan rubber over the mouth of a canteen and throws the canteen at Leonard. The canteen hits Leonard on the side of the head. Sergeant Gerheim bellows, "Marines *do not cry!*"

Leonard is ordered to nurse on the canteen every day after chow.

During bayonet training Sergeant Gerheim dances an aggressive ballet. He knocks us down with a pugil stick, a five-foot pole with heavy padding on both ends. We play war with the pugil sticks. We beat each other without mercy. Then Sergeant Gerheim orders us to fix bayonets.

Sergeant Gerheim demonstrates effective attack techniques to a recruit named Barnard, a soft-spoken farm boy from Maine. The beefy drill instructor knocks out two of Private Barnard's teeth with a rifle butt.

The purpose of bayonet training, Sergeant Gerheim explains, is to awaken our killer instincts. The killer instinct will make us fearless and aggressive, like animals. If the meek ever inherit the earth the strong will take it away from them. The weak exist to be devoured by the strong. Every Marine must pack his own gear. Every Marine must be the instrument of his own salvation. It's hard, but there it is.

Private Barnard, his jaw bleeding, his mouth a bloody hole, demonstrates that he has been paying attention. Private Barnard grabs his rifle and, sitting up, bayonets Sergeant Gerheim through the right thigh.

Sergeant Gerheim grunts. Then he responds with a vertical butt stroke, but misses. So he backhands Private Barnard across the face with his fist.

Whipping off his web belt, Sergeant Gerheim ties a crude tourniquet around his bloody thigh. Then he makes the unconscious Private Barnard a squad leader. "Goddamn it, there's one little maggot who knows that the spirit of the bayonet is to *kill*! He'll make a damn fine field Marine. He ought to be a fucking general."

On the last day of our sixth week I wake up and find my rifle in my rack. My rifle is under my blanket, beside me. I don't know how it got there.

My mind isn't on my responsibilities and I forget to remind Leonard to shave.

Inspection. Junk on the bunk. Sergeant Gerheim points out that Private Pyle did not stand close enough to his razor.

Sergeant Gerheim orders Leonard and the recruit squad leaders into the head.

In the head, Sergeant Gerheim orders us to piss into a toilet bowl. "LOCK THEM HEELS! YOU ARE AT ATTENTION! READDDDDY . . . WHIZZZZ . . ."

We whiz.

Sergeant Gerheim grabs the back of Leonard's neck and forces Leonard to his knees, pushes his head down into the yellow pool. Leonard struggles. Bubbles. Panic gives Leonard strength; Sergeant Gerheim holds him down.

After we're sure that Leonard has drowned, Sergeant Gerheim flushes the toilet. When the water stops flowing, Sergeant Gerheim releases his hold on Leonard's neck.

Sergeant Gerheim's imagination is both cruel and comprehensive, but nothing works. Leonard continues to fuck up. Now, whenever Leonard makes a mistake, Sergeant Gerheim does not punish Leonard. He punishes the whole platoon. He excludes Leonard from the punishment. While Leonard rests, we do squat-thrusts and side-straddle hops, many, many of them.

Leonard touches my arm as we move through the chow line with our metal trays. "I just can't do nothing right. I need some help. I don't want you boys to be in trouble. I—"

I move away.

The first night of our seventh week of training the platoon gives Leonard a blanket party.

Midnight.

The fire watch stands by. Private Philips, the House Mouse, Sergeant Gerheim's "go-fer", pads barefoot down the squad bay to watch for Sergeant Gerheim.

In the dark, one hundred recruits walk to Leonard's rack.

Leonard is grinning even in his sleep.

The squad leaders hold towels and bars of soap.

Four recruits throw a blanket over Leonard. They grip the corners of the blanket so that Leonard can't sit up and so that his screams will be muffled.

I hear the hard breathing of a hundred sweating bodies and I hear the fump and thud as Cowboy and Private Barnard beat Leonard with bars of soap slung in towels.

Leonard's screams are like the braying of a sick mule, heard far away. He struggles.

The eyes of the platoon are on me. Eyes are aimed at me in the dark, eyes like rubies.

Leonard stops screaming.

I hesitate. The eyes are on me. I step back.

Cowboy punches me in the chest with his towel and a bar of soap.

I sling the towel, drop in the soap, and then I beat Leonard, who has stopped moving. He lies in silence, stunned, gagging for air. I beat him harder and harder and when I feel tears being flung from my eyes, I beat him harder for it.

The next day, on the parade deck, Leonard does not grin.

When Gunnery Sergeant Gerheim asks, "What do we do for a living, ladies?" and we reply, "KILL! KILL! KILL!," Leonard remains silent. When our junior drill instructors ask, "Do we love the Crotch, ladies? Do we love our beloved Corps?" and the platoon responds with one voice, "GUNG HO! GUNG HO! GUNG HO!," Leonard is silent.

On the third day of our seventh week we move to the rifle range and shoot holes in paper targets. Sergeant Gerheim brags about the marksmanship of ex-Marines Charles Whitman and Lee Harvey Oswald.

By the end of our seventh week Leonard has become a model recruit. We decide that Leonard's silence is a result of his new intense concentration. Day by day, Leonard is more motivated, more squared away. His manual of arms is flawless now, but his eyes are milk glass. Leonard cleans his weapon more than any recruit in the platoon. Every night after chow Leonard caresses the scarred oak stock with linseed oil the way hundreds of earlier recruits have caressed the same piece of wood. Leonard improves at everything, but remains silent. He does what he is told but he is no longer part of the platoon.

We can see that Sergeant Gerheim resents Leonard's attitude. He reminds Leonard that the motto of the Marine Corps is *Semper Fidelis*—"Always Faithful." Sergeant Gerheim reminds Leonard that "Gung ho" is Chinese for "working together."

It is a Marine Corps tradition, Sergeant Gerheim says, that Marines never abandon their dead or wounded. Sergeant Gerheim is careful not to come down too hard on Leonard as long as Leonard remains squared away. We have already lost seven recruits on Section Eight discharges. A Kentucky boy named Perkins stepped to the center of the squad bay and slashed his wrists with his bayonet. Sergeant Gerheim was not happy to see a recruit bleeding upon his nice clean squad bay. The recruit was ordered to police the area, mop up the blood, and replace the bayonet in its sheath. While Perkins mopped up the blood, Sergeant Gerheim called a school circle and poo-pooed the recruit's shallow slash across his wrists with a bayonet. The U.S.M.C.—approved method of recruit suicide is to get *alone* and take a razor blade and slash deep and vertical, from wrist to elbow, Sergeant Gerheim said. Then he allowed Perkins to double-time to sick bay.

Sergeant Gerheim leaves Leonard alone and concentrates on the rest of us.

Sunday.
Magic show. Religious services in the faith of your choice—and you *will* have a choice—because religious services are specified in the beautiful full-color brochures the Crotch distributes to Mom and Dad back in hometown America, even though Sergeant Gerheim assures us that the Marine Corps was here before God. "You can give your heart to Jesus but your ass belongs to the Corps."

After the "magic show" we eat chow. The squad leaders read grace from cards set in holders on the tables. Then: "SEATS!"

We spread butter on slices of bread and then sprinkle sugar on the butter. We smuggle the sandwiches out of the mess hall, risking a beating for the novelty of unscheduled chow. We don't give a shit; we're salty. Now, when Sergeant Gerheim and his junior drill instructors stomp us we tell them that we love it and to do it some more. When Sergeant Gerheim commands: "Okay, ladies, give me fifty squat-thrusts. And some side-straddle hops. Many, many of them," we laugh and then do them.

The drill instructors are proud to see that we are growing beyond their control. The Marine Corps does not want robots. The Marine Corps wants killers. The Marine Corps wants to build indestructible men, men without fear. Civilians may choose to submit or to fight back. The drill instructors leave recruits no choice. Marines fight back or they do not survive. There it is. No slack.

Graduation is only a few days away and the salty recruits of Platoon 30–92 are ready to eat their own guts and then ask for seconds. The moment the Commandant of the Marine Corps gives us the word, we will grab the Viet Cong guerrillas and the battle-hardened North Vietnamese regulars by their scrawny throats and we'll punch their fucking heads off.

Sunday afternoon in the sun. We scrub our little green garments on a long concrete table.

For the hundredth time, I tell Cowboy that I want to slip my tube steak into his sister so what will he take in trade?

For the hundredth time, Cowboy replies, "What do you have?"

Sergeant Gerheim struts around the table. He is trying not to limp. He criticizes our utilization of the Marine Corps scrub brush.

We don't care; we're too salty.

Sergeant Gerheim won the Navy Cross on Iwo Jima, he says. He got it for teaching young Marines how to bleed, he says. Marines are supposed to bleed in tidy little pools because Marines are disciplined. Civilians and members of the lesser services bleed all over the place like bed wetters.

We don't listen. We swap scuttlebutt. Laundry day is the only time we are allowed to talk to each other.

Philips—Sergeant Gerheim's black, silver-tongued House Mouse—is telling everybody about the one thousand cherries he has busted.

I say, "Leonard talks to his rifle."

A dozen recruits look up. They hesitate. Some look sick. Others look scared. And some look shocked and angry, as though I'd just slapped a cripple.

I force myself to speak: "Leonard talks to his rifle." Nobody moves. Nobody says anything. "I don't think Leonard can hack it anymore. I think Leonard is a Section Eight."

Now guys all along the table are listening. They look confused. Their eyes seem fixed on some distant object as though they are trying to remember a bad dream.

Private Barnard nods. "I've been having this nightmare.

My . . . rifle talks to me." He hesitates. "And I've been talking back to it . . ."

"There it is," says Philips. "Yeah. Its cold. Its a cold voice. I thought I was going plain fucking crazy. My rifle said—"

Sergeant Gerheim's big fist drives Philips's next word down his throat and out of his asshole. Philips is nailed to the deck. He's on his back. His lips are crushed. He groans.

The platoon freezes.

Sergeant Gerheim puts his fists on his hips. His eyes glare out from under the brim of his Smokey the Bear campaign cover like the barrels of a shotgun. "Private Pyle is a Section Eight. You hear me? If Private Pyle talks to his piece it is because he's plain fucking crazy. You maggots *will* belay all this scuttlebutt. Don't let Private Joker play with your imaginations. I don't want to hear another word. Do you hear me? Not one word."

Night at Parris Island. We stand by until Sergeant Gerheim snaps out his last order of the day: "Prepare to mount . . . Readddy . . . MOUNT!" Then we're lying on our backs in our skivvies, at attention, our weapons held at port arms.

We say our prayers:

I am a United States Marine Corps recruit. I serve in the forces which guard my country and my way of life. I am prepared to give my life in their defense, so help me God . . . GUNG HO! GUNG HO! GUNG HO!

Then the Rifleman's Creed, by Marine Corps Major General W. H. Rupertus:

This is my rifle. There are many like it but this one is mine. My rifle is my best friend. It is my life. I must master it as I master my life.

My rifle, without me, is useless. I must fire my rifle true. I must shoot straighter than my enemy who is trying to kill me. I must shoot him before he shoots me.

I will.

Leonard is speaking for the first time in weeks. His voice booms louder and louder. Heads turn. Bodies shift. The platoon voice fades. Leonard is about to explode. His words are being coughed up from some deep, ugly place.

Sergeant Gerheim has the night duty. He struts to Leonard's rack and stands by, fists on hips.

Leonard doesn't see Sergeant Gerheim. The veins in Leonard's neck are bulging as he bellows:

MY RIFLE IS HUMAN, EVEN AS I, BECAUSE IT IS MY LIFE. THUS I WILL LEARN IT AS A BROTHER. I WILL LEARN ITS ACCESSORIES, ITS SIGHTS, ITS BARREL.

I WILL KEEP MY RIFLE CLEAN AND READY, EVEN AS I AM CLEAN AND READY. WE WILL BECOME PART OF EACH OTHER.

WE WILL . . .

BEFORE GOD I SWEAR THIS CREED. MY RIFLE AND MYSELF ARE THE MASTER OF OUR ENEMY. WE ARE THE SAVIORS OF MY LIFE.

SO BE IT, UNTIL VICTORY IS AMERICA'S AND THERE IS NO ENEMY BUT PEACE!

AMEN.

Sergeant Gerheim kicks Leonard's rack. "Hey—*you*—Private Pyle . . ."

"What? Yes? YES, SIR!" Leonard snaps to attention in his rack. "AYE-AYE, SIR!"

"What's that weapon's name, maggot?

"SIR, THE PRIVATE'S WEAPON'S NAME IS CHARLENE, SIR!"

"At ease, maggot." Sergeant Gerheim grins. "You are becoming one sharp recruit, Private Pyle. Most motivated prive in my herd. Why, I may even allow you to serve as a rifleman in my beloved Corps. I had you figured for a shitbird, but you'll make a good grunt."

"AYE-AYE, SIR!"

I look at the rifle slung on my rack. It's a beautiful instrument, gracefully designed, solid and symmetrical. My rifle is clean, oiled, and works perfectly. It's a fine tool. I touch it.

Sergeant Gerheim marches down the length of the squad bay. "THE REST OF YOU ANIMALS COULD TAKE LESSONS FROM PRIVATE PYLE. He's squared away. You are all squared away. Tomorrow you will be Marines. READDDY . . . SLEEP!"

Graduation day. A thousand new Marines stand tall on the parade deck, lean and tan in immaculate khaki, their clean weapons held at port arms.

Leonard is selected as the outstanding recruit from Platoon 30–92. He is awarded a free set of dress blues and is allowed to wear the colorful uniform when the graduating platoons pass in review. The Commanding General of Parris Island shakes Leonard's hand and gives him a "Well done." Our series commander pins a RIFLE EXPERT badge on Leonard's chest and our company commander awards Leonard a citation for shooting the highest score in the training battalion.

Because of a special commendation submitted by Sergeant Gerheim, I'm promoted to Private First Class. After our series commander pins on my EXPERT's badge, Sergeant Gerheim presents me with two red and green chevrons and explains that they're his old PFC stripes.

When we pass in review I walk right guide, tall and proud.

Cowboy receives an EXPERT's badge and is selected to carry the platoon guidon.

The Commanding General of Parris Island speaks into a microphone: "Have you seen the light? The white light? The great light? The guiding light? Do you have the vision?"

And we cheer, happy beyond belief.

The Commanding General sings. We sing too:

> Hey, Marine, have you heard?
> Hey, Marine . . .
> L. B. J. has passed the word.
> Hey, Marine . . .

Say good-bye to Dad and Mom.
Hey, Marine . . .
You're gonna die in Viet Nam.
Hey, Marine, yeah!

After the graduation ceremony our orders are distributed. Cowboy, Leonard, Private Barnard, Philips, and most
of the other Marines in Platoon 30–92 are ordered to
ITR—the Infantry Training Regiment—to be trained as
grunts, infantrymen.

My orders instruct me to report to the Basic Military
Journalism School at Fort Benjamin Harrison, Indiana, after
I graduate from ITR. Sergeant Gerheim is disgusted by the
fact that I am to be a combat correspondent and not a grunt.
He calls me a poge, an office pinky. He says that shitbirds get
all the slack.

Standing at ease on the parade deck, beneath the monument
to the Iwo Jima flag raising, Sergeant Gerheim says, "The
smoking lamp is lit. You people are no longer maggots. Today
you are Marines. Once a Marine, always a Marine . . ."

Leonard laughs out loud.

Our last night on the island.

I draw fire watch.

I stand by in utility trousers, skivvy shirt, spitshined combat
boots, and a helmet liner which has been painted silver.

Sergeant Gerheim gives me his wristwatch and a flashlight.
"Good night, Marine."

I march up and down the squad bay between two perfectly
aligned rows of racks.

One hundred young Marines breathe peacefully as they
sleep—one hundred survivors from our original hundred and
twenty.

Tomorrow at dawn we'll all board cattle-car buses for the
ride to Camp Geiger in North Carolina. There, ITR—the
infantry training regiment. All Marines are grunts, even
though some of us will learn additional military skills. After
advanced infantry training we'll be allowed pogey bait at the
slop chute and we'll be given weekend liberty off the base and
then we'll receive assignments to our permanent duty stations.

The squad bay is as quiet as a funeral parlor at midnight. The silence is disturbed only by the soft *creak-creak* of bedsprings and an occasional cough.

It's almost time for me to wake my relief when I hear a voice. Some recruit is talking in his sleep.

I stop. I listen. A second voice. Two guys must be swapping scuttlebutt. If Sergeant Gerheim hears them it'll be my ass. I hurry toward the sound.

It's Leonard. Leonard is talking to his rifle. But there is also another voice A whisper. A cold, seductive moan. It's the voice of a woman.

Leonard's rifle is not slung on his rack. He's holding his rifle, hugging it. "Okay, okay. I *love* you!" Very softly: "I've given you the best months of my life. And now you—" I snap on my flashlight. Leonard ignores me. "I LOVE YOU! DON'T YOU UNDERSTAND? I CAN DO IT. I'LL DO ANYTHING!"

Leonards words reverberate down the squad bay. Racks squeak. Someone rolls over. One recruit sits up, rubs his eyes.

I watch the far end of the squad bay. I wait for the light to go on inside Sergeant Gerheim's palace.

I touch Leonard's shoulder. "Hey, shut your mouth, Leonard. Sergeant Gerheim will break my back."

Leonard sits up. He looks at me. He strips off his skivvy shirt and ties it around his face to blindfold himself. He begins to field-strip his weapon. "This is the first time I've ever seen her naked." He pulls off the blindfold. His fingers continue to break down the rifle into components. Then, gently, he fondles each piece. "Just look at that pretty trigger guard. Have you ever seen a more beautiful piece of metal?" He starts snapping the steel components back together. "Her connector assembly is so beautiful . . ."

Leonard continues to babble as his trained fingers reassemble the black metal hardware.

I think about Vanessa, my girl back home. We're on a river bank, wrapped in an old sleeping bag, and I'm fucking her eyes out. But my favorite fantasy has gone stale. Thinking about Vanessa's thighs, her dark nipples, her full lips doesn't give me a hard-on anymore. I guess it must be the saltpeter in our food, like they say.

Leonard reaches under his pillow and comes out with a loaded magazine. Gently, he inserts the metal magazine into his weapon, into Charlene.

"Leonard . . . where did you get those live rounds?"

Now a lot of guys are sitting up, whispering, "What's happening?" to each other.

Sergeant Gerheim's light floods the far end of the squad bay.

"OKAY, LEONARD, LET'S GO." I'm determined to save my own ass if I can, certain that Leonard's is forfeit in any case. The last time Sergeant Gerheim caught a recruit with a live round—just one round—he ordered the recruit to dig a grave ten feet long and ten feet deep. The whole platoon had to fall out for the "funeral." I say, "You're in a world of shit now, Leonard."

The overhead lights explode. The squad bay is washed with light. "WHAT'S THIS MICKEY MOUSE SHIT? JUST WHAT IN THE NAME OF JESUS H. CHRIST ARE YOU ANIMALS DOING IN MY SQUAD BAY?"

Sergeant Gerheim comes at me like a mad dog. His voice cuts the squad bay in half: "MY BEAUTY SLEEP HAS BEEN INTERRUPTED, LADIES. YOU *KNOW* WHAT THAT MEANS. YOU HEAR ME, HERD? IT MEANS THAT ONE RECRUIT HAS VOLUNTEERED HIS YOUNG HEART FOR A GODDAMN HUMAN SACRIFICE!"

Leonard pounces from his rack, confronts Sergeant Gerheim.

Now the whole platoon is awake. We all wait to see what Sergeant Gerheim will do, confident that it will be worth watching.

"Private Joker. You shitbird. Front and center."

I move my ass. "AYE-AYE, SIR!"

"Okay, you little maggot, *speak*. Why is Private Pyle out of his rack after lights out? Why is Private Pyle holding that weapon? Why ain't you stomping Private Pyle's guts out?"

"SIR, it is the private's duty to report to the drill instructor that Private . . . Pyle . . . has a full magazine and has locked and loaded, SIR."

Sergeant Gerheim looks at Leonard and nods. He sighs.

Gunnery Sergeant Gerheim looks more than a little ridiculous in his pure white skivvies and red rubber flip-flop shower shoes and hairy legs and tattooed forearms and a beer gut and a face the color of raw beef, and, on his bald head, the green and brown Smokey the Bear campaign cover.

Our senior drill instructor focuses all of his considerable powers of intimidation into his best John-Wayne-on-Suribachi voice: "Listen to me, Private Pyle, You *will* place your weapon on your rack and—"

"NO! YOU CAN'T HAVE HER! SHE'S MINE! YOU HEAR ME? SHE'S MINE! I LOVE HER!"

Gunnery Sergeant Gerheim can't control himself any longer. "NOW YOU LISTEN TO ME, YOU FUCKING WORTHLESS LITTLE PIECE OF SHIT. YOU *WILL* GIVE ME THAT WEAPON OR I'M GOING TO TEAR YOUR BALLS OFF AND STUFF THEM DOWN YOUR SCRAWNY LITTLE THROAT! YOU HEAR ME, MARINE? I'M GOING TO PUNCH YOUR FUCKING HEART OUT!"

Leonard aims the weapon at Sergeant Gerheim's heart, caresses the trigger guard, then caresses the trigger . . .

Sergeant Gerheim is suddenly calm. His eyes, his manner are those of a wanderer who has found his home. He is a man in complete control of himself and of the world he lives in. His face is cold and beautiful as the dark side surfaces. He smiles. It is not a friendly smile, but an evil smile, as though Sergeant Gerheim were a werewolf baring its fangs. "Private Pyle, I'm proud—"

Bang.

The steel buttplate slams into Leonard's shoulder.

One 7.62-millimeter high-velocity copper-jacketed bullet punches Gunnery Sergeant Gerheim back.

He falls.

We all stare at Sergeant Gerheim. Nobody moves.

Sergeant Gerheim sits up as though nothing has happened. For one second, we relax. Leonard has missed. Then dark blood squirts from a little hole in Sergeant Gerheim's chest. The red blood blossoms into his white skivvy shirt like a beautiful flower. Sergeant Gerheim's bug eyes are focused upon the blood rose on his chest, fascinated. He looks up at

Leonard. He squints. Then he relaxes. The werewolf smile is frozen on his lips.

My menial position of authority as the fire watch on duty forces me to act. "Now, uh, Leonard, we're all your bros, man, your brothers. I'm your bunkmate, right? I—"

"Sure," says Cowboy. "Go easy, Leonard. We don't want to hurt you."

"Affirmative," says Private Barnard.

Leonard doesn't hear. "Did you see the way he looked at her? Did you? I knew what he was thinking. I knew. That fat pig and his dirty—"

"Leonard . . ."

"We can kill you. You know that." Leonard caresses his rifle. "Don't you know that Charlene and I can kill you all?"

Leonard aims his rifle at my face.

I don't look at the rifle. I look into Leonard's eyes. I know that Leonard is too weak to control his instrument of death. It is a hard heart that kills, not the weapon. Leonard is a defective instrument for the power that is following through him. Sergeant Gerheim's mistake was in not seeing that Leonard was like a glass rifle which would shatter when fired. Leonard is not hard enough to harness the power of an interior explosion to propel the cold black bullet of his will.

Leonard is grinning at us, the final grin that is on the face of death, the terrible grin of the skull.

The grin changes to a look of surprise and then to confusion and then to terror as Leonard's weapon moves up and back and then Leonard takes the black metal barrel into his mouth. "NO! Not—"

Bang.

Leonard is dead on the deck. His head is now an awful lump of blood and facial bones and sinus fluids and uprooted teeth and jagged, torn flesh. The skin looks plastic and unreal.

The civilians will demand yet another investigation, of course. But during the investigation the recruits of Platoon 30–92 will testify that Private Pratt, while highly motivated, was a ten percenter who did not pack the gear to be a Marine in our beloved Corps.

Sergeant Gerheim is still smiling. He was a fine drill instructor. Dying, that's what we're here for, he would have said—blood makes the grass grow. If he could speak, Gunnery Sergeant Gerheim would explain to Leonard why the guns that we love don't love back. And he would say, "Well done."

I turn off the overhead lights.

JAMES CRUMLEY
One to Count Cadence

*James Crumley (1939–) was born in Texas
and served for three years in the US army
as an enlisted man. His subsequent novel,*
One to Count Cadence *(1969), is one
of the first and finest books of the Vietnam
War. Crumley is also the author of several
volumes of acclaimed private eye fiction,*
The Wrong Case, The Last Good
Kiss *and* Dancing Bear.

The extract below is from One to
Count Cadence, *and is set at the Clark
Air Force Base in the Philippines in 1962,
where the 721st Communication Security
Detachment is being trained preparatory
to Vietnam. The Detachment is led by
Sergeant Jake "Slag" Krummel, the nov-
el's hero and friend of the rebellious Joe
Morning.*

T ETRICK'S ADMONITION TO STEP EASILY with Lt. Dottlinger commanding the Company proved all too correct.
During the set of days after my lengthy initiation into the
seminal rites of Town, a small incident, the breaking of four
cases of bottles, touched off the events known as The Great
Coke Bottle Mystery, or Slag Krummel Rides, Howsoever
Badly, Again.

It was a Wednesday or Thursday morning—without the
limits of an established weekend period of rest, we seldom knew
the day of the week. Lt. Dottlinger always checked the Day
Room first thing each morning. He counted the pool cues and
balls, and the shuffleboard pucks, examined the felt of the pool

tables for new nicks or tears, and made sure the Coke machine
was full. These things were nominally his responsibility since
the equipment had been purchased from the Company Fund
and the Coke machine was a concession of the Fund. All
seemed well until he felt a bit of glass crunch under his
spit-shined shoe. He picked it up, and found it to be the lip
ring off the rim of a bottle. He knew the trick: two rims hooked
together, then jerk, and a neat little ring of glass pops off one or
both. He didn't see any others at first, but when he examined
the trash in the houseboy's dust bucket, he found dozens of
rings. Also, he noted, there were hundreds of cigarette butts,
in spite of his standing orders against extinguishing them on
the Day Room floor. He checked the four cases of empties.
All except for one had been broken. Dottlinger took the
dust bucket and dumped its contents in a neat pile in front
of the innocently humming Coke machine. He shooed the
houseboy out, closed and locked the double doors opening to
the outside passageway, unplugged the Coke machine, which
burped twice like a drunken private in ranks, rolled shut the
louvers on both walls, turned off the lights, then locked the
entrance from the Orderly Room.

He took the pass box from the 1st Sgt's desk and placed it
in his desk which he always kept locked. Then he called the
Criminal Investigation Division.

The CID officer who came was a heavy Negro captain
in a baggy suit and 1930s snap-brim hat which shouted
"Copper!" He nodded his head when Lt. Dottlinger explained
the situation and showed him the evidence, but said nothing.
The CID man dusted part of one case of bottles at Lt.
Dottlinger's insistence. There were over two hundred partial,
smudged and clear prints on them. When Lt. Dottlinger
demanded that he run a check on the prints, the CID
officer shook his head and said, "Lieutenant, they are Coke
bottles. For treason, perhaps even for a murder, I might be
able to run the ten thousand or so prints on those bottles,
but for Coke bottles . . . sorry about that." He shrugged
and left. Tetrick heard Lt. Dottlinger mumble, "Damned
nigger cops. Can't expect them to understand the value of
property."

Shortly before noon a notice was posted on the bulletin

board. There would be no passes pending confession of the bottle-breaker.

In theory mass punishment is against the Uniform Code of Military Justice but since a pass is a privilege rather than a right, it can be denied at any time for no reason.

Most of the men were extremely annoyed at first, but they quickly settled down, thinking, as did Lt. Dottlinger, that the guilty party would confess. During those first few days they found it almost refreshing not to be able to go to Town. They had the Airman's Club and the Silver Wing Service Club to pass the nights, or they could bowl or go to the gym or the library. A new, exciting kind of party evolved in the large storm ditches on the edge of the Company Area, called Champagne Ditch Parties. Mumm's was cheap at the Club and did not count on the liquor ration. The ditches were concrete lined, about five feet deep and shaped like an inverted trapezoid. A man could sit in the bottom, lean back and drink Mumm's from a crystal glass, and hope it didn't rain if he passed out. A kid from Trick One broke both arms trying to broad jump a ditch one night, but took little of the fun out of the parties.

So they did these things for one, two, then three weeks, but no one ever came forward. I noticed that Morning who had been the loudest and longest griper at first seemed to be resigned to the lack of Town. By the end of the fourth week the only hope was the return of Capt. Saunders. Tetrick had given up trying to persuade Lt. Dottlinger, and had taken to playing golf three afternoons a week, drunk before the tenth tee. The men were quiet, but uneasily so. They, like Morning, had stopped talking about it. They gathered shamelessly around the older dependent girls at the pool; they who had vowed to a man at one drunken time or another never to sully their hands on a leech. Even Novotny shouted from the high diving board, strutted his brown body before them and let them pity his scarred leg. He had taken an eighteen-year-old one to the movie one night, but Trick Two was waiting in ambush and hooted him out of the theater. "There are some things a man just doesn't do," Cagle snorted when Novotny complained to him.

Every room had its personal copies of *Playboy*, and they were closely guarded. Closed doors were respected with a warning knock, and men took alternate cubicles in the latrine out of deference to the *Playboy* readers. All the seed which heretofore had been cast into the bellies of whores, now flushed down larger, wetter holes, until it was a wonder that the sewage system didn't clog or give birth.

I kept busy during this time, helping the sergeant from the Agency outfit who was going to coach the football team draw up plays and practice routines. He had asked me to coach the line as well as play. Tetrick and I had tried to go to Town twice. Both times we ended up at old movies and felt guilty for two days afterward. Oddly enough I had the best run of luck I had ever seen during this month. I won over seven hundred fifty dollars in four nights at the NCO Club playing poker, then went to Manila with Tetrick and took out three thousand pesos shooting craps at the Key Club while a quiet, fat Filipino dropped ten thousand on the back line against my string of thirteen straight passes. He looked as if he wanted to kill me when I quit after thirteen. But still I didn't have enough money to get passes for the men.

Then word came that Capt. Saunders was going to take a month's leave after the school. That meant another six weeks without Town, and that was unbearable for the men. It is one thing to be a soldier, to live in a world of close order drill, of Physical Training each morning, equipment maintenance, maneuvers, training lectures, and another thing to be a clerk, a changer of typewriter ribbons, a cleaner of keys. Being a soldier gives you the feeling of accomplishment no matter how stupid you think the whole idea is: you survive in spite of everything they can do to you. Being a clerk has all the stupidities, all the same injustices as being a soldier, but none of the pride: anyone can survive being a clerk. It is the same problem which attacks men on assembly lines and in paper-shuffling office jobs when they discover that their life is as senseless as their work. They take to the bottle, join lodges, coach little league teams, have an affair—anything to forget what they are. The men in the 721st had Town to cover all these areas of memory-killing. Oh, sure, some of them made their tours in the Philippines on library books, camera trips and butterfly collections, but most needed Town. That is why it was there. And Lt. Dottlinger had taken it away. So what happened had to happen. (Or at least I like to tell myself that it did.)

If Morning had come to me with his idea in the beginning, I would have, as he so aptly noted, stopped him, but he came near the end, when it was ready for enactment, and it was too late to stop him.

He came in my room the night before the mass confession, grinning and excited, popping his fingers and pushing his glasses back up on his nose. "We got him," he said, opening my door without knocking.

"Who?"

"Slutfuckingfinger, man. Lt. Big Butt Dottlinger. Pinned to the wall by his mangy cock. Betrayed by his own words."

"What? Who? . . ."

"I got every one of them, man, every last swinging dick." He danced around my room as if he needed to pee.

"Wait a minute. Slow down. Sit down and let me know who has got whom where."

He swung a chair in front of the bunk, straddled it, and said, "The man said, 'No passes until the guilty one confesses.' Right? Right! Tomorrow he is going to confess."

"You know who it is?"

"No, but it doesn't make any difference."

"You elected a savior to sacrifice?" I laughed. I wondered who.

"No." He smiled and rubbed his thighs as if he had a magnificent secret. "Tomorrow morning at 0700, beginning with the day-trick before it goes to work and ending with the mid-trick, every enlisted man in the Operations section will go see the commanding officer and confess . . ."

"Don't tell me. Not another word."

"What do you mean? We got that son of a motherfucker dead. Dropped him down, man."

"Don't tell me. Jesus, Morning," I said, getting off the bunk. "This kind of crap is . . . damnit, it's mutiny or inciting to mutiny or conspiring to mutiny or something. I don't know the name, but I do know it is Leavenworth talk. Don't you know that? Goddamn don't tell me. I don't want to know. I can't know. Get the hell out of here. Now!"

"What's with you? He can't touch a hair on our heads. He

hasn't got the guts to court martial the whole outfit, and he can't get me unless somebody breaks."

"Morning, don't you understand, somebody will shit out. Somebody will! Somebody always does. Even a single trick couldn't pull this off, much less forty men. They're going to send you to jail, babe, forever."

"Somebody shits, they get busted!" He popped his fingers loudly, and I knew it would happen. There was no doubt in his voice. "Besides, it will never get that far. Dottlinger will blow his stack, hit an enlisted man or have a heart attack or something. I go in first, and you know how he hates me, and he hasn't got the brains to think that I've got the guts to organize this and still go in first. He thinks I'm crazy."

"What if he takes just you."

"So fucking what? I only have one stripe to lose for my country."

"But what about . . ." I moaned, waving my arm in the general direction of heaven and hell. "Do any of the other trick chiefs know?"

"You're not even supposed to know. But I thought you'd want to."

"How sweet. I don't know! I don't know you! Get your ass out of here!" I took the cigarette he offered. "At Leavenworth, kid, they got even a literary magazine, but no women, no beer, but lots of walls. You won't like it there."

"It'll work. What are you afraid of? It will work."

"Don't tell me. I don't want it to work. I hope you guys never get your passes back. Never. You're all crazy. I hope they lock you up forever. Jesus, what a mess. Don't do it. Don't do it."

"What!" he shouted. "And let that half-assed Arkansas farmer do this to us. Man, we have to fight back, and now! What kind of men are we if we let him do this to us and we don't fight back."

"Write your congressman. Consult the chaplain. Shit in the air. But don't try to fight the Army. Don't." . . .

. . . Only Joe Morning had the personality, the voice and the gall to convince so many men to even agree to such madness, much less carry it out. But he did it. He talked in private to every enlisted man in the Operations section, and then hit them again with a band of converts. I learned from Novotny that Morning had first mentioned the idea during the wee hours of a ditch party, but only mentioned it. Then the next day, when everyone had forgotten, he spoke about it again in the back of the three-quarter going to work, and then again coming back. He convinced Novotny in a long talk that night. Quinn and Franklin wondered why they hadn't thought of such a great idea. Cagle was ready for anything. The rest of the Trick was easy to convince. Once he had the Trick, he had their close friends on the other tricks, then their buddies, then the whole damned Company. That they only had to use physical persuasion on two men is an indication of the mood of the Company. And keeping it quiet was even easier, since the men were already security conscious because of the work.

It was beautiful and funny and I loved and feared the whole idea, but stayed in my room, sleeping with the door locked, while it took place.

I was blasted out about midmorning by Lt. Dottlinger on the handle of a bull horn. It was so loud I didn't understand what had been screamed, and I charged out in my shorts, thinking partly of Pearl Harbor and partly of a public execution. Lt. Dottlinger stood at my end of the hall calmly announcing, "Company formation in fifteen minutes!" He had known what was up when he opened the door to Morning and saw the line, but he didn't say anything. He had already given a blanket permission for anyone knowing anything about the broken bottles to see him without going through the 1st Sgt. He let them all in, asked questions about the bottles, made notes, and took names. Outside Tetrick was racing up and down the line, bald, sweat-shining head in hands, pleading with them to break it up and go away before they were all killed. He remembered a pile of heads he had seen in Burma left by the Japanese. But Lt. Dottlinger was calm and controlled through it all, though his control must have been the absolute hold which marks the final stage of hysteria. He quietly ordered each man back to his quarters after the interview. The men in the back of the line were frightened, as well they might have been, by this quiet approach of the lieutenant's. Many might have broken line, but Morning, intrepid, wily Joe Morning, had placed men he could trust on either side of those he couldn't; and he knew just exactly which were which. But he hadn't counted on Lt. Dottlinger's anger taking this form. More than men have hung on the nature of another man's mood in the morning. When I saw Lt. Dottlinger in the hall, speaking pleasantly into the electric megaphone like a daytime television game-show announcer, I knew Morning's plans had failed. I wondered what was going to happen, as I got into uniform; I should have wondered who was going to pay. When Lt. Dottlinger had first seen me in the hall, he had smiled, nodded, and said, "Good morning, Sgt. Krummel." How little he knew.

The Company had been assembled on the volleyball court between the barracks and the drainage ditches for nearly an hour before Lt. Dottlinger came out. He was walking from the waist down, a smug, arrogant strut like Brando in *The Wild One*. Ah, he was loose. I thought for a moment he might mumble too, but he had added an English undertone to his Southern accent to strut a bit more. He accepted Tetrick's "Hall pre'nt an' 'counted for, sir," with a salute of languid grace. I wanted to laugh. But it would have been a nervous giggle. I, the whole Company too, was caught by that creepy version of fear which only comes when you're faced with someone who is crazy. It isn't so much that you're frightened that you might come to physical harm, but that you're faced with something not human anymore. You don't know what it is, and you don't care because you realize what it isn't, and you can only run and run until you wipe the face of insanity from the deepest regions of your memory; but as you run, you understand that some unsuspecting night you will dream that tormented, twisted face, and wake, oh my God, scream for the savior you had forgotten, and scream again, for the face is yours. Dottlinger scared us like that. If he had taken a rifle and shot the first rank of men or snatched a rose from his shirt and sniffed, none of us would have blinked.

"Well," he began, striding along the Company front, his hands clasped casually behind him. For once he didn't have his ball-point swagger stick. "It seems we have a small mutiny on our hands, troopers. Or at least a conspiracy to mutiny, troopers, which carries an equally harsh penalty. I would only guess, but I could probably put each and every one of you behind bars for the rest of your natural lives." He pivoted, paused and reflected. It wasn't a particularly hot day, but two large sweat stains were slowly creeping from under Lt. Dottlinger's arms like cancerous stigmata. He wasn't quite so frightening now. He was beginning to lose his edge, and was forced to begin to play himself. It had taken too long to write his speech. "But I'm not going to do that," he continued. "At least not right this minute. I'm sure most of you men didn't mean to cause this much trouble, or face such a stiff charge. Certainly your leaders lied to you about this—you're surprised I know there were leaders. Don't be, don't be. It was obvious. Yes, I'm sure there were leaders, perhaps even a single organizer." He paused, "And I would like to put him behind bars. I really want that. I want him!" He could barely control himself now.

"But I'll let that go. Let it go," he said, smiling suddenly, a forced, theatrical smile. "Yes, even that. Just to let you know I'm a fair and understanding officer. Yes, I'll forget this whole little affair ever took place, and I'll even lose the names of the men. Yes.

"But I want, I still want, and I will have the man whobrokethe . . . bottles." He took a deep breath before continuing. "I have an idea, mind you, just a hint of an idea, that he will be the same man who organized this childish little demonstration." Morning grunted with anger behind me. "This same whining disrespect for authority applies to property too and comes out of the same Godless overeducated under-spanked children.

"Until such time as the man who broke the four cases of Coke bottles, the ninety-six bottles, confesses, you are restricted to the Company and Operations Area, and to your quarters when not working, eating, or relieving yourself," he said, very businesslike now. A communal moan drifted up from the men. Morning grunted again, this time like a frustrated wart hog preparing to charge.

"At ease!" Tetrick growled.

"The day-trick will relieve the mid-trick after noon chow,

and then make up the lost time by going to work at 0400 tomorrow morning." Nice move. The day-trick was going on Break, and my Trick would have to make up the time.

It wasn't good, but it wasn't disaster either. Then I heard another grunt from Morning, a furious exhalation, and he started to say, "Request permission . . ." But I overruled him.

"Request permission to speak to the Company Commander, sir," I sang out. Dottlinger wouldn't hold to his word about forgetting about the mutiny charges if he got hold of Morning. Why he hadn't figured it out by this time was a wonder to me.

"Certainly, Sgt. Krummel."

I said dreadful things to myself as I walked toward him, but I wasn't afraid of him anymore. I just didn't know what I was going to say.

"Could I speak to you in private, sir?" I asked after saluting. The sweat blackened areas of his shirt had grown, and his face was pale, but his eyes still glittered with fire enough for one more encounter. He told Tetrick to have the men stand easy. I followed him a few steps toward the barracks.

"Yes, Sgt. Krummel?"

"Sir. Sir, I know I'm off base, but the events of this morning seem to call for unusual actions."

"They are unusual events."

"Yes, sir."

"Well, sergeant, what did you want?" he inquired when I hadn't spoken for several seconds.

"Well, sir, it's about the restriction to the Company Area."

"What about it?"

"Well, sir, ah, I'm worried about the quality of the work at Operations. It is already low due to the tension, and this harsher restriction, sir, will probably lower it even further. The Filipino liaison officer has already threatened to go to the major if the work doesn't pick up." One lie. "And the men are terribly on edge, sir, already. Might even say they're horny as hell, sir." I giggled like a high school virgin. I was willing to be anything.

"I think the men can curb their physical appetites, sergeant. There's too much of that sort of thing happening in this

Company anyway. And as for the quality of the work—send them to me if it doesn't pick up. This outfit is getting soft. It needs a little iron, and I intend to see that they get it."

"Yes, sir, I agree." Two lies. "But the men feel that if the man who broke the bottles . . ." (God, I thought, is this really about some broken bottles.) ". . . is in the Company, sir, then he has confessed and, sir, no matter how silly this logic sounds, or how much a play on words it is, that's the way the men feel, sir, and . . ."

"Well, if they think I'm going to be threatened . . ."

"Excuse me, sir, but they don't mean that, I'm sure." Three lies. "They're just desperate, sir, and I'm afraid, sir, that we might have a real mutiny on our hands. I saw one in Korea, sir, and it was bad." Four lies. "Everyone's record took a permanent blemish, sir."

He nodded. He knew who was threatening whom, and he didn't like it. He thought for a bit, then smiled slowly as if he knew something. "You're perfectly correct, sergeant, a real mutiny would be quite disastrous. But I don't see how I can go back on my word, do you?"

"Sir?"

"Well, everyone hasn't confessed."

"Sir?"

"You haven't confessed, Sgt. Krummel. You might have done it, for all I know." He smiled again, a smile which said, "I've got you Mr Master's Degree."

"Sir, I'd like to make a statement. I'm the one, sir, who broke your Coke bottles in the Day Room." Five lies. "I'll make restitution to the Company Fund, sir, and plead guilty to any charges you would like to make in connection with the actual destruction of the bottles, sir."

"Were you drunk, sergeant?" Oh, he was loving this.

"No, sir."

"Then why did you do it?" His best fatherly tone.

"Momentary loss of perspective, sir. The machine took my coin and refused me a Coke, and since the machine was unbreakable, I avenged myself on the innocent bottles, sir."

"Sounds as if you might be mentally unbalanced, sergeant." How he would like me to plead that.

"No, not at all, sir. Like all good soldiers, sir, I have a

quick temper and a strong sense of right which, under the direction of competent officers, can be a formidable weapon in combat, sir."

For a second he had forgotten whom he was playing with. "Well . . . Well, this isn't combat. Return to your Trick, and report to me after this formation."

"Right, sir." I saluted sharply, whirled and marched back.

Lt. Dottlinger turned to Tetrick, told him to dismiss the Company after informing the men that all prior restrictions were lifted and the pass box would be open immediately. The Day Room would be reopened after proper cleaning. The men had already heard the lieutenant's words, and they cheered when Tetrick dismissed them. Most ran for the barracks to change for Town, but a few paused to ask unanswered questions of me.

I told Tetrick what I had done before I went in to see Dottlinger. He assured me that Dottlinger would not dare any more than an Article 15, Company Punishment. Tetrick seemed resigned that someone would be slaughtered for the greatest good, and seemed not to mind particularly that that someone was me. His attitude seemed to say, "It's for the best."

"To hell with it," I said. "Maybe I'll kiss the bastard and let him queer me out, or maybe bust his pussylick face for him and let him hang my stripes for teeth he ain't going to have."

"If you do, holler, so I can be a witness that he hit you first," Tetrick laughed.

But I had already thought of the worst thing he could do: ignore my confession, let me go, and then single out any enlisted man and bust him with evidence he would say I'd given; and if I didn't agree to this, then the Company would be back on restriction again. I was surprised how much I hated Dottlinger at that moment, but even more surprised to discover that I wasn't worried about my stripes and that I cared about the respect of my men. I had said, when I reenlisted back in Seattle, that God couldn't involve me with anything or anybody again; I wanted to be a happy, stupid, payday drunk. But what God couldn't do, Joe Morning managed.

Dottlinger did, as Tetrick had predicted, give me Company

Punishment: two hours extra duty for fifteen days. One hour policing the Day Room and one hour marching in front of the barracks as an example with full field pack and blanket roll. "To begin immediately," he had said. He unlocked the Day Room, had me open the louvers, and gloated while I swept the floor with a short broom.

So for fifteen days no one spoke to me for fear I'd take their heads off. The whole thing was so public, marching in daylight, squatting in the Day Room like a recruit. Once at a particularly bleak moment Tetrick had said, "Tell him to fuck himself. He hasn't got a leg to stand on. He can't touch you within the regs."

"For a man with no legs, he's stepping on my toes pretty heavily," I answered—but thought about his suggestion more than I care to admit.

I had nearly decided that what I had done wasn't worth it when the only good thing of the time happened. This kid from Trick One came out of the barracks one day when the sun was pouring into my fatigues like lava, and at that dark, sunblinded moment, had said, "Look at the little tin soldier. It walks, it talks, it's almost human." I don't suppose he intended that I hear him, but I had. Someone else had too. From the second floor above the door an invisible voice roared like the wrath of Jehovah. "Shut your wise mouth, fuckhead!" The kid jumped, looked around, then dashed back in the barracks, perhaps wondering if God hadn't spoken to him.

I glowed. I sparkled. I felt heroic for a change, instead of dumb. (I'm not ashamed: pride has turned better heads than mine.) Someone understood.

"Ah 'tis a kind voice I hear above me," I said, but only a deep laugh answered me.

But by the time my hour was over I had lost that quick lift under the sun. The sun wasn't merely in the sky, it was the sky. From horizon to zenith the heavens burned in my honor, and in my chest and back and head. And in the shattering light all clear things lost themselves. Colors faded into pale imitations of themselves and became dust.

I had come back to be alone, to find simplicity, and had found trouble, and in this trouble found I must fall back on that which I was, that which I would be, that which I had always tried not to be.

I am the eldest son of generations of eldest sons, the final moment of a proud descent of professional killers, warriors, men of strength whose only concern with virtue lay in personal honor. But I still misunderstood a bit that day, I still confused being a soldier with being a warrior. That small, mean part of me which had wanted to care about rank and security and privilege was dying, and with the death of order began the birth of something in me monstrous, ah, but so beautiful. My heritage called, and though it would be many long moons before I answered, the song had burst my cold, ordered heart and I hated in the ringing sweep of the sun, and I lived.

DONALD BODEY
This is War, Man

Donald Bodey (1946–) served in the infan-
try in Vietnam before becoming a writer.
In this excerpt from his Vietnam novel
F.N.G (1979), Gabriel "Chieu Hoi"
Sauers's squad has just ambushed a Viet
Cong patrol. F.N.G is Vietnam slang for
"Fucking New Guy".

BLOOD.
      Like cottage-red paint shot from a fire hydrant, blood
everywhere: sprayed all over the leaves and rocks and running
in the rainwater that trickles off the rocks. *Jesus-fuckinchrist.*
      "Oh, muthafucker, they're dead."
      "We musta got 'em all."
      "Let's go. We're lucky this didn't draw a tiger last night."
      As we came up, some rodents scampered away and as we
are standing there I look away and meet two little eyes looking
at us from under a rock. I feel like I hate the goddamn rodent.
I hate everything. There are four dinks. Two of them were cut
in half by our claymores. *How goddamn much blood is there in a*
person? I might faint. It seems like everything should be still
but there are flies by the hundreds and the birds in the canopy
are squawking. There must be an animal in the matted grass
behind the bodies because there is noise there too. At first I
can't identify the other sound I hear; then I realize it is the
static of the radio.
      I have been breathing fast and I'm sweating, but I can't
turn away. The rain is drizzle now, but it seems like it would
have washed more blood away. I smell something besides wet
jungle, but it doesn't smell dead. *Does blood have a smell of its own?*
Is that what the vultures smell? I feel faint again: like my mind is

swinging up there in the canopy, like *I'm a vulture seeing us look at the bodies. I see Pops break the silence.*

"Four of 'em. That's all we want to know. Let's go back to the top and call it in. I don't want to stand around here. Pick up the rifles." *And I can see me pick up a gun. When I feel it* my mind comes back to earth. We go back up where our rucks are.

The rifle is an AK. I can't forget the sound after the day Chickenfeed got hit. The rifle is beat to pieces. It only has half the original stock; the back half is a piece of wood with twig marks on it still, carved on the end to fit a shoulder. *Which of the four did it come from?*

"Greenleaf, this is Titbird. How's your copy?"

Pops has the radio up on a rock, and the way he is standing there talking makes me flash on a cop, *downtown Cincinnati,* calling in from a beat box. I feel fuckin' drugged. OK, *this is war, man. This ain't Cincinnati. You're part of this, Gabriel.* Everybody looks the same—empty. Muthafucker, *can this be?* I smell the rifle to see if it was fired last night but there isn't any smell but metal. This ain't the fuckin' movies; you ain't John Wayne. I wonder if it had shot any GIs. It's heavier than my rifle. The ammo clip is curved. The more I stare at the gun the more it looks unreal, toy-like. No, it actually looks more real than my plastic M-16 but there is something childish about it. *The fucking thing looks homemade. That carved butt piece, the way it's wired together. Homemade.*

Pops is scooting the radio up the rock now. It occurs to me that I haven't been watching the bush. Eltee gets up and goes to help Pops. He seems to have regained his composure but his face is tight-looking. Peacock is picking his nose with one hand and toothbrushing the feed mechanism of the Sixty with his other.

"We got four rabbits out here. Coming back to your position. Over."

"Titbird, Greenleaf."

"Stand by."

"Them dinks caught our claymores letters-high," Pea says, to nobody in particular.

"Think of how much dinky damage they musta done to the Z."

"Titbird, how's your copy? Over."

"Good copy. Go ahead, dammit."

"Titbird, Higher says cut a chimney, they'll be out. Over."

Prophet angrily slams his hat on his thigh and Pops bangs the microphone with his free hand.

"No way," Pops says to Eltee. "Fuck those lifers. You tell 'em, we can't cut a chimney through that canopy. All they want to do is make sure we counted right, and I ain't fuckin' doing it."

I can't imagine how we could cut a hole, big enough to let a Loach down, and I can't imagine why.

Pops reads my mind.

"They wanna bring a Chieu Hoi out here and see if he can tell what unit the dinks are from."

"There isn't enough left of the four dinks to tell anybody jack-shit."

"Eltee, tell the fuckers to walk out here. We did," Prophet says.

Lieutenant Williams is standing up with his arms folded across the radio. He is rocking back and forth on his heels and toes. He never looks our way. The radio is low-volume static. If I can read Eltee's mind, I know he is torn, tortured, confused. He's going to be caught in the middle.

"Well, do something, for chrissakes. We can't cut 'em a hole, and we sure as fuck don't want to stay here much longer. Charlie is gonna be looking for these guys."

"Greenleaf, Titbird. Code name William."

"Go, Titbird."

"Greenleaf, too much canopy, too high. We'll bring captured weapons to your papa. These rabbits are in parts. Repeat, in parts. Not enough left for ID. Copy?"

"Code name William, code name Beaver. Wait one."

Pops flips through the code book.

"It's that short red-haired fucker, Billingham."

I didn't know his name, but I figured that's who it was. He's some kind of aide to the colonel and he carries a Car-15. A few days ago I saw his radioman taking his picture. He had a flak jacket and helmet on then, and the asshole probably hasn't ever been to the Bush. This is beginning to get real shitty. I'm becoming afraid again. We blew these guys away and their pals must be around here somewhere. If we don't get going we'll be sitting ducks. I feel my anger and fear mount together. I have a quick fantasy of taking a swing at that fat little fucker.

"Titbird, Greenleaf."

Even the radio seems alive and against us. It must be my fear that makes me think that way all of a sudden. Unfuckin' fair to be out here in the middle of nowhere and scared, talking long-distance and visualizing Billingham sitting in a sandbagged conex telling us to do something we already told him we can't fuckin' do.

"Titbird, it is essential that you provide us a way of identifying your rabbits. Many lives may depend on it."

"Many lives! Our lives are the only ones relevant to them dead dinks; where does he get off giving us a lecture like we're still in The World? This ain't practice. There ain't enough of them dinks left to tell anything. Make the fucker understand they're using us for bait."

Peacock is standing beside Williams now, struggling to keep his voice under control. Eltee looks at him blankly, puts a hand on his back, then pushes his own helmet back on his head. Eltee looks five years older than he did yesterday, and he looks confused.

"Oh, fucker . . ." Callme moans.

Prophet has been sitting with his elbows on his knees, looking away from us. Now he looks up at the canopy and shakes his head.

"Greenleaf, code name William, over."

"Go."

"I repeat. No can do."

"Titbird, that's affirm. Transport your rabbits to Checkpoint Bravo. Out."

No! *Bullshit*. I'm dreaming. Or is this a movie?

Peacock slumps down into the mud and begins stabbing at it with his knife. He is soon using both hands to stab with. He's nuts. I feel crazy too. Everybody else *looks* crazy. Eltee lets the microphone drop against the rock and stands staring at us. He looks like he's trying to get his mind to work.

"OK—" he starts.

"OK, so let's go to Bravo and they can fuckin' walk

back up here without us. We'll tell 'em right where the ambush is."

"Listen up," Eltee says. "This is some real bullshit, but there's no alternative."

"No alternative? Let's just fuckin' refuse to do it."

"Pops, you're a short-timer. If we don't do it we're all guilty of disobeying a direct order and we're all going to get court-martialed. You know that. Not just me. They'd bust us, send us all to jail, then send us back out here, and that jail time is bad time. You won't rotate out of here until *next* year. Think about it."

Pops's face is stretched round with red anger. He looks like he's ready to explode. I expect an outburst, but instead he slumps down to his knees and turns his face upward to let the silent rain hit him. He sighs.

"Eltee is right," Peacock says.

"If we're gonna do it, let's do it. We'll get even with them fuckin' Higher-highers," Prophet says.

Lieutenant Williams looks at him and opens his mouth but doesn't say anything.

"You never heard me say that, Eltee, for your own good. We like you and I know what you're thinking, but just forget it. You're one of us, for now."

Jesus, this is escalating. I don't know for sure what Prophet is saying, but his tone is severe and he isn't about ready to back down from anything the Eltee can offer.

"I won't hump no dead guy," Callme says.

"Dinks don't weigh much," Pea says.

Callmeblack makes his big black hand into a big black fist and drives it into his wadded-up poncho. Then he half buries his face in the poncho and either sobs or sighs.

Dear Dad: You won't believe this. Dear Brother Bob: Go to Canada. Dear President Johnson: Could you do this? Dear God: For my mother's sake, numb me. (Fucking jail! . . . Everybody knows the horror stories about military prisons, especially in The Nam.) There's nothing fair about some Army officer three kilometers away telling us to obey this insane order or go to jail. But why should I expect fairness? I'm in the Army, and the Army is in a war. It's simple. I don't have any choice.

So I'm the first one to move. I stand up and unroll my

poncho. I'm conscious of the rest of them watching me but I don't look at them.

"Are we supposed to call 'em when we get there?"

"Yeah," Prophet says, "call 'em and say send a taxi after we dragged the muthafuckin' corpses all the way through this damn jungle while they meanwhile sit back there getting dug in, then fly out to meet us."

He stands and is talking loud but not yelling.

"Then, goddammit, then they'll turn that helicopter around and we'll goddamn have to walk back too!"

"Those hardcore Shake-and-Bake officers don't even think about us killing these poor bastards, let alone have to haul around what's left. They probably can't think of it, just have wet dreams about being a hero when they get home."

We're psyching ourselves up. Everybody but Peacock is getting ready now. Eltee already has his ruck on. He goes over to Callme and squats alongside him. They don't even say anything but I can see Callme's courage—or whatever it is—coming back. I feel a little jealous of Eltee right now. I'm ready. My ruck doesn't feel so heavy and I'm not as tired as I was before it got light.

"Pray for luck," Peacock says. "If Charlie is around here close and sees this mess, you know he ain't gonna goddamn worry about big guns out here. He's gonna have our shit on a stick. He'll be hawking my goddamn watch in Hanoi if he knows what we're carrying and just happens to see us clod-hoppin' American boys here in his jungle. Them lifers think about the wrong things, that's all. They call the war by numbers. They're gonna say them four dinks only had one arm anyway, so we really blew eight away."

"Peacock," Pops says, "I never heard you be so right."

"Man, I'm just talking to keep from seeing, because seeing is believing."

"That's more like your old self, you asshole. That doesn't make any sense."

Jesus the flies.

We have two sets of ponchos snapped into pairs and are going to gather the bodies onto the ponchos, then split the weight up so four guys can carry the two slings. Even then, two guys will have to hump the radio, the machine gun, and the extra weapons, so really we'll be fuckin'-A useless if anything happens. Prophet goes to look for the best way by himself; we want to keep him as light as we can because he will be walking point. When he leaves, the rest of us go back to the site together. The flies are so loud I hear them from behind the first set of rocks, ten meters away.

We spread the ponchos out. Nobody talks. At first we all stand still. Then Callmeblack begins humming "Swing Low, Sweet Chariot" and Pops drags most of a body onto one of the ponchos. The guts drag along between the body's legs. The flies swarm in one extra-loud sound and land again when the body is on the poncho. Pops goes off from us a bit.

Right at my feet is an arm. It's short but it looks like what there is is almost all of what there ever was, like it came off at the shoulder. There are green flies around its bloody end. Callme is still humming and has tossed a couple pieces onto the poncho. I pick the arm up by the unbloody hand and it is like shaking hands with a snake. I'm careful not to touch the fingers. I fling the arm onto the pile that must be most of two guys now. Or women. Pops is back, white and old-looking.

Callmeblack sits down and spits a lot between his boots, but doesn't puke. The head that had been hanging by a thread of skin onto the body Pops carried is between Callmeblack and me and we both see it at the same time. It is most of a face, but half of it is turned into the muddy trail so it looks like a mask except for the flies. Callmeblack and I both look at it and then at each other and he looks back between his boots and half spits, half retches. I kick the head good; the face sails a foot off the ground and lands at the top of the pile, then rolls over the top. I'm glad it doesn't end up looking at me.

Eltee and Pops are about to fold the poncho over their pile and tie it shut.

"Let's be damn sure they're about the same weight."

"I pretended I was splitting a hundred pounds of Cambodian Red weed, man. I eyeballed it like I didn't know which half was mine, I—"

"OK, OK, OK. Shut up."

Peacock looks hurt. His tattoo is showing. I don't think it's raining. I think what is coming down is dripping off the canopy. Peacock's face is an eggshell color. In fact the light is all like that, the color of a dirty white dog.

I take as much air into my lungs as I can. I walk second, behind Prophet, who is carrying one of the captured rifles. Peacock has the other end of the poncho; then Pops and Callmeblack carrying the other sling, and Eltee is walking last. We tried slinging the weight on vines, in hopes that it would be easier carrying, but that didn't work because the trail is so sharp in places that the vines were too long to turn without the lead guy having to stop and turn around. So I twist the corners of the poncho together and use both hands to shoulder my end. Prophet helped me sling my rifle with shoelaces so it at least hangs in front of me and will be possible to get at, if it comes to that.

Eltee stays quite a ways back from the rest of us. Incredibly, he has the radio, the Sixty, and an extra rifle, and he has to pull rear security. I can't breathe normally—it's more like taking a gulp of air in and walking until it's used up, then gasping again, like I've swum too far away from shore. The going is slow and seems noisy. For a while we walk on a fairly level trail and our footing is solid, but the weight gets to us and we have to rest. When we set the poncho down the flies all seem to catch up and swirl into the holes between the snaps on the ponchos. The blood still isn't dried, so when I pick up the knot that makes my handle the blood squeezes out, and some runs down my arms.

After fifteen minutes my back begins to throb. Trying to walk mostly downhill now and still trying to keep the poncho fairly level to make it easier on Peacock strains my muscles and makes me aware of the spots I slept on last night. I'm constantly gasping for breath, and the bag keeps swinging, so I have to struggle to keep my balance. I come to the edge of my endurance. I want to cuss and throw something. I want to destroy. Finally, the slippery knot comes out of my grasp and the sling falls. Without looking back, because I am so goddamn out of touch, I keep walking, dragging the poncho behind me. It slides easily enough through the mud and makes a small sound like a brake rubbing against a bicycle tire. We don't go on like that very long before Prophet stops us and points at a swale below: Checkpoint Bravo. I simply fall down, gasping so hard I wonder if it's possible to catch up on the air I'm missing. I lie there with my eyes closed, listening to the others catching their breath and the buzzing of the flies.

It is almost as though I am asleep, momentarily, because the sound of the flies begins to sound like a song. Honest to God: song. I hear snatches of nursery rhymes, and church choirs and classical music, and the ditty that is the commercial for life insurance. . . . When my breathing gets closer to normal the smell of reality fights its way back, and once again the predominant sound is that of the bloodthirsty flies swarming. I could puke in my own lap and it wouldn't make any difference right now.

From a sitting position I can see cleanly through the foliage. Checkpoint Bravo is a small, almost round, hollow. It looks marshy. Instead of jungle it looks like tall grass. I wonder how deep the water is. My breath has come back now. I see that one of the arms has worked its way partly out from the bundled poncho. I'll be damned if I'm going to touch it again to shove it back in. I don't care if it gets lost.

Eltee is making radio contact; otherwise there isn't any sound except for the goddamn flies. It takes skill to use an Army PRC-25 radio so that it isn't like hearing a supermarket speaker, and Williams is good enough that I can barely hear the transmissions from five meters away. I semi-want to smoke a cigarette, but my hands smell like the blood that is drying black now. I try to think of what it resembles, having squeezed out of the poncho, but it doesn't look like anything but what it is. Thinking about carrying these pieces of dinks to a helicopter landing in a small clearing makes the fear come hard, but who is there to tell I'm scared, and what good would it do?

"Wait till we hear the birds coming," Eltee says. "Pass it on."

We whisper it ahead and Prophet nods. His face is rock-hard and dirty. The way the light is hitting his face I can see the rivulets of sweat running over the wax we use to camouflage our faces. He must have mostly used the stick of green. I used brown. The camo sticks are precious; it is one more thing the Army never has enough of. Prophet sits quietly looking around all 360 degrees, spitting silently between his teeth. I'm glad the rain has quit, at least for now; I'm still cold, or shivering from fear. It isn't long before we hear the helicopters coming. We don't want to give our position away any sooner than we absolutely have to, so we don't move until the birds are in sight. As high up as they stay, their sound is no louder than the noise of the flies. Everybody chambers a round, ready to pick up the ponchos for the last time.

"Pray, baby," Peacock whispers. I nod. I do. I breathe as deeply as I can.

The clearing is a shade different in color than everything else around, darker green. From this distance, it looks like briars, but I've never seen briars over here. I can tell the grass is too tall for a bird to come down in, that we'll have to hack some of it away. My question is what we're going to do with these fucking bodies in the meantime.

Eltee is working his way up the line, whispering to everybody as he goes by. It strikes me as absurd, although not stupid, for him to be whispering. I don't know, maybe he isn't whispering: it's as though all I can hear are the goddamn flies, like a radio station off the air for the night—a low *hummmzaat.* As Williams moves up he walks hunchback to carry the weight of the radio and his ruck. My ruck straps cut into me all the way down the trail but I didn't notice the ache much until now. Fuck it. All we have to do is get these slings another thirty meters, cut a hole, and catch a ride back to the LZ.

Before I know it Eltee is at my side.

"We're about ready to move," he says. His face is like a clock, so exact is the intensity of his expression. I notice his nose looks wider on one side than the other. I listen to what he says, and it seems to echo through my mind even after he's gone. We'll be up and move fast. We're dropping the ponchos on signal. Three of us go out for security and the other three hack a hole in the weeds, good enough for a bird to come down long enough to pick up the pieces; when that bird is gone another will come in to get us. I'm going to be one who cuts.

My mouth feels like I've been sucking a rubber band. The nylon pads in my shoulder straps look freshly painted, and I feel conscious of every one of the five hundred more seconds we sit there. Eltee is still up front with Prophet. I can see them both through a hole in the trees. Eltee is talking on the radio some of the time. First one of their faces shows in the hole, then the other—like watching TV.

We're up. I get the signal from Prophet and pass it on to Peacock, who passes it on. Now we pick up the sling. Heavy. This time I'm very conscious of my rifle swinging in front of me. I've gotten used to having it in my hand when I want it, and right now I want it.

We hustle. Everything hurts—my back, my head where the steel pot has bounced, my arms from having the sling behind me, my feet, my chafing asshole, even my goddamn eyes from sleeplessness. I hurt inside too. I feel like a piece of shit, like nobody. But on we go. In five minutes we're into the swamp. The water is quickly up to my shins, finally up to my balls. It doesn't feel warm or cold, not thick or clean, just wet and one more thing to fight against. We drop the poncho and it half sinks. The flies are there, like they're pissed off. They swirl in a wave like paint flung off a roller. I hate them. Air escapes from the poncho and comes to the surface, and the water turns the color of aged leather from the mud we stir up and the blood.

By pure luck, we stumble upon a hard bottom so we can stand up and hack away at the bushes exactly at water level. It's me, Prophet, and Peacock. We don't speak. We give it hell, our machetes swirling. The bushes are mostly easy to cut, and it doesn't take long to hack a ten-foot by ten-foot hole down to the waterline, and it isn't long after that that the bird arrives.

It comes over the tree line like a hotrod cresting some country hill, then settles over us with the motion that only helicopters have, a gliding sort of motion, with its tail swerving from side to side. The machine gunners give us a long peace sign. We half carry, half float the ponchos over. It takes four of us to get them out of the water and into the bird. As we're loading the second, trying to keep the chopped-up grass and water out of our eyes and struggling to keep our footing, rounds begin pelting the windshield of the helicopter and either the pilot or the copilot gets hit. I dive into the water and weeds and futilely try to keep my rifle up.

Rounds begin to ricochet all over hell. The gunners open up, firing directly over our heads into the tree line. The shell casings come off the gun in a perfect arc, and some of them land on the grass we have cut that floats on the water. I'm disoriented and afraid to fire because I don't know where anybody else is, but I get my safety off and try to be careful to keep the barrel pointed up while I work my way, staying oh-so-low, away from where the bird is. I glance quickly at it and I can see the gunner taking the vibration of his gun with exact concentration. There is scurrying behind him and either the other gunner or a crew chief is leaned into the cockpit, probably aiding the pilot. I catch sight of Peacock, who has his Sixty at shoulder height. He is pouring rounds out toward the tree line.

The helicopter gets up and hovers for only an instant before it banks slightly and takes off away from the tree line we're facing. It circles and comes back over, low, stirring up the water and cut weeds. It passes over the tree line and both gunners fire continually. Then it comes back again and keeps a steady stream of rounds slashing into the tree line.

Eltee is yelling and signaling to make a circle. He has the radio mike in his hand. His rifle is slung downward and the AK is strapped to the radio. Prophet and Callme come out of the weeds behind him and run as best they can through the water until they reach the edge of our cut. Pops and I begin making it toward the cleared spot from opposite sides. Pops's face is covered with blood. I can't tell if he has been hit or not. Just as I get to where I intend to stop there is an explosion a few meters on the other side of Peacock, then another one, then two more. Mortars. The bursts hit the swamp in tandems now. First, two beyond us; then two in front of us. Peacock is trying to move back to our position but he has to get down every time a mortar lands. They bracketed, and have the range on those tubes now, so I expect the next rounds to come right on top of us. The helicopter is still hanging above the tree line, blasting it.

Four more mortars. The first two are off target but the second ones land almost right on top of Lieutenant Williams, maybe twenty meters away from me on the other side of the clearing. He screams. The wave of water from the mortar's concussion passes by me and there is still shit in the air. Pops slips out of his ruck and begins to work his way toward Eltee.

546

Everybody else begins to pump rounds into the tree line. I fire about where the helicopter is working out because I thought I saw a muzzle flash come from somewhere near there. As I am looking I see one for sure, a few feet off the ground. I squeeze three or four rounds off at where I saw it, then have to change magazines and when I look up again, the spot is being torn apart by the bird's Sixties. I cheer to myself. *Kill the fuckers.* I expect more mortars any time.

Pops is coming back toward us. He has the radio in one hand and is dragging Eltee behind him in a sort of backward-walking fireman's carry. Eltee is no longer screaming. A second helicopter comes over the opposite tree line. Eltee is dead.

The first helicopter continues working on the tree line and the second one comes at us rapidly. We all make a break for it. I go to Pops to help him. Together, we manage to get to the bird with our gear and the body. He didn't live past the scream. More than half of that handsome black face has been ripped back toward his skull. As long as the body was in the water the blood didn't show much, but when we are loaded and drag the body in after us, a pool of blood the color of fire spreads across the floor. We're all in, we're up, we head away from the tree line, high above which the bird with the ponchos full of bodies now hovers. Exhaustion hits and my body feels like a wet paper bag.

Jesus, there's no way to describe the ride. We get up fast, over a set of mountains, then up again. Riding along on the vibration of the bird is like being wind-rocked in a hammock. The five of us are sitting toward the front. I am leaning against the aluminum wall that defines the cockpit; the machine gunner is between me and the open door; past him I can see a patch of sky and beyond that mountains, mountains, mountains.

The sound of the rotor is steady: *rum thump thump rum thump thump.*

God, I stink. I've been sweating into these same clothes for at least ten days; I've been wallowing around in swamp water.

My mind just roams around like my eyes. The door gunner on my side is dark-complexioned and stocky. His mustache is trimmed and just a dab of black hair shows below the headset helmet. The back of his helmet has something painted on it but I can't read it. Across from me, against the wall on the other side of the doorway to the cockpit, Pops is slumped in a heap. He's filthy. There is a line of mud that runs from the top of his head, over his face and through his mustache, through the hair on his belly, and down to his pants. His shirt is unbuttoned and his flak jacket isn't hooked. Just a trace of a paunch hangs over the belt loops. He looks thinner now than he did just a month ago.

The others are leaning against whatever there is to lean against, and toward the back is Eltee's body. I stare at it, and it doesn't seem like he could be dead. I can't see his head that is half mincemeat now and I can't really believe he will never move again. Dead. Goddamn dead. It could've been anybody. He got a mortar; the dinks weren't going for the radio and they weren't going for him because he was an officer. They were just going for anybody and trying to disable the helicopters. I wonder who will have to write a report up on this mission, and I wonder what Lieutenant Williams's family will find out.

Thump rump kathump kathump. We are descending. I have to sit up straight to see the Z below us and I feel so tired. As we come down we scoot toward the door. It isn't easy because the bird isn't level and the ruck seems to weigh more than ever. I'm so tired. I just want to lie down. It seems like there should be more waiting for us than this goddamn hill full of holes. This, my man, is home for now. Eltee doesn't even have this.

Fifty feet up, then thirty. It's like working on a high, high ladder. The guys on the ground all move away from the pad and cover their eyes. Parts of C-ration cartons whirl up as high as we are and dive through the crazy air currents like bats going after insects in a porch light. All the dudes on the ground are wearing flak jackets, and a lot of them have helmets on. The landing pad is built out of sandbags, and from a few feet up it reminds me of a caned chair seat. We settle between two big slings of ammunition. After the bird shuts down to a low speed, guys start again at unloading the slings and carrying the ammo away. Most of it is for our mortars and artillery. The rounds come in wooden boxes about two feet long.

Over by the big guns are stacks of ammo crates, and guys are carrying these empties away to fill full of sand and build hooches.

The CO comes over to the bird with his face down. He is a stern-looking guy, maybe thirty years old. His expression isn't mean-looking but it sure as hell isn't joyful. He reaches up and helps us off the bird, just puts his hand under our rucks. When he helps me off he is already looking at whoever is behind me.

"There's coffee over there," he says to all of us. "I want to see the whole squad in a few minutes."

We all drop our rucks as soon as we're far enough away from the pad. Getting the ruck off is like taking a good shit. It's cloudy and there's dust in the air from something. Since we've been out, there has probably been a couple thousand sandbags filled. Some are laid into flat parapet walls and some of the hooches are getting to be deep enough for roofs. Ammo crates and full sandbags make squat, solid walls.

Most of three companies are on the Z now and it has spread out like a carnival parking lot. When we started to dig in, we were on the outside of the perimeter but now the perimeter has moved out in all directions.

There are two guys sitting near the coffeepot smoking and waiting for us. They have been humping ammo from the pad. "Hey, what is it."

"It is a muthafucker," Pops says. It seems like a long time since I have heard his voice.

"You guys the squad that got some dinks last night?"

"Yeah, four. How bad was it here?"

"Bad, man. Mostly incoming, but they almost broke through on the other side of the hill. Over there." The guy points to our right.

"Charlie put some shit in here last night," the other guy says. He emphasizes "put" by pounding his rifle's butt plate against the ammo crate he has his feet resting on.

"Eighty-twos?"

"Mostly."

"He was keying on that side of the hill. We were over there, the other side, and everything went over us, wounded one guy out on LP. Alpha Company got it the worst. I heard six KIAs and twenty wounded."

"Our Eltee ate an eighty-two round."

"Dead?"

"Fuckin'-A dead."

"Anybody else get hit?"

"Nope. Freaky. We were loading those goddamn dinks and Charlie walked about a dozen rounds in."

"Bravo Company is going to move out that direction."

"You guys from Bravo?"

"Yeah. We aren't even dug in, but they keep trying to stick us on ammo detail."

"Well, man, Charlie's out there. Even though it musta been bad here last night, I'd rather be here tonight."

"Dig it, but at least our whole company's going out."

I'm surprised the coffee tastes good. C-ration coffee sucks; this came from a big urn shaped like a fire hydrant. There are some shit-green food cans lined up behind the coffee, but it looks like the food must have come in sometime yesterday because some of the cans have shrapnel in them. After I get my coffee I sit down on a pile of sandbags that have been filled but not tied off yet. I can see the bad side of the Z, where there must be twenty shallow craters. The thing I didn't expect to see is the shrapnel holes everywhere and even a few pieces of shrap. There's none nearby but I can see it glint in the sun in a few paths.

Big guns sound somewhere. I wonder what time it is. The sun is still a little above the west ridge of mountains. I'd guess it will be dark in four hours. I wonder if these guys from Bravo are going to try to get dug in tonight. I look at them and try to see the fear that I know is somewhere in their faces.

One guy is Italian-looking. He is sitting on one of the melomite cans, sipping coffee from his canteen cup.

"Eltee didn't have a shot at it," Callme says.

I don't feel like saying anything. I helped float his body through the water. I flash on the body over there in the bird in a pool of blood. The CO is just starting back from the pad. Even though there isn't any dust flying now, he still walks with his face down. Somebody is leaning into the helicopter. Slowly, the rotor starts to turn, and when the CO gets to us the bird is starting off. We all have to shield ourselves from the shit that flies around. When I look up, the CO is looking at Peacock, who's still looking down. So the CO looks right at me.

"What's your name, soldier?"

"Gabriel Sauers, sir."

"Tell me about it."

"About the patrol?"

"Yeah, from the time you made contact."

"Well . . ." I don't know what to say. Talking to an officer always bothers me. Eltee was an officer though, too. "Well," I say again, "it all happened awful fast. We were set up on a trail, and me and Callme were pretty close together and the rest of them were spread out. Peacock was ahead of us with the Sixty. We heard them coming and somebody blew the claymores. I could see the explosion and action. I emptied a clip and reloaded. That's all I know."

"Did you hear anything afterwards?"

"Nothing, sir."

"Who's the squad leader?"

"I am," Pops says. He doesn't add "sir."

"What's your name, Sergeant?"

"Pops," he says. He has undone his pants and is standing there talking to the CO with his dick out, rubbing one finger all around the jungle rot on his balls. I notice the CO has rot too, on his neck.

"You have anything to add, Pops?"

"I don't think Eltee Williams should be dead."

"What are you saying, soldier?"

"I think somebody fucked up back here. Those dinks were in pieces no bigger than these damn sandbags and there was no reason to bring 'em back here, but we hadda goddamn carry 'em down the fuckin' hill and into that clearing. Any-fuckin'-body woulda known the dinks were gonna drop some shit in there, but if we coulda got right in and right out of the edge of it, then Eltee wouldn't have gotten fuckin' killed. They walked 'em right in on us."

"Sergeant, your squad killed four enemies who might be responsible for killing ten GIs. That's what you have to think of. And"—he puts his hand on Pops's hand, which is still on his nuts, and looks around at all of us—"I understand how you feel. There's nothing I can do about it. Echo Company didn't make the decision, you know that. Listen, I *know* how you feel."

The way he says it, the way he looks around at all of us with a tiny little frown, the way he gives Pops's ball-handling wrist an additional shake . . . something makes me think he *does* know how Pops feels, and probably how I feel even if I don't. I feel something in my throat. Prophet spits, Callme spits, Peacock spits. The CO turns to leave and spits. I spit.

TIM O'BRIEN
Stocking

The American writer Tim O'Brien (1946–) is the author of the Vietnam classics If I Should Die in a Combat Zone (1973), and Going After Cacciato (1978), a National Book Award-winner. He served in the infantry in Vietnam, and is an ex-national affairs reporter for the Washington Post.
"Stocking" is a short story from his collection The Things They Carried (1990).

HENRY DOBBINS WAS A GOOD MAN, and a superb soldier, but sophistication was not his strong suit. The ironies went beyond him. In many ways he was like America itself, big and strong, full of good intentions, a roll of fat jiggling at his belly, slow of foot but always plodding along, always there when you needed him, a believer in the virtues of simplicity and directness and hard labor. Like his country, too, Dobbins was drawn toward sentimentality.

Even now, twenty years later, I can see him wrapping his girlfriend's pantyhose around his neck before heading out on ambush.

It was his one eccentricity. The pantyhose, he said, had the properties of a good-luck charm. He liked putting his nose into the nylon and breathing in the scent of his girlfriend's body; he liked the memories this inspired; he sometimes slept with the stockings up against his face, the way an infant sleeps with a magic blanket, secure and peaceful. More than anything, though, the stockings were a talisman for him. They kept him safe. They gave access to a spiritual world, where things were soft and intimate, a place where he might someday take his girlfriend to live. Like many of us in Vietnam, Dobbins felt the pull of supersition, and he believed firmly and absolutely in the protective power of the stockings. They were like body armor, he thought. Whenever we saddled up for a late-night ambush, putting on our helmets and flak jackets, Henry Dobbins would make a ritual out of arranging the nylons around his neck, carefully tying a knot, draping the two leg sections over his left shoulder. There were some jokes, of course, but we came to appreciate the mystery of it all. Dobbins was invulnerable. Never wounded, never a scratch. In August, he tripped a Bouncing Betty, which failed to detonate. And a week later he got caught in the open during a fierce little firefight, no cover at all, but he just slipped the pantyhose over his nose and breathed deep and let the magic do its work.

It turned us into a platoon of believers. You don't dispute facts.

But then, near the end of October, his girlfriend dumped him. It was a hard blow. Dobbins went quiet for a while, staring down at her letter, then after a time he took out the stockings and tied them around his neck as a comforter.

"No sweat," he said. "I still love her. The magic doesn't go away."

It was a relief for all of us.

DAVID HUDDLE
The Interrogation of the Prisoner Bung by Mister Hawkins and Sergeant Tree

*The American writer David Huddle (1942–)
served in the US Army from 1964 to 1967,
first as a paratrooper in Germany, later
with Military Intelligence in Vietnam. His
books of poetry and short stories include* A
Dream With No Stumps In It, *and*
Only the Little Bone.

*This short story was originally published
in 1971 in* Esquire.

THE LAND IN THESE PROVINCES to the south of the capital
city is so flat it would be possible to ride a bicycle from one
end of this district to the other and to pedal only occasionally.
The narrow highway passes over kilometers and kilometers
of rice fields, laid out square and separated by slender green
lines of grassy paddy-dikes and by irrigation ditches filled with
bad water. The villages are far apart and small. Around them
are clustered the little pockets of huts, the hamlets where the
rice farmers live. The village that serves as the capital of this
district is just large enough to have a proper marketplace.
Close to the police compound, a detachment of Americans
has set up its tents. These are lumps of new green canvas,
and they sit on a concrete, French-built tennis court, long
abandoned, not far from a large lily pond where women come

in the morning to wash clothes and where policemen of the compound and their children come to swim and bathe in the late afternoon.

The door of a room to the rear of the District Police Headquarters is cracked for light and air. Outside noises—chickens quarreling, children playing, the mellow grunting of the pigs owned by the police chief—these reach the ears of the three men inside the quiet room. The room is not a cell; it is more like a small bedroom.

The American is nervous and fully awake, but he forces himself to yawn and sips at his coffee. In front of him are his papers, the report forms, yellow notepaper, two pencils and a ball-point pen. Across the table from the American is Sergeant Tree, a young man who was noticed by the government of his country and taken from his studies to be sent to interpreter's school. Sergeant Tree has a pleasant and healthy face. He is accustomed to smiling, especially in the presence of Americans, who are, it happens, quite fond of him. Sergeant Tree knows that he has an admirable position working with Mister Hawkins; several of his unlucky classmates from interpreter's school serve nearer the shooting.

The prisoner, Bung, squats in the far corner of the room, his back at the intersection of the cool concrete walls. Bung is a large man for an Asian, but he is squatted down close to the floor. He was given a cigarette by the American when he was first brought into the room, but has finished smoking and holds the white filter inside his fist. Bung is not tied, nor restrained, but he squats perfectly still, his bare feet laid out flat and large on the floor. His hair, cut by his wife, is cropped short and uneven; his skin is dark, leathery, and there is a bruise below one of his shoulder blades. He looks only at the floor, and he wonders what he will do with the tip of the cigarette when the interrogation begins. He suspects that he ought to eat it now so that it will not be discovered later.

From the large barracks room on the other side of the building comes laughter and loud talking, the policemen changing shifts. Sergeant Tree smiles at these sounds. Some of the younger policemen are his friends. Hawkins, the American, does not seem to have heard. He is trying to think about sex, and he cannot concentrate.

"Ask the prisoner what his name is."

"What is your name?"

The prisoner reports that his name is Bung. The language startles Hawkins. He does not understand this language, except the first ten numbers of counting, and the words for yes and no. With Sergeant Tree helping him with the spelling, Hawkins enters the name into the proper blank.

"Ask the prisoner where he lives."

"Where do you live?"

The prisoner wails a string of language. He begins to weep as he speaks, and he goes on like this, swelling up the small room with the sound of his voice until he sees a warning twitch of the interpreter's hand. He stops immediately, as though corked. One of the police chief's pigs is snuffing over the ground just outside the door, rooting for scraps of food.

"What did he say?"

"He says that he is classed as a poor farmer, that he lives in the hamlet near where the soldiers found him, and that he has not seen his wife and his children for four days now and they do not know where he is.

"He says that he is not one of the enemy, although he has seen the enemy many times this year in his hamlet and in the village near his hamlet. He says that he was forced to give rice to the enemy on two different occasions, once at night, and another time during the day, and that he gave rice to the enemy only because they would have shot him if he had not.

"He says that he does not know the names of any of these men. He says that one of the men asked him to join them and to go with them, but that he told this man that he could not join them and go with them because he was poor and because his wife and his children would not be able to live without him to work for them to feed them. He says that the enemy men laughed at him when he said this but that they did not make him go with them when they left his house.

"He says that two days after the night the enemy came and took rice from him, the soldiers came to him in the field where he was working and made him walk with them for many kilometers, and made him climb into the back of a large truck, and put a cloth over his eyes, so that he did not see where the truck carried him and did not know where he was until he was put with some other people in a pen. He says that one of the soldiers hit him in the back with a weapon, because he was afraid at first to climb into the truck.

"He says that he does not have any money but that he has ten kilos of rice hidden beneath the floor of the kitchen of his house. He says that he would make us the gift of this rice if we would let him go back to his wife and his children."

When he has finished his translation of the prisoner's speech, Sergeant Tree smiles at Mister Hawkins. Hawkins feels that he ought to write something down. He moves the pencil to a corner of the paper and writes down his service number, his Social Security number, the telephone number of his girl friend in Silver Spring, Maryland and the amount of money he has saved in his allotment account.

"Ask the prisoner in what year he was born?"

Hawkins has decided to end the interrogation of this prisoner as quickly as he can. If there is enough time left, he will find an excuse for Sergeant Tree and himself to drive the jeep into the village.

"In what year were you born?"

The prisoner tells the year of his birth.

"Ask the prisoner in what place he was born."

"In what place were you born?"

The prisoner tells the place of his birth.

"Ask the prisoner the name of his wife."

"What is the name of your wife?"

Bung gives the name of his wife.

"Ask the prisoner the names of his parents."

Bung tells the names.

"Ask the prisoner the names of his children."

"What are the names of your children?"

The American takes down these things on the form, painstakingly, with the help in the spelling from the interpreter, who has become bored with this. Hawkins fills all the blank spaces on the front of the form. Later, he will add his summary of the interrogation in the space provided on the back.

"Ask the prisoner the name of his hamlet chief."

"What is the name of your hamlet chief?"

The prisoner tells this name, and Hawkins takes it down on the notepaper. Hawkins has been trained to ask these questions. If a prisoner gives one incorrect name, then all names given may be incorrect, all information secured unreliable.

Bung tells the name of his village chief, and the American takes it down. Hawkins tears off this sheet of notepaper and gives it to Sergeant Tree. He asks the interpreter to take this paper to the police chief to check if these are the correct names. Sergeant Tree does not like to deal with the police chief because the police chief treats him as if he were a farmer. But he leaves the room in the manner of someone engaged in important business. Bung continues to stare at the floor, afraid the American will kill him now that they are in this room together, alone.

Hawkins is again trying to think about sex. Again, he is finding it difficult to concentrate. He cannot choose between thinking about sex with his girl friend Suzanne or with a plump girl who works in a souvenir shop in the village. The soft grunting of the pig outside catches his ear, and he finds that he is thinking of having sex with the pig. He takes another sheet of notepaper and begins calculating the number of days he has left to remain in Asia. The number turns out to be one hundred and thirty-three. This distresses him because the last time he calculated the number it was one hundred and thirty-five. He decides to think about food. He thinks of an omelet. He would like to have an omelet. His eyelids begin to close as he considers all the things that he likes to eat: an omelet, chocolate pie, macaroni, cookies, cheeseburgers, black-cherry Jell-O. He has a sudden vivid image of Suzanne's stomach, the path of downy hair to her navel. He stretches the muscles in his legs, and settles into concentration.

The clamor of chickens distracts him. Sergeant Tree has caused this noise by throwing a rock on his way back. The police chief refused to speak with him and required him to conduct his business with the secretary, whereas this secretary gloated over the indignity to Sergeant Tree, made many unnecessary delays and complications before letting the interpreter have a copy of the list of hamlet chiefs and village chiefs in the district.

Sergeant Tree enters the room, goes directly to the prisoner, with the toe of his boot kicks the prisoner on the shinbone. The boot hitting bone makes a wooden sound. Hawkins jerks up in his chair, but before he quite understands the situation, Sergeant Tree has shut the door to the small room and has kicked the prisoner's other shinbone. Bung responds with a grunt and holds his shins with his hands, drawing himself tighter into the corner.

"Wait!" The American stands up to restrain Sergeant Tree, but this is not necessary. Sergeant Tree has passed by the prisoner now and has gone to stand at his own side of the table. From underneath his uniform shirt he takes a rubber club, which he has borrowed from one of his policeman friends. He slaps the club on the table.

"He lies!" Sergeant Tree says this with as much evil as he can force into his voice.

"Hold on now. Let's check this out." Hawkins' sense of justice has been touched. He regards the prisoner as a clumsy, hulking sort, obviously not bright, but clearly honest.

"The police chief says that he lies!" Sergeant Tree announces. He shows Hawkins the paper listing the names of the hamlet chiefs and the village chiefs. With the door shut, the light in the small room is very dim, and it is difficult to locate the names on the list. Hawkins is disturbed by the darkness, is uncomfortable being so intimately together with two men. The breath of the interpreter has something sweetish to it. It occurs to Hawkins that now, since the prisoner has lied to them, there will probably not be enough time after the interrogation to take the jeep and drive into the village. This vexes him. He decides there must be something unhealthy in the diet of these people, something that causes this sweet-smelling breath.

Hawkins finds it almost impossible to read the columns of handwriting. He is confused. Sergeant Tree must show him the places on the list where the names of the prisoner's hamlet chief and village chief are written. They agree that the prisoner has given them incorrect names, though Hawkins is not certain of it. He wishes these things were less complicated, and he dreads what he knows must follow. He thinks regretfully of what could have happened if the prisoner had given the correct names: the interrogation would have ended quickly, the prisoner released; he and Sergeant Tree could have driven into the village in the jeep, wearing their sunglasses, with the cool wind whipping past them, dust billowing around the jeep, shoeshine boys shrieking, the girl in the souvenir shop going with him into the back room for a time.

Sergeant Tree goes to the prisoner, kneels on the floor beside him, and takes Bung's face between his hands. Tenderly, he draws the prisoner's head close to his own, and asks, almost absentmindedly, "Are you one of the enemy?"

"No."

All this strikes Hawkins as vaguely comic, someone saying, "I love you," in a high-school play.

Sergeant Tree spits in the face of the prisoner and then jams the prisoner's head back against the wall. Sergeant Tree stands up quickly, jerks the police club from the table, and starts beating the prisoner with random blows. Bung stays squatted down and covers his head with both arms. He makes a shrill noise.

Hawkins has seen this before in other interrogations. He listens closely, trying to hear everything: little shrieks coming from Sergeant Tree's throat, the chunking sound of the rubber club makes. The American recognizes a kind of rightness in this, like the final slapping together of the bellies of a man and a woman.

Sergeant Tree stops. He stands, legs apart, facing the prisoner, his back to Hawkins. Bung keeps his squatting position, his arms crossed over his head.

The door scratches and opens just wide enough to let in a policeman friend of Sergeant Tree's, a skinny, rotten-toothed man, and a small boy. Hawkins has seen this boy and the policeman before. The two of them smile at the American and at Sergeant Tree, whom they admire for his education and for having achieved such an excellent position. Hawkins starts to send them back out, but decides to let them stay. He does not like to be discourteous to Asians.

Sergeant Tree acknowledges the presence of his friend and the boy. He sets the club on the table and removes his uniform shirt and the white T-shirt beneath it. His chest is powerful, but hairless. He catches Bung by the ears and jerks upward until the prisoner stands. Sergeant Tree is much shorter than the prisoner, and this he finds an advantage.

Hawkins notices that the muscles in Sergeant Tree's buttocks are clenched tight, and he admires this, finds it attractive. He has in his mind Suzanne. They are sitting on the back seat of the Oldsmobile. She has removed her stockings and garter belt, and now slides the panties down from her hips, down her legs, off one foot, keeping them dangling on one ankle, ready to be pulled up quickly in case someone comes to the car and catches them. Hawkins has perfect concentration. He sees her panties glow.

Sergeant Tree tears away the prisoner's shirt, first from one side of his chest and then the other. Bung's mouth sags open now, as though he were about to drool.

The boy clutches at the sleeve of the policeman to whisper in his ear. The policeman giggles. They hush when the American glances at them. Hawkins is furious because they have distracted him. He decides there is no privacy to be had in the entire country.

"Sergeant Tree, send these people out of here, please."

Sergeant Tree gives no sign that he has heard what Hawkins has said. He is poising himself to begin. Letting out a heaving grunt, Sergeant Tree chops with the police club, catching the prisoner directly in the center of the forehead. A flame begins in Bung's brain; he is conscious of a fire, blazing, blinding him. He feels the club touch him twice more, once at his ribs and once at his forearm.

"Are you the enemy?" Sergeant Tree screams.

The policeman and the boy squat beside each other near the door. They whisper to each other as they watch Sergeant Tree settle into the steady, methodical beating. Occasionally he pauses to ask the question again, but he gets no answer.

From a certain height, Hawkins can see that what is happening is profoundly sensible. He sees how deeply he loves these men in this room and how he respects them for the things they are doing. The knowledge rises in him, pushes to reveal itself. He stands up from his chair, virtually at attention.

A loud, hard smack swings the door wide open, and the room is filled with light. The Police Chief stands in the doorway, dressed in a crisp, white shirt, his rimless glasses sparkling. He is a fat man in the way that a good merchant might be fat—solid, confident, commanding. He stands with his hands on his hips, an authority in all matters. The policeman and the boy nod respectfully. The Police Chief walks to the table and picks up the list of hamlet chiefs and village chiefs. He examines this, and then he takes from his shirt pocket another paper, which is also a list of hamlet chiefs and village chiefs. He carries both lists to Sergeant Tree, who is kneeling in front of the prisoner. He shows Sergeant Tree the mistake he has made in getting a list that is out of date. He places the new list in Sergeant Tree's free hand, and then he takes the rubber club from Sergeant Tree's other hand and slaps it down across the top of Sergeant Tree's head. The Police Chief leaves the room, passing before the American, the policeman, the boy, not speaking or looking other than to the direction of the door.

It is late afternoon and the rain has come. Hawkins stands inside his tent, looking through the open flap. He likes to look out across the old tennis court at the big lily pond. He has been fond of water since he learned to water-ski. If the rain stops before dark, he will go out to join the policeman and the children who swim and bathe in the lily pond.

Walking out on the highway, with one kilometer still to go before he comes to the village, is Sergeant Tree. He is alone, the highway behind him and in front of him as far as he can see and nothing else around him but rain and the fields of wet, green rice. His head hurts and his arms are weary from the load of rice he carries. When he returned the prisoner to his hamlet, the man's wife made such a fuss Sergeant Tree had to shout at her to make her shut up, and then, while he was inside the prisoner's hut conducting the final arrangements for the prisoner's release, the rain came, and his policeman friends in the jeep left him to manage alone.

The ten kilos of rice he carries are heavy for him, and he would put his load down and leave it, except that he plans to sell the rice and add the money to what he has been saving to buy a .45 caliber pistol like the one Mister Hawkins carries at his hip. Sergeant Tree tries to think about how well-received he will be in California because he speaks the American language so well, and how it is likely that he will marry a rich American girl with very large breasts.

The prisoner Bung is delighted by the rain. It brought his children inside the hut, and the sounds of their fighting with each other make him happy. His wife came to him and touched him. The rice is cooking, and in a half hour his cousin will come, bringing with him the leader and two other members of Bung's squad. They will not be happy that half of their rice was taken by the interpreter to pay the American, but it will not be a disaster for them. The squad leader will be proud of Bung for gathering the information that he has—for he has memorized the guard routines at the police headquarters and at the old French area where the Americans are staying. He has watched all the comings and goings at these places, and he has marked out in his mind the best avenues of approach, the best escape routes, and the best places to set up ambush. Also, he has discovered a way that they can lie in wait and kill the Police Chief. It will occur at the place where the Police Chief goes to urinate every morning at a certain time. Bung has much information inside his head, and he believes he will be praised by the members of his squad. It is even possible that he will receive a commendation from someone very high.

His wife brings the rifle that was hidden, and Bung sets to cleaning it, savoring the smell of the rice his wife places before him and of the American oil he uses on the weapon. He particularly enjoys taking the weapon apart and putting it together again. He is very fast at this.

BOBBIE ANN MASON
Memorial

Bobbie Ann Mason (1940–) was born in Mayfield, Kentucky. Her works include the prize-winning Shiloh & Other Stories *(1982), and the novel,* In Country *(1987), which has recently been filmed under the same title.*

The following excerpt from In Country *takes place in Washington D.C. in 1984, when seventeen-year-old Sam, her uncle Emmett and her grandmother Mamaw visit the Vietnam Veterans Memorial.*

A S THEY DRIVE INTO WASHINGTON a few hours later, Sam feels sick with apprehension. She has kept telling herself that the memorial is only a rock with names on it. It doesn't mean anything except they're dead. It's just names. Nobody here but us chickens. Just us and the planet Earth and the nuclear bomb. But that's O.K., she thinks now. There is something comforting about the idea of nobody here but us chickens. It's so intimate. Nobody here but us. Maybe that's the point. People shouldn't make too much of death. Her history teacher said there are more people alive now than dead. He warned that there were so many people alive now, and they were living so much longer, that people had the idea they were practically immortal. But everyone's going to die and we'd better get used to the notion, he said. Dead and gone. Long gone from Kentucky.

Sometimes in the middle of the night it struck Sam with sudden clarity that she was going to die someday. Most of the time she forgot about this. But now, as she and Emmett and Mamaw Hughes drive into Washington, where the Vietnam

Memorial bears the names of so many who died, the reality of death hits her in broad daylight. Mamaw is fifty-eight. She is going to die soon. She could die any minute, like that racehorse that keeled over dead, inexplicably, on Father's Day. Sam has been so afraid Emmett would die. But Emmett came to Cawood's Pond looking for her, because it was unbearable to him that she might have left him alone, that she might even die.

The Washington Monument is a gleaming pencil against the sky. Emmett is driving, and the traffic is frightening, so many cars swishing and merging, like bold skaters in a crowded rink. They pass cars with government license plates that say FED. Sam wonders how long the Washington Monument will stand on the Earth.

A brown sign on Constitution Avenue says VIETNAM VETERANS MEMORIAL. Emmett can't find a parking place nearby. He parks on a side street and they walk toward the Washington Monument. Mamaw puffs along. She has put on a good dress and stockings. Sam feels they are ambling, out for a stroll, it is so slow. She wants to break into a run. The Washington Monument rises up out of the earth, proud and tall. She remembers Tom's bitter comment about it—a big white prick. She once heard someone say the U.S.A. goes around fucking the world. That guy who put pink plastic around those islands should make a big rubber for the Washington Monument, Sam thinks. She has so many bizarre ideas there should be a market for her imagination. These ideas are churning in her head. She can hardly enjoy Washington for these thoughts. In Washington, the buildings are so pretty, so white. In a dream, the Vietnam Memorial was a black boomerang, whizzing toward her head.

"I don't see it," Mamaw says.

"It's over yonder," Emmett says, pointing. "They say you come up on it sudden."

"My legs are starting to hurt."

Sam wants to run, but she doesn't know whether she wants to run toward the memorial or away from it. She just wants to run. She has the new record album with her, so it won't melt in the hot car. It's in a plastic bag with handles. Emmett is carrying the pot of geraniums. She is amazed by him, his impressive bulk, his secret suffering. She feels his anxiety. His heart must be racing, as if something intolerable is about to happen.

Emmett holds Mamaw's arm protectively and steers her across the street. The pot of geraniums hugs his chest.

"There it is," Sam says.

It is massive, a black gash in a hillside, like a vein of coal exposed and then polished with polyurethane. A crowd is filing by slowly, staring at it solemnly.

"Law," says Sam's grandmother quietly. "It's black as night."

"Here's the directory," Emmett says, pausing at the entrance. "I'll look up his name for you, Mrs Hughes."

The directory is on a pedestal with a protective plastic shield. Sam stands in the shade, looking forward, at the black wing embedded in the soil, with grass growing above. It is like a giant grave, fifty-eight thousand bodies rotting here behind those names. The people are streaming past, down into the pit.

"It don't show up good," Mamaw says anxiously. "It's just a hole in the ground."

The memorial cuts a V in the ground, like the wings of an abstract bird, huge and headless. Overhead, a jet plane angles upward, taking off.

"It's on Panel 9E," Emmett reports. "That's on the east wing. We're on the west."

At the bottom of the wall is a granite trough, and on the edge of it the sunlight reflects the names just above, in mirror writing, upside down. Flower arrangements are scattered at the base. A little kid says, "Look, Daddy, the flowers are dying." The man snaps, "Some are and some aren't."

The walkway is separated from the memorial by a strip of gravel, and on the other side of the walk is a border of dark gray brick. The shiny surface of the wall reflects the Lincoln Memorial and the Washington Monument, at opposite angles.

A woman in a sunhat is focusing a camera on the wall. She says to the woman with her, "I didn't think it would look like this. Things aren't what you think they look like. I didn't know it was a wall."

A spraddle-legged guy in camouflage clothing walks by with a cane. Probably he has an artificial leg, Sam thinks, but he walks along proudly, as if he has been here many times before and doesn't have any particular business at that moment. He seems to belong here, like Emmett hanging out at McDonald's.

A group of schoolkids tumble through, noisy as chickens. As they enter, one of the girls says, "Are they piled on top of each other?" They walk a few steps farther and she says, "What are all these names anyway?" Sam feels like punching the girl in the face for being so dumb. How could anybody that age not know? But she realizes that she doesn't know either. She is just beginning to understand. And she will never really know what happened to all these men in the war. Some people walk by, talking as though they are on a Sunday picnic, but most are reverent, and some of them are crying.

Sam stands in the center of the V, deep in the pit. The V is like the white wings of the shopping mall in Paducah. The Washington Monument is reflected at the center line. If she moves slightly to the left, she sees the monument, and if she moves the other way she sees a reflection of the flag opposite the memorial. Both the monument and the flag seem like arrogant gestures, like the country giving the finger to the dead boys, flung in this hole in the ground. Sam doesn't understand what she is feeling, but it is something so strong, it is like a tornado moving in her, something massive and overpowering. It feels like giving birth to this wall.

"I wish Tom could be here," Sam says to Emmett. "He needs to be here." Her voice is thin, like smoke, barely audible.

"He'll make it here someday. Jim's coming too. They're all coming one of these days."

"Are you going to look for anybody's name besides my daddy's?"

"Yeah."

"Who?"

"Those guys I told you about, the ones that died all around me that day. And that guy I was going to look up—he might be here. I don't know if he made it out or not."

Sam gets a flash of Emmett's suffering, his grieving all

these years. He has been grieving for fourteen years. In this dazzling sunlight, his pimples don't show. A jet plane flies overhead, close to the earth. Its wings are angled back too, like a bird's.

Two workmen in hard hats are there with a stepladder and some loud machinery. One of the workmen, whose hat says on the back NEVER AGAIN, seems to be drilling into the wall.

"What's he doing, hon?" Sam hears Mamaw say behind her.

"It looks like they're patching up a hole or something." *Fixing a hole where the rain gets in.*

The man on the ladder turns off the tool, a sander, and the other workman hands him a brush. He brushes the spot. Silver duct tape is patched around several names, leaving the names exposed. The names are highlighted in yellow, as though someone has taken a Magic Marker and colored them, the way Sam used to mark names and dates, important facts, in her textbooks.

"Somebody must have vandalized it," says a man behind Sam. "Can you imagine the sicko who would do that?"

"No," says the woman with him. "Somebody just wanted the names to stand out and be noticed. I can go with that."

"Do you think they colored Dwayne's name?" Mamaw asks Sam worriedly.

"No. Why would they?" Sam gazes at the flowers spaced along the base of the memorial. A white carnation is stuck in a crack between two panels of the wall. A woman bends down and straightens a ribbon on a wreath. The ribbon has gold letters on it, "VFW Post 7215 of Pa."

They are moving slowly. Panel 9E is some distance ahead. Sam reads a small poster propped at the base of the wall: "To those men of C Company, 1st Bn. 503 Inf., 173rd Airborne who were lost in the battle for Hill 823, Dak To, Nov. 11, 1967. Because of their bravery I am here today. A grateful buddy."

A man rolls past in a wheelchair. Another jet plane flies over.

A handwritten note taped to the wall apologizes to one of the names for abandoning him in a firefight.

Mamaw turns to fuss over the geraniums in Emmett's arms, the way she might fluff a pillow.

The workmen are cleaning the yellow paint from the names. They sand the wall and brush it carefully, like men polishing their cars. The man on the ladder sprays water on the name he has just sanded and wipes it with a rag.

Sam, conscious of how slowly they are moving, with dread, watches two uniformed marines searching and searching for a name. "He must have been along here somewhere," one says. They keep looking, running their hands over the names.

"There it is. That's him."

They read his name and both look abruptly away, stare out for a moment in the direction of the Lincoln Memorial, then walk briskly off.

"May I help you find someone's name?" asks a woman in a T-shirt and green pants. She is a park guide, with a clipboard in her hand.

"We know where we are," Emmett says. "Much obliged, though."

At panel 9E, Sam stands back while Emmett and Mamaw search for her father's name. Emmett, his gaze steady and intent, faces the wall, as though he were watching birds; and Mamaw, through her glasses, seems intent and purposeful, as though she were looking for something back in the field, watching to see if a cow had gotten out of the pasture. Sam imagines the egret patrolling for ticks on a water buffalo's back, ducking and snaking its head forward, its beak like a punji stick.

"There it is," Emmett says. It is far above his head, near the top of the wall. He reaches up and touches the name. "There's his name, Dwayne E. Hughes."

"I can't reach it," says Mamaw. "Oh, I wanted to touch it," she says softly, in disappointment.

"We'll set the flowers here, Mrs Hughes," says Emmett. He sets the pot at the base of the panel, tenderly, as though tucking in a baby.

"I'm going to bawl," Mamaw says, bowing her head and starting to sob. "I wish I could touch it."

Sam has an idea. She sprints over to the workmen and asks them to let her borrow the stepladder. They are almost finished, and they agree. One of them brings it over and sets it up beside the wall, and Sam urges Mamaw to climb the ladder, but Mamaw protests. "No, I can't do it. You do it."

"Go ahead, ma'am," the workman says.

"Emmett and me'll hold the ladder," says Sam.

"Somebody might see up my dress."

"No, go on, Mrs Hughes. You can do it," says Emmett. "Come on, we'll help you reach it."

He takes her arm. Together, he and Sam steady her while she places her foot on the first step and swings herself up. She seems scared, and she doesn't speak. She reaches but cannot touch the name.

"One more, Mamaw," says Sam, looking up at her grandmother—at the sagging wrinkles, her flab hanging loose and sad, and her eyes reddened with crying. Mamaw reaches toward the name and slowly struggles up the next step, holding her dress tight against her. She touches the name, running her hand over it, stroking it tentatively, affectionately, like feeling a cat's back. Her chin wobbles, and after a moment she backs down the ladder silently.

When Mamaw is down, Sam starts up the ladder, with the record package in her hand.

"Here, take the camera, Sam. Get his name." Mamaw has brought Donna's Instamatic.

"No, I can't take a picture this close."

Sam climbs the ladder until she is eye level with her father's name. She feels funny, touching it. A scratching on a rock. Writing. Something for future archaeologists to puzzle over, clues to a language.

"Look this way, Sam," Mamaw says. "I want to take your picture. I want to get you and his name and the flowers in together if I can."

"The name won't show up," Sam says.

"Smile."

"How can I smile?" She is crying.

Mamaw backs up and snaps two pictures. Sam feels her face looking blank. Up on the ladder, she feels so tall, like a spindly weed that is sprouting up out of this diamond-bright seam of hard earth. She sees Emmett at the directory, probably searching for his buddies' names. She touches her father's name again.

"All I can see here is my reflection," Mamaw says when Sam comes down the ladder. "I hope his name shows up. And your face was all shadow."

"Wait here a minute," Sam says, turning away her tears from Mamaw. She hurries to the directory on the east side. Emmett isn't there anymore. She sees him striding along the wall, looking for a certain panel. Nearby, a group of marines is keeping a vigil for the POWs and MIAs. A double row of flags is planted in the dirt alongside their table. One of the marines walks by with a poster: "You Are an American, Your Voice Can Make the Difference." Sam flips through the directory and finds "Hughes." She wants to see her father's name there too. She runs down the row of Hughes names. There were so many Hughes boys killed, names she doesn't know. His name is there, and she gazes at it for a moment. Then suddenly her own name leaps out at her.

SAM ALAN HUGHES PFC AR 02 MAR 49 02 FEB 67 HOUSTON TX 14E 104

Her heart pounding, she rushes to panel 14E, and after racing her eyes over the string of names for a moment, she locates her own name.

SAM A HUGHES. It is the first on a line. It is down low enough to touch. She touches her own name. How odd it feels, as though all the names in America have been used to decorate this wall.

Acknowledgements

As ever my thanks are due to Nick Robinson, Alex Stitt and Stephanie Maury at Robinson Publishing. I am also grateful for the help and advice of Nigel Matheson, Julian Jenkins, Beryl Griffiths, Helen Joy, the staff of the British Library and, most of all, Penny Stempel.

Permissions Acknowledgements

"The Boat" is an extract from *U-Boat* by Lothar-Günther Buchheim. Translated by G. Lawaetz. Copyright © 1977 Alfred A. Knopf Inc. Reprinted by permission of HarperCollins and Alfred A. Knopf Inc.

"The Unknown Soldier" is an extract from *1919* by John Dos Passos. Copyright © 1932 John Dos Passos.

"Not Substantial Things" is from *The Selected Stories of Dan Davin*. Reprinted by permission of David Higham Associates.

"An Egg for the Major" by C. S. Forester. Copyright © 1944 C. S. Forester. Reprinted by permission of Peters Fraser & Dunlop.

"Bombardier" by Paul Gallico. Copyright © 1942 the Curtis Publishing Company. Copyright renewed 1969 Paul Gallico. Reprinted by permission of Harold Ober Associates.

"Svejk and the Stable Pinscher" is an extract from *The Good Soldier Svejk* by Jaroslav Hasek. Translation copyright © Cecil Parrott. Reprinted by permission of William Heinemann Ltd.

"The Spirit of the Bayonet" is an extract from *The Short-Timers* by Gustav Hasford. Copyright © 1979 Gustav Hasford. Reprinted by permission of Bantam Books Inc.

"Wheels of Terror" is an extract from *Wheels of Terror* by Sven Hassel. Copyright © 1959 Sven Hassel.

"Yossarian and the Psychiatrist" is an extract from *Catch-22* by Joseph Heller. Copyright © 1955 Joseph Heller. Renewed 1961. Reprinted by permission of Candida Donadio.

"The Trick of El Sordo of the Hilltop" is an extract from *For Whom the Bell Tolls* by Ernest Hemingway. Copyright © 1940 Ernest Hemingway. Reprinted by permission of Charles Scribner's Sons and HarperCollins.

"The Interrogation of the Prisoner Bung by Mister Hawkins and Sergeant Tree" by David Huddle. Copyright © 1971 David Huddle. Reprinted by permission of the author.

"Two Soldiers" by Chester Himes. Copyright © 1943 Chester Himes. Reprinted by permission of Virgin Publishing.